Rise of the Alliance III

The Hunters and the Hunted

SARTORIAS-DELES BOOKS

HISTORICAL ARC
"Lily and Crown"
Inda
The Fox
King's Shield
Treason's Shore
Time of Daughters (two volumes)
Banner of the Damned

MODERN ERA
The CJ Journals
Senrid
Spy Princess
Sartor
Fleeing Peace
A Stranger to Command
Crown Duel
The Trouble with Kings
Sasharia En Garde

AND
THE RISE OF THE ALLIANCE ARC
A Sword Named Truth
The Blood Mage Texts
The Hunters and the Hunted
Nightside of the Sun (late Feb 2022)

Rise of the Alliance III

The Hunters and the Hunted

SHERWOOD SMITH

BOOK VIEW CAFE

Published by Book View Café
304 S. Jones Blvd., Suite #2906
Las Vegas, NV 89107
www.bookviewcafe.com

ISBN: 978-1-61138-981-4

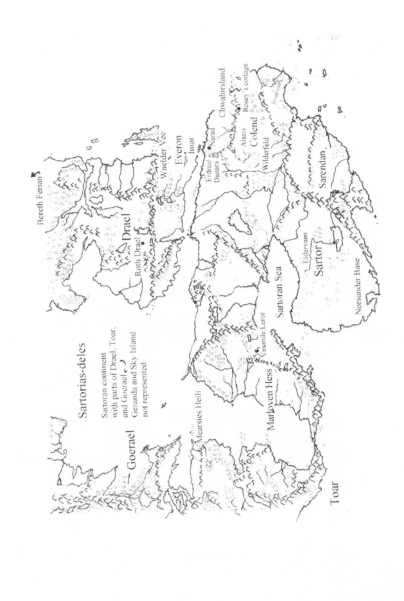

Sartorias-deles

Sartoran continent
with parts of Drael, Toar,
and Goerael ~
Geranda and Sky Island
not represented

Goerael

Mearsies Heili

Marloven Hess

Toar

Bereth Ferian

Drael

Roth Drael

Whelder Vee

Everon

Imar

Erdrael
Danara
Narad

Alsais
Colend
Wilderfeld

Chwahirsland

Roscy's cottage

Sartoran Sea

Vasande Leror

Eidervaen

Sartor

Sarendan

Norsunder Base

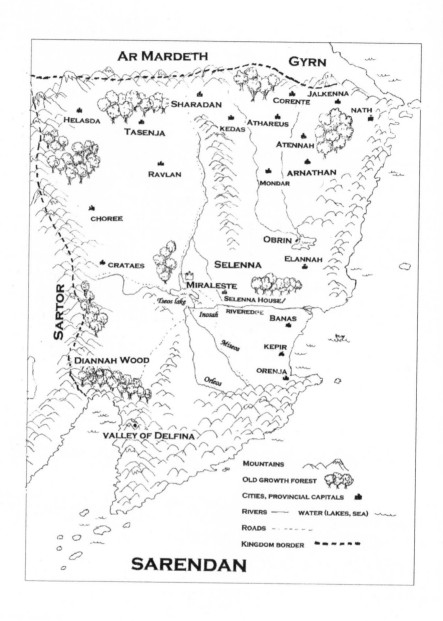

Dramatis Personae for
The Hunters and the Hunted

(For more information there is a Sartorias-deles wiki at
http://reqfd.net/s-d/)

NORSUNDER

Benin: Ambitious mage, his specialty the soul-bound (people caught at the point of death, their wills bound to the command of whoever holds the soul-bound magic). Benin tends to not wait until potential soul-bound are dead in order to experiment.

Bostian: Ambitious Norsundrian military captain.

Dejain: Mage specializing in dark magic, one of a succession of Norsunder Base commanders, who tend to be summarily replaced by violence. She has no objections to others dying by violence, but she'd prefer to keep her hands clean.

Detlev: Chief visible mage and sometime military leader, answerable to Norsunder's Host of Lords. Born four thousand years ago, has lived in and outside time ever since. Like his nephew Siamis, has **Dena Yeresbeth**. (A teacher and trainer, his boys are introduced in this volume)

Efael: Considers himself one of the Host of Lords, the authors of Norsunder. Has a penchant for cruelty. He is the Host of Lords' chief assassin, bloodhound, interrogator; he and his sister **Yeres** consider Detlev their rival for a seat among the Host of Lords.

Henerek: Ambitious low-ranking young Norsunder military captain, originated in Everon. Wanted to be one of the Knights of Dei, but was cashiered due to excess cruelty, drunkenness, and inability to follow orders. Wishes to be a king.

Host of Lords: Authors of Norsunder, existing beyond time, readying for a second try at taking the world. Or worlds. Why, and who they are, will become clearer in the succeeding volumes.

Kessler Sonscarna: Renegade Chwahir prince with considerable military abilities, forced into Norsunder as a result of treachery by the mage **Dejain.** Hates Norsunder. (See **Chwahirsland** below)

Lesca: Apparently lazy steward in charge of Norsunder Base. Overlook her at your peril.

Siamis: Nephew to Detlev, recently emerged (it is believed for the first time) in four thousand years, as a young adult. Formidable mage, and like Detlev, has **Dena Yeresbeth.**

Yeres: She and Efael, her brother, were born off-world, and so thoroughly and spectacularly corrupted that they caught the attention of Svirle of Yssel, one of the authors of Norsunder. Yeres is a powerful mage. She and Efael gladly execute the errands that the Host of Lords, steeped in evil, consider too distasteful.

LIGHT MAGIC MAGES AIDING THE ALLIANCE

Tsauderei: Oldest of the senior mages, independent of the two leading mage schools, living in a historic mage retreat located in the mountains bordering Sarendan and Sartor in the Valley of Delfina.

Erai-Yanya: One of a long line of mages dwelling in the ruined city of Roth Drael. Trained partly by the northern Mage School at Bereth Ferian, and partly by Tsauderei, she works independently, her specialty magical wards. She has one son, '**Arthur'**, who was adopted by Eveneth and became the titular Prince in Bereth Ferian. Erai-Yanya's student mage is the Marloven exile Hibern Askan.

Evend: One-time colleague of Tsauderei, King of Bereth Ferian (a courtesy title only) and head of the mage school there, he surrendered his life to bind rift magic from being used in Sartorias-deles by Norsunder. His place as titular king was taken by **Arthur**.

Lilith the Guardian: She was a lower ranking mage and what might be called an officer of rites and rituals in Ancient Sartor, which was as close to a government as they got. She had one daughter, Erdrael, who was killed along with most of the rest of the population when Norsunder tried to wrest control of the world, for reasons explored in a volume to come. Her name is a modern adaptation, and she found herself trying to combat Norsunder on this and other worlds around the sun Erhal; she comes out of hiding beyond time whenever she finds evidence that Detlev has been in the world, acting for Norsunder's Host of Lords.

Murial of Mearsies Heili: Recluse mage, living hidden in the western wilds of Mearsies Heili. Born a princess, she supported the transfer of the throne to her niece **Clair** on the death of her sister. Protecting the kingdom from a distance, she has seen to it that Clair gets magical training.

THE YOUNG ALLIES and OTHERS, Listed by Kingdom

BERETH FERIAN

Arthur: Named Yrtur, he adopted the name Arthur after his rescue by young world-gate crossing friends. Son of mage Erai-Yanya, he early showed great ability in learning and magic, but he was unhappy living in isolation. He was adopted as heir by **Evend**, the head mage of the Bereth Ferian Mage School, and presiding King of the loose federation headquartered at Bereth Ferian, a title he shared with Liere Fer Eider in her persona as Sartora, the Girl Who Saved the World.

Evend: (see Light Mages)

Liere Fer Eider: Also known as the Girl Who Saved the World, she was the first of her generation to be born with **Dena Yeresbeth**. At ten years old she left her small town to escape being captured by Siamis, who had extended an enchantment over the world, which Liere later broke. The enchantment is generally known as The Lost Year, as most lived in a dream world while it lasted. She was lauded by all, and given the courtesy title of Queen in Bereth Ferian, a title with no powers or responsibilities whatsoever — but which still chafed her unbearably. Liere is the poster child for Imposter Syndrome.

LAND OF THE CHWAHIR (aka CHWAHIRSLAND)

Jilo: Son of a lowly sergeant, heir to elderly **Prince Kwenz Sonscarna**, he finds himself acting king of Chwahirsland, after Norsunder's removal of the previous king, who had ruled for more than a century. What that means is, he is slowly poisoning himself in trying to remove the toxic accretion of dark magic enchantments over Chwahirsland, and especially its capital.

Prince Kessler Sonscarna: The single living descendant of the ruling Sonscarnas, who were systematically killed off by Wan-Edhe, blood relations notwithstanding. Prince Kessler escaped at a young age, made his way to a martial arts group, where he mastered military arts. He allied with a Norsundrian mage, Dejain, and began to assemble followers for his plan to remove all the hereditary rulers of the world, and replace them with his followers, chosen solely on merit. When defeated, he was forced into Norsunder by Dejain, who betrayed him.

Mondros (Rosey), Mage: His origins are a mystery, his intent to battle Wan-Edhe from a distance. He has looked out for some of the Young Allies Wan-Edhe has tried to suborn, and to kill. He lives in a cottage on the border of Chwahirsland; recently repatriated with his son **Rel**. (see **Sartor**)

Wan-Edhe, King of the Chwahir: Descendant of the ruling Sonscarna family, has ruled for close to a century. A powerful dark magic mage, he has managed to create a powerful citadel in the heart of his kingdom, where time itself is distorted.

COLEND

King Carlael Lirendi: Regarded generally as Mad King Carlael. He is as beautiful as he is strange. He seems to exist in a world of dreams, from which he emerges now and then, very alert and very aware. There is a loose council made up of the chief nobles who oversee the kingdom when he is unable to respond to the world around him.

Prince Shontande Lirendi: Son of Carlael, King of Colend, and crown prince.

Karhin Keperi: She is a teenage scribe student in a small town in the west of Colend, who volunteers to function as the center of the young allies' communication network. An indefatigable letter writer, she first met Puddlenose of the Mearsieans, and gradually got drawn into the Alliance.

Thad Keperi: Red-haired brother of Karhin, also a scribe student, but much less passionate about the scribe life. Very social, and friend to all the Alliance.

Little Bee and Lisbet Keperi: Younger sister and brother of Thad and Karhin. Little Bee is blind, has Dena Yeresbeth, though the family is not aware of it.

EVERON

King Berthold and Queen Mersedes Carinna Delieth: King and queen, survivors of rough earlier years. Mersedes, daughter of a con man, became one of the Knights of Dei, dedicated to protecting the kingdom.

Prince Glenn Delieth: Heir to the throne of Everon, and convinced that a strong army solves all questions, especially the threat of Norsunder attacking.

Princess Hatahra Delieth (Tahra): Younger sister of Glenn, passionate about numbers.

Roderic Dei: Commander of the Knights of Dei, once defenders and protectors of the realm. Decimated in the war Henerek brought, and Kessler Sonscarna finished.

MARLOVEN HESS

Senrid Montredaun-An: Young king of Marloven Hess, a mage studying both dark and light magic. First friend to **Liere Fer Eider**, and second to make his unity in **Dena Yeresbeth**.

Retren Forthan: A young man from a farm background, he is the best of the leaders to come out of the military academy. Senrid, the young king, hopes that Forthan will one day lead the Marloven army.

Commander Keriam: Career military man, now head of the Marloven military academy, also titular head of the Palace Guard. Acted as guardian and foster-father to Senrid, protecting him from the regent as much as possible.

Hibern Askan: Light magic student, tutored by Erai-Yanya of Roth Drael, who learned in the northern mage school. Hibern was exiled by her family.

MEARSIES HEILI

Clair of Mearsies Heili: Young queen of Mearsies Heili, a small agrarian polity on the northeast corner of the continent Toar. Niece of the hermit-mage **Murial**, and cousin to the wandering boy known only as **Puddlenose**, she has adopted a group of girls, most of them runaways. Her right-hand and designated 'heir' is **C.J.**

C.J. (Cherenneh Jenet): Found by Clair, who traveled through the World-gate, C.J. is from Earth, adopted into Clair's gang of runaways and rejects. She learns magic fitfully, and is generally regarded as the leader of Clair's gang of girls.

CJ's Gang of Girls: Falinneh and Dhana currently wear human form but are not actually human, Seshe has a mysterious past, Irenne thinks the world is a stage and she is the heroine of the play, Diana is a martial artist and forester, and Sherry and Gwen are followers. Clair adopted all of them.

Mearsieanne: Once Queen of Mearsies Heili after she walked in and took an empty throne and renamed herself. She was taken by Norsunder, and existed beyond time for nearly a century, while her son and granddaughter ruled. Now returned, she has stepped in and in the nicest way possible, shouldered aside Clair, her great-granddaughter and the girl queen, in order to show her how ruling ought to be done.

Murial: (see Light Mages)

Puddlenose of Mearsies Heili: Bereft of family at a very young age, and used by The King of the Chwahir in his compli-cated plots, he was rescued several times by Rosey (Mondros, see Mages). He wanders the world, determined to have fun. His chief companion is a world-gate wanderer from Earth named **Christoph**, but sometimes he's joined by **Rel**.

SARENDAN

Peitar Selenna, King of Sarendan: Reluctant king who would rather study magic, he came to the throne after an especially vicious civil war. He, nephew to the former king, Darian Irad, was one of the leaders of the revolution, but advocated non-violent means. His accession was a compromise between the commoners, who adore him, and the nobles, who recognize that at least he is nominally one of their own.

Lilah Selenna, Princess of Sarendan: Younger Sister to Peitar. She, with friends **Bren** (artist), **Innon** (a noble-born accountant at heart) and **Deon** were deeply involved in the revolution.

Derek Diamagan: Charismatic leader of the revolution, a commoner who wished to overthrow all the nobles, and institute common rule. He was a far better speech maker than he was an organizer; his revolution was a disaster. Close friend of Peitar Selenna.

SARTOR

Queen Yustnesveas Landis V (Atan): New young queen of Sartor, after the oldest kingdom in the world was removed from time by nearly a century. She was found on the border by Tsauderei the mage, and raised by him before the enchantment was broken. She began her queenship as a mage student, with little training in statecraft, but well-read in history.

Mistress Veltos Jhaer: Head of the prestigious Sartoran mage guild, until the enchantment the foremost mage school in the world. Now a century behind. She is further burdened by guilt for having lost the kingdom to enchantment.

Hinder and Sinder: Morvende (cave dwellers), friends of Atan.

Rel: Known as Rel the shepherd's son, and more widely as Rel the Traveler, he was happily raised by a guardian in Tser Mearsies until wanderlust caused him to leave home. Met **Puddlenose** of the Mearsieans and consequently became tangled in some of the Mearsieans' adventures. Friends with **Atan**, and one of the **Rescuers**. He was the only outsider ever invited to join the **Knights of Dei** in Everon; in the previous volume he discovered his parentage, which he is still trying to process.

Rescuers: The name given to a band of children who had lived in a magic-protected forest during the enchantment. They sheltered Atan before the enchantment was broken. Ostensibly highly regarded as heroes by the Sartorans, there are the aristocratic Rescuers, and the non-aristocratic, Rel among them.

VASANDE LEROR

Leander Tlennen-Hess: Like Senrid, a young king, though of a tiny polity that historically belonged to the Marlovens, then broke away four centuries previous. Leander and Senrid have a lot in common, and would be friends, except for Leander's jealous step-sister:

Kyale Marlonen: Adoptive sister to Leander, relishes being a princess, and is jealous of Leander's attention.

Llhei: Sarendan-trained nanny (sister to Lizana, nurse to the royal children of **Sarendan**), governess to Kyale, remained after evil Queen Mara Jinia defeated.

Alaxandar: Captain of royal guard, quit under evil queen Mara Jinia, protected Leander.

PART ONE:
HUNTER

Firejive

/gyve: to fetter, to shackle, to bind/

THIS CHRONICLE BEGINS WITH Detlev, who emerged from Norsun-der Beyond into the center of a violent struggle for power at Norsunder Base. He stepped over the dead and entered the command center, currently deserted as the mage Dejain and the military commander Bostian stalked one another elsewhere in the fortress.

Because there is no time measure in the Beyond, he found the date—and calculated how long he'd been gone—via the accumulation of messages in the dispatch tray. There was no sign of Siamis, nor any report.

He reached the last, considered the lacunae, then sat down to write a coded note.

> *Why was I not alerted about the blood mage text?*
> *Did any of you try to secure it?*

A short time later came the answer:

> *Jilo of the Chwahir was either given it, or was given the location by Kessler Sonscarna. Senrid Montredaun-An took it away. I wrote a report immediately. I found out through gossip that Kessler*

> *took the texts back, and I reported that, too. Since we*
> *received no new orders, and information was long*
> *after the fact, we stayed tight with standing orders.*

Detlev wrote:

> *Our relay is compromised. Reports to be made in*
> *person, through you. Commencing with your*
> *conveying these orders, face to face.*

At the other end of the world, in a place of mutable time, occasionally—cruelly—some trick of light in a changing sky evoked in Siamis's memory the cloud ships of Yssel, the last of which he witnessed sinking slowly to a fiery death nearly five thousand years ago: dragon-ribbed keelson, spars of glowing crystal, and vast sails iridescent as wasp wings.

The glimpses into past times were never quick to last. The world had changed so vastly, and he was no longer a terror-stricken, bewildered boy. But echoes of those long ago emotions sometimes lingered: astonishment, harrowing realization, the numbness of betrayal, and finally a long-smoldering anger.

"I will someday destroy the entire world," he had shrieked when summoned to the Garden of the Twelve early after he was taken, and all the Host had laughed but one.

Ilerian tipped his head, regarding Siamis with mild interest. "How will you go about it?"

Later, Detlev had said, "Existence will be far less painful if you say nothing to catch Ilerian's interest. But if that cannot be avoided, have an answer. And always have a plan. "

Siamis had scorned his uncle's too-late advice as he'd scorned everything his uncle said and did, until it was proven—excruciatingly, and lasciviously prolonged—to be true.

So his real training began. In Norsunder-Beyond, where time was nearly meaningless, marked by occasional and brief emergences into the real world for either training or a lesson, he had no age markers to measure by except by guesswork.

He might have been the equivalent of fourteen when he figured out how to combine the two—flout and stealth. Flouting Detlev when he could be perceived by the Host or their minions had amused them, and each time he'd been caught he'd suffered the consequences philosophically. While

Norsunder's lords, who rarely stirred from their timeless citadel, began to regard his errors as a typical for callow youth, he had learned from each.

The lesson he kept closest: the mind gained in strength along with the body only in the physical realm, where time resumed its natural progression, where there was sunlight and the fresh air that renews itself as it sweeps over pure water. But those excursions had to be brief, and always in obedience to someone else's plan.

When at last he dared venture on his own to explore the immeasurable realm between Norsunder's ageless, arid center and the world, he knew how to leave no physical trace or magical shadow. Detlev called that the hand through the water.

Finally, the most dangerous of all, he essayed single visits back in time, using the great window in the Garden of the Twelve at Norsunder's center. It was vital to be unperceived; an error meant far worse than the idle cruelties of those who found entertainment in such pursuits, it meant being forever lost in a fold of time.

And so, it transpired, learning to maneuver in Norsunder had prepared him for dealing with the anomaly the mages of Old Sartor had named the Moonfire.

He moved with practiced stealth, the stages of his plan ranked mentally in meticulous order, but found that this anomaly was far more slippery than Norsunder's magic-straitened boundaries. He had the *where*, but not the *when* . . .

One

Late summer, 4743 AF
Delfina Valley to the Border of Chwahirsland

MONDROS'S BEARD BRISTLED AS his eyes widened with horror.

"When I think," he said to Tsauderei, as thunder rumbled low in the distance, "how very close we came to knowing nothing whatsoever about this blood mage text, I'm afraid I am going to have nightmares for months. Years."

Tsauderei shook his head slowly. He, too, felt that unsettling roil in the gut that came with a sense that they had lost control of something important. "This is, in a way, worse than the time the youngsters took themselves off to Geth-deles without consulting any of us. What do you suggest we do?"

"What *can* we do?" Mondros asked, broad hands extended to either side on the word *can*.

Tsauderei said, "Jilo, Senrid, the Mearsiean girls — it's their alliance again."

"Which was a benighted idea."

"But don't you see, I feel confident in stating that, except for Kessler Sonscarna, whose motivations are impossible to guess beyond an apparent animus against Norsunder, at every stage they thought they were doing their best. Jilo turns to Senrid of Marloven Hess, who turns to young Leander in Vasande Leror, who turns to his friends in Mearsies Heili, all using those young Colendi scribe students as a communications clearing house. The way they've been trained to serve."

"I see ignorant youths acting without due consideration, especially for their guardians." Mondros's deep voice rumbled low in his massive chest.

"Oh, and they're the first generation to do that," Tsauderei said sardonically.

"Granted." Mondros uttered an unwilling laugh. "My ire is entirely bound up in my sense of personal failure. I thought I'd established a good enough understanding with young Jilo to enable him to come to me. He faces a monumental task, one might as well say an impossible task. He cannot possibly succeed alone, and he seems to know it, yet there he is, laboring alone in that vile fortress where no one can get in to aid him in dismantling Wan-Edhe's architecture of evil."

"Mondros. Don't you see the problem?" Tsauderei said. "I do. At far too late an age."

"What problem?"

"The very reason we have mage schools, to provide a hierarchy as fallback. A trusted hierarchy. None of these young folk seem to have the luxury of trusted hierarchy, representing cumulative wisdom. Several survived by learning early they could not trust those in authority over them."

"So they trust each other instead. Yes, I see it." Mondros glared into space.

Tsauderei opened his hands. "When youth turns to youth for wisdom, it makes good sense to hare off the world to Geth-deles without telling anyone, and to translate and hide a blood mage text that Norsunder is seeking."

"But you had them living in your valley all last summer. You mean they don't trust you?"

"Atan does," Tsauderei said slowly. "Hibern as well, though I suspect she communicates with me on direct orders from Erai-Yanya. As yet, only a few of them know her well enough to trust her opinion. In any case, I think the problem runs back farther than last summer. It runs back before they were born, to when I turned down the offer to head the northern school because I was impatient of negotiation and compromise. My old friend Evend was more patient, but he's gone. I'm seen for what I am, standing outside the hierarchy, acting on my own, which suffices to justify Senrid and Jilo and the rest in acting on their own."

"So what do we do? Warn them?" Mondros asked.

"As if they don't know their dangers? I think they do, at least in part. The part that they don't understand is the perspective that comes with age, which leads me to suspect that they would take our cautions as more finger wagging. I think we need to convince them that they need us."

Tsauderei sighed heavily. "And the need is only going to get worse. We must establish good communication with all these youngsters as soon as possible, so that trust will come."

Mondros eyed him, hands on knees, elbows out. "Speaking of trouble, what do you make of these magical trespasses in Bereth Ferian? Local trouble brewing in the north?"

"Been pondering that." Tsauderei grunted. "Without further evidence, my instinct is to refrain from thinking politically. Chwahirsland, Bereth Ferian — my Delfina Valley. Look at the connections. Why would any mage venture past Oalthoreh's wards in Bereth Ferian, after all these centuries of relative quiet? Since nothing has gone missing, Oalthoreh's fear that the mage is after the Moonfire seems an unsettlingly good guess. At the very same time, why would Kessler Sonscarna dig out a blood mage text obviously secreted in Chwahir archives for at least as long?"

Mondros's heavy brows shot upward. "You think there might be some connection with the Venn?" His voice was a low rumble in his chest, unsettlingly echoed by the distant thunder; he heard it, and uttered an unwilling laugh. "Sinister, aren't I?"

"The Venn have always had that effect." Tsauderei stroked his mustache, which Mondros noted was beautifully groomed. "I would have said it's far more likely that the connection has to do with the Chwahir, and Wan-Edhe, except Bereth Ferian is way up north, one would think too far for anything of use to the Chwahir."

"But not far enough away for the Venn," Mondros said.

Tsauderei pursed his lips, head back, and Mondros observed him as the elder mage stared upward in reverie. Rumor had it the old boy had been handsome and dashing in his day — popular with lovers, though he'd never settled with one. He still wore the long, closed robes of his young manhood, sporting that diamond in his ear, and the long hair of those old fashions. Laughter flared in Mondros at the realization that we are never truly old inside our heads.

"So why now?" Tsauderei finally said, and Mondros's humor extinguished. "Let's assume the connection is the Venn. Norsunder has certainly wanted the Venn and their magic for centuries. Maybe it's become a primary goal now that they've been defeated again in trying to establish rifts big enough to bring their armies over from Norsunder-Beyond. But I don't believe the Venn have rift magic."

"We don't know that. We don't know what they've been up to inside their borders for the past six or seven centuries," Mondros said grimly, chill gripping the back of his neck. "You think it's a Venn renegade mage? Risking the treaty?"

They both knew that the ancient treaty stated that any Venn mage caught practicing magic outside their border could be executed on sight. That is, if that the Arrow wards didn't destroy them first.

"It's possible, after all these centuries. I think we need to find out."

"But no mage is permitted inside their border any more than their mages are allowed out in the world. Only traders can enter their harbors, and those apparently don't get into the Venn cities." Mondros swooped his hand, suggesting a dive into tunnels.

"*We* couldn't," Tsauderei said slowly, "but someone young might. Someone used to travel. Learns languages fast and gets along well. Skilled in the ways the Venn once admired, and probably still do . . ."

Mondros stared back uncomprehending, and then thrust his fingers through his beard. "You mean Rel? You want me to ask him, scarcely a month after he found out who I am? I feel guilty enough leaving him asleep to sneak away for this conversation!"

Tsauderei waved a hand to and fro, hiding how astonishing he'd found his old friend's confession that Rel was his son. As old as he was, he could still be caught by surprise. But now he comprehended Mondros's reluctance to talk about his past. "I understand. He's your boy. But Mondros, I did listen to the youngsters last summer, even if they didn't turn to me for advice. I believe he'd like to be asked."

"Humph."

Tsauderei said provocatively, "If I'd known who he was, I might have made an attempt to become better acquainted."

Mondros, stung, said, "I never told anyone but Raneseh. It

seemed safer. You know how deadly Wan-Edhe is." He shook his head.

"This was not an accusation, merely a reminder of the effects of keeping secrets for what seem to be the best of reasons," Tsauderei said gently, and seeing that tough, wary, reclusive Mondros was genuinely upset, he went on. "So you didn't know where Rel was. Or that he was in the midst of the fighting, until after the fact. That was a necessary ill. You were vitally employed in making certain that Norsunder's war did not become a mage war. And rescuing Roderic Dei. Which no one else could have done."

Mondros's angry flush died away, leaving the downward gaze of remorse. "I could not find the queen. I still do not know if she lives."

"This is the price we mages pay," Tsauderei reminded him.

They both reflected on the fact that however much governments argued with one another, they were pretty much all agreed: mages must stay out of politics. It was an ancient prejudice, far too ingrained to overcome. Mondros's efforts on behalf of Everon would never be known by more than a few, and certainly never acknowledged.

"You really think I ought to ask Rel to go to the Land of the Venn?"

"I think he would be complimented by the trust implied, and I believe he would enjoy the challenge. He's an excellent observer, and travelers are often the best placed people to hear general talk of events inside a country. If there are great changes talked of by ordinary people inside the Venn kingdom, then that might warrant further exploration, including diplomatic pressure."

"True enough."

"Further, if he tells his allies that you are entrusting him with a crucially important task, perhaps they, in turn, might begin to extend their trust past him to you."

"All right, then," Mondros said. "I'm willing to try that, since I have so obviously failed with Jilo, struggling alone in that damned city. And Rel doesn't know any magic, so there's no residue around him." Mondros slapped his knees. "I'll put it to him when he wakes."

You would think that father and son reuniting would be an

occasion for joy.

In a sense it was, but Rel was aware that he should be happy, that one day he might feel happy. It would be a mistake to say that finding his father was a disappointment, because that was not at all true. It was more that "father" in Rel's mind took an amorphous, ideal form. Until he found him his father could have been anyone.

But now "father" had a face, a form, and his own goals. His own life. As the days went by, they worked together, and studied Ancient Sartoran together, both preferring quiet. On the surface they got along well, but then Rel got along well with most people, and Mondros strained every nerve to anticipate what Rel might want, from choice of food to subject of study.

There were times as the days turned into a week, then a month, that Rel would catch himself as he sat across from this strange man at his rough table, or watched him poring over his books, or listened to his deep breathing in the other bunk in the loft bedroom—his overwhelming emotion was a sense of unreality. And at times, awkwardness.

Mondros felt the awkwardness when he saw it in Rel, and each hesitation, each down-and-away glance, hurt him. But he strove to hide the hurt, grateful because he sensed no anger or resentment. Perhaps Rel, who might have lain awake thinking he could be anyone from anywhere, was having a rough time adjusting to the fact that he was not only half-Chwahir and a descendent from one of the most infamous families in that kingdom, but his other parent was a disinherited exile from a kingdom with a sinister reputation.

After the conversation with Tsauderei, Mondros intended to get right to the Venn problem, but he spent a couple of days trying to find a way to bring up the subject without it seeming as if he wanted to rediscover his son in time to use him.

Over breakfast one morning, after a disturbed night, he finally forced himself in what he considered an uncomfortably snaky way to mention Tsauderei wanting to find an experience-ed traveler for a scouting mission.

Rel's chin cut upward no more than the width of a grass blade, but the reaction caught Mondros by surprise. Tsauderei was right, he thought grimly. I don't know my own son at all. "I do not want you feeling any obligation," he said anyway, because that much he'd planned. "But if you want to hear it, I'll give you a report."

"Please," Rel said.

And Mondros did. Rel's obvious interest caused him to think that Rel was like him after all, liking a defined goal, and the prospect of action.

He was partly right. Rel gazed down at the breadcrumbs on his plate, almost giddy with relief. As soon as he recognized that inward release, he tightened up again with remorse. He shouldn't be so grateful for a natural exit, but he was. The past night or so he'd been wondering how long he was supposed to stay. Winter would be arriving soon in these high mountains, making travel impossible. He didn't know if he was expected to call this cottage home, even though he didn't feel any more at home here than he did at Raneseh's holding.

Less.

Raneseh had trained him in etiquette, but there was no rule for this situation.

". . .there are Destinations in the lands at either side of the Venn border, but I'm told the patrols are formidable, as are the penalties for being caught crossing. I know the Venn trade with other lands, but that is limited, and every scrap searched."

"It sounds interesting," Rel said. "I've never been up that far. Captain Heraford said once that there's plenty of ship trade. Captains who can deal with the constant storms, and pass Venn inspections, stand to make a lot bringing out those porcelain stoves they make, with the enameled knotwork decoration. And they take in grains and foods they can't grow underground. I can always get work on a ship, as I can hand, reef, and steer."

"Shall I send you by magic?"

Rel smiled into Mondros's dark eyes so much like his own, and guilt harrowed him again at the anxiousness he saw there, almost a plea.

"No need. If they are as wary as you say, I'll want to learn my way, and I'll do that better traveling as I usually do. Since there doesn't seem to be urgency."

Mondros agreed, understanding what was not said: Rel would be gone before he could be mired in the cottage over winter. "But I'll still give you a transfer token. For in case."

Rel thanked him.

Over the following night, Rel was subliminally aware of the whispering drone of Mondros's voice, rather than the deep breathing of sleep. When he woke, Mondros was still at it, his voice a low, hoarse rumble. As Rel washed up and packed his things, he reflected that if all that magic work was the spells for a transfer, no wonder those things were so costly.

Mondros set out fresh bread, shirred eggs, three kinds of fruit, and a stoneware jug of pear cider. As Rel loaded his plate, Mondros laid a Sartoran coin between them. "You can always trade that for the gold in it. Before you do, be aware that you have a not only a transfer spell on it, it's warded in every way I could think of. That's the hard part, the protective wards. To complete the transfer, simply hold it and repeat Tsauderei's name twice. You don't even have to keep a Destination in mind—it will safely bring you back here."

Rel perceived in that tired gaze that any guilt he felt was a candle flame to the guilt of a father who had left his child, safety notwithstanding. Impulse prompted him to stretch his hands over the table and clasp Mondros's heavy shoulders. The muscles under his fingers were rock hard with tension.

They both stood, and Rel came around to pull Mondros in for a rib cracking hug. He heard in the slight catch of breath from Mondros that this was right, it was better than any words.

Before the sun had lifted a finger off the eastern horizon, he was on the road south.

Mondros watched him until his tiny figure vanished for the last time around a fold in the lower valleys, then trod heavily inside his cottage. He sat down, scowling at a piece of paper, considering. Finally he wrote:

Jilo, what have I done to cause you not to trust me? Why did you not bring the blood mage book to me?

He sent that off, walked back out, and stood on the edge of the cliff, staring down at the empty road.

When Jilo found the note in his golden case, he scowled at it owlishly. He'd utterly forgotten about the blood mage texts, which he was sure Prince Kessler still had. That was probably how he'd broken that spell over CJ's arm.

Then he remembered that Leander Tlennen-Hess had been planning to translate the books. That meant he might have made a copy.

He brooded for a time, then wrote to Karhin in Colend for the sigil to Leander's golden notecase. Because he was a Chwahir, who knew little of the rest of the world's politesse, he wrote in careful Sartoran: *Leander, did you translate that text I brought? Jilo.*

At the other end, Leander took the note out. It was late at night, and he had been wavering between sleep and a little more study.

He considered how much to tell Jilo—and more importantly why.

He walked to his window and stared sightlessly out into the dark courtyard, as night birds swooped and drifted against the peaceful stars. With those few words he was thrown back to the horror he'd felt as he got further into the translation, and the conviction that had caused him to rise and chuck the entire thing into the fire.

He liked Senrid. He trusted Senrid—no, he wanted to trust Senrid, but he knew what a burden Marloven Hess's crown was. Even without the threats Detlev had made against Senrid.

Leander could too easily see Senrid, driven to desperation, wanting to use that blood magic for the best of reasons . . .and using it again. And again.

And so he'd stood over the fire until the last vestige of his painstakingly made copy had turned to ash, so that if the day came bringing Senrid to ask about the book, he could tell the truth: it was gone.

What should he say to Jilo? He glanced at Jilo's blunt note, deciding the simplest truth would do. He sat down and scrawled, *It was evil so I burned my half-finished translation.* And send the note off.

But there was no satisfaction in so doing, even if he'd kept the thing out of Senrid's hands. (And Senrid, so far, had never asked about it.)

Because the original book still existed out there somewhere.

Mondros stared in bemusement at the hunch-shouldered, awkward figure in rusty black who sat on the bench where Rel had eaten his last breakfast that morning, lank black hair hanging like claws in his eyes.

". . .and so he said he burned it. Wherever it is, I don't have it," Jilo was saying. "It wasn't a matter of trust, but habit."

""Habit," Mondros said gently, "develops out of trust. I'm not leveling any accusations at you, Jilo. I admire you for what you're doing, but at the same time I fear for you."

Jilo's head dropped, so all Mondros could see was the tops of his ears, and his thin, knobby hands as he worked them on his knees. He mumbled something that seemed to be some sort of apology.

Mondros did not let him tangle himself up further. "There is also the matter of Wan-Edhe's infamous enemies book, which I've learned third-hand actually exists. And in your possession."

Jilo's head came up. "Yes." He stiffened warily.

Mondros sighed. "I'm not going to attempt to take it. Can you tell me how it functions?"

"It tracks the magic transfers of enemies. It has limits," Jilo said. "One limit is, it only traces Destinations that Wan-Edhe was able to ward. I think there might be other ways around its spells. Because there are gaps. Like, it will say that Detlev is at Norsunder Base, and then again at Norsunder Base, and then a third time. Without any sign of where he went between those times."

"Maybe he goes to Norsunder-Beyond. I should think even Wan-Edhe was unsuccessful in laying wards *there*." Mondros thumped his fists on his knees once, twice. "May I put a request to you?"

Jilo's shoulders hunched a notch higher.

"If you see any patterns of movement in the world by Detlev or Siamis, will you let me or Tsauderei know?"

Jilo's expression cleared. "Yes," he said. "That's easy enough. Though Siamis hasn't shown up at all for a long time."

"I expect it's too much to hope he's dead," Mondros said on a sigh.

Two

Spring, 4744
Everon

SPRING ARCED GENTLY TOWARD summer.

Dawn's bright sun promised a glorious day.

When Prince Glenn woke to clear light, he tore out of bed, chuckling with anticipation. Good weather *finally*. They could take the horses up north of the city and hold their thrice-postponed war game!

He dashed through his cleaning frame, pulled on his clothes, and ran downstairs to grab a hunk of bread-and-butter.

"Are you going off?" Tahra asked, resigned.

"Only overnight." In a burst of generosity, he added, "And when I come back, you have everything ready that you wanted us to work on. I'll get right to it. I promise."

Her expression eased, but only a fraction. She took promises seriously, and she wasn't sure he did. "Why do you have to go now?" she asked.

He sighed. "You know. Demonstration. When I invite Senrid, I think he'll listen to me—to us—if he has some respect for us. And he'll have some respect if we can make a decent showing in the ways he knows best." And then, back to his favorite statement, "We won't be able to lead an alliance of allied armies if our Everoneth are not worthy of being the leaders. We have to be better — we have to be the *best*."

Tahra looked down at her plate. Her brother kept talking about Senrid, what he'd like and what he wouldn't, but Glenn never got around to sending a message directly. Or even through Karhin, if he was worried about his language skills. Senrid had become an excuse for war practice, it was a simple as that. Even though Senrid had talked about the importance of communications. And he never bragged about military stuff. He barely even talked about it.

But Tahra knew her brother. He would only get angry if she said anything, and right now, unless their mother escaped Norsunder (because Tahra refused to believe she was dead) all they had was each other. So she said, as off-hand as she could, "Have fun."

Glenn ran all the way to the stables, slowing when he saw no one there but lackeys. At the other end, near the door to the salle, stood a small knot of his noble-born followers, but no dark curly head among them. Laban was not there waiting. Frustrated and irritated, Glen wondered why Laban didn't take orders like the rest of the future honor guard. Sometimes Glenn wasn't even certain the newcomer understood the prestige of being invited to an elite guard.

Glenn contained his impatience as three or four more of his group showed up, breathless and apologetic. The sun was now strong, sitting atop the far roof. Glenn, looking up, felt his impatience turn to apprehension.

On the pretext of inspecting the gear on each horse he postponed the order to ride out, but that couldn't last forever. He was reluctantly considering giving the order when he heard the noise of arrivals at the other end of the stable yard.

Glenn grinned in relief. There was Laban — with another boy. The group fell silent, inspecting this newcomer.

Laban leaped off his horse with the unconscious ease that reinforced Glenn's conviction that Laban'd had some kind of training, somewhere. "Glenn! Am I glad you haven't gone yet. We've been riding since before sunup." He waved at the two sweaty horses, which stable hands immediately took in hand.

The newcomer Laban had brought with him was tall, and lean. Not thin. Lean: he looked about sixteen and the curve of thigh at the saddle and the bulge of bicep outlined by the spring breeze toying with the loose black sleeve of his long tunic shirt were those of a warrior in training. His face was all sharp planes, his skin brown enough to render his yellow-flecked eyes a startling contrast. Sardonic humor bracketed his thin mouth. His straight black hair was, like Laban's, long on top, and cut in a military square-off above his collar in back.

"I went to see a contest over the border into Imar," Laban explained. "MV here was the winner. Brought him along, since he said he'd been to Khanerenth in disguise, for their last games. He won."

MV grinned. This was going to be fun.

"Very well." Glenn nodded, struggling to hide the leap of pleasure in his chest. He was a prince. He should be expecting his people to seek new recruits. It showed loyalty, and (he had to admit, though only to himself) he wasn't all that sure of Laban's loyalty. "We can see how we measure up, then." He turned his head. "Denold! Two fresh horses. Shift their gear."

The servants accomplished this order while the rest mounted up, and then Glenn raised his hand. They galloped through the still-ruined (but guarded) palace gates, across the park paling and up the main street. One day they wouldn't just be boys playing, he vowed as he citizens backed away, horses sidled, and carts hastily veered to either side of the road.

One day they'd be in battle tunics, all wearing his colors, with banners streaming, and the people wouldn't scramble aside looking annoyed, but they would back off and bow with respect the way they had for the Knights back in the good old days.

His pleasure lasted exactly half a day.

Midmorning they reached the traditional practice site, a broad expanse of fairly flat grassland bordered by hedgerows. This land had belonged to the Knights of Dei for uncounted years; Glenn had had to ask permission from Commander Dei to use it. He longed for the day when it would be his, dedicated to his personal honor guard, who would be the elite of the elite.

Glenn glanced around the peaceful meadow, still struggling mentally with his inner dilemma: in his vision, he led the battle, as did the mighty kings in the songs, stories, and tapestries. And yet if you were fighting at the front, how could you watch the battle at the same time in order to lead them to victory? Maybe the honor guard let only one enemy through at a time. They protected you so that you can see the battle, and command. But you still had to be a great swordsman in order to inspire your followers.

He laughed as a couple of the boys ran whooping toward a copse of trees, sending birds shooting upward, squawking raucously. They unloaded their gear in a rough circle next to a stream. Servants would be along presently to set up a cook tent and a fire.

Glenn waited until everyone had his gear unpacked, then he said, "Let's get started."

As his group pulled on chain mail and gloves and neck gear, he flashed a quick glance at Laban's friend MV, who stood watching, hands on propped on his skinny hips. He didn't wear a sash over that long tunic-shirt, only a blackweave belt riding low—a knife belt, though no sheath or weapon was attached. His blackweave riding boots were cut like Senrid's with cavalry high heels, for locking down in the stirrup. Maybe MV had been training with lances.

"Want the loan of gear?" Glenn asked. "We have extra mail and padding along."

MV's gaze shifted his way. A trick of the light struck highlights in the yellow-flecked amber, making his eyes seem on fire. It was just the contrast to his dark lashes and brows, of course, but the effect was kind of sinister.

"Nah," MV said, with a careless wave of his hand. He grinned briefly. "Just the ash stick. You ristos always run soft."

Not us, Glenn wanted to say, but he'd learned from watching Senrid, during their adventures on Geth-deles, that action was much more convincing than words. If you had to defend your rep with words, you'd already lost it.

He forced himself to shrug, and to finish gearing up. Maybe, he thought grimly as he picked up his wooden blade ("ash stick" MV'd said, not even "practice sword") MV would regret his pose of expert. These ash swords weren't lethal, unless you cracked someone's skull or broke their neck, but they raised horrible welts.

When everyone was ready, Glenn divided up the boys. He kept Laban on his team, for he still suspected that Laban was a lot better than he let on. MV he put on the other side, under the command of one of his favorites.

They formed a line, trotted to opposite ends of the field, and when Glenn raised his hand, charged.

Oh, Laban was good, all right. He rode like he'd been born to it, and his sword work betrayed a supple wrist and a lot of practice. He knocked the weapon out of the hand of his opponent and wheeled his horse effortlessly to look for another.

Glenn tried to watch them all. But he couldn't get a clear sight past the dust, and everyone was milling in different directions. He heard a couple of curt shouts from that MV, the result of which a few more of Glenn's team gave cries of disappointment and had to withdraw.

Meanwhile, Glenn was still trying to evade being attacked. He was hot, and his arms hurt. Finally he gestured to his opponent (who was also breathing like a bellows, and secretly reluctant to whack the prince) for time out. He definitely required an honor guard, at least until he got stronger.

Glenn turned his head as MV rode down the wind, white teeth bared in a slashing grin as he closed on one of Glenn's bigger recruits. And with two fast, powerful blows with the flat of his ash blade he knocked the boy right out of the saddle. Not his weapon. The boy himself. Who landed yelling in pain and protest, which sent his horse skittering, ears flat.

But MV was already off for the last two — last two! One of those last two was Laban. Glenn hadn't even noticed his team getting slaughtered.

Forgetting about his dry throat and aching ribs, Glenn jammed his knees into his horse's sides and rode to defend the nearest, but MV was faster. Three blows — a look of dismay — and Fraelec toppled over his horse's rump. Fraelec knew how to fall, or he might have been badly hurt, so fast they'd been riding.

Glenn turned aside, a stitch agonizing in his ribs at every breath. MV bore down on Laban, and their horses circled tightly, as the two exchanged blows. It was a fast exchange — faster than any of the other scraps by a wide margin — the feints and blocks quick and practiced, and then Laban's sword went flying. Laban laughed and threw his hands over his head as if to protect it.

MV veered and thundered back toward Glenn, who was now encircled by enemies.

Glenn made the signal for halt, knowing that he couldn't let himself be knocked out of the saddle. He'd lose his prestige for certain. Because of his rank it would be an insult to them all.

"You won," he said, as off-hand as he could. And as MV reined up, grinning, Glenn lifted his voice, striving to sound commanding. "Water break!"

The boys chased down their horses and brought them back to the campsite, some exchanging comments under their breath, and sending long glances MV's way.

MV seemed sublimely unaware.

When they had their breath back, Glenn called out for the sword work. There, at least, they ought to make a good showing. He had two or three who even Commander Dei said showed promise.

MV whipped every one of them. He did it so fast, and so hard, and without once losing his breath, that the boys fell silent, making it easier to hear MV's hoarse, voiceless snicker—he was having fun. Everyone tried against him, except Laban, who insisted he'd wrenched his wrist losing his ash sword. Glenn watched, deciding that his place as commander did not require him to face that stinging ash blade.

By then the servants had come and the smells of a savory soup drifted on the balmy afternoon air. Glenn declared a meal break, after which they'd pair off for the wrestling, but by then they knew who was going to win.

The boys trudged back to camp to get their soup and bread-and-cheese.

Glenn decided he'd better get it over with, and before the others heard. He stepped up next to MV, who walked with long strides that he abated for no one.

"You were at Khanerenth? For the Games?" he asked.

MV lifted a shoulder. "Why not? It was fun."

"How do we compare?"

MV's mouth twisted. "You really want to hear it?"

Glenn shook his head, his internal vision of impressing Senrid vanishing like smoke. "Will you teach us? Can you?" he asked, all pretense at pride gone. So much for leading from the front! MV's style was utterly unlike drill, everyone moving in unison to well-remembered calls.

MV raised a long, capable hand to wipe back the black hair that fanged his brow as he squinted at the line of boys waiting for soup, some of them hunched to protect wrenched muscles and joints. They were sore now, and would be a lot sorer when they woke.

"I can," he said finally. "And I will, but only till I get bored. I'll get bored fast if they whine about clean beds, or how duchas' boys aren't treated with respect, or any similar horseshit."

Glenn pressed his lips together. "Right. I'll speak to them."

He did. And saw that they were impressed enough not to grumble.

He gave orders to the servants to return to Ferdrian and bring tents, in case of rain, and food for a week.

Already his promise to his sister was forgotten, in the face of what he saw as far greater need.

Three

Colend

THE ROYAL PRINCE'S ENORMOUS staff had recently completed the yearly journey to the isolated palace at Skya Lake.

"I hate leaving Alsais," the cook's new girl mourned.

Cook and Jasvar the under-steward gave her tolerant glances.

"Of course you do," Cook said, drying her hands on her apron as she sank with a sigh into her chair next to the fire. "But you'll find that it's comfy here. This is our own parlor. No one else can use it. The rest of the palace staff has never been here, so we can say what we like, and no one overhears."

"Are They settled, then?" Cook asked, with a glance ceiling-ward.

Jasvar nodded, sitting backward in a chair and leaning his forearms across the chair back. There he was, bulky, sixty if a day, gray-haired, and he still had the habits of boyhood — at least, when off duty. Astounding, how invisible so large a man could be when on duty.

"They weren't happy to be back," Jasvar ventured.

This news earned shrugs and ironic looks from the downstairs staff. Everyone in Prince Shontande's staff had to work together, but those servants upstairs, specially trained by the heralds, were a close set, kept themselves to themselves, and in the considered opinions of those who kept the household running, gave themselves worse airs than any noble.

But their job was also the hardest, for downstairs only had the palace to run. The upstairs staff—generally referred to as They or Them—had it to guard. It, and Him, the crown prince, beautiful as the picture of the Old King, but seldom glimpsed by the downstairs people.

Downstairs knew they weren't permitted to speak to Him, and they suspected He wasn't supposed to speak to them either, though sometimes, on those rare occasions when there was an encounter, He did. He was so polite, so well-behaved, so *interested.* His few words were repeated often, and discussed among them as much as if they had been royal proclamations.

The stable master came in, carrying the big tray, the cook's assistant behind with everything that didn't fit. At the welcome entrance of the Sartoran steep everyone looked happy.

"Ten years it's been," Cook spoke with satisfaction. "Ten years, and wasn't it that second year that summer-steep came back?"

Jasvar said, "Sartor was freed in '34, near as I remember."

Cook thought back to her childhood, and the tiny dried leaves from Sartor that her grandmother had saved for either very special occasions, or for comfort after disasters. Was vivid memory of Grandmother's earnest look, her careful hands, the best crockery, the anticipation, part of the wonder of its sunlit aroma, its blissful taste? "There's nothing like it in the world," she said after savoring a mouthful.

"Nothing," the stable master agreed, carefully pouring out his cup. They used the same gold-edged porcelain as Upstairs, another benefit of isolation. The beautiful—exquisite—porcelain had been left from some earlier royal sequestration generations ago.

That was usually the opening for a good, comfortable gossip about things they didn't discuss in the capital, where they were merely adjuncts to the King's Household, and might be overheard. Here, they were safe from intrusive ears, and one of the great pleasures of returning was the sharing of treasured-up report, following which they might spend weeks in cheerful conjecture.

After dishing the entire royal court, out came the memories, the eldest chuckling. "I remember the turn of the year 700. Oh, the festivals! Nothing like since. But life zigs and zags, whatever they call the year."

And so thoroughly did the Skya Palace downstairs staff embrace their old routine that at the week's end, when Thad Keperi and the newcomer Curtas reached the coast of the great lake, winter had settled into the past, alive only in gossip; otherwise it seemed as if they'd never been away.

Late on a spring morning of spectacular beauty Curtas and Thad stood on the northern shore of the lake, trading off staring to the southeast through the spyglass Curtas carried in his gear.

This appeared to be a very good one; Thad had only looked through one once before. That one had flattened everything into distortion. He swept the glass along the opposite coastline, picking out fine houses amid century-old tended gardens, lawns, and ordered forest. Then, when he trained it eastward again, and focused on the pearlescent towers gleaming there atop the island in the middle of the eastern arm of the lake, it struck him that this was a very good spyglass, as good as you probably got in the military.

He didn't like to ask, but he suspected Curtas must have stolen it.

The castle—made of the palest granite—was sharp as a painting against the deep blue of the sky. Thad studied the castle with half his attention, wondering what Curtas's life had been like , raised by thieves. The eastern side of Skya Lake was completely empty, except for royal herald posts hidden from casual view. It was all crown land.

Thad handed back the glass. If you were a thief you would know how to get in and out of places forbidden to everyone else.

He turned to Curtas. "What do we do now?"

Curtas had been waiting for questions that he wasn't sure how to answer. The trip so far had been fun. Curtas hadn't had to think ahead at all. Thad came from a family accustomed to the inner byways used by scribe messengers, and all it had taken was the right word spoken at guild houses along the way, and they had food, horses, and good beds. When the weather turned nasty there were even plain clothes of various sorts, all things left behind by travelers for others to use and in turn pass on.

Now it was Curtas's turn to know the way.

"Cross over."

"I hope not a boat," Thad said. "I don't know much about this area, but I do know it's forbidden to cross the lake. They'd have to see us, and we'll be arrested, most assuredly."

"It's a tunnel that goes beneath."

Thad drew in a breath. "I've heard stories about tunnels under the castle! My oldest cousin says he read about one in an old history, when he was studying to become an archivist-scribe, up in Ymadan. I've got to do more reading! So it's real, not a story, and you found it, is that what you're saying?"

"Someone showed me," Curtas ventured. "To be exact."

Brief, vivid memory: the unremarkable hazel gaze, the quiet voice, *Here is the access way. Here is how you open it. And close it. The knowledge is now yours. It can either help you or destroy you, depending on how you use it.*

The memory faded, and there was Thad's expectant face. When Curtas said nothing more, Thad wondered if thieves had their own form of melende.

"Shall we go while the weather is holding, then?" Curtas suggested, and Thad put his hands together in assent.

It was a relief to follow orders. The next three days, so tense, so scary for Thad, were extended proof just how far outside his experience he'd strayed. The entire world seemed different as they lay side by side on a slanted roof, Thad shoved up against the edge of the pale stone of which the castle was made.

He kept silence, because it had been made clear that Curtas did not share his apprehension. Not after that first day when they camped in the tunnel so far down it was neither cold nor warm, and Curtas gave him a quick grin. "It'll be easy. You'll see. They're all so used to their routine. As long as we take care never to leave any sign, or make any noise, we'll waft right through. A picnic."

A picnic? Thad's idea of a picnic was a shared basket of food in a summer glade. But he would never think of going back.

As the crown prince methodically practiced his archery directly below them, Thad cautiously lifted his head to take in the jumble of roofs above four courtyards at different heights. The one they lay above was the highest, built above the royal rooms. Beyond the wall in the other direction lay the lake, reflecting with wind-stirred ripples the gray-streaked sky.

Slam! Below, the crown prince lowered his bow. A servant ran to pull arrows from the target at the other end of the court, and brought them back, laying them on a little table next to

Prince Shontande, who murmured a word of thanks, then picked up an arrow and fitted it to the bow. He drew his arm back in a single smooth motion, straight from elbow to fingertip. When he shot his arm snapped back, swept down to the arrows, and brought up another in a smooth circle. He never once looked down.

"He's good," Thad breathed.

Curtas turned his head sideways, his mouth long. "Promising form, though slow. But he'll never actually have to use that skill — it's entirely art here, because of the Covenant of Civility."

The cold wind took their words up over the roof and beyond. The sentries on the walls below were far out of hearing.

The first day, they spent just observing. "We'll bring food for four days, if we can," Curtas had said. "I know their schedule in the capital, but it might vary here." By the end of the second day, Curtas had declared that the variation was insignificant. Prince Shontande was more in evidence, in a way he never was in the capital. Here there was no one to see him but his household.

Pang! Another arrow. Pang! Steady, methodical, and each if not a perfect shot, certainly close enough within the four rings of the target not to be shameful — or so Thad thought, but this time he did not voice his opinion.

A tiny noise made them both freeze, Curtas's hand vanishing among his clothes and coming out with a wicked two-edged dagger. Where had he kept that?

A plump cat walked delicately along the roof edge, tail high. They pressed down flat. The animal minced up to them, sniffed each, flicked its tail, then dropped down to the court.

Thad watched the prince become aware of the animal. Until then Shontande Lirendi had appeared intimidatingly remote, flawless in dress and feature, so very much a ryal that Thad could not believe the prince would do anything but call the guards on them if they dared to make themselves known.

But at the sight of the cat his smile transformed his face, making him seem less a prince from some distant tale out of history and more like a boy of scarcely ten. As Curtas and Thad watched, Shontande chirruped to the cat.

Who sat down and began a slow, complacent grooming session.

And so it was the prince, and not the cat, who had to cross

the distance in order to make contact.

Curtas drew in a breath that Thad heard. "This is it."

Thad's mouth dried.

Curtas moved again, and the knife vanished. Curtas rolled something between thumb and forefinger as below them the golden head bowed over the purring animal, who butted up against the prince's silk covered leg.

One last check of the skyline, and then Curtas raised himself on one elbow, squinted, and with a sharp sling of his wrist tossed down the little stone.

It struck Shontande's arm. The prince stilled, and the cat, sensing something wrong, swarmed fluidly around his ankle and shot off across the court. Shontande looked up, the boys looked down, and once again Thad sustained a shock as the wind fingered through the prince's long what-colored hair, sunlight limning the contours of his perfect face. Thad had always heard that he was the most beautiful of all the Lirendis, as beautiful as the infamous Mathias the Emperor, and maybe even as beautiful as the first Lirendi king, Martande. But it wasn't Shontande's beauty that made Thad feel almost dizzy, it was the intensity of the prince's change in expression from wariness to a smile of surprise, of joy.

Shontande swung to his feet, as fluid and unconsciously graceful as the cat. His liveried servant stood at the wall side of the target, gazing out over the lake, as he had been ever since the prince had knelt to pet the cat.

Shontande chirruped again, this time louder. The servants glanced up, then away again. Two, three, no, four cats appeared from the various places they'd been roaming, trotting toward Shontande, tails high.

"I think they're hungry," Shontande called to his servant. "Perhaps the kitchen staff forgot to put their bowls out. Please fetch some fresh fish."

The liveried servant bowed and withdrew. Shontande moved a step nearer, then knelt and stroked another cat that the boys hadn't noticed.

"You must not be seen," he said, lightly, so his voice would not carry.

Thad and Curtas elbow-crawled forward the better to hear the soft-spoken words.

"The Council will have the guards killed along with anyone caught here," Shontande said. "They will insist you are a threat, and the guards negligent. This is their lives."

"I know," Curtas responded, also lightly. Thad didn't dare speak. "There's an old tunnel. We spotted the routine first."

"Very well. And thank you."

"I shall talk fast, this time." Curtas leaned forward, low-voiced. "Next time, more stories about life out there. Right now, Terry—Prince Tereneth of Erdrael Danara—wants you to know that there is a secret youth alliance against Norsunder. Thad here is a part, as well. They want you to join."

"I can do nothing. I cannot even order when we come here, or how long we stay."

No one mistook the bitterness in that quiet voice.

"Yet," Thad ventured, agonized on the prince's behalf. How unfair this imprisonment was! And it had gone on all his life. Why? Part of the unspoken, of course: The King's Madness. "Until then, everyone wants you among us."

Shontande lifted his head, and Thad's eyes met that dark blue gaze, earnest, intense, so intense it seemed as if the prince could hear his thoughts and read his anguish on the prince's behalf, his love for his country, even for the king, mad as he was: sustaining that gaze felt dizzying, almost painful—as if one stared at the sun. "Who is everybody?" Shontande asked, which broke the strange spell.

Thad rattled off names as the prince listened, his head high as if he concentrated. No hint of recognition lifted his brows— of course he didn't know anyone of them, kept prisoner as he was—but at the end he touched his fingertips together courteously. "Please tender them all my greetings and gratitude." And to Curtas, "You'll return?"

"Yes," Curtas said, and to underscore the promise, he restated the obvious: "When they've settled into a routine, they won't be as vigilant."

Shontande touched his fingertips together again, then turned his dense blue gaze Thad's way. "Your name?"

"Thad Keperi."

"I'm honored. But you must never be seen."

Thad dipped his head in acknowledgement, as close to a bow as he could manage while lying flat.

"I'll bring you more news when I can," Curtas promised.

"Then I—"

They all heard the footsteps coming up the last of the stairs on the opposite side of the court, and Curtas and Thad had barely enough time to scrunch back before the liveried servant reappeared, carrying a silver tray with two-hundred year old gold-edged porcelain dishes piled with fresh-caught fish.

Prince and servant set out the dishes for the eight or ten cats who had silently gathered. Then Shontande stood up, dusted his fingers and said, "I'm done for now, I believe." He left without a backward look, the servant following.

Thad did not speak until much later, after a sometimes terrifying descent to the tunnel. There, in the dark, he let out his breath in an exclamation, "He's not mad."

He could not see Curtas, but heard his amusement. "Never said he was."

"But we all have worried. Because why else would he be kept in a cage?"

"You didn't think his father's madness inherited, did you?"

Thad hugged his arms against himself. Though he'd met several princes by now, and followed with sickening tension the distant reports of the Everoneth battle, it wasn't until now — in this tunnel below the handsome prison sheltering Colend's crown prince — that he felt a sense of being lost in vast events he only partly understood. "But what else is there?"

"Dark magic." Curtas's voice was flat. "From Norsunder."

Four

KARHIN KEPERI WOKE SUDDENLY, filled with joy. It was odd, how sometimes she knew when certain people neared Wilderfeld. She did not believe it was Dena Yeresbeth, at least not as she understood it from talk about Liere Fer Eider, who could hear your thoughts, and who could walk in your dreams from half the world away.

Karhin occasionally heard thoughts, or at least she thought she did. It might only be her imagination, which she knew was vivid. She was more certain about this knack for knowing who was coming, because they always showed up.

Today, it was going to be Rel.

She rose, and instead of stepping through the cleaning frame, she took a bath, filled with her favorite herbs. She dressed carefully, then sat down to her accumulated correspondence, finding a letter on top from Terry.

The awkward scrawl was invisible to her by now. Terry was funny, and wry, and friendly — everyone who visited him came back talking about how much they liked him. She hoped they would meet again soon, and in the meantime, as she chose a fresh sheet of Dawn's Gleam paper in order to answer, she felt that this would be a good day.

As for Rel, he tramped the last distance, as always appreciating Colend's pretty roads that looped gracefully alongside canals and hills.

There was no reason to go to Wilderfeld, except that it had become habit after he had been traveling for a while. It wasn't in any sense a home any more than that little cottage up in the mountains. The concept of home still brought the image of people, not places — except for Sartor's capital city.

Raneseh and his daughter were childhood home — safety — and Atan's palace in Eidervaen was the anti-home, because those guarding Atan had made it clear that his stays must be infrequent, and never last longer than three days. And yet his friendship with Mendaen, Hannla, Hinder, and Atan felt more like what he understood home was to feel like, a sense of belonging. Wilderfeld was where he could catch up on alliance news over winter while he'd been in Erdrael Danara. But as familiar landmarks appeared on the river road, he recognized the tightness in his neck as apprehension.

He knew the cause. And he was conscious of regret. No blame to CJ if she'd told everyone in the alliance about his successful search last summer. He hadn't thought to ask her not to, and he knew those Mearsiean girls shared everything with each other, and with the world, whether the world was interested or not.

It was all reasonable, but by the time Wilderfeld lay beyond the next bend, the necessity to think of various explanations in hopes of warding questions he did not want to answer had succeeded in putting him in a mood he could not shake.

When he saw the little town nestled between placid waters and forested hills, he experienced a sudden, intense desire to turn around and leave.

No. It was better to get the worst over. Otherwise he'd keep brooding about it, and there were few things more boring than endless questions in his head.

When he saw the familiar low, rambling scribe house on the pleasant village square, he crossed the square, ducked under the low awning into the shadows still holding winter's chill. Inside, he heard the lilt of polite Colendi voices. The soft lighting, placed so there would be no shadows, was pleasant on his eyes.

One of the young duty scribe students smiled in immediate recognition and opened his hand toward the stairs.

His heart hammered his ribs. At the top appeared a wand-slim girl with a cloud of red hair and wide blue eyes. Karhin

Keperi was usually the one to greet visitors.

She saw at a glance that he had still not released the Child Spell, and was astonished at the intense flare of resentment against the unknown Atan of Sartor.

Determinedly Karhin squashed that unworthy reaction. "Be welcome! I hope and trust you do not carry anxious news?" Her gaze was searching—quickly shuttered—but there was in that glimpse no bright gaze of knowledge, of question.

Was it possible she didn't know?

"It was a very quiet winter," he said, consciously avoiding using the word *no*.

"Ah-ye. And we too have had a quiet winter." Her smile was faint, even tremulous, but it was not the smile of secret knowledge.

She didn't know.

She saw in him the subtle signs of released tension in his splendid shoulders. Perhaps he was bracing for bad news from her! Or . . .did he somehow intuit her unworthy emotions?

She was so dismayed at the idea that she extended her hand toward Thad's room, and whispered something about refreshments before she fled.

Rel didn't notice. He was immediately confronted by Karhin's and Thad's noisy, bouncing half-sister Lisbet. Brown braids flapping, she gestured for Rel to come in and take the nicest mat on the floor, while bombarding him with questions. "Rel! Were you in Everon? Did you see Princess Tahra? Did you meet any other royalty or famous people?"

None of her questions were about searches or fathers. Rel's smile was real as he said, "I spent most of the winter with old friends."

"Lisbet," Thad said. "Shall we permit Rel to take a seat?"

Lisbet sighed as she clapped her hands in the peace.

Rel greeted Thad, then noticed Adam in the corner, using the slanting late morning light to sketch by. "Adam! Still here?"

"He was gone, but then came back," Lisbet said.

"I've been studying vitrine art." Adam scratched his head under his light brown mass of hair, which looked curlier and more unkempt than ever. Rel could see at least four different paint splotches clotting in it. "But I don't know . . ."

"He can't get shades," Lisbet said briskly, flopping down in the center of the room. "I *told* him. I tried prenticing to three different glass makers, so I warned him."

"A person sometimes has to see for himself," Adam said equably. "And I did finish a window."

"Which broke, alas," Thad spoke up from where he sat on his bed, a lexicon at hand as he worked on a translation assignment. "So we did not get to see it."

Rel moved his mat closer to the wall, having learned that this was a politeness in Colend. The middle was left for those so important in rank that everything must flow around them.

Karhin did not reappear. Instead, the duty page brought up a tray of food, and they amicably passed around tiny sandwiches and minute bites of fresh fruit cut up so that one could eat noiselessly. The conversation was general, Lisbet putting herself in the center of talk. Apparently she had changed her prenticeship yet again, having become bored with the latest.

As Rel ate, he listened to the quality of their voices — the lilt of Colendi, patient and friendly, even in Lisbet, though she spoke with a quick energy that reminded him of CJ when she was determined. But CJ never worked to make herself the center of talk. The Mearsieans formed around her with her as their center, a different thing. And she didn't crave attention as Lisbet did. Whatever else you could say about CJ, she did not want to be regarded as the center of interest. There was always a goal, toward which she tried to draw everyone around her in her enthusiasm.

He was lost in a reflection on motivations (from Lisbet to Mondros) when Thad's head came up sharply. "Little Bee is in the square." He turned Lisbet's way. "It is your turn."

Lisbet cast a dramatic sigh as she rose. Clearly nothing of interest was going to happen that she might be left out of, so she neatly stacked her dishes on the tray and scampered noiselessly out.

Thad shut the door, and turned to Rel. "You wanted to know what communication there is, but I haven't much to report. King Tereneth — Terry — of Erdrael Danara writes regularly to Karhin, but she says it's mostly local news, and I gather you would have heard it?"

Rel assented. He'd spent a good part of winter with Terry, working with the mountain guard as he researched possible ships going up the north side of Drael, which was new territory to him.

Thad went on, "Princess Hatahra of Everon also writes to Karhin regularly, but that is mostly, ah, concerns over how to pay for her brother's plan to build his army, as Everon is still recovering from the devastation of the Norsunder attack. We have not heard from Hibern at all."

"What about the Mearsieans?" Rel asked, holding his breath.

"Nothing since they returned. King Leander writes to Arthur of Bereth Ferian about mage studies, and his sister writes a great deal, but that is entirely local news."

Thad considered mentioning that Curtas had twice sneaked through to talk to Prince Shontande, but decided not to unless Rel asked. Neither he nor Karhin liked talking about the royal family to outsiders—specifically their beautiful, mad king.

Thad glanced out the window, a gesture Rel understood. Aware that Lisbet would return as soon as she could, Rel gave a quick report, shortened when he saw that the news about Jilo and the mage Dejain had already reached them. And then, because he could not resist a last test, "Since I was in Chwahirsland, I visited the mage Mondros, who oversees the land-ease spells over Chwahirsland. And watches over Jilo from a distance."

Thad exhibited no reaction to the name Mondros. "The scribes heard a distressing rumor that the Chwahir king had let the quake-easing spells lapse, except where he lives. Lived. I trust this mage knows that?"

"Indeed," Rel said. "And I understand has addressed the problem."

Then it was true. For whatever reason, CJ had kept her discovery to herself. "There is another thing. Mondros is one of Tsauderei's many allies, and passed on to me a message from Tsauderei. It seems they want someone to travel to the Land of the Venn . . ."

As soon as he said 'Venn' he not only had Thad's but Adam's attention.

Downstairs, Karhin stumbled half-blindly into the hallway, shying back when she heard the low murmur of voices in the shop. She hovered uncertainly, then her eye was caught by Nalisse, the courier who had arrived that morning.

Nalisse, a sturdy girl recently bathed and changed out of her travel clothes, had been looking for Karin or Thad, old friends since her days as an apprentice courier tagging along behind an adult.

Nalisse was on her second circuit between Eth Endra, where she'd been born, and Colend, as a lone courier. Conscientious about time, ordinarily she would have left after the customary meal, but she had hurried the last two stops so she could linger a little in Wilderfeld with her friends. When she saw Karhin's unhappy face, she set down her plate on a shelf and crossed the space between them in three steps.

"Karhin?"

In silence Karhin drew Nalisse to the formal salon used by her mothers. It was nearly always empty on work days. Her eyes burned with tears. Stupid tears. She walked to the wall and leaned her forehead against the carving of larks and laurels in one of the goldenwood lesenes, breathing in the faint, lingering aroma of honeysuckle and the rustle of silk favored by her stepmother.

Nalisse asked soberly, "What is amiss?"

"Rel," Karhin said. "He's back. And . . ."

Nalisse was the only one Karhin had told about her growing feelings for Rel. Though she knew her family would sympathize, somehow the idea of sympathy was unbearable.

Nalisse sighed. "My dad would say, 'Invite him to the crane chamber.' He's old enough, isn't he?" Nalisse had not yet met Rel, though she'd heard plenty about him.

"He is, but he isn't," Karhin said, thumbing a tear away.

Nalisse's brow furrowed. "Oh, did you not say he did that Child Spell?"

"Yes. But he is very close to the dance of the cranes, as close as you can be. You'd know it if you saw him. And yet he looks at me, talks to me, as if I were thirteen."

Nalisse said tentatively, "You appear younger than you are." And on Karhin's gesture of regret, for she was still young enough to resent instead of appreciate that, Nalisse went on in a tentative tone, "They always tell us that the first fancy is the worst."

"It is more than mere fancy," Karhin stated, her chin lifting. "My heart has wakened to love."

Nalisse was a year younger than Karhin, and so she accepted this statement as knowledge from someone older and more experienced.

Karhin went on in a low, passionate voice, "The worst of it is, I know who he thinks about. Not that he has ever said. It's the way he asks about news, listening without breath at mention of the Queen of Sartor. The way his voice drops when he says her name."

Nalisse tipped her head, one hand signing regret.

"It's all so useless," Karhin whispered. "*She*'ll one day marry a prince, and he will never be more than a traveler. He deserves more than to be a mere royal favorite, he deserves . . ."

"Someone like you," Nalisse said sincerely.

"Oh, what is the use of such talk? I meant to enjoy it, because my mothers will say that it is only my first fancy, it won't endure, I'm too young, I ought to think of the emotion as practice even if we never so much as kiss. But it cannot be mere fancy. It hurts so much."

Nalisse put her palms together. "My grandmother keeps saying that our heads can listen to wisdom, but hearts have no ears."

A sob welled up inside Karhin. She suppressed it. "The worst is, I have come to hate Atan of Sartor. She could have anyone else, but there she sits on her mighty throne, too lofty to perceive his steadfastness . . ."

Nalisse had been to Sartor, and had glimpsed the young queen once, at a distance. Atan was a tall girl, build like a draft horse, with plank brown hair that she could certainly afford the magic to color to a more interesting shade, and a kindly smile beneath those famous Landis gooseberry eyes. Though judging someone at a distance was untrustworthy, that queen — who it was said everywhere liked the simplicity of Atan rather than the full weight of Queen Yustnesveas V — did not at all appear the lofty type, much less someone who would be mowing down lovers like summer grass.

Nalisse stared at Karhin, trying to smother her appalled reaction, but unsuccessfully enough that Karhin said quickly, "Oh, I know none of that is true. But I cannot help thinking it all the same."

Nalisse said in a low voice, "Is your melende requiring harmony? Perhaps a visit to the healer, for some time in the chamber of blossoms?"

Karhin's head bent as her palms came together. "Melende" was not just personal harmony, or honor. There was also an obligation to do one's part in achieving familial and social harmony. She was nearly seventeen, too old to be sent to the healer to comb out tangled emotions. She ought to be regulating herself better.

"Sometimes," Nalisse said with the conviction of experience, "it is good to let oneself be ministered to. But if you prefer to restore your spirits in private, may I suggest a touch of orange blossom tincture to elbows and forehead as you reread Etais on King Martande and the Riverside Egrets?"

Karhin bowed, palms together in the peace, and departed, thinking aggrievedly that it was all very well for the handsome and brilliant first king of Colend to find beauty in the mating dance of egrets, when he could have anyone he wanted. But she knew her friend was right.

The conversation about Land of the Venn was pretty much universal agreement about how little anyone knew about them, other than gruesome tales out of history. Rel finally said, "No one seems to have advice on how best to get there, only dire warnings, so my instinct is to stick with the sea."

That was cut short by the reappearance of Lisbet with Little Bee. The latter became the subject of talk, as they shared the midday meal and asked what Little Bee had been learning.

Lisbet writhed with impatience, bored with her little brother being the center of attention. She wanted to know why Rel was really here, if he was on a secret mission, if he had been visiting any important people. She was too well trained to interrupt, but she was glad at that at least Adam had wandered off, so there were only the two left to blabber on and on about Little Bee's day.

When the duty page reappeared to carry down the tray of dirty dishes, Lisbet popped to her feet, ready to get rid of Little Bee. The faster she got him back to his tutor, the quicker she could return and catch something interesting going on.

As soon as she was out the door, Adam appeared scrubbed clean, his hair even clipped, so that it rose in short curls all over his head.

He blinked and looked around as if he'd lost something, then startled everyone when he said vaguely, "I really would like to see the Land of the Venn." He hefted his pack, in which his paints and brushes and pencils rattled lightly, and they all knew the context of the word *see*. "Rel, do you want company on this journey of yours?"

Rel had found Adam easy to travel with, able to walk

without tiring, happy with silence when there was nothing to say, and not the least choosy about sleeping in barns or out in the open when necessary. And the way he looked at the world, primarily through color, was so different from anything Rel had experienced that though they'd walked for days through some of the dullest terrain in the south, he had never been bored. "How are you with ship travel?"

"Ships? You won't go up the western side of Drael?"

"From what I've gleaned, there's no getting over the Venn border from the land side. If the weather doesn't get you, the terrain will. That's if their roving guards miss you. Better chance if we come in by sea."

"I like ships," Adam said equably, reflecting that he was ready for a blue month. He favored shades of green—such an infinitude—and brown was almost as enthralling—but it was perhaps just as well that he be required to bestir himself. He must not fall into the obliviousness of habit.

"Have you traveled on the water?" Thad asked enviously.

Adam waved a hand. "Oh, yes. I didn't get sick." He smiled with mild triumph and pointed to his travel-worn pack. "I'm ready anytime you are." And he observed the mild green light around Rel.

Spoken like a traveler, Rel thought, glad to have the company. "Come along, then."

Rel got to his feet, made the peace to Thad, and said, "If we're going to sail, we'll want to reach the western end of Drael before the winds shift. We might as well leave now. Thad, please give the rest of your family my thanks and farewells."

Thad agreed, Rel hefted his pack, and the two slipped down the back stairs, and away.

A short time later, Karhin appeared, finding her spirits much refreshed after reading the long, rhythmic verses. She was relieved to find her brother alone, and exhorted herself to remember King Martande's words, that civilized people can learn from the egrets, where passion meets grace.

Thad looked up. "You were gone a long time."

"I was with Nalisse," Karhin said evasively. "Where is Adam? And Rel?"

"They left. For Land of the Venn. Adam decided to go with him. I wondered why he'd tidied up his things this morning. He must have been restless again."

"He's been traveling so much!"

"Ah-ye, so he has. And yet he was eager to go off with Rel."

"To the Land of the Venn?" Karhin exclaimed, groping for understanding. "Are the Venn not proscribed? Why would anyone go all the way to the very north of the world, just to be turned away again?"

Thad spread his hands. "Rel has a task, and you know Adam. A new place and people to draw."

Karhin drew a cautious breath, the lingering scent of orange blossom and distilled listerberry soothing. Yes, it was better that Rel was gone. She looked down at her brother, and said, "Then we shall have Adam's new drawings to look forward to."

Five

Sarendan

A STING THROBBED IN the cuticle of Liere's thumb. She yanked her fingers away from her mouth and stared in disgust at the thin welling of blood along the bed of her nail.

She rubbed her fingers against her clothes and looked around furtively, but she could have been screaming and bouncing around and no one would have noticed as the last of the slow parade made its way up Miraleste's royal road toward the newly-renovated palace.

Among those leading the parade walked stocky, fox-faced Lilah Selenna, her hands clutching a pole with a banner on it as she lifted her tear-blotched face ardently and sang with the rest of the crowd. At her side walked her closest friends, who also had done the Child Spell, looking like four twelve-year-olds.

Liere rejoiced to see them looking like children, as she did. She felt *safe* in the Child Spell, though she knew it really did not stop aging, but it stopped whatever it was that lengthened bodies into adult shape, which in turn caused emotions like the sharp, hidden sorrow when Peitar Selenna, Lilah's brother and king of Sarendan, thought about Atan of Sartor or talked about Derek Diamagan.

Liere understood Peitar's grief about Derek, who had been

a beloved hero to the entire kingdom of Sarendan, as well as Peitar's lifelong best friend in spite of the differences in their birth. The two had nearly been executed by the old king, in the revolution that almost failed. She found more unsettling, painful, and incomprehensible the idea of opening whatever door it was that caused people to "fall in love" and hurt the more because the other person did not fall in love back. Staying in child form could at least save one from *that*.

> . . .*Diamagan's honor is sung from the borders*
> *To Miraleste palace, by king and all commons,*
> *Because of his courage in leading the people.*

> *In daring to face the evil Si-YAH-mis*
> *He gave his heart's blood in saving the kingdom.*
> *So honor and fame grows ever stronger*
> *Wreathing the name of Derek Diamagan . . .*

As those at the front crossed under the gate to the palace, the long line dissolved into a crowd that packed into the parade court, voices rising toward the last verses of the poignant hero's ballad with its internal triplet chords, harking back to Ancient Sartor.

Liere gritted her teeth against the onslaught of emotion from all those people.

The song came to an end, and Peitar, standing within arm's distance away from Liere on the balcony overlooking the parade ground and the street beyond the gate, lifted his arms.

"I brought back Heroes' Day to honor Derek Diamagan, my friend and my brother in heart, Commander of Sarendan's Defense and hero to the last. But now, I invite you all to go out and celebrate all your heroes, ancestral and those who fell during our own strife, and that which Norsunder brought upon us. All inns and eateries are to feed any who come: tonight. The crown pays."

A huge roar rose, and with an alacrity prompted perhaps as much by good appetite as by good will, the crowd began to disperse.

Liere said as Lilah joined them, "Brought back Heroes' Day?"

Lilah wiped her eyes on her sleeve, sniffed, and grinned fiercely. "Oh, yes. It is an old festival. Ancient. But when my uncle's family, the Irads, took over the throne, they stopped it — they didn't like anyone celebrating anybody but them."

Peitar gave her a rueful smile. "Lilah, that's not quite how it went. The festival had become an excuse for the nobles to complain about the crown at crown expense, but when our great-grandfather tried to get the nobles to pay their share of the festival, they refused, and the tradition lapsed."

Lilah shrugged sharply, her slanty brows even more aslant. "The Irads were a bunch of clotpoles," she stated. "And my uncle Darian the worst of them. Except maybe for his grandfather. Come on, everybody, let's go inside and celebrate Derek." She looked around. "Is this all? I thought the Mearsieans were coming."

Peitar said, "Some are already inside. The Mearsieans, alas, are not among them."

Lilah had written to invite CJ, but had made the well-meant mistake of adding that Rel wouldn't be there—no one had heard from him in months. CJ had written back (with vigorous underlining) to say she would have liked to see Rel, and it was a shame she couldn't come. Of course the rest of the Mearsean girls stayed away as well.

"The alliance is falling apart, "Lilah said morosely to Liere as they followed Peitar inside the palace. She looked around in pride at the newly-refurbished gold marble floor and the black marble insets in the walls, framed by arabesques in plaster, painted green with bunches of stylized crimson blossoms. In the early days after the revolution, she had helped with the painting herself. She'd wanted to show the finished chambers to the Mearsean girls, whose adventures she admired.

Then she spied Atan's tall form on the other side of the room, where she sat on pillows around a low table, with Arthur and that jug-eared mage student from Geth-deles, Roy. Talking magic studies, no doubt.

"Atan," Lilah exclaimed happily, freckled arms outflung as she rushed to greet them all. "You missed the parade for Derek, but I'm so glad you are here!"

Liere, following more slowly, was glad once again that no one but her could hear the thoughts that the others forgot to shield as Atan said, "I would've loved to see the parade, but you know how difficult it is for me to get away. I cannot stay long as it is."

It was all true, but Liere sensed the intense dislike of Derek

Diamagan that Atan sought to hide.

Peitar's dark eyes narrowed in question as he moved to join the group. Once again, Liere wondered if he might have some kind of awareness, if not Dena Yeresbeth. He was not shielding his thoughts, but he didn't send them like a mental shout, the way everyone else did when they forgot about shields.

Liere struggled hard enough to shut out the mental realm. Reaching past someone's instinctive barrier was wrong, except in self-defense. And she did not have to defend herself now.

Peitar barely limped as he joined the group, and sat on a pillow next to his sister.

"You haven't missed the *important* part," Lilah said earnestly. "We can go round the circle and share our best memories of Derek. If you want to begin, Atan, please do."

Liere held her breath, but Atan smiled back at Lilah, who scrubbed her eyes impatiently on her dusty sleeve.

"I'd be glad to," Atan said, in what Liere thought of as her Queen of Sartor voice. "I admired the way Derek took those orphans left from the civil war and gave them all purpose."

Derek's Sarendan friends exclaimed in agreement then stirred, each wanting to talk first.

Liere's knuckles twinged, and she discovered she had been crimping her hands tightly. She forced herself to relax them as Lilah and her three friends vented overflowing emotions in rambling, heartfelt streams of memory.

Liere had learned early, when listening to her younger sister, that people did not always remember how things actually happened. They sometimes mixed emotions with actual details, or memory would mix up what had happened and what they wished had happened, or what they thought had happened.

She'd learned early to regard other people's memories like stories, except that her own memories were always relentlessly clear, sometimes excruciatingly so. She'd discovered that around the time she became aware that she was different from others, because nobody else heard thoughts, or other people's dreams.

And so she listened in silence as people talked about Derek Diamagan, their sincerity blurring the details — the ones that never had happened, but perhaps ought to have happened — that replaced what Liere had actually seen that horrible summer.

Peitar was last, saying in a husky voice that resonated with emotion, "When you sit through the night with someone before what you believe will be your execution, everything changes. Aside from Lilah, Derek was the one I trusted most."

Atan crossed her arms, head bent. Arthur's eyelids flickered. Peitar, usually so sensitive, gazed unseeing beyond them — beyond the walls — into the past as his voice lowered to a whisper. "His entire life was dedicated to Sarendan and its people. We had our disagreements, but even then I always knew he wanted the best for Sarendan. He was the brother I should have had, *we* should have had." He smiled at Lilah, who smiled tearily back. "I don't believe we will ever recover from his loss."

He lifted his head. "But life does go on. He would be the first to insist. We shouldn't let the food go cold. That would be ungrateful, when I know the kitchen has been preparing a special meal."

"Including Derek's favorites," Lilah said, jumping up to lead the way.

Arthur and Roy joined Liere at the far end of the long table. "When this is over, are you coming back to the school with me?" Arthur said to Liere.

Roy glanced up, awaiting her answer. He had come to Bereth Ferian prepared for anything from the much-talked-about Liere Fer Eider but what he'd found.

Whereas Liere had been dreading that question. "Are you truly sure it wasn't Siamis trespassing in Bereth Ferian?" she asked.

"Erai-Yanya could have told you that there's been no sign of Siamis's presence." Arthur was so rarely sarcastic that it looked strange on his round, pleasant face. "And further, the *entire school* has made it their first priority to create a webwork of wards and tracers."

Liere flushed, and because no one else was paying attention to them, she said, "Arthur, the truth is, I hate magic lessons. I don't mean there's anything wrong with the teachers, or what they teach. It's just that I'm so *stupid*."

Her voice had risen. She saw Lilah staring wide-eyed, and sensed Arthur's hurt as he muttered, "You're not stupid. You know that."

Liere struggled with the familiar gnaw of self-hatred. "I like learning the *history* of magic. In the basics class, I loved the stories about how an angel first came to women by the river, as givers and keepers of life. It makes so much *sense*, how the form and intent of magic came about — but as for its practice, I just can't get the simplest spells right." Her thumbnail worried at a ragged cuticle, then she snapped her fingers down to her lap as if she'd been slapped.

Roy said in his accented voice, "It is the purpose for basics to take it slow, is it not? It is so with our study on my world, which, I know, it approaches magic differently."

Liere couldn't stop herself. "The teachers go slow as ice. With me. But nothing helps the fact that I am really *stupid*. Maybe it's my being merely a shopkeeper's daughter, though when I said that to Senrid he got angry with me. Being born in towns, or castles, or tree houses, has nothing to do with how we learn, all they might limit is access, that's what he said. But try as I might, magic *never* works right for me. I mean the simplest basics, the ones the first year students get to learn. No matter how hard I try. They . . . fail. All I can manage is illusions."

"Then surely," Roy said, "the fault lies with the teacher?"

Arthur thumbed his temples. "We've talked endlessly about it," he admitted. "The head mages, Erai-Yanya. Oalthor-eh. Tsauderei, even." He made a helpless gesture. "No student has a perfect a memory like Liere's. No one's as diligent. But no one is as consistently bad at managing basic spells. We don't understand it."

Atan listened with sympathy, but inwardly measured the inexorable slipping away of time. Officially she was in a conference back in Sartor. Sarendan's restoring a festival day had nothing to do with Sartor, and her high council, so often fractious, especially these days as they argued endlessly about ways to get the Music Festival back to Sartor, would have united in saying she would do nothing to heighten Sartor's prestige by attending.

But she had two purposes here. The first had been met on her appearance. Peitar and Lilah were personal friends. She knew how important this day was to both, and their invitation had been a personal one, from friends to friends, not to the Queen of Sartor.

Her second . . .

She was distracted by Lilah leaning out, her voice rising, her tilted eyes wide as she faced down the table. "Well, isn't it?" she asked. "When Derek was alive, the alliance was really strong. That's why we all went to Geth-deles. But ever since we got back, it's like nobody cares anymore. Bren here thinks it's because the ones who think the Child Spell is stupid are turning against us."

Her thumb indicated the bony boy with the shaggy hair sitting beside her, his posture tight with incipient hostility, and then herself.

Atan said, "Speaking as one who would rather release the Child Spell, but hasn't yet, I don't believe there is any division between those releasing it and those not releasing it so much as other causes entirely."

Liere looked relieved at the change of subject. "I know that Senrid tries to write to everybody now. He writes to Leander every morning over breakfast, he says, and Hibern, a lot, too, when he has time to study magic. But he doesn't always have the rest of the day free." She turned her earnest face, dominated by those enormous eyes that looked golden in certain kinds of light, toward Atan. "Is it not the same for you?"

Atan smiled at this unexpected, graceful out. "Indeed. In fact, I'll have to transfer back very soon, if my absence isn't to be discovered. I think the problem might be busy lives in places so distant from one another, and a lack of . . ." She glanced at the row of ardent young faces who had come together to celebrate Derek Diamagan—the young leader who had despised Atan simply because of her birth. She bit back the word "hierarchy," and tentatively offered, "leadership."

In the small silence that met these words, Arthur suspected he was not the only one thinking of Prince Glenn of Everon, who wanted nothing more than to assume command of the alliance. On his terms.

But clearly no one wanted to say it.

Into that silence, Roy said pleasantly. "I apologize if my being from Geth makes me out a nose-poke, but I have myself a friend, a fellow mage student. He is like me from Geth, very good at organizing. Think you he might be useful here? David is interested in your world."

"Duh-FEED?" One of Lilah's friends asked, making a face. "Is that a name or a thing?"

"It is a common name, on Geth," Roy said. "I am told, you even have it here, but said differently."

"I've heard something like it in Marloven Hess," Liere said. "They have a lot of names that end in *id* and *ed*. DAY-vid, DAY-ved, something like it."

"Daved and David are familiar names at the west end of the

continent, too. It's Dau-vith in Colend, and parts of Sartor," Atan said, because she had been raised by a mage with a fierce love of knowledge. And because she was Queen of Sartor, nobody ever said — out loud — that she was a tad pedantic.

The row of faces smiled, though nobody cared two breaths about the linguistic footprint of the name David.

Atan said with determined politeness to Roy, "Any friend of yours is welcome, especially a mage student." She didn't want to say that bringing in some stranger was not going to organize them, but from the total lack of interest expressed by the others, she suspected they were all thinking the same thing.

Peitar sensed Atan's distraction, and disappointment was so sharp he held his breath. The younger ones maligned his uncle as an evil and wicked king, and while it was true that Uncle Darian had made terrible mistakes, Peitar was coming to understand how slippery such concepts of power, control, and order could be. Like now. He was a king, he had dedicated and loyal guards within shouting distance, but the person his heart had chosen was on the verge of transporting back to her home.

And there was nothing — *nothing* — he could do to change that.

He tried desperately for a subject that would keep Atan a few moments longer, though he knew before he spoke that it was a waste of time, that he was a fool. But he tried anyway. "Tsauderei told me that Venerable Mage Ynizang has written another book. I've been reading it — "

"There they go," Lilah whispered. "It's going to be history of magic, politics, kings, and boredom. Let's take the pie and go tell Derek-stories."

Her local friends bobbed up instantly, the skinny girl who looked like she didn't eat much more than a butterfly grabbing not only the berry-pie, but a tray of custards as well.

Liere watched them go, thinking sadly that they were like a family. The word turned around and around in her mind. Family. Family, your own family. One you're not thrown into, but one you make . . .

Atan was instantly distracted. No one at home talked history and magic with her — either they agreed with everything she said, because she was the queen, or they told her what to think, if they were counselors. Half the court looked glassy-eyed if she mentioned Venerable Mage Ynizang, who had been elderly before Sartor was removed for a century behind enchantment.

Many Sartorans now did not like the conclusions she was drawing between Sartor and the rest of the world . . ."Did you read what Venerable Mage Ynizang says about empires?"

Peitar said, "'When rulers make empires, they are mirroring the predator animals who take other animals' territories at the cost of blood. When those ruled seek to join territories, we may use the term *civilization* without irony.'"

"You saw that!" Atan exclaimed. "Tsauderei says . . .'

Her excitement sharpened Peitar's exquisite pain. Useless to admonish himself that crushes always burned out if not returned, that it was too early to assume this was a lifelong passion, that he didn't understand what love even was. Useless also to insist that Atan's cleaving to the Child Spell widened the distance between them. She wasn't a child though she was no nearer the threshold of physical womanhood. But her eyes, her speech, were not those of a child. Ageing wasn't halted, just. . . altered.

No one would ever call Atan beautiful. She was tall, sturdily built—one day she would be square. Those distinctive Landis eyes were anywhere else called goggle, gooseberry, frog, with the droopy under-lid. Her chin was masterful—would have been handsome on a fellow—her brows thick and straight in her bony face. To Peitar she was beautiful. He cherished the strong line of her jaw, the sweet curve of her ears, every subtle quirk of humor in her high, intelligent brow. The entrancing shape of her lips.

She leaned forward, elbows on the table, her expensive gown crushed unheeding as she tumbled headlong into speech, quoting the wily old mage whose words Peitar knew well.

At the far end, Arthur whispered to Liere and Roy, "Shall we follow Lilah and Bren?"

Liere said, "I think they want to reminisce about Derek. I saw him so very little."

Arthur let out a breath of relief. And with the ease of association—for he and Peitar had been meeting at Tsauderei's mountain cottage for magic tutoring for a couple of years now—"Then why don't we just go?"

Roy, who had not missed the lack of interest in his proffered candidate for leadership, was very ready to shift away from his blunder.

David was coming anyway.

Arthur said to Liere, "Are you returning to Bereth Ferian?"

"I will after two promised visits," she said evasively.

Arthur handed her the transfer token he had made for her. "For when you do." He nodded to Roy, and they went to the nearby Destination chamber and transferred to Bereth Ferian.

Alone in the hallway, Liere let out her breath in relief. She'd felt the disappointment—the sense of failure—that Arthur tried to hide. He was like his mother, Erai-Yanya, an instinctive tutor, and when the student didn't learn, they felt at fault. She pocketed Arthur's token and fingered the token Senrid had given her, then whispered the words as she braced herself for the wrench of transfer.

As soon as she saw they were alone, Atan did her best to hide her own breath of relief. "I do want to talk about this," she interrupted herself. "Oh, indeed I do, and I trust we'll be able to meet at Tsauderei's, when you can get free as well as I. But not here, anymore, which is why I hoped to speak to you alone."

Peitar's nerves chilled. "What's this?"

Atan flushed. "It makes me ill to admit it. I wasn't going to tell you, but I feel I owe you the truth. I came late not because of—well, yes, I did sneak away. I know I ought to stand up to them, and I have been. But not about this, because it would have given them fuel for . . ."

She looked away, jutted out her jaw, and then said, "I'm tired of seeming a child—I feel out of balance. But I'm going to stick it out until I get my throne, in the real sense. They want me to reach the age of maturity so they can begin negotiating marriages," she said quickly, breathlessly, almost running the words together. "My friendship. With you. Now is gaining approval because they think if they can match us, Sarendan will become a satellite to Sartor, and solve all our trade and treasury problems. Because the truth is, in spite of our illustrious traditions—some even say because of them—Sartor is backward, and still struggling to catch up. The outer evidence is in how easily Colend has managed to keep hold of the *Sartoran* Music Festival, which had taken place in Eidervaen for *centuries*. But empire-building, even through peaceful means, is not the way to solve our problems. And that's why they really hate Venerable Mage Ynizang, because she says that empires lead to wars."

The sheen in her eyes made Peitar feel even more helpless.

But what could he say? "Thank you for telling me."

"So official visits are off." She blinked rapidly, and the tears did not fall. She lifted her chin. "But we won't stop visiting in secret. At Tsauderei's. Be sure to tell Lilah," she added, hammering the last nail in Peitar's hopes. "Because I know she'll want to be there, too, and I'd miss her horribly if I couldn't see her! Hinder says the same."

Six

Marloven Hess

LIERE FOUND HERSELF ALONE in Senrid's study, and plopped down on the rug to recover.

Chill air enveloped her, the sky outside the four tall windows the intense blue of dawn. Liere breathed in the pungent smells of horse, dust, and grass as she got to her feet and walked to the window.

The academy swarmed with activity. Alarm spiked through her, then she huffed her breath out sharply. She shouldn't be afraid of these Marlovens, it was stupid and babyish. Nobody was waving swords or attacking anyone.

She leaned her hands on the windowsill—Senrid left his windows open for most of the year, as he couldn't abide stuffy rooms—and peered out. Was that him? There were so many yellow heads. But nobody else wore a white shirt without a tunic jacket over it in that academy. Liere found it so odd that Senrid wouldn't let himself wear a uniform he didn't feel he was entitled to, but he dressed in the next thing to it.

Despite the chaos around him, Senrid looked up sharply, and then beckoned to Liere to come down and join him.

By the time she had run down that long hall, descended three flights of stairs, and dashed under the mossy tunnel below the massive palace wall, the milling swarm of horses and boys had resolved into columns marked off at intervals by boys bearing beat-up pennons on poles.

She hesitated beyond an archway, hating to emerge with all those eyes facing forward, though she knew nothing would happen to her. From the back came unintelligible shouts, the final shout from the boy carrying the black and gold screaming eagle flag at the front.

Then the boy on the horse next to the flag bearer turned Senrid's way and saluted, fist thumping his chest. "All ready."

"Ride out," Senrid said, and saluted back, fist to chest.

The boy commander turned his head. "Ride out!" he bawled, and somewhere along the line trumpeters blew quick notes, almost overwhelmed by the sudden thunder of horse hooves in motion.

Dust spiraled up in the mild early morning breeze, and Liere backed up, pulling her age-softened shirt up over her nose. As Senrid joined her, she said, "I thought they do that in summer."

"The senior houses earned this outing. They're going to take on the city guard out on the plains."

Liere hid a grimace. Strange, how very differently people thought about the word 'earn.' She would have thought it a punishment. But Senrid would probably say next that he wanted to go.

Sure enough. "*How* I wish I was riding with them." He sighed the words.

Though Liere could not comprehend how anyone would want to spend days living outside in all weathers, playing at fighting all day, she still found it sort of comforting, knowing what Senrid would say. It meant everything was as it should be — no surprises. She loathed surprises. They were always bad.

"How was the memorial?" he asked as he led the way into the gloom of the tunnel beneath the wall, Liere trotting to keep up with his quick step.

"They're restoring a festival day, though Derek Diamagan was honored most," Liere said. "There was a parade all around the city, guards and artisans and lake fishers mixed with court people. They carried things belonging to heroes. After it, in the palace, they talked about Derek, but nobody else."

Senrid snapped his palm away, then closed it into a fist. "I wish Siamis was here right now so I could put a bolt through his heart."

Liere remembered that Senrid had been there when Siamis shot Derek dead. Heart-sick, she said, "Lilah cried so hard. That was one reason why I had to leave. The emotions, it was . . ." She didn't want to say horrible, because it seemed disrespectful somehow.

Senrid grimaced her way. "Couldn't shut 'em out?"

She gave her head a shake.

Though Senrid was better than most as shielding his thoughts, she still felt the unspoken question, *Then why did you go?* And far, far down underneath, where only memory images lived with emotions, a flash so clear that it may as well have been her own memory: looking up at the towering adults, their faces ruddy from the light of two tall torches either side of a great bier. On it lay Senrid's father, and why was he so still, why did he not hear, and get up, and smile? *Papa, Papa . . .*

But that desolate cry was not her voice. She shut Senrid's inadvertent memory away quickly so that no echo of it might reach him. As they ran upstairs, she steadied herself with reality. Senrid had been small when his father was murdered. Liere's own father was alive, but she never had to see him again, ever, ever, ever.

Something must have alerted Senrid, for she sensed a sharp look, and she said quickly, "Lilah doesn't want to be Peitar's heir. She was telling me before the parade started. She's trying to talk him into trying the Birth Spell to get an heir, especially as it might stop their aunt from pushing marriage partners at him."

Senrid shrugged sharply.

"And I thought, well, *I* could be old enough to do the Birth Spell, I think. Barely, but still, and wouldn't it be wonderful to have a daughter of my very own? She and I would have so much to share!"

Senrid waited until they had passed his armsmen at their posts, and the occasion runner, before speaking. Once the door to his study was shut, he said, "I don't know anything about that. But I do know this, after the way my own life has been: Don't expect any brat to be what you want. It's going to be what it wants to be."

She said firmly, "I *know* that. Any daughter of mine will have *perfect* freedom. Not like it was for us Fer Eiders when we were little."

"You're so sure you'd have a daughter?"

Liere shrugged. "I can't imagine anything else." Her inner view was of a quiet pale-haired child who would love doing whatever Liere was doing.

"If you really do anything that crazy, I hope you have twin boys. Triplets!" Senrid laughed. "Come on, let's try to figure out why the basics won't work for you."

Liere groaned. "I already went through that with Hibern. And Erai-Yanya. And Arthur, a little, as well as those teachers . . ."

"But you didn't with me. So let's start with an illusion. . ."

Seven

Summer, 4744 AF
Vasande Leror

LEANDER TLENNEN-HESS, KING of tiny Vasande Leror,
returned from his visit to the summer festival in Crestel, having
enjoyed the mellow air, the ride, and the craftspeople.

He wished Kyale had not refused to attend. He'd assumed
that if she forgot she was a princess, she'd have fun, and maybe
even meet a friend or two, but she'd insisted on transfer tokens
so she could visit the other girl princesses in the alliance,
especially those with fine palaces.

He heard her voice downstairs. At least whichever princess
it was had come here, for once. He hoped it might be Tahra of
Everon, whose palace was still so war-damaged that Kyale
couldn't disparagingly compare their own home to Everon's
royal palace. Kyale needed friends. Tahra needed friends.

Everon needed friends. It needed . . .

Never mind. No one wanted his opinion, least of all Glenn
of Everon.

Leander walked into his study, very aware that there was
plenty right at home to occupy his mind. Even a king of an
inkblot-sized kingdom had work. Especially if the inkblot was
a blot on the enormous border of Marloven Hess. Ancestral

squabbling had handed him his name and his rank and his responsibilities, and in Vasande Leror having a king meant you got his personal attention when you had a problem, and not a flunky's. In fact the royal castle had a serious dearth of flunkies.

On his desk lay a note from Alaxandar, his steward, briefly stating the problem (the mines again) with a location, and the transfer token Leander had made for him against emergencies. Leander winced when he saw the heavy metal disk. That meant TROUBLE RIGHT NOW.

Leander braced himself, picked up the transfer token, and said the spell, which he knew would take him directly to where the steward was. At least it was bound to be a short transfer.

The two lines gathered tensely on either side of a dramatic trough in the ground each stepped back when a sudden gust of wind and a flicker of light announced the arrival of a weedy dark-haired boy who blinked rapidly, then opened eyes of a rare, bright green.

"And here," Alaxandar declared grimly, "is our king himself."

Alaxandar the steward looked like what he was, a lifetime warrior. Ordinarily this was the only type Marlovens respected, but there had been bad blood between the Marlovens and the Lerorans for too long.

"I'm terrified. Will he blast us into stone, then Laxdren, here, for presumption?" one of the Marlovens asked caustically.

Leander blinked the black spots from his eyes. "A-*lax*-andar," he said, though he knew he should be diplomatic. "You can say it, surely, if you try. 'Andar,' or 'ander' still means 'trees' even in your language, I believe. My name in your tongue used to be Anderle. You just put the 'lee' for 'green' at the end, not the beginning. 'Lax' in old Iascan meant 'tall' and the 'a' at front turns it into 'tallest,'" he finished in a mendaciously instructive tone.

Leander's Marloven was accented but perfectly clear, and though the quick words flitted by swiftly, his sarcasm caused flushes and shuffles among the Marlovens. All of whom were armed, Leander noted belatedly.

But he made himself look away from those swords and bows, to the ruined ground. Carefully nurtured rows of white mulberry trees had fallen, undermined from below. Withered leaves had been wind-scattered everywhere.

Alaxandar bowed. "They're trying to tell us that this is a

collapsed morvende geliath."

Leander held his breath, regretting his sarcasm, which never helped even when there weren't twenty-seven armed Marlovens—what they called a flight—ranged on one side, their bodies tense to act. Leander's dozen Lerorans gripped their shovels and tools, drawing instinctively together.

Leander stepped toward the Marlovens, striving to keep his tone even as he met the eyes of each. "It's not a geliath," he said. "There is no geliath in our mountains, which are not actually mountains as understood by those who live underground. These are hills to anyone with real mountains, whose caverns are larger than our highest peak here. Did you know the morvende don't actually tunnel much, except to connect caverns?"

A pause. No one spoke, though the youngest fellow's fingers gripped the hilt of his sword, and the oldest, who seemed to be in charge, shifted his gaze away. Leander hoped he wasn't about to give the order to attack.

Leander could escape by magic, but he could not leave his people to be slaughtered.

Leander lifted his voice, drawing the man's attention back to him. "Therefore. Any caves or tunnels in these hills are evidence of mining. Some of them are centuries old. This one is not. I believe that your own Captain Senelac will recognize a very recent mining tunnel."

As Leander had expected, attention snapped back to him when he mentioned the Marloven second in command at the East Army garrison. The Marlovens might have no respect whatever for the tiny populace of Vasande Leror, but they had great respect for their local captains. Especially this Senelac.

"And I also happen to know that he really, really hates magic transfers, almost as much as I do." Leander raised his hands. "But I'll be happy to summon him to inspect."

They had all seen Leander appear. He whispered some illusory light around his raised hands. Let them think he could winkle Captain Senelac from wherever he was. Few people understood the boundaries of magic . . .

Swords lowered amid uneasy glances exchanged. "No need, no need," their leader said hastily.

Leander let the light fade. He kept his voice pleasant. "We have a treaty with King Senrid. This treaty specifically forbids your digging ore on our side of the border. This tunnel, on this eastern slope, is on our side of the border. Do I need to summon Captain Senelac to report to your king what has happened, or are you going to be repairing the damage?" Leander asked.

Another set of exchanged looks, then the leader spat into the ground. This insult caused hisses and mutters on Leander's side, but Leander ignored it and waited.

"What do you expect from us?" the leader said truculently, avoiding Leander's gaze.

Leander turned to the old woman whose orchard had been collapsed. "What needs to be done?" he asked her.

She rubbed gnarled hands, spat deliberately — on the west, or Marloven side — and though the Marlovens stirred, they were not going to raise their weapons against an unarmed old woman. Especially since their own flight-captain had landed the first insult.

She stepped up to the leader, and squinted up into his face. "You can start by righting every one of these here trees . . ."

A short time later, Leander followed Alaxandar to where the horses were held by one of the farm folk's children.

Leander pulled himself gratefully into the saddle of one.

"They'll probably try to wiggle out of it," Alaxandar said.

"Then Senrid will be hearing about it."

"Good."

It was not a long ride back. Leander's headache cleared off in that time, and while Alaxandar took care of the horses, Leander entered the castle.

Light streamed in the windows, catching in Kyale's long silver hair as she stamped in, the ribbons on her gown quivering with her indignation.

"Leander!" Kyale's voice was pretty as a voice, but that imperious tone certainly could grate. "*Finally,* you're back! Why did that stupid harvest thing take so long? Liere is here. And the Mearsiean girls. It's *important.*"

Leander turned his steps away from the direction of his study toward the room Kyale used for visitors, as she lowered her voice. "*Why* won't you *at least* hire footmen? It's so embarrassing, having an aproned kitchen maid answering the door."

Leander did not bother pointing out that the Mearsieans had no footmen either, and Liere would probably shrivel up like a prune if anyone ever told her she needed a servant. This argument was old — and he knew Kyale knew it.

Kyale finished up the familiar speech without the usual force. She believed that if she kept at it, he would one day listen, but even the lack of suitable royal display in her home couldn't ruin her delight in being the center of attention, especially for alliance business. Then she got to the point. "They're here because of that *annoying* Glenn of Everon . . ."

As soon as he heard the name, Leander sighed inwardly.

". . .and further," Kyale wound up her peroration without seeing his reaction, her wide gray eyes catching the light so they looked silver, "Glenn still hasn't done the Child Spell yet, though he promised he would, and Tahra wants to do what her brother does, but she's afraid it might already be *too late.* How can he think that growing into a disgusting overgrown hulk is going to defeat Norsunder? From what Tahra says, a lot of grown men died in that battle, including his own father . . ."

In the next room, CJ shifted on her bare feet as Kyale and Leander spoke, their voices only murmurs, but her nascent Dena Yeresbeth sensed a tension she could not define. She saw it corroborated in Liere's downcast gaze.

"I can't talk to Glenn," Liere said, shoulders hunching. "He despises me." *And Tahra still thinks me the Girl Who Saved the World.*

"He despises everybody who isn't a war-mad bully of a *boy.*" CJ spat the word out. "Liere, you should use that weird command voice on him, the one where you can make somebody's body do stuff. *Make* him listen."

Liere shook her head. "It only works for a heartbeat or two. And I have to have their range. I don't know Glenn's range, even if I would use it against him. What would be the use? You can make somebody hear you, but not heed you."

"*You* should talk to him, CJ, if Sartora won't." Kyale appeared, having heard the last few words, Leander behind her. "*All* you Mearsieans."

Liere's forefingers dug into the inflamed beds of her thumbnails. CJ scowled.

"Not me," said Irenne, flinging back her ribbon-tied ponytail.

Kyale turned her way. Irenne was easily the best dressed of all the Mearsiean girls. She dressed the way a princess should dress, and Kyale liked her the most.

Except now.

"I'm never going back to Everon. We helped out after that

horrid war, and for what? A bunch of snobs. If this visit is just to that putrid Glenn, I'm going back home." Irenne tossed her hair, and reached for the medallion around her neck. She transferred out.

Several of the others didn't even wait until the displaced air had finished stirring. No one, it seemed, wanted to face Prince Glenn.

CJ watched her friends vanish one by one, and struggled against the desire to go with them. But guilt kept her rooted, a residual regret for how much she'd managed to make people despise her when they'd all gone to Geth-deles.

"I'll go with you," she said to Kyale. After all, communication was important, wasn't it? And to Liere, "You don't have to say anything if you don't want to, but I know Tahra would like you there."

Liere knew that was true, though the reasoning made her feel more like a fraud. Because Tahra wanted *Sartora* there. She didn't even know Liere.

But that was business as usual. "All right."

Kyale turned her glare on Leander. "*You're* coming, right?"

Leander shook his head. "Much as I value the alliance, it's in spite of Glenn's desire to turn us into an army. And Glenn knows it. Also, something as personal as the Child Spell is . . .personal. I'd never discuss it with someone without their leave. This errand is yours, Kyale."

The girls flashed into Ferdrian castle's destination chamber, which was in a roofed but open-walled annex to the half-destroyed castle. It took them all a short time to rid themselves of the transfer malaise.

Funny, how different the air smelled in different places, CJ thought as Kyale promptly sneezed. CJ sniffed, trying to identify the scents on the breeze. It was cooler here than home, and wetter, smelling more like really old, old forest.

A page recognized them, and ran off. Shortly thereafter Tahra appeared at a run, her usually somber, sallow face almost unrecognizable with its bright-cheeked grin of delight. The girls had recovered from the transfer malaise by then, and Tahra invited them to her own rooms, though those were still fire damaged from the recent war—scrubbed clean, but furnishings sparse, and the walls bare in the light of a glow-globe.

Kyale noticed Tahra's attention on Liere, who walked with her shoulders hunched, her gaze on her feet. Kyale assumed that the famous Sartora was still feeling transfer malaise, and *she* was hostess of his expedition, so she stepped forward. "Tahra, I promised you I'd bring help."

Tahra turned her serious gaze from Kyale back to Liere. "Thank you," she said. "I hope you'll talk to my brother. He won't listen to me."

Poor Liere was already struggling against the emotional blare of Tahra's distorted admiration, made nearly unbearable by an inchoate longing that neither girl as yet had the experience to define.

Kyale marched forward, followed by the others, Tahra saying, "They're worse than ever. All because of that new boy, the one they call MV. Glenn is going mad trying to impress this no-family drifter, I don't know why. They're drilling again, though the sun set an hour and a quarter ago, and he should be . . .No, I won't complain."

From the practice area, Glenn Delieth saw them.

"CJ?" he asked, coming forward. He ignored Kyale, and nodded at Liere. She might be useless in a war, but at least she'd faced down the villain Siamis all by herself. She had courage. He respected that. "Welcome, Sartora. What brings you here?"

But Liere only shook her head, her stringy short hair obscuring her face.

So Glenn turned back to CJ. She was short and spindly; he could not understand sticking with that Child Spell. Further, she was not born to her rank, but the tangles she'd gotten into — and out of — with Norsunder had earned his respect. He wished she would spend more time with Tahra, instead of that tiresome, prissy Kyale.

"This is CJ of Mearsies Heili," Glenn said to a boy CJ didn't recognize, with curly dark brown hair and blue eyes. And to CJ, "This is Laban. I don't think you two have met."

"No," Laban said, his winged brows rising to a steep angle. "But I've heard stories. Let's see. According to you, boys are stupid, Norsunder is stupid, adults are stupid, and . . .does that leave anyone else out?" Laban gave CJ an up-and-down, his lip curling, then he indicated the practice mats. "Surely so great a defeater of Norsundrians can take the time to give us a lesson in how to be smart?"

CJ flushed, completely thrown by this unexpected attack. If

another girl had said it, she would have been hurt, but since this was one of Glenn's bullies, she crossed her arms defiantly. "Did you hear *me* say those things?"

"No," Laban said, but in exactly the same derisive tone, his words accented in a way she didn't recognize. "So you never said any of that? Someone made it all up?"

Kyale's face heated, and her gaze sidled away.

CJ snorted. "Adults *can* be stupid. So can boys—and girls. Norsunder IS stupid—or do you think they are great, wise, and wonderful?"

Laban retorted, "What I heard was, you think them easy to defeat."

CJ rolled her eyes. "I *never* said that! Just thinking about that crazy Kessler, and our close calls—" She flung her arms out, trying to think of insults cosmic enough to express her horror, when she caught sight of Kyale's miserable, guilty expression.

Oh, no.

"So modest?" Laban asked, hands to his heart. "Then the stories of your prowess can't possibly come from you." As the boys laughed, his vivid blue gaze rested on Kyale.

"No," CJ said cordially, determined not to expose Kyale to this obnoxious twit. "What you'll hear about from me is how we Mearsieans treat bigmouths. And by the way, being a muscle-popping grunt is not what I call being smart." She kicked the edge of a mat with her bare toes.

The boys laughed again.

All except Laban. "Yes?" Laban rounded his eyes. "Do tell me how to be smart."

CJ glared, completely thrown. She'd come in hopes of atoning for her past mistakes. He was an ally. They were all fighting Norsunder.

"Glenn," CJ said, turning her back squarely on Laban. Skipping over the Child Spell issue, she went to surer ground: the alliance. "Clair says we should talk about communication, the way we started before Siamis's last attack. Senrid says the same thing."

"Senrid," Glenn repeated. If he could impress MV, then surely he could impress Senrid. If.

CJ let out a breath of relief at Glenn's altered tone. He was listening! CJ went on, "He says communication is the first thing to break down if there's trouble."

Glenn rubbed his hands through his hair. "Senrid's right—

of course. If he wants to set up a system, I'm all for it."

CJ said, "Great. I'll let him know."

"You do that," Laban said in a cheery tone. "Be sure to tell him how to treat bigmouths."

"Bigmouths," Tahra said, losing her struggle, "can be left to my brother, CJ. Let's leave the boys to waste time playing warrior while we get to the real work."

"Right," CJ said.

Liere hunched into a ball, braced against the nightmare of tangled emotional conflicts.

Kyale stuck her nose in the air. All right, so she'd been bragging about CJ too much. Leander had warned her about that. But that Laban was just like Senrid, only worse!

The girls left, Kyale's skirts flouncing with dismissal. "How rude that Laban was," she stated, all the more heated because of the pulse of guilt. "Glenn ought to turn him away without pay or recommendation. Tahra, I know when I'm not welcome." And before Tahra could nerve herself to invite the famous Sartora to stay, Kyale turned to Liere. "Why don't you come visit in Vasande Leror? I know you like my cats."

Liere wanted to think about her secret plan, away from Senrid (who she knew thought it was a crazy idea) and ...well, she just didn't want to be in Bereth Ferian for a lot of reasons. "I would like that," she said.

As soon as they were out of earshot, Glenn said, "Senrid could have told *me*."

"Why didn't he?" Laban asked.

Glenn scowled in suspicion. But Laban didn't look mocking. His expression was interested.

So Glenn said, "I think it's because he wants to run us. That's what Marlovens do, isn't it? Well." He forced a laugh. "Maybe I'll take his advice, and begin putting together my own chain of command. We really need to get Morgeh to set aside that stupid lute and pay attention to his royal duty in Wnelder Vee. Also, I might write to Terry in Erdrael Danara."

"I'll go to Wnelder Vee if you like," Laban said.

Glenn smiled, gratified. This was the first time Laban had — well, not taken orders, but volunteered to execute one of Glenn's wishes. "That would be excellent," he said, thinking: I'm already building my command.

Eight

A WEEK WITH KYALE in Vasande Leror's small castle had begun to feel like a year.

Liere had not been able to think about her secret plan as
Kyale demanded her company, her attention, from breakfast to
retiring.

Liere struggled not to tense up at Kyale's tireless nagging at
her brother. When Leander wasn't around, the princess was
actually good company. They practiced riding, and played
endlessly with a new batch of kittens, which Liere could not get
enough of, reveling in their warmth and softness, and the
contented, purring response when they cuddled the small
creatures. Kyale would never scold her for kissing their tiny
ears and paws, their cute little muzzles and their round
tummies — she did it herself. But all this outpouring of affection
seemed to create a yawning hole inside her.

She appreciated Kyale's sense of art and style, and she
could sympathize with someone sensitive to light and color
having to live in an ugly granite castle. They read together in
Kyale's collection of journals written by princesses who had
had interesting lives, some of the books being a couple
centuries old and very expensive. Liere discovered she really
enjoyed these — though she felt like she was cheating, and ought
to be putting her time into learning something useful.

But when Kyale tried to wheedle, caution, and scold "Sartora" into convincing Leander to do things he obviously did not want to do, Liere wanted to run.

On the tenth day, a letter for Leander arrived.

Over dinner, Leander showed them the letter. "Karhin says that Lisbet has lost another prenticeship, and could use sympathetic company. Kyale, you like visiting in Colend. Shall I send you there?"

Kyale had been thinking that Liere, for all her fame, was kind of a tiresome guest. She refused to dress the way Sartora the Girl Who Saved the World should dress, refused to talk about her adventures, especially in front of others, and in short, seemed to want to act like a shopkeeper's apprentice rather than a world-famous mind reader who had defeated the Evil Siamis. She had even insisted that Kyale not tell anyone locally that Liere was Sartora, and when Kyale had accidentally let it out to a visiting guild representative, Liere had hid in her room, saying her head hurt.

It was so *weird*. Why would Liere not want to be the heroic Sartora? And also, why did she have more of those annoying streamers of colored light writhing and whirling in the air around her than anyone else? Kyale had learned early in life to ignore them, as they were not only useless, no one else could see them. Most of the time they were easy to overlook, but the ones around Liere were so distracting.

So Kyale was very ready for the visit to be over. Even better, going to Colend! Land of art, fashion, music, and beautiful things!

The next morning, Leander gave them transfer tokens, saying that it would be later in the day in Colend, perfect time for arrival.

The three girls were soon ensconced in Lisbet's room, where she proceeded to vent about having failed the first level of first-year mage studies. As it happened, she couldn't have chosen a more sympathetic audience.

"Learning magic would make sense if you could learn spells for things you actually wanted," Lisbet said. "What was the use in chanting all those nonsense sounds, that don't even do anything?"

"That is so *very* true," Kyale exclaimed, her silvery eyes wide. "That is *exactly* what I told my brother. But would he listen? *Of course* he would not listen, he just went on about how

I had to memorize the basics, and then practice spells that no one would even want. And I couldn't remember them, *ever*."

"Even if you could remember them," Liere said sadly, "it might not be any use. I'm living proof of that."

Kyale and Lisbet turned her way. Well! If Sartora, the Girl who Saved the World, had no use for magic studies, then it vindicated their lack of interest.

Kyale tossed her hair back. "Arthur probably doesn't know how to teach right. Or he's just too busy with that Roy."

Liere looked away, wishing she hadn't spoken. She could hear in Kyale's tone that she wanted — expected — approval for what she thought of as loyalty. But what she said wasn't true, and further she could hear in Kyale's voice that she knew it.

Liere looked down at her hands, hating her own failure. Hating the jealousy she couldn't fight, not because Arthur was friends with Roy, but because she hadn't understood how hard Arthur tried with her until she saw how Arthur behaved with Roy — the laughter, the quick jokes, the genuine interest in magic and history. With Liere, Arthur was always patient, kind, and polite.

It was sickening to realize that she was not only a failure, she was an obligation, a duty. Then she hated herself for whining inside her own head.

And it wasn't as if Liere didn't have friends of her own. There was Senrid, of course, and these two girls right here. It was just that she had so little in common with either Kyale or Lisbet, except for feeling like an outsider. She wanted to be their friend, but how did you go about making yourself a friend if you didn't truly feel it? Friendship wasn't just having things in common. With Senrid, she'd had almost nothing in common, but friendship had just happened without any effort on either of their parts.

Liere tried to listen as Kyale lectured them in a complacent tone, fully expecting agreement and sympathy, about how magic should be taught — interesting spells first — and Lisbet agreed, as expected. Liere found herself nodding, and hated herself for her hypocrisy. Lisbet and Kyale weren't going to like her any better for it.

Liere made herself stop, and considered the other two. It was clear from the way Lisbet sat, facing Kyale, that she loved having a princess visiting as much as Kyale loved being a princess. She took comfort in her superior rank, but she was still on her best behavior; everything she loved in art and clothing was Colendi in origin.

In spite of her frequent airy references to the trouble of royal rank, Liere could sense Kyale watching anxiously for any sign that they despised little, out-of-the-way-of-anything-interesting Vasande Leror.

". . .might try to learn magic if I didn't have to spend so much time child-minding my little brother," Lisbet was saying.

Liere blinked. The conversation had shifted again.

"Child-minding?" she repeated. "You know something about little ones? Babies?"

"I do," Lisbet claimed. "Why, I've been minding Little Bee since he was born. The others always got out of it, claiming they have scribal duties. Sometimes I think I'm a better mother than either of our real mothers."

This was not the least bit true—and Liere understood that it was not true—but Liere heard the undercurrent of longing to be important.

Now was the time.

Now she knew what to do!

"You can help me," she said, thrilling to decision. Senrid had only expressed skepticism at her idea, and she understood his reasons, but she kept coming back to her most secret wish, impelled by the loneliness and sense of not belonging anywhere that shadowed her days.

These girls, she knew, would adore being singled out for this important moment, and Lisbet, at least, could help!

"I," she said, savoring the words, "am going to have my own family."

"What?" Kyale squeaked.

"Ah-ye!" Lisbet's hands clapped in the peace. Her eyes rounded. "Can you? Without talking with anyone grown?"

"The Birth Spell comes when it will," Liere said.

"How do you know?" Kyale asked, hands clasped tightly to the flat lace-and-ribbon bosom of her gown.

Liere's nerves sparked. "I thought about it ever so long. And there the spell is, in my mind. It's . . .different from that other magic I tried to learn. This spell is so clear I can see it as well as say it."

She shivered with the glory of her idea, then said after a pulse of doubt, "Do you know about the care of really small infants?"

Lisbet longed to claim expertise, but she recollected how difficult infants could be. So she said in an authoritative voice, "No, not newborns. But I know who does. Princess Tahra is friends with the morvende orphanage leader Piper, in Everon. I've stayed there twice, when they needed help with the orphans. Piper will tell you everything you want to know."

Lisbet and Kyale stared at Liere. Babies seemed something . . .alien, something to be thought of in the far future. The idea of now stunned them both. But after all, Liere was Sartora, the Girl who Saved the World, she was different from everybody with that amazing Dena Yeresbeth you heard about.

Liere softly uttered the spell, the room seemed to fill with light as space and time thinned, and there was a baby lying pink and wriggling in Liere's short, thin arms.

"She *is* a girl," Liere exclaimed in delight.

"She has black hair," Kyale marveled.

Liere was startled by that, but maybe it would change. Of course her daughter would be nothing like her pretty sister Marga, always noisy and the center of attention.

"She's bee-yoo-tiful," Lisbet crooned. "Did you think of a name?" Her mind crowded with suggestions.

Liere had thought that out, too. "Her first name will be Lyren, for a friend I met from another world. That way, no one's feelings will be hurt here. After that, she will have names from all of my friends in the alliance, the longest name in the world!"

"And at the end?" Lisbet asked, who could not imagine anyone without a family name. "Fer Eider?"

Liere's first impulse was denial. She wanted nothing to do with her father and his angry sarcasm, or her indifferent brothers, or her sister, who was nice enough, but always the favorite. Liere remembered her mother, and guilt twinged at her. In a fit of self-abnegation, she said bitterly, "Why not start a new family name? What would be better than Sartora?"

Neither Kyale nor Lisbet perceived the irony.

"That's perfect," Kyale exclaimed, and Liere's insides pulsed with the familiar self-hatred, except it didn't last long, because the baby wriggled, eyes opening as little fists waved. Then the baby opened her mouth and made a noise that sounded like a kitten mewing.

"She needs to be wrapped up," Lisbet said practically. "Look, her skin is getting mottled from the cold air."

"It's not cold," Kyale exclaimed.

"It is when you just got born."

"From where?" Kyale asked, for the first time considering the matter. "She wasn't inside Liere."

Liere at that moment felt a weird pulse through her middle, a flash of something that was gone again in a moment: her body had responded to some signal, but then it subsided again.

Liere said slowly, "In the reading I did, some mage said that the baby grows beyond time, then comes here. Another mage said that in all the possible worlds, the baby might have been inside another version of you, which is why it only comes when you lived a certain number of years. It might be a you who did not do the Child Spell."

"Except men can do the Birth Spell," Kyale said. "Or Lilah wouldn't be telling Peitar to try it."

"There are several theories," Liere said. "I told you two, but I don't know if either is right. The only thing the mages agree on is that the babe draws on inherited traits from all your ancestors inside you."

"I don't understand any of that," Kyale stated.

"I don't either," Liere admitted. "All I know is, if I hadn't done the Child Spell, I would now have enough of a grownup form to be able to have children the regular way, so maybe it becomes possible?"

"Ugh," Kyale said, wrinkling her nose. "That subject is so disgusting."

Lisbet's lip curled, but at that moment Lyren's face flushed a rosy purple and she let out a yell.

"What's wrong?" Kyale gasped.

"Here, I'll take her," Lisbet said. "She's probably cold."

Awkwardly, stiffly, Liere handed over the writhing infant. Lisbet took her even more awkwardly, her sense of expertise fading like steam as the baby's cry abruptly scaled up higher. "Here. She wants you." She pushed the baby back into Liere's thin arms.

Liere shut her eyes, braced against the emotional onslaught: yes, the babe did want her, but Liere could not parse what she needed.

Lisbet looked around her bedroom, then exclaimed, "Just the thing." She dove toward her trunk, and lifted out a soft cotton wrap.

Between them both, she and Liere got the wrap around the baby, then Lisbet said, "Princess Tahra's friend Piper would know. I think we'd better talk to Mother about a transfer token, because Lee-ran—"

"LYE-ren," Liere corrected.

"Ly-ren is going to want to nurse, and then she's going to need diapers at the other end."

"Diapers," Liere repeated, appalled. "Nurse?"

None of the mage books about the Birth Spell had mentioned *that*.

Kyale backed away a step. Her desire to hold the baby had vanished at the first cry. Babies were nothing like cats, which were so easy to cuddle, then they used their little house, where the droppings were wanded away. This baby was going to demand all Liere's time, she could see it already, and it might wet at any moment and ruin her lace and silk.

"Good idea," she said, adding, "I wish I could go, but Piper's in Everon, and Prince Glenn hates me. You all saw it when we were there a week ago."

Lisbet didn't bother pointing out that Prince Glenn was unlikely to visit the orphanage, except to scout for boys for his army. As the baby continued to cry, kicking her feet, Lisbet was also thinking that the sooner Liere got that baby safely to Piper, the better.

Liere caught their emotions, looked down at that screwed up face, thinking in bewildered joy and anxiety and wonder: *This is forever*.

Nine

Beyond Place and Time

SHIFTING AND BLENDING IN color, the long-limbed Pir moved with slow and graceful intent, their high, arched feathered crests rippling. Backward-jointed knees flexed as delicate three-toed feet lifted and arched, counterpoint to the exquisite rise and fall of six wings.

Pir combined and separated as no mammal, reptile, or insect from outworld ever could: Siamis stared, unable to move for an anguished thrum of his heart.

He had come too far, back to the days of his childhood on the eve of war. This world was gone, at least to human access, maybe forever.

He stilled, aware of exhaustion deep within, far away: though it seemed he stood in a room of ever shifting mirrors, that was only symbolically, his mind's way of imposing human order on . . .not chaos. That was at least as vast an error as mistaking symbol for reality. It was more eternity and evanescence, nearly impossible for the mind to comprehend in totality.

Stillness. Stillness. Still . . .

No mental movement until that flare of panic snuffed.

Still.

A mental twitch, as subtle as the lift of an eyelash — and the images faded. No emotion must leak, no memory, because the mind reaches for them and there is another lost time, beckoning though there might be no mirror to step through.

Back, back. Focus on place had not worked. Focus on symbol — Arrow — in any form had not worked. Focus on the three northern light-mages who had bound the Venn had not worked: he had seen glimpses of their robes from the Moonfire access, distortions as if he watched a reflection in water. That meant they had somehow bound not only the 'Arrow' into enchantment, but they had also bound their binding.

Each of these glimpses reflected in the Moonfire's mental plane mirrors, which were also doorways — one way.

Stepping through — at best — would mire one forever in another time. And if the mirror were fashioned by memory, there would be no time, only the dreams of someone long dead. Siamis had gained the training, and the coinherence once called Dena Yeresbeth gave him the wherewithal, but the Moonfire still proved to be dangerously elusive.

The one possibility left was the most perilous of all: to locate the mirror from the Venn side. First *where*, and then *when* . . .

Autumn 4744 AF
Everon

Hanold Wemegan, a boy who'd found himself the new baras after his father's and his older brother's deaths during the Norsunder attack, felt ambivalent when that tall, blade-lean MV showed up again. Hanold and many of the others had been secretly, then not-so-secretly, relieved when MV had abruptly vanished, and months had passed.

But here he was again, with a husky dark-skinned, dark-haired boy he introduced simply as, "Rolfin. He's going to show you slackers how to handle a bow."

"A bow! But arrows are directly against the Covenant of Peace!"

"Is that what you're going to tell Norsunder if, no, when they come again?" MV held up a hand. "Wait, Norsundrian captain," he said in a shrill whine. "You can't give an order to shoot — that's against the Covenant! Which Norsunder never agreed to," MV said, dropping back into his own voice as he lounged over to inspect the bow in Rolfin's hand. "Not bad. Not bad." He turned his head. "So are you slackers going to moan and blub as they shoot you down, or are you going to shoot back?"

The response of disbelief and derision would have been louder, Hanold suspected, if Prince Glenn's future honor guard had not learned a wary respect for MV, who scorned them as pampered slackers! Yet the prince said nothing in defense of his own people. Instead, he regarded MV with a huge smile of delight.

They studied the powerfully built newcomer in silence, as Rolfin stared back, his mind-shield tight, and behind it his mind calculating distances between each, stances, balance. Though he sensed no threat in anyone, long habit formulated both attack and exit strategy. Nothing in his life had been easy, and he exerted himself to never be taken by surprise.

The others had no idea what to make of this boy with the wary stance, and shoulders like a man in that plain, undyed tunic-shirt. Hanold could not even determine if "Rolfin" was a family name, a territorial name, or merely a given name; he studied that impassive gaze, sensing . . .not threat, precisely. His instinct, surer than his conscious thoughts roiling around titles, and status, sensed the patience of the hunter.

Prince Glenn cleared his throat. "That scar. On your face. How did you get that?"

"Fell."

"But it looks like a knife scar."

"Fell on a knife blade," Rolfin said, in exactly the same tone.

Laban had gone off somewhere, but Hanold could easily imagine him rolling his eyes.

MV uttered his voiceless snicker. It sounded sinister to Hanold, but then everything about MV was sinister.

Before anyone else could speak, Rolfin picked up one of the bows, restrung it, reached for arrows, and then— turning precisely on the worn heel of his riding boot four times—he sent four arrows zipping to each corner of the practice salle. One by one the arrows nailed the wood-carved gargoyles up under the ceiling, each squarely in its grinning teeth.

The result was a thoughtful silence.

Hanold could see his own reaction mirrored in his prince's sallow face. Here was another apparently no-family vaga-bond—because otherwise surely he'd mention a rank or title—

showing them up. You could call them mere arms masters—
hirelings, sworn to serve—but Hanold did not lie to himself.
MV had not sworn anything to anyone, or he'd have heard.
More importantly, the rest of Prince Glenn's carefully chosen
elite, all with impeccable lineage, did not feel in command of
either MV or the big, quiet newcomer Rolfin.

As a summer storm crackled and boomed overhead, and
boys sweated in the humid air, Rolfin taught them how to string
and pull their bows. He did not let them shoot. They had too
much to unlearn. He made it clear that it was personally painful
to watch them, until they could get their hands, elbows, and
shoulders in a straight line. They practiced that until their
upper-body muscles trembled like loosened strings. As the sun
sank, one, then two, then all watched the shadows lengthen.
They were hungry and wanted to go home.

Prince Glenn noticed the looks, and hoped MV hadn't.
Glenn dreaded hearing him or the newcomer saying something
about self-discipline. He suppressed his own hunger and said,
"Now for some fighting practice."

"Is that supposed to impress him?" Hanold's cousin Meric
whispered, wiping back his sweat-darkened fair hair. "We're
going to be commanders, not foot warriors—"

"Sh." Hanold warned Meric.

MV propped his fists on his hips and looked askance at
Glenn. "You have something against dinner?"

Glenn's cheeks reddened. "You said we were weak."

MV's lip curled, but he said mildly enough, "Makes sense
to grab a meal when you can."

Prince Glenn lifted his voice. "Be back at the bell change."

Hanold winced at the sharpness in the prince's voice. Meric
wiped his freckled nose on his sleeve, and groused as he
followed Hanold out, "Who is really in command?"

Hanold had no answer. The question continued to bother
him as they walked down to the cavernous mess hall where
once the Knights of Dei had dined together. Here he was, now
a baras, and he should be at home, learning what his brother
had been raised to know. But he was stuck here. Meric was in
the same situation.

They were not the only ones glumly considering questions
they dared not ask. Glenn, seeing their faces, assumed they
were tired, and mentally sorted words for a speech when they
reassembled. He would never say so, but he wanted that MV to

see his leadership, to be impressed. To be respectful.

Everything depended on respect, that his father had tried to teach him, and Glenn thought he understood now that he was the heir, almost a king. If people respected you, they respected your orders, and they obeyed them. Life would go back to normal.

He walked into the palace, and found his sister halfway through her dinner.

Tahra made a face. "Why aren't you eating with your . . ." She waved a hand toward the barracks. "Playmates?"

He ignored her sarcasm with the ease of habit. "I did. For a while. But I think if I'm too familiar, they'll see me as one of them, not their commander. The hierarchy has to be preserved." Besides, he'd noticed that MV rarely went to the Knights' mess. Nobody knew where he ate when he went off, or where he stayed.

"I wish you'd use a cleaning frame before coming in here," Tahra said, wrinkling her nose. She loathed the rank stink of sweaty boys, but this was really her way of reminding Glenn that he was supposed to be a prince, not a spear carrier. A prince who ought to be governing, instead of leaving it to Roderic Dei, with Tahra trying to learn what she had never been taught.

Glenn tipped his chin up and cast a disparaging look around the barren dining chamber. It was clean — that testified to the vigor of the Sandorals, the chamberlain family for generations — but the walls still bore the marks from fire. And nothing had been replaced beyond table, chairs, dishes. "Why? The barracks mess looks better."

Tahra's lips thinned. "You know why. Until Mother comes back, we have to decide these things together, and that means beginning with sitting in king's court."

Glenn sighed. He had less interest in fooling around with wall decorations, paints, or carvings than he did in listening to a lot of guild blowhards and town officials blabbering on about taxes and the empty treasury.

But Tahra did not understand. "She's not coming back," he said, hardening his voice as disappointment, frustration, and the anger of betrayal hardened his heart. "She's dead. Like all the others. She and Father trusted Uncle Roderic more than anyone. He does a better job with king's court than we ever could."

Tahra scowled. "Mearsieanne says Mother isn't . . .dead." She hated saying the word, as if saying it would make it true.

"How would Mearsieanne know? Unless she's still under Norsunder's spell?"

"It was because she was a prisoner in Norsunder that she knows," Tahra said, her voice unsteady as she tapped a letter beside her plate. "Mearsieanne insists that Mother was taken prisoner, maybe to the Norsunder Base, or maybe into Norsunder Beyond-time. Or someone would have seen her body. Bodies don't Disappear on their own."

"And I don't believe she's alive," he stated.

He saw how much his words upset her, and relented. They both had seen their father lying dead in the courtyard beyond those windows, his honor guard slaughtered with him. Two of their sons were eating over at the mess now.

He didn't *want* to believe their mother was alive without proof, because he hated hope. Hope *always* betrayed you.

"I see you've been writing letters." He indicated her neat piles of folded paper that she carried around with her everywhere, arranged around the golden case that she never seemed to stop touching.

"Karhin says that Terry's friend Curtas took Thad to see Shontande Lirendi again. Curtas has sneaked past the guards twice. Shontande Lirendi wants to join the alliance, he told them."

Glenn forced himself to say what was proper, but he grimaced. Shontande Lirendi, why did everyone care so much? At least *Glenn's* father wasn't mad.

But that was the sort of thing you could never say out loud. "Anything else?"

"Yes. The most surprising thing. At least, Karhin wasn't there, but her sister Lisbet was, and I also received a letter from Piper," Tahra said, her long, sallow face closed as she shuttered away her disappointment. "Sartora was here, in Everon, for an entire week."

"Why did she not come to us?" Glenn asked, though he still felt ambivalent about that girl and her mind-reading powers— the more because his sister clearly admired her above anyone else.

"Because she used the Birth Spell, and has an infant. And needed Piper's help."

"What?" He was so astonished he dropped his bread.

"Lisbet and Kyale were there." Tahra tapped another neatly folded letter, and would have read it out, but Glenn knew his sister's penchant for exact detail, which could be as tiresome as her constantly counting things like steps, and how many times she had turned right or left, or the way she carried those letters around as if they were an invisible honor guard.

"Never mind, never mind," he said, and laughed as he retrieved his bread.

"What is so funny?" she asked.

"It's just that now I'm certain there is no wise Other Beings in command of that spell, or anything else. Or, they could be in charge, but they have to be as stupid as snails to let *her* bespell a baby. She's got no family, no home even, and still has that idiotic Child Spell on her. What a disaster! She'll probably hand it off to Piper when she gets tired of the wailing and the diapers, and our kingdom will be responsible for yet another no-family brat, this one not even a result of war."

"She."

"What?"

"The baby is a she."

Glenn shook his head. "Really, really stupid. Arthur will just love all that howling getting in the way of his mumbling over his books . . ."

He continued to complain about Liere's decision from time to time, another evidence of the stupidity of performing the Child Spell. But most of his attention was on getting through his meal as quickly as possible. He was eager to get back to the salle; when he arrived, he was in time to see the others emerge in a body from the mess hall. MV strode in the lead, Rolfin with him.

Chagrin squeezed Glenn's heart, but he straightened up, determined to conduct himself like a future king.

"Now then!" he shouted. "One last session for the day."

Meric and Hanold were silent as they trudged back to the salle. Why had MV taken it into his head to join them for the meal? He had a caustic way about whiners, so no one had dared vent their feelings.

The prince as usual had not been there, but MV had presided as if he were in command, increasing the ranking boys' resentment. That resentment translated into a sharpened determination when they were paired up for hand-to-hand matches.

MV and Rolfin thrashed their way through them all.

Hanold was resigned, but each humiliating defeat angered Meric, so much that when it was his turn, he threw himself at Rolfin, ignoring the practice rules — to be efficiently yanked off-balance. In desperation, he fought for purchase, refusing to be slammed to the mat. Angrily he gripped Rolfin's tunic as the latter snapped Meric over his hip. Lightning fired up his arm, igniting a sun in his shoulder.

He crowed for breath, barely aware of Rolfin letting go.

Meric tumbled to the mat, his arm torqued out of the socket.

Glenn and the Everoneth crowded around squawking at each other MV's long fingers reached for his shattered arm. Meric tried to scream, but he couldn't breathe. He twitched, fighting to escape.

"Lie still, idiot," MV said impatiently. His implacable grip tightened on Meric's wrist, a foot planted itself against his ribs, the fire burst in Meric's brain, then abruptly subsided to a red, dull ache as his shoulder locked back into place.

"Why didn't any of you do that?" MV glanced around. "You lot really are ignorant. What if you're out there in the field, who's going to patch you up? Right, you'll prance out onto the battlefield trailing servants, cooks, and healers. Will they do your fighting for you, too?"

He flipped up the back of his hand to them all, and walked out.

Meric sat up, hand to his reset shoulder, his limbs trembling too much to trust to standing. Hanold helped him up, wondering who was really in command. How could there be civilization when everyone looked to the strongest and the most violent to lead them?

"Going home." Meric forced the words out.

Prince Glenn nodded vigorously. "Right. Right. Take a few days."

But Meric was going home for good.

Ten

On Goerael Continent

SIX MONTHS AFTER SETTING out, Rel and Adam reached the crown mountain dividing Alcandamer from Ralanor Veleth. The slope to the west below was, according to the map Rel had studied at Mondros's cottage, the province once called Glenereth.

Rel had told Adam that Mondros wanted them to travel through Alcandamer, listening for any gossip about Norsunder nosing around, or rumors of mysterious magic. This was true enough, given their mission, and in any case they hadn't heard a thing.

He did not tell Adam why he wanted to climb the bridge over the chasm that the locals said was the border, or why he'd struck up conversation with a gabby baker's apprentice. Adam thoughtfully remained on the verge, velvet-grassed with spring growth, and sketched the tangled budding vines of tree-like creepers trained to form the supports of the ancient bridge as Rel and his acquaintance walked to the top of the curve.

Adam studied the creepers, which had gradually thickened and hardened to the strength of oak, though the mighty branches still lived. That was apparent from the last of the wine-colored leaves that had stubbornly clung through the long winter, sticking up along the carefully trained lengths, one or two giving way at last to spiral down to the waterfall thundering on the rocks far below.

The baker's assistant, a scrawny fellow somewhere between boy and man, wiped his hands absently on his apron, and pointed off to the northwest. "You can see the castle there, no? Four towers, two of them new? Ho! My grandfer used to scare us with stories about the Velethi when we were small, though they seem to be settled somewhat now. If you can trust that."

Rel gazed at the land sloping below, haze wreathing the trees. It dropped away toward plains, pale gold in the sinking spring sun. "That is Glenereth castle?" Rel asked.

The baker scratched his head. "No longer. The old family is gone."

While he'd been talking, the baker assessed his inquisitor, who spoke with an accent he did not recognize. The fellow was very tall, and dark-haired, with deep-set eyes that reminded him of some families in the area.

Everyone knew the old rumors that the Velethi were descended from Venn, who had married among the darker peoples of the south. That Venn background surely explained their preoccupation with war, and how good they were at it. But anyone might have eyes like that, and he was dressed like a traveling artisan. He was polite, quiet, and tipped well, so the baker asked only, "Anything else? I should get back to turn out my pans."

Rel thanked him again, and they walked back down the bridge, where they rejoined Adam at the foot.

The baker loped on down a side path dug into the patchy new grass along the slope, leading to the back end of the village built into the side of the rocky hill.

Rel picked up his pack that Adam had been minding, and they set out along the wider path that skirted the village.

Adam stared down at his walking boots, taking in each scuff, gap, and discoloration in the road-stippled, sun-bleached brownweave. Then he looked at his hand clutching the strap of his pack. He had drawn it so many times he knew every pore and hair, every tiny skin fold in the knuckles, the thin scars pinking the sun-brown.

He breathed, listening to the hissing inside his lungs, and whooshed the air out, feeling the coolness on his lips. The air smelled of wool, of wood, a bit like wet dog.

Will I ever remember this moment? He concentrated on each sense in an effort to fix the whole into memory. He did not want it to slide out, as had many uneventful moments, hours, days. Nor did he wish to touch anything, and gain an unwanted memory not his, or leave a memory there for another inadvertent hand.

In the north here, the songs were completely different from those of the southerners as people went about taking down the winter storm shutters after a very late, rainy spring, and planting food and flowers to catch the benefit of impending summer.

Was there a common theme, way underneath, or was that intrinsic to music? He would find someone to ask. Several someones. A variation in explanations would be as interesting as the truth.

"Did you climb yon bridge to a purpose?" Adam asked after they had walked in silence for a time.

Rel glanced at him, considering. People talked in front of Adam, he'd noticed. Adam seemed so dreamy, as if he didn't hear much of the world around him. And yet his drawings made it clear he was a very close observer.

Adam was also ready to talk, at length, about everything around him, and to ask questions, and yet Rel still didn't know where Adam came from, or much of anything about his past. A couple vague mentions indicated a brother or two, maybe cousins, or even village friends, but the only person he consistently referred to was his former art master. Who didn't have a name, or even a place.

Maybe Adam hadn't had all that great a start in life. Rel himself wasn't ready to talk to anyone about the family he had discovered: on one side, descent from the worst king in the entire world, and on the other side, a clan disgraced and displaced.

So he answered Adam's question with a deflection. "Curiosity. But we've discovered nothing of use to Tsauderei or the mages. Let's cross the stream by the lower bridge. The baker told me that we can catch a boat there. It'll feed into the river. Take us all the way to Alcandamer's harbor. Get used to being on the water, before we try joining up with a trade ship."

"What is that bird? There, with the white underside, and the long beak? That can't be a sea bird, not so far inland, can it? Oh, where is my chalk . . ."

Rel laughed to himself. "There's a big lake in the mountains south of here. My guess it's a water bird, flown north."

When Rel and Adam hefted their packs and stepped off the riverboat, it was to find a harbor filled with ships. Not just any ships: at the far end, isolated as if proximity might damage ordinary traders, floated five ships with startling profiles in upward curving prows suggesting dragons' heads, the sides straked. All five floated with bare poles, yards uncrossed, obviously not going anywhere.

"Those are Venn drakan ships," Rel said, peering under his hand. He'd only seen drawings of them in very old books until the bleak winter's day he'd lain on a bluff above a nearly frozen bay, and watched several of them pop out of nothingness, sending water surging up onto the shore and nearly swamping the Norsundrian warriors about to embark for Everon.

These were the very same ships.

Rel's breath caught. He looked upward, trying to banish the memories of the attack on Everon.

Adam whistled slowly. "I'd like to draw one," he said unsurprisingly.

They threaded along the crowded pier, Rel fighting the instinct to flee. The Norsundrians who had torn up Everon were long gone. They couldn't possibly be here now — they'd merely used these ships as transport. But he was reluctant to go anywhere near those drakans.

Then he noticed the guards posted between gawkers and the vessels, and he caught Adam's pack by the strap. "I mistrust the look of those guards."

Adam sighed. "Do you think they're going to the Land of the Venn? It would make our journey so easy!" And he raced off toward the closest inn as the best place for gossip.

The grizzled ship's carpenter-turned-innkeeper was perfectly ready to talk after the boys ordered a substantial meal. "This parcel o' madmen sailed into the harbor a month past, can you believe it? Plain as plain, came right up here, not ten paces from where you sit, a-jabbering old-fashioned Venn. The guard mustered faster'n you can bend a stormsail, and hauled 'em up to the garrison. My nephew, a night guard, says they kept saying things like they thought Alcandamer was a Venn colony, and they expected supplies!"

"Were they indeed mad?" Adam asked.

Rel was distracted by the way Adam always seemed to hesitate over his food, as if he couldn't quite see it. Or maybe he was reluctant to touch it. Then he gently picked up the rolled tart dripping with iced orange sauce. His expression flickered, too quick to catch, before he took a bite.

"No one knows! Still clapped up in prison," the innkeeper explained. "Until the queen decides what to do with 'em. The Venn can't come down out o' the north, everybody knows that. Not for centuries. These piss-haired crazies claimed they don't know nothing about no proscription, nor even what year it is, if you can imagine that. What's more, them ships is full of gear you wouldn't find outside of some treasure trunk, buried since Peddler Antivad was a pup!"

He paused to laugh, and Adam laughed agreeably because the man laughed, but Rel wanted nothing to do with those ships, whoever had been on them. "We still have to find ourselves a berth," he said to Adam once the innkeeper turned away to wait on someone else.

They paid for their breakfast, picked up their packs again, and began to work their way down the harbor.

Rel was very good at spotting likely ships. He figured well-kept (non military) ships were his best choice. These usually meant a captain not too mean with pay, but ships that looked like royal yachts too often had tyrannical captains who cared more for the bunting of sails than for the lives of crew in high winter winds. And though the summers were generally mild, up here in the northern part of the world, the peninsula on which the Venn lived was infamous for its year-round storms.

Rel said, "Let's look for ships rigged fore-and-aft. They may or may not be going north, but for certain anyone rigged square is running south."

And Adam said, "What?"

"Fore-and-aft. The triangular ones. Ships can sail closer to the wind, and going north, we're likely to be tacking." Rel traced a finger zigzag in the air. "If not beating the wind altogether. Square is for deep-ocean, with the wind on the beam. I expect when these traders come south again, they rig square."

Adam's bland expression convinced Rel that Adam's experience with sailing had been brief, and as a passenger. That would make it somewhat more difficult to find work for two, but many ships needed extra captain's rats, the boys or girls who served as errand runners as they learned ship skills.

"Maybe I should do the talking," he suggested to Adam, who shrugged.

They walked along the docks, as Rel asked the destinations of tied-up fore-and-aft rigged ships.

"First choice," he said to Adam, "is something going all the way to Khiven Harbor in Lorise. That's west of Florianth—which lies straight across from the Land of the Venn—but I don't want to go there if we can avoid it."

"Because?"

"Florianth used to be called Westvenn. Everything I read, it's more army-mad than the Marlovens. At best they might try summary recruitment." He flicked a hand down his body. "Happened before."

"They probably wouldn't want me," Adam ventured, scratching his head with a chalk pencil through his wild hair.

The pencil left a green mark. Rel hid a smile as he marched up to the first ship he liked the looks of, and asked the mate of the deck whither it was bound, and if they hired crew.

"Dolhir, Has Peri, Alma, Khiven," said the first mate, a pleasant gray-haired woman. "And yes. We lost two top-hands, a carpenter's mate, and a sails mate, all wanting to ship south."

Rel liked the clean lines of the ship, and the first mate's sensible tone. He could do any of those jobs.

He opened his mouth just as Adam, who had been looking around, pointed to some barrels being rolled up the ramp, and said, "Is that wine?"

The mate said in amusement, "That'll be flour."

She turned back to Rel, but before he could speak, Adam said, "Don't you have wine on board? How much do you allow the crew?"

She answered, but her tone was reflective, and Rel's heart sank. He wasn't surprised when she said regretfully that she might see clear to fit Rel on board, but she hadn't room for a land rat. She didn't say "drunken land rat" but she may as well have.

They took polite leave, left the captain's deck, and made their way down the ramp to the next ship. Rel said, "Adam, she thinks you're a drunk."

"She what?" Adam's eyes rounded in surprise. "I'm not! I just wanted to know."

Rel sighed. "Consider saving questions about wine until

after we get hired, all right?"

They climbed the next ramp, found the first mate—to discover that they always rigged fore-and-aft, but the ship was sailing south. The third was not ideal. It was working its way from tiny harbor to tiny port, but the final destination was Khiven. Rel said, "We're looking for—"

Adam sniffed, then grimaced. "What is that stench?"

"This is a fish trader," the old mate of the watch said, chuckling. "We put 'em in the tanks, to trade north where they don't normally swarm. People put 'em in ponds. Moats. Pools."

"Oh," Adam said on a low note. "Does it always stink like this?"

The chuckle died. "You get used to it."

"I bet the reek is worse in summer. Or do you fish for ones that don't whiff so bad?"

Rel sighed, wondering how many words for "stench" Adam was going to come up with.

"Well, you won't know, as we're full up." The mate spat to the side—barely.

Rel said as they tramped down the ramp, "They know about the stink. Pointing it out won't get us hired."

"Oh," Adam said with an air of discovery. "I guess they *would* know, wouldn't they?"

The next one was another southern trader, and the following had no need for crew.

The sun was beginning its dip toward the west, and Rel was hungry again when they found another ship going north to the right harbors. Rel liked Adam, but promised himself if the cloud-brained artist said one more idiotic thing to put them off a possible hire, he'd tie a kerchief around his jaw to gag him.

The mate of the watch was a cheery fellow Rel's own age. He said with obvious regret, "We lost one, almost two. But he came back." He shrugged and rolled his eyes, conveying his opinion of the one who'd returned. "So what we're really looking for is a ship's cook."

Adam piped up, "I can cook."

The mate squinted doubtfully at him. "You can?"

"You can?" Rel gazed at Adam in astonishment.

"Only for about twenty-five at most," Adam said, blushing and hanging his head. He mumbled something in which the word "school" could be made out.

The mate smiled broadly. "We sail five to a watch, the

captain, the carpenter, sails, and a cook, with a ship's brat as general aid." When Adam just shrugged, the mate's smile increased. "Bide here, will you? The captain spent all yesterday trying to find a cook who wasn't too old, or too drunk, or demanded too much pay." He frowned. "What do you expect?"

"Anything is fine," Adam said. "Work for passage. As long as I can draw when I'm not in the galley." He brandished his wrinkled, edge-curled sketchpad.

"Well." The mate drew a deep breath. "Bide here! Don't move!"

Rel whistled. "You never told me you had a skill to offer."

Adam gazed at his scruffy shoes. "I had to learn to cook. But I want to be an artist."

"Weren't you training to be an artist?"

"Yes, but prentices also had to learn to cook. I don't like to do it," Adam added. "But I can."

Rel's misgivings increased sharply.

But unnecessarily: the captain came up to interview them, said that Adam could fix their evening meal on trial, and if the crew liked it, he was hired. As for Rel, a tall, strong-looking fellow who could hand, reef, and steer was always welcome.

Much to Rel's surprise, Adam took a long look around the little galley, setting a tentative forefinger to the wood here, then there, as the other two looked on in puzzlement. But then he set to work, and when he emerged again, it was to serve up an excellent batch of corn cakes, crispy spiced greens, and fish grilled with a splash of wine, all ingredients he found on hand.

When the trader had finished loading its cargo, it set sail, Adam and Rel on board

Eleven

Colend

IT TOOK THREE TRIES before Curtas could get back to see Shontande Lirendi, scarce days before the prince's household was to pack up for the return to Alsais for the winter.

Three tries because on the first, Thad — who had never been trained to climb walls — slipped and began to fall from the lowest roof. Curtas caught his wrist, and Thad's arm nearly pulled from his socket as he stared up, face strained with pain and the need to keep silent.

Curtas managed to get Thad pulled up and over the lip before the guards, alerted by a servant who heard Thad's heels hit the wall, passed below, weapons ready. Thad's arm was strained, his face and hands cut and bleeding from scraping over the rain gutter. They were forced to turn back, Thad bitterly disappointed in himself.

Neither had spoken at all until they retired at a scribal inn that night, a safe distance away. Then Thad had said, "It might be better if I write letters. He can always burn them."

And Curtas, relieved, said, "Good idea."

Thad scrupulously kept his promise when he got back home. He had been sufficiently intimidated by Shontande Lirendi, in spite of his young age — maybe because of it — to feel that only the most formal letter, on the best paper, written in a court hand with fine ink, would do.

Karhin, who loved writing letters, gladly added hers to Thad's. Because it took a couple more tries for Curtas to get past the vigilant guards — whose lives were forfeit if anyone got past them and was caught — he had a bundle of letters thrust inside his tunic when a storm blasted through, making it impossible for the guards to see an arm's length beyond their faces.

Curtas never told anyone how long it took to worm his way upward in that sleeting storm, with lightning stabbing all around. But at last he made it, his feet tapping the lit window of the prince's suite on the top floor until Shontande himself opened the mullioned window, which flashed a hundred crystalline reflections of the lightning silhouetting Curtas's hanging figure, before he swung inside the window and dropped, shivering, to the beautiful marquetry floor.

"I almost thought I imagined the sound," Shontande said, for he was hesitant about describing the mental prod that insisted someone hung outside the window, thinking desperately of him. "How did you manage that?" he asked, looking from Curtas to the end of the rope in the open window.

"P-pulley and l-line." Curtas's teeth chattered.

"Come to the fire," Shontande said. "You will be safe. They are all retired for the night."

"So I'd hoped," Curtas said, his mocs sloshing and his clothes dripping as he crossed to the fireplace, where he crouched so deeply in the hearth he was nearly in the flames, whereupon his clothes began to steam.

Shontande pulled the window to, then surveyed the pool of water on the floor. He walked off to his stately bath chamber to fetch towels. By the time he'd mopped up the evidence and festooned the towels over the backs of chairs near the fire to dry out, Curtas had stopped shivering so violently.

"For you," Curtas said, reaching inside his tunic and pulling forth a scribal pouch, magically warded against wet.

Shontande took it, but his interest remained on his visitor. "It seems a shame you could not wear it to protect you instead of whatever is inside."

"Letters," Curtas said. "Thad tried to come with me earlier in summer. We were nearly caught."

Shontande had sensed something of the sort, but as always kept his own counsel as Curtas continued, "So he wrote. So did his sister, Karhin. A couple times, as I wasn't able to get past the guards last time. And it seemed dangerous to lurk around too long. They also sent those two books."

Shontande pulled out the letters, and two slim books.

Curtas said, "Karhin thought you ought to have books suitable for a prince, but Thad thought you probably already had those, and you might like what people beside princes read. If you don't like old folk tales and the like, they'll find what you do want."

Shontande set the letters and the books on a beautiful, highly polished table worked with thin threads of gold. "Thad is right about books suitable for a prince. I believe I have every cautionary and instructive tome aimed at princes that has ever been written, each more earnest than the last." He grimaced. "And nothing else, save very carefully chosen histories, suitable for the son of a madman."

"Do they really believe you might be mad?" Curtas asked.

Shontande made an airy gesture. "I am beginning to believe it suits them to say so. What they believe, I cannot guess."

"But your father didn't inherit madness," Curtas exclaimed.

"That is true," Shontande said throwing himself into the chair so he could stare across the two arm's lengths into Curtas's face as if trying to read it. "As you said once before. But how do you know that?"

Curtas's gaze dropped as he considered what to say.

Shontande sat back. "It's easy enough to blame Norsunder. But I believe you cannot possibly know any more than I do the true cause, so it can only be conjecture."

Curtas did, in fact, know the true cause, but he reached for diplomacy anyway, because of the pain that Shontande didn't try to hide. "There is no madness in the Lirendi family. Everybody who can read history knows that. But it seems to suit your regency council to believe otherwise."

"So the world knows that, too?" Shontande's gaze was direct, his pupils huge.

"I don't know what the world knows," Curtas said, shifting to warm his other side, and incidentally breaking that unwavering gaze.

"I know that they are always watching me for signs of madness," Shontande said.

Curtas shook his head. "All I see is you here, effectively imprisoned. I don't know any of those people or their motivations."

Shontande got to his feet and reached a hand to brush over the books. "Colend does well," he said. "I have no complaint, save that I have no freedom of movement, but they insist it's for my own safety."

Curtas spoke recklessly, "Do you want to escape? I could get you out. You could go anywhere you want. Be anyone you want. Except maybe the Crown Prince of Colend."

Shontande threw back his head, his gaze going upward. He'd begun to grow, hints of the emerging bones of manhood no more than shadows in the wavering light. Yet his expression demonstrated the self-control of someone much older.

He barely breathed as he gazed sightlessly, nothing moving about him except the reflection of the firelight in those enormous pupils. "Thank you," he said finally, as the fire leaped and crackled. "I thank you for the pleasure imagining that will give me."

"But?" Curtas said, surprised. He'd sent his mind headlong down the path of extreme difficulties, for hiding Shontande would require more work than the prince had any idea of. And his orders had nothing to do with stealing a prince.

"But sometimes my father has moments of sanity. And I must be there, if I can," Shontande said. "I know there is something he wishes to tell me, but the . . .the madness always closes over. I have to be there if he fights free. My place is here. My purpose. Though sometimes I think . . ."

He waved his hand in another of those airy gestures. "Sometimes I am afraid too much time will pass before he sees me, and I won't be his son. I'll be grown. And as it says in so many of the old histories, he might see me as a threat."

Curtas said, "I told you on my second visit about the Child Spell, and hiding in plain sight."

Shontande touched his fingertips together and opened his hands. "And you illustrated that by talking of Senrid of Marloven Hess, who hides this way in plain sight. I've read about the Marlovens since then. Have you met him?"

*You will stay away from Senrid Montredaun-An . . .*Survival, Curtas had learned when very small, required keeping thoughts in private little boxes. Anything about his upbringing was locked in the deepest box. "No. As for escape, if you happen to change your mind—" His voice suspended as his chin came up.

They both stilled, and the prince understood: the only noise was the fire.

"Damn," Curtas muttered.

As fast as the storm had come on, it had blown past. He had to get out before the guards figured it out and came forth from their shelter to begin their rounds.

In three long strides he reached the window and threw it open, Shontande on his heels.

As the prince watched, Curtas leaped out into the air, with that terrible drop below, and caught the rope with a splatter of rain drops. He swung on the rope as he climbed rapidly hand over hand up it, then vanished from sight.

Shontande turned away, knowing that, carefully trained as he was, he would never have been able to manage that trick, and yet Curtas's assumption that he could not leave without aid — that he was incapable of escape, had he wished — required pondering. Curtas had confessed that he had been brought up as a thief. That certainly would explain the acrobatics, and his ability to hide his thoughts, but did thieves also have education and a sense of honor?

He felt that he had handled the discussion ineptly. That, too, required pondering. Perhaps it would be a good idea to discuss it when Curtas returned.

Right now, he had the letters and books. Shifting a couple of the gently steaming towels, he sat down to examine them. One was stories of the Peddler Antivad, which, from the illustrations, were probably humorous. The other was a traveler's tale about the mysteries of the northern lands.

He set those aside for later, and turned to the letters.

Thad's beautiful, formal missive was short. Shontande read past the formality, invisible to one raised to a formal life, to the lines offering friendship. The words were entirely conventional, but he remembered that red-haired boy perched so uncertainly on the roof, and he was inclined to believe the motivation genuine.

Karhin's letter was written in perfect court hand, and used court phrasing, but he immediately saw past that to the unknown writer who, in her turn, attempted to look past the trappings of princedom to the person behind. She wanted to know what made him laugh, what stories he favored, whose music and poetry he turned to.

Then she went on to describe the others in the alliance. Her careful words about Prince Glenn of Everon matched Shontande's memory of the glowering boy posturing away. He was also caught by the very careful words about "Atan" of Sartor, who — if he was reading the hints correctly — might be as constrained as he was by her regency council, with no mad father in the question.

Could he write directly to her? No. So much of his life was lived third-hand. He must meet her first, face to face. But he would listen for mentions of Atan of Sartor.

Karhin finished with a description of the mysterious Sartora, the Girl Who Saved the World, who had recently had a daughter by Birth Spell, and now everyone was wondering if there were three in the world who had Dena Yeresbeth, the second being Senrid. But she had not seen Liere in the months since the babe's appearance, so as yet that question was unanswered.

At the bottom of her letter, she had even written her golden notecase sigil. It was hidden under her signature, and he suspected she was uncertain it was appropriate.

He had never wanted a golden notecase. The one cousin he would have enjoyed writing to didn't care for writing at all. Anyone else, he knew would share his missives with ambitious relatives, if they weren't ambitious themselves. It was the way courtiers were raised.

But now he had a project. He could make one, using the magical training he had worked so hard to accrue. It might take a few tries, but he certainly had the time. And eventually, he would have someone to write to.

As he glanced down Karhin's letter, his gaze caught on those words about Dena Yeresbeth, a concept he'd come across in his historical reading, but imperfectly understood. How would you know if . . .things you couldn't explain hearing . . .was it that, or something else?

Not madness. Not madness.

Bereth Ferian

Reality, Liere discovered, was all the little things she had never before noticed in life, though they had always surrounded her in South End, the small town in Imar where she had been born.

She, who thought herself observant, had been completely

unaware of an important layer of life. She now suspected she was unaware of a lot of layers, but as some of those belonged to adults—and those details she shied from contemplating— she confined herself to what was before her.

Like diaper buckets.

The water purification spell was precisely the same as the one on the rain barrels, and the dish buckets in the kitchen, and the baths. The water was exactly as pure in each. But no one would dream of carrying a diaper bucket into a kitchen. Or drinking from the dish bucket.

These little rituals of everyday life had been uninteresting, but she thought about them now that her life was bound to a small scrap of humanity. There was no going off to visit Senrid, or Hibern, because the baby liked routine. And there was no place for a baby in her friends' homes. Babies required bedding, and baby clothes, and diapers and buckets.

At first Liere had been nearly overwhelmed, but she had listened carefully to Piper at the orphanage in Everon. Then, when she turned up in Bereth Ferian with the infant, many of the servants had been thrilled, and Lyren was passed from hand to hand.

The head steward had found Liere a nursemaid—one of Piper's lessons. For about four months, Liere handed her infant daughter off to a woman and shut her mind from the mental sounds of contentment. Lyren was supposed to regard *her* that way, but Liere couldn't give Lyren what she wanted most.

At five months, Lyren drank goats' milk, and began to crawl, but she was no longer mostly sleeping, and her mental cries could rip through Liere's consciousness like a knife.

Her sweet dream of a doll-like baby with wispy blonde hair who adored Liere, and would somehow swiftly grow into her best friend, had vanished like fog before the reality of an amazing being crowned by thick, silky dark hair, with thoughts as quick-changing as sun on water, and moods like the colors of the sea. Sometimes words drifted through: Liere sensed which words Lyren was interested in, and all of them were baby things.

As Lyren slept less and demanded more, it became harder to deal with her, and Liere's sense of guilt grew with every smile Lyren gave her. Because now she understood her own mother a little better.

And so she finally wrote her a letter—after six or seven

drafts—begging her to visit. Liere expected rage, insult, anger, anything but a thin woman not much taller than Liere arriving in Bereth Ferian by expensive transfer token.

Elen Fer Eider took over Lyren's life so naturally that it was a relief when Liere's anxious days suddenly became an orderly schedule that contented everyone.

Until Liere's father showed up.

When a palace runner arrived to summon her, saying the name Lesim Fer Eider, Liere's first reaction was sick anxiety, and she ran downstairs to the receiving room off the transfer chamber.

Liere had not seen her father for several years, and was shocked at how much older he seemed. The smoldering anger that breathed off him had grooved the lines deeper into his face, and his pale hair had thinned more, revealing more of his tight, angry brow.

As soon as he saw her, his head jerked back as if he'd encountered a terrible smell, and he said, "What have you done to yourself?"

The old fear paralyzed Liere. She could scarcely breathe. Though they stood in the elegant marble and gilt receiving room of one of the world's finest palaces, her emotions blasted her back to the bare, cheerless front room in their small house in South End. "Child Spell," she whispered.

"So you've ruined yourself playing around with magic, aping your betters," Lesim Fer Eider said caustically. "And when your high-and-mighty 'friends' get tired of your tricks to get attention and send you back to South End, what are the neighbors going to say? They will laugh us off the street!"

Arthur had frozen inside the doorway, his hand half-raised in greeting. He looked from Liere to her father, utterly unable to speak, or even move.

Behind him, Elen appeared, with Lyren on her hip. "Lesim," she said, and Liere hated how her mother's face looked anxious again. Until that moment she hadn't noticed how gradually it had smoothed over the weeks of her visit. "Is there trouble at home?"

"Yes, there is! You've been wasting time here, when from the looks of this place there are servants a-plenty. Why have you been gone so long?"

Arthur backed up and retreated down the hall, as did the transfer host, as Elen said quietly, "This is your granddaughter

Lyren. She looks exactly like my grandmother Margala, she who was beloved by everybody." Her voice trembled with conviction.

"Lyren! What kind of name is that?"

Elen turned to the daughter she had never understood, who looked unchanged from the day she had vanished from their home, though she ought to look nineteen instead of twelve.

Liere unconsciously stepped closer to her mother, aware that her mother had never been able to protect her from her father's corrosive bitterness. But Liere, until she had learned to shield her mind, had always heard her mother's longing to shield her children.

She said, "It's the first of Lyren's names. She's named after all my friends." And with a tremble-voiced show of bravado she reeled off those names, ending with, "Sartora."

Lesim Fer Eider reddened. "'Sartora'? What preposterous, pretentious foolery is this? Fer Eider is a good name, a respected name in South End. Or are you pretending to be something better than you are? Sartora!" He spat that out contemptuously. "Show me the Sartora family you've adopted into." And when Liere just stared back, "I thought so. You made it up. What are they going to say in South End? We're already the butts of gossip."

"If Liere had adopted into another family, the babe would still have another name," Elen said softly.

Lesim turned on her. "And I would see evidence of that family. Everything in proper order. Except that they never deigned to call upon us. Respected merchants of South End aren't good enough, no doubt." He jerked a stiff hand toward Liere. "Yet here she is, looking like a street rat. Are you the kitchen maid here? The shoe girl?"

Liere could not move her lips. She was already ashamed enough of the pretense of being "Queen in Bereth Ferian" and her father's excoriating tone threw her right back into the anxiety of early childhood.

"She's well respected," Elen said, unexpectedly coming to Liere's aid. "She has a place here. They don't do things the way we do, but they all work just as hard, in different ways."

Lesim looked disbelieving, but another glance around the fine room caused him to "Humph." Then, "When are you returning home, Elen? You have two other grandchildren, and from the looks of this place, they can afford help."

"Nobody, rich or poor, buys a grandmother," Elen stated. "I will return home anon." Her voice lightened. "This darling charmer has kept me here with her smiles."

Lyren, sensitive to the warmth in her grandmother's voice, cooed and rewarded her with a dimpled grin, in which one tooth gleamed.

Lesim said in a stiff undertone, "You've got another just as charming."

Elen's face lit. "Darling Marga's surrounded by helpers who want nothing more than to love her. But Lyren, so far away . . ." Then she turned to her husband, and said in a quiet, firm voice. "Here, I felt I was needed."

Twelve

Along Goerael Coast

NORTH OF GOERAEL IS the infamous Sea of Storms, from which most of the wind and weather patterns of the world originate. To explain it, ship captains often use the example of a clock — for those who come from places where clocks are known. Inside is a coiled spring, which slowly loosens over the seasons, the winds and storms spiraling out over half a year, then breaking up into smaller whorls of storm as winter closes in again in the north.

Before it breaks up, the outer curve of wind flow hits the warm air banding the world, and when the summer season begins in the south, the winds swoop from west to east, which in turn is important to the cycle of southern trade and ship travel.

These northern ships had adapted to their own cycle in which they worked their way northward from port to port along the continent of Goerael until reaching the last peninsula directly west of Land of the Venn, now called Florianth. Once they traded southern goods for the exquisite porcelain stoves of the Venn, and other fine artifacts made by people who mostly lived underground, the ships rigged for square and rode the winds in a fast, often exhilarating, sometimes dangerous, run all the way south—when the wind was right, in days rather than the weeks it had taken to work northward along the coast.

Rel had learned this from Captain Heraford of the Mearsieans. Thus he knew some of what to expect.

The ship set sail, beating into fractious winds, which called for a great deal of attention to the set of the sails. As always, Rel was aware of the rhythm of shipboard life. The entire world reduced itself to the boundary of wooden walls.

He was given a night watch, which was usual for newcomers. A week or so of adjustment, and he settled into sleeping by day and walking the deck by night, occasionally climbing to the masthead to scan for ship lights, at the behest of the mate of the watch. There were a number of local ships that made their living sailing east enough to catch those northward-laboring vessels who might not have touched land for weeks, and would be in need of fresh food, and sometimes cordage and spars if the storms had been exceptionally rough.

This was also the way news passed up and down the coast, including warnings about pirates plying the seas on the watch for certain kinds of traders. "Seeing as we're carrying flax," the captain said one evening, "we ought to be safe from pursuit, but we'll still keep a weatherly eye for those desperate enough to want a wide-bodied trade ship."

"Desperate?" Adam asked Rel, as he collected the square mess plates for dunking into the cleaning bucket. "Don't pirates want a big ship to keep all their loot in?"

"Pirates have to be fast," Rel said. "Long and lean. They turn their loot into gold, or spend it. And when they're hungry enough, set out to get more."

"Sounds kind of boring," Adam said as he took up his knitting—it was far too wet for sketching, and scarfs, hats, and mittens were always welcome.

The night shift was the easiest, and the quietest. Rel noticed straight off that most of this crew had been together for a long time. Captain Mathen, the first mate, and the carpenter seemed to be some kind of a family, with mutually discussed newly grown children between them, often referred to as "our," as in "How d'ya think our Jinnap is doin', navigating her first cruise?" and "I trust we'll be seeing our Poll when we reach Whiterock Harbor." The rest were pleasant enough, but they shared friends as well as history, if not family.

At first Rel was scarcely aware of the quiet boy they called

Cor, clearly new to sailing, who lived apart from everyone else as much as anyone could in so small a space. Rel began to suspect that the crew member who'd almost left the ship but came back had to be Cor, who seemed . . .odd.

Rel saw how the others slowed their words down and emphasized simple orders with gestures whenever they talked to him. Cor was about Puddlenose's age and size—maybe fifteen—and as well-made physically. There the similarities ended. Cor's tightly braided light hair had odd greenish streaks, and there were brown creases in his skin as if he seldom bathed. Where Puddlenose chatted easily with everybody, fitting himself to whatever company he found himself in, Cor was awkward, silent, often watching the horizon and brooding tight-lipped. He never met anyone's gaze.

Rel tried to be friendly, to be met with one-word responses to questions. All right, Cor didn't want company? Rel left him alone.

Adam had free time between meals, as he was not part of a watch. He only had to come on deck in response to "All Hands," which happened fairly rarely, as the weather so far had been clement, and the mates were all experienced, always aware of the hum of the rigging, the pull of sail and the pitch of the ship.

Adam often sat on the capstan with his knitting or—on rare fine days—his sketches. On one occasion, after the crew had their late meal he sat sketching the tattered clouds that looked like flames above a glorious sunset, when the wind caught a handful of his papers and sent them spinning and turning down the deck. Adam gave a squawk and leaped to catch them.

Rel happened to be strolling the deck as he waited for the bells to announce the watch change, so he put his longer legs to good use and swept up most of them.

"Here," he exclaimed in surprise. "You drew up those drakan ships."

"From memory," Adam said, and in an apologetic tone, "I know I don't have them right. Something is missing. Maybe many somethings."

Rel frowned down at the drawing, knowing that Adam liked talking about his work, and never minded opinions. "The shields down the rail, for one thing."

"Oh! Yes, now I remember. You are more observant than I," Adam said cheerfully.

"I saw those ships once before," Rel admitted. After all, the attack on Everon was not a secret. He just hated even thinking about it, much less talking.

"You did?" Adam asked. "When was that?"

"Some time back. Briefly."

Adam studied him, his vague gaze acute for once, or maybe it was the clear light. Because his head turned as he tracked a sea bird riding the current overhead. "There they are again. Different colors above and below. That, I can paint. But how can I paint how . . .they . . .move?" Adam asked, his hand swooping and diving through the air.

He wandered off, clutching his drawings. Rel smothered a laugh — then turned quickly, one arm coming up in a defensive block when a shadow darkened the periphery of his vision.

It was Cor. "The ships." He crooked his forefinger, emulating the prow of a drakan. "Where you see?"

His accent was odd to Rel, who had heard many accents in his travels. It reminded him a little of Senrid. A Marloven?

"It was south of Sarendan," Rel said slowly.

"You talk they?"

"No. I spied them from atop a cliff."

Cor's blue eyes widened.

"They were brought out of nowhere by magic," Rel said, remembering the startling sight of those strange high-prowed ships shooting into the icy water, nearly foundering on the rocks. "I don't know how."

Cor's breath hissed in. "You talk they? Them. I want — "

"All hands," the watch commander bawled, as the ship began to heel in a wind shift. They ran to take their place along the forming line in order to change sail.

The subject of the Venn ships did not come up again until a few days later; Rel was mildly bemused to find Cor working beside him.

"Venn drakans," he whispered. "You speak they?"

Rel shook his head. "Just watched."

As that day turned into another, and time streamed on, he found himself often working next to Cor. Rel's curiosity sharpened, but he had learned to wait.

Sure enough, one rainy day, as water hissed down all around and they were the only crew at the forecastle, Cor said, "I want. Go back. Speak they. Venn, prison." He looked around furtively, though the helmsman — the only other crew member on deck—stood at the wheel aft, the long length of the companionway between him and them. "Need help." Cor touched his lips. "Speak. Speech?" He touched his lips again, and then his ears.

They were both drenched to the skin. Rel noticed that Cor's skin still showed brown at the creases—not dirt, then, but dye? Fad or disguise? Skin painting was popular in a lot of places, but usually in patterns, not all over. "You want someone to interpret?" And when Cor looked back at him helplessly, Rel bit back the question, *Why are you here if you want to talk to the drakan ship crew?*

The answer was obvious—Cor was hampered not only by language, but by the invisible doors between an ordinary sailor and royal prisoners. He might even have been warned off, if he'd tried at the prison. Possibly chased off, which might explain his retreat to the ship.

Leaving the question: why would he be desperate to talk to people who, if Tsauderei was right, had vanished from the world eight centuries ago?

"I think I know what you need," Rel said slowly, " or rather, who." Though Sartor was unlikely to have any embassy on this continent, Atan surely would know how to get around the doors of diplomacy. She was probably getting lessons in this kind of maneuvering at that very moment.

He envisioned her sitting patiently in one of those fabulous anterooms, her serious gaze turning toward each speaker, her hands quietly expressive. The rest of the Sartoran inner circles of government saw her as the last of a long line of rulers—as a cipher to be spoken through—as an ignorant girl. None of them saw her for who she was: smart, honest, and very, very determined.

He blinked and there was Cor's hopeful face.

Lightning cracked overhead. The wind shifted, causing the ship to heel dangerously.

The mate of the watch popped up from the hatch, tossing away the bread he had been eating, and bawled, "All hands!"

Over the following weeks, Rel considered how to approach Atan on Cor's behalf, without creating another difficulty in her life. Between those mental wrestlings he did his best to teach Cor some Sartoran, as the green slowly washed out of the boy's hair, and the brown stain vanished from his flesh.

The ship touched at Dolhir — which meant they stayed out in the harbor and rowed in half of the barrels and barrels of flax beautifully hackled in the strong sun over the belt of the world, going west and north to be incorporated into the mountain weavings, where the sun seldom appeared and the weather was too cold to grow flax.

Then they replaced those barrels with good ordered by others along the route. By now Rel had learned that the ship belonged to a family consortium, and it carried goods to be handled from their stores along the coast.

They set sail immediately on the turn of the tide for Has Peri, where the rest of the flax was unloaded, and in came bales of fine woven cloth from the morvende in the western mountains of Koteli, again to go north.

Cor and Rel were in different watches, and due to the fretful weather that required everyone in a watch to constantly be on deck, or laboring with the loading and unloading, Cor and Rel did not have significant time alone. While in company with others, they talked Sartoran that rapidly became less laborious — at least Cor was a very fast learner. His accent remained strong, at times reminding Rel of Senrid's accent, but at others, not. Rel had never heard that accent before, but when he tried asking where Cor came from, the answer was even more evasive than Adam's.

Well, Rel had his own secret about his origins, so he wasn't about to judge.

They were on the way to the important trade city of Alma on the Almeiran peninsula when at last there came a calm day — so calm the winds died, and left them rocking on the water. At last it felt like summer.

This warm balm was enjoyable for a day.

Cor sought Rel out when the latter emerged in the evening for his first meal of the day. They climbed up onto the foremast-head, Rel thought to continue another lesson in Sartoran, but instead, Cor launched into a carefully planned speech.

"In next harbor, you go back with me. Talk for me, talk to drakan sailors? I pay. All my pay." Cor withdrew from his coarse-woven tunic a bag that clinked promisingly. It had to contain his entire earnings.

Rel considered. At Alma, they could easily catch someone going south. With that money, they could even pay for passage.

As for Mondros's quest, it would be a mere matter of starting out again, but so what? It wasn't as if Rel had any deadline. The Venn, penned up for centuries, were not about to break out, and Rel had always heard that mages thought in terms of decades. Not days.

The most pressing reason, he admitted to himself, was that it gave him an excuse to contact Atan, and for a reason no one could possibly object to.

"I will," he said.

He figured he'd meet up with Adam again some other time, the way he encountered Puddlenose now and then on his travels, but it was an unspoken etiquette among those who lived on the road to tell their traveling companions before shifting in another direction.

He found Adam and explained in Kifelian, which he knew no one local would understand, as none of them had been anywhere near Colend. As expected, Adam said, "Sounds interesting! If you actually get on board the drakans, look at them closely so you can describe them when next we meet."

After that Rel was called to work, and Cor retired to sleep.

Over the next two days, as the heat climbed exponentially with the sun, they cleaned the ship from topgallant yards to the hold. The only break in this laborious stretch occurred when they spoke two ships floating slowly by on the southward tack, where the airs were infinitesimally more favorable. Then, at last, the glassy water rippled, the slack upper sails shivered, then slowly filled.

The captain came out of his cabin, looked skyward and seaward. Everyone waited for the order to head northwest — which didn't come.

"Set main and topgallants, north-northeast," he said tightly.

If Rel hadn't already discovered who was related to the captain and who was not, he would have seen it in the way the relatives mirrored that grim expression, while everyone else looked puzzled. But obeyed.

They tacked their way into the outer edges of what were called the Floating Islands. Rel had read on one of Captain Heraford's charts that some were actually believed to float — that no two maps showed them in exactly the same positions or the same size.

He'd thought that fanciful until he overheard covert grumbling: no one wanted to sail into the Floating Islands.

Pirates—lee shores—no night sailing, too dangerous—rocks and reefs. By the next day lookouts were posted at the highest trucks of all three masts, constantly on the watch for hazards as they passed the first two small islands.

On the fourth day, as intermittent rain flattened the sea, the captain conned the ship himself, guiding them by a chart that looked newly sketched.

Rel found Adam in the galley, putting away the dishes after early mess. "What you want to wager," he said in Kifelian, "the captain's got one of those gold notecases?"

"Someone certainly wants him to do something," Adam a-greed. And as shouts echoed around the deck, "Sounds like—"

"All hands!"

Everyone had a place at a rope or on a yard as the ship navigated between two narrow islands. It was like sailing up a river.

At the far end, they spilled their wind and anchored. "Boat down," the captain ordered shortly, tension radiating off him like summer heat.

Watched by the entire crew, Captain Mathen and his nephew, the first mate, rowed into a shallow stream, where someone in another boat could be made out through a field glass. As everyone watched, something was loaded into his boat, after which he rowed back, his brow in an angry crease.

As soon as the boat and the barrel were loaded onto the deck they set sail immediately, bending westward to get out of those islands. When they'd sunk that pair of islands beyond the horizon, the captain approached the barrel, which the first mate had been watching.

He raised his voice. "My sister prevailed on me to take this and guard it, as she says she's being chased by thieves. She claims it's a rare wine, but no wine ever acted like this." He jiggled the barrel, his muscles bulging. "If there is liquid in it, then I'm a Venn."

Cor's breath hitched. Rel cast him a glance. But Cor seemed to be concentrating on understanding the captain's rapid, angry speech.

Then he set about opening the barrel, whose top was not only nailed, but there was a layer of pressed metal below it, and then another cover beneath.

That, too, was pried up, revealing—

"Sand?"

Captain Mathen plunged his hand into the sand, then came up with a handful of something as sand poured between his fingers in a thin tan stream. He opened his fingers onto the deck, and they all stared down at gloriously iridescent stones about the size of grapes as they rolled and rattled.

"Halair," breathed the oldest crewman on board, the captain's great-uncle, who functioned as sail maker.

"Land pearls?" Rel said, translating *hal* and *aer* or *air* into Sartoran.

All heads turned. The first mate had gone pale. "You don't know what those are?" he asked, as the captain rapidly brushed the halair together and shoved them deep into the barrel.

Rel opened his hands. "First journey to this continent."

"The price for having one is death," the first mate said heavily. "Much less selling it."

One of the younger cousins said, "You can get the price of a ship for three of those things. If someone outa the lake lands don't get you first."

Captain Mathen turned Rel's way, but spoke so everyone could hear. "They are called land pearls because they are found on the west side of the mountains some distance north. I don't know land distances, but I do know they are ground and mixed up so they make enamel, which in turn laid on buildings and the like makes 'em shine like pearls. They aren't allowed out of those kingdoms. At all. Pain of death."

He paused, meeting eyes. "This here barrel, my sister, who's been trouble all my life, lied about. She wants it going to some smuggler, but it's not going to be. I'm going to get rid of it in Alma, to my dad, who'll know what to do without getting us all killed. Did you hear that? *Without getting us all killed.* So we're going to forget we even saw it, and when we dock at Alma, it'll be the first thing off. And gone as soon as I can make that happen. Understood?"

Variations on "Yes sir!" echoed all over the ship.

Shaking his head, the captain rolled the barrel into his cabin, and shut the door.

They soon had to spill wind and drop anchor for the night, as navigation was far too dangerous. When the sun came up the next morning, it was to another siege of light, variable airs — mostly blocked by the hump of the island to the northeast.

Three ships glided by on the opposite tack in as many days. They spoke the first ship, as the custom is on the sea. As the second came into view, Adam went to the captain. "Could we signal for fresh greens? I'm afraid we're out, after all this time floating."

The captain sighed. "Can't you pick something off one of these islands? I see stuff growing all over them. Take a boat, and as many hands as you need. They may as well be working."

"I see only nettle, stickle-weed, and a variety of grasses whose effect on the stomach would be very bad," Adam said apologetically.

So they hailed the second ship by signal, and Adam rowed over to request fresh food in trade, but came back empty-handed.

The next day they fared better — he rowed back in triumph with carrots, beans, radishes, turnips, and two colors of potatoes. No sooner had he cooked up a careful portion of these into a savory soup than the wind picked up once more, and by nightfall built into a gale.

Once again they had to lie up in the lee of an island, rolling on waves reaching up well past the jib. The storm howled around them for a day and a night, the clouds so low it seemed the frantically arcing masts pierced the surging undersides.

At last the sleet softened into summer rain, and then passed to the southeast in a silver curtain, leaving them to rock once more on a glassy sea. The island that had protected them again blocked the wind.

All this time the captain stayed shut in his cabin, angry and brooding over their dangerous contraband. When at last a capricious west breeze flirted with the sails, the captain roared hoarsely for all hands, hungry as they were. Their stores had diminished at a sobering rate.

Having ordered topsails and topgallants drawn tight, and determined to wring as much distance out as he could before the winds either changed or died, Captain Mathen demanded they go east, clear the islands, and make a straight run north. "But we're out of the patrol area, Uncle," the first mate began.

"Do it. I want us in Alma by week's end, and no touching shore before then. We don't dare, when a single loose word could get us all killed."

Tension gripped everyone as they went about their tasks. Even the surge of the ship on the blue waters and the cold, clean wind did not raise spirits. This fretful, untrustworthy wind struck forward of the beam, calling for finicky sail combinations and tightly handled tacking.

With relief they counted off each island that slid past. It was full dark when they anchored.

Next morning, the golden sun glinting on the horizon between the slate-gray sea and equally gray clouds limned what everyone feared second to prowling patrol ships: a rake-masted, narrow-hulled pirate.

Thirteen

Land of the Venn

THEY HAD ONE POSSIBLE defense: speed.

Everyone worked, watch on watch, as they piled on studding sails until the masts creaked in warning and the ship heeled at such a slant that the water foamed along the rail. The pirate, though built for speed, was hampered by a thick mat of seaweed attached to its bottom. Pirates could not sail into harbors and hire scrapers, as had Captain Mathen in Alcandamer two harbors ago.

Rel worked alongside his crewmates. He remembered his golden coin, but he wouldn't leave the rest unless he was forced to. He thought of his sword in the crew's quarters, the hilt hidden with a dirty cloth around it. He hadn't done sword drill for months—but one thing you could say for work on the yardarms, it kept up your strength.

That night the winds were so strong everyone on watch had duty. As soon as he was dismissed below, instead of going to the wardroom with the rest of his watch for breakfast, he made his way noiselessly to the crew's quarters, where he found himself alone.

He checked to make certain his sword was loose in its scabbard, then felt for his coin to reassure himself . . .

It was not there.

He had a special pocket in his pack for things he did not want to lose. It lay against an inner seam. No one would have known it was there unless searching for it. He felt more urgently, and finally upended his entire pack, shook every piece of clothing before refolding it, and examined each pocket and seam.

Mondros's coin had vanished.

Furious, Rel repacked everything, too annoyed to notice how difficult it had become to keep his balance, until a sudden, deep plunge threw him into a bulkhead. He secured his pack and dashed to the ladder, aware of the noise he'd shut out: the rising wind.

One of the infamous deepwater storms howled straight off the Sea of Storms to the north and hit them hard. Sea, sky, and a sense of direction vanished into gale-force darkness.

Day and night, time and bearing lost meaning. They dared not strip to a scrap of sail just wide enough to keep them pointed into the wind, not with the occasionally glimpsed pirate ship, like some kind of evil ghost, shadowing them closely.

They ate in turns, dripping wet, and snatched bits of sleep wherever they could; no one had time to go below to the hammocks, which banged and smashed anyway. Once Rel was dismissed for a break, his hands so numb they felt like two sacks of sand tied to his wrists. He looked in vague surprise at a sluggish cut on one palm from hauling the foresheet. He was too exhausted to feel anything but indifference.

He stumbled into the galley to discover the captain had arrived not long before, judging by the pool of water sloshing beneath him. The captain hunched in exhaustion as Adam deftly served out the scrapings of oat-slurry that were about all that was left of their stores.

"Why are they after us?" Sails asked the bulkhead. "Why us?"

The captain had been glaring through his bowl, through the pull-down table, the hull, the keelson, the uncountable fathoms below. But at this he raised his head sharply. "I know why." He stabbed a finger at Adam. "You were the only one talked to anyone outside our ship. Only one, when we spoke that trader. You blabbed about those damned land pearls."

"I didn't," Adam protested, then grimaced. "I might have asked something when they talked about painting. There was a girl aboard that trader, doing a mural in the cabin, and —"

"What did you say?"

"I only asked if she knew how paint was made with land pearls. See, she said —"

"If you weren't keeping us alive with *this*." The captain banged his square wooden mess bowl onto the galley shelf that served as a table. "I would fling you over the rail right now. Damn you for an *idiot*."

"At least he can cook," old Sails said as he put his awl away. "As for blame, I say that rests square on young Marit, who never shoulda brought you into her schemes in the first place."

Rel gazed at Adam, not believing the same boy who could talk about the subtleties of Colendi shadow vernacular could have done something that stupid.

Adam sighed, looking so unhappy that Rel could not meet his eyes. He gazed at his bowl, discovered he'd eaten everything and was scraping the bowl in futile search for more. Without speaking Adam set a biscuit before him, and Rel wondered how he could be so observant and yet so oblivious.

The biscuit was gone in two bites. He leaned back, closed his eyes . . .and was shaken awake by an apologetic crew member.

He forced himself to his feet, and braced himself to bend into the howling wind for another endless nightmare.

One bleak dawn the ship's bell clanged wildly. Those asleep and in the stupor that passed for wakefulness shook themselves, rubbed ice crystals from eyebrows and whatever hair straggled from their yeath-fur hats, and stared in horror at the pirate nearly alongside.

Rel vaulted down the hatch, and reappeared with his sword, which he swung to warm up cramped muscles as he scanned the deck for the best defensive position against the likeliest angle of attack.

As he did, he took in his crewmates, strong people all, but exhausted, and worse, the lack of drill on this cruise showed in the way they stood looking to one another and the captain for guidance. Rel knew the only hope they had would be if the pirates were equally untrained, counting on fright and the noise of boarding to intimidate their prey into surrender.

Time suspended as the two ships heaved on the mountainous green-gray seas. The pirate boarding party looked down at the deck of the trader as their captain swept his expert gaze over them—and stopped at the tall, broad-shouldered youngster whose stance revealed a trained fighter.

The pirate captain pointed his sword at Rel, his lip curling in anticipatory triumph. "I want that one alive. He might be useful."

The pirates gave a roar—out swung grappling hooks—and pirates swung over.

Rel had a heartbeat's time to notice Cor taking up a fighting stance at his left, a cutlass gripped in one hand. "Stay back." Rel motioned Cor behind him.

Then the first pirate dropped to the deck.

Rel didn't wait for the pirates to catch their balance. He struck low and hard, having been taught by Captain Hereford that knees are the weakest point for anyone standing, and if you are reluctant to kill outright, whacking enemies' legs from under them could be compassed by anyone, especially under threat.

Emboldened by Rel's effective defense, the crew rallied behind him, belaboring pirates with a variety of weapons or carpentry tools. A secondary wave of pirates prepared to swing over when screams from their lookout caused all heads to whip around.

Someone else had sailed up on the pirate's weather side, stealing their wind.

The rain had lifted at last, though the sky was still low and threatening; beyond the pirate's foremast rigging Rel made out the upward slant of a jib that curved a lot like those ancient Venn drakans.

Nearby Cor froze, his breath hissing.

Rel ducked a swinging boarding axe, thrust at the big pirate trying to get past him, and said over his shoulder, "Get behind me!"

Cor started, lips compressed as two pirates charged. Fighting beside Rel, he whipped up his cutlass. Block, strike— and his pirate fell, curled around the stab wound in his gut, as Rel broke his pirate's right kneecap, then brought his sword in an uppercut on the hot-nerve place in his left elbow.

Then it was over. The newcomers swung across on the pirates' grappling lines. With lightning-fast efficiency they struck down the pirates, and ranged up, facing the horrified traders, most of whom had retreated to the aft deck, leaving Rel at point. Cor stood at his left shoulder.

Then came the strangest part of the lengthy nightmare. A bony fellow with hair the color of butter began to gesture toward Rel and Cor. He took a step and stilled. His eyelids flashed up so dramatically that Rel could see the pale blue of his irises five paces away. He turned his head sharply, shouted something or other, and half a dozen sailors surrounded Cor and took him away.

Rel heard Cor's teenage honk protesting, but not what he said. Then a pair of armed and armored men faced Rel. One commanded him to surrender his sword in . . .

Venn?

The Universal Language Spell is untrustworthy with languages difficult for mages to access. Without access they cannot bind equivalent spells into the overall enchantment. Chwahir tops the list, but Venn is second, and thereafter some of the Venn-related languages, plus some tongues spoken on Toar, whose borders are dangerous to cross.

Rel's captors separated him from Daelender, the sword Atan had given him, but with a sort of rigid respect, and he was directed by an opened palm instead of shoved.

He'd fallen into enough adventures to differentiate between being treated as an enemy, a suspect, or a criminal. Everyone had rules for handling prisoners.

Perhaps because he was so tired, memory seized him in spite of his precarious situation, and he had to shake his head to remain present. But even then the question persisted: Did Kessler know who he was or didn't he?

We're not done with one another yet, Rel thought as he was motioned below-decks with the rest of the traders. Soon came the unmistakable sounds of their own ship being handled by someone else as it heeled.

"The new pirates are taking my ship," Captain Mathen whispered. Then he glared at his old uncle. "Keep that damn traitor away from me."

Rel glanced about him, but didn't see Adam. At least he had enough prudence to stay out of the captain's reach.

Rel cleared his throat. "I don't think they're pirates. That is, I'm fairly certain they speak Venn, whatever they are."

"Venn!" The exclamation all around him was more of an epithet.

The gloomy crew, exhausted almost beyond endurance, retired to their hammocks and fell asleep one by one. Rel glanced tiredly, not seeing Adam in his hammock. Maybe he was hiding in the hold.

Rel shrugged as he fell into his own hammock, which swung peacefully. His last thought was, Well, Father, it seems I've reached my target after all . . .

His dreams careened between storm-wild seas, Mondros's mountain cabin, and Kessler's flat blue stare.

Rel might have slept through an entire day. There was no knowing.

He woke to gnawing hunger and a desperate thirst. Mess tables had been let down, and from the hum of conversation he discovered that someone—Adam? Their captors?—had left fresh bread, green-stalks, and grilled fish for them to eat, as well as a cask of fresh water.

There was enough for everyone, after which Rel retreated to his hammock again. He slept.

When the hatch was thrown at last, they clambered to the deck to find themselves in a harbor in which ice chunks floated, bumping up against the ship with gently insistent taps. The only sign of summer was the pinpoint sun hanging up there in the sky, though it was very late in the day—early evening farther south. They had all pulled on their winter clothes, clean due to the cleaning frame below, but still feeling frowsy and uncertain.

Rel was convinced this had to be the Land of the Venn by the unrelieved grimness surrounding him. Everything was gray: the low, cloudy sky, the restless sea the color of pewter, the thick bulwarks carved out of rock rising above the granite-flagged wharf. The harsh, cold wind scraped the stone clean, denying the scene the touch of color that moss might have lent it. The towers stood starkly against that grim sky.

Tall Venn waited for the armored guards to motion the fearful, shivering trade crew down a long stone jetty toward two figures in thick greatcoats of midnight blue, with what looked like some kind of hammer with a crown over it worn on the breast. The escort guards struck right hands to chests and paused, perforce causing the traders to shuffle to a stop, worried and sullen glances interchanged.

One of the waiting figures lifted a hand, forefinger pointing out Rel. "We will take the tall one," she said in barely understandable Sartoran.

The traders' guards separated out Rel and took his pack with motions that invited no argument. He was led in one direction, the crew in another. As they parted, he looked back for Adam. When he did not see that familiar curly head, he tried to count the crew. His last glimpse of the traders was of Captain Mathen sending a weary, hopeless glance back at his ship, then they vanished beyond the walled jetty.

Rel's heart thumped as the two in midnight blue stepped to either side of him and set a brisk pace. Even if he hadn't seen at a glance how heavily armed they were, he recognized from their walks that both women — as tall as he — had been trained as warriors.

They led him to one of the forbidding gray buildings, one leading and one following behind Rel as they passed through a massive iron-reinforced door. The ease with which the first one opened that door convinced Rel that his decision to cooperate was wise, besides, he had no idea where to go even if he'd managed to fight free.

If they'd wanted to kill him outright, they could have done it aboard the ship, or out on that wind-scoured wharf under the bleak, wintry sky. Well, he was supposed to investigate the Venn. Looked like they wanted to investigate him.

They entered a short hall and turned sharply to one side, where waited another heavy door. It opened to a stairway lit by glow-globes set in iron sconces. Down they traveled, down and down.

Gradually the bitter cold gave way to warm air wafting from somewhere.

Another doorway, etched with intricate knots looping and weaving in compelling patterns, did not prepare him for the shock of color. Light, bright as noonday, in the spring made the most of gilt vaulting curving high overhead, to join with complications of arches that evoked the knotted patterns he'd seen in the door. Arches, carvings, and beyond the intense cobalt of a painted sky, with what he suspected was the northern starscape.

He could not gauge distance anymore than he could dimension, then he was urged through yet another door.

Here the stonework was all in pale colors to waist height,

and above that plastered walls of sky blue, the curving ceiling marked at intervals by the sort of glass insets he'd seen in some ships, meant to gather light to enhance what reached below-decks. Only while those were dim except at noon in summer, these glowed with what appeared to be strong morning light, as if the ceiling lay directly under the surface. He knew they were far underground, which meant the stones had sunlight gathered by magic.

He was handed off to armed guards in gray. The pairs spoke in formal ritual, the only word he was certain of being "Crown."

Shortly thereafter he was gestured into a room with a platform bed, a small table set on short legs bent inward to suggest an arch, stone floor and flat blue plaster above. Over the door had been set a single glow-globe.

The door closed.

The origins of blood magic lie in the healing arts.

It was one of the most volatile of all magics, and while dark mages usually did not mind the high rate of fatalities in experiments, even they eventually ran out of prisoners or criminals before mastering the more grandiose plans.

Light mages had for centuries been forbidden to venture there. Healers stayed strictly within the bounds of their training and oaths—and healer mages in what was called the high arts trained longer than most other branches of mage learning.

As Siamis crossed the border into the Land of the Venn, he reflected on the similarities between the healer mages and the mysterious Eyes of the Crown, the mage descendants of the dags of a thousand years ago.

The mages called Eyes of the Crown had incorporated blood magic into their arts, using it as magical enhancement and personal wards through complicated ink patterns stippled onto their bodies with steel needles. Ritual equaled control. In the rest of the world, those drawn to healer magic were the idealists, and he wondered if a similar motivation drew the Venn Eyes.

It couldn't be completely the same, because the Eyes also were granted permission to kill invading mages, especially any who crossed the border into the Land of the

Venn. They were therefore more lethal than the Arm of the Crown, the military defenders, because they were sneakier.

After spending a full month studying the border wards from one of the most difficult mountain passes in the north of the kingdom, well out of human reach, Siamis decided the best plan was to plant transfer tokens at a number of places along the border, break the tracer wards, and while the mages raced to investigate all those breeches, cross by foot at the most desolate and difficult to reach. He'd walk into the Land of the Venn on foot, performing no magic, which would make him impossible to trace by magic, though if he was not careful, he could be tracked.

This he did, under cover of a blizzard. Two weeks he stumbled half-blinded down a valley, which gave him barely enough protection from the howling winds and horizontal shafts of icy snow to keep him from being blown off his feet. When he reached the lower region, he sensed, rather than saw, that he was being tracked.

Exhausted as he was, head-light from hunger (for he'd had to carry what he could eat), he now had to use everything he had learned about stealth.

But Norsunder was the deadliest of schools.

Fourteen

Summer, 4745 AF
Colend

THE BOY NICKNAMED LITTLE Bee until a recent birthday yelled in delight, "Adam! You're back!"

"Heyo, Bee. What colors do you smell?"

"Green! But green is almost gone," Bee said. "Yellow sky time is coming when the bells sing hot the longest."

"Summer?" Adam guessed as he set his pack down beside the bench where Bee sat with strings of memory beads.

"Yes!" Bee lifted his face happily, as a face appeared in the open window above.

"Adam?" Karhin called, and added in as natural a voice as she could, "Is Rel with you?"

"Still sailing," Adam called up. He added ruefully, "I did something really stupid, and I'd forgotten my promise to sketch at the music festival. So I made my way back."

Karhin turned away, hiding her disappointment in a bustle to arrange an added place at their midday meal.

Down below, Bee shivered with delight. "They let me go to hear the first day of the festival, and I guessed who would win."

"I already missed it?" Adam asked. "Oh, I always seem to be late. I shall have to run to catch up with myself."

Bee thought that a prime joke, and as Adam went inside to join Thad and Karhin to find out news, Bee repeated it to himself a couple times, "Catch up with myself, catch up with myself." But with the words came the sense of two Adams, the one with the voice Bee heard in the air, and the one with a voice he heard in his head.

His humor died away as he pondered that, while upstairs, Karhin said, "Thad is on duty. You are most welcome to wait. What adventures did you have at sea?"

"I was a good cook and a bad sailor," Adam said cheerfully. "They were glad to see me go. Cooking I can do anywhere, and easier. If I leave today, then I can listen in all the towns, and when the festival is over, make my way north. Any news here? Do you have any messages for me to carry?"

"Life has been quiet, I am happy to say. I did meet again King Tereneth of Erdrael Danara, who, like the others, prefers his short name, Terry." Her face lifted. "Now when I read his letters, I hear his voice."

"Laughter in it," Adam said. "When I met him, he told me a day isn't a good one if he hasn't had a chance to laugh."

Karhin put her palms together in agreement, thinking of the faint lines in Terry's face, evidence of terrible pain. But his gaze was so . . .so *true*. She said aloud, "As for other news, everyone is using notecases now. Hibern made them for those who cannot buy one."

"Not everyone." Adam shook with silent laughter.

A month later, as summer reached its height, in the Altan duchy in northern Colend, the capital swarmed with musicians. Four performers on the verge of adulthood had arrived early that morning, dusty and travel-worn but hopeful, as they had made it this far in the competition.

This round would decide who went to Alsais for the final contest.

"*He's* here," Jande, their leader, said in a tone of displeased discovery.

Three of the Colendi quartet turned to face Jande, who was also the oldest. Jande's broad, pleasant face had tightened, his lips thin.

"Who's here?" Elisse, the single woman, looked around.

"The foreigner. With the farmer's whistle."

Elisse knew whom Jande meant before she spied the familiar blond boy on the other side of the green, talking to a tall, thin fellow with a tiranthe, and a girl with a proper flute. She sighed. "Jande, he must be good, or he wouldn't be here, one step away from Alsais."

Her brother said behind his hand, "Or he might have been chucked out of the last round, and he's here to listen and to learn. We did that, our first time. Don't you remember?"

"Why," Jande said heavily, "must he be here at all?"

No one argued. All four felt varying degrees of resentment that foreigners came to compete in the Music Festival, which should by rights be confined to Colendi—and oh, sure, Sartorans. And perhaps kingdoms neighboring Sartor. But anyone else, why didn't they hold their own competitions? Next thing you knew, Jande had said in private, moon-faced Chwahir would be turning up, burbling through their noses in their stupid hums.

It didn't help that the previous year's Silver Feather had gone to some choral group from islands nobody in Colend had even heard of. "Though they were wonderful," Elisse had admitted.

Her brother and their friends had no answer to that; they all knew that place of origin was irrelevant to the unknown judges.

Jande scowled at the blond boy now sitting alone on a bench before the guild house, working at his marsh cane flute with his knife. A marsh cane flute! He did not even have to grace to be apologetic for such a crude instrument.

At the first competition, Elisse had first noticed the boy because of the dark mottle of bruises under his honey-brown skin, and his swollen knuckles. His hands hurt to look at, and yet he seemed determined to play his simple cane flute. She had respected that, though she'd kept her opinion to herself.

"Probably kicked out of one of these half-civilized kingdoms for his presumption," Jande had said, lip curled. "At least the judges, whoever they are, will surely have the good taste to rule against someone who could not be bothered to obtain the very best instrument possible."

The others agreed. The only excuse for a flute any non-musician could make would be as accompaniment for singing, and he couldn't be singing if he was playing that wretched cane flute.

Perhaps it was pity, perhaps the judges were fools, which was why they had been chosen to judge at the earliest levels, for the fellow had been selected twice.

"I'd like to hear him play," Elisse said, noticing that at least this time the boy's bruises were gone, and his hands looked normal. "He must be good, if he's here."

Jande had suggested they ignore those they considered beneath them, and as the Altan festival competition would run over two days, with people performing at inns and eateries as well as in the open air (and on stage if they could manage to arrange it) it was more difficult to hear all one's competitors than not.

"I," Jande said, "would not go two steps out of my way to endure the tootle of a marsh cane flute." Irritated at others' lack of standards, he said, "We have been sitting in that wagon all night. We should find a place to warm up."

Since his music master had included exercise in the first part of warming the voice — the body had to be strong to sing well — that meant removing themselves from the public eye.

He did his best to shake off the irritation, which never sounded well in voice. They found a spacious enough room for four, and set aside their packs.

Jande hummed under his breath as they began the strenuous physical warm-up that sent the blood singing through all limbs, muscles glowing from within. As Jande added in extra pushups in an effort to shed his bad mood, he contented himself with a little dream about all foreigners being constrained to watch from the sidelines.

In music there was no room for pity (surely it was misplaced pity that allowed for cane marsh pipes, which you couldn't even call flutes) or being generous to outsiders. Music, his master had said, requires the superlative in effort, dedication, and material. Talent was only the starting place.

They broke to clean up, put their stale travel clothes through the cleaning frame for their next journey (each privately hoping that it would be to Alsais, and not back home), then don their performance tunics, trousers, and thin summer over-robes.

Last they rebraided each other's hair with tiny silk

blossoms. It would never do to go out in public sweaty or mussed, like a day laborer given leave, Jande had said once. Elisse and her brother—from a family with a long tradition in shoemaking—had absorbed Jande's lofty standards as they had absorbed their music teacher's training.

They left to seek breakfast, during which they broke up to chat with acquaintances, or to review; Elisse, on seeing the blond flute player again, said nothing to Jande, but to her brother, "I'm curious about the foreigner."

Her brother shrugged. "Not me. Unless that flute gets him to Alsais."

Elisse respected Jande. Few sang better, or were more serious about music. His family was rich—he could be at Lake Skya shore now, enjoying the summer on the water with the rest of the wealthy, instead of wandering the dusty roads and singing in streets. She and her brother had worked very hard to be chosen for this quartet. But Jande had a tendency to direct their lives as well as their music.

She waited until Jande fell in conversation with some people they'd met in Ranflar, and crossed the grassy space before the guild house where lived the local aged population who had no homes of their own, or who preferred to live with their age mates, having handed down their homes. Guild retirement homes were usually nicer than government houses, she reflected as she glanced at the old folks wandering about, and you didn't have to do community service for your bed and board. Of course, some liked doing community service.

She wondered if the judges for the present competition had been picked out from the guild home population. That would be fun for them!

She approached the boy, who sat alone on a rock, his head bent over the marsh cane flute. Like most foreigners, he seemed unaware of where his shadow lay, but politeness caused her to approach from the side, within his view, so that her shadow safely melded with the dappled shadows of the candle-chestnut nearby.

He worked with a knife at his flute's sound hole, carefully carving tiny curls thinner than a blade of grass.

He glanced up briefly. He had sleepy brown eyes, and corn-colored hair a shade lighter than Jande's, but clipped short like a commoner's, curling slightly on his neck above the collar of his shirt.

She touched her palms together in the peace, then asked, "Did you make your flute?"

"Yes." He spoke the single word with an accent.

"I'm Elisse," she said. "And you?"

"David."

"Duh-feed?"

"Close enough." A pause, during which he turned the knife expertly, and shaved it over the edge of the sound hole. His droopy brown gaze lifted to her almost as if it took too much effort, then returned to his task as he said equably, "I am from Geth. You could say sister world, the one you never see in the sky. We do not see this one, either, from our islands — we call you Darksiders, or Nightsiders."

"I once heard a song about that," Elisse said. "'Nightside of the sun.' I thought it meant that they lived always in night."

"And so we thought about you." He smiled.

"How did you come to hear of the Colendi Music Festival from so very far away?"

"My teacher." David added in his slow voice, "I am given to understand, this festival, it was Sartoran, yes? For centuries?"

"It is true, but that changed in my great-grandmother's day," Elisse said, glancing across the glade. On the other side, under the oldest and broadest chestnut tree, Jande stood, wearing his performance robe, his golden hair with the tiny cerulean night sky buds etched against the cream-colored wall behind him. He was glancing around. She could tell from his posture that he wanted to begin.

She hesitated, looking down at the boy in the common laborer's plain, high-collared cottonweave shirt — the best you could say about it was that it was clean — and the dusty riding trousers and worn mocs. Then she put her hands together in the peace, saying, "I wish you clear air," and hurried away without waiting for his response.

Too late. Jande had spotted her; his brows drew together in a line. But he said nothing as she twitched the folds of her performance robe into place, and breathed the readiness pattern. If she sang well, he might forgo scolding.

They had decided not to join the bustle for stages. Some places gouged a swingeing price for the opportunity to tread a board scarcely better than a door set atop a pair of tables. And real theaters seemed to always favor local, or well-known performers. They walked the streets in two pairs, their steps keeping the beat.

The judges had two days to circle among all performers, and so far, Jande's idea of mimicking the old-fashioned traveling bards, singing to the air, had done well for them.

As the two days wore on, some of the contestants vanished. Others stayed to listen, as there was no public announcement when contestants were eliminated.

Elisse managed to be by when David played, while the others were busy elsewhere. As she expected, he played unfamiliar music, and she very much liked the quick melodic lines, the evocative shifts in keys, and he fingered well, but not brilliantly. The marsh flute in his hands did not alter into an instrument of high art or transformative emotion. She suspected he wouldn't make it to Alsais, but she kept that to herself.

Late on the second day, Elisse and Jande's quartet had gone all day without any quiet messengers approaching them, which they knew meant they were somewhere in the final selection: only the winner would be made public.

Their moods ranged from triumphant to hopeful as they took a break to eat an early supper, in order to ready themselves for their next set. They were walking under the trees toward the guild hall when a white-haired man greeted them politely, saying, "Are you the quartet from Erais?"

Despite his kindly countenance and the scrupulous politesse, they knew as soon as they saw him that once again, they had been ruled out of the running. He spoke the words, they thanked him, each party with hands in peace mode and then the messenger retreated along his own shadow without disturbing anyone else's. Everything discreet, polite, respectful.

Jande, savage with disappointment and a sharp sense of failure looked anywhere but at his fellow singers as Elisse sighed and said, "We can still sing tonight. Maybe even better, as the worry is over."

Jande, who had often mouthed out platitudes about singing for the joy of making music, was too angry to think about music for its own sake. He had to know who had seen their humiliation. The Colendi nearby walked by or sat in their groups, so scrupulously oblivious that he knew they were pityingly pretending not to notice, the same way he would have.

All, that is, all except that foreigner.

Over all three of the competitions that David had attended, Jande's scornful looks his way had not gone unnoticed. David, always aware of his surroundings, had kept a prudent distance. He was here in Colend to have fun. However, Jande's attitude had been obvious enough that David smiled at the evidence that the Colendi toff and his group had been eliminated.

It was not a grin, but a mild, even gentle smile under those sleepy eyes, still Jande sensed in that steady regard the hidden challenge. He was far too disappointed, and angry, to reflect that his own behavior had sparked that challenge.

He spoke to his friends, but his voice, trained to pitch in a room, carried. "I fail to see how allowing every wanderer to swell the numbers does anything to benefit the festival."

David rose from the carved bench where he had been sitting, his expression altering to mock surprise. "Was that," he asked, "addressed to me?"

Of course it was. To speak before someone using the third person was considered rude to Colendi. If deliberate, it was an insult not quite as deliberate as stepping on one's shadow, but halfway there.

A Colendi would have pretended not to hear inadvertent rudeness. Deliberate insult could be answered in a variety of ways, but David decided it was time to test the direct answer. He sauntered forward two steps, looked measuringly down at the long late-afternoon shades, and placed his foot squarely on the shadow of Jande's head.

Then raised his gaze. And smiled.

All Jande's pent up frustration and disappointment fired into rage. Good manners, the music, everything was forgotten. He snapped a look left and right in unspoken order, and charged.

David's sleepy smile widened as the three came at him, two fast and Elisse's brother lagging, unsure about this, but he always followed Jande. Only Elisse stood where she was, appalled and embarrassed.

Quick steps, a gulp of breath, a flash of lightning and the next thing Jande knew he lay on the grass, crowing for breath past his throbbing ribs. He hazily recollected the elbow that had impacted them, and turned his head. There lay their tenor, curled up clutching his twisted knee, and the third groaned on the other side, limbs jerking as he tried to get up in spite of a broken collarbone.

"Don't you know anything about blocking?" came the accented voice before guild peace guardians appeared to disperse the shocked crowd. Three of them led the unresisting David away, and others went to the fallen, helping them to the guild house, so that order and decorum might be swiftly restored.

Inside the guild house's north wing, which had been turned into a stage, a frizz-haired young artist's apprentice sighed, put away his chalks, and rolled his sketches. When he got up, the other artists gathered there in order to draw the performers shifted to fill his space.

It was night when David emerged from the House of Repose. "Adam," he said. And in the language of Geth-deles, "What're you doing here?"

"Running messages." Adam had been scrutinizing the reflection of candlelight in the water of the pond in the central square. "I got in a fine afternoon sketching, while *you* got yourself jailed."

"Jail," David repeated, waving his hand in a little circle. "In Colend, there is no jail. It was interesting, all of it. Starting with the shadows. It really does hot them up, stepping on a shadow. I thought that was talk."

"You're an idiot," Adam said equably. "Did they boot you out of the competition?"

"That happened this morning. I wanted to hear who made it to the end."

"It was that string group from Sles Adran. They announced it right after the evening carillon. While you were contemplating your uncivilized actions in the non-jail."

"The three women, harp, tiranthe, viol?" David said, rolling his 'r's appreciatively. "These Colendi will hate that. What's your message?"

Instead of answering immediately, Adam flipped a heavy metal token into the air.

David caught it, ran his thumb over it, then said, "Transfer token. World transfer. I just got here a few weeks ago."

Adam's expression was impossible to read. "You'll be back," he said. "There's . . .someone new you should meet."

David philosophically stuck his cane flute into his pack, sliding it in next to a sword wrapped up in cloth. He grimaced in anticipation, and the transfer took him out of the world, leaving Adam stepping back from a sudden blast of cold air.

Fifteen

Land of the Venn

FOR TWO DAYS SIAMIS laid himself up with his water flask filled with snow, which he knew would melt to water. Not enough water. He'd been forced to exert all his control to survive that winter descent alongside the frozen stream in that valley, leaving him nearly delirious with exhaustion.

When his body was no longer dangerously cold, he discovered in the throbbing ache where icy shards of stone had cut his flesh on his descent. He ripped up his extra shirt to bind tightly around the cuts, made certain that he scrubbed the blood from the place he'd lain with melted snow.

Then he made his way through ancient accesses to the underground city, and groped down the mossy old tunnels, his strength fast fading. He forced his mind to stay sharp enough to sense the living as he approached the newer tunnels and levels of the city.

He stole food from what appeared to be gardens and orchards, their life-giving light shed from coruscant points overhead, where captured sunlight had been stored in diamond-like gems that were not diamonds at all.

The Venn, effectively shut away from the rest of the world for centuries, had bred fruits and vegetables to evolving tastes:

apples so tart his tongue crimped (these apples, he suspected, would bake extraordinarily well); carrots of a paleness and sweetness unknown in the south; perfect chestnuts from trees never bent by any wind, or troubled by occasional drought. He chose carefully, so as not to leave evidence of his passing, and set out to learn his way around.

Exhaustion requires recovery. He found a place to lie up, yet even with his care he was nearly discovered. Only his habit of keeping his mind open to his surroundings saved him. Nearly too late, he discovered that his pursuers had somehow found his trail despite the blizzard in that mountain.

But this was their territory. The Arm of the Crown, the military protectors, apparently knew every step of those mountains, and that weather was customary for them. The Eyes of the Crown had their own formidable methods of tracking.

And one of those nearly tripped him up. His physical senses perceived nothing, but on the mental plane he made out red shadows closing in from several directions.

A lot of them.

He forced himself to lie where he was, breathing slowly as he widened his focus. Ah. Their circle of enclosure lay one level above, and a short distance to his right.

Another breath, and a different scan: his surroundings through the eyes of the denizens. This mental search was, in its way, as dangerous as trying to navigate in a blizzard, but he could not afford to blunder underground where there was no sense of direction, and everything was alien.

How many? At least a hundred searchers, methodical, organized, disciplined. As he gathered strength for the necessary trip, he considered Venn history. He knew what had happened to many of their kings. To command them must be akin to controlling the vast power of that blizzard overhead, which might shred you to your components in a moment's inattention.

The red shadows afforded a kind of illusion that had to be bound to the blood magic spells inked by pinprick deep into the skin of the Eyes of the Crown. Siamis had once seen the terrible Erkric when he was brought to Norsunder, and glimpses of the Erama Krona, the sea dags of his time whom Erkric had corrupted with his quest for power.

These mages and their forebears, so dedicated and so loyal, had spent centuries recovering their prestige, and now they went about robed in black and white, forbidden to own property besides the clothing they stood up in, forbidden even to handle money. They had to beg for their meals.

Except he could sense, as he sifted minds, they didn't beg: most memories made it plain people thought it an honor to invite them to share a meal. Further, they had recovered their prestige enough to be regarded as the queen's voice in local judicial matters, and he could find no surface thoughts, or easily sifted memories, that doubted their probity.

These were the dedicates who hunted him now—to them, he was an unknown invader who had slipped across their border and made his way straight to their capital. The worst sort of threat without even knowing what he was after.

If he were the hunter and he had seen this vector, he would not make the mistake of assuming the goal was anything trivial.

He knew how much strength he had left—little enough—and how fast the threat was coalescing. He could transfer, but surely a magical trap lay in wait.

No. The time to move was now. Breathing to control the dizziness and the bone-ache, he rose, searched sleeping minds until he found memory of an old thrall tunnel that people still avoided centuries after the thrall system was outlawed, and made his escape.

The Venn guards opened Rel's cell door at intervals, a guard setting a tray on the table, then coming in a bit later to take it away again, as another armed guard stood at the door. They never spoke. The food was spicy, today yellow rice, some kind of fish-and-pepper sauce, crunchy greens. Water to drink.

He clapped out the glow-globe when he wanted to sleep.

At first, sleeping and eating was all he did, after the exhaustion of the storm and chase. But as energy returned, so did thought, foremost a sharp worry about Adam's disappear-ance. As he considered that, he recollected his missing transfer coin.

He knew he should not assume that Adam had stolen it. Anyone could have, anyone very good at searching. That was the aspect that mitigated suspicion from Adam—Rel couldn't believe that Adam would be so adept at searching.

He tried not to feel betrayed. He tried not to think at all. Conjecture sometimes was worse then ignorance, especially with few facts. He knew he had done nothing wrong. Moreover this was not the first time he'd been summarily grabbed, which inevitably led to recruitment attempts. He'd always talked his way out of these, except that once with Kessler, who'd wanted to recruit young assassins to take out the world's kings.

But these were Venn, shut away from the world except in trade, for centuries. He tried not to guess reasons, and began counting his meals in an effort to decide how many days were passing. Between meals he began doing sword drills without a sword, lying under his bunk and pressing it upward until his arm muscles trembled with the burn of fatigue, one-handed pushups and fighting kicks, a hundred a side. Sit, and repeat. In this way he tried to pass the time, and tire himself out enough to sleep away the killing boredom.

Communal areas, Siamis found as he slipped from hiding place to hiding place over the course of successive days, were kept lit. The living areas, especially the upper levels, reflected the diurnal cycle with those diamond-bright fire stones given to human mages uncounted centuries before.

Each day he forced himself to rise and move, though exhaustion still dragged at his limbs and vice-clenched his skull. He could not afford true sleep. His mind must remain vigilant. But his body recovered enough for him to make his way up a level, down two levels, always bearing westward toward the great towers of the ancient days.

Twice he was nearly caught, until he figured out the magical tracers, again bound to blood. If one is sensitive enough on the mental plane, bloodshed leaves its mark just as indelibly as in the physical world.

He learned to discern these markers, and the invisible nets extending therefrom. And sensed in the hunters that they had lost him again.

To lead them off, he forced himself toward the royal enclave, a vast complex that lay aboveground and below. There he deliberately crossed a marker, and then hurled himself down a dank, mossy thrall tunnel that ran with bitter water.

But not before he unexpectedly found in a memory — the old queen's no less — the place he sought: no mere hall of gathering, as existed with similar tapestries and paintings all over the Land of the Venn, but what had once been the Hall of Judgment in the long-ago Anborc tower, now nearly relict.

Siamis retreated down and away as the trap closing above

altered into a disturbingly fast and efficient widespread search.

The Hall was not the same as it had been when the seer who'd mothered the present ruling family had reportedly sustained a Yaga Ydrasal vision—the great banner becoming a window to something beyond cloth and gold and stone walls.

Erkric had been stunned by horror, then he had cloaked himself with the comfort of skepticism, but that memory had so burned into his mind that Siamis, curious to see the evil blood mage everyone sought, had rifled that memory from the Garden of the Twelve.

That cavernous hall was now used for state purposes of the most grave, but the present queen knew its history.

He was going to have to be even more vigilant now. Though the remains of Anborc were all but uninhabited, the symbolic importance of the place pretty much guaranteed it would be laden with tracers, traps, and wards.

Sleep vanished. Tiredness gripped. He was going to have to be fast, because he knew that while he could detect and remove wards from access tunnels, he couldn't replace them—and somebody was going to check them, sooner than later.

Further, that Hall would be loaded with centuries of spells. It would take him months to remove them all.

He stopped only long enough to refill his water flask in one of the stone pools with water pouring from time-smoothed statues of mighty, armored Norna bearing jugs in their hands.

Honor guards paced in twos through the vaulted halls. Siamis slipped behind one pair, listening on the mental plane for the pattern of patrol. These men and women were on alert, but as yet not ordered to the chase.

He found the massive doors wildly splendid with gemmed mosaic, and so perfectly hung that one man could open them—but it took much effort to halt the movement and reverse it without them booming shut.

He slipped in, and felt a webwork of magic.

He turned around slowly, orienting on the queen's memory and Erkric's until they overlay.

That way. And . . .that was the alarm.

Knowing that he'd been discovered, he threw up a ward that he hoped would require some effort to break, and paced slowly, gazing upward at the stone as he tried to see the ancient banner, tattered by two centuries . . .

A flicker.

They're coming.

There. He moved back a step. Another flicker, like a distant reflection on glass, and here was the window he'd glimpsed from the Moonfire.

They're closing in — magic attacked his ward, but he forced himself to stillness as he watched the last of the Erama Krona suffer the binding enchantment on . . .

On their own great treasure, another of those firestones, this one called The Dragoneye, given by an ancient Venn king to his queen when they were crowned, after which it was displayed in this room. The Venn, in capitulation, had ritually surrendered their greatest treasure . . .

Which was then taken away by a grim-eyed mage who wore the robes of one of the long-outdated northern mage guilds. This was one of the three mages who had bound the Arrow, as seen so murkily from the time vault of the Moonfire.

But now Siamis saw two things that had been hereto hidden. First, he recognized that face staring straight at him across the centuries: the famous (or infamous) soon-to-be head of the Sartoran Mage Guild. So this was the event that motivated that promotion, and also proved that the southern mages *had* been involved.

But even more chilling, a shadowy figure behind the three, unperceived by them: a man above medium height, gray-green eyes, gazing directly at Siamis across the centuries.

Detlev, why didn't you tell me you were there?

Of course he wouldn't. This was both a test, and a warning.

Damnation. At that moment all around him, transfers flickered as black and white robed Venn mages appeared, hands already glowing green.

He gave them a rueful salute, his head pounding with pain from his effort, and transferred away, to a place he had prepared for such an emergency. He fell back onto the narrow bed in the small, abandoned house, his eyes closing, his bleeding nose shoved into the crook of his elbow.

He was safe, but right back where he had started. Or very nearly. For that disguised Sartoran mage had taken away The Dragoneye. It wasn't anywhere in the north. All the records were lies. Of course they were lies.

That meant he faced a much harder task than breaking into Land of the Venn: he was going to have to breach the Sartoran Mage Archives, the only place to find the truth.

Sixteen

AT LAST THE GUARDS reappeared outside Rel's cell, but not with a tray.

He was motioned out, and taken on another long walk down faceless corridors of stone and blue, then up stairs to another beautiful room with a complication of vaulted ceilings. He almost got dizzy, trying to look upward while crossing the shining marble floor to great carved doors with a stylized sunburst radiating out in beaten gold.

Inside a room with a fabulous mural painted on one wall waited a man and a woman. Both looked somewhere around Mondros's age, the woman a guard, the man wearing a plain black robe over white. On the breast of his black robe had been stitched a stylized falcon eye under the arch of a crown. He sat behind a table. The woman, fully armed, stood behind the man, who had no weapons. She wore the dark blue he'd seen before, but no greatcoat; barely visible beneath the high collar of her tunic, the edges of a pattern-etched iron torc. Her collar gleamed with tiny representations of the hammer and crown.

On the table lay everything in Rel's pack, neatly folded or lined up, and next to his pack, his sword.

"This sword, it is a prince's weapon. In gold," the man said in heavily accented Sartoran, a finger pointing to the chased hilt, "the three-point crown common to the southern empire."

"It's an heirloom," Rel said. "Given me by someone who had a lot of heirlooms."

"Are you then a prince?"

"No," Rel exclaimed. Then he frowned down at the subtle interlocking circle pattern of stone, light gray and white, in the floor. What was he? He couldn't get his mind around "Chwahir prince." And really, what did that kind of title mean, if all the trappings were long gone?

Nothing.

"No," he said again, more firmly. "I'm a traveler. I earn my way by working. Sailor on seas, caravan guard on land."

"Who gives you an heirloom sword?" the woman asked.

"A friend."

Though neither moved, he sensed by a stiffened shoulder, a tightened brow that neither interlocutor liked this answer. "For what royal interest do you spy?" the woman asked.

Rel was about to retort that he was not a spy, but hesitated. Wasn't that by some definition exactly what he was doing? What was the difference between scout and spy?

Start with the fact that Mondros and Tsauderei do not intend any harm to the Venn, he thought, and since vagueness had not served, he'd shift to specifics. "The sword was a gift from the Queen of Sartor, directly after Sartor was freed from a century of enchantment. At that time she was just a girl raised by a mage, and she had no idea whose sword this had been. It was given in friendship."

The man had been looking at something in his hand. He murmured in Venn; Rel caught the word *truth*. The Universal Language Spell knew that word, at least.

They then began with questions about the trade ship, why he'd chosen that one to hire onto, how he knew Captain Mathen, and then a host of questions about the boy Cor. Thoroughly bewildered at the direction of the questioning, Rel answered readily enough, finally admitting that it was the queen of Sartor he'd intended to request help from on Cor's behalf.

As soon as the words were out, the questioning abruptly ended.

The two exchanged glances, the woman gave a brief nod at the guards behind Rel, and he was taken out again. He sighed, thinking regretfully of his clothes back there on the table, and how very much he wished for a change.

But scarcely had they reached his cell again when a runner

dashed up and whispered something to the guards, who did an abrupt about-face.

Back to the vaulted ceiling again, but this time he was taken into another vaulted room made of gold-veined marble. A vast mosaic covered the floor, an astonishing complexity of interlocking knotwork in a succession of bright colors that drew the eye to the golden center, then brought it out again in an explosion of color.

He scarcely had time to look at it when he was gestured to a tall door with carvings that continued the effect of the floor, drawing in all the color to a golden tree with complicated stylized branches knotted around a sinking sun. A crown? He was so dazzled by the colors and interwoven knots that he blinked, unable to comprehend scale — then he stepped into another room of gold-veined white marble, but this time the stylized decoration was made of a glassy black stone.

White and black: severe, somehow intimidating, especially with those black-robed people standing silently at either end of a glossy black stone chair. Above it again that golden tree with the branches interwoven below a sun or crown, he was not certain which. The tree was framed by an elm on one side and an ash on the other, the silver branches interlocking with those of the golden tree between them.

He blinked, forcing his eye down to the person sitting in the chair: an old woman, white of hair, dressed entirely in black and gold and white. Thin, gnarled hands rested on the polished black arms of the chair. The *throne*.

His heart banged against his ribs, and his neck tightened.

The guards halted, Rel perforce with them, as from a side door another of the black-and-white people came in, carrying Rel's pack, belongings, and on top, the sword.

He laid them before the throne. Rel was distracted by color at the fellow's wrist as his sleeve dropped back. More of that complicated knotwork had been inked by needle from the top of his hand up his wrist to disappear into the sleeve.

Rel had seen such body art. In various parts of the world it was the fashion, and he had learned that it had been fashionable at one time here and there in the south, but never had he glimpsed those compelling knots.

The fellow straightened up, the sleeve covering his hand. His thumb caught the hem of the sleeve as his hand pressed to his chest. He backed to the door then slipped silently through.

The old woman said in slow Venn, "My Eyes say you have the spell of speech upon you."

Rel said warily, "I do." He braced for more accusations about being a spy, knowing that in essence it was true.

But then she took him completely by surprise. "My son, now under Sinbor shadow, speaks well of you." *Sinbor shadow* seemed to equal disgrace.

And as Rel gazed in astonishment, a discreet door in back of the throne opened, and here came a tall, boyish form wearing midnight blue silk embroidered in gold, his long, shining blond hair faintly streaked with stubborn green. Around his head he wore a thin gold band similar to the queen's.

And that, Rel thought grimly, is why I hate the idea of being a prince.

Between one breath and another his completely disinterested offer of aid had suddenly become political.

The queen, taking in Rel's surprise that faded into puzzled chagrin, said with slow irony, "My son, Kerendal Sofar."

Cor—Kerendal—flushed, then his chin came up. "They treated you with respect?" he asked Rel in his stumbling Sartoran. "You were given a table, a bed, as a guest?"

Rel assented, nerves chilling at the indirect threat.

The queen lifted a finger, and Kerendal fell silent.

"My Eyes inform me your queen is young, no more than a girl. New to her rule, as her kingdom is newly emerged again into the world?"

"Yes," Rel said, not quite making it a question.

"And so it might have happened in chance, and not by intent, that you, bearing this sword, join the ship my foolish son chose for his perilous misadventure—that you would aid him in his forbidden quest out of good will, and most telling you fought to defend him during this attack on the seas?"

At each point, Rel assented.

"And that all these things occur, by chance, after one of your countrymen is found invading one of our oldest, most sacred halls?"

Rel could not hide his astonishment. "One of my countrymen? From Tser Mearsies?"

"Sartor." The queen pronounced the name carefully, with gentle reproach.

Rel flushed. "I am not Sartoran. I speak the language because it's common in the south, the language of trade." And scribes and diplomacy, but he had nothing to do with those. "I was raised in Tser Mearsies."

The queen lifted her gaze to one of the mages in black and white, who muttered softly and gestured.

An image flashed in the middle of the floor. Fresh horror pooled in Rel's gut when he recognized Siamis, whose head whipped around. He gazed outward, looking haggard, then vanished.

The queen and her attendants took in Rel's blanched expression, the half step he backed from that image, before Rel said, "That is no countryman of mine. You know who that is?"

"Yes," the queen responded. "The young man who forced his enchantment on us not so long ago."

"He *was* Sartoran," Rel said grimly, trying to recover. "Four thousand years ago. Now he's Norsundrian."

"I would not have believed the four thousand years," the queen responded. "Until it transpired that people of our own from eight centuries ago have wandered into a port on the western continent."

Kerendal flushed to the ears.

"And you have seen their appearance?" the queen asked. "These are many coincidences. But the sailors from your trade vessel all tell a similar tale, and so we have sent them south again, to carry on with their trade. As for you." The queen opened her hand to the side. "You are now my son's responsibility."

Kerendal and the other Venn remained standing, hands flat to their chests as the old woman rose, stepped to the other side of her throne, and vanished quietly through that discreet door.

Kerendal leaped down as if shot from a bow. "Come, Rel," he said. "I shall conduct you on a tour. You would like, yes?"

"Yes," Rel agreed, thinking that anything was better than being imprisoned again. Not that he was certain he was safe yet; as Kerendal flung open the door, the two guards there fell in behind Rel, and paced silently almost within arm's reach.

"I saw your face," Kerendal said. "He is mad!" The word carried the old connotations of *berserk*. "I was mad," his voice dropped ruefully as they walked swiftly along a vaulted hall carved with trees and birds and other figures. "When we heard about the drakan-ships, I *had* to know. To see them. To talk to them. To ask questions about a time when so many records were destroyed."

"So the Venn, that is, your people know about them?"

"It was a rumor at first. And there are so many, ah rules? In my language —" The word he said came out *constraints*. Rel was not surprised that that translated. "We are not permitted this, and so we do not permit outsiders that. We are not allowed out, except certain among us, and under established rules. We say, no one is allowed in at all."

He shrugged as they turned a corner, passing rapidly through a series of amazing high-vaulted rooms, some with complications of brilliant diamonds suspended from high ceilings, shedding captured sunlight. Trees grew in giant pots, their limbs carefully trained to rise in orderly symmetry, evoking that banner Rel had seen. These were connected by very, very long halls. Rel was just as glad of a chance to stretch his legs, though he wondered where the prince might be taking him; it felt like they were traversing an entire underground city.

Kerendal did not look around once. To him, the wide world was much more interesting than the familiar boundaries of his home. "I knew I must see them. And so I planned it carefully," he said finally, as they entered another tunnel. He did not seem to want to speak inside those silent chambers. "I left a message, yet they thought me dead. I must do no magic, see. They must not trace me, not that I know much of any help to me."

They ascended finally, and walked through an archway framed by clinging vines with drooping trumpet lilies of pale gold, and to a new hall. "And so, I find, I have a sister! Old as my mother is—and she was old when she did the spell that brought me—Birth Spell worked again for her. Significant, or happenstance, nobody knows, yes?"

"That's my understanding," Rel said as they entered another hall whose carvings seemed to bear the patina of age.

"My mother is angry with me. Very! Says she might still disown me, and make little Erenlara heir. I do not tell her to do so, though I want to. Duty, I feel it here." Kerendal struck a fist lightly to his chest. "I felt it was duty to find the drakan-ships! And I failed in that." He sighed as at last, he came to a halt.

The guards stepped around them and each took hold of the carved knotwork handles to the massive doors they faced. Rel blinked, trying to take in the wild mosaic, glittering with gold and gems, in the high doors.

He could see that these were expertly hung—the guards exerted no extraordinary effort—but there seemed to be a ritual in their opening.

When Kerendal stepped inside the space beyond, Rel followed cautiously, unprepared for the vast chamber in pale stone, with complicated vaulting overhead. The wall behind them had been carved into a enormous tree, the lower branches still twelve, but wild in their loops and turns and branchings. Those doors he'd thought so massive on the inside fit into a far larger tangle of roots that narrowed to an immense trunk which, in its turn, ramified outward into a sky-scraping tangle of branches above.

Kerendal strode farther into the chamber with the air of one accustomed to the place. He abandoned Sartoran, and spoke rapidly in his own tongue. Rel understood the gist. The lacunae in the Language Spell was roughly equivalent to Kerendal's rudimentary Sartoran.

"They believed I had been taken prisoner when they discovered me so suddenly on what they thought a pirate chase. It *was* a pirate chase," he amended. "But they saw you defending me, at first thinking you wanted me alive for a prize — or in concert with he who had breached our border. Now they know it is not so."

He stopped at the other end, and gazed up at a balcony above them, the wall displaying the finest of any of the mosaics Rel had glimpsed so far. Magically burning torches at points along the balcony struck glints and glitters of fiery color so that the great tree with its branches woven around a crowned rising sun seemed alive, moving in a wind that blew from beyond the world. And again, ash and elm were present at either side.

"That man, Siamis," Kerendal whispered. "He was found here. At the heart of the Land of the Venn, in the Hall of Ancestors. He evaded the Eyes of the Crown and the Arm, and yet he vanished, having touched nothing. They have bound the chamber against him, and he has not since attempted to return."

"What is the purpose of this room?" Rel asked.

Kerendal meant to define it simply, but he got caught up in the long history of Anborc Tower, and how this chamber had once been the Hall of Judgment until the mother of his line — falsely accused of treason by the Erkric the Betrayer — had sustained a vision so powerful that all had witnessed it. The mosaic, he explained, replaced exactly — every stitch represented by a gem or mineral — the great banner of the Tree of Ydrasal that had hung there until it rotted.

He talked on, compelled by emotions he did not understand, except that he had failed in his quest, he had failed his mother who had worn the colors of grief, he had failed those whose task it had been to guard him.

He had failed himself, because he desired above all to travel into the world, and he knew he would never leave again. And so he was given this chance to talk to the young man who had traveled the world, who had taught him Sartoran, and who had fought to save him. He talked until his voice gave out, unused for so many months, because he found himself unable to put the question that had come to matter a great deal.

But there were the guards, and he knew the time. Duty had reclaimed him.

He faced Rel. "You are a very good warrior," he began.

Rel thought immediately of Kessler, shorter and slighter, who had defeated him twice. Could have killed him. But he said only, "I'm learning."

"Will you stay here? Become one of our Arm?"

Rel saw past the appeal, suspecting the same sort of constrained life he had felt before he left Tser Mearsies, only the prince's situation was far more stringent. Kerendal longed to be out in the world, and perhaps keeping Rel here would give him the next best thing, someone who could talk of the world outside Venn.

"I can't," he said, and to make it easier on Kerendal, who was after all just a boy, "I have a duty elsewhere."

"Of course." Kerendal flushed, then raised his head. "Ah. To the queen of Sartor?"

Rel hesitated. Anywhere outside of the Land of the Venn he would never assent to such a thing—misunderstood gossip could only hurt Atan. But here? Who would ever care a heartbeat after he spoke?

"Yes," he said.

Kerendal's expression cleared. "They halted a trader from departure, in the chance you would not stay."

When Rel was conducted back through the halls, he sensed a little of Kerendal's emotions, but did not know what to say to a prince who had resigned himself, out of duty and loyalty, to a lifetime of imprisonment.

Never more intense was Rel's gratitude that he was not a prince.

No one spoke until he was brought back to that black and

white chamber, where he found his pack waiting on the table, his things still there. Kerendal then strove to regain a normal tone, reminiscing about sailing as Rel methodically repacked his kit, then picked up his sword.

No one said anything as he slung it into its baldric.

"Fare well," Kerendal said, touching his fingers to his breast, his expression one of sorrow and resignation.

Rel mirrored the sign, heart-felt, as he knew that in other circumstances the two of them could have become fast friends.

The guards conducted Rel on a long walk back through the halls, up the stairs, and out onto the wharf.

It seemed no time had passed at all. The sun hung in the western sky once again, only this time striking the fiery colors of the long northern twilight in the shredded, racing gold-edged violet-hued clouds. That lurid sunset, he observed, had been reflected in some of the mosaics he'd seen below.

He was escorted to a trade ship, where he discovered his passage had been arranged. Avidly curious sailors watched him as the guards saw him to the deck, and then departed wordlessly.

Rel scarcely listened to the captain, a red-haired fellow from Ghanthur whose Sartoran accent was so bad that little of his speech was intelligible. Rel watched the dark mountains of Venn slowly sink away.

He sighed inwardly, missing Mondros's transfer coin. It was going to be a very long trip.

Seventeen

Early summer (autumn in the south) 4745 AF
Bereth Ferian

"RAH," LYREN DECLARED IN her piping little voice, and took off running barefoot in the warmth of early summer in the north.

Liere chased after, reaching mentally to stop the toddler, but Lyren had already learned a kind of shield. Or maybe it was that toddlers were so single-minded they heeded nothing else.

Liere wished for the hundredth time that her mother had been able to stay, but her father had insisted on Elen's return to South End when Lyren turned a year old. After all, she had other grandchildren. It had been a long, a very long, several months since.

As Liere followed helplessly behind the twinkle of fast little feet, she missed those days with Elen. Though she and her mother would never understand one another, it had been so comforting to have her there. Liere had been able to pretend that Lyren was a little sister. In fact she even looked more like Marga, her actual sister, than she looked like Liere. And she had the same sudden smile that made everyone smile back.

In short, Lyren, barely talking, was already more well-liked than Liere had ever been in her entire life. Just as Marga had been, back in South End.

"Rah!" Lyren said.

Voices echoed faintly, and Liere listened on the mental plane — Arthur and Hibern, talking to . . .Roy. The latter was the only one who remembered his mental shield.

Hibern was actually laughing. Liere slowed as Lyren approached the heavy door, and scrabbled with fat little hands to open it. Liere had not heard Hibern laugh since they were on the sister world. Ever since, she'd been, oh, not a different person, but a lot more Marloven. Like Senrid, when he was focused on something.

They laughed as Lyren jumped, groping for the door latch. Liere caught her before she was about to wail. She suppressed the urge to send a mental command to stop crying — she had learned the hard way that connecting on the mental plane had so confused Lyren that for a while she had stopped talking or listening in the physical world. The mental plane was so much easier.

Liere lifted the latch, and Lyren sped inside, shouting in triumph, "Rah!"

The three looked up from magic texts. Studying, Liere realized as she entered behind Lyren. She hated the pulse of guilt and near-resentment that constricted inside her chest at the sight of Roy's mild smile and jug ears. Roy was now a top student at the magic school. He's taken my place, Liere could not help thinking. No, the place she might have had if she hadn't been the world's worst mage student.

The two boys smiled as Lyren ran to them, pointing a fat finger. "Buk!"

"That's right, bo-o-o-ok," Arthur said with every evidence of delight.

Hibern rolled her eyes. "If it's vocabulary time, I'll take these wards with me. I want to look up what Erai-Yanya's foremothers have written on the Venn."

Arthur gave her a flap of the hand, and Hibern transferred away.

Arthur beamed as Lyren ran through her vocabulary in the happy triumph of knowing. And when Arthur opened his book and pointed to various letters, sounding them out, Lyren was quick to echo him.

"Listen to that," Arthur said. "At this rate she'll be reading younger than I was. And she can start at the magic school!" He

beamed at Roy and Liere, clearly expecting them to be delighted.

Roy smiled back, and Liere tried to smile. She didn't want
to point out that Lyren had no interest whatsoever in the book,
or the meaningless marks on the page: she was mimicking
because Arthur smiled.

Arthur was too kindly to even think that Lyren might
become the student that Liere hadn't been — that Liere was a
disappointment. She struggled with the awareness of that
disappointment, how everyone accepted her running after
Lyren as a kind of sister, governess, anything-but-mother, but
at least she had a place, a role. She had disappointed everyone:
she was no longer the Girl Who Saved the World.

Liere did not miss that. At all. And yet she still felt like a
failure.

She could almost hear Senrid scoffing. *So do something else!*
Or he might say, *Isn't this better than running in fear from Siamis
or Detlev?*

That much was true. As for "something else," right now
that seemed to be Lyren, and also writing letters. Senrid would
be pleased with her having received three letters so far that day,
the most she'd ever gotten in day. Or even a week.

When Lyren tired of repeating Arthur's lesson, she ran out,
her steps noticeably slower. After lunch came nap time, and
while Lyren slumbered, Liere looked at her three letters. The
first, from Kyale Marlonen, she made herself deal with right off.
It was hard work to maintain a friendship with Kyale, but Liere
was determined to keep at it. The letter was all about Kyale
herself, except when she complained about Leander.

Liere answered it, asking after every one of Kyale's cats,
aware that naming them took up more space on the page.

Second was Lilah Selenna's letter. That was much more fun,
all about life in Sarendan, and all Lilah's friends, and a little
about King Peitar's magical studies. Liere filled two pages
easily in response to that.

Third was from Karhin Keperi, who corresponded with
pretty much everyone in the alliance, as if it still existed the way
it had when it was first formed. The part that caught Liere's
interest the most was near the end, when Karhin wrote:

> . . .*and after all this time, I've given in to Thad and
> I'll accompany them on their next journey to visit*

Prince Shontande. Curtas and Thad each insist the danger is minimal now — they know exactly how to get around the guards . . .

Liere remembered the royal Lirendis, father and son, from her journey around the world to release Siamis's spell. The father had had the strangest mental signature she had ever encountered.

The prince — little older than Lyren at the time — had been lonely, his thoughts full of roses.

Colend

It was not three, but four who traveled to Lake Skya in late autumn in the south.

Karhin had been postponing traveling with Thad to meet the prince (it was always the wrong time, too much work, bad weather) until her mothers had granted her wish to take on her mastery project early.

Curtas had returned from Erdrael Danara. Thad was ready. It was now, or never: from New Year's onward, she would be far too busy.

And so, though she disliked the discomfort of travel, she packed as little as possible ("Everything you bring you must carry," Thad had warned her) and readied her mind for endurance.

Adam arrived the morning the three were to depart, and on discovering their intention, promptly hefted his pack and said, "Oh, that sounds like fun."

Three voices said with genuine enthusiasm, "Come with us!"

That night, when they camped after a long day of travel in the bitter cold, Adam sat by Karhin. "How are all our friends?"

The question wasn't idle talk. Adam asked about people specifically. On hearing that Rel still had not returned, he frowned into the crackling fire, then said, "I trust he's all right."

"If anyone is all right, it's Rel," Karhin stated, the faint pulse that his name always caused falling away swiftly. "He never communicates, at least through us. His way is to come and go."

"I trust he'll return soon," Adam said as he pulled out his battered sketchbook. "I was hoping he might take me along on his next trip south. I would very much like to meet Peitar Selenna."

Curtas glanced up then. Karhin would not have noticed, had not the flames reflected in his gaze as it met Adam's. Then he returned to his conversation with Thad, and Adam opened the sketchbook. "Would you like to see the sketches I made of the music festival last summer?"

It was scarcely even a moment and yet it remained in Karhin's memory. Perhaps it was because Adam and Curtas rarely talked to one another as they traveled and camped. They didn't ignore each other, or pretend the other was not there. It was more like the four of them had fallen into two parties, Adam with her, and Curtas walking and talking with Thad.

And two parties they remained, until they were caught in the sleet storm. Karhin had been too cold and miserable to do anything but follow the pounding footsteps in front of her, but as soon as they entered the barn, she shivered as she and Thad watched the two work swiftly to set up the fire. It was smoothly done, no wasted movement—as if they had practiced together.

Maybe they had. Curtas was a traveler, too. Karhin stretched cold, aching hands gratefully to the fire, pondering the fact that she knew absolutely nothing of Curtas other than the fact that he had been raised as a thief, then somehow became one of King Terry Larensar's many wandering friends.

The night before they reached Lake Skya, Karhin, bored by the sleety rain falling outside the barn they'd sneaked into, asked Adam if she could look through his latest sketches.

As always, he readily surrendered the sketchbook. She saw expert renditions of herself and Thad from various angles, the shading sometimes dramatic, as if sketched by candle light, and sometimes subtle, in daylight colors. But there was no sketch of Curtas.

She handed back the sketchbook and said, "Why don't you draw him?" She nodded at Curtas, whose pleasant, ordinary face was animated as he and Thad dug through their packs to find something they could warm over the fire for a meal.

"Oh, I have," Adam said. "Those drawings are in another sketchbook."

So they had traveled together. Of course they had.

That became more apparent to her when they reached Skya the next day, and commenced the nerve-wracking sneak-and-climb up to the palace roof. Karhin had assumed that Adam would be no better than she at sneakery, but he surprised her with his strength and speed, and with the similarity in the patterns of direction and encouragement that both he and Curtas spoke on the long, arduous climb.

She—who prided herself on her stamina and strength training in fan dancing, and who had been a better climber than Thad when small—was slowest and most awkward.

But she gritted her teeth and pressed on grimly, for there was no going back alone. Scraped elbows, knuckles, and barked shins elicited no more than a sharp breath, until at last, heart laboring in her chest, she crawled onto the roof next to her brother.

She beheld Prince Shontande, and every other thought went straight out of her head. When Shontande saw Thad and Curtas, a smile transformed his face. He was already beautiful—unlike boys of his age, there was nothing awkward about him, his face like a carving.

In ten years, Karhin thought, the prince was going to become the most beautiful man in the world. And I will be there to serve him, she vowed.

She braced herself when Thad indicated her, saying, "And my sister Karhin, your highness. She's the one who unites the alliance."

It had become habit for Karhin to assume a mind-shield, once she'd learned about them, for she had not wanted any of Rel's mind-reading friends to know about her useless crush. As Prince Shontande's eyes met hers she felt a moment of vertigo, much like that she had felt on meeting Liere the first time. It was brief, more like the slight shock or startlement, as when a bird bumps the window glass.

Then it was gone, and her mouth responded with a lifetime of training in politeness.

"Thank you for your letters, and for the books," the prince said. "If I could write to anybody, it would be King Tereneth—what did you say he likes to be called?"

"Terry, your highness," Karhin said, bowing with her hands in the peace, though she saw the others did not perform protocol. But her muscles were too well trained.

Shontande's smile flashed again, and her heart stuttered in her chest. "I liked him so much when we met. He made me laugh. It banished the tedium." He opened his fingers suddenly in the starburst gesture. "Would he write to me? The council says I must not. I am not yet educated enough to represent Colend well. But he would not mind my errors, surely?"

Karhin caught twin expressions of surprise in Thad and Curtas. Adam sat silently, sketching on a wrinkled bit of paper he'd thrust inside his clothing earlier. He always had chalk somewhere about him.

"Of all those in the alliance, Terry would number among those who would notice such things the least," Karhin stated with confidence. "Do write to him! I believe you will enjoy it. But perhaps we ought to bring you a golden notecase, as the rest of us use. It would save so much time and travel." The impulse brought a ghastly thought: how could she possibly afford one suitable for a their crown prince? Senrid had made the others, which were very plain.

He then surprised her. "I have made one. But it is useless until I obtain the sigils of correspondents."

"It would be my pleasure to furnish them," she said, bowing. "If you wished, your highness."

He bowed in thanks, then turned to the boys, and they held a swift conversation, all awareness turned outward in case they might be discovered. Karhin listened to one word in twenty — most of it was repetitions of conversations the others had had, never third hand news, always first hand — as she struggled with the evidence of the prince's loneliness, in spite of his beautiful surroundings.

By some signal she did not perceive the others decided it was time for the long, tense, arduous retreat. The prince formally thanked them all by name, and the two Colendi bowed with equal formality. Curtas and Adam dipped their heads.

Karhin grimly forced herself through the taxing motions of retreat, as a wind smelling of ice rose off the lake, which had darkened to the color of pewter. In the distance, before they reached the tunnel entrance, the screeling of winter birds indicated some kind of stir. But then they were safely enclosed in the darkness.

"That was a first," Thad commented, as their feet crunched the thin layer of ice at the bottom of the tunnel. "I wonder why he never asked me to put him in contact with Terry? I'm a scribe, too, and he knows it."

"You're not the one writing to everyone," Curtas pointed out. "You told him from the start that Karhin does that, and he seems to proceed with care. I think he needs to see people one at a time before he asks for things. He's either been told what people think he wants to hear, or else what others want him to believe. Why do you think he listens to me blabber on about weavers' songs in Eth Endra, and the old glover I met who had the twenty-two goats? It's because they are people living lives that have nothing to do with him."

Karhin exclaimed, "Ah-ye, true," mittened hands coming together. Another thought: she'd seldom heard so much speculation from Curtas. He usually confined himself to the immediate.

Everyone fell quiet as they splashed their way down the tunnel, doing their best to avoid the sucking mud. Karhin became aware of her tiredness in the weightiness of her limbs, the way their firestick torch's flicker bothered her eyes.

When they emerged, it was to a world of white: it had begun to snow at last. That meant footprints. They walked in single file until they found a road full of ruts, which meant getting their shoes caked with chilled mud.

But at last the long, strange day ended in another barn, with sheep milling close-packed below, and sweet-smelling hay from recent harvest around them. They'd cleared a space for the firestick, shared out the last of the stale travel bread and dried cheese, knowing that the next day would mean hot, fresh food.

Everyone curled up. Karhin dropped off so fast she didn't remember falling asleep, but sometime later she woke abruptly when the wood above her head gave a creak.

She lay where she was, knowing that if she moved at all, winter air might seep into her cocoon of blankets. She became aware of the slow rhythm, almost a snore, of her brother's breathing nearby. But farther away, soft voices — speaking Sartoran, not the Kifelian of Colend.

"Everything one person away," Adam was saying. "And with Shontande, protocol, because that's a given in his life."

"That's what he knows," Curtas observed.

"That's what he trusts," Adam said.

"Yes." Curtas sighed, barely audible. "The regency council lies to him — no, that's too easy. They tell him one thing. It makes sense. He's told another thing by us."

Adam responded, "It's a strategy."

They know each other well. Karhin waited for Curtas's response, but the pause became a silence, during which she slid back into sleep.

Eighteen

New Year's Week, 4746 AF

RETURN TRAVEL WAS SLOWER, as two snowstorms pinned them down. Consequently they reached Winterfeld the day before New Year's Firstday, and walked into the scribe house, which was filled with the delicious scents of New Year's Week baking.

Tired and gritty, the four of them walked straight to the downstairs cleaning frame. It felt like an iron band released her when Karhin stepped through and the frame snapped away the accumulation of mud on her shoes and coat and trousers.

A quick step presaged the appearance of Bee, one hand out with a finger upraised, though he rarely needed to touch any surface inside the house. "You are back—how many?" he asked happily, turning his head back and forth as he listened to breathing. "Adam?"

"And me," Curtas said. "Heyo, Little Bee."

"I'm Bee now," he said. "I'm not little," he added—he was nearly as tall as Karhin, though much more weedy.

"Bee it is."

"Thad, Karhin, Rel is here," Bee said as he scurried up the stairs ahead of them.

Karhin checked, then walked on, hiding the rapid surge of

her heartbeat. They reached Thad's room, always the center of their lives and there was Rel sitting on a cushion, his clothes so worn-looking the cuffs were frayed, the knees shapeless.

As everyone exchanged greetings, Karhin found herself searching Rel's countenance for roughness, for signs of weakness or discord. He looked tired and worn, not grubby only because he, too, had gone through the cleaning frame. He looked back at her with the same absent kindness as always. Nothing more.

He was nothing more. He would never, at his very best, be as superlative as Prince Shontande promised to be—Colend's future king.

A fleeting awareness of the need for self-examination—why ought he not slide from crush to friend?—passed through her, and was gone. He might have chosen her, instead of that far-off queen whose only attraction, from everything she'd heard, was her title.

"I'll see to a meal," she said, made a general peace to preserve *melende*, and left.

Thad watched her leave, puzzled at its abruptness. But Karhin had always had her moods. As did he. "It's good to see you back," he said to Rel. "An interesting journey?"

"Very," Rel said. "Except for the past eight months, fighting winter up north, then arriving at the strait for the last gasp of the summer currents and hitting storm after storm. So I'm back just in time for another winter," he finished, his deep-set eyes emphasizing the grim twist to his smile.

Then he turned his head. "Adam, you vanished at the right moment."

"I had a token," Adam said with his vague smile. "I'm always trading for things."

Trading what for magic transfer tokens? They were costly. Rel had imagined many different conversations if and when he next saw Adam, but now his mind filled with new questions.

Adam glanced up at him, his lazy brown gaze good-humored and guileless. "Everyone on board was angry with me for my mistake. Even you, were you not?" he added with a rueful smile.

Rel could have said a lot of things. Puddlenose would never have transferred out like that, nor would he have stolen anything from a friend. But Rel did not know for certain that Adam had stolen his token. He might very well have possessed his own, or even traded for it, somehow, when he was arranging stores for the galley.

Rel wasn't going to ask because he wasn't certain he'd believe the answer.

One thing he'd learned was never to tell someone possibly untrustworthy that you didn't trust them. That was handing them a weapon. But Adam couldn't be an enemy, and this thinking trod too far down that path.

Rel gazed uncertainly as Adam shook out his chalks and paper from his battered travel bag, his expression under his mat of unruly brown curls the customary good will.

Rel said to Thad, "I arrived yesterday. Lisbet said that one of the two of you have transfer tokens that Leander donated for alliance purposes." He noticed glances from Adam and Curtas, and went on, "Might I lay claim to one?"

Thad scrambled off his mat, uneasy at the tone of Rel's deep voice. He had never heard Rel angry before. His deep voice somehow deepened more, and Rel seemed even bigger than he was. "I will fetch one at once."

"Alliance business?" Curtas asked, in his mild voice. "Anything we should know?"

Thad reappeared, the token on his hand. Rel had meant to stay for the midday meal, and catch up with news, but he had to get his temper away before he said something stupid. "If it's important," Rel said, "it'll get around."

He took the token with a word of thanks, gripped his gear tote, stepped politely outside Thad's room, concentrated on Mondros's Destination, and transferred.

When the magic finished turning him inside out, he found himself swaying on Mondros's cliff, up to his knees in fresh snow. He stood there watching his breath as he let the anger seep away.

He was here. He wasn't going to solve the mystery of the missing token. Time to move on with his life.

He chuffed through the snow to the heavy front door, fully expecting Mondros to be gone, beginning yet another long delay. But he ducked under the lintel to find himself in a room filled with light from glowglobes, and the smell of frying onions and garlic.

Mondros stood in the kitchen alcove, an apron bound around his middle. His head turned, and his beard seemed to bristle as a grin split his face. "Rel!"

All the old awkwardness rushed back. How should Rel greet him?

But Mondros didn't wait for him to speak. "Put your knapsack anywhere, and come help me. If we get these pies baking, we can talk while they cook — and eat the sooner."

Rel soon found himself rolling out pastry and pressing it into the ceramic bowls, after which Mondros layered in browned onions, herbs, cheese, tomatoes, and repeat, until the bowl was full, after which came another layer of pastry.

Those went into the stone oven, Mondros hung up his apron, and gestured to the table. "So. What have you to report?"

This, too, Rel had thought over endlessly while laboring on six separate ships, and in four different harbor towns during a series of storms that halted all sailing. He'd come out of that with some new carpentry skills and two Venn dialects, and half of a third.

He delivered the report he'd mentally prepared. Mondros listened all the way through without interrupting. At the end, he said, "How long since you were interviewed by the Queen of the Venn?"

Rel told him.

Mondros whistled. "I think," he said, "I had better let Tsauderei know right away." He turned to fetch his scry stone, then shook his head. "No, this had better be in person. Keep an eye on those pies. When the top is golden, pull them out."

"Glad to," Rel said, with the intense sincerity of one with a vested interest in the perfection of fresh-baked pies.

His shoulders eased as he breathed out. Mondros was clearly not demanding a father and son relationship, after a lifetime of avoiding being a father.

Mondros was very aware of Rel's ambivalence — he'd seen it the moment Rel entered so warily — but he, too, had had time to think. As he braced himself for the long transfer to Sarendan, he was glad he'd decided to take his cues from Rel. If friendship was all Rel could give, Mondros would take that, and gratefully.

He expected Tsauderei to be at his cottage, or else down in Miraleste, the capital city of Sarendan. The wards Tsauderei had laid over the mountain accesses to his remote village passed him through, which meant Tsauderei was in residence, and Mondros dropped into the guest chair in the mage's warm cottage overlooking the frozen lake.

When he'd caught his breath, he repeated everything Rel had said, ending with, "Why would Siamis disturb the Venn?"

"Has to be the Arrow," Tsauderei said.

Mondros snorted. "Our mage histories are full of failed attempts to locate it—theirs as well as ours. And hints of Norsunder's."

They both contemplated what they knew of the Arrow's history: the northern mages who'd bound it had vanished afterward. No one knew if they had been murdered, had killed themselves, or had gone through the world-gate to begin new lives. There was no record of them after they had been selected for the final binding. Which meant there had been no one to interrogate.

What little record there was had been warded centuries ago, kept in the mage archives in Eidervaen's Tower of Knowledge. No one got in there without leave from the head mage of the Sartoran Mage Council.

It was written that those who tried also vanished.

"All right," Tsauderei said, smacking gnarled hands on his bony knees. "Tell your boy he did well. You two are finished. I see this as my quest from here."

Mondros shook his head. "Be glad to help you."

"No," Tsauderei said. "You've a family now, and young Jilo is eventually going to see the wisdom of seeking your guidance. You might even have to intervene."

Mondros said slowly, "But you're not going to pursue the Arrow."

"No. Waste of time."

"You're going after Siamis."

Shadows deepened in the lines beside Tsauderei's mouth. "If this is my last mad quest, maybe I can make it significant."

Nineteen

Erdrael Danara

JILO OF CHWAHIRSLAND AND Terry of Erdrael Danara on Chwahirsland's western border got together to talk over lemon cakes with almond paste and cold glasses of root brew high in Terry's favorite castle overlooking Erdrael Danara's largest lake.

"There's a last thing," Terry said. "It's not advice. Not my business to do that. I'm like you, still learning how to be a king. Never wanted to be one. But here we are." He gestured with his good hand, as always keeping the one with missing fingers curled close to his body. "Something Rel said last time he was here, ah-ye, I thought I might pass it along if you want to hear it."

Jilo snorted a laugh. "If Rel has a suggestion, I'd better hear it."

"Yes. He's kind of that way," Terry said with his twisted grin. "Is it because he's so much bigger than any of us?"

Jilo thought of Rel's quiet strength and competence, wishing he had a tenth of it. "What did he say?"

"We were talking about my mountain guard, and how much better they are after learning from Senrid's Captain Forthan. Then Rel said he thought the Chwahir would benefit

from something like that—and then he added that if you were
to start the old parade competitions again, only with rewards,
not killing the losers, it would keep your fellows busy."

"Without killing the losers." If only it were that easy. Wan-
Edhe had reveled in watching masses of soldiery lined up
before him on an enormous parade ground, responding in
unison to his commands. Drilling for those competitions had
taken up most of the army's time, as everyone knew that the
losers would be punished in various terrible ways, depending
on Wan-Edhe's whim. "It keeps them sharp," Wan-Edhe had
said. "And when we march over the mountains, they will be
like a sword to the throat of the world, perfect in executing my
will."

Jilo had suspended those competitions because of what had
happened, in front of everyone, to the losers. At its worst in
Wan-Edhe's latter years, the humiliations had taken as much as
two days, with Wan-Edhe presiding to watch ever agonizing
moment. Yet everyone else had watched, too, and had carried
out those punishments even after Wan-Edhe was gone.

Jilo said, "I suspended them, and for a time, put the army
into the fields. My idea was to get them competing to grow
better crops, then everyone benefits. At first it worked. But a
year or so back, I learned they resented being subjected to such
labor, once it got boring. They resented it the more when they
personally saw the effect when drought would strike, or
something else caused crop failure. The summer Norsunder
attacked Everon, we had mass drought, and famine. The army
always gets fed first, of course, so they never had to experience
about how it hurts to labor so hard for nothing. Thinking back,
I believe it's no accident that the assassination attempt
happened right after, though at the time I didn't put them
together."

Terry nodded, his curtain of long hair swinging forward to
hide the scarred part of his face. "Did you set them back to their
marching drills?"

"I had to. It was clear they expected it. But I postponed the
competitions, and have never set a date."

Terry observed Jilo's somber face, his distant gaze, then
said, "One thing I've learned. If it seems you don't care, then
they won't care. And if they lose purpose, they begin to look for
purpose in the only way they know how. This is very hard
when it comes to armies."

And everything in Chwahirsland centered around its army.

Jilo grimaced, remembering that day when Rel and CJ so unexpectedly appeared to help him. "But Senrid's a real king. Of course the Marlovens care what he thinks. You're also a real king. I know you don't want to be one, but your people want you. I'm not a king, and I don't want to be a king. As for the people, what they want is no more Wan-Edhe."

"So until he dies, what are you, Jilo?" Terry asked.

"I'm a . . ." Jilo flopped his arms out. "A mage student?"

Terry laughed, rocking back and forth on his chair there in the plain room in his castle. Then he scrubbed his wrist across his eyes, and his smile vanished. "Nobody will believe Wan-Edhe's dead until someone sees his rotting corpse, right?"

"Right," Jilo said grimly. "This is what I'm certain of: when he returns, he'll be coming for me first. And his second command, after my execution, will be to undo everything I've done."

"But you're doing it anyway."

"I'm doing it anyway."

"Why?"

Jilo hunched inward, and Terry regretted the question.

But his tone hadn't been accusatory. Jilo knew that Terry struggled with kingship—he was frank about his failures—so he said, "Because there is always hope. And even if it turns out that hope wasn't enough, every day I win a small change for people is a victory right now. I can't promise them a future, but I can give them something right now that they would not have had."

"Fair enough." Terry shook his head; he admired Jilo, but knew better than to say anything that would make Jilo feel more awkward. "Look, I'm so glad to have you beyond my eastern border, and not him, or any of his worst followers. I don't want to see anything happen to you if he doesn't come back. But Rel did mention pretending to be a Chwahir soldier, before he came to rescue me from Wan-Edhe after he tried to invade Colend."

Jilo said, "That's right. I'd forgotten that."

"So Rel knows what your soldiers talk about."

Jilo agreed, and after he transferred back to the dusty, dank fortress in Narad, reflected on how weird it was that the soldiers would sweat for six months to get their long, complicated marching patterns perfected in hopes of winning the shoulder badge that would belong to each division, brigade, battalion, company, and squadron in the winning army for only one year.

If losing was not going to cause mass deaths, he needed to provide a reward.

The obvious reward was being first to receive any new supplies. In an eternally hungry kingdom, that was important. Jilo summoned a runner to warn his generals that this year, they would resume the drill competition, and he would preside.

Unknown to Jilo and Terry, Rel himself was on his way to Erdrael Danara, having traveled Chwahirsland's southern border after he left Mondros.

A week and three traded horses later, Rel reached the Danaran border. He relinquished the last mount to the local Chwahir, and set out across the border—a concept, he reflected, that mostly lived in people's heads. The vicious magic of Chwahirsland's border wards, once a poisonous wring of nausea and a scrape along the bones, was now no more than a sting and a whiff of hot metal. Jilo seemed to be peeling away the worst wards, one by one.

Rel wondered how many remained as silver birch and arrow pines clustered thickly on either side, boughs coated with snow. A white owl drifted long and low on an unseen current, flickering between the trees, as Rel set out walking.

Eventually the Danaran mountain guard should come across his footprints. He counted upon his name—Rel the Traveler—earning him a mount and a pass to the king, if this particular patrol didn't recognize him. He'd earned the commander's good will by training and riding with them the winter before his departure. Nothing to do with birth.

As his feet crunched and squeaked over the snow, he contemplated the illusion of titles, so much like the illusion of borders. To his left, in Tser Mearsies, Holders still elected their counts, who were traditionally tax gatherers. Holders tended to elect descendants of previous counts unless they'd been egregiously bad. And the counts elected the monarch.

Rel watched the loping grace of some deer, who vanished into the hazy woods, as he wondered what the descendants of Erdrael Danara's new duchas would do with their new titles. Hierarchy was supposed to mean order, and that meant someone had to make the final decision, which everyone else followed. And if it wasn't the right decision . . .

Rel glanced back at the hazy purple juts of Chwahirsland's rocky heights.

I never want to be a king.

The sun had moved a thumb's width across the sky when the patrol galloped up and surrounded him.

"Rel," he said to the leader, for the first time aware of the two unspoken family names he could not, and would not, use. "Here to visit the king."

As he'd hoped, the captain's face cleared with the easing of recognition. "I thought I recognized you. We're on our way back to the post. Ride with us? We can send you on up."

Rel doubled up behind the smallest of them, as the captain went on, "The truce is holding, but we still need to patrol."

"Truce?" Rel asked.

"Between our king and the Chwahir. Their raids, mostly, since The Hate went away. They went for supplies."

Someone else said, "We're paying 'em in foodstuffs not to attack us."

"Picture that," another spoke, thumbing the ridge along his horse's neck. "Chwahirsland has to be five times our size. More."

"Definitely more," several said.

"But their soil is not much better than dust."

"So the king said, maybe if we feed 'em, they'll stay on their side of the mountains. Their new king was here a week ago, everybody said gobbling lemon cakes like he'd been starving all his life."

The others laughed, and Rel smiled because it was expected, but he winced inwardly, thinking of the Chwahir scrabbling for existence for several generations as Wan-Edhe's wretched magic slowly poisoned land and even the air above it. And Jilo, whose life had not been much better. Yet he still risked that life on a daily basis to try to turn the benighted kingdom around.

By nightfall he sat in a comfortable room, now fully tiled, in the royal palace that on his last visit was still under construction.

Terry sat across from him, his grin lopsided because of the scar marking his face. "I was beginning to wonder if we'd ever seen you again!"

Rel said, "It was a long journey. What can you tell me about the alliance?"

Terry and Halad, his half-Chwahir friend, exchanged looks, then Terry's smile turned wry. "You haven't talked to the Keperis?"

"I was there, but they had company, and they both had just returned from their own journey. So I left."

Terry felt a blush coming, and because he couldn't fight it, he got up and limped to the window to look out. "As it happens, we met with the Keperis. No news, really. Everything is the same," he said to the window glass.

Halad said, "We did a border ride with the guard. And it really isn't that far down along the river to Colend, and the weather was perfect. So we took a detour to Wilderfeld."

Rel smiled. "I've walked it a number of times. One of the nicest roads I've ever traveled."

Terry wasn't thinking of the road. His mind filled with Karhin, so graceful and brilliant with that red hair and those blue eyes, her pretty figure in those light-colored robes she wore, that smelled so good. The meeting had scarcely lasted an hour, filled with the dullest talk, but he'd been over every word in memory since, knowing that there was no chance that she would feel the same way about a sorry object such as him as he felt about her.

Then Halad said soberly, "We aren't certain that there is an alliance anymore."

The reminder of all the old problems helped Terry to catch himself up mentally, and he turned to sit down, as Rel studied Halad. His hair, Rel noticed distractedly, was the same blue-black as his own: the color common to Chwahir.

"More like three separate alliances," Halad went on.

Terry lifted his good hand, three fingers spread. "There's Atan of Sartor's alliance, which includes Peitar and Lilah Selenna, and you could count Arthur in Bereth Ferian in with them, as he's often studying with Peitar Selenna these days. Call it a magic alliance. Then there's the Mearsieans, which includes Vasande Leror, and maybe Senrid, though he tries, like the Keperis, to keep everyone together. When he has time. And finally . . ." He paused to draw a breath.

"Glenn of Everon," Halad said, low-voiced. "Who wants to lead an allied army."

Later on they talked about Jilo, and Terry said, "He really

seems grateful for any help he can get. I gave him my sigil so he can write to me if he wants. Nobody believes he'll last, until there is news that Wan-Edhe is truly dead." Terry sighed. "But everyone with half a brain on either side of the border thinks Jilo the best thing to happen to the Chwahir in centuries."

Rel stayed on in Erdrael Danara, joining Terry and Halad in working out with the mountain guard (whose drills had sharpened to a remarkable degree, especially horseback fighting) and playing winter sports, until the first frost melt.

Rel had never had the least interest in the work of monarchs until this past two years. Now he watched Terry from afar, whose kingly duties during winter, at least, were not all that arduous. Much more insidious, Rel thought, was that deference he was surrounded with, but Terry never seemed to regard it as his right. It seemed part of a role he played. When Terry was alone with friends, he shed the role the way others would shed a heavy coat they weren't particularly fond of wearing, but needed to keep from freezing.

When the melt seemed likely to last more than a couple days, Rel departed for lower elevations, where winter was significantly milder, then worked his way across the strait.

Twenty

Sartor

THE MOMENT SIAMIS HAD seen the truth of the Arrow's enchantment, he had known it was time to vanish from the magical world. Though his name was widely known, his face wasn't.

While Rel had sailed so arduously southward, Siamis traveled equally arduously over land, laboring side by side with ordinary people, choosing physical labor that kept him fit and left no magical traces as well as no trail to follow. He changed his clothes and his accent and his gait to blend with the locals, traveling alone or in company, sleeping at common hostelries or pleasure houses frequented by the working world.

It gave him plenty of time to reflect.

The material and magical worlds are so entwined that it's easy to forget that either can become effectively invisible to the other. Just as Norsunder-Beyond is invisible to the material world, so someone in the material world can become invisible to magical watchers.

Assuming, of course, you know how to effectively sense and avoid wards designed to reveal transfers, or entry past a warded perimeter.

It was no surprise to discover that the written records had

carefully colluded to leave behind a lie. What the world called diplomacy was so often a fabrication, illustrating in fulsome language and excellent courtly handwriting what those in power wanted those who came after to believe had happened, in place of what really had.

It should not have been a surprise to discover that the Sartoran Mage Guild had forced the northerners to accept one of their own when the Venn were magically bound. The real surprise had been the discovery of Detlev there.

It meant he had known at least a portion of the truth all along.

About the time Rel reached the Keperis in Colend, Siamis slipped across the border into Sartor.

It was time for stealth.

Moving mostly by night, he slipped across the kingdom while the innocent slept. He knew the patterns of those also moving by stealth, for he had been trained by the best.

It was time to discover what was going on at Norsunder Base, two weeks' hard ride to the south. Using extreme care, he located two spies, and matched paces with them before risking contact in the mental realm. That was always a danger because one cannot be physically conscious when one's mind is elsewhere for extended periods.

Both were plants, reporting to someone else: the first was one of Bostian's. Useless. That idiot Bostian would never give up his desire to make himself king of Sartor. The second was a roaming spy reporting to one of the ever-changing plants in the capital, who in turn reported regularly to whoever commanded at Norsunder Base.

Siamis entered Eidervaen on a cold night after a storm, trailing the roaming spy. Drifts of mushy snow lay in windswept piles against buildings. The stunning sky of scattered stars glowed around the faintly iridescent Tower of Knowledge.

But first, a situation report. The mole might be a few months into her stint—no one left them in place long enough to settle in. Too easy to lose them to the other side. But news three months old would be better than nothing.

The spy bypassed the royal palace and the tower without a glance, proceeding into the older part of the city, then stopping at a shop selling second-hand gloves, coats, and the like. Siamis waited in the shadows as the spy knocked at a side window in a specific pattern.

Golden light flared in the cracks of the shutters, and a short time later a woman appeared at the door, a lantern in hand, revealing bulgy blue eyes and a wide grin. "Cousin!" she cried, though Siamis could have told her that no one in the little square paid the least heed.

He crouched below a dark window at the side of the house, trusting to the deep shadows, and reached mentally. The woman's mind was a rat's nest of spitefully relished covert pettiness, and as she listened was already reshaping what she was told in a manner meant to make her indispensible to Dejain.

Trusting to her preoccupation with the spy, he sank below the miasma of her conscious thoughts to recent memory of Norsunder Base.

Emotion sharpens memory. It also distorts it, but he was practiced at disassembling the mind's symbols. Fear keeps memory close to the surface. Adrenaline spiked through the woman—echoing in Siamis—when she saw Detlev enter the command center, where she'd loitered with three other spies exchanging gossip. The room had been empty except for the dispatch desk runner, but suddenly here was Detlev, after months away. They stilled, prey before predator.

And not a heartbeat later transfer magic stirred the air, smelling of winter and smoke, and here was Efael of the Host, the sharp bones of his face emphasized by a childhood and youth of rapacious cruelty, his black-dyed man-leather coat swinging at his heels, subtly glistening in a world that did not know leather, man or beast.

"It seems," Efael said to Detlev, "you neglected to report that you'd sent Siamis to find the Arrow."

Detlev set down the dispatches he'd picked up. "Why report nothing?"

"So he's failed in that, too?"

"I don't know," Detlev said. "I've been in the Garden, and then busy on Five. So I was about to see if there's something here . . ." He turned away to leaf through the dispatches. "Nothing." He picked up the papers and dropped them with a dismissive gesture. "He seems to be in the wind."

Efael's eyes narrowed in his pallid face, and Siamis wondered when Efael had last stood in sunlight or breathed fresh air. "You've lost control of him." Efael's lip curled, eyes contemptuous.

"Yes." Detlev shrugged. "Like you said, another failure. As far as I'm concerned, he's all yours."

Vindication, anticipation, the ugly lust peculiar to Efael, which had nothing to do with attraction and everything to do with domination, emphasized the sneering mouth.

Efael was no strategist. He lived for the hunt, and the lingering humiliation of his prey afterward.

But he wasn't stupid. "Want to watch, once I find him?" He stilled, gauging Detlev.

Detlev said with light irony, "Already have."

Efael closed his fist and vanished. Detlev returned to the dispatches.

Siamis stayed in the woman's mind only long enough to find the when: four months ago.

He abandoned the contact, and sat against the wall to restore his equilibrium as he breathed slowly. Four months ago. Could have been worse, but it wasn't good. Worst case: Efael would unleashed his Black Knives, hunter-killers all. They would start up in the north, as he had. But Siamis would be a fool to trust to that. If Efael brought his sister in, she was capable, even enthusiastic, about using innocent people as bait in her magical traps.

The entire city could be filled with people forced to watch at windows by magical compulsions, and unless he touched every mind, he wouldn't find them. The only chance in his favor was Yeres's obsession with preserving her youth, and how she hated the drag of time aging her even so much as a day. She loathed coming out of the Beyond for more than a few hours here and there.

Siamis slipped along the alleys until he glimpsed the great parade square before the royal palace, where he paused behind a weather-worn archway to fight back a headache caused by hunger and the long hours of sustained exertion. He scanned the palace, seeing nothing. But that didn't mean someone wasn't there, out of sight behind one of the many windows. He did not have enough strength to mentally reach behind each one.

He'd have to trust to the fact that Yeres was rarely subtle, and the well-ordered palace life would have noticed one of their number abruptly behaving like a puppet pulled by strings.

He turned his attention toward the Tower of Knowledge gleaming ghost-pale against the stars.

Detlev had brought him there on his first visit outside of Norsunder Beyond-Time. The shock of familiarity imposed over unfamiliarity had rammed home the remorselessness of passing time. Three thousand years had nearly eradicated the well-remembered lineaments, replacing them with this jumble of a palace squatting awkwardly around the Tower.

There were two facts he knew about the Tower in these times: the oldest treasures of the Landis family were kept in it, and he could not enter it.

The herald archives kept careful note of everything in that tower, and the Arrow had gained no mention. Years of spies had already ascertained that much, which was no surprise considering the fact that Sartor was not supposed to have been involved with that binding.

Siamis would begin on the assumption that The Dragoneye—renamed the Arrow—wasn't there. That meant penetrating the magical archives, wherever they were. Nearly four thousand years of accumulation were located all over the kingdom, but magical and royal records were kept close.

He backed up and ghosted through the quiet streets to the old five-story blocks of houses on twisting streets behind the grander buildings still reflecting the curve of the long-gone first ring of the city. These lesser buildings now mostly belonged to crown employ, scribes, heralds . . .and mages.

The oldest buildings in the center housed the senior mages who did not possess other homes. It was here that Siamis paused, leaning against damp, mossy-smelling stone in a narrow alley with rainwater still trickling down the bricked gutter from the earlier shower. He braced himself, then sent his mind to test the building for any new wards.

During his two enchantment experiments, he had taken care to learn the dreamscapes of the senior four mages. By these he could cross the boundary into memory without force or compulsion, and without their conscious awareness: in the same way he violated their mental privacy he also protected them, as there would never be any trace of him should they fall into the hands of the more avaricious.

He began with Chief Veltos, the head of the Sartoran mages. Mind and memory were fissiparous with years, the whole tainted with the bitterness of what she regarded as a failed life.

Sustained mental contact from a distance would drain him, tired as he was. He needed proximity, though that was risky, too. A quick search revealed sleepers who liked fresh air even in stormy weather. He eased open a window and vaulted inside a small room.

The figure on the bed snorted and stirred, but a touch on his forehead, a mental suggestion to return to the dreamscape — this was merely a new dream — a pause to listen for the deep breathing of renewed sleep, and he opened the door and passed into a warm hall that smelled of wood polish and a trace of baking honey-buns. The kitchen staff was already awake.

Up the stairs Siamis ran, four at a time, until he reached Veltos's suite, comprising a book room, a work room, and a narrow bedroom. The suite was warded. He could remove them and replace them when he left, but a mage of her caliber would recognize replaced wards made by someone else. And she would know his magical signature after the world enchantment experiments. So he would have to do this from a distance.

Trusting to her penchant for solitary living, he slid down the wall, drew his knees up, put his forearms across them and rested his head on his forearms.

Then he send his mind into Veltos, who lay deep in sleep. He skimmed recent memory, catching glimpses of her still-fruitless search for the magic that Detlev had used to smite Sartor out of time for nearly a century. It seemed she sought a mirror to that magic, to be used as defense if Norsunder came again, a search she entrusted to no one.

He reached farther into memory. The secret archive was only known to the most senior mages. He walked with her as she taught the young man she had chosen as her replacement, and once Siamis gained location, ward keys, and her general explanation of what lay where, he broke the contact without her ever leaving the dreamscape.

Success. He had just saved himself weeks, maybe a month, of searching. He rose to his feet, waited while his head swam unpleasantly, and withdrew from the house, leaving no trace of his physical presence: the hand through the water.

The stars had already begun to fade in the east. He walked past a local pleasure house, these being places where questions were never asked. A young person appearing at any hour must have only one thing on their mind. But he could not hole up there to wait for nightfall. If one of the Black Knives stumbled onto his trail—and it was likely—there must be utterly no trace of him interacting with anyone.

When the sun rose at last, he walked down a hall past room after room of coded archives penned by long gone Mage Council leaders.

Now the real search would begin.

Twenty-one

Spring 4746 AF
Everon

WINTER WAS BEGINNING TO loosen its grip on Everon by the
time Rel arrived. The vivid memories of traveling these familiar
roads still hurt, though Everon was slowly healing, both land
and people.

He passed through three rings of patrolling guards on his
approach to the capital. They passed him through without
trouble. It was good to see rebuilding, either completed or
begun everywhere but the royal palace. That looked pretty
much as it had, though at least the grounds had been swept.
One unused wing still had a gap-toothed look, broken windows
open to the wintry air.

Near the side entrance he was greeted by one of the many
Shendoral stewards, who had been taking care of the palace for
as long as the Delieths had ruled. Though it was as clean as they
could get it, without repair to stone and wood and glass, the
palace was still a silent testament to violence.

He was escorted to inner chamber where the king and
queen used to relax away from royal duties. Here he found
Tahra seated at the long table, which was covered with neatly
squared papers.

She looked up, taller and bonier than the last time he'd seen her, her dark, protuberant eyes evidence of her ancestral connection to the Landises.

"Rel," Tahra said, her solemn face lighting to a friendly smile. She flicked back lank, unkempt dark hair, and said, "They said you went all the way to the other side of the world."

"So I did," he replied, and because this was Tahra, "to come back to find the fire damage just as bad. Why haven't you fixed it? Treasury still empty?"

"It's better, after two good harvests. We won't do anything here until Mother returns," Tahra said, then looked away. And back, her shoulders tightening. "*I* won't forget her. Things remind me of her. Glenn . . .everything he does is so it won't happen again. He says."

"Army?" Rel asked.

"You'll find him at the Knights garrison most every day, which is where the building has happened," she responded, then her expression lightened. "Until Mother comes back, we decided to share her duties. I like accounting. There's purpose to numbers." She clasped her hands to her still-scrawny chest. Though she'd aged, she was still a few years shy of maturity.

Her straight, dark brows drew together. "Glenn will want to see you, of course," she said in a tone of resignation.

Rel dipped his head in a nod. So far, he hadn't seen anything that furnished understanding of Terry and Halad's hints. But then he hadn't expected to find whatever it was with Tahra. He knew the answer lay with Glenn.

He started out, then turned back. Not sure why he was asking, except that Tahra always told the truth as she saw it. "Have you had a visit with Adam of late?"

"Not since summer," she said. "He was here long enough to make some sketches for Glenn."

"You like him?"

"Oh yes," Tahra said with mild pleasure. "Everybody likes Adam."

"That's true," Rel said.

"He understands colors and mood. He knows what I mean about mud days. Though he *likes* brown. He said one afternoon the light poured like honey. I don't see it that way. Colors are . . .are feelings, for me. But I know what he means." She sighed, squaring her carefully mended pens to exactitude. "I like him much more than the new ones."

"New ones?"

"I don't mean our people. But the ones from foreign places. Like David, the latest, came a few days ago. Adam got Glenn to talk about other things besides war, war, war, and Glenn never wanted to recruit him because he's an artist. I *hate* the ones Glenn thinks he has to recruit. Glenn never stops talking about how good they might be, how to get them to become loyal — if they've ever killed anyone. This last one wouldn't answer. Maybe he was trying to impress Glenn. And he *was* impressed. Ugh." Her eyes drifted toward what she'd been doing, so Rel lifted a hand and left.

Tahra glanced up briefly, watching him go. She liked Rel for a lot of reasons, beginning with his help during the Norsunder attack, but mainly because he didn't talk about war and fighting, and he didn't want to join Glenn. She hoped that was still true, and returned to her guild reports.

Rel hefted his gear — not sure if he'd stay or go — and headed toward the enclave that had traditionally been reserved to the Knights of Dei. He considered his reaction to Tahra's words about Adam. He felt unsettled, as if he'd been chastened. Not by Tahra, but by his own question.

Adam had had his own transfer token, Rel decided. He hadn't mentioned it any more than Rel had mentioned the one Mondros gave him. One of the pirates somehow got his, and sold it for the gold, not knowing the transfer phrase.

Not surprising, the ring and clash of steel met his ears before he reached the big salle, whose door was set open. That meant they'd been at it for some time, and needed the cold air.

He paused in the doorway, utterly unaware of what a figure he made, his head two fingers lower than the lintel, his shoulders a hand-spread from either side.

To his eyes, things looked the same, and yet not: for one thing, more boys, gangling youngsters to tall boys in their late teens. And not just boys. There were a few girls scattered among them.

Glenn walked down the middle, calling out single-word commands. He'd shot up, filling out in the chest, though his elbows were still bony. Rel sensed that Glenn had seen him and was aware of being watched — and the angle of his bent arm, the two stiff fingers resting at his hip signified self-consciousness. Pride.

Glenn was doing what he loved most, and the sharpening

of his voice as he barked another command made it clear that Rel was to be the impressed audience. Rel made his way to where a handful of watchers sat or leaned, and took his place on a bench, setting his gear down beside him as he took in the practice.

The drills were complicated combinations. They looked good — they looked impressive. The Chwahir drilled like that, but for them it was vitally important to match one another to exactitude: swords rang at precisely the same moment, feet stamped, heads snapped left or right, bodies angled to the same degree. The Chwahir had been trained to act as one. For the Chwahir, one short command could unleash a complicated routine that might take a full quarter — sometimes even longer — of the hourglass. The slightest divergence could net you a bloody back, at the least.

Glenn seemed to be reinventing the Chwahir training strategy, Rel hoped without the floggings.

A flicker to his left caused Rel to glance up. One of the watchers lounged his way, hands loose, step a shamble that almost disguised the cat walk of martial training. Whoever he was, he had skills, though his sleepy expression under an unruly cap of blonde hair belied that.

"You must be Rel," this newcomer said, lounging to a stop an arm's length away. "Bigger than anyone, and besides, it is clear to the eye his highness knows you."

He spoke with an accent — Geth, Rel recognized belatedly. "His highness." If Glenn had imposed honorifics, Rel would comply, but he was aware of irony. Honorifics were supposed to signal respect and prestige, but if Rel had to call Glenn *your highness*, his opinion of him would lessen.

"And you?" Rel asked, though he suspected this was Tahra's newcomer.

"David."

"What brings you here?" Rel asked. "You're a sword for hire?"

"No, no. I learn many things." The newcomer tapped the top of a wood flute sticking out of a travel pack much like his. Rel made out the length of a sword also wrapped up in the pack. "But I heard, such were being sought. And me, I am curious."

From the far end of the salle, Glenn watched sidelong. The two people he wanted most under his command were talking, which had to mean they were more bored than impressed.

He waited for the present combination to end, relishing the sweep of swords, the loud clash, the sparks here and there. He made certain to nod approval at those who struck with enough force to spark. That would carry well to the battlefield.

At the end, he said, "Enough warming. The parade ground has been swept. How about a melee?"

He knew they much preferred the games to the drill. His own delight was in the drill, for everything was orderly — they were all extensions of his will. Everything he'd read pointed to the truth: that the more drill, the faster they carried out the commander's will.

As he expected, shouts of pleasure rang to the rafters, and when someone shouted, "Foot or mounted?" he said, "We have time enough for both."

"Who commands?"

"Besides MV," someone else cracked, to general laughter.

Glenn flicked a look Rel's way, aware of a sense of relief that Rel was still talking to the newcomer David and not paying attention to the fact that no one was clamoring for "Prince Glenn!" to lead.

At that moment David glanced up, not at Glenn but at MV, who lifted his chin almost imperceptibly, mouth quirked to suppress laughter.

They know each other. Immediately doubt set in. *Do they?* David was new, from Geth-deles. MV certainly wasn't — his accent was the same one found all along the wharves and farms and towns at this end of the continent.

A sickening roil of doubt impelled Glenn to say, "MV it will be, but let's not let him get lazy. Why don't we try to make him sweat a little? MV, you'll have no more than nine, the usual number for a patrol. The rest of you, divide into two teams under . . .Silvanas and Alfrec."

Rel broke off the conversation that had barely begun as noise erupted all around, and the boys began swarming for the door. Rel followed more slowly, and when he heard a snatch of words in Geth, he listened only because it was unusual to hear that language on this world.

". . .your suggestion?"

The boy who spoke was slim, with large deer eyes, cedar-brown skin, and long, glossy dark hair tied back. His face was expressive as he waited for an answer.

David replied, "Sword master is right-handed? These drills pretty much all broke right."

"They are when Glenn runs them."

"Enough to be habit? If so, try clearing off the other team fast by putting your lefties up front. Oblique flank attack, and scatter them like roly-pins."

The dark-haired one cracked a laugh, raised a hand, and vanished into the crowd.

Rel followed more slowly, having decided he owed it to Terry and Halad to stay and watch for a while. He regretted the impulse not ten heartbeats later, when Glenn joined him, a flock of followers at his heels.

Rel bowed correctly. "Your highness," he said, deciding to get the inevitable over with.

Glenn flushed. The lift of his chin revealed pleasure instead of embarrassment, but he said, "Just Glenn. Never more, not from you, who was there when my father was killed. And you who saved us."

Rel thought for a heartbeat that Glenn had adopted the royal 'us' of monarchs who spoke formally for the entire kingdom. But the tip of the prince's head toward the north wing of the palace made it clear that Glenn meant Tahra as well as himself.

So far, it seemed to Rel that Glenn had not turned into a caricature of his worst side. But he remained wary, remembering Terry's and Halad's extreme reserve. He still didn't know if the problem was Glenn, or his followers.

"I was thinking too small," Glenn said in a low voice, as he waved the others on ahead. "Great as any one man is, he cannot defeat armies on his own. I read as much as I could. Unfortunately, Senrid's records are all in his language, and there's so much historical reference that it's slow going trying to learn from their best. But I did get this much: command is more effective when your captains are all trained by you."

Rel said, "It sounds reasonable. Though I admit I've never studied the subject."

"*You* don't have to," Glenn said, dark eyes narrowed. "*I* do. I'm trying to get local princes to join. I suspect I'll have more success if we suitably impress them. Right now we've that wretched defeat at the hands of Norsunder against us. Admittedly Wnelder Vee is scarcely governed, but I've sent Laban to scout there. Did you meet him? And to the south,

Conrad is all but powerless."

Rel grimaced privately, remembering the difficult, moody Prince Rusalsflad Conrad, with whom Rel had dealt with briefly early in his travels.

"I know that as soon as we achieve some success, our alliance will grow," Glenn said. "That's what Matthias of Colend did, when he built his empire. And what Leskandar Dei did for my royal forebears in making the Knights of Dei into greatness. Success begets success."

"I can't argue with that," Rel said.

Glenn smiled at Rel, aware of how the difference in their heights had diminished. His admiration for Rel felt more like appreciation, now that Glenn was gaining height and physical strength. Rel didn't seem as tall as a mountain anymore. And there was the matter of his lack of birth. No, his wish to get Rel under his command had abated—but his appreciation never would.

"Come watch, and tell me what you think," he said, indicating the enormous parade ground where there used to be a cluster of small buildings, and garden.

The air was too cold to smell, but Rel suspected the stable had been moved back, as well as expanded, from all this talk of "mounted" and "cavalry" rising on the still air.

So far Glenn sounded more reasonable than he ever had.

While Rel was absorbed inwardly, Glenn watched the groups dividing up. Griping him under the friendship and appreciation for Rel was the conviction that a future king partly descended from the great Leskandar Dei should be able to win Rel's loyalty. All the great commanders inspired by their words, their actions. They used praise when it was due. They did not lower themselves to flattery and pleading.

But he kept resorting to flattery and pleading to keep MV around, and he hated that weakness in himself. No one was to find out that he got up early every morning for two hours of practice with the sword master before breakfast. He ran drills, but he didn't fight with anyone, and wouldn't until he knew he would be able to defeat Uncle Roderic's sword master.

At least MV was here, and not in Marloven Hess, or Khanerenth. And so far nobody else could beat him. So he served as a standard. Glenn had to get that strong, and he also had to master command, and choose those he'd trust as future captains. He wavered about MV. Only those he knew would be loyal would become his inner circle of commanders, he resolved for the thousandth time.

He hated it that the very best—MV, Rolfin, the horse master Silvanas, right now laughing with his team, even that obnoxious little blond Noser who followed Silvanas around — were here because they liked fighting, not because the wanted to defend Everon, or because they wanted the notice of Everon's future king.

Glenn was still undecided about the newest one, David.

Rel took a seat on one of the stone benches that used to look into the garden Glenn had ordered ripped out. It now faced the parade ground. Glenn walked on, and spotted David leaning with his forearms on the back of the next bench.

Glenn said, "You've watched. You want to join? The others will show you the way."

He meant to be encouraging and generous, but he heard his voice in his own ears sounding more like entreaty.

"Oh, I watch better, I think," David said in his Geth accent.

"As you will." Glenn gestured open-handed the way his father used to. Though David hadn't so much as touched a weapon, the way he held himself—the way he moved—made Glenn wonder how good he was. And then, there had been that look. Did he know MV?

"Though there's no age limit," Glenn said, testing. "We all have to begin somewhere."

But David gazed blandly back at him out of sleepy light brown eyes.

Glenn cleared his throat, and gestured toward his future Knights. "They will soon be the best." As soon as the words were out, he again felt they were the wrong ones, or his tone was off.

Then came the pulse of irritation: he shouldn't have to try to impress anyone. Prospective warriors ought to be exerting themselves to impress *him*.

So he had to be impressive, he had to command a field exercise and win. And Senrid had said that the more you watched, the more you learned.

As soon as the weather cleared, he'd plan a three day war game, he decided. If he asked Tahra to find the funds to supply it, maybe even a week. He just needed *experience*.

Glenn moved to the stands, and took his place on the royal platform, from which he could see everything with beautiful clarity. He assessed the three teams. MV, not surprisingly, had chosen Rolfin and his cousin Leefan, or Leef, who was even more silent. Between the two of them, Glenn didn't think he'd heard a hundred words spoken, and from Leef, fewer than ten. Leef wasn't the archer his cousin was, but he had turned out to be the best at the two citywide hunt-and-search games.

MV had also chosen Erol, who Glenn strongly suspected had Chwahir blood in him, he was so pale, with blue-black hair every bit as dark as Rel's. (Which meant of course that hair that black was not confined to the moon-faces, because someone with Rel's heighth, strength, and looks could never be related to any Chwahir.) Glenn hadn't wanted Erol at first, not because of his round, pale Chwahir-looking face, or because he was so quiet, almost furtive in the way he drifted along perimeters, but because that awful stutter had made him sound stupid.

But Erol wasn't stupid at drills. Few were as strong. And MV consistently chose him first.

The rest of his team he made up of good fighters, paying no attention whatsoever to rank, unlike Alfrec, captain of the Blue Team. Silvanas, captain of the Red Team, not surprisingly first chose that disgusting little rat Noser, and with his usual lazy smile accepted everyone Alfrec hadn't wanted. All six girls, including Uncle Roderic's oldest daughter, ranged up in Silvanas's team.

Glenn leaned forward, hands gripped together as he concentrated. It didn't do to show how hard he was working as he tried to watch how they organized for their attack. He watched MV, who sauntered toward the far corner, one long hand gesturing as he addressed his eight. Glenn couldn't make out the words, and MV merely pointed with his chin, rather than waving arms and gesturing to illustrate his strategy.

So Glenn switched his attention to Alfrec, who was dividing his force in an immediately recognizable pattern, just as Uncle Roderic's weaponsmaster taught: faster and lighter fighters on the wings, strongest at the center.

Laughter rose from Red Team, drawing Glenn's attention as Silvanas joked with his group. The formation they were in made no sense to him. Was Silvanas playing one of his practical jokes during a game? Well, talented as he was with knife and contact fighting, as a captain it seemed that he'd get trounced.

Glenn mentally shut him out, and waited until the captains saluted him the way he'd taught them, indicating readiness.

Then he raised his right hand, fist up: begin.

And they launched into action as if released from a bow.

Glenn breathed slowly, exhilarated. *This* was command, one of those rare, breathtaking moments when he felt the power that was his by birthright. But it wasn't real command, because he'd merely started them. He wasn't directing the battle.

So watch and learn.

So far everything made sense, Alfrec's battle order most of all.

But as soon as the teams met, there went his understanding — yet again. He sensed he was a heartbeat behind, always looking in the wrong direction, which put him further behind when he should be anticipating the next move.

He'd mentally shut Silvanas out, assuming he was clowning, but when Red Team sliced through Team Blue in a flanking wedge from the left, they cut Alfrec's team to pieces. Nearly all Alfrec's boys gave cries of anger, or disgust, clapped hands to death wounds, and trooped to the perimeter to watch out the remainder of the game. Not one of Red Team had a wound.

Alfrec was one of the dead, so Silvanas waved the remainder of Blue Team into Silvanas's group, saying something that made them laugh, and now it was Red Team against MV, the latter having veered off with his group to watch.

Tactical retreat, Glenn thought — but again, he was naming it after the fact, not calling it.

Then MV gave that characteristic sharp jerk of his chin, and his team launched at the others — and again, all became confusion.

Watch the leaders, Glenn thought. The rest is chaos. He tried to track MV and Silvanas, but it was difficult to keep both in view, much less anticipate their actions. However, switching fast between them revealed something odd, glances off-side. At?

Instinctively he turned Rel's way. Rel sat on the bench, elbows on knees, hands loose as he watched. Beyond Rel, David had chosen to sit on the back of another bench, feet on the seat, which put him almost at horseback-riding height. His head moved as subtly and minutely as a predator bird — and —

Surprise burned through Glenn, chased by fury when he saw Silvanas flash a grin at David, then veer off into the scrum. MV's sharp-boned face turned David's way, and a brief grin flared before he, too, caromed away, Erol, Rolfin and Leef caroming with him as if they all shared one mind.

Then Silvanas's front runners broke apart, and the back formation charged in a tight wedge to cut MV out from his three flanking guards, or at least attempt to. MV's team fended them off, but lost their offensive, forcing a change in their tactics.

One look. Another look—

Signals of command *from David*?

Glenn stopped watching the game, and turned all his attention to David, who sat almost motionless, except for those tiny jerks or nods. And each one of those caused a change in the game, ripples that affected the chaos and caused more death wound slaps. For a short time the game intensified, swiftly winnowing down to the best fighters. MV evaided capture again and again, rallying and driving into Red Team to divide them. Would you do that on the battlefield? Judging by the death wounds, only if you wanted to sacrifice that strike team.

When at last it was down to MV, Erol, Rolfin, and Leef against Silvanas, a tiny gesture from David caused Rolfin and Leef to abruptly switch sides, evening up the two teams. Then David sat back, propped his elbows on his knees and his chin on his hand, a passive watcher like Rel, as the four battled it out with their wooden swords and knives.

By the time MV won—as always—Glenn's emotions had coalesced into resentment, and hatred. Who was this posturing nobody who walked in and commanded the very people Glenn was trying to win?

When MV stood alone as Erol (the last combatant) tapped out, faces turned expectantly toward the royal stand. Glenn forced a smile and spoke a few words of praise that to his ears fell flat in the cold air. Then he said, "Why don't we break for midday?"

He had to get control of this fury. He'd look like a fool if he showed it. A commander—a king (a future king, he had to remember that)—was above that. He left the stands, and walked toward the benches, wondering next if he ought to eat with his men in the mess hall, demonstrating a warrior comradeship. He didn't want anyone to think he was lowering himself.

Like poking at a wound, he could not resist looking David's way, to catch a narrow, considering gaze. Immediately David's

expression resumed that sleepy, vague look that no longer
fooled Glenn.

"You know MV and Silvanas," he said, then heard his
question as weak — showing too much interest.

David lifted a shoulder, and Glenn's irritation spiked into a
sharper hatred in the lack of answer, the lack of deference — of
order.

Before he could frame a reaction that would not further
erode his prestige, David took a sidestep and vanished in the
crowd.

Another sidestep between two groups of talking people, a
third, and he slipped around the corner of the weapons annex,
to find MV lounging against the wall, arms crossed, flanked by
Leef and Rolfin.

"You idiot," MV said, uncrossing his arms and poking
David in the chest.

David grabbed MV's forefinger and twisted, to catch a hard
forearm across his neck. Fast and silent they traded light blows,
MV occasionally wheezing a snicker.

Then David stepped away and their hands dropped.

MV clawed his black hair out of his eyes. "You've had a year
of bad temper. Result?"

David didn't have to say it. They all knew that he could
never return to Geth. Likewise, nobody pointed out that Geth
had been the practice ground.

David rocked back on his heels, then sighed. "Yeah, I'm an
idiot." His tone altered, signaling a change of subject. "So Adam
says that Laban found us a rat-hole."

"I did what I could," MV said. "How about you finish it.
And when you return —"

"Right. I don't know you."

David eased around the side of the building and walked
away from the royal palace, using the blind spots in the sentry
rounds.

While he did that, the others separated and returned to join
the rest for the midday meal, where Glenn sat beside Rel after
asking what he thought, and listening to the typical short Rel
answer: "Where'd MV and those others get trained? Best I've
seen."

Glenn had to say, "I don't know." He resented, bitterly, not
knowing.

So commenced a very long meal during which Glenn

alternately bragged and asked questions that were not-very-subtle hints for reassurance that revealed more to Rel than Rel's answers did to Glenn.

As Glenn talked, Rel looked around for those boys who'd fought so well. He'd had enough experience by now to have recognized immediately that they'd been trained by someone different from Roderic Dei's sword masters. Because Rel kept looking for them, he noticed them slip in one at a time, each from different doors.

He had no idea what was going on, and in the larger sense he didn't care. Glenn might sound more reasonable in some ways, but in others he was exactly as single-minded as ever. His vision of the alliance was clearly a military empire, dedicated to fighting Norsunder, with him in command.

Rel had never forgotten something Tsauderei had said about Sarendan's dead hero, Derek Diamagan: when you spend all your time forming an army that does nothing else but train, eventually — if your enemy doesn't conveniently come to you — you're going to go looking for someone to fight.

When the meal broke up preparatory to more war games, Rel took his leave of Glenn, who saw at a glance that he'd lost Rel once again. Well, that was no surprise. And it wasn't as if he didn't have better prospects. For the sake of the past, Glenn gave Rel a friendly farewell, and they parted, Glenn to plan more war games, and Rel to heft his gear over his shoulder and head out into the open air.

He'd done his duty. He'd earned a visit to Sartor. Chief Veltos and the rest of them could hardly accuse him of crowding Atan after all this time away.

But the idea of visiting Atan again didn't mitigate the residue of disappointment, of the sense that something had gone wrong, and Glenn's army was a part of it.

One thing he was sure of. As he stepped onto the broad road leading southward out of the city, he wondered how to tell Terry that he was right. The alliance they had tried to build was effectively dead, killed by Glenn with the best intentions.

Twenty-two

Sarendan

> *It's been a month since that David left, so I trust he
> is gone for good, and Glenn will eventually stop
> complaining and speculating endlessly about him.
> Spy? Conspiracy? He is sure that Senrid never has
> to face such threats.*

> *Once I told him instead of imagining all these
> situations that are unlikely and probably impossible
> he could help me with the tariff situation, but no, he
> calls his endless worrying strategic thinking and
> says I don't understand it. . .*

Karhin looked up from Tahra's letter and regarded Senrid.
"And that's the last one. Do you think there's any danger here?"

"Don't know." Senrid gestured with his palm up. "I'm
thinking about that letter you read first."

"The one from last month?"

"Older than that. The one that mentioned something about
Khanerenth. Tahra might not know it, but they've a military
school there. Trains their navy as well as their home guard.
Outsiders welcome. So this David and the rest of them must

have gone there. I don't see anything sinister in that. A lot of people go for a season, or a couple years, then find out they want to do something else. Hey, Rel went there for a time, if I recollect something Derek Diamagan told me right before Siamis shot him."

Karhin let out her breath. She had been feeling as if she'd missed something, and of course she knew nothing whatsoever about military strategy. And cared less. She hated any mention of war's destruction, especially these days when she could scarcely keep up with meaningful work.

"Good," she said. "Thank you. I shall report to Tahra what you said, and I trust and hope it will ease her mind, even if it does nothing for Prince Glenn."

Senrid didn't miss how careful the Keperis all were to use Glenn's title, but Tahra was just Tahra. As Karhin slid her letters back into her pocket, and led the way across the terrace overlooking the lake, Senrid renewed his determination never to return to Everon. Likewise, if Glenn wrote to him, to keep his answers short.

Before following Karhin through the archway into the Miraleste's royal palace, he paused at the stone rail and looked out over the lake reflecting the balmy spring sky. It was significantly warmer on this side of the continent than it was in Marloven Hess.

On the lake, little boats of various sizes floated about, their curved white sails like wings. Senrid missed sailing with Puddlenose on the *Tzasilia*, looking out at the ever changing sky. No, he could see plenty of sky on the plains below his own capital, and the sea was just the sea. It was that sense of freedom he missed.

He laughed at himself as Karhin gave a polite touch of her palms to whoever it was opening a carved door for them. If he were to go on board a ship, he would start fretting about whatever was going on at home.

They re-entered the antechamber decorated by silken hangings with paintings of blossoms. Lilah's, CJ's, and Kyale's high girl voices rose as they cooed over the newborn Prince Darian Selenna. The rest of the private Name Day party stood on the other side of the round bassinette, looking down with various expressions at the infant whose tiny fists jerked and waved.

Peitar stood over his little son, an expression on his face that Senrid had never seen, and couldn't name, as tenderness was not part of his conscious vocabulary. But he sensed the depth of Peitar's feeling. The whole idea made Senrid feel weird, but this was nothing new. He'd been keeping the weird feeling strictly private ever since Liere had suddenly produced Lyren — who from the beginning was not a miniature Liere, and with each season ever less so.

Lilah stood in the center of the knot of girls, her frizzy red braids seeming to bristle with her obvious delight and good will as she described the official Name Day celebration earlier. She and Peitar had paraded through the city showing the new heir to the cheering citizens, who all threw bright-colored flowers. "Darian will be like a little brother to me," Lilah finished. "He'll never call me Aunt. Yuk! I've had enough of aunts!"

"Lyren is already kinda like a sister to Liere," CJ — who was on her very best behavior — said.

"He's so bee-*yoo*-ti-full," cooed Kyale Marlonen, holding out a finger for the infant to grab. "He's got tilty eyes like yours, Lilah."

"Does he?" Lilah glanced down doubtfully. "I can't tell. All babies look the same to me. I can hardly wait until he starts talking, so I can teach him how to insult Norsundrians."

That got the expected laugh, as Kyale plucked the infant from the bassinette and cradled him, watched by Peitar, whose stiff hands betrayed his unease.

The baby scrunched his face, obviously preparing to wail, and Kyale rather hastily handed him to Arthur at her right. Senrid was surprised to see how expert Arthur was, then remembered he'd had plenty of practice with Lyren.

"You named him after the deposed king?" Roy asked. "Yes?"

Lilah made a face, but Peitar said, "My uncle was not a bad man. But he became a bad king in trying to force the kingdom to prepare for war with Norsunder."

Like Glenn?

Senrid wondered if every person there was thinking the same thing. Of course Glenn was not (yet) a king, and even when he reached adulthood in a year or two, if they decided the queen was not returning, he would co-rule with Tahra, who was doing all the real work.

But the name was in the air until Roy said, "I think I misspoke."

Peitar lifted a hand in negation. "It was a reasonable question." He liked Roy and been studying wards with him once a month for the past year and a half, so he turned the subject as on the far side of the room the girls were deep in conversation.

"No, Dejain is much worse," Kyale was saying in a voice of doom, her tone begging for questions.

"I hate thinking about that," CJ said, shuddering.

Lilah turned from one to the other. "What? Oh, tell me!"

"Dejain . . .and blood magic," Kyale uttered in a stage whisper — then looked around. Oh, but everyone was in the alliance. So she settled herself, spreading her skirts, and said, "It all began with my brother . . ."

"May I sketch you?" Adam asked.

Kyale smiled — nothing could be better. She had the attention of two princes, she wore the prettiest dress in the room (except for Atan, of course, but she was next thing to a grownup, as well as Queen of Sartor), and she was the heroine of this story. Yes, the heroine — if it hadn't been for her, Senrid and Leander would be *dead*. Kyale drew the story out, dramatically describing every one of her thoughts and actions as CJ fidgeted, more and more uncomfortable, until Kyale reached the Mearsies Heili portion. "And so it ends," Kyale finished, as she was not the center of this portion.

"Not quite." CJ rubbed her arm unconsciously. The shocked, interested gazes of the other two girls brought out her part of the story, faltering only when Lilah said, "Rel was in Chwahirsland? Why?"

CJ had her mind-shield firmly in place, knowing she skirted a secret not hers to tell. She reddened, saying, "Well, you know, Rel travels. And he had something or other to tell Jilo . . ." And then in a rush of relief-impelled memory, "Some army junk or other. Anyway, there we all were in horrible Chwahirsland, and Dejain got booted out by magic but Kessler got those nasty books."

Adam held up his sketch. "What do you think?"

It was good. Maybe too good? Lilah and CJ both took in Kyale's complacent smirk, excellently sketched, whereas Kyale saw only that the beautiful ribbons and embroidery on her gown were barely hinted at. Trust a boy to not get it right! "Very nice," she said.

The other two echoed her, then Lilah jumped up. "Maybe it's time to bring out the cake?"

"Oh, yum," CJ said. "What kind?"

Refreshments had been set on a side table, unseen until now because all attention had been centered on little Prince Darian. But an infant is only interesting to outsiders for a short time, and the shift in conversation indicated that that time was over.

As the cake plates got passed, sparking chatter about deliciousness and favorites, Senrid—whose attention had begun to wander—found Karhin's distracted gaze turned his way as she sat with her plate unnoticed in her hands. Senrid glanced at the layered cake, which smelled of vanilla and some kind of seed, then back to Karhin, whose gaze stayed blank until Thad nudged her.

She blinked a couple times, then her face flooded, contrasting with her bright red hair.

She glanced at the others, appalled at her lapse in manners. It was proof, as if she needed it, that she was always too tired. Too many letters—not just alliance, but she had taken on a full share downstairs in hopes that their mothers would promote her by the next year. But first, of course, she must complete her archival task, which demanded yet more time.

"Karhin?" Thad whispered, wondering if here in Sarendan the custom of hosts serving guests themselves was the highest honor, as it was in Colend, or a result of the revolution not long ago, when the nobles had been overthrown along with the former king.

Then the thought vanished when Karhin whispered back, "I think I know who."

Thad knew what she meant: for half a year they had talked in a desultory way about getting her help in answering alliance letters, as her scribe work had taken over so much of her life.

Of course she would continue to write to her personal friends, and it was an honor as well as a responsibility to write to Prince Shontande. Those letters took thought and care, and young as he was, he always wrote back formally, in royal blue. (It didn't occur to her that that was all the ink he had available to him.)

But for the rest of alliance matters, who knew everyone the way she did?

She glanced across the gathering toward Adam, and Thad followed her gaze, mouth open. Of course! Now that Adam had gotten his wish and met Peitar and Lilah, he, too, seemed to be connected to everybody in the alliance.

As if aware of their gazes, he glanced up.

Peitar, seeing that Adam was not absorbed in sketching, asked, "Are you an artist? Lilah's friend Bren is. You might like to meet him."

Adam said, "I don't think of myself as an artist. Art is most serious, and I'm never serious if I can help it."

Arthur glanced up from his book, his fingers inky. "Adam, an artist makes art. Every time I see you, you're making art." He wiggled his smudged thumb and third finger. "I wouldn't say I'm not a mage, just because I'm still learning."

"Yes," Lilah exclaimed. "Bren says, a learning artist is still an artist, not a potato."

Everyone laughed except Karhin, who watched Adam with an arrested look that caught Senrid's interest. Karhin, he'd discovered, was aware of that net of communication *as* a net. People, in his experience, usually only thought about their particular strand.

Adam set aside his chalk. "No, art is a way of seeing the world. Surely you've read Adamas Dei."

"You mean Adamas Dei of the Black Sword," Peitar said.

Karhin turned his way, distracted by the fine bones of his sensitive face, his dark eyes shadowed by years of pain. They reminded her a little of Terry, who otherwise was sadly rather unprepossessing to look at. But Peitar Selenna was arrestingly handsome.

He quoted, "'Art is harmony of all things perceivable, our finite attempt to express the sublime — the infinite. True art strives to break the bonds of the finite, and the effect of art makes us part of that harmony for a time.'"

"Art *is* truth," Adam stated. "It's the only truth. As soon as you try to define it in words, it muddies. I am not yet an artist because I might capture a moment the way I see that moment, but I am unsuccessful at *making* it truth. As a . . .a larger thing."

Under his breath, Senrid muttered, "Whatever that might be."

"Art is ineffable," Peitar observed. "Is truth?"

"Here it comes," Senrid said with a sigh. "Next up is how truth is good and untruth is evil, and once we get onto good and evil, we're in for forty verses of lighter moral superiority, rhymed in three places."

Peitar's sudden slash of a smile completely transformed his somber countenance, a gleam of reflected light in his dark eyes.

Adam absently wiped his fingers on his chalk-dusted pants

and got to his feet. "Before we get to the poetry, a question."

He looked around as Lilah bounced up to fetch the cake and knife to take around for any who wanted seconds.

"Let's hear it," Senrid said.

"As long as it's not poetry," Arthur put in, with one of his rare grins.

"No poetry." Adam laughed silently, shivering inside at the brilliance of all their colors, so very different, from Senrid's steel to Kyale's bright green, then gold shot with a thin strand of red. Karhin's deep violet, deeper by the moment.

He shuttered away the distracting auras. "A question. When I last left Colend to visit Terry, I met a girl on the border between Erdrael Danara and Chwahirsland. You know how everyone says that the Chwahir look alike, well, she didn't look like a Chwahir. But she was one. I found out her story."

He opened his hands, his smile so charming that Karhin thought, of course he found out her story. She had never met a better listener, or anyone more interested and sympathetic than Adam. Who knew everyone. . .why was that important?

"It seems," Adam said, "that she was chosen by her village when very young to not be put in a twi. I don't quite understand if a twi is family or friends or a combination, but she wasn't given one, because she was taught to speak flawless Kifelian, then taken south and apprenticed to one of the silk guilds. At end of each summer, when many of the prenties are sent home to help with the harvest — "

"I thought they kept the prenties like prisoners in those silk houses," Senrid interrupted. "It's high treason if they breathe a word of their secrets."

"It's part of one's vows to keep the arts within the walls," Thad said.

"But this isn't one of those houses, that cater to the wealthy." Adam made a dismissive gesture. "It's useful silk, not the transparent or the shimmer or the patterned stuff with all the fancy names." He sidestepped Lilah, who passed Senrid, offering cake, to be waved on. "Anyway, she teaches her village everything she spent the year learning. So, is that evil?"

"If she promised not to, that's a betrayal," Karhin said, palms down in a gesture of reserved judgment that actually means *Convince me not to condemn.*

"Ah." Adam turned to her, working to keep the colors at bay. "What if she insists that the Colendi in fact stole those secrets from the Chwahir, long ago, and they all believe that they are getting their own back again?"

Karhin and Thad put their hands flat on their thighs in polite, silent repudiation, and Peitar's brows lifted.

Arthur cut in unexpectedly. "Ever since we met Jilo, I've been reading about Chwahirsland. Did you know that they were the leaders in flax weaving until about ten centuries ago? *Everybody* else learned from them."

"And then?" Roy asked, his Geth accent strong at that moment.

"And then," Arthur said, "they had a series of really bad kings, or mages, or both, and somewhere in there a Sartoran prince was sent up to marry a Chwahir prince."

"What?" Lilah squawked, her head jerking back—and the sharp knife slid off the big cake platter.

The rest didn't even have time to react as the knife spun toward the bassinette. Adam nipped the blade up before it could land. His breath hitched for a heartbeat, then he laid the knife on the plate as he said, "That girl told me the Chwahir invented the complicated weaving patterns."

Arthur shrugged. "What I read is that that queen brought Sartoran experts and artists to Chwahirsland."

"Where they didn't do well," Peitar said, blinking at the bassinette as his mind caught up with his eyes, and processed the near disaster. "Lilah, please put the cake back on the table. People can help themselves. As for the experts taken to Chwahirsland, according to the more recent Sartoran histories, they didn't do well."

Senrid gazed at Adam with interest. Nobody besides Peitar seemed aware of the close call that wasn't one, it had been so deftly done. Senrid laughed to himself. It seemed somewhere, sometime, someone had managed to get a little self-defense into Adam's cloud of a brain. Because he certainly wasn't afraid of plucking a spinning knife out of the air.

"What might not be in those more recent histories is that earlier Chwahir escaped south during unsettled times, taking their skills with them," Arthur said, as always trying to see both sides. "Two became wealthy and changed their names, adopting their new kingdom and language. One returned home, unable to live long away from his family. And one—a silk weaver—vanished. Many believe she was killed after revealing her secrets."

"In Sartor?"

"That's not clear," Arthur picked at his cake absently — like someone, Adam thought as he watched them all, who had never gone hungry. "There are rumors she sold her secrets to the Adranis. Others insist she was taken to Toar, which communicates little with the Sartoran continent."

Karhin found herself so caught up in the discussion — and her effort to resist the temptation to defend what she perceived as an attack on Colend — that she lost the train of thought she'd been pursuing. It would come back. Something about Adam knowing everyone. She'd recover it later, and could also ask if he might be interested in taking on some letter-writing, especially to the younger alliance members, like Kyale Marlonen.

When the cake had been demolished, the Name Day party was done.

Those who had come a long way began to leave, either escorted by Peitar and Lilah to the Destination chamber, or politely walking into the hall if they had transfer tokens. CJ lagged behind in order to snag a last of the chocolate pastries; moving silently on bare feet, she was half-hidden by the cluster of tall-backed chairs as she followed the last of the guests toward the door.

She was there to see Adam and Roy pause to let Arthur through the door. When Arthur had vanished into the hallway, Adam turned a wide-eyed, rueful grin toward Roy, saying on an outward breath, "Firejive."

Roy waggled his head as he led the way out.

CJ, now alone, touched the medallion around her neck and transferred home, where she reported everything to Clair. "I'll write a thank you to Lilah," she finished. "But I wondered, what does 'Firejive' mean — what language is that? Because it almost sounds like you-know-what."

Clair knew that CJ still hated any references to her Earth origins, as if a mention would force her back to a life of abuse and fear.

"You know there are all kinds of words that sound like other words, but have different meanings," Clair said. "Adam said it to Roy? I didn't know he knew Roy."

"Adam knows everybody," CJ said, and laughed. "I guess I'll ask him, next time I see him."

Twenty-three

A LITTLE LATER, SHE was not thinking of Adam, or babies, or even the alliance as she pottered in the underground hideout the Mearsiean girls called the Junky, neatening her room. While she hated cleaning, she loved her room so much she saw to it that her forest-green bedcover lay smooth over the bed, and her journals lined up neatly in her bookcase.

She stood in the doorway, looking with contented appreciation at the curving brown walls overhead, the dirt smoothed by magic, and the tracery of tree roots in the ceiling. She'd made pictures to brighten the walls, mostly sketches of the other girls in the group, but one of Hreealdar transforming from the form of a white horse into lightning. She'd tried three times to get it right, and had to admit it just looked weird. Maybe it was time to make a new picture.

"CJ!"

She couldn't tell who was yelling, so she waited, squinting at the wall and trying to recollect what Adam had said about underground rooms and how if pictures were to be like windows, then the lighting in the pictures ought to blend with the lighting in the room.

"Okay," she said, her heart sinking. "The lamp is here, so the shadows are there." Every one of her pictures had different lighting. Ooops.

"CJ, what are you doing?" Red-haired Falinneh was at the door, hands on her hips. She didn't wait for an answer. "Mearsieanne's here!"

Small, blonde Gwen popped up at Falinneh shoulder. "To stay!"

"I thought she was going to stay in Wnelder Vee and help ol' Troiad get used to throne-warming."

"She did, and he did," Falinneh said briskly. "But Mearsies Heili is home, she says."

"Of course it's home," CJ stated proudly.

Gwen added with equal pride, "All the alliance rulers offered to have her live with them. Sartora, Atan, Kyale. All of 'em. But she wanted to come home."

"Wow," CJ exclaimed, rubbing her hands. "Let's go upstairs. It's not often a queen gets to live with her great-grandmother and neither's a grownup — " she began, and then her expression changed from pride to puzzlement, even uneasiness.

Two queens?

Well, but it would work out, she thought. After all, Clair was wonderful, Mearsieanne was wonderful, and Clair's Aunt Murial, though a grownup, and who should have inherited ahead of Clair, preferred living isolated in the western wild, so surely, surely, everyone would be okay. Right?

CJ did the transfer spell to the white palace on the mountain, ran upstairs to the library, which she thought of as Clair's study.

And there was Mearsieanne! She appeared to be around fifteen, long black hair, blue eyes, a contrast to Clair's snow-white hair and hazel gaze. The two shared square jaws, broad foreheads and straight brows.

Clair was smiling at Mearsieanne, who twirled around, scanning the throne room. "Your styles are so much simpler than ours — " she was saying, then she saw CJ. "Cher-*enn*-eh!" she exclaimed with obvious pleasure.

CJ loved her name, Cherenneh Jenet, which Clair had picked out for her, but she was so used to CJ that it was slightly unsettling to hear her name, all drawn out in all three syllables like that. It felt formal, somehow.

"Hi," she said, shaking off the feeling. "Welcome back!"

"It's wonderful to be home at last," Mearsieanne said.

"Hungry?" Falinneh — of course — asked.

Mearsieanne shook her head again, her hair swinging

against her silken skirts as she turned about.

Here she was again, back in her home kingdom after a century, thanks to Norsunder, specifically Detlev and his hateful experiments. She prided herself on having survived, and had often reminded Morgeh Troiad gently of that when he seemed the vaguest. Well, she'd brought him to a sense of his duty. In spite of that irritating, smart-mouthed snip Laban.

The truth — that she would never admit out loud — was that she had discovered that Morgeh Troiad preferred Laban's company to her own. Perhaps it was to be expected that a teenage boy would prefer the company of another teenage boy. And so it was time to return home, though the truth was, she loathed all the changes.

"Thank you," she said, squaring herself to make the best of things. "I'd much prefer getting acquainted with my city again. So very odd, to find it fitted down along the mountain like this. Did you ever find out why the cloud lowered?"

Clair heard *my city*, and was surprised at how it unsettled her.

Quickly, before anyone might notice her unworthy reactions, she said, "That was so frightening, I hate to remember it. Aunt Murial has consulted Tsauderei and other mages, but no one knows anything. I think that's what's so frightening, though no one was hurt. Just a lot of windows smashed, and dishes falling off shelves."

CJ, with her new, wayward sensitivity, side-eyed Clair, who smiled and led the way outside.

The tour extended to the underground hideout the girls called the Junky, which they were eager to show off. Mearsieanne looked about with a fixed expression, uttered polite compliments as the girls talked over one another, explaining every picture and trophy, relating past adventures, and offering to double up if she wanted one of their rooms.

Mearsieanne's smile did not change when Sherry asked questions or Irenne flounced about, dramatizing anecdotes. She didn't flop onto the cushions scattered about on the multicolored rug in the main room; she sat carefully, disposing her skirts close by her, as if she feared they would get dirty.

And afterward, as the days began to drift by, she never went back.

Vasande Leror

Leander Tlennen-Hess rode into the small stable of his royal castle, dismounted, and exchanged some chat with the stable hand who came for the horse.

He walked inside, whacking dust from his clothes, secretly relieved that he could dress in his favorite forest garb while Kyale was visiting in Sarendan. He wished he could find a way to convince her that outward forms didn't confer respect, but a semblance of respect. From there his mind wandered to an equally familiar path, wondering if the Child Spell was a mistake.

No, that was too simplistic. He thought back over his visit to Sarendan. While it had been excellent — Arthur and Roy and Peitar always had new magic books that Leander otherwise could never have found on his own — when Peitar fell into reverie, Leander had seen . . .

What? Not happiness, except when he was with the infant prince, or his sister bounced in so eagerly, her good will radiating around her like a sunny day. He had never seen that adulthood really afforded that much more insight or wisdom. Nor happiness.

Leander reached his desk, and checked his golden notecase. He found a letter from Senrid. A short time later they sat in Senrid's study, the four tall windows wide open to the spring air. High voices shouted in cadence from the academy below.

Senrid said, "I went to the Name Day celebration."

Leander gave a nod. "I left right before it. I had some things to see to here."

Senrid picked up a letter from the desk and tossed it to Leander, who recognized Karhin Keperi's beautiful handwriting. "She thinks there's *another* alliance?" He looked up at Senrid. "What's this, are we left out?"

"No." Senrid flat-handed the air. "At the Name Day thing, she showed me a letter from Tahra."

Leander sighed. "Glenn and his army pretty much killed the alliance. We all know that. Nothing new there."

"Wrong. Karhin was worried about some of Glenn's new-comers, who might have trained at Khanerenth."

Leander suppressed the impulse to shrug. Senrid kept himself on a tight schedule, and wouldn't take this time over mere military training natter.

"When you sort through all the Colendi politesse, what Karhin is seeing is, there might be a new alliance forming, and Adam is at the center of it."

"Adam!" Leander exclaimed. "The painter?"

"Yes."

"So? He travels. Until Rel took off somewhere a year or so ago, we could have said *he* was at the center of the alliance. As Karhin is at the center with her pen."

"You're still not getting it." Senrid rubbed his chin as he gazed out his window. "Liere told me once that Karhin has some kind of Dena Yeresbeth potential. Doesn't seem to know it. Liere decided not to tell her because she feels her own abilities made her into an outcast."

Leander felt sorry for poor Liere, who at least had Lyren now. That chattering two-year-old made even the gloomiest people smile. "You could tell Karhin."

"And?" Senrid spread his hands. "It's not like *I* know how to control it. Anyway, Liere told me once that it didn't surprise her that Karhin would do so well with the alliance because she always seemed to know who was coming, who might come — she sees . . .patterns, I guess you'd say. The way I've learned to see patterns out on the practice field."

"All right, with you so far. So?"

"So Karhin wanted to know how many newcomers have appeared since Adam did, and how many of them are connected to him. Is there another alliance, and if so, why don't we know about it?"

"Huh. I don't know. It seems natural that Adam, like Rel, would be friends with travelers like Puddlenose and Curtas."

"And those boys up in Everon," Senrid said. "And apparently Roy, the mage student studying with Arthur."

Leander looked startled at that. "I've seen a lot of Roy. He's come here with Arthur while we were studying wards, before all that about the Venn. I don't think Adam ever mentioned Roy."

"Well, apparently CJ overheard them at the Name Day celebration, talking like old friends. Anyway, she wants us to ask Adam when next he turns up, because he hasn't been back in Colend for a while."

"All right, that's easy enough."

Senrid paused, still, chin up, as he listened to the change in the cadenced voices outside. Whatever he listened for seemed to be all right, because he turned to face Leander. "There's something else, that bothers *me*."

Leander's interest sharpened.

"You weren't there, but while they were jabbering about art, Lilah was carrying around the cake, and let the knife slip — right over the baby."

"What?" Leander sat up.

"Oh, I don't think it would have landed on him. Angle was wrong for anything but falling flat on the blankets, but my point is, while Adam was blabbing, he caught up the knife. By the blade. I don't think he was really looking, and he put it back without a hesitation."

Leander waited, and when Senrid didn't say anything more, he spoke. "Is that all? It sounds like the sort of thing you'd do."

"But that's just it. I can't." Senrid slipped free the knife he always wore up a sleeve, and brandished it. "This isn't a cake knife, but I've tried it. A number of times."

He held the knife up and dropped it toward the floor. With his other hand he made a swipe at it, grasping the handle.

"So? You got the handle. Where are you going with this?"

"I got hold of the handle after some practice. When I forced myself to grab the blade, this was the result." Senrid held up two fingers with straight pinkish scars slanting across them. "Have you ever seen Adam's hands?"

"Only covered with chalk."

"Yeah. I wonder what sort of scars might be under that chalk. Anyway, what I do is contact fighting several times a week, and knife throwing. What he did shows . . ." Senrid shrugged. "He really knows how to handle a knife."

Leander thought back to his days as an outlaw living in the forest, and the weapons practice he'd felt it was his duty. He still tried to get in some basic drills once a week with his small guard, so he wasn't unfamiliar with handling weapons. But he knew that he would never catch a dropped knife by either hilt or blade. That Adam could seemed less like a trick you learn over a couple of weeks of practice, and more like long habit. He couldn't put that together with Adam the artist, who seemed vague about everything except new shades of color.

"All right," he said. "When I see Adam next I'll let you know, and you can ask him about knives and secret alliances. Meanwhile, I'm glad Karhin is writing to everyone. Who knows, maybe that'll get things started again. And best of all, it has nothing to do with Glenn's army."

Senrid grinned. "That's true."

They parted, each to their own affairs.

Weeks slipped by without Adam showing up to be asked any of those questions, so in time both boys forgot all about the birthday cake knife. After all, it wasn't as if anyone equated Adam with dangerous conspiracies.

Twenty-four

Eidervaen, capital of Sartor

IT TOOK SIAMIS PATIENCE and exhausting care to remain unseen while he searched.

Days dragged, turning into weeks as he forced himself to be methodical. At last he found the record he sought. He dared not remove it from the premises, for that would require an entire day of sensing and removing wards and tracers, which in turn extended the possibility of himself leaving traces.

He crouched on the stone floor below the stack of boxes belonging to that year, and carefully lifted and turned the brittle pages until he reached the right date.

If he had not seen what he'd seen via the Moonfire's mirror into time, he would have passed by the entry, which was coded yet a third time. The Sartoran mage masked his dangerous journey into the past as a personal trip. The Arrow was listed as a carved tree so singular that the king decreed it must be kept in royal governance. The mage then returned to the past and there remained, vanishing from the records. Subsequent mages preserved the secret until they died out one by one.

The Arrow, still listed as carved wood, remained in the Sartoran royal archive while the Venn were still ruling the high seas, and Erkric the Bloody had not yet been born. There it rested until some newly crowned monarch, in cruising through the archive to see what he'd inherited, happened to spot a fine gem that somehow had been overlooked by his predecessors, and demanded to know why it had been mis-catalogued. Kings and their greed!

The supposed wood now vanished from the records, reappearing as yet one more of many, many royal jewels. Which required Siamis to shift the search to the royal archive.

He knew precisely where the royal archives lay, as he'd had plenty of time to explore the royal palace at his leisure while occupying it before the failed attempt to gain mass transfer wards from Geth-deles's mages. He also knew how difficult the search would be, as generations of the Landis family were raised to record everything they did and thought, and they never threw anything away. Every blathering scrap (if penned by a Landis) was scrupulously preserved . . .somewhere.

Upstairs duty scribes talked and laughed, their voices dim as Siamis made his way into the older archive.

He found the king, he found the year. He found the day the new king rummaged through the family loot and chose for his regalia a set of stones, including a most exquisite fire-diamond he named the Morningstar, which would grace his winter informal crown.

And... nothing, nothing, nothing, through three succeeding books until he wrote his will—bequeathing the Morningstar to his younger daughter.

She had not ruled. Where would her records be? Siamis remembered the basement level archives where lesser Landises' papers were stored.

And so commenced his third search.

The Morningstar Winter Crown, he discovered, came to be considered part of the royal regalia, and so was left by the princess to her niece, the next generation's youngest Landis when she was chosen as heir.

Siamis tracked it through succeeding generations until a chatty old prince mentioned having the old-fashioned, awkward crown taken apart and the Winter stone hung from a necklace with diamonds alongside.

This was bequeathed to yet another Landis princess . . .whose diary was full of sorrow when her beloved Martande Lirendi left Sartor, taking her heart's most precious diamond with him as her gift. With it went the diamond, and its tangled provenance, more than four hundred years before the conflict that bound the Venn.

Siamis looked up, the diary with its faded purple ink lying forgotten on his knee, and thrust aside the question of how the Arrow could exist in two places at once—Land of the Venn and Sartor. It was a magical artifact, which had different properties than actual stones. If you studied magic, you learned early that places and races in this world did not always obey the same laws governing time and space that humans and their artifacts must.

No, the stunner was this: Martande Lirendi was the first king of Colend.

The Arrow is in Colend.

Siamis was even certain which one it was: the Lirendi Diamond, which was later brought out of a Colendi vault and given to Lasva Skychild by her besotted royal suitor, and worn during Colend's empire days.

Damn it. Detlev *had* to know. Siamis breathed hard, contemplating the threat, the hunt.

He looked down at the book, and briefly considered cutting the relevant pages out. But what would be the use? If Detlev knew, then this knowledge was not secret. If in Colend's fair capital lay the other half of a trap, it was merely a question of who would spring it.

Before the sun came up he was well out of the city and riding fast for Colend.

Norsunder Base

Not everyone understood that in Norsunder-Beyond, nothing is really private.

Of the Host of Lords, there were two who did not possess Dena Yeresbeth or something similar. Efael and Yeres prided themselves on being counted among the Host, without understanding that the architecture of Norsunder Beyond-Time was predicated on Dena Yeresbeth.

To Efael and Yeres, the world was a plaything, full of living toys to be destroyed at their pleasure. They could not, or would not, comprehend that they were mere flunkeys to Ilerian and Svirle, the architects of Norsunder.

When Efael received a private signal from his sister, the two met in what they thought was their secret citadel beyond the Garden of the Twelve, from which those with the ability could watch through magically placed windows into the world. Yeres, whose skills with magic surpassed those of her brother, greeted him with a smacking kiss on the mouth, but seeing that he was not in the mood for dalliance, sighed and shrugged.

"Have you found him?" Efael said

"Siamis? Yes and no." When her brother's expression turned vicious, she said smugly, "In Sartor."

"Sartor," Efael repeated, astonishment replacing wrath. "So he gave up on the Arrow? He certainly isn't the first. But what was he doing there?"

"I don't know what he *is* doing there."

"Is?" Efael took hold of her wrist in a bruising grip. "He's there? Right now?"

"I can't tell you that. I've been busy — as you are well aware — with Detlev's army base project on Five." She stopped there, gazing down at his hand until Efael loosened his fingers and dropped his hand to his side.

Yeres knew he was in a temper, and it would only get worse when he had a chance to reflect on all the time he and his hunters had wasted in the north, where others had fruitlessly searched for centuries. But she couldn't help taunting him, as she always had.

So she took the time to rub at the marks he'd made in her flesh, while he waited, still and poised and very deadly. She liked him best that way.

Finally she said, "Since you did not want to risk Detlev or any of the others catching my tracers as they cross the Norsunder ward, I've been forced to visit personally to pick eyes for my compulsions, and then to revisit them to find out what they've seen. And highly unpleasant I find it."

They had both worked magic on themselves to halt aging, but even in Norsunder, time did move at incremental speed, and there was a cost when they stepped into the real world. When she emphasized what they both knew, it was always because she wanted something.

She went on. "This is your game. Not mine. But I forced myself on your behalf to visit the outerworld, specifically an old palace servant I'd put a compulsion on before the war, so she was easy enough to add another to. I went to Sartor just now, and the tracer revealed him crossing her sight."

"Into the city? When?"

"I don't know. Could be an hour, or a year. No, not that long; the same season."

He grunted. "Same season? Then the trail is still warm. I'll assume he raided the mages' HQ. Good enough. Who's your eyes? I don't want anyone else finding out what she saw." And when she'd told him—the old wreck was next to useless anyway—he said, "Good job. Once I get the Arrow, I'll let you have Siamis first."

Yeres simpered sweetly. Siamis had been so easy to torment as a little boy, but gradually it had become more difficult, which was a different sort of fun. "He's an idiot, but a pretty one."

"Leave him pretty for me," Efael said, but absently. "Sartor. Is it possible the Arrow is in the *south*? How could we not know that?"

"Have you considered that they might have lost it?" she asked, knowing that whatever could be taken into what the Sartorans so pompously termed the Tower of Knowledge (which ought to be the Tower of Old Lumber) could have been taken out again at some point over the stream of years. Magical the stones of the tower might be, but it was still a construct, and did not possess infinite space inside. And those Sartorans were pack rats.

Efael had a better sense of the slow tide of world politics than Yeres. Her interests lay in the magical realm, except when she entertained herself with sporadic exertions on behalf of one of her pets.

"Impossible," he said. "I can name half a dozen Sartoran kings who would have used it in power plays by now. I think the mages hid it."

"If the Arrow has ever been in their possession," she said confidently, "they'll have records. They keep track of every book and ring and button, if it has enough magic on it, or if a Landis ever touched it. The Arrow would qualify."

Efael grinned. "I'll prise it out of them."

"No, you won't," she retorted. "Remember they wear those death rings—"

But he was already gone. Of course he'd do what he wanted to do.

So she'd return to laying the magical groundwork for the eventual transfer of armies to holding stations on Five, a task of surpassing tedium and exactitude, especially as she was determined to accomplish most of it without having the cross the boundary into that arid, dust-choked, dead world. Though it might be slightly less tedious now that she was aware of maneuvering behind Detlev's back while cooperating with him face to face on the war preparations.

Ah. She performed a tracer, and found her current pet, Henerek, drilling at Norsunder Base. It was time for him to make his move, and take the place before either Siamis or Detlev returned.

She contemplated transferring to Norsunder Base, to dismiss the idea when a message would be as good, and less costly in the physical realm.

Snap!

Henerek felt the strike of magic, and hastily disengaged from what he was doing. Whatever Yeres sent would be waiting in his own chamber. He made haste to get there, read it, and laughed aloud.

Norsunder Base? He considered, wavering. Yeres had sent the note rather than coming, which meant she was staying safely in Norsunder-Beyond. That gave him time: he knew that preparing Five was supposed to require a couple of years' work at least.

Meanwhile, he could stay here maneuvering against Bostian and Dejain while his pair of suborned mages worked on his plans . . .

Yes. It was time to act. He'd brooded for several years, waiting to get recompense for Siamis's betrayal. He summoned Benin and Vasz, and said, "Now is the time to start bringing the soul-bound to the Dars site."

"We got orders?" asked Vasz, the younger, impatient mage. Benin, the grizzled one, looked askance.

"Yes," Henerek said. "*My* orders. Right now. Are you going to argue?"

"No, no," Vasz said with oily obsequiousness.

Benin raised a hand. "We agreed to work with you. But Dars is Detlev's supply cache for the war. It's taken decades to prepare those Destinations and the caches."

"Yes, and? He should have released them to me years ago, and I would have taken that entire area. Instead, he flounced off to Geth-deles to get their rift magic. And failed. Well, Siamis is apparently renegade, and Detlev is dancing to Yeres's tune over at Five. So we're going to pick up right where we left off.

Soul-bound, to Dars."

The mages exchanged a glance, then Benin said, "The Destinations are not stable without rift magic, and anyone who tried to make rift magic burns to ash."

"Which is why you send soul-bound by regular transfer, one or two at a time, until they burn up. Then we'll know not to use that particular Destination. We can afford to lose a few, eh? You'll be making more!"

Benin's expression closed. He did not like mentions of his secret blood-magic experiments. You never knew who might be listening. "But . . .then those Destinations will be utterly unusable," he cautioned. "It could be years — even centuries."

"That," Henerek said, "will be Detlev's problem."

"It'll still take time. Maybe even months, as *we* have to move safely between the Destinations."

"Use what time you need. I want an army ready to move once the ice melts up there next spring. When I retake Everon, I'll be in a position to come back here for more. And if you're with me, instead of wasting time arguing, you'll be able to do what you like to Dejain and the rest of them."

Benin licked his lips. He'd get back at Dejain for not sharing that news about the blood-mage texts, and then losing them.

Vasz smirked. She'd caught him spying on her work, and the result had been extremely painful. He owed her for that.

They left, talking in urgent undertones.

Henerek laughed. No one in Norsunder Base was going to find out until it was too late. Except, of course, for his prisoner.

Oh, yes. This was going to be fun.

Twenty-five

AS SIAMIS WALKED THE gently curving brick sidewalks along-side the canals in Alsais, Colend's capital, he reflected on how a royal palace was the perfect place to hide something like the Arrow. Centuries after anyone (except Detlev) would recognize it, it was safest in plain sight.

Had anyone other than a monarch tried to keep it, the secret was far more likely to come out, unless buried and forgotten. But kings tended to have caches of jewels, which went in and out of fashion.

Alsais had changed slowly over the centuries, but there were certain constants: curves, glass, mosaic patterns, gardens matured over the centuries. Bay and oriel windows in pleasing proliferation, garden framed, as were the many arched bridges over the curving canals.

It was one of the few cities in the world in which everyone who visited wanted to live, so growth was controlled by royal decree—which was firmly supported by the guilds. Though Colend regarded itself as the embodiment of melende—of civilization, honor, and the life of art—in Alsais, the competition was far too fierce for slackers in any service to last long.

That included its court, though in recent years, who was invited to return and who was politely but firmly pressured to grace their estates, was controlled by a regency council.

On his hard ride north, Siamis had thought about the best way to enter the city without gaining notice. He could break his no-magic imperative only so far as making illusion, the lighter the better. Illusory magic, which rendered no change, was the most tenuous of all, and the city was full of it, mostly enhancing light sources, which made the place stunning at night. He wove the most ephemeral of illusions around his gear, deflecting the eye from the hilt of his sword sticking out.

He needed to be overlooked, and no one was more unnoticeable than a servant. He dared not assumed the guise of a scribe, as they all knew each other and thought nothing of stopping to chat to a newcomer.

The days were long-gone when Colend's fashions had so stratified life that people were constrained to eat behind screens. Nowadays Colendi ate together as was done anywhere else, and restaurants flourished. Even more important, vendors selling food provided dainty containers for those taken by the whim to eat out in the pleasant air, and runners carried tastefully covered baskets to the canal boats and back.

While changing horses at the border, Siamis obtained the loose clothing and over-robe currently worn in Colend. Outside the city he stopped at one of the bakeries competing to gain enough renown for a move inside Alsais, and bought a variety of spiced cakes and tarts, chosen because they had just come hot and aromatic from the oven.

He entered the city on foot, and strolled along with a basket of savory-smelling baked goods on his arm, his gear over his other shoulder, blurred by the illusion. No one paid heed to a messenger with a fragrant basket.

When he neared the palace, he chose a cluster of teenager canal boat tenders, handed the basket to the eldest of them, and said, "A surprise sent by a secret admirer."

The group turned to the blushing girl, and everyone started guessing who that might be. Siamis withdrew without any notice and slipped around a corner and into a pocket garden, careful not to disturb so much as a blossom.

The low wall beyond the little garden bordered on the east wall of the royal palace, beyond the stable complex, which meant it was secluded from the main buildings. Siamis carried no magical objects that would trip a ward. He slipped in, making certain no one saw him.

He knew that the patrol routine left no unwatched halls around the king and prince. But now—between the hours of Lily and Harp, as the sun set—was the busiest time as courtiers began summoning servants to ready them for evening entertainment, and the entertainers themselves arrived at the palace. Everywhere kitchen staff readied sumptuous refreshments and servants walked everywhere in lines bearing covered silver trays.

Siamis ghosted through them all, in patience-testing increments. It was full dark when he reached the secluded garden outside the royal suite. He left his gear under a flowering shrub and climbed a trellis of starliss. A leap to the middle branch of pleached golden aspen, another leap to the window sill, and he was in.

The king sat alone in a room filled with lilies and citrus blossoms. Carlael liked fresh air: all his windows stood wide open to the fragrances of the royal garden.

He could have been a marble carving, so still he was, candle light glowing softly along the age-blurred line of his cheeks and jaw, and striking golden highlights in his thinning, silver-touched auburn hair, which had been neatly combed and lay loose on his shoulders. Carlael was nearly fifty, but in this forgiving light looked closer to twenty, which had been the age he'd reached when Detlev laid the enchantment over him that confirmed the whispers of madness. The only other sign of age was his thinness, shrouded beneath the perfectly tailored midnight blue velvet clothing he favored.

The whispers about Prince Carlael's madness had begun before Detlev's spell. As Siamis crossed the silent room and paused, sensing protective wards and spells, he remembered a brief glimpse of the youthful Carlael as he struggled with mental awarenesses not demonstrated by anyone else. Detlev had not permitted Siamis to interact at all with Carlael, or even to stay past the sweetly ringing carillons marking the hour, as he meticulously laid the enchantment that the world reviled as so cruel.

Not cruel enough for Norsunder, or more correctly, a stupid blunder, condemning the king to a madness that no one could effectively use. Carlael was regarded by Norsunder as one of Detlev's relatively few failed experiments.

Siamis sat cross-legged before the king's carved chair, propping his head on his hands, and reaching mentally past the miasmic barrier of the magic to the dreaming mind below.

He dared not risk physical encounter with the oblivious king, for a tangle of wards lay over him. A single touch and a horde of heralds and mages would come on the run. But as music drifted through the open window, and soft laughter rose from the night-shrouded garden, Siamis found Carlael in the dreamscape he'd created over the years of enchantment, a mirror to the world Carlael knew.

Dream-Carlael had been dancing in a long line of youths, a dance the Colendi had taken from an Ancient Sartoran sword warm-up and reinvented to emphasize muscle control and grace. Music played, plangent melodies in strings and wood.

Dream-Carlael turned at dream-Siamis's approach. Dreams have their own logic; Carlael regarded him with interest, but no surprise.

"The gem worn by Lasva Sky Child," dream-Siamis said to dream-Carlael, gesturing with his hand—and the carved marble screens vanished, replaced by the famous magical capture of the living woman, and the glittering gem at her throat.

"Ah, my favorite. The Lirendi Diamond." Dream-Carlael sighed—no surprise at his immediate recognition.

Siamis suppressed an inward laugh at the predictability of humans and their gemstone cathexis.

"I want it," dream-Siamis said.

And waited while Carlael struggled against the enchantment by concentrating on the mental image of his Diamond. The magic thinned and receded like fog, leaving Carlael blinking in his chair. The dreams vanished.

Siamis rose to his feet. "I want that gem," he said again.

"Why?" Carlael, the owner of so much treasure he did not know the half of it, gazed back as if he were about to be robbed of it all.

Siamis had considered what to say if he got this far. The inevitable hunt would not be far behind; there was no reason not to speak the truth. "Long before it came to you, magic was bound onto it. Release of those spells will free the Venn mages."

"The Venn," Carlael said with a faint lifting of his brows. "But the Venn were bound long after Martande Lirendi, my ancestor, came here with that diamond and crowned himself king."

"Yes."

Carlael's hauteur altered to a head-tilt of deliberation, then he crossed the room to a cabinet, and returned with the gem lying on his palm. The candlelight glittered and refracted over its surface, responding to an inner light so intense a cobalt blue that it was almost, but not quite, painful; the structure of the gem was far more compelling than ordinary diamonds, enchanting the eye in a way that had nothing to do with spells.

These stones that were not stones reflected light from a source impossible to perceive, and mages had known for millennia that they were alive in a way difficult to define: the closest analogy was the difference between how an ancient redwood and a human were alive. But even that was too limited to be useful.

The one thing known for certain was that any violence — such as prising the stones out of the walls of the caves — extinguished that light, and the magic that resonated through them. Even violent intent had been known to snuff the living gems into lifeless stone.

"Did you know," Carlael said, looking down at it, "that the last person to wear it before I rediscovered it, was the Lasva who married and went to the other side of the continent? She wore it on her wedding day, then left it behind. It's said that my ancestors who came after could not wear it well. It was set aside as vulgar and gaudy, until I rediscovered it in the vault."

The gem rolled on Carlael's thin palm, causing the light to glimmer over and in it, seductive as a lover. Siamis reflected briefly on the long-dead, revered Venn king holding it in his hands. How much it must have hurt the Venn to surrender it — one of their curious notions of honor.

"This kind of gem," Carlael's soft voice drifted dispassionately, "widens awareness of the world. Did you know that? If one contemplates its depths long enough, one sees the turning of the sun, and can almost hear a sound, very like music . . ."

Cold shock ran through Siamis. The gems did not in fact confer that ability: Carlael had been born with that skill. That, Siamis had not known about.

Now he knew why Detlev had never told him, and why.

". . .where no human living goes, "the king whispered. "Where there are no palaces or crowns. Or shadows." Carlael looked up at Siamis. "It is this that enables me to fight that fog and rejoin the world."

To the physical eye, there was no fog in the clean, beauty-fully apportioned chamber, though the sensitive might feel a chill in spite of the balmy air of spring ripening toward summer. But in the mental realm, the fog of enchantment encircled them both, clammy tendrils wavering toward Carlael with each breath.

"I know," Siamis said.

Carlael's eyes narrowed. "I have met you before, have I not?"

"It was when Norsunder attacked, a few years back. I bound you and the rest of the kingdom under another enchantment, and the warriors withdrew."

Carlael said softly, "That is a war we cannot win."

"Perhaps not, though the question rightly belongs to the future. As regards this gem, it is not the physical stone that enables you to break free of the enchantment for a time, not any more. You know it so well in memory and dream that you can grasp it there and still break free."

Carlael's breath stilled. "As I just did."

"Yes, and as you instinctively did when your kingdom was threatened. And at other important times." Siamis locked his hands behind him, to still the impulse to snatch at the thing. If he did, he knew he would then see gem's integrity wink out — taking the complication of spells with it.

So close, so very close.

Siamis cleared his throat. "The truth is, I am probably the first of those soon to be coming for it."

"You mean Norsunder," Carlael said.

"That," Siamis said, "is a given. Go ahead. You can feel the enchantment closing around you, can you not? Set the gem down, and reach for it in mind, as you've done by instinct until now. I'll wait."

Carlael regarded him impassively as his breath rose and fell, the candlelight shimmering over his midnight blue velvet. Then he laid the stone on top of the carved jewelry case, sat down — and stilled.

Siamis watched the remorseless enchantment grip Carlael. He turned his gaze to the cobalt fulgence of the gem, fighting the nearly overwhelming instinct to run.

"You spoke truth." Carlael's voice, hoarse with the effort of fighting the enchantment back a second time, startled Siamis. "Take it. Take this magical battle that has nothing to do with us, and carry it elsewhere."

He rose, wincing, picked up the stone from atop the casket, and laid it in Siamis's hand. Siamis's fingers closed convulsively over the gem, which sparkled between his fingers. "I hope I'm in time."

Carlael acknowledged the danger with a slight nod. Courage he had always had, as well as grace. "Even relative freedom is . . ." He turned his hand in a fluid circle. "I wish I'd known. My son would not be so much a stranger."

"A piece of advice," Siamis said. "The longer you can hide your sanity, the longer you'll be able to stay free of a tighter layer of new spells."

"Why?" Carlael asked, voice strained with desperation. "Why me?"

But that, Siamis could not possibly answer. In three steps he was at the window, then dropped directly into the garden. In spite of the way he had left the king, there was no angry face at the window, and no voices disturbed the quiet night: Carlael had to be considering what he'd said, before the inexorable fog of enchantment bound him once again into the relative safety of the dream world.

Siamis retrieved his gear, then stood in the garden considering what to do next. He hadn't permitted himself to think much past this moment, though he should have: retrieving the Arrow was not a success, but a decision point.

Until now, there had always been a chance of going back.

No, there wasn't, really.

He ghosted through the garden toward the river. Now to do his best to lead the trail away from Carlael, in hopes of saving his life.

He slipped through the fence, and away.

Twenty-six

Western Wnelder Vee

"I LIKE IT HERE," David said, relaxing back in a hammock Laban had scouted from somewhere.

Adam shook his head as he leaned over the new fire, expertly toasting bread on a stick. "You've got to go back to Everon and start over."

MV, newly arrived for the same purpose as David, couldn't resist a jibe: "There's Adam again, the king's conscience."

"Queen," said Adam. "You do remember that the Queen of Everon is very much alive."

"You know you're completely mad, don't you?" MV asked, snatching the toast from Adam and crunching into it.

Adam smiled as he reached for more stale bread. "Everyone is mad. The only difference between them and me is that I know it."

"Speak for yourself, shitbird," Laban said, making a swipe at Adam, which the latter easily evaded.

David lifted his hands. "We're out of supplies anyway, and the wards are finished. I'll ride in the morning."

MV jabbed the bread in his direction. "And I'll be there to see that you do." He glared at Adam. "As for you?"

Adam twirled a newly loaded stick above the fire. "I'm

staying here. For now. I don't think my blunder with Karhin Keperi can be undone except by time."

"While we've still got it," David said, eyes nearly shut, ruddy pinpoints flames reflecting in his pupils.

The bonfire crackled and spat in the silence, then Adam reached into a pocket and pulled out a coin, which he flipped to David, who caught it mid-air. "That's my last transfer token," Adam said. "I'm not going back to Wilderfeld in Colend anytime soon, so you may as well keep it for whoever goes to visit the Keperis."

"I'll pass it to Curtas," David said. "They like him. Trust him."

"Enough yap." MV whacked Adam's back, and lifted a foot to kick David's hammock. "What do you say to a night run?"

Instead of answering, David flipped onto his feet and took off, the others bolting in his wake.

MV and David reached Everon's capital in the wake of an early summer thunderstorm. They went straight to the room at the back of the stable that Silvanas shared with Noser. As soon as they showed up, Noser ran to summon the others, and by the time the two had changed into dry clothes, Leef, and Rolfin arrived at the run, Noser trailing behind, his constant grin smug as he vaulted from the top bunk to the bare support beam under the slanted roof.

David looked around at them, then said, "Where's Curtas?"

"Goes b-b-back. And forth. W-w-wilderfeld. C-c-capital. Skya L-l-lake," Erol said.

Rolfin looked up, and because he spoke so rarely, everyone turned his way. His black eyes reflected the light as he said, "Karhin's been relaying letters about how Terry thinks Glenn destroyed the alliance."

"He did," David said. "Isn't that why we're here?"

"Yeah. But now rumors are flying about how we might have something to do with it."

"That stinks," David said. "Especially since Glenn's managed that all on his own. But it makes things tougher for us, especially after Adam's blunder. I'd hoped they'd all forgotten by now."

"Adam's an idiot," Noser squeaked.

They ignored him out of long habit, as Erol said, "Wh-what.

Happened?"

"Latest letters, Karhin might be onto us. *All* of us. Including Roy. Adam as coms. Senrid backing her up. You know he was there watching Adam."

Erol whistled. "Adam *is* c-c-c-coms."

"I've got Adam's last transfer token to the Keperis." David flicked the side pocket of his gear bag. "For Curtas, whenever he turns up. He can fix the damage." Then he sighed. "Anyway, we've now got our own rat-hole, there in Wnelder Vee, if we're forced to fall back. It'll keep out anyone older than we are, dark magic or light."

This complicated and difficult enchantment was not new to any of them. There was a small city populated by children and teens who had yet to reach puberty on Geth-deles. Adults could not enter. To set that kind of enchantment properly meant casting the spells step by step around a perimeter. It had taken an entire season for three of them to get it done to David's satisfaction.

"But we shouldn't need a rat-hole," David said. "We've got a new start on this world, and we've got orders. We need to get it right."

"*You* need to get it right," Noser shrilled from his perch on the beam. "*We're* in good here. He jabbed his thumb into his skinny chest. "That Karhin blabs too much."

"So Curtas will deal," David said equably.

Handling Noser was practice for fitting in among difficult personalities. And yet it obviously hadn't been practice enough. On his previous visit to Everon David had let Glenn irritate him into running the winners during that stupid war game, and even worse, he'd let the prince see him doing it.

Now it was time to undo the damage. *Deal.*

When the watch change bells rang, Noser yelled, "Chow time!" flipped backward over the beam, and somersaulted before landing barefooted in the midst of their circle.

They left as a group.

Silvanas explained as they walked that Glenn had asked questions about David, to which they'd answered that they didn't know him — thought he was inexperienced — and Noser proclaimed in his piping squeak, "Van slathered on the butter."

"We've been filling his ears with how much we want to be here," Silvanas said.

"Learning," Erol put in. "From him."

"And letting him win," Silvanas said, grinning. "But not *too* easy. The rest of the boys have been doing the same. Everybody sees how much his mood improves when he trashes someone."

"And we know *nothing* about *that*," Noser drawled nastily.

A few glances flicked David's way, but he shrugged. "Gone is gone. And we're better off. Back to Glenn. If it's flattery he wants, that's what I'll give him. Rest of you —" David jerked his thumb outward. "MV and I will say we met on the road, and he talked me into coming back. Remember, you don't know me."

They ran off, separating.

None of them understood the depths of Glenn's single-mindedness — or the turmoil driving it — that Glenn had been hiding behind a determined mind-shield ever since he'd been taught how to keep one, so horrified he had been to discover there were people who could hear thoughts.

Much as he respected Sartora, the Girl Who Saved the World, he didn't want her *ever* hearing his self-doubts. So his mind-shield was the first thing he thought of on waking each morning, and the last thing before he turned in for the night.

When Glenn saw the newcomer walk in with MV, the boy he admired the most, but had come to trust the least, it was all he could do to hide his fury.

He struggled against regret and resentment and anger driven by shame whenever he thought of those inward visions of the best fighters dressed in his own personal livery. How close he had come to wheedling them with the privileges they would have — far more even than the Knights.

But Uncle Roderic had said recently, "One thing Grandpa Saddlesore was famous for saying was that loyalty had to be given, not bought. They earn their privilege by pleasing you. If you have to bribe them with privilege, then your loyalty is going to them. And someone always offers a higher price."

Glenn had heard about Grandpa Saddlesore — Leskandar Dei — since his earliest years, one of the most famous of the famous Deis: handsome, clever, and a natural leader.

Unlike me, Glenn was thinking as the ready anger ignited. Unlike me.

He watched suspiciously as MV and David approached, and to his surprise, they bowed like the Everoneth boys. "I've come back to join your beginners, like you suggested," David said, hands out.

"Met him on the road," MV put in. "Talked him into it."

"I'm really impressed with what you've done here," David said. Then hastily added, "Your highness."

David was tired after the long trip, and because he despised Glenn, he dared not look directly at the prince lest Glenn intuit his true emotions. So he didn't see how closely, how desperately, Glenn watched for the subtle signs that he most dreaded seeing.

"MV's back!" someone yelled from inside.

Another voice joined. "Now we'll have some fun."

Glenn forced a smile, and an even tone. "We'll see what you've got, come morning drill, shall we?"

"Where shall I stay, your highness?" David asked, his sleepy brown eyes earnest.

"Wherever you like. We've plenty of room. I thought MV would have set you up," he added, and couldn't help his sharp tone, "since you met on the road."

He turned away, knowing he was losing his grip on his temper, leaving behind an exchange of looks: this was going to take some work.

At the end of the meal, Glenn stood, and the entire mess hall promptly fell silent. This obedience pleased Glenn enough to spark a genuine smile. "Morning drill, real swords. We'll go back to practice wood for skirmishing."

He walked to the palace wing to sit with Tahra, because that was duty, though he much preferred eating with his men (he loved thinking of them that way, though he hadn't quite aired the words yet), especially as they showed the emerging bones and muscles of the men to be. Soon — *finally* — there would be no more boys.

Tahra's dislike of physical proximity had turned into a disgust whenever she went anywhere near the garrison area. It was pretty clear that she would only like girls, if she ever got close enough to one. She found boys repellent.

Glenn knew it, so he always stepped through a cleaning frame before he crossed to the still-ruined residence. Weird, how what disgusted his sister exhilarated him. Sex was a new feeling, unexplored so far because he didn't feel it for any person so much as situations. Like watching MV win fights — the snap of his clothes, the powerful precision of his moves. MV was never going to look like Rel, Uncle Roderic had said, when he got his full height. He'd always be lean. But Glenn was willing to wager any amount of money that MV was as strong as Rel.

Glenn had no desire to see MV naked, and the thought of kissing him was horrifying. The lure was in his strength and skill. Nor did he feel attraction for the best of the girls, Carinna Dei, whose long horse face looked so much like Tahra's they could be sisters instead of distant cousins. But when she was riding and shooting, she was as good as Rolfin, and both stirred him the same way MV did. He also got it from the clash and clang and sparks of sword play, especially when they managed drill in perfect unison. And he got it when he raised his fist to see every man in sight obedient to his order.

He wished he could have sex with that feeling of power.

The real thing could wait, he decided as he joined Tahra, who immediately began droning on about money matters in that accusatory tone she was beginning to use all the time. He listened long enough to determine that she had nothing new to say, and fell into reverie. Yes, sword drill on the morrow. That meant David would have to ask for a weapon, and Glenn could be magnanimous. If David really wanted to start with the beginners, to be obedient, loyal, then everything would proceed in the proper order.

As soon as he could, Glenn left Tahra — most of what she'd said unheard — and went off to his suite, where he did a hundred sword lifts, each arm, and lunged at his own shadow until he was tired enough to sleep.

He woke to sticky heat. Summer was here with a vengeance. The boys would be complaining about the heat. As he dressed, he considered how to ask Tahra to find money to hire mages to bring cold air down out of the sky for the practice salle.

He hurried through breakfast, avoiding Tahra for now. Once a day was enough of a duty visit. He ran out to the salle to be there when David showed up without a weapon.

He stopped short when he spotted David, who wore his usual old shirt, riding trousers, and forest mocs. But in his right hand, a sword. That wasn't any Everoneth saber, Glenn could see at a glance. The guard was old-fashioned, like in very old paintings, with no decoration, and the blade black. With rust?

He walked over. "Come inside. I can give you a better blade than that."

David looked down at the sword in his hand as if discovering it for the first time. He lifted it, and said, "You needn't, your highness. It'll do. I'm used to it."

When the blade caught the light, Glenn saw that what he'd taken as rust was the ripples of many, many foldings and reforgings. Ugly—common, really—but a very good blade despite the dark color. Glenn glanced from that to David, distracted by the damp curls on his brow, and the clammy look to that old tunic shirt. Glenn turned to MV, to notice a sheen of sweat high on his temples. Already overheated? No.

They'd already been drilling. The thought unsettled him, as if they'd been somehow caught cheating, but it wasn't that. It was that sense of conspiracy again. How many of the others? No. He knew how many of them overslept, dragging themselves to breakfast, or even showing up sticky-eyed and frowsy to the salle, skipping breakfast altogether.

Glenn turned his head. He couldn't tell if Rolfin had also been drilling, as he wore his black hair slicked back from his brow, but Silvanus 's curly hair hung in damp rings. Even that irritating urchin they called Noser was crimson in the face.

"Who *are* you people?" The words just came out.

"We're here to learn." The moment the word *we* passed David's lips, he knew it was the wrong one. If he could have reached to snatch it back, he would have.

Glenn's eyes narrowed. Color flooded his face. "So there is a conspiracy."

MV's eyes widened. "Conspiracy?" he repeated in a tone of surprise, and looked around as if masked conspirators lurked behind every corner.

Defensive and resenting it, Glenn went on the attack. "You people obviously have your own private drill that you haven't bothered to teach *us*," he shot at MV. "Why is that?"

"Because you run 'em," MV said, trying to sound reasonable. To *be* reasonable, a tough thing when you despise someone. "You asked me to teach fighting on horseback. And some grappling, until that one baron's boy dislocated his shoulder. After that, just to captain some of your war games while you sit and watch."

Glenn knew that was true, but that only made him angrier. It was so unjust. *Everything* was unjust. He worked so hard, but MV and Erol and Rolfin were so much better than he was. Even that lazy Silvanas. Even the brat!

He glared at David, standing there with that old sword. Shorter than Glenn, slighter. Younger.

All Glenn's work had finally paid off. He was bigger than they were, therefore he was stronger, and all those silent hours sweating in his room meant that it was time for a thrashing. It was time to *take* command.

He pulled free the sword his father had died with, with its beautiful swept guard and jeweled cap to the grip, and slashed down at David.

Who met the stroke with an expert deflection. "Hey!" David protested, stepping back. "Shouldn't we be inside?" He jerked his thumb over his shoulder.

"First, you need to learn." *Clang!* "To follow orders." *Crash!* "Not give them." Glenn was the prince. He had the right, the honor, and the duty, and order arose out of due deference. *No one* worked harder at being a future king than Glenn.

He struck again, and David jumped back after another block. "Be reasonable," David pleaded, his point out wide. "Cool down, Glenn. Your highness."

"You don't give *me* orders," Glenn whispered, and swung again, harder. "This is my army. My alliance. My vision."

"Talk to me," David said, backing once more, until his shoulders hit the wall. "Teach me. What's your vision here?"

Glenn hesitated, and David said in a coaxing voice, "I know you've been reading up. You know that successful wars have specific goals. What's your military goal here?"

Glenn checked, breathing hard. The urge to speak of his grand plan edged aside the urge to beat David to his knees. "The utter defeat — the eradication — of Norsunder."

David's brows shot up as he stood there, back to the wall. "Does that mean you're going to march your army across two continents to attack the Norsunder Base? But what about Norsunder-Beyond?"

Glenn's eyes shifted to gauge the others' reactions. They stood apart, not in a group, but there was that shared sweaty state. "*Clearly* my purpose is defense, the next time they cross our border."

"But that could be in another fifty years." MV shrugged.

"You don't know that," Glenn retorted, and David shot MV a look, at which the latter backed up, palms briefly out in a deference that Glenn had never seen, ever, from MV. David really did command them!

Fury boiled up again as David said in that coaxing voice, as if Glenn were five years old," You know people who've studied magic. Until Norsunder regains the rift transfers in order to bring armies out of Norsunder-Beyond, Everon would not be first, or even third, target."

Glenn's voice rose. He couldn't stop it. "We were first when my father was killed."

"True," David said, still in that coaxing tone. A coddling tone. "But that was personal, that idiot Henerek acting on his own." Before Glenn could demand what David knew of Henerek, David lowered his voice even more, as if gentling a skittish horse. "Listen, here's the real question you can answer. I'm ignorant here. How can Everon support this army you're building? Don't you need a population three or four times as big as Everon's is now to supply a standing army of a size to take on Norsunder Base?"

"That's why we need an alliances of princes," Glenn said, hotly resenting David's presumption in questioning him, and yet it felt good to have the right answer.

Then short, snub-nosed Noser gazed truculently up through his messy hair and said snidely, "You mean you're gonna be a emperor?"

MV's mouth flattened, as if suppressing a grin, and from that stuttering twit Erol came a cough that didn't hide a laugh.

David silenced them all with a look.

And Glenn lost his temper at last.

Their instant obedience, which Glenn had never won from them, despite all his hard work and his hopes, flared blood-hot, jealousy boiling into rage. He went for David, his one thought to challenge the leader who dared to interfere in his domain: defeat the leader, and they *must be his.*

Three strikes, fast and hard. David deflected them with a cool expertise that pounded white fury in Glenn's ears. He had the younger boy against a wall—he had to win if he had to *kill* him.

David fought for his life, his mind spinning back a year to when he fought for his life against a young man determined to silence him, to silence the truth that David had figured out, beneath all the rhetoric about freedom and justice for the under-aged. Proof that the lighters who supposedly honored truth only revered it when it served their own purposes . . . Emotions he'd thought conquered opened like an old wound, throwing his mind into freefall as trained muscles reacted fast as fire.

Glenn was fast but David was so much faster.

Both Glenn and David stared in utter disbelief as the sword slid between Glenn's ribs. David yanked his blade free but it was too late. The pain hit and Glenn coughed but could not breathe past the blood filling his lungs. His last sight was of David's wide, shocked gaze that reminded him curiously of. . . of. . .

And his consciousness, cut free, fled.

David stared as Glenn's murderous intent widened into surprise, then contorted into pain, then slackened into puzzle-ment, and then he fell forward on top of his own sword — as chance would have it, not a hundred feet from where his father had fallen.

"You." The hoarse, high voice snapped them all around. "What . . ."

"Shit," MV muttered as they perceived a knot of young Knight trainees standing in a shocked row, led by earnest, loyal Carnold.

David blinked, aware of Glenn's blood splashed down his front, but before he could speak, Canold charged, fury driving his sword arm.

With brisk efficiency, MV stepped in, deflected the blow, kicked Canold's knee out, and when the Knight trainee slammed to the ground, MV tapped him behind the ear with the hilt of his boot knife.

David's boys took on the rest of the Knight trainees, leaving them unconscious on the ground. Then David looked from Glenn's lifeless body to his would-be defenders, enough wits returning to recognize a situation impossible to finesse.

"We're done here," David said. "Run."

They ghosted around the other side of the building, avoiding the windows, and separated back to their various rooms. When David reached his pack, he paused long enough to look at the congealing blood on his sword, and dunked it over and over into the cleaning barrel at the end of the barracks.

The others showed up . . .one, two three . . ."Silvanas, where's Noser?"

Vana's gaze jerked up. "I thought he was with you."

They all scanned. Nothing. David plunged his hand into his pack for that transfer token, though he couldn't have said what prompted that search. When the pocket turned up empty, he said, "He could have gone anywhere."

MV sighed. "We're for it now."

At the Same Moment
Wilderfeld, Colend

Noser paused in the doorway, having at last located the tall red-haired girl who had to be Karhin.

Girl? She was next thing to grown, sitting so silent on her cushion.

Karhin had been getting through her morning's work while trying to figure out what to say to Terry of Erdrael Danara, who wanted to visit again. She liked Terry very much as a correspondent—he was one of her three favorites—but as a correspondent. How do you avoid someone you can't look at without that hitch of breath? It would be hurtful and rude to look at his hand, but his face—which would never have been handsome—was dominated by that purple-red scar, then that lurching walk . . .

Her head panged, and she hated herself for such thoughts. Did people avoid staring at Bee's blank gaze? But it wasn't the same. For one thing, Bee couldn't see rude stares. That was it, she was afraid to be caught, that Terry might see the aversion she could not avoid, especially when he seemed to like sitting next to her.

That pang hit her again, a feeling of wrongness, almost like an incipient headache. Of course it was her lack of melende, and yes, she would invite Terry to visit. But she'd invite others, too, so the eye had somewhere to go—

She was utterly unaware of the boy lurking at the side of her doorway, glaring in under messy blond hair.

She was the reason they'd been outed. *She* spread the rumors. David said they had to deal. David did deal, and Glenn lay in his blood to prove it.

But now that Noser had found her, he scowled. He wouldn't be dealing if there wasn't even a fight. She wouldn't give him any fight. Look at her. Cosseted and rich, soft as those fancy silk cushions, the wall hangings with birds and things, her robe with all that embroidery. He found the anger he needed in resenting her wealth and life of ease, which made her an easy target because people like her never had to defend themselves, they had it so easy, they never got punched and hit and kicked before they even knew how to walk and talk, never got locked in a box if they dared cry, never got burned inside and out . . .

Rage propelled him into the room. She heard his step and turned, looking up in surprise. "You and your big mouth ruined everything," he yelled, because a hero always had a reason.

Karhin stared wit-flown at the boy's wild eyes. "Who *are* you? Ruined what?"

He struck. "That's what."

That much he'd planned, but the knife didn't go in cleanly. She gasped, twisting. Sucked in a breath to yell. This was supposed to be fast! Silent! He kicked her chin so hard her neck snapped and she fell back in a welter of pearlescent silk, her loose red hair like rivulets of blood, her eyes stark and lifeless, gazing beyond the ceiling, beyond the sky.

To be sure, he stabbed her twice more. The third time he was certain got to her heart.

He pulled out his knife, his entire body shaking the way it always had after a violation in the days before light, and food, and safety, when he became Little Brother. His head even swam as it had then, and still did in his dreams, as he fumbled for the transfer coin . . .and it didn't work to take him back.

Like the nightmares.

He tried the spell three times, choking on the words. But there was no magic on it. Of course there wasn't. One way. Because Adam always traveled out with one of the targets . . .

Noser wiped his knife on her clothes and backed to the door, then he got out, and pulled the door shut, his mind running, running, he'd done it for the group. He'd saved everything. He wouldn't just be Noser anymore, he'd be Knife, yeah, that sounded good, though MV might laugh, so he'd be Killer . . .

He saw the people only as shadows as he made his legs get him downstairs, and out, and away, away, away.

Once Tahra got over the shock of seeing her dead brother, something she had been dreading ever since he'd been talking up the army, she listened to Canold and the others.

David. Of course. She'd disliked him from the instant she'd seen him, though not as much as she loathed that smart-mouth Laban. While the Knight trainees set about picking up the dead prince, and arguing in fierce whispers about where to take him to be laid out properly, she bolted back inside and threw herself down at her desk.

She wrote to Karhin. Then waited. But for the first time in memory, Karhin did not write back.

She wrote next to Mearsieanne in Mearsies Heili, and then to Terry in Erdrael Danara, and finally to Arthur, in hopes he might send Sartora, who could surely do what she had done before, and save the world?

By then Commander Dei had arrived, and took charge of the angry, grieving trainees, who had almost talked themselves into forming a lynch mob to go searching for the assassin and his friends.

Meanwhile, the bad news spread through the almost moribund alliance, letter by letter.

Twenty-seven

Sartor

VELTOS JHAER, HEAD OF the Sartoran Mage Guild, paused on her way to the guild's principal building, her chin lifted as she listened to the rise and fall of young voices chanting a mnemonic for basic spell combinations. The melody was a very old weavers' song, adapted to aid first year mage students.

Her mind reached back to her own childhood, rather than paying attention to her surroundings in the city she'd dwelt in all her life, so she was taken by surprise when a strong hand closed around her wrist hard enough to grind skin and tendon against bone.

She looked up at a sharp-boned face dominated by unblinking eyes as affectless as that of a snake.

Shock, fear, anger—regret—churned in her as he said, "Where is it?"

"Where is what?" her voice husked as her body began to tremble.

Instead of answering, he began to muscle her toward the door. She struggled with all her strength. He twisted her arm up behind her until white pain half-blinded her, and she rose on her toes in an effort to ease that grip.

In the empty foyer, he snapped her around to face him.

"The Arrow," he said. "Where is it."

"The what?" she exclaimed.

His eyes widened at the genuine surprise in her face, but then she faltered as a memory flickered: hadn't she dreamed about something . . .

Whatever it was, she wouldn't talk about it with the likes of him. He saw the decision in her face, and shifted his grip as he pulled a long, thin-bladed knife.

She saw death in his cruel gaze, the parted lips that showed the tips of strong white teeth. "Talk now, or after I have some fun. Your choice."

The death ring was said to be painless. She hadn't believed it, of course. If anyone had come back to corroborate that, she would have seen the records.

But she'd made the vow, and took the means, just the same. It was another duty, like many, whose yoke she accepted as the price of the power she had learned over the years would never be enough to protect Sartor: when you reached a certain level of secrecy, you wore a death ring night and day, so that if some moment like this came, you would not have to endure being tortured to death for what you knew.

This vow was not unknown, certainly in Norsunder, and they all wore a gaudy ring with plenty of wards laid over it. The ring's wards were useful in day-to-day affairs, and its bright sapphire drew the eye.

She had a heartbeat or two to take in that merciless gaze, ludicrously framed by a fall of soft dark hair, before her heart thumped once then pattered frantically against her ribs. His black clothing, gleaming with a sinister oiliness, smelled of stale sweat as he sawed off the finger bearing the sapphire with three deliberate strokes.

Her heart lurched and then the first lance of pain wrung through her as he said, "Your protection is gone." He kicked the finger and ring spinning across the tiles, pausing to watch it smear faint arcs of red. "Where is the Arrow?"

Black spots blooming across her vision. The vice-like fingers forced her upright, but she ignored them, ignored everything except the thought that she would take away her death from him.

Yes, seen that way—I choose—it was a triumph in a life of failure after failure.

Cool conviction eddied in and out of the faintness. She

smiled up into the young man's face, not hearing a word he said as he glanced aside, and his mouth moved.

"No it's not." She exhaled the words with her last breath, flexed her toe with the magic-laden little ring, and the coolness seized her body, and freed her mind to lift and drift outward, as if she floated like dandelion on a current of air.

How odd, how very odd . . .

Tsauderei sat in his old friend Evend's chamber as snow beat against the mullioned windows, obscuring the barren birch trunks not twenty paces away. While waiting for the arrival of the Venn mages, after weeks of delicate back-and-forth, he'd taken on the task of sorting Evend's personal papers, as it was clear that Arthur had not been able to bear entering this chamber even after all this time.

How his old friend's handwriting brought back their young days! All those crises and celebrations, each so immediate, so world-shaking, all folded into the past now . . .

The inward ping of his notecase made him sigh. He read the last few lines of a personal letter from an lover long dead, and laid it on the fire before reaching into his pocket.

The note said: *Scry now. Mondros.*

Tsauderei groaned. He had not brought his scry stone. But he could use Evend's, as they had practiced on it together seventy-five years ago.

He grunted to his feet to retrieve it, sat back down and squared himself in the chair, then touched the stone and muttered the spell.

Mondros's bearded face appeared. "Tsauderei, they just found Veltos Jhaer's body."

"What?"

"Murial contacted me, and Erai-Yanya. They need you."

Tsauderei lifted his hand, forcing his mind to focus — to shut out the chatter of questions he couldn't answer. Diplomacy required him to transfer to the Destination in Sartor's royal palace, but then he'd have to haul his decrepit carcass somewhere else.

Or. He could damn the diplomacy and go straight to the queen, as one who had been given the right. The Sartoran first circle and head mages had agreed on little, but in hating him they had united.

It had been Veltos who distrusted him most.

With a wince of regret, he used Atan as a Destination. She had never warded him, and so he found himself snorting for breath and clutching at a wall in a place he had never been permitted: the foyer of the guild's building.

A semi-circle of faces turned his way as he fought the twinkling lights and clouds at the edge of his vision.

Atan looked distraught, her large, protuberant eyes wide as they had been when she was a curious child, her mouth pressed in a line of pain and anger. "Oh, you're here," she breathed, the violet mois-stones woven into her coronet of braids glinting with her rapid heartbeat. "I was just about to . . ." She waved a hand toward him.

"Send for me," he finished for her, comprehending that she had as many emotional reactions as she had demands for her instant attention. "What happened?"

Atan turned her back, and he tottered after the sweeping brocade over-robe she wore, as the blue-robed Sartoran Mages backed out of their queen's path.

Veltos lay on the tiled floor, splashed with blood still fresh. Tsauderei grimaced when he saw what someone had done to her hand — but a missing finger was no death wound.

Atan sent looks over both her shoulders that made the silent watchers fall back several paces, before she said in an undertone, "Maybe it's the same in the north? You never told me. But in our mage guild, the guild master wears a suicide stone."

He raised a hand, remembering. "I know." He glanced around. "Was it Detlev?" Cold gripped him. "Siamis?"

"We don't know. But Tsauderei, she's not the only one. Two other senior mages are dead, and they had no suicide stones. They were . . ." She shut her eyes, her face blanching as she swallowed.

"Tortured," Tsauderei said. "For information? Have you any idea for what?"

"There's more. An old palace servant, who'd been wandering mentally for years, was found dead, throat cut, in the palace. All she did was dust the archives."

"Was anything disturbed?"

"I just now found this out, and sent people to investigate."

Tsauderei closed his eyes, testing for magical residue around Veltos's body. There was none. Whoever killed her had been able to catch Veltos off-guard outside the wards, then dragged her inside, which enabled the killer to negate the protective wards and tracers. No doubt it was the same for the senior mages. "I've seen enough," he said.

Atan glanced at some of the hovering mages in their dark blue overrobes. A red-haired man of about thirty gestured to a couple of minor mages, from the lack of embroidered rank markings on their robes. One retrieved the severed finger and laid it gently beside Veltos's hand, then they reverently straightened and covered the body.

Tsauderei saw the redhead step toward Atan, and knew that the jockeying for position had already begun, for if one of the two dead was Leiclan, whom Veltos had been training as the next mage chief . . ..

Atan straightened her shoulders, faced the mages, and in a hard voice, said, "I am appointing Tsauderei as interim chief mage of the Sartoran Mage Guild."

Tsauderei was aware of a brief, bleak pang of humor, which he was able to keep from his face. Poor Veltos, ghost-ridden by her own sense of duty! She had kept a stranglehold not only on the guild, but on the high council, made up of survivors of the war a century ago, before Sartor was enchanted and removed from time. Her intent had been to wrest backward Sartor into modern times, keeping Atan (as a child not raised to her position) and Tsauderei (as an outsider) out of decision-making.

It seemed that Atan was beginning to assert herself at last.

Tsauderei bowed to his former ward and student, for the first time.

Belatedly, the mages all bowed as well.

He said for Atan's private ear, "Can you do everything that's right for the memorials and Disappearance, while I return to the north? I've been chasing Siamis," he said. "Who is no doubt responsible for this. I must meet with a Venn diplomat and wrap up some other affairs, then I will return and give all my attention to figuring out what happened, if I possible can."

Atan was physically still in her middle teens, due to that age-abating spell, but it was the pain of an adult that gazed back at him out of her dark blue eyes as she dipped her chin in assent. "Come back as soon as you can."

Tsauderei wrote first to Mondros.

In Chwahirsland, Jilo sat on a balcony overlooking First Army's vast parade ground, the stones weather- and boot-worn to a smoothness that had all but polished them to shininess over the centuries. Here Wan-Edhe had held the bloodiest Courts of Rule in the past few decades, handing down ever more draconian punishments for ever smaller transgressions in his mad effort to weld the Five Armies into one mindless body that acted only according to his will.

Knowing this aim—having grown up with it—Jilo loathed the drill competition. He'd avoided it, permitting the five generals decide it however they wished, since Supreme Commander Henjit had vanished with Wan-Edhe.

Now Jilo sat alone on the king's platform, trying not to shiver. Everywhere else on the continent it was summer, but here low clouds and a bitter wind serried through the perfect squares gathered down below.

Loathing the total falsity of his position, Jilo stood and stretched out his arms parallel to the ground, then tapped his two fists together.

THUD! Ten thousand iron-shod right heels slammed to the stone: the two thousand best from each army, chosen after intense competition.

Jilo flopped back down as four of the vast squares marched to either side, melting in precise steps into lines, leaving one alone in the center. At a silent signal from the brigade captain, they pulled their swords, each moving exactly in time with his neighbor, swords held up then striking right and left in perfect unison. The evolutions had arisen out of regular morning drill, Jilo knew that much, as he'd been doing them as a boy before he was chosen by Wan-Edhe's brother, Kwenz, to learn magic.

But the way the square broke abruptly into smaller squares, men wheeling and stepping and recombining as the swords swung in arcs and overhead, and sliced down and around, would be utterly useless in battle.

As the pattern went on, the steps sometimes syncopating, Jilo began to wonder if some of the rhythms beneath those stomping, hissing, heel-tapping feet were in some way a part of the Great Hum, the rhythm to Chwahir life that Wan-Edhe had tried to utterly eradicate. He wondered if they felt that rhythm the same way, or if he was imagining it. He wondered what they were all thinking. Couldn't be the pattern. From what he remembered, it would probably be rote now, but heartbeat, fear of an error, maybe hope and pride, those were most likely.

Then the familiar stomach roil began: he had no idea what he going to do with them, since his great idea about turning them into farmers had been a disaster.

His breath shuddered in his chest. This was why he hated coming out of the workroom in Narad. There was so very much yet to do there to dismantle that well of evil, and yet, on his coming out, and escaping the still-strong sucking of life and the distortion of time, the weight of decision pressed on him.

What do you do with a vast army that drills forever? Did that life have meaning for them? The kingdom was beginning to wake up, to his mind like a dragon so ancient that its bones had become covered with dust, which grew trees and shrubs and became mountains.

Once it roused, the world would rumble —

The internal flick of his notecase startled him.

He kept his head still, aware of the impact of all those eyes watching him sidelong, as he took out the note. But he was so high above them all they couldn't see his hands.

Mondros! Had to be more bad news.

Jilo: Has Siamis been mentioned in your book?

Jilo slipped a pencil from his pocket and wrote on the back: *Not since BF last yr. I look every day.*

The answer came back promptly. *If you see his movements mentioned, will you let us know at once?*

Jilo answered yes, and made a mental note to write to Senrid as soon as he got back to Narad.

In Tsauderei's mountaintop cottage, under the crash and roar of summer thunder, the newly appointed head of the Sartoran Mage Guild sat with Mondros and Erai-Yanya, while in Sartor, Atan oversaw the preparation of a suitable memorial for the former guild head, and the entire mage school deployed in teams, busily laying down intersecting wards with all the vigor and determination of people who knew that they could be next on the list of victims.

Tsauderei said, "I have gone through Veltos's desk, once I broke the wards. I also discovered why she had not formally appointed a successor, and kept Leiclan at a distance."

Here Erai-Yanya surprised him. "She promised her senior mages that whoever duplicated Detlev's spell removing Sartor from the world would get that position. That was to be their defense, if and when Norsunder attacks. Her plan was to take Sartor away from them summarily."

Tsauderei exclaimed, "She told *you?*"

Erai-Yanya shook her head, and the quill holding her hair up into a loose bun shook loose. She made an exasperated noise, sounding like a kitten sneezing, and as she bound the neglected locks up again, said, "She came to me for certain kinds of research. I put it together. Easy enough as Murial of the Mearsieans and I had already trod that road with Evend. That was before he branched into studying the rifts."

"I figured someone would try," Mondros said. "I did. In the process of trying to worm my way into Wan-Edhe's wards."

"Secrets upon secrets." Tsauderei scowled. "It's understandable, I suppose, but it leads to so much duplicated and unnecessary effort. Anyway, so far, the Sartorans have failed to find that magic."

Mondros had been studying the grubby piece of paper in his hand. "Jilo will report next time Siamis transfers." He tossed the paper onto the fire and wiped his pencil-smeared fingers.

"I don't understand how the magic functions in that book of his," Erai-Yanya said. "Are we all in it? Can we do anything about it?"

"Possibly, and no," Mondros said. "Dark magic transfer spells and alerts work differently in this matter as in so many others. I put in considerable effort detecting and removing spells off the Destination in Sartor, at Tsauderei's request, just to discover that they somehow reformed. Wan-Edhe has to have taken decades secretly laying them, and Jilo still hasn't found the mage book containing Wan-Edhe's notes on those. If it even exists. Jilo thinks there is a great deal that Wan-Edhe was so determined to keep secret that he burned them after establishing the spells."

Erai-Yanya shuddered. "He really did think he would live forever."

"And he is still alive," Mondros reminded them both. "Also: time still is untrustworthy in Narad. Jilo's answering right away means that he was not in the capital. If he goes back, six months could pass, or more, before he answers."

"Which brings us," Tsauderei said, "to what we *can* control. I'll have to return to Sartor soon, but I am not giving up this chase, especially if Siamis is somehow connected to these murders and assassinations. I'd rather find Siamis before he hits us with some new plot. Erai-Yanya, can we use the dyr to track him?"

"Those objects are useless." Erai-Yanya paused as a crash of thunder reverberated through the cottage, and pulled her shawl more tightly around her. "Whatever virtue they once had, all they do now is distort magic. Even simple magic."

Tsauderei rubbed his throbbing forehead. Too much change too fast—he felt it as a physical wrench. "And yet illiterate, ten-year-old Liere managed a complicated spell that could have defeated a senior mage student when she first brought that thing out of the Never," Tsauderei said, "and then she used it to defeat Siamis."

"Well, to be exact, she used it to tear apart Siamis's enchantment," Erai-Yanya replied, fighting a yawn. It wasn't the shorted sleep so much as the disturbing dreams that woke her during those brief rests, that made her eyes feel gritty. "Which was actually quite flimsy—for someone with Dena Yeresbeth." She sighed. "My magic . . .slides off the dyr in, oh, a way similar to how poor Liere seems to slide away from mastering elementary magic. But 'slide' is an inexact term. Explains nothing, really. Nor do the two circumstances show any useful similarity."

Erai-Yanya dropped the dyr onto the table and glared at it. "Except for this: I wonder if the thing only works for someone with Dena Yeresbeth."

"Then give it back to her," Tsauderei said.

Erai-Yanya pulled her shawl tight. "While ordinarily I would never condone learning magic with a crutch, maybe that's what's needed for Liere."

"Yes." Tsauderei sighed, glad to have something decided. "Ask her to try elementary magic again, with this dyr thing in hand."

"I'll get Arthur to bring Liere to me," Erai-Yanya said. "In fact, I feel they'd both be safer in Roth Drael, with this shocking news from Everon, and Colend. Do you think Siamis sent those boys?"

"Let us not assume anything until we know more. My meeting with the Venn Eye—mage—they call themselves Eyes of the Crown—was a whole lot of nothing. But I could see that they are as disturbed about the prospects of Norsunder getting the Arrow as we are. Oalthoreh promised to follow up with the Venn."

"Good," Erai-Yanya said.

"So. Back to us. If Siamis is somehow closing in on the Arrow, which I think we had better assume, then his next step will surely be to launch the Venn at us in some kind of new and more deadly enchantment. Once he alters the bindings on Arrow to his control. We are going to need every advantage we can possible grasp in order to find him first. So let's divide up our tasks. . ."

Efael ripped through several useless lighter mages before he found one who put him on the trail of a catalogue of magical artifacts from outlanders.

His minions infiltrated Sartor's archives, and worked through night and day in teams until they put together the connection between the Arrow, the Morningstar, and the Lirendi Diamond. When at last they located the key text, he transferred to the airless archive vault, read it, threw it to the floor and used magic to burn it.

Then he sent the Black Knives after Siamis, and transferred to Colend himself. The Colendi were so complacent in their safety that their defenses were laughably flimsy.

He hid while waiting for the king to finish listening to a group scraping and tweedling musical instruments, as he observed the sentry patterns of the decorative idiots the Colendi flattered themselves able to guard their king.

By the time the scrapers had finished their noise and were led off in one direction, and (from the smells of food) the king had withdrawn to his solitary meal, Efael knew the guards' pattern of interlocked fields of vision, which at two seldom-used corners every third round were only one guard deep.

He garroted one of those guards, and stashed her body where it wouldn't be found until long after he was gone. In the time it took for the next two guards to reach that hall from either end, he'd already slipped inside the king's suite.

The dining alcove was set in an oriel window overlooking a bend in the canal. Efael stopped, swaying, partly in physical fatigue due to the strain of being in the material world for so many uncounted hours, and partly because no one had told him this particular Lirendi was so beautiful, after a few centuries of toads. They'd only said he was mad.

If this one had been thirty years younger . . .

"Who are you?" the king asked.

Efael approached. "Where's the Lirendi Diamond?"

"Gone."

"To?"

The king did not answer, but sat back, head averting slightly, upper lip crimped. Efael uttered a laugh. "Don't like the stink of sweat and blood?"

The king set down his goblet and reached for the golden fruit-peeling knife. Efael slammed his hand down across the king's, pinning it to the table.

At once distant shouts rose, and Efael sensed magical tracers. Fuck! He hadn't thought a king would tolerate being warded. "To?" he demanded.

The king reached with his left for his fork, and Efael drove his knife through that hand, pinning it to the table. "To?" he demanded, and when the king's eyes closed — thin lids blue-veined — his fine lips pressed into a line, Efael leaned as close as a lover and whispered, "I'll kill every idiot coming through that door —"

"Blonde. Tall."

Siamis has it.

Three doors opened, and a horde started in at a full run. Furious, Efael yanked his knife from the king's hand, and in a last burst of petulance drove it straight into his heart. Then he transferred back to Norsunder to recover.

Twenty-eight

Elsewhere in Colend

"THE TRUTH IS," THADKeperi said to Curtas as they walked down the familiar path, Wilderfeld's rooftops shimmering in the heat to the southwest, "when I consider my future, something I've only begun to do, I don't see myself sitting at a desk with my scribe tools at hand and endless stacks of paper before me."

There. The words were out—and spoken to someone who wouldn't betray a shocked hitch of breath, and the under-the-eyebrows glance reserved for layabouts. Curtas tucked his thumbs in his belt, his mild grin deepening the shadows at either side of his mouth as he said, "I figured that much."

"You did? How? *I* didn't, really, until this trip."

"Because it's this trip," Curtas said. "Because you seize every chance you can to be on the road, and because you keep talking about your mastery project as something to be decided some day in the future. But your sister had already proposed hers, right?"

Thad sighed, not wanting to put into words the silence growing between him and Karhin on the subject. Karhin never argued. That was the trouble. They used to share the work without thinking, but in the last year or so, as she stayed up later in the evenings, and took more shifts downstairs, she talked to Thad about everything *but* scribe affairs. The silence, a relief at first, had of late began to hurt, because it had become a wall between them.

"I wonder if my mothers know," Thad said as he kicked a pebble. Dust spurted up from each tumble on the ground until it spun away in the grass. "Ah-ye," he muttered in a put-upon voice. "I expect I'll hear some questions when my Name Day comes round again, and I still haven't chosen a mastery project."

Curtas gave him another of those sideways glances, the late summer sun casting highlighting greenish tints in his brown-gray eyes. "If I'd had mothers like yours," he said, "I wouldn't be here now."

Thad opened his mouth, then the import struck him. He'd forgotten Curtas's past as a thief. "You've never said anything about your early days."

"Nor will I," Curtas retorted.

Thad ventured a question. "Not even to Shontande?"

Curtas lifted his chin. "Least of all to Shontande." And after tracking a low-flying redbird all the way to the hazy northern horizon, where the shadowy juts of the Chwahir border mountains shimmered in the summer heat, he added, "He'd hate that kind of story. Would want to do something about it."

"Shontande likes stories about travel, not so much why people might have to be traveling," Thad said, feeling his way. It was odd, how gradually the prince had ceased to be *the prince* in his mind, and had become *Shontande*.

Curtas said in the tone one uses when quoting someone, "He wants stories about freedom. Not confinement. Of any kind." And in a more natural voice, "You've heard him. It's not just politeness. He really does like hearing about people we've met on the road. Every detail."

"He likes the way you tell them," Thad said.

"Because I give him the details. I've been saving them up. Shontande will want to hear about this singing blacksmith. He'll want to hear about the city-sanctioned snowball fight to settle a guild conflict. The night the hissing lights of the north fingered all the way down to the mountains above Wnelder Vee."

"Saving the details up," Thad repeated, then the next thought vanished when they reached the river bend toward town, and the first person they encountered was a young carter whose eyes widened at the sight of Thad.

Then she dropped her reins between her knees, put her hands together and bowed over them in a profound peace.

Thad bowed back, thoroughly puzzled, and alarmed. You only bowed like that to people you knew when . . .

He began to run, Curtas pacing easily at his side. Each person Thad recognized bowed like wheat in the wind, silence separating him off from the world. His breath rasped in his throat by the time he reached home.

The first sound he heard through the open upstairs windows was Lisbet sobbing in that high-pitched, attention-craving tone that he found so difficult to deal with. The downstairs, usually packed with scribes, couriers, and customers, was empty—something usually only seen on festival days.

When he smelled lilies and roses on the air, he stuttered to a stop, looking around wildly. "Karhin? Mother?"

His birth-mother emerged from the formal antechamber, her gray-streaked red hair disheveled, her eyes puffy and swollen.

His vision flashed white. People flattened to shadows. Voices distorted to the high caw of birds: framed in the open door was the rose and lily decked bier on which Karhin lay, hands folded on her breast, her hair tenderly combed over her shoulders in orderly locks, glowing ruddy in the light of the candles set at her head and foot.

Sounds passed over him in waves as he struggled to under-stand. Shock made him shiver, and he knew the agony was coming, but he could only stand there, until Curtas, who had been holding him up, looked directly into his face.

Thad stared back at distended hazel eyes, pain and regret in every small muscle of Curtas's face as his lips shaped the words, "I'm sorry, I'm sorry."

Thad collapsed slowly, until both his mothers' arms twined around him, holding him up as the first sob ripped mercilessly through his chest.

Sound and sense returned with the sound of Bee's voice. His skinny body pressed into their circle, and on the other side, Lisbet cried on, a thin, exhausted sound.

"Why?" Thad's throat was raw, but he forced the words out. "What happened?"

Bee's entire body trembled. "I heard it," he whispered. "All. He did not know I was there below."

"He?"

"A high voice, not a girl," Bee said. "'You and your big mouth are ruining everything.' 'Who are you? Ruining what?'" Bee, training as a listening scribe, not only memorized the words he heard, but the tone of voice, even the way the person spoke, and hearing an echo of Karhin's characteristic speech pattern in Bee's recitation wounded Thad anew.

"'That's what.' Then she tried to cry out, but it went thin, like this." Bee reproduced a wet, gasping noise that scraped Thad's nerves. "Then she fell down."

Thad knew what he had to ask next. It hurt yet again – like a knife, but this one did not cut bone and flesh, it cut the heart, soul, and mind – but he owed it to Karhin. "Did you hear his thoughts?" he asked gently.

Bee's blind gaze would always be blank, but his chin lifted. "Did Karhin tell you? That I can do that?"

"Yes," Thad said.

"She doesn't hear people talking in their minds, like I do," Bee admitted. "She hears . . .*heard* . . .differently. She said people were diverse lights. I wish I knew what light is! But she told me, what I hear, it's not wrong, if I don't *try* to hear them. If they just come. But that time, I tried to hear."

"What words did you hear from the killer's mind?"

"'It's not the way we talk. It's . . .things I don't understand, and feelings, and snips of words. This is all I understood: 'Now I won't be Noser, I'll be Knife. No, Killer.'"

"Noser," Thad repeated, though his head pounded so hard his thoughts seemed to come from a long way away. "I've heard that before. But there could be a lot of people called that. This one was a boy shorter than Bee, with yellow hair –" And as always, he caught himself up, remembering that his brother would not have any idea what any of that meant.

"One of the foreigners," Lisbet said, sniffing. "I remember him. A bratty snot. He came with some other boys that Curtas and Adam brought ages ago, but you two were busy with your secrets and all, so I only saw them before they left again." She scowled at Thad, remembered what had happened to Karhin, and her chin trembled as fresh tears ran down her cheeks.

Thad turned. "Curtas?" He looked around. "Where's Curtas? He was with me."

"He left." His mother's voice broke.

"Without offering any grief respects." Lisbet's voice shook.
"You'd think—"

Everyone stilled when the carillons began to ring the rarely-
heard, low toll that the young people had never heard before,
and which made the older people look at one another with
frightened eyes: it only sounded at the death of a monarch.

Marloven Hess

Senrid woke early to notes so tightly packed in his golden
notecase that they exploded out when he clicked it open.

He sorted through them, reading rapidly, then gazed
sightlessly at his darkened windows, for he always rose early
in order to get in some practice before breakfast. He mentally
calculated times—yes, this last one, from Lilah Selenna, had to
have been the latest, only a short time before.

He knew the transfer Destination in Miraleste, braced, and
magic wrenched him to the other end of the continent, where
the sun was sinking gradually toward the west.

He ran to the familiar den where Peitar usually gathered
with his friends, and paused in the doorway, noticing who was
there and who wasn't. His first thought had been that the
alliance was together again, but it wasn't true: Liere was
missing (he knew she was in Roth Drael with Erai-Yanya and
Hibern, her little daughter in tow); Arthur was there, but
without his shadow, Roy; Leander and Kyale were there,
uncharacteristically silent, or rather Kyale was uncharacteristically silent as green-eyed Leander gave Senrid a small nod;
Atan was missing, as was Rel; nobody from Mearsies Heili or
Everon or Colend was there, and that included the wandering
artist Adam.

Instead of Roy, a familiar stocky, pale-haired boy stood next
to Arthur, wearing a brightly colored, long silky tunic-robe
thing over loose trousers. A green snake's head peeked out of
one wrist cuff, then withdrew: Senrid remembered him now.
Dak! The boy who had guided them on their quest against
Siamis the summer of '42, when the alliance had all gone to
Geth-deles after the Norsunder attack on Everon.

"Dak?" Senrid said.

Dak gave him a wan smile.

Arthur, standing next to him, turned his gaze Senrid's way. Senrid didn't think he'd ever seen the usually vague, always scholarly Arthur angry. But Arthur was angry now, as Senrid said, "Where's Roy?"

"Gone," Arthur said, bright spots of red mottling his cheeks. "With a whole lot of our senior mage teachings with him."

"So?" Senrid asked.

Arthur turned to Dak. "Tell him."

"We've had a leaky boat in high seas, yes, in some of our islands," Dak said slowly, as if he were listening to the Translation Spell changing his words. They heard him in Sartoran, the words shaped by the distinctive, graceful Geth accent. "We truly did not know they were here. Or that Roy was one of them. Or we should have warned you."

"They?" Senrid asked, since it was plain that the others were already ahead of him in news. To make things go faster, as his mind was still partly on all he ought to be doing at home, he said, "This is what I know so far. Glenn Delieth of Everon was murdered by somebody named David, one of Adam's friends. Also murdered, Karhin Keperi. And the Colendi king. Not known, if all were done by the same hand."

Everyone talked at once, and Senrid heard the names *Detlev* and *Siamis*, then Peitar raised a hand.

The others fell silent.

"Glenn was definitely killed by David," Arthur said. "Tahra reports that there were eyewitnesses."

"Killed by the same boy," Dak said earnestly, "who murdered our hero, Les Rhoderan."

"Who had discovered a new form of magical illusion," Arthur put in, and would have said more, but he could see that no one at that moment was interested in new forms of magical illusion.

"We all loved Les Rhoderan and his sister Charis-Merian, who grieves to this day." Dak looked as if he still grieved as well. "We thought Detlev took David and his gang back to Norsunder when they were declared outlaw by so many —"

"Wait, wait," Senrid said. "Detlev? Gang? *Back?* They're not from your world?"

Dak scowled. "They came to Geth oh, a few years ago. David, their new leader; his lieutenant, the one with the initials, MV. Laban —"

"Don't forget what CJ said, that Adam knew Roy. They even had some kind of secret code word. *Firejive*." Lilah waved a piece of paper. "I have her letter about it right here. Adam said it at little Ian's Name Day. But we didn't think it *meant* anything." She blinked back tears.

"Then we shall count in Roy with David, MV, and Laban, unless proved different," Arthur said in a hard voice as unlike him as his angry expression. "Those three are the most advanced in magic. Dark magic, at least David and MV are. Roy might very well be, too." He gritted his teeth against that sickening sense of betrayal, that he'd been taken for a fool where he had seen only friendship.

Dak sidled a look his way. "Ferret, the tracker, Adam, the painter, Erol, Curtas, Rolfin, Leefan, Silvanas, and the horrid little one they call the Nose."

Senrid cursed under his breath.

"Detlev's boys," Dak said, his cheerful brown countenance altering to a scowl under his shock of pale hair. "He raised them, and now they are loose in *your* world."

Senrid said, "Then we all go home, check wards and protections. And keep a sharp watch for them."

He transferred soon after, expecting a row of grinning enemies waiting with spinning knives. When he arrived home to find it the way he left it, he ripped down his magic books and began the arduous process—it was going to take weeks, he thought bitterly—of warding Detlev's boys, name by name, from entering Choreid Dhelerei.

PART TWO:
HUNTED

Firejive ll

/Fire: to heat clay and glazes hot enough to fuse them into a new form/

I MUST TAKE THE reader beyond space and time, to where Siamis sat with the "dragoneye" stone in his hands, its cobalt center reflecting light from somewhere beyond the dim cavern surrounding him. As he gazed into the gem's depths, he considered the headlong stream of time outside of Norsunder-Beyond, and yet how time could seem inex-orable, slow and deliberate as a tide, and as irresistible.

Emotional distortion appeared to operate on a similar principle. Was it because exertion in Norsunder-Beyond seemed to impel months, even years to pass? But there was no sensible measure.

It was very much like watching a play. Time outside seems still, while within the two or three hours of physical effort it takes to watch the play, time ranges over hours or years or even centuries. He stopped there, refusing to permit the simile to become metaphor: it had already been trite before Colend tried to make art of the concept.

The time had come to assume his role.

He set the stone carefully on a heavily warded support, settled into a comfortable position and took a cleansing breath.

Here, then, was the third level of the complex of spells making up "the Arrow": first there had been the Moonfire, which granted vision into time and place, then the binding of the enchantments onto this stone. Now he had to sift through those enchantments from the inside.

This was going to be a long, dangerous labyrinth to walk in that equipoise between the magical and mental realms.

One

DETLEV'S BOYS LAY LOW in their rat-hole, their days spent in training, their nights going round and round in review and speculation, as summer waned to autumn.

The day after Noser finally turned up, shivering and gibbering about how *Next time I'll do it better, Next time*, they woke up to find a stack of transfer tokens waiting.

With a minimum of discussion, they took the time to clean up, for Detlev hated slovenly habits. Even Noser brushed the hair out of his eyes, revealing his round, freckled face, snub nose, and chewed, chapped lips, his stunted body scrupulously buttoned into a shirt and trousers. He even up-dumped his gear bag and excavated a pair of shoes, though he mostly lived barefoot except when it snowed.

One by one they transferred. They knew better than to bolt. At one time or another someone had done a runner, and either Siamis had chased them down, or Detlev had contacted them on the mental plane. It never came out well.

They found themselves on the top of a cliff above a scree-covered slope, and everyone's heart sank. Mountain-top. They knew what that meant.

At the extreme edge of a cliff sat a huge boulder, against which Detlev leaned, silent until the last of them appeared. The air was so cold and windy that the smells and summer heat snapped away instantly. In the shadowy folds of ground here and there lay blue streaks of winter snow, sparkling icily.

Detlev waited motionless, the only sign of life the wind toying with his short brown hair, and flagging the loose fabric of his white sleeves.

When the last of them had gathered, and they sat in a semi-circle, he said, "David, push this over the edge." As he spoke he straightened up and turned his palm toward the boulder.

David sprang up, took the time to walk around the boulder as far as he could, then pressed his palms against it, placed his feet well back, and pushed with all his strength. The rock didn't shift. So he brushed his hands down his pants, tried a different angle, and this time braced a shoulder against it, grounded his feet, and focused his strength on the point of contact between flesh and rock.

Nothing.

He straightened up. Detlev flicked a glance to the side. "Mal Venn?"

MV sprang up, flickering a grim side-eye at David. The mountain-top was bad enough, but even worse was when Detlev used their given names. MV tried from three different angles, with no more success than David'd had.

Next was Rolfin, who, with his powerful upper body and somewhat lower balance point, still was unable to move it. Nor could Leefan.

If those four couldn't, the others hadn't a hope, but still they were called up one by one, and they dared not give it anything but their best try — Noser providing grunts and sighs of extreme effort in a (forlorn) hope of convincing Detlev of his earnestness.

When they were done, Detlev indicated a smaller boulder a few paces away, then opened his hand toward the slope behind them. "Fetch that limb over there."

Farther up, some straggly oaks clung to life. A storm-torn branch lay below one. It took two of them to fetch it, and at a slight sign from Detlev, MV and David pulled their knives and stripped away the twigs and smaller branches, because by now they knew what was to come.

When the limb had been as planed as straight as they could

make it, at a gesture from Detlev, they dug under the big boulder and shoved the planed end there as far as it would reach, balancing the middle on the smaller rock. Then Detlev gestured to Noser, saying, "Edde."

Noser's shoulders hunched under his ears. Hearing his given name was never good.

"Alaki."

Ferret's eyes flickered, and he slid up next to Noser on the long end of the plank. They went in size order, lightest to heaviest. By the time Noser had backed up to the highest point, Leef put his foot on the plank, and pressed. The boulder, which had already shifted, tipped and they sprang down to watch it topple with a mighty crash, causing a rock fall as it bounced and spun away below.

When the noise had abated, and a cloud of gray dust hung in the air, whirling slowly in the wind, Detlev snapped his fingers and they sat down again.

"What did you just see?" he asked.

Noser sighed loudly. "Working together. But we *have!* We *did!*"

Laban's bright blue gaze turned his way, lip curled. MV's narrow-eyed glance was more venomous, and Noser sat back, huffing.

"What," Detlev asked gently, "did you just see?"

The quiet tone was a far more effective threat than any rant would have been. Noser said, "We did it together."

"You did it together," Detlev said, "under direction. Would it have been as successful if Rolfin had gone first?"

"Of course. Or maybe him'n'Leef. And Erol," Noser blustered.

"The branch would have broken," Curtas the builder said to Noser.

"Oh." Then Noser flushed. "So David didn't send me after that red-haired Karhin. But he'd just done for Glenn, he said we had to deal, that was dealing, so I thought, finally, what we been training for, and I dealt with the threat!"

"With what result?"

"But she knew about us! She blabbed!"

Detlev said, "I can think of at least three ways to finesse that, and keep the plan intact. David?"

"One of us could have told her the truth, but not all of it: yes, an alliance within the alliance."

"Mal Venn?"

"Tell her she got it wrong, she's seeing what isn't there."

"Laban?"

"Fog," said Laban with a derisive glance Noser's way. "Point out someone like Rel, ask if *he's* the center of a secret and sinister conspiracy. Or Puddlenose of the Mearsieans. Or Senrid."

Detlev turned back to Noser, who said defensively, "You taught us first thing that no plan survives first contact with the enemy."

"True," Detlev said, turning to David. "When I found out that Adam's reports on alliance communications were being intercepted at Norsunder Base, I sent an order for Adam to report to me in person, and relay orders to you in person. As a result, you remained undiscovered."

They all remembered the mysterious affair of Jilo's text that had been written in blood, which seemed to have vanished, with no one in the alliance — including the Keperis — knowing what had happened, until Adam overheard Kyale's and CJ's stories on Prince Darian's Name Day.

Detlev said, "Next point to consider: when deviation from orders is the result of stupidity, the target wins at the outset."

Stung by the word "stupidity," David began to expostulate, beginning with Glenn's utter lack of ability to command.

Detlev cut in, "Are you attempting to justify your blunder by using your loss of self-control as your chief defense?"

David let out his breath in a hiss. "No."

Detlev said, "Maintaining your guise with Glenn Delieth would have been far less onerous than the prospect before you now: finding yourself before Efael of the Host, he with a whip in one hand, a knife in the other, and you with nothing but your wits as he says, 'Run.' That's how his test for recruitment to his band of assassins begins, and it will get worse from there. It is also a test you cannot refuse, should he choose to take an interest in you."

That silenced them.

He went on, "Until now, Efael assumed you were being trained as spies, and he has little interest in spies. At this moment he's hunting Siamis. If he fails, he will be looking to take it out on someone, and you've now caught his eye."

Stupid and loss of control or not, the boys all knew that Glenn's death had been an inadvertent blunder. But Karhin's was far worse. Covert looks, angry and brooding, flashed Noser's way.

He crossed his arms, expression mutinous, though he could still feel the pressure on his palm from shoving that knife in. In his nightmares, he was shoving it into himself, pressing harder and harder, but it wouldn't budge, until he woke up in a sweat, with his head pounding.

Detlev continued. "You are not mere assassins. Norsunder is full of assassins. Some of them excellently trained. Their utility is limited."

Noser scowled, but he was listening, wincing against an echo of the headache.

"Part of your training as future commanders is to master all aspects of strategy, including intelligence gathering. Each of you, put in exactly the right place, and doing what you were ordered, could eventually have earned your targets' complete trust. Which would have put you in positions of influence when Norsunder does attack. Instead . . .David? MV?"

David flushed. "I neglected to post a watch when Glenn came after me. So Canold saw us."

MV's blade-sharp cheekbones mottled with dull red. "Should have established a perimeter. Which could have deflected Canold and the rest of 'em turning up for morning drill."

"Try again." Detlev's expression didn't change, or his voice, but David and MV both stiffened, the others shifting uneasily.

"I should have knocked his weapon out of his hand as soon as I saw him go for me," David said.

MV mumbled, "Shoulda finessed."

"Yes. Each of you—all of you—know at least five ways to effectively end a fight and maintain your cover. So instead of carrying on with your orders." Detlev tipped his head toward Leef, who had set his foot on the lever. "Instead—after all these months of effort—you lost your targets' trust in one day's work. And your timing," his consonants sharpened, "could not have been worse."

Silence.

"You have lost the effectiveness of the hand through the water. The strategy for now will be mitigation. Edde. When you get to ground level—"

"Don't make me work wood," Noser moaned. "I *hate* working wood. I learned my lesson: follow orders."

Once he'd been the boys' mascot, some even calling him Little Brother. Only Silvanas called him that now, though Noser still regarded himself as everyone's pet.

Detlev said, "When you reach ground level, you will transfer back to Five, and carve me a chair. Diamond back, lion claw legs. High polish."

"Why isn't David getting sent to do wood?" Noser whined.

"Why do I require wood-carving?" Detlev asked in a deceptively gentle voice.

Noser's shoulders hitched up, and he recited in a small voice, "While strengthening arms and hands, focus and precision, wood-carving above all trains patience."

"Excellent. Then you will only be required to add leaf pattern supports. Unless you have any other observations to offer?"

Noser flushed and hung his head.

"Roy."

The awkward boy with the jug-handled ears had been studying his hands. He looked up as Detlev said, "Hole up and write out everything you have learned at the northern mage school, while it is still fresh."

"I saved my notes," Roy said quietly.

"Excellent. Rewrite them focusing on what you've learned about wards, comparing the strengths and weaknesses of dark and light magic. You've been on the inside of their best training, something no one else has managed. One of the most regrettable results of that day's work was having to pull you out."

Roy's head bowed, his dark hair hiding his eyes. David winced.

Detlev turned to the rest. "Fall back to Norsunder Base for now, while I find out why Efael is leaving a trail of dead bodies."

The name Efael caused the restless, disappointed boys to sober into stillness. "When I left for the Beyond last, there were three factions struggling for control at Norsunder Base. I suspect it's no different now. The only thing they'd agree on is that you lot are easy targets. About all you have going for you is your still being underage. The worst ones will see you as boring. The smartest ones will remember that you're under my protection. But that's little enough. Keep up your drills where no one can see you. Be wary, move always in pairs or threes when you have to. Do not be caught alone."

He vanished, leaving them staring disconsolately down into the canyon below.

It was going to be a very long climb.

Colend

Thad had never paid much attention to short, sturdy, unremarkable Nalisse, except in the general way of goodwill toward a sibling's close friends. But at the Karhin's memorial, Thad found himself standing next to Nalisse, who shook with silent sobs as the entire town of Wilderfeld gathered in the town square to sing the Lily Lament, which was only sung for the young whose lives had been cut short.

The poignancy of the high voices soaring in descant above the lower voices singing the ancient triplets hurt Thad so much with their beauty that he couldn't sing, though he tried.

Afterward, Nalisse said in the low voice of a vow, "Your sister told me I should act on my dreams. She said life should be lived doing what you love, not what is easiest. When I go home, I'm turning in my courier pouch. And old as I am, I'm prenticing out to any pastry cook who'll have me."

Thad understood that sometimes vows had to be heard by someone else, and not a mere stranger. Nalisse needed to speak her vow to Thad, because that was the closest she could come to making her promise to Karhin.

He made a formal peace. "I hope, when you remember Karhin, you might share those memories with me. And I would like to hear of your progress."

Nalisse gulped, and turned aside her red eyes and nose. "So I shall."

"Then I, too, will make a vow, to speak to the elders about relinquishing the scribe trade. Though I don't know quite what yet I will do. But I promise to find it."

They bowed again to each other, hands in the peace.

As it happened, the royal memorial was scheduled for a few days after Karhin's memorial, allowing for those traveling from the outer reaches of the kingdom. The upper ranks (and the servants) knew that negotiation and compromise, demand and withdrawal, all the more fierce for the outward requirement of seemly sorrow and silence, went on behind closed palace doors so that the new power would be ready with a smooth transition to new government.

In history, it had been the new king or queen, making concessions or demands while putting together the all-important First Decrees from the Throne. Now, everyone wondered if Prince Shontande, so seldom seen, would walk alone, or with the regency council—and when the coronation would be declared. In other words, who truly held power?

Thad used his tiny saving of coin and hired a horse. He knew it was foolish and frivolous, but urgency drove him on anyway, as he passed through a kingdom still in mourning, blue and white and lilies displayed everywhere, the carillons muffled when playing the hours, all business but absolute necessity halted.

Thad knew only this: he had to be there, though he had little hope of catching a glimpse of the new king processing from the Gate of Silver Willow to the Gate of Gold. But he had a better chance of seeing Shontande now than on Martande Day, when he'd be formally crowned—if the regency council let him.

Grief and urgency drove Thad onward. He kept seeing Curtas's wide, shocked eyes, and hearing him say over and over *I'm sorry, I'm sorry.* Next to his breast Thad carried the crumpled, tear-stained grief letter from King Terry of Erdrael Danara, which Thad was determined to put in Shontande's hands.

He had run entirely out of money by the time he reached the outskirts of the capital. The roads were filled with people dressed in mourning white and Lirendi blue, locals all heading inward. Thad walked with them, stopping occasionally to drink from the many public fountains in order to kill his hunger, until he reached the inner city. Many merchants and some of the nobles had chosen to express their grief—and their welcome of the new king—by offering free food and drink to the pilgrims who kept coming, without number. Thad was oblivious to the nobles' generosity signaling the shift in power. He was simply grateful to see someone holding out a basket of buns.

That single hazelnut bun quieted the gnawing of Thad's stomach and cleared his head enough for him to stand on tiptoes to peer about him. People who didn't know the byways of the capital had crowded along the main canals, or outside the eight gates of the city, especially Gate of the Silver Willow, from which the royal procession would emerge.

The crowd was thinner along the winding pathways leading to the Gate of Gold, through which the new king-in-name would walk, ending the period of mourning and signaling permission for life to resume. Thad found a spot and wedged himself between two of the ceramic pots of lilies that had been set along the royal prince's route.

Thad's sorrow had never abated, and though he knew about mind-shields, he rarely remembered them. No one knew that Shontande Lirendi was struggling to master Dena Yeresbeth. He'd told no one, having feared it was father's madness emerging in him.

Thus it appeared to Thad as the most astonishing chance that Shontande, walking alone in the midst of his vigilant herald guards as everyone made the full formal peace bow, would turn his head and meet Thad's upturned gaze.

Shontande raised his hand.

A subtle riffle of surprise passed through the procession, which halted.

Shontande beckoned Thad from the press along the walkway.

Trembling with hunger and fatigue, Thad squeezed past those who parted to let him through. He pressed his hands together, bobbing the peace right and left, blushing in shame at being seen in his rumpled, stale clothes. But he pulled out Terry's letter, and approached Shontande, remembering belatedly to make the royal peace as he braced himself against the moral weight of all those watching eyes.

Shontande gestured the heralds back a step. When the two boys were alone, Shontande said, "Is Curtas with you?"

Thad shut his eyes. "I'm so sorry, your highness. But . . .here. This letter will explain. I know you will forgive Terry — King Tereneth — for his lack of formality, for he did not know I would share this letter. He wrote to me after Karhin was killed, and to report that Curtas is a spy, one of the murderers. Here. It's all explained, and I probably should have sent it but I felt I *had* to come. To put it into your hands myself." Thad felt the pressure of the entire parade's gazes as he slid the letter into Shontande's hand.

"Karhin? Killed?"

Thad's miserable, mute tip of the chin above his tightly pressed palms was all he could bring himself to communi-cate.

Shontande lowered his voice. "So Curtas's friendship was

false?"

"I can't believe it myself. But that's what they all say," Thad said, and Shontande braced mentally to withstand the intensity of Thad's grief, sorrow, and bewildered sense of betrayal.

"But your friendship is true."

"Mine is true," Thad whispered.

"Will you write to me? And return to the rose garden?"

Thad's reddened eyes lifted, to see his own grief mirrored in the prince. "Yes," he said voicelessly, but in the mental realm Shontande felt the impact of Thad's promise as a vow.

Then Thad noticed the stiff heralds a few paces away and hastened backward, still bowing.

When Thad's red head vanished in the crowd, Shontande forced himself to move. One of his only two friends a spy? He stood there alone, shocked. Then came the disbelief. He felt somewhere down underneath a kindling of betrayal, of anger.

He was not bereft. He had Thad. And he had the alliance, too, if he wrote back to King Tereneth. A soft hiss of fabric, the sound of a single footstep, reminded him that he stood in the middle of the path, the crowd silent, staring. He could feel the pressure not of the crowd, but those individuals walking behind him, who had given him that scroll to read as First Decrees from the Throne.

He slid the precious letter into his inner sleeve next to their scroll, glanced at the lead herald, and they walked on.

Behind him, the Count of Ariath lifted her fan and murmured to the Duchas of Altan, "What was that?"

His fan moved to a plangent angle. "I hardly know."

"We shall have to make certain nothing of the sort occurs again."

"It is not seemly."

"It is not safe."

"Yes, very true, not safe at all."

The two resumed their courtly demeanors as they paced slowly behind their very young king, who clearly would need much closer guidance, for his own safety and education.

As for Thad, he avoided gazes—questions—shock and surprise, fading back and back until he reached the rear of the crowd, who had seen nothing. After that, it was easy to slip away, and begin the long journey home.

Norsunder Base

Life at Norsunder Base was as grim as usual.

Roy was effectively off limits while he had specific orders, so David and MV had to deal with the magic. Once they'd searched for traps, tracers, and wards in the smelly, cramped, airless space over the stables at the far end—five and six to a room—where they'd been stuck on previous visits, they crowded into the corner room for a meeting.

"Mitigation," David said. "That's strategic orders. I see it leaving us some tactical maneuvering."

"Like?" Laban crossed his arms, mouth derisive.

Everyone's mood was rotten. Before he and MV had begun the tedium of their search and secure sweep, David had taken Ferret and Adam aside to find out what they knew. "Ferret," he said now, "tell them what you found out."

"Siamis has gone renegade." Ferret waited for the exclamations and disbelief to die down. Anyone too loud got a kick from MV, who sat in a chair in the doorway, tipped back at a dangerous angle as he watched down the stairs.

When the mutters of disbelief died down at last, David said, "Ferret, go on."

"That's what I'm hearing in the mess hall and the courier annex."

"I thought Detlev sent him to get that Arrow thing, whatever that is," Curtas said.

"Did. Some think he might have it, others that he's on the run. But like Detlev said, Efael is hunting him down."

Rolfin let out a low whistle.

"I can find him," Ferret whispered.

Everyone turned to him. Leef, Ferret, and Erol were the quietest, the latter because of his stutter, Leef because he was naturally laconic, and Ferret because remaining invisible had been his survival strategy all his life. Good as they all were at stalking one another in their hunting games, Ferret was the best.

MV and David slewed around, gazing from him to each other. David said slowly, "Can you find out where Siamis was last?"

"Already did." Ferret shrugged a shoulder.

"Start there." MV propped his fists on his hips.

"What do you mean, start there?" Laban glared at MV.

"We're stuck here. Weren't you listening?"

"HQ here, but no specific orders," MV stated. "Leaves us maneuvering room. Prove ourselves." He waited, but no one argued; they all wanted out. MV tipped his chin at Ferret. "First transfer token is yours. Where to?"

"I'll start from Colend's capital," Ferret said, again surprising them all.

David scratched his head as Ferret slipped to his feet, sidestepped once, twice, and vanished out the door to pack his gear.

Adam glanced up. "There's still the blood magic text."

David said, "I've got that one." And a glance to either side.

No one argued. None of the others wanted to tangle with mad, murderous Kessler Sonscarna.

Laban said, "What about the dyr? Everyone was after it at one time."

"Arthur and Liere were sent to Roth Drael," Adam said. "She has the dyr again."

No one bothered asking how he knew. Whenever he tried to explain how he found out things from people's dreams, it sounded like nonsense, but it always turned out to be true.

David said, "She's useless, right? Those of you who've met her say she's afraid of her own shadow. So it should be easy to get the dyr. Three different plans, each getting us out of this shit-hole. Mitigation."

No debate.

David set Adam and Erol to serving as runners in the command annex where the Destination book was kept. When they were alone, Erol guarded the door while Adam sketched all the Destinations in their target areas.

MV made transfer tokens, cursing the while. Magic was laborious for him. Ferret got the first, and Curtas the second. He was sent to scout Roth Drael, where Hibern and Erai-Yanya, used to being alone and living in a building full of cracks, talked freely. Curtas scarcely had to lurk about a day before he overheard them wondering if Arthur, Liere, and Lyren had made it to "the coast" yet. Curtas was joined by Leef in scouting the trail the shortest distance from Roth Drael to the coast.

When the famous *Berdrer* was sighted touching at Hael Morvendrion's main harbor by some retired privateers, Leef brought the news back. Didn't take a great leap to assume that Liere and Arthur would sail with Dtheldevor.

David stayed up through two nights to get transfer tokens ready while MV located a ship fast enough to chase the *Berdrer*; its captain claimed to be a trader, but MV knew a pirate when he saw one. Excellent. A pirate meant speed first of all. He cast a tight illusion over a small bag of rocks, transforming them to what looked like diamonds, and offered this reward to the captain to chase the *Berdrer*, promising a lot more where that came from.

Two

Deep Ocean North of Sartoran Continent

LIERE AND ARTHUR HAD only been in Roth Drael a day or two when Erai-Yanya received further bad news that made her look *old* as she said to Hibern, "Get them out of here. No magic. We have no idea if they're targets, but we're going to assume so right now, until we know more."

Her voice, breathy with disbelief, shadowed Liere after that, as Hibern helped the two of them pack, load on winter gear, then trek northwestward out of Roth Drael, Hibern's voice echoing in their ears, "Keep the mountains on the right, and the lake on the left, and when you pass it, you'll be in Hael Morvendrion, where you can hire horses to get to the coast." And she'd given them local coinage.

The night before they sighted the ocean, Arthur got a note from Hibern directing them to the north-facing bay, where they would find none other than the famous (some said infamous) Dtheldevor and her privateer crew awaiting them.

While Liere, Arthur, and little Lyren made their way down into Hael Morvendrion's rocky bay, Arthur said about Dtheldevor, "She's got no interest in stories or history because she's been too busy living them."

"I know!" Liere said. "We heard stories about her all the

time." Most parents disapproved of Dtheldevor tales, her father especially, which had just made them more interesting.

Arthur said, "You have to remember she was born a pirate. She took over her father's ship when he met a pirate's end, and at a real young age. This was a year or two before she did the Child Spell. She stopped sailing against merchants and went against the ships supplying the Norsundrian ally holding Wnelder Vee in those days."

"So she's a girl and yet not a girl," Liere said, a subject she had been contemplating as the Child Spell held her body firmly where she wanted it: the way she'd been at twelve.

And yet her mind wasn't twelve in so many ways. In others, it was.

Out on the wintry, greenish-gray water a rowboat headed toward the low breakers, and Lyren hopped on her toes, watching seabirds wheel and dive as Arthur's breath steamed. "Senrid says Dtheldevor's great to have at your back in a fight. All those years of practice with her rapier has made her fast and formidable, and she was always fearless. Fearless, and reckless, she and her crew."

Liere got to what interested her most. "The Mearsieans told me once she has a centaur on her crew."

"Yes, and a dawnsinger. She's loud about her prejudices, which can be counted on two fingers: Norsunder and adults. She makes an exception for her first mate, Carsen, who sailed with her as a boy off the wharves, went away, grew old, then came back recently. The other adult is Lilith the Guardian, who put wards on her hideout island that Norsunder has never been able to break."

The rowboat splashed up on shore, and Liere and Arthur climbed into the sternsheets. A pair of teens pushed them back into the water and began to row. Liere clutched the sides, hating the rocking and splashing. Once they got to the deeps, she tried not to look below the surface of the water. She could sense curious mers down there, and remembered all the warning stories about people who fell into the sea never coming up again.

But she and Arthur got on board with no problems, and Dtheldevor's privateers, used to taking on youngsters on the Wander as crew, were easy to get along with.

Liere, who had loved sailing with Captain Hereford, happily settled into ship life—until the night she woke with a gasp, the grip of the dream so real she still saw Roy's mottled face, his angry eyes boring into hers as he shouted, "Run!"

She wasn't aware she'd made a noise until Arthur's whisper came out of the thick darkness, "Liere?"

Liere's head swam dizzily. She clutched at the bedclothes, then remembered she was swinging in a hammock, and the chaotic horror of dizziness resolved into order and sense, the back-and-forth of her hammock countered gently by the rolling swell beneath the ship.

She steadied herself, breathing with the motion.

Liere reviewed all that she had learned, cherishing each fact as she breathed in the aromas of wet wood and brine and hemprope.

She remembered was on the schooner *Berdrer*, a three-masted ship, though smaller than trysails and raffees, but like them built for speed. She'd learned that it was gaff-rigged, with a square topsail. Its captain was Dtheldevor, who was no legend, but a real person.

Every detail loosened the hold of the dream.

"Liere?" Arthur said again. From the sound, he was sitting in his hammock.

"Bad dream," she said. "I think."

A brief silence ensued, during which he reflected on how Liere was the only one who would say "I think" after admitting to a bad dream, and for reasons few would guess. He waited to see if she'd add anything as she listened to the wash-splash of water against the hull, the patter of footsteps on the deck overhead, and the creak of timbers from somewhere.

Presently Arthur gave up. He muttered a spell and a tiny snaplight glowed, its weak blue-white glimmer throwing his face and pale, tousled hair into high relief as he looked around to see if they were alone.

Except for the hammock on Liere's other side, where little Lyren slumbered in a welter of blankets, the rest of the hammocks swung empty, so he said, "Light," and made the two-fingered gesture that caused the glow-globe swinging overhead to illuminate the narrow cabin.

Liere shut her eyes to orient herself firmly before she sorted the memory-roots from the nightmare, then opened her eyes, and found Arthur waiting patiently for an answer. "I don't know if it was actually Roy or only my fear of him coming to attack us. He was suddenly there in my dream, and yelled *run*.

It might only be me . . ."She waved a hand, trying to find the words.

Arthur said, "I think I get it. It's somehow so much worse that we thought he was a friend, but he was only faking it. He keeps showing up in my dreams, too. As soon as I see him, I throw spells at him."

Arthur's lip curled with resentment, which Liere found unsettling. In all the time she'd known Arthur, she'd seen him in every mood but she hadn't thought he had wrath in him. Until now.

One thing she was sure of, it hurt so much worse to be betrayed by a friend than by a stranger.

"It might be a real threat," Liere said, hating each word, as if speaking it made it true. "It's just that the dyr makes everything so very intense, and it also makes it easier to walk in my dreams to others' dreams. Though I wasn't doing that."

"Well, if you wandered into his dreams, it makes no sense for him to warn you, unless it's a taunt," Arthur said. "For that matter, was he saying it to *you*?"

"Yes."

Arthur thumped one fist lightly on his knee as the lamp swung overhead. "Run, so they can chase us? Or run, to reveal our hiding place? If they really are hunting us, we still don't know if they can somehow trace the dyr. Even after all the test spells Erai-Yanya tried."

Liere nodded. Her magic lessons with the dyr had proved to be even more of a disaster. The dyr seemed to draw elementary magic spells into it like ink poured into water. Or maybe oil. Not quite part of it, but useless and smeared. Its properties made emotions loud and distinct, and distorted distance. Liere could feel that the dyr required some kind of . . .structure, but how do you make structure without physical tools, or even words?

The only comfort she had was that Erai-Yanya had been working with the dyr for nearly a year without anyone evil showing up to demand it. So she didn't *think* it was warded to lure Norsundrians. But she didn't *know*.

"What can we do?" Liere asked. "We can't transfer. We're too far from land to swim."

Arthur wanted very badly to sink back into his hammock. His eyelids itched with the need to sleep, after his having stayed up late writing letters. He longed for Liere to dismiss her nightmare as nonsense, but she kept rubbing the dyr over her dry palm, scratch, scratch, scratch, and she stared down at it as if it would give her an answer. He knew if he tried to sleep that scratching sound would drive him mad—already it made him restless. It wasn't a loud sound. Like a baby's cry. Taken alone, there were worse sounds, but these kindled a need to do something at once.

How he'd come to hate that dyr. Whatever use the thing had been four thousand years before, it was useless now. "Let's see if anyone's awake," he said, flipping out of the hammock.

The hatch contained a cleaning frame, which snapped away the physical frowziness, even if it didn't clear tried brains. They scrambled up the ladder to the slightly curving flush deck, into cool air.

Liere breathed deeply. Over the past week, each day had brought them into significantly warmer weather, though she knew that autumn was ending in the south, bringing the cold of winter. Above them, the sky pressed low, the underbellies of thick clouds highlighted with weak blue light from the smeary orange-purple in the east.

Dtheldevor stood next to grizzled old Carsen, the single adult crewmember. He leaned on the wheel, gnarled hands dangling as he squinted up at the set of the sails. Dtheldevor peered aft through her glass.

Diana of the Mearsieans swung down to the deck after reefing a sail. It still surprised Liere to see dark-skinned Diana away from that tight-knit group of girls. Diana never said why she was sailing apart from the other Mearsieans, and Liere didn't quite dare ask.

Sharly, the centaur, had a deer-like body, covered with red-brown spots against white. Her hair was red-brown, and she trotted easily along the deck, her hooves making a dainty click click sound that delighted Liere, and so enraptured little Lyren on first meeting that the toddler had insisted on riding Sharly. The centaur hadn't minded at all.

She approached Liere and Arthur. "Storm is coming," she said to them, as far in the north a purple glare flickered. "Wind's going to freshen."

Dtheldevor lowered her glass and thumped it closed against her palm. "You two's up fer some reason?"

Arthur turned to Liere. "Tell her."

Liere ducked her head, afraid that she was utterly wrong,

stupid, jumping at shadows. Afraid, but not certain, so she got the words out as quickly as she could.

Dtheldevor turned her head, the lurid dawn light glowing on the side of her tilted eyes and weather-browned face, striking a ruddy pinpoint of light along the golden hoop of the earring peeking from under one of her long, glossy black braids. Dtheldevor cared nothing for fashions, and never wore shoes, but she was very proud of her knee-length hair like a river of black silk with ruddy highlights. She'd bound it up in a coronet of braids, which meant she was expecting action.

As soon as Liere finished talking, she said, "By damn, we been running through the night since that there raffee hove hull down on the horizon last night. And, see, it's still there."

"It's chasing us?" Liere asked, terror clawing at her throat. "Is it Norsunder?"

"Well, now, dunno 'bout that," Dtheldevor said, her Dock Talk accent strong. "This here is what you can call a road, that is, where anyone goin' for the strait begins the curve round Nathur an' Llynthur, and so you might see any number o' ships hull down on the horizon. Or hull up." At their twin puzzled looks, she said, "Closer. That raffee, they's rigged for chases, see? I call that pirate-riggin'. And so, I been drivin' us hard, in hopes a catchin' the last gasp of the summer winds afore they die down for winter."

"How do we know if they are chasing us?" Arthur asked, peering northward, where a blot could barely be made out against the dark gray of sky and sea.

"We don't, 'less we haul wind an' wait on 'em to come up alongside."

"Not if it's *them*," Liere said.

"Here's what I'm thinkin'," Dtheldevor said. "'less you really want to be on the other side o' Drael, why don't you take the cutter on west t' the Mearsieans? Ain't you friends with them?"

"Won't they see us from that other ship?" Liere asked.

"Not if we wait till that there storm hits. We won't see ten paces," Dtheldevor predicted. "It'll be a mite touchy t' get ya over the side, but we'll manage. I'll send one a the Warrens with ya, and if Diana wants t'go home, she can go, and between the four of ya, you'll get there two, three weeks, tack on tack. We got plenty o' stores, and if ya need, the Delfin Islands is right on yer way. Got friends there. They'll treat ya good, and they won't sell off me cutter. Meantime . . ." She laughed heartily as she flipped up the back of her hand rudely toward that ship in the north. "I'll give them a chase t' remember."

Liere looked around, oppressed by an eddy of mimosa carried off the distant shore: the smell, once so pleasant, always threw her back to her time as Detlev's prisoner on Geth-deles.

The skin between her shoulder blades crawled, and she said to Arthur, "I think we should do it."

Arthur looked back, his tired eyes serious. "So do I."

Dtheldevor said to Sharly, "Let's turn up all hands. Soon's the first rains hit, get the cutter over the side. Stock it, eh?"

Sharly trotted toward the broad steps someone had built so that she could get down to the waist, and she disappeared belowdeck as she called to the sleeping watch, "All hands! All hands!"

Liere ran to the ladder to get hers and Lyren's things together, Arthur on her heels to collect all his study materials.

On coming back up, it was to find the curtain of rain approaching, big fat drops splatting on sails, deck, rigging, and crew. Diana was there, helping to get the cutter onto the booms for swinging over the side.

The rest of the day disintegrated into a maelstrom of wet, howling wind, and tossing waves. Lyren was delighted, Liere terrified for two. But the three of them were bundled safely into the cutter, which rose on a wave almost flush to the bigger ship's deck.

They scrambled below, into the little cabin to shiver and drip, as Diana the Mearsiean leaned into the tiller, and Joey Warren, a lithe teenage boy almost as dark as Diana, wrestled the thundering sail taut, whereupon the wind seemed to lift the craft almost out of the water before it plunged down again. Liere peered out from time to time, her terror held in check by the sight of Diana standing at the tiller, feet spread in a strong stance, two thrumming ropes aiding her in keeping the cutter with the wind driving them.

Liere gazed at her, scarcely blinking, as if to shift her sight away might somehow cause them to founder. As she watched Diana grinning into the storm, she wondered what had happened to break the magic circle of the Mearsiean girls' gang, a circle she had longed to join until she understood it was unbreakable.

Just before nightfall the last of the storm vanished into the east, leaving a restless sea full of frothing whiteheads and no ships anywhere in view. They began the arduous task of tacking in zigzags in the direction of the continent of Toar.

Behind them, the *Berdrer* ran before the wind, sails drum-tight, masts taut. Dtheldevor stood at the wheel herself, the ship's vibration under her bare feet guiding her as she pushed the ship to the brink: if one sail split, or a spar broke, they might broach to in the massive waves, which would sink them instantly.

She lived for this kind of thrill. Every subtle alteration in wind, sea, and the color and smell of the air streamed through her. She spared a sympathetic thought for that poor shadow-ridden Liere, first of those who had begun to change the world out of all recognizing. There was nothing Dtheldevor could do against mysterious mind powers, but this kind of run? Ah, this she understood.

The sun had long since sunk behind them when the last of the storm eddied around them and whirled away toward the south, dwindling to a rainstorm striking the Brennish headland. Under the emerging stars she pulled out her glass, and carefully scanned the horizon. The chase was gone, or hull down beyond the horizon, which was far enough away for her to catch a snooze.

She turned the wheel over to old Carsen, who had taken a caulk, as sailors called a quick nap, in the lifeboat, once it looked as if the storm was going to break up.

"Day watch to the hammocks," Dtheldevor said to the ragged, red-eyed crew.

They were too tired to cheer. They racked their weapons in the locker and shambled below. Carsen tucked his cutlass into its place in the binnacle. He always felt better with it by.

By midnight the wind had died down enough for Carsen to tell the exhausted night watch (who had spent all day on deck with everyone else) to reef all sail except one, and catch some rest. He'd finish the watch on his own.

They all knew Dtheldevor didn't like one person on night watch, but they were exhausted, Carsen was her oldest friend, and the wind and water were calming into a peaceful, star-strewn night. So they stretched out or curled up on folded sail or coiled ropes, falling asleep the moment they laid their heads down.

Carsen leaned at the helm, gazing forward at the distant

stars. He, too, was tired, but he refused to acknowledge it: he wasn't getting old, wasn't getting past it. He had plenty of good years left in him, yes he did. These aches and pains that catch behind the ribs on his left side, eh, pretend they ain't there and they'll stop yammering.

The soft slapping of water against the hull, the whisper of wind through the rigging, the steady silken breeze, smelling of salt, that buffeted his weathered face, all lulled him into reverie—as three figures clambered silently up the aft tumble-home.

Three

BEFORE THE ROWBOAT SPLASHED down from the raffee chasing Dtheldevor's ship, MV thoughtfully renewed the illusion over the false diamonds so it would last past their return to Norsunder Base, then he jumped down after the other two of his team, and cast an illusion over the rowboat.

They'd become expert rowers during their time on Geth, pulling fast and silent toward the three-master, then quietly shipped their oars when they reached its stern.

MV, Rolfin, and Laban climbed over the *Berdrer's* taffrail, to see a sparse-haired geezer leaning half-asleep on the wheel. MV cast an approving gaze at the ship's well-tended ropes, the exact set of sail.

He would have liked to poke around, but Laban, who loathed ship travel and wanted this over with, went up to Carsen and said, "Where's Liere?"

Carsen snorted awake and whipped around, his hand scrabbling for the hilt of his cutlass. "Who're you?" he demanded, looping a brace-rope over a spoke of the helm's wheel as he hefted the sword.

MV started toward the hatch.

Pirates, Carsen thought, and charged him.

MV pulled two of his knives, and grinned.

Playing with sharpened steel is a game for the young,

Carsen thought as he and the young pirate exchanged blows. This young pirate was very fast. Very skilled. And he wasn't even breathing hard.

That whining pain in Carsen's side howled for attention. Carsen's breath wheezed, his hand began to sweat, and the sword's hilt slipped in his fingers. MV's knife slid over a bad block and sliced along his ribs, a cut Carsen barely noticed because he couldn't lift his arm. His entire left side was on fire and he couldn't breathe.

"No," Carsen gasped, the deck rising gently to meet his face.

"Ah, shit." MV backed away.

Down below, Dtheldevor, deep in sleep, registered the thump of feet on the deck in no sail-tending pattern. She whirled out of her hammock, grabbing up a sword from the rack beside the cabin door as she plunged outside and took Sharly's steps four at a time.

She spotted Carsen lying aft in the pool of light made by the helm lamp, blood on his shirt, his old face slack, starlight glittering in his sightless eyes. Her mind numbed. Defeat—grief—had become alien emotions, shut away long ago, locked unseen in her heart after her father met his end.

She spotted MV with the two knives and charged him, her emotions crystalized into the desire to kill.

It was a death-dance of superlative skill, a rare treat for them all; neither MV nor Dtheldevor often got to fight an enemy worthy of their steel. They were close enough in size (she was shorter than he by three fingers' thickness or so, true, but still she was taller than either Laban or Rolfin) and built more or less alike.

Whang! Stamp. As the sleep-sodden crew on deck woke, shaking heads, Rolfin stepped up on guard.

Laban slipped below and began a fast search.

On deck MV laughed hoarsely from sheer pleasure, then said, "Where's Liere?"

"Eat shit and die."

Damn she was good! MV feinted twice, then whirled in. Dtheldevor blocked him hard enough to raise sparks, then lunged in a furious attack, causing him to back up two, three steps.

She knew several tricks that he didn't, calling forth exclamations of surprise, and the occasional laugh. Once she very nearly disarmed him; if he'd been slightly less quick and she slightly stronger, his blade would have flown but even so he slammed back against the taffrail—jeered lustily by Rolfin as he fended off one of the wakened crew now trying to brain him with a belaying pin. The other girl ran for the weapons locker.

"Time to move," Rolfin called.

Dtheldevor grunted with a last effort to ram her sword through the murderer's heart but she had fought night and day all through that storm. As her rage cooled and tiredness leeched away her fury, she saw that he was holding back. Watching for . . .?

Laban appeared topside, chased by rousing crew, and held out his empty hands as he ran.

"Damn," MV said. "So she *was* here."

Searching for Liere! Dtheldevor couldn't resist. "*Long gone.*"

There was no withdrawing unnoticed, and they'd lost the trail.

When Dtheldevor gathered her strength for a last wild lunge MV shifted with blinding speed to the attack, and then, with a move that she'd never seen, used the knives in a whirling bind that wrenched the blade from her sweaty fingers and sent it skidding down the deck.

She gazed after it in bellows-breathing astonishment. "Well, shit *fire*, I never seen *that* move," she exclaimed—promptly convulsing the three boys.

Laban and Rolfin held up their transfer tokens, then vanished. Still laughing, MV gave in to impulse. He used the token that had been meant for Liere, clamped a hand on Dtheldevor's arm, and dark magic wrenched them both out of the world, to Norsunder Base. . .

. . .where a short time later David, frustrated at his total lack of success in gleaning any useful clues about what coast CJ of the Mearsieans had been on when encountering Kessler Sonscarna, glared at MV.

"Don't give me that look," MV warned. "You said you were going after the blood mage text."

"I had a trail," David said. "I thought. Adam heard CJ of the Mearsieans tell the Sarendan girl that Dejain sent her by magic to the coast of Roth Drael. Kessler was *there*. Lone tower. No other inhabitants. Impossible to miss, right? I was up and down that coast. No towers that aren't in the middle of fortresses or cities. I'm beginning to think it was all illusion, Kessler Sonscarna playing with Dejain." He sighed. "You took a prisoner? Why?"

MV said with a shrug, "She knows where Liere is."

"She knew where she *was*," David corrected. "She could have put Liere off in a boat anywhere. And the only prisoners we were agreed on were Kessler, and maybe Liere, if she has that dyr."

MV shrugged again. "Dtheldevor's fast. Good with her hands. Wouldn't it be fun to turn her, and send her back against 'em?"

"How long is it going to take to do that? Especially when she thinks you just did for the old man."

"But I didn't! I backed off as soon as he started wheezing. Barely a scrape." MV touched his ribs.

Rolfin spoke up from the background. "That's right. Whatever dropped him wasn't MV."

They were talking in the end room, directly over the stable, quarters given the lowest of the low. The stink of manure made the eternal dust even heavier, the stench and dust scarcely lessened by the bitter air of impending winter.

David sighed again. MV was the best of them at carrying out plans, but he was no planner.

"So we'll leave her for Detlev." Laban shrugged.

David jerked his thumb toward the door. "And we've got our search to begin again."

Dtheldevor expected that being a prisoner at Norsunder Base would be bad, and it was.

The first time her cell door opened, she launched straight from the ground into the woman who'd come down to get a look at the famous Dtheldevor. The nose-poke's glimpse was of a dark blur, then stars as she sustained the head-butt of a lifetime.

But that was the last good blow Dtheldevor got in, because the woman's cronies crowded in behind, peeled Dtheldevor off, threw her into the opposite wall, and slammed the door.

The woman took a great deal of chaffing, which caused word to spread faster. Dtheldevor's next visitor—the duty guard decided to leave her in there a day or two without food or water—was a party of Henerek's favorites, restless while waiting for transfer.

They'd seen Detlev's babies around, and the idea that these idiots had the brass to take prisoners was considered an instant invitation to make the hierarchy very clear.

And the best way to make it clear was to take apart their prisoner bit by bit.

The leader of this lynch mob, who'd been the lifelong victim of a sister as vain as she was vicious, had the bright idea of starting the fun by cutting off those long shiny braids, after which (of course their victim would collapse sobbing and begging) they would start in with fingers and toes, then see where inspiration took them.

It took all five of them to hold Dtheldevor down, and the ringleader, sniggering with anticipation, had just triumphantly sawed off the second braid when Erol—silently drifting around—overheard laughing duty guards commenting on the commotion echoing up the stone corridor from the cells, and he ran to get the others.

MV and David knew that their prestige was at stake. They roused Rolfin and Leef, the two strongest, and the four took off for the dungeon, to discover their prisoner trying her best to heave off those holding her down so that the smirking ringleader could taunt her with his knife.

But she hadn't been cooperating. Sawing off her braids had just made her angrier.

MV slammed open the cell door, and ripped his blades across the ringleader's ears as David said, "That's Detlev's prisoner."

The ringleader turned on him, knife out. A short, vicious exchange took place, during which the advantage of two knives was witnessed bloodily by all, and when he staggered out into the hall, hands clapped to his ears, MV grinned. "Who's next?"

The others might have interfered had they not been busy stepping on Dtheldevor, who had never stopped thrashing about. The nearest, his boot grinding into her shoulder, commented, "Detlev isn't here."

"I'll be sure to mention you wanted him to visit you in specific as soon as he shows up," David retorted.

The big foot lifted, and the lynch party retreated, collecting their ringleader to take him to the lazaretto.

By then Dtheldevor had struggled up from the floor, and readied to attack with her bare hands. To her there was no difference between any of them. But MV slammed the door in her face. With a pulse of regret, as he respected anyone who put in that much resistance. He had no idea what to say to mitigate what he now knew was a stupid idea, so he said nothing.

As soon as the four reached the end of the corridor, David said, "You're going to have to guard her."

MV had already figured that out. Everyone knew the duty guards didn't care what happened to the prisoners beyond basic food and water, unless given specific instructions.

MV said, "And those wolf turds are going to be looking for a dust-up."

"Yes. So we go around in threes, fours with Noser."

Mentally they braced for a long, grim haul, to be surprised that night by Detlev turning up. By the time he'd swept his office for wards and tracers they'd all crowded in. "Your report?" he asked.

All eyes swiveled to David as speaker.

While he related everything, down in the prison cells, Dtheldevor forced herself to sit in a corner of the bare cell, back pressed into it, knees up, hands cradled between her thighs and her stomach.

Her entire body throbbed from the beating she'd taken before the sniggerer's pals had flung her down and stepped on arms and legs. Bad as she felt, she figured worse was to come, so her plan was to fight so hard they'd kill her fast.

She was ready when the door opened once again, and a couple of huge guards entered. Once again she launched at them, but they were expecting her attack. A sidestep, a grab at her arms, a lift, and she found it much harder to fight while her feet dangled above the ground.

They took her out of the cell, she kicking and writhing until she was out of breath, each bruise and scrape agonizing.

The silent guards let her loose in an office — desk, chair, window — and slammed the door shut. She heard the thump of shoulders outside the door.

She limped to the window, to see a pair of sentries outside, and a slice of a busy courtyard beyond. No escape here, at least not now.

She turned her attention to the desk. Bare. She limped to the other side, found drawers, and looked through them. Ink, paper, pens, and a letter opener!

This was no knife — scarcely sharp enough to slit seals — but it was better than nothing. She slid it up her sleeve moments before noise outside the door indicated someone coming.

She hopped around to the other side of the desk, wincing at every step, as the door opened, and Detlev entered, threw down the latest collection from the dispatch desk, and sat on the chair.

"What is that," he asked, "an old schooner you're running now?"

Dtheldevor gaped in surprise.

"Where'd you get it?" Detlev continued.

"Took it offa some pirates tryin' to start up the Brotherhood of Blood again, down offa Mardgar," she said, seeing no reason to lie.

Detlev said, "They never seem to give up, do they?"

Nonplussed—thirsty, hungry from no food for what seemed an eternity—aching in every bone and muscle, she said, "I'll be gut-stabbed an' blasted before I tell you anything."

"Right," Detlev said, and started looking through the papers.

"Damn and blast it," she exclaimed, furious. "Why'd you sic your bully-boys onta me ship, so's they killt Carsen, me oldest friend?"

"I didn't. This is their exercise. A learning experience. Your Carsen died, I believe you'll discover, from heart-failure," Detlev said, and he returned to reading.

Dtheldevor swayed, and because she knew she hadn't much strength left, but a clear duty before her, sidled slowly, one hand reaching for the other sleeve . . .

Without taking his eyes off the paper he was reading, Detlev said, "Put the letter-opener down."

Dtheldevor clapped her hands to her head, the letter-opener clattering to the stone floor. "Keep outa me mind!"

"It's difficult to avoid your thoughts. You're as loud on the mental plane as you are in person," he said, and continued looking rapidly through the reports, as news of his presence burned through the entire Base.

Dtheldevor stood there, waiting for . . .something, but Detlev only read through the papers until he reached the last one. Then he gazed reflectively at the opposite wall, and in another wing, two stories down, the ringleader of the would-be lynch mob screamed and fell to his knees, blood coming out of his nose as his cronies backed away, looking around wildly.

Detlev blinked a couple times before saying to Dtheldevor, "Since you are here, we'll keep you as leverage. But I believe we've sufficiently established your custody."

He glanced at the door, and it opened by a rough hand.

Dtheldevor kept her hands over her ears, as if that would shield her mind. The duty guards took her away, and once she was out of sight, David returned.

Detlev said, "I must return to Five. Carry on."

He vanished, leaving David with the reports.

Meanwhile, Dtheldevor was muscled back to the prisoner cells, but this time shut into one with a cot, and a jug of water sitting on the floor next to it. A meal (leftovers from the mess hall, slopped together into a bowl) arrived a short time later, and the door clanged shut.

Four

Marladath (Twelfthmonth), 4746 AF
Eidervaen, capital of Sartor

REL ENTERED THE ROYAL palace, sensing a subtle difference as one of the pages politely led him upstairs to Atan's private dining room. He saw three places set, and, knowing that Atan's morvende friends were deep in their geliath with Atan's cousin Julian, wondered who their third would be.

Atan joined him almost at once, a smile transforming her long face when she saw him.

His smile faded first, and she said, "Something amiss? I thought your guard friends would be happy to get a little space back, even if I can't yet restore them to the old quarters in First District. I know the guilds will be delighted not to have to be paying for shop guards, come New Year's Week."

Rel said, "Word on the street is, they hope the guilds will remember to lower prices as they promised, if they no longer have to hire guild guards to patrol their shops."

Atan said, "The guild chiefs all know that they will be summoned to Star Chamber to report, come second-month."

"That'll please 'em." Rel made a wry face. "But they all seem to think I'm responsible for the new expansion of the city guard, when I had nothing to do with it. You'd already faced down the high council before I got here."

"They don't need to know that," Atan said, hugging her elbows against her as she sat down. "The guard feels you belong to them. Let them give you credit, if it raises their spirits. For too long they've been taking the blame for losing the war when the mages are just as culpable."

"There's something else that bothers me more," Rel said. "Mendaen won't believe me when I tell him that I had nothing to do with that letter about his father's shipwreck a century ago, after Sartor vanished. I put in queries in Mardgar, and Remalna, and the port at Ela. I've never been to Sles Adran."

Atan leaned forward, the candlelight running in a golden fire down the braiding edging her brocade overdress, and gleaming in the rich violet folds. "I wish you'd told me. I could have put out requests so you wouldn't have to search."

"But it was easy for me because I could stop at scribe archives on the road. Actually, he didn't ask me. Hannla did," he said, referring to his fellow Rescuer, who worked at her the family restaurant and pleasure house. "None of them wanted to burden you with it, or risk the search becoming political. You know how the high council would have reacted had they'd known."

Atan gritted her teeth, then gave her head a shake. "If you didn't, who did?"

"That's what gripes me," Rel admitted. "The only person who knew I was asking about Mendaen's father was poor Karhin, who had said she'd try to help, but she apologized to me for letting the search lapse, due to her workload, about the time Mendaen got his letter. Oh, and Adam. He was with me when I made those initial inquiries."

"Adam! That painter, the one they say is part of Detlev's pack of assassins?"

"The very one."

Atan fingered one of her coiled braids, then dropped her hand. "I still find that so difficult to believe. He seemed like a typical artist. Wouldn't be able to defend himself against a mouse, much less attack people."

"So I thought at well," Rel said grimly. "And I traveled with him for months. Never got a hint of anything sinister, but then you'd expect a spy trained by Detlev to be really good."

"But—supposing it was Adam who made the request— what could Norsunder possibly get out of discovering that

Mendaen's father had survived a shipwreck ninety years ago, and started a new family on the other side of the Sartoran Sea, becoming a saddler?"

"None. You'd think. But Tsauderei keeps saying that Detlev makes long plans. Very long. And I remember Senrid telling us how Detlev threatened him once, saying that he wasn't worth his time yet, and he'd come for him someday. That sort of threat indicates long planning, doesn't it?"

Atan set down her goblet. "When you put it that way, what seemed a generous gesture becomes . . .ominously personal."

"Personal," Rel repeated as the door opened. "Like the attack on Karhin."

Tall, gaunt Tsauderei walked in, his snowy beard swaying with his fine robe. "Attack on Karhin?" he repeated. "Is this related to the news about Liere?"

The two dark heads turned toward him, Rel and Atan saying in unison, "What?"

Tsauderei lowered himself carefully into the third chair. At first glance they seemed so incongruous: Rel, tall and striking on the verge of manhood, dressed in worn old riding garments; Atan, exquisitely gowned, her plain brown hair elaborately dressed. No one would ever call her beautiful, but stamped into her bones as firmly as a goldsmith's mark were the distinctive Landis features.

"So you haven't heard? Those boys of Detlev's apparently attacked Dtheldevor's ship. One of her crew dead. And Dtheldevor vanished with them after they ascertained that Liere was not on board."

"Why would anyone chase poor Liere?" Atan asked. "She has no political position, and she can't master the simplest magical spell."

"Revenge?" Rel asked. "Is Siamis involved?"

"I know no more now than I did last summer," Tsauderei said with an exasperated sigh. "In spite of a great deal of effort. But. I am off to Roth Drael for a meeting about these and other matters, specifically a treaty — or truce — with the Venn, which Oalthoreh has negotiated."

Atan paused in the act of spooning rice balls onto her plate. "Something's happened."

Tsauderei placed his hands on the table, as if to steady himself. "Yes. A week ago word reached me that the heralds, in cataloguing the former king's possessions in Colend, discovered that the something called the Lirendi Diamond was missing. Nothing else."

"And so his murder was by a thief?"

"A thief who seems to have netted the Arrow."

Atan shook her head. "Wait, that's the name of the Venn magical enchantment, right? How could it possibly be in Colend?"

"I doubt I will ever get similar cooperation from the Colendi regency council again, but they were desperate enough to discover who had murdered their king to permit a couple of senior mages into their records. They traced the thing all the way back to Martande Lirendi, who was given this diamond by an ancestor of yours, Atan. And her records led us back here, to one of the lesser archives, visited maybe once a year, usually by beginning students doing a sweep for dust and mildew."

Atan gripped her hands together tightly when she saw Tsauderei's grim expression. "Where we found a missing record. Putting everything together, including the pattern of the murders, we're fairly certain that some king or queen with sticky fingers used their royal status to filch the gem from the mages, who, apparently, held the Arrow in secret. In short, after centuries of light and dark mages scouring the north for magical arrows, real and symbolic, turns out the thing was here all along. Well, here and in Colend, worn in plain sight."

"And the missing text?"

"It's gone, but we're fairly certain it furnished a clue to the mage-killer. A very old tracer lies on those old texts, an illusion, so easy to miss. Anyone tampers with the text, the illusion captures the moment. We have a glimpse of a young man, dark hair, wearing a long black coat made of a heavy, smooth fabric they could not name. They made a sketch—distinctive face, sharp bones, wide temples—a triangular face, one herald said, with a mouth like a shark." Tsauderei sketched a ∧ shape in the air. "Using fire to destroy the text."

"That's not Siamis," Rel said.

"No." Tsauderei sighed. "Though anyone can wear black shiny fabric, Siamis is fair-haired, his features more regular. The image was too clear for him to be wearing an illusion. There would be a distortion effect, the heralds insist. They know that particular ward better than I."

Atan nodded slowly, having had during her first year on the throne had to sit through long lectures on the centuries-old layers of archival security.

Tsauderei went on. "For now I've given up pursuing Siamis in favor of finding out the identity of this possible suspect, so we can weave hard wards against him."

The old mage turned to Rel. "Tell me everything you know about Detlev's young assassins."

Roth Drael

As soon as Senrid heard via Leander that Liere had been targeted by three of Detlev's gang, he forcibly dealt with his schedule so that he could be there to hear what the world's senior mages were planning. He cared nothing for light mage grand strategies, treaties, and the like. If Detlev's gang was going after the alliance members they'd been spying on so successfully this past couple of years, it was time to do something about them.

It was barely noon in Marloven Hess. When he recovered from the transfer to Roth Drael, he found himself in standing in ochre light, the strange ruined city striped by the long shadows of trees. The setting sun had bounced not only behind him, but closer. In the north, spring was ripening toward summer.

He looked around the familiar terrace, which doubled as the city's Destination, and drew an unsteady breath. The last time he'd stood in this place had been when he and Liere had been on the run from Siamis, after she'd brought the dyr successfully out of what the light mages called the Never.

That magic had been powerful, complicated, and successful, managed by a girl barely eleven — who now could not manage the simplest spell. It's got to be the dyr, he thought as he walked up the shallow, gently curving white stone steps of the terrace, and approached the jagged, broken door that led inside Erai-Yanya's domicile.

Except that, until recently, Liere had apparently been experimenting with the thing, and she still couldn't manage elementary spells.

He heard voices inside.

"Boneribs! You here, too?" CJ of the Mearsieans appeared, long black hair flapping on her scrawny back, green skirt swinging above bare feet.

"I got a letter from Lilah in Sarendan," Senrid said. "Who

heard from her friend Deon, sailing with Dtheldevor. Liere was with them, until they got chased."

"And Carsen got killed," CJ exclaimed indignantly. "Just like Karhin! And Glenn. Who's next?"

"Liere," Senrid said sardonically. "Which is why I'm here. To find out if anyone is doing anything about Detlev's gang of assassins."

"We are, too, Clair and me," CJ exclaimed. "I mean, here to find out who's going after those creeps. We're afraid the adults are going to adult all over everything, and ignore what's important. Like, how those stinkers were spying on all us. Are they supposed to get rid of us one by one? We should get rid of them first! My vote will be to turn them all into petunias."

She jerked her thumb over her shoulder toward one of the inside rooms, some of which had partial ceilings, but had been sealed by magic centuries before.

Senrid's gaze searched among the various figures until he found tall, dark-eyed, dark-haired Hibern. Once they'd studied together every week, but since she'd stopped coming he'd scarcely seen her since that mess with the blood-text.

Senrid suspected something had died in Hibern when her idiotic family had thrown her off for something that was entirely her father's fault, but he also knew that people who had families — which he didn't — could have emotions that made no sense to anyone else.

So he said only, "Hibern. How go the studies?"

"I put my project aside for the dyr experiments, and then there was the Arrow search, and now . . ." She turned her flat palm up, a Marloven gesture, though she wore the blue robe of a mage student over her summer tunic and loose riding trousers. Senrid realized for the first time that her blue was not the dark color favored by the Sartoran mages, nor the sky blue of the northerners. She had her own distinctive shade of blue.

"Thought I'd see how far I get listening in on any plans in motion," Senrid said.

"They're going to start soon." Hibern turned her back and walked away as if they'd seen one another that morning, and not more than a year ago.

Senrid followed her to an almost complete room with two tables put together, and a variety of chairs and a bench placed around them. Erai-Yanya, her flyaway hair jumbled on the top of her head and stuck through with a quill pen, moved about stacking books and clearing space. She glanced at Senrid and CJ with the sort of distracted expression that meant they were on the periphery of her interest.

But old Tsauderei, neatly dressed in the robes that had been the fashion in his day, smiled under heavy white brows at Senrid, and gave a nod from his seat underneath a jagged crack in the ceiling above which extended a branch of a leafing tree. Senrid wondered if in autumn its leaves piled up on the ward magic, like on glass, or if they slid off.

"At least the geez isn't going to bung us out," CJ muttered out of the side of her mouth. "Where's Clair —"

The sound of an indignant older boy's voice reached them from the opposite side of the room. They spotted Clair's white hair gilt with sunset color as she stood listening to Terry of Erdrael Danara, taller now, rangy in build. His scarred face was flushed.

Neither CJ nor Senrid remembered ever seeing easy-going Terry angry. They skirted the table, catching Terry's words as they neared. ". . .Shontande's regency council wrote back. Under all the Colendi lace and flowers they told me he didn't have any time to write letters. To anyone, and they would be delighted to send an emissary to me to convey personally any message to the new king."

"He doesn't have time to *write a letter?*" CJ asked.

Terry glanced her way. "That's what they said."

Senrid snorted. "How far did your letter get?"

"I don't know. I'd already tried the notecase, but got no answer, and since it's magic, you have no idea if the spells wore out, or got compromised, or he really did get it and hasn't time, or the case got lost."

"Or they pinched it," CJ said snidely.

"Yes," Terry said. "But I know he wanted an answer. He wrote to me. By that same sigil. Responding to my letter, after Karhin died." His voice roughened as he looked down, swallowed, then he looked up. "Then I never heard from him again. So I sent Halad."

Senrid said, "What exactly happened?"

"I sent Halad with a bag of coins so he could buy fancy clothes, and say he was my royal emissary, if that's what they expect. He thinks they didn't let him much past the visitors' gate because he looks like a Chwahir. Anyway a senior herald came out with a senior scribe to take the letter, all with a parade of ceremony. They put him in some kind of side building with a lot of food. Said to wait. With an army of big, armed heralds standing around, like he was about to sneak up and start knifing people left and right. After a while the same two brought back a verbal answer, all the flowery talk, as I said before. I really hate to think that's on Shontande's orders. I *won't* think it."

CJ crossed her arms across her scrawny front. "I'd go snout out what was happening myself."

"I did," Terry said. "And the same thing happened to me, except they put me in a room made of rose colored marble, and sent a musical group of nine or ten people in to play music at me, before some duchas came in and yammered at me about how sorry she was that Shontande was not present in the royal city, and when I asked when he would return, told me that they did not know when his young majesty would desire to grace them again."

"Did you get the food, too?" Clair asked.

Terry flashed a one-sided grin, the scarred side of his face corroding. "Yup. And I have to say, it was really good."

"Then it's just as bad as the days under Creepy Carlael," CJ pronounced in disgust. "Only you didn't get a snobby, crazy king staring at you, you got a snobby duchas instead."

Terry winced, and Clair sent CJ a troubled look.

CJ scowled. "Well, he *was* creepy." She looked up. "He looked right *through* you. How about Thad?"

Terry shook his head. "I haven't been able to make myself write back to him, after the first letter, which he has not answered. I can't get past recollecting that it was I who sent Curtas to them. Thad might be too angry with me. Can't blame him."

"Did *Curtas* kill Karhin?" CJ asked, eyes round. "We've heard a bunch of different stuff."

Senrid spoke up. "I went to see Thad myself. Curtas wasn't there when it happened. He was with Thad the entire time. Bee says it was Noser, the runty one tagging after the horse-trainer Silvanas, who Adam introduced in Everon."

Terry turned an anxious face to Senrid. "How is Thad? I'd do anything if you thought it could help."

Senrid sighed. "It's bad. He was about to be sent off somewhere. Not sure what was going on, except he was leaving the scribes, and he said he couldn't bear right then to write to anyone. Said he didn't know what to say. Refused to use any of the appropriate gradations, is what he called it. I suspect that means polite fart-noise."

A short, uncomfortable silence followed this, then Erai-Yanya said, "Ah, you came!"

The four turned to see a new arrival: a stout, gray-haired older woman with a kindly face. Senrid's nerves flared hot and cold when he recognized Lilith the Guardian, with whom he'd had the strangest conversation while the alliance was on Geth-deles.

"I cannot stay long," the mage born in Ancient Sartor said. "Detlev seems to be negotiating with the Norss of Songre Silde-deles, our third world from Erhal."

"Norss?" CJ squawked, her blue eyes stark. "That sounds like Norsunder! Are they evil guys?"

"Come," Erai-Yanya broke in. "Sit down. We've fresh-baked bread, and there's fruit and cheese and citrus-punch."

People took places at the table, then Lilith said, "You have it backwards, young Mearsiean. Norss is the very much like the mage councils here, and the Gathering of Ones on Geth-deles, only it's older. Far older. Being a body dedicated to harmony and peace, the Norss move slowly, valuing consensus as part of harmonic existence. Those who opposed the Norss were Norss-en-dar, or 'Norss-not-hearing,' a term which was adopted by the Sartorans and altered into Norsunder, as something to call the enemy, in my day." She added with a brief dip into irony, "A name they subsequently adopted."

"So you, like, talk to people on other worlds all the time?" CJ mimicked holding a phone receiver to her ear — a gesture no one at that table recognized, except Lilith.

Lilith said, "Let us begin at the beginning. The universal world-gates brought humans to Erhal's seven worlds millennia ago, scattering them across time as well as geographical space. The wanderers discovered that Erhal's seven worlds supported various forms of indigenous life, but not all of which they recognized as *aware* and *communicative*, which is how we have defined human."

"Okay," CJ said, hoping the lecture wouldn't go on too long before getting to the good stuff, like how to get rid of Detlev's assassins.

Lilith, very well aware of CJ's thoughts, hid her pulse of amusement. "Some indigenous beings took care to stay unrecognized. On two worlds, others either eradicated the invaders or forced them back through the world gate. And a third set attempted to modify humans, on Songre Silde, the third world, and here on Sartorias-deles."

She paused, studying the youngsters. She had all their attention, though their expressions were so characteristic: Hibern serious, Senrid impatient, Clair thoughtful, Terry grief-stricken still.

"What you have come to call the Fall of Ancient Sartor actually involved this world and Aldau-Rayad-deles, the fifth world from Erhal."

She paused, looking down at the untasted citrus drink she cradled in her hands. Old hands — it always surprised her to see them.

Senrid was also staring at her hands. She, like Detlev and Siamis, had been young when that war happened over four thousand years ago. After he met her on Geth, Senrid had read everything he could about her. It seemed she had aged more than the others because she had appeared in the physical world a lot more, in her efforts to guide and to save.

Not written was that she'd had a daughter, before that war. She'd told him herself, when the name of that daughter had been used in a strange ruse at the worst moment of his life — one that still recurred in nightmares. He, king for less than a day, had stood on a cliff forced to watch Detlev's cruel demonstration of the meaning of power, until Senrid shouted *Erdrael!*

He still wondered while tossing and turning during nightmares about that day what would have happened if he hadn't shouted the name. That had been his first introduction to world politics. Bad as his civil war had been, there were bigger conflicts, and it seemed he'd briefly served as a game token in one of those.

Therefore, much as he esteemed Lilith the Guardian, he suspected that her presence here was no good thing.

He was half-aware that she had gone on.

". . .women, washing clothes by the riverside, were the first to make successful contact with those whose physical forms were most comfortable in water. Introduced to magic potential, those women put their emerging skills into improving quality of life. And so became the earliest mages."

"There's a lot you're skipping, right?" CJ asked. "Kyale told me there's stuff about angels."

Senrid rolled his eyes. Lilith cast him a look of amusement, and said, "Another time, perhaps. For our purposes now: when they weren't fighting each other, humans formed a loose confederation, and because humans can't do without their hierarchies, it took the form of, oh, if I use the term empire, you'll get the wrong idea. There was a queen—always a queen—but her reign was largely symbolic, though ritual was vitally important." She saw impatient shifts of posture and gazes, checked, then said, "Years fled into centuries, the early habit of war and destruction gradually giving way to fruitful existence, which included travel between the three worlds where humans flourished: Sartorias-deles, Songre Silde, and Aldau-Rayad."

"But magic transfer hurts so much."

"Magic had a much different form then," Lilith replied. "There was a great deal more of it. Indigenous magic also enhanced human potential. By the time the Sartoran polity— empire is really the wrong word in every way except geographical reach—by the time Sartor stretched round the southern half of the world, and along the coasts in the north, most people spoke mind-to-mind, and controlled the aging process from within, which meant one could take decades to age if one wished.

"They recognized the coinherence of body, mind, and spirit, which they called *Dena Yeresbeth*, 'unity of the three.' They regarded death as a translation to another existence, though exactly what that meant was debated in council, poetry, and art."

So far, the adults knew all that, and waited patiently. But Tsauderei's attention sharpened as Lilith went on, "They were still human, so not everyone was equally happy or tranquil. As their abilities were enhanced, so too were their healers. Those healers trained to use dyra—aids to healing—were called *dyranarya*."

"But those things are gone, right?"

"Correct." Lilith glanced down. "And there is only one dyranarya left: Detlev."

Erai-Yanya looked her way, and addressed the group, as if to spare Lilith pain. "You cannot truly understand the history of magic until you begin to perceive what we lost more than 4700 years ago, when Ancient Sartor fell."

Lilith turned to Senrid. "The Fall was to us a conflagration of destruction. Life — magic — nearly everything was gone, the indigenous beings withdrawn deeply. Many of the survivors on Sartorias-deles fled to the archipelagos of Geth-deles to start anew, and slowly developed a different approach to magic there. On our world, over the years since, the indigenous beings have returned to the present plane, and more slowly than that, magic, mastered in the forms you know. And there you have things as they are today."

CJ sighed. "So now Norsunder wants to attack the Norss, is that it?"

"I beg a little more patience! I'm almost done with the history lesson. In everyday life, we regard Norsunder as 'the ancient enemy,' as if those who choose that path have a single mind and motivation."

"Well, aren't they?" CJ asked, arms crossed.

"Norsunder *is* our enemy. They united nearly five thousand years ago to bring about the fall of Ancient Sartor, so the word *ancient* is not inapt. But there is a vast difference between the warriors holding Norsunder's fortress in the south, and the Host of Lords commanding them from their timeless citadel. The fortress is an ongoing threat, but until they can recover the rift magic, that threat is mostly local to Sartor. The Host of Lords appear in the world maybe once in a thousand years. Their attitudes, their plans, are not the same. That includes Detlev, whom they made their agent in the physical world."

"Okay, but if you ask me, they're all a bunch of stinkers. So, these Norss. If they aren't evil, they won't give Detlev what he wants, right?" CJ asked.

"It's not as simple as give or not give," Lilith said.

Senrid rolled his eyes, and CJ groaned. "I *hate* hearing that."

Lilith went on as if she hadn't spoken. "There is evidence that Norsunder, through Detlev, has been formulating a way to take what they need."

"Another form of rift magic," Tsauderei put in. "A way to shift armies from Beyond to world, without burning everyone up."

"That is perhaps the best definition," Lilith said. "The magic of the Norss involves time and space in ways very difficult to understand. Those who know most are not human, and have trouble expressing themselves in human speech. The descendants of humans on Songre Silde are those treating with us — including Detlev — in an effort to explain themselves. I am trying to circumvent him as best I can without a direct encounter."

Senrid's skin crawled.

"In addition," Lilith added, fingers steepled, "there are signs that Aldau-Rayad is being prepared. Some years ago Detlev established there a heavily protected base. Their next move seems to be a significant expansion."

"They're bringing out armies from Norsunder-Beyond?" Tsauderei asked.

"This is what I fear," Lilith answered. She blinked down at her cup, and drank. "Which is why I need to be there."

Senrid wondered what it was like to slip in and out of time as centuries passed. Why one would do it, when each time you came, everything would be different, and everyone you'd met at the last visit was gone? "So I take it you can't do anything about his gang of spies," he asked, and watched the expressions of those turning his way. Only Erai-Yanya looked impatient, and that was a moment's reaction.

Tsauderei said slowly, "My concern right now is the Arrow, and preventing Norsunder from forcing the Venn to their will. Our ancestors, in trying to bind the Venn against attacking their neighbors, might inadvertently have created a vast problem for their progeny."

"So what you're saying is, dealing with Detlev's boys is our problem?" Senrid asked.

Tsauderei tapped his fingers on the table. "What I'm saying is, the boys might be a diversion from these more pressing concerns."

"A diversion." Senrid sat back. That sounded just like Detlev. And further, Senrid wagered himself that Adam and the rest of them didn't regard themselves as mere diversions. They were game tokens just the same. "But their first decoy plan seems to be chasing after Liere and that dyr thing. Why did you give it to her if it paints a target on her back?" He turned his gaze to Erai-Yanya.

"There was no evidence that it drew attention," she said, her cheeks mottled with color, and Senrid recognized worry and even guilt, underscoring the fact that no one really did know much about those ancient artifacts. "The dyr didn't do anything useful. We tested it in a number of ways."

Senrid glanced at Lilith, expecting her to at least correct

Erai-Yanya, if she wasn't going to explain more about the thing that Senrid had carried for a time himself. But Lilith said nothing. But then she wasn't a *dyranarya*. Could be she didn't know herself.

"Can you find her?" CJ asked him, tapping her head.

"I could try," Senrid said. "But if Detlev is anywhere on the mental plane, he'd hear me in a heartbeat. I'm not very good at that. And Liere, who is, has stayed out of contact, so I figure it's for a reason." He turned to Clair and Hibern. "My suggestion is, we start up the alliance again, in the old way — an inside line of communication — and keep everyone apprised. Sightings reported to all. Detlev's moles spent a lot of time with some of us. There has to be a reason beyond diversion."

Lilith gave Senrid a smile and a small nod. She turned that benevolent gaze to everyone and said, "So to it." And vanished as abruptly as she'd come, one to whom time was an ever-present burden in the physical world.

Tsauderei and Erai-Yanya began talking low-voiced, the words "Venn" and "Oalthoreh" distinct.

The younger allies drew together at the other end of the table.

CJ said, "When we were there for little Darian's Name Day party, I heard Adam say something to Roy that sounded like 'firejive.' Clair says it doesn't mean anything in the languages here."

"I checked," Clair said. "And Mearsieanne told me she's never heard of it, including in the Norsunder language, which she was forced to learn during her time as their prisoner."

CJ scowled. "But on Earth — " She paused to make a spitting motion. "In the language I grew up in, there was a word, *jive*, but it was slang for a kind of music. Fire music doesn't make any sense."

"Maybe it's some kind of code," Terry said.

Senrid flashed his toothy, challenging grin. "When we corner one of them, we can always ask."

CJ grinned back, and Clair looked troubled. *I checked.* Senrid remembered that Clair had been recently superseded by her great-grandmother, which gave Clair the time for things like researching the world's languages.

Senrid's stomach clenched at the thought of one of his long-dead ancestors turning up after a long stint in Norsunder and saying, "I'll have my throne back now, thank you." Only in

Marloven Hess it was far more likely that Senrid would wake up to an assassination team, from what he'd read of his own great-grandfather.

Anyway he *did* have a much older relative waiting in Norsunder, Ivandred Montredaun-An, leading his unbeatable First Lancers . . .

He shut *that* down hard. "So what do you want to do?" he asked, turning to each.

"If they show up . . ." Terry hit a fist into his hand. "Get them first."

"What do you mean by 'get'?" Senrid asked. "Kill?"

Terry's gaze faltered, then he flushed and said grittily, "Yes. If it keeps them from murdering any more of us. So?"

Before Senrid could answer the challenge Clair said, "I think they ought to get a fair hearing. By who, and what to do about them, maybe we'll have different ideas, and I can't . . ." The others could all see her catching herself up. "I have to consult with Mearsieanne," Clair said, and Senrid watched CJ's gaze dart to the side, then upward, before her face smoothed into blandness.

A pause ensued as everyone became aware that this was the point at which someone would suggest reporting to Karhin, who would write to the alliance. Faces turned away, mouths grim.

Senrid said, "I'll let Leander know. Jilo as well." On the periphery of his vision he was aware of a flicker of attention from Tsauderei. When Senrid glanced that way, the old mage nicked his chin down in approval. Senrid turned back. "I'll also write to Thad. If he writes back, we can go from there."

"I'll write to Lilah," CJ said.

"And I to Arthur," Hibern spoke up for the first time.

Senrid said, "If any of your consultations result in a plan, you know where I am." As he walked by Hibern, he said to her, "Same to you."

She shook her head. "I'm staying out of the alliance. Trying to get ahead in my studies." She finished on a low, fierce note.

Senrid studied Hibern's wary black eyes above her tight mouth, and decided to keep his yap shut. He didn't know for certain what had caused this decision. Maybe it was the Siamis chase, or the Arrow, or any number of the world magic affairs that Erai-Yanya was clearly training her for. Maybe it was Karhin's senseless murder. But it was clear she didn't want to talk about it.

He flipped up his fingers in a salute and passed on by to the terrace, where he braced for the return transfer.

CJ watched him go, wondering what that look of his meant. She hoped he would come up with some sort of plan for smiting those lying, sneaking traitors. She knew she had trouble with grudges, and struggled hard to control them, but she found herself brooding about that snot Laban and his insulting tone way back when she'd gone on a mission of diplomacy to Everon.

She loathed all of them, but Laban was definitely the worst.

Five

CJ AND CLAIR TRANSFERRED back to Mearsies Heili. They found Mearsieanne finishing breakfast. CJ remained in the background as Clair reported the conversation.

Mearsieanne wore a fine gown of blue and soft shades of green, with embroidered clusters of tiny grapes in a pattern at the square neck and the half-sleeves. She didn't dress to flatter a figure she didn't have, but to look queenly, a style Irenne copied happily. Irenne used to be fun to do plays with, but now it seemed as if she preferred playing the role of lady in waiting, wearing all her prettiest dresses, and swanning about when petitioners and visitors came.

Just the sort of behavior that Diana hated most. And so she'd gone off sailing with Dtheldevor.

CJ backed away another step, hating how things had changed, but what could you do when there was no villain to blame? All she knew was, ever since Mearsieanne came, the girls who had been so tight were drifting in different directions.

"Detlev," Mearsieanne said in a tone of corrosive hatred. "Of course he's behind it all. I think we need to institute regular patrols, in case these assassins of his decide to make trouble here."

"Why would they make trouble here?" Clair asked. "We don't have anything they'd want, I should think."

"Why do they make trouble anywhere? Everon ceased being a place of importance even before my day, and Wnelder Vee and Imar are the same. And yet there they were, attacked by Detlev in his vicious mind control enchantments. I believe we ought to summon the governors to a council."

And as always, Clair said, "All right."

CJ backed away further; there was nothing to say now. Clair would always agree with Mearsieanne in order to keep the peace.

This is something I'll have to look into myself, CJ decided. And the person to ask (though Mearsieanne despised him) was Senrid.

CJ had not been back to Choreid Dhelerei since the terrible days she'd spent as Senrid's cousin Ndand, when Senrid's horrible uncle was still king, and Senrid busy studying dark magic. She blinked away the dazzling dots in front of her eyes, and pressed out the bee-sting feeling from lips and fingertips and toes before she registered voices, and though she knew that she wasn't necessarily in danger, she still hunched up as she looked around.

It was true, what Clair had said: the Mearsieans were on some list that enabled their transfers to bring them all the way to the Destination inside Senrid's gigantic castle, rather than forcing them out at the one outside the city walls, where you had to wait until a roving patrol got to you.

A runner in the familiar black and tan uniform poked his head in, and CJ said loudly, "I'm here to see Senrid."

A short time later she was shown to a room that seemed to have Senrid imprinted all over it: a desk and chair the size of someone short, a carved case containing maps. CJ remembered that he not only liked maps, but he'd made most of his himself, with precise detail. There were also books, and on the opposite wall, four tall, open windows through which came the sound of voices. Kids' voices. Had to be that army school of his.

She hated to look nosy, then remembered that it was a school. *How secret can that be?* She walked to the window. Being three stories up, she could see a gigantic field, with stone seats on one side, stone walls that marked off a warren of one story buildings. The voices came from beyond the field's far walls, along which she glimpsed a stone archway that led into a courtyard.

Senrid's quick step approached, and she turned. "Is that big field part of your school?"

His eyebrows shot up and he said, "It's for demonstrations and games."

CJ said, "I was just thinking it would be perfect for a giant pie fight."

"Pie fight?" Senrid repeated.

"Yes," she said. "I might not be any good with a sword, and terrible with a knife or bow, but the Art of the Flying Pie — the underhanded face-smash, or the over-hand neck-smear, or the feint-and-ear-splap — I'm the best."

"You really do that? With food?" Senrid asked.

"No, it's illusion food. It melts away pretty fast. Otherwise it would be disgusting to clean up." She snorted, off-balance. "Why is this castle so big, anyway? Did you used to have to put all your army guys in it?"

Senrid set his golden notecase down on the desk, next to a neat stack of papers. Shooting her a sarcastic grin, he said, "What? Interested in Marloven history all of a sudden? I have a roomful of records you can study — "

"Which can sit and rot," CJ retorted. "Is it? Or is it just for show?"

"Only used certain times of the year is the briefest answer," he replied. "Convocations traditionally required armsmen and liveried servants. Practicality, too, when there was politicking to be done."

"You mean dirty work," she said. "Like assassinations and executions. I remember *that* from your uncle's day."

Senrid twirled a finger in the air. "So you took me away from wrangling with the blacksmiths' guild to pass comments on my ancestors?"

CJ reddened to the ears. "I came because I want to know what you think we ought to do about Detlev's gang of villains. Mearsieanne wants to kill them on sight. She even wants us to have, like, patrols, sort of like an army. Terry wrote to Clair saying that Tahra wants them dead."

"No surprise there."

"What are we going to do?" she asked. "I think . . .I think Clair is worried," she said in a rush. "Like, what if it's Adam we see? Or Roy? Clair was *friends* with Roy. She traveled on Dtheldevor's *boat* with him. She says he even saved her life. Mearsieanne keeps saying he was a spy, and only pretending friendship, and Clair might be next on the murder list, because why would anyone possibly want to kill Karhin, who was a scribe?"

"What do you want to do?" Senrid asked, not ready to admit that he'd been wondering the same thing.

"If no one accepts my petunia plan, and I don't see why not, I guess it wouldn't work to make them so miserable they'd want to go . . ." She waved a hand.

"Back to Geth-deles, and carry out their killing there?" Senrid asked, and when CJ grimaced, shaking her head, he went on less sarcastically, "From what Dak said, there are capital warrants out against at least some of them on most of their islands." Then he paused, eyeing her. "This conversation isn't about them, it's about Clair, right?"

Her blue eyed widened. "How did you—" She flapped a hand.

Senrid walked to the window and looked out somewhere beyond the empty arena. "I'd offer to help, but we both know that Mearsieanne would take against any suggestion I made, on principle. You'll remember our brief meeting, when she looked at me as if I'd puked on her shoes. My great-grandfather, or maybe his father, made quite an impression, it seems."

CJ ground her bare toes into the floor. "Everything is . . .weird, and I know it's because of her being forced into the present from the past—losing all her world—"

Senrid's gaze flicked to her, then returned to the view through the window. She joined him, saying, "I can't talk to the girls because it feels like I'm being a traitor. And I sure can't talk to Clair, because anything I say will put her in the middle."

"What's your specific worry? Is it this talk of patrols? You fear it's going to become an army, and lead to war? That's why you're here. Talking to *me*."

CJ didn't deny it, but gazed out at the walls and roofs, and the sentries visible on the curve of the city walls far to the left. Then she made out figures in the far courtyard. Sunlight glinted on steel in one's hand. A duel? Kids? Maybe it was some kind of practice.

Senrid stared intently that way, the light falling on his profile, highlighting the emerging bones of his face so that to CJ he looked grim. His sleeves were rolled up to his elbows, and she noted the whitish pink scars round his wrists. He'd never told anyone she knew how he got those scars.

He let out a short breath. "Tell Clair that military culture doesn't happen overnight. But if she wants to help keep patrols and government apart, then let the governors organize their own people. Make it a virtue not to mix with politics. You lighters all go for virtue. If they have to swear oaths, let it be to the country and not to the queen."

"So if I suggest that to Clair, to, like, mention to Mearsie-anne, we won't end up . . ."

"Like us?" His lip curled, but his gaze returned to that far courtyard, and she wondered where he would be if she hadn't arrived and forced this interview on him. Though he could have refused.

He said to the window, "Why do you think it's taking me so long to make any improvements here? Separating power over civilians from the hereditary provincial commanders is like trying to spoon my way through rock. A warrior kingdom is organized to support the warriors, who then protect the kingdom. That's the fundament of government here. Has been since our earliest days. Marlovens despise militias, seeing them as farmers and tool workers playing warrior."

He faced her. "But from what I've been reading in outside histories, militias have their own pride, in being able to pick up weapons when they must, and down them again as soon as the threat is gone so they can get back to their real work. Work that matters—as they spout from the pinnacle of Mount Moral Superiority—that builds instead of destroys."

CJ drew in a breath. "That's it. That's what Clair and I were trying to figure out. Militia," she repeated, drawing the word out.

Senrid's expression tightened. He shook his head slightly, then turned away from the window; in that far courtyard, a bleeding figure was being carried away by other uniforms, while the opponent stood there watching.

CJ's stomach roiled. It *had* been a real duel. And she could not resist blurting out, "You *like* watching that? Your uncle sure did, I remember."

His head snapped to face her, his mouth a white line, and she stumbled back a step, blushing. "I didn't mean . . ."

"Yes, you did," he said on an outward exhale. "I don't like it. Nor do I permit it. But it's the traditional place for duels, and their traditional right. And I had to know what was happening."

So 'wrangling with the blacksmiths' guild' had been a

deflection. He'd expected to watch that alone.

CJ muttered, "Okay."

Senrid jerked his thumb toward the window. "As for Detlev's spies, if we want violence, seems to me they're ready and willing. But violence escalates fast. So the question is, do we let them act first, or do we?"

His words unnerved CJ because the last few echoed something Clair had said: *Do we let them kill another of us and then retaliate, or do we kill one of them first? And if we do, who really is the villain?*

"I'll tell Clair what you said. About a militia," she mumbled. "Thanks."

As she fingered the medallion around her neck that would transfer her safely home, she wanted badly for things to go back to the way things used to be. Back when they knew who the villains were, and fighting them was fighting evil.

Six

DEEP IN THE MIDLAND plains, Jilo was glad to see that his
family had been slowly taking stones from the hopelessly ruined part of the old way-station castle to reinforce their living
quarters. As he sat with a mug of hot boiled sweetgrass, he
listened carefully to his uncle's recounting of the weather
patterns.

Jilo felt good when he stayed away from Narad. He'd discovered that when he first visited Senrid. He would never forget that first night of sleep, and the taste of their food, such simple things, but so vital. So important. Simple, vital pleasures
denied everyone in the fortress at Narad, capital of Chwahirsland, because their lives were slowly being leached from them
to increase the power of Wan-Edhe.

It was going to take a long time to dismantle that, but
meanwhile, Jilo had discovered that when he could spend time
away his head cleared, and when his head cleared, he could
work better. Like the series of spells he had put in place while
he was away from Narad to reflect back and forth, making it
seem he was always elsewhere. In the rest of the world that
would never convince anyone past a day, but in the horrible

constraint of Narad's inner city, where time distorted so badly, it had proved to work.

Even so, he knew he must return and get back to the endless list of urgent tasks.

His Uncle Shiam sat down across from him. "Jilo, we shall observe the Great Hum for New Year's Firstday. I want you to know that."

Jilo did not try to suppress the chill those words gave him. It was not a bad chill, like threat. It felt more like pride, mixed with fear that the cause of pride would be snatched away. And yet he had seen the power in ordinary people — everyday flatfoots, and those who served the army — making quiet resistance to Wan-Edhe's poisonous laws, and life, one by one.

"I hope you do," Jilo said.

Jilo's cousin smiled as she passed through the room, and Jilo considered her smile. It wasn't surprise, it was . . .conviction? He thought of word spreading from person to person, all across the country. How Wan-Edhe would hate this unspoken but unmistakable defiance!

"I hope everybody does," Jilo said.

"And yet there is no rescinding of the law?" Uncle Shiam asked.

"I'm not a king."

Uncle Shiam leaned forward. "We see you as a king."

"People wish I was a king, because that would mean The Hate is gone. But we don't know that. So I preside over army inspections and competitions because that is the life the military understands. I continue to let the word spread that Narad will take no notice when specific laws are broken. And I work, every day — whatever that means in Narad — on breaking the poisonous magic that Wan-Edhe created."

"That," said Shiam quietly, "what makes you a king."

Jilo shook his head, hating the stuffy, hot feeling such words gave him, and turned his thoughts toward magic. At least he understood that. "I have a long way to go. The capital is still under the pull of the time and life spells. I don't think New Year's Week has any meaning in Narad yet." Jilo touched the front of his tunic. "I only notice time and seasons when I'm away. But it's getting better," he added.

Though he knew they had scarce supplies, he took a meal with them, because it was important to families to eat together. And after the meal they walked down to the basement and stood in a circle to share a small hum.

It always made his eyes prickle, though he could not say why: the deep fremitus of his uncle on one side, chanting "Hrum, hrum, hrum," and on his other his cousin Kinnit's high voice mimicking birds, insects, and wind. Behind him a discreet rattle of beads made it rain if only in their minds: purifying rain, evoking the fresh smells of moist earth, redolent of life.

Sometimes all the family was there, sometimes one or another with their twi. When he prepared to leave, he wondered if he would ever have a twi of his own — eight people in a circle of trust, more precious than mere jewels. But twis began in childhood, and grew up together.

He would always be alone, he thought as people departed quietly.

If he even lived.

When he returned to Narad, he walked to his work room to check for messages. He found one from Senrid asking if he could transfer over to visit Jilo, who answered with *I'm back.* Then Jilo fetched the enemies book and checked it, because that was invariably Senrid's first question. Nothing about Siamis or Detlev. The only mention of those boys was Norsunder Base.

There were fewer mentions altogether. He frowned at the book, wondering if someone was dismantling some of the tracer spells.

The inward pulse of magic caused him to blink: Senrid had arrived. "This place isn't quite as bad," he said, looking around the familiar gray stone. "Still bad, but I don't feel like I've got a boulder in my chest when I try to breathe." *Unless I move,* he thought. When Jilo shrugged awkwardly, he added, "What's the latest you heard?"

Jilo repeated what he'd seen in the enemies book first. Then: "Mondros writes to me regularly. It's how I hang onto time." He thought that over. "As much as that means here. Which is still, ah . . ." He waved his hand in a vague circle. "I've been going through Wan-Edhe's books one by one. I found his invasion plans."

Senrid's fair hair, bleached to straw in the glaring light of Jilo's glow-globes, glinted with what Jilo realize were drops of rain. Like crystal. Oh, to see pure rain again, not the thin, bitter wetness that fell too infrequently.

"What kind of plans?" Senrid asked.

Jilo blinked, and pointed to a set of maps and papers at the other end of the table. "Everything worked out. Army, division, brigade, down to what company goes where and does what. Everything. I think the only thing that protected Colend from its being executed was the time distortion. I believe even he was losing awareness of time."

Senrid glanced with interest at the maps, and though he did not read Chwahir, he'd seen enough military maps to guess the gist. "Plans always look good on paper," he said. "That much I've learned from my grabby ancestors." He grinned. "This is actually smart: take out the scribe and herald centers, destroy the inside line of communication, but otherwise . . ." He pushed the plans back. "What are you going to do with that?"

"I read it all. Try to understand it so that I will understand the army commanders' talk. Then burn it. Though they might have copies of these."

"Can you send out orders? What's your relationship with the army?"

"It's . . .strange," Jilo said. "There's the time distortion here, so even if they come to make trouble, it affects them. Then there was an attempt on me that got foiled. I think it scared them."

Jilo still didn't understand why Kessler had interfered, only that he had. He sighed, shoulders tight in guilt. "I've listened in on the captains from time to time, through the spy eyes, though I said I wouldn't. Wan-Edhe didn't trust anyone, especially those right around him. He has spy eyes everywhere. I demolished a few, but . . .a few I didn't. Three of the five army commanders hate me, but they know Wan-Edhe would flay anyone who took initiative."

"You don't mean that metaphorically."

"No."

"I had to ask." Senrid grimaced.

"About the army. Summer. I did something Rel suggested. I think it was a good idea," Jilo said slowly. "But . . .we all know it's temporary."

"Everything is, if you want to look at it that way." Senrid grimaced again as he turned his own transfer token over in his hands. "So here's the latest from the rest of the alliance. Not that it's much . . ."

Senrid gave a quick report, then transferred away.

Jilo got to work on his new project, which was to attempt to disassemble the horrific wards on the border that prevented specific people from ever crossing. That took tremendous power, which in turn leached life somehow from air and water and land.

But at some point he felt rather than heard a subtle thrum, and lifted his eyes from the musty page. It must be New Year's Firstday. His gaze fell on Mondros's last note, with the date underscored as always at the top: the 32nd of the twelfth month, year 4746.

Jilo did not try to count the days since. He'd eaten. He'd slept. It was silent in that huge, arid tomb of a fortress, and yet as he lifted his head he felt as if he heard a wordless sound, as if the landscape itself hummed: a weaving and thripping and undulating serry of noises that together ignited color and light, openness and air, fashioning a healing spell that had nothing to do with the hard-wrought controls of magic, and everything to do with upwelling, outflowing peace spiraling skyward to spread across the limitless stars.

It was the Great Hum, it had to be. In basements and caverns, closets and attics, twis of eight and sixteen and maybe even twenty-four gathered, no one daring the open air as in days of old because *He* might come back to smite them with fire and flaying knife. But it raced lifeward just the same—from heart to heart—with the speed of the wind. Conviction thrummed, resonating in his chest.

Did anyone in the city know what day it was? Might some be gathered in stone-protected alcoves, adding to the sound? He dared not walk out to discover; the drum beat of footsteps would shatter them into furtive, fearful singles, hiding separate and alone until the interloper safely passed.

He tipped his head back as tears burned under his eyelids and slipped down his cheeks, knowing that in the farthest reaches of the kingdom, people dared to gather and sing. After a time went to rest, rose and ate, and returned to his labors, a little lighter, easier.

Days slipped by. Then, as often happens, the worst dread will follow on the best surprise: he got some breakfast and went to check the enemies book.

As soon as he touched it, he sustained the internal poke of one of Wan-Edhe's tracer spells.

An enemy had entered the city.

Food forgotten, he ran for the enemies book and slapped it open, then stared down in horror: Arech, Wan-Edhe's torturer, had entered the city on foot. Wan-Edhe had trusted no one at all, even Arech, except in his dungeons, so he'd transferred to the border and walked in.

Jilo's mind was clear enough for him to remember his promise to Mondros. He sat down and wrote a quick note, then sent it off. Jilo had always known that this day would come, and he'd figured that Wan-Edhe would send someone ahead to clear the way before he arrived to wrest back magical control.

And he'd win. Too much of his work remained to be dismantled.

But Jilo wouldn't make it easy.

He thrust the enemies book inside his tunic and retreated to the workroom. Arech would be sent for two purposes: kill Jilo, and fetch the enemies book, so that Wan-Edhe could locate enemies before he returned.

Jilo began working through the ladder of spells he'd set up to complete if he had enough warning.

While he was doing that, Arech waited for the rest of his team to arrive, all having had to travel in the long way from the border.

And far to the south, in Sartor, Rel moved with his friends among the city guard as they took up their stations along the parade route.

Rel's spirits soared. This would be the first time he'd be able to celebrate New Year's Week in Sartor. At noon the first circle nobles would be led by Atan in silence around the Grand Chandos Way, which marked what had in ancient times been the city wall, as Eidervaen's inhabitants watched in silence, everyone carrying a candle.

"It used to be called the Twelve," Atan told him over breakfast. "At noon all the city—all Sartor—would stop what they were doing and shut their eyes and be together in the mental realm. All the histories I've read make it out to be some kind of poetic semblance of harmony. But after I learned about Dena Yeresbeth, I wonder if there really was something being shared."

Rel thought of the Chwahir Great Hum, which he had read about in histories of the Chwahir on Mondros's shelves. But he was ambivalent about mentioning the Chwahir, lest he be asked about his interest. He wasn't ready to talk about that yet to anyone—

"Rel! Where's Rel?"

A page in purple and pale rose livery dashed up, breathless. "Rel, the queen requests your attendance," the child said in a rush.

When Rel got inside the palace, where nobles milled around checking stylish hats, mittens, and warm robes, he dodged past them to the side-chamber where a couple of maids put finishing touches on Atan's elaborate winter walking outfit and her loops of braided hair. "Rel," she said. "Mondros sent a transfer token. Needs you. Jilo is in trouble."

She spun it in the air to him. He caught the metal, which was warm from her hand, as she said, with an upward twitch of her straight brows, "I do wish you would consent to carry a notecase."

"If the world would cooperate in letting me keep them," he answered, and they exchanged smiles — each regretting yet another separation, and each determined not to give voice to it — as he whispered his father's name.

As soon as Rel recovered from the transfer reaction, Mondros said, "You remember Arech."

"Wish I could forget," Rel said grimly. "He's going after Jilo?"

"Yes, and I still cannot cross the border," Mondros said. "But I can send *you* straight to the city walls."

"Let me change into my flatfoot uniform," Rel said. He was already shrugging carefully out of the fine shirt Atan had given him, having laid aside his calf-length winter tunic of fine wool.

He was shrugging his way into the dusty black Chwahir tunic when he paused. "Damn. I left my sword in Sartor."

"Take mine."

Rel followed as Mondros stumped up the ladder to the gloomy loft bedroom, plunked down the candleholder on a table and thumped to a trunk at the foot of his bed. He flung it open and rummaged under a neatly folded quilt, then — to Rel's surprise — he lifted out a splendid sheath of patterned weave, from which protruded a gracefully made hilt engraved and gem-studded. It was the weapon of a prince.

Rosey pulled the sword free and made a couple of experimental passes in the air. "Old wrists still holding out, I see," he observed.

"You never told me about that." Rel indicated the sword.

"I told the Mearsieans, long time ago," Rosey said with a

grin. "Puddlenose went through my trunk once, after I first rescued him from Wan-Edhe. The boy needed some cheering, so I told him I won it from pirates, and the next year I told him I'd stolen it from a magical statue that came alive every thousand years to fight heroes —"

"And if Puddlenose ever asks, you want me to corroborate that?" Rel asked as he did up the laces on the tunic.

"No, no, just remembering the last time I had the thing out," Mondros said hastily, as Rel shook with silent laughter. "Truth is, it came from Berthold's hand, back in the days when the queen and I fought together, right before I met your mother. Carl, Queen Mersedes Carinna, that is, was a Knight back then." His humor vanished. "And Raneseh. Good days, that vanished altogether, so I made stories that didn't end sad. Puddlenose had a terrible enough life, which he'd never asked for."

He handed sword and sheath to Rel, then his finger flickered as he cast a simple illusion over it, which dimmed down the jewels and decorations.

"What do you want me to do with Jilo?"

"Defend him. If it's just Arech, he should be able to ward him off by magic, unless Wan-Edhe has armed him with triggers to hidden spells in that damned death-trap of a fortress. Hard as Jilo works, he's not going to undo eighty years of evil while he's still learning himself."

Rel shook his head. "I'm impressed he's lasted this long."

"Everyone is," Mondros said. "This is probably an exploratory run on the part of Wan-Edhe. See who survives Arech, before he risks his accursed carcass in returning," Mondros ended fiercely, his voice guttural with loathing. "But if it's worse than that, pull Jilo out. If he balks, use this." Mondros had two transfer tokens waiting. Considering how long it took to make these, he must have planned for such an eventuality a while ago.

Rel nicked his chin down in a nod. They'd always known Wan-Edhe would return, a prospect that would spread misery everywhere. It was hard to believe in justice at such moments.

So, Rel thought as transfer magic began shredding him, you behaved as if it existed.

Jilo had so thoroughly expected the numerous castle guard to abandon him at the first sight of Wan-Edhe or any of his minions that when he heard the clash and clang of steel echoing down the stone corridors, he was certain they were coming to kill him first.

But when he got to the second floor and glanced out one of the moisture-frosted windows, he was astonished to discover the castle guard attacking eight newcomers. Wan-Edhe's personal guard fought viciously, but there were a lot more defenders. One by one they dropped, until Arech began running from one to another of the castle defenders, tossing something that glowed greenish when it hit the guards. Each man arced as if stabbed, then crumpled. The stink of intense dark magic rose to Jilo on the balcony as below, Arech moved from one slumped, groggy man to another and began to knife them, helped by the remaining three of Wan-Edhe's personal guard.

The castle guard backed away, swords still raised. Arech raised his head, an ugly smile creasing his thin face below his broad shiny forehead. He touched his hand to something on his black clothing, and vanished —

To reappear steps away from Jilo. Who scrambled back, throwing up an illusion as he darted into an archway. The scrape and clatter of footsteps behind meant Arech checked only long enough to test the illusion for traps, then started in pursuit.

He was maybe fifty, tall and stringy, and much stronger than Jilo. Everyone was. From below, before Jilo darted down a corridor into the warren of inner rooms, he heard fighting break out again.

As he ran, Jilo cursed himself for not thinking of magical traps for Arech the dungeon master, who he had never seen permitted upstairs in Wan-Edhe's own wing. All the traps and tracers Jilo had labored over so long were centered around Wan-Edhe.

He stopped by his room long enough to snatch up the sword lying in a corner, that he always meant to exercise with when he had time.

When he started out again, he heard another set of footsteps running along the hall. That had to be one of Wan-Edhe's personal guards, who had somehow broken past the defenders below.

Worse, as Jilo feared, Arech knew the inner warren as well

as he did. Jilo, chivvied by two pairs of running footsteps, kept twisting and turning, knowing he was being forced toward a dead end. When he reached the last corridor he turned around, bitter with despair, as Arech slowed, breathing hard, his shiny face mottled an ugly color in the grayish light of the magically enhanced torches.

And, being who he was, he could not resist toying with his prey. "Where shall I begin first?" Arech said, licking his lips with anticipation. "Wan-Edhe wants you alive, but he never said how much."

Jilo gripped the hilt of his dull-bladed practice sword in his hand —

And then the second set of footsteps arrived.

It was Rel.

Arech turned, his teeth baring in fury. He whirled again, raised his knife, which glowed with an ugly greenish edge. Blood magic, Jilo thought in despair, desperately trying to ward the blade.

But he was too tired, and too slow. Two hard beats and Jilo's blade flew from his fingers. Arech's blade slid, cold and shivery and terrible, into his shoulder.

Arech yanked the poison blade free and turned to face his opponent. Dimly Jilo watched as Rel attacked, his intent to kill —

But Arech slid his free hand into a pocket and vanished.

Jilo closed his eyes. Felt the burn of salt. Heard Rel's steady breathing. "Come, Jilo. We're going to Mondros."

"No," Jilo whispered. "I can't just leave . . ."

"Jilo, you know that wound will never heal in here."

Cold metal touched Jilo's free hand. He tried to grasp it, to get his dry mouth to move, but it seemed he didn't need to concentrate. Magic wrenched him from the world and threw him back in, where he sank unconscious to the ground.

"Arech hit him with a cursed knife, and vanished," Rel said tightly, laying aside Mondros's blade and bending to pick up Jilo's gangling form.

"That's bad." Mondros whooshed out a breath. "Very bad." He held up a hand, and when Rel paused, he patted Jilo all over. The boy moved slightly and moaned when Mondros's fingers thunked on a flat shape inside Jilo's clothes. "He's got it. At least that much is denied Wan-Edhe." Mondros sighed, shaking his head. "But cursed knife? We've never been able to do anything about the blood magic on those."

So much had changed in Rel's life that day he'd come to Jilo's aid, and discovered CJ there, marked by a bloodknife.

"You can't," Rel said. "But Kessler can."

"Kessler!" Mondros shook his head. "That's as bad as no solution."

Rel said, "CJ found him in some tower, after which she wandered lost for days somewhere west of Roth Drael."

"That covers a significant area. And he's got to have formidable protections. Assuming he's even still there."

Rel glanced down at Jilo, who had curled up on the bed.

By mutual agreement the two went downstairs, and outside. Rel said, low-voiced, "I'll go."

"You!" Mondros thrust his fingers through his beard, causing it to bristle wildly. "You don't think the boy can withstand their magical torments?"

"Not night after night. Without fail. No sleep, just dread, until you find a knife and start cutting at yourself to get that mark off you, but that does nothing because the magic is in your blood."

Mondros grimaced. "I know about the spell in theory. Haven't seen it in action."

"I have. Getting back to the point . . ." Rel still couldn't quite get out *Father.* "If Kessler wanted me dead, he's had plenty of chances."

Mondros scowled ferociously, then his heavy shoulders slumped. "How do we even contact him? All I know is half Norsunder has been hunting him."

"True. But he seems to be watching out for Jilo in some way," Rel said. "At least, he showed up that day in Jilo's defense, though that may have been only to thwart Dejain. The thing is, if there is any way to contact him, my guess it would be in that castle. Send me back. I know my way around it. I'll go sit there. See if he shows up."

Mondros glanced back at the cottage, as if he could see Jilo, then stabbed his fingers through his beard once more. "I hate this. But I'll do it, on the condition you'll use a transfer token at the first sign of betrayal. I'll have it bring you straight back to me."

Rel agreed, and so a day later — after Mondros had spent the rest of a day and a night working on one of his transfer tokens — Rel found himself wandering the stuffy, dank, dark halls of

Narad's royal fortress.

On his other adventures there it had merely been an enemy stronghold, until these last two excursions in aid of Jilo. Neither of those times he'd had time to reflect, but as he walked alone through the magical lour of the third floor, careful not to touch anything, he tried to fit himself into the context of his ancestors having grown up there.

His mother having been a girl there.

Where would she have stayed? He wouldn't bother looking. Of course there would be nothing to discover. Wan-Edhe would have destroyed any trace of anyone but himself.

How had he come to be such a monster? Had he always been —

Rel turned a corner and found himself face to face with Kessler. Despite his pompously casual words to Mondros, alarm flashed painfully through him, one hand going to his sword, the other clutching tightly to the transfer token.

Kessler uttered one of his short, humorless laughs, his blue eyes unsettlingly shaped like Atan's. Rel stepped back, though he knew it was no defense.

Kessler said, "You looking for Arech? He and the three survivors of his strike team left by magic."

"I took Jilo away," Rel said.

"I know. I've tracers all over here, and I use the spy eyes Jilo avoids." Kessler's teeth showed briefly. "Arech's appearance was a foray. Assuming Efael lets Wan-Edhe go, he'll not return here until he thinks he's perfectly safe."

"Is he?"

"Jilo has layered traps and wards all over. As it happens, few of those will disturb our respected ancestor."

Rel could not hide his shock. "You know who I am."

Kessler's eyes narrowed. "You have somewhat a look of your mother. I must have been about four. She'd learned enough magic to come for me. I saw her, down in the first courtyard there, but Arech had me in his grip, and she ran. Never came back. I'll kill him, and Wan-Edhe, both someday," Kessler added in that soft, emotionless voice. "I reserve that pleasure for myself."

Then, suddenly, he changed the subject. "You're here for an ancestral tour?"

"I'm here to find you. Arech marked Jilo with a bloodknife. You know how to remove the spell."

Kessler uttered another of those soft laughs. "Yes. And the tracer no doubt added. I'll do it, because it will anger both Arech and his master. But only if you give me the transfer token you no doubt have, with all its protections and wards to waft you safely back."

Rel suspected Mondros would be angry, but again, if Kessler wanted Jilo dead, he could have done that any time. Another thought occurred, something CJ had not seen when she'd blurted out her horror story after Dejain had forced her to serve as a target: Kessler, after a lifetime of betrayal, had an obsession about trust.

Rel moved before he could have second, and third, and fourth, thoughts. He opened his hand and disclosed the token.

Kessler took it, and began whispering.

Before Rel could frame a question, Kessler made one of those lightning-fast moves of his, struck Rel on the shoulder, and Rel found himself wrenched out of the world and thrown violently back in again.

He staggered, nearly falling over a rough-hewn table, and found himself in a room full of people. The heady aroma of beer lying over the stuffiness from too many people in an enclosed space caused him to grope for the bench he glimpsed nearby.

"Rel?"

Rel blinked up, recognizing Puddlenose of the Mearsieans, who was picking himself up off the floor. Others as well, or rubbing the backs of heads where they had been slammed against a wall. Rel breathed hard against the surge of nausea caused by the dark magic transfer spell, followed by the realization of just how dangerous it was to transfer someone into a room full of people. But it seemed no one had been killed by his violent emergence among them.

"Puddlenose?" he said witlessly. "Where am I?"

"In a wharf dive, while we wait out yon blizzard, and hope the ships out in the roads don't get smashed to splinters," Puddlenose said, indicating the windows, which were pure white. "We're in the main harbor. Delfin Islands."

Rel shook his head slowly. He was now halfway around the world from Mondros, Jilo, and their unexpected visitor. With Puddlenose, who had been a victim of Wan-Edhe, and one of Kessler's would-be assassins what seemed a lifetime ago.

This wasn't an accident, but Rel couldn't even begin to imagine what Kessler had meant by sending him here.

Then he remembered his gear lying back in Mondros's cottage. And people wondered why he never carried a golden notecase?

"Um, Rel, why are you dressed like a Chwahir flatfoot? Why are you *here?*"

"Long story."

Puddlenose dropped onto the other end of the bench, his cheerful face rueful. "Looks like we've got plenty of time to hear it."

Seven

Winter's End, 4747 AF
Two Long Chases

THE ONLY GOOD MEMORIES in Ferret's life had been among the boys, with enough to eat and a bed he could call his own. Shoes, too. But even then life had not been easy, and so he survived on the periphery, watching every detail.

Tracking Siamis stressed all his skills.

But he'd done it. The king's old wing in Colend's royal palace was empty, and would remain so until Shontande was officially crowned. No one allowed in or out. That enabled Ferret and Adam to explore minutely, drifting below the windows until Adam, using his bare fingers, felt Siamis's presence in the brush of a twig against his cheek. The touch of Siamis's fingers among the remains of broken stems where something such as a knapsack might have been set, and picked up in haste by a bare hand.

Ferret understood the cost of this strange skill of Adam's that overlaid memories on physical things, and how hard Adam worked to shut it out normally. But Adam stayed with Ferret long enough to provide a vector, then transferred back to Norsunder Base to resume his job as lowly kitchen aid and message runner in the command annex.

That vector was enough to enable Ferret to invent mild questions to put to possible witnesses, always with preternatural patience, and a face and voice soon forgotten. Where the Colendi would avoid someone exuding threat, a small boy dressed in servant gray with a story about a lost halter, or a missing cloak, or a message gone astray, prompted willing speech.

And so he hunted as autumn turned to winter: Colend to Barhoth, thence southward to Loss Arken, then abruptly northward up the Margren River, with side-jinks for no reason Ferret could understand, except maybe as deflections.

Here, a blond man seen near horses; there, a hooded cape exchanged for an old jacket and a patched scarf. In this place, nut oil for dyeing sold to the nicest young man, so fair, but he spoke of a New Year's masquerade.

Siamis had traveled fast, every day getting farther ahead, but Ferret had to watch for two targets. He had taken care to break off the twigs in the garden and to pull up the broken stems, in case the Black Knives returned again to search more thoroughly. This was to be expected when people had to travel fast without magical aid. Nobody could pass with total invisibility through the physical world, no matter how experienced they were.

Ferret had run obstacle courses while training with Siamis, so he had a sense of how long a strong young man could go before he must stop to eat, or to drink, or to rest, and at these approximations were where he would stop to begin his search — always while being on the watch that he was not shadowed.

But Ferret had to eat, and rest, too. More often.

On the edge of an utterly undistinguished small town in Bermund, called Searn, he had to rest as he was getting clumsy. He followed his training in going up with at least three separate avenues of escape, rather than down where he might be trapped.

His most prized possession was a water-resistant cloak of a soft gray that seemed to slough color. Exhausted, he swathed himself in it. With his sturdy, warm woolen tunic and trousers under it, he could sleep in comfort anywhere as long as he was not directly in falling snow or rain. He had wedged up under an eave on a roof garden to catch a much overdue short nap one night when he woke with a start, a hand clapped over his mouth.

From somewhere a faint gleam of light caught in fair hair.

"Oh, yes." Amusement lightened Siamis's voice. "Ferret, is it not? You always paid attention when I told you boys to sleep high, with a full field of vision. But you forgot the vision."

Ferret waited to find out if he would live long enough to correct the error.

"Are your orders to attack me?" Siamis asked gently.

Ferret gave his head the tiniest shake, all that the strong grip would permit.

The hand lifted. "Find and report, then?"

"Yes."

"Efael?"

"David."

"I assume then that you boys have managed to stay out of Efael's notice, in spite of your idiocy in Everon and Colend."

Ferret flushed, though he was not responsible for either of those deaths. "Detlev warned us that Efael was hunting you down." Ferret swallowed in a dry throat. "I haven't seen anyone."

"There are two of his Black Knives, actually. Well, there were. Menlas was half a day off your heels. The second should find Menlas's body tomorrow."

Ferret gave an involuntary shiver. Everyone had heard of Menlas, and what he liked to do to targets. That included anyone interfering with one of his stalks.

"You'll be free to carry on soon, but first, you are going to aid me," Siamis went on, as Ferret made subtle movements, checking his weapons and his notecase for reporting: all missing. Siamis had managed to search and disarm him before Ferret woke.

Or was permitted to waken; he understood then that Siamis had been lying in wait for someone to fall into his trap.

Ferret swallowed again. "What must I do?"

All the time Ferret had been traveling overland, the *Berdrer*'s little cutter endured a long sea journey.

The winds that had so exhilaratingly pushed the *Berdrer* ahead of the chase had been the cutter's enemy from the start. Liere and Arthur learned how to interpret every shift of the wind, every trick of rope and sail and tiller as they zigzagged endlessly back and forth, sawing against the wind as the great mass of water beneath them carried them relentlessly eastward.

They were spared boredom by a series of storms, each one successively colder, until the worst storm of all during a night that never seemed to end, with purple lightning all around, glaring on the silhouettes of a black, mountainous sea.

Lyren was tied into her hammock and told to stay. Of course she struggled mightily until Liere, frightened more than she had ever been, shot a desperate thought at her — *Lie still!* — which shocked the child into quiescence. Guilt wrung Liere, but the situation was too desperate for any more than that as she clung tightly to her part of the tiller, a rope wrapped twice around her waist.

Endlessly they endured wave after wave, Liere gasping between each dousing, flickering checks mentally on Lyren until the tears gave way at last to the deep sleep of the very young.

Liere returned to the weather deck, expending her spindly, fast-dwindling strength as they fought to keep the cutter climbing each monstrous wave. Water cascaded in monstrous black cataracts down the deck, half-submerging it. They were all tied by the waist to the mast, Diana and Joey forward, hanging on the taut boom, Liere and Arthur aft, numb, bleeding hands on the tiller, which was also tied down.

Though the continuous noise crashed about them, they could not be said to be witless with terror. Fragile skulls sheltered equally wild storms of memories, wishes, yearnings, fears. Joey, perhaps the most straightforward of the four, fought every new surge, and regarded every drop into the canyon between waves as a victory. This was not his first storm, and as far as he permitted himself to think beyond the moment, he hoped it would not be his last.

Diana struggled with regret. She had not been ready to return to Mearsies Heili, because she knew she returned to the same situation she'd left. The endless days of fun with the girls had . . .ended, when Mearsieanne returned. As her medallion clunked against her chest each time the cutter plunged down into another trough, she sometimes thought about transferring home. It was only a thought. She would not leave Joey to deal with the storm single-handed, as the other two were next to useless.

Liere did what she was told, trembling with cold and fatigue, though each was encased in magically water-resistant jackets and trousers that Dtheldevor equipped all her vessels with. She fought not the usual fears, but the nearly overwhelming temptation to cut free mentally, escape the terrifying physical plane altogether, and maybe even explore the strange mind-lights below the surface of the water, so very different from the humans of the surface world and the deep mountain caverns.

Arthur wondered grimly if drowning would come before being snatched below by the mysterious life forms of the deeps, or if you had to drown first, and if so, did everyone go not to somewhere out of the world beyond after death, but into the sea? Did they learn magic in the sea? He could bear it if they did . . .

He was slumbering briefly between waves, great snorting, beyond-exhaustion brief naps, when he roused enough to see that the waves were somewhat smaller, the canyons between the waves larger.

Then Joey loomed up, loosened from his lifeline, and said, "Go get some rest."

When Arthur and Liere stumbled onto the deck, still aching and gritty eyed, Joey looked tired but alert. "The winds shifted," he said.

"What does that mean?" Arthur asked.

"It means we're being blown back up toward Goerael. Look."

He took them into the little aft cabin, and spread out a chart that showed the edges of four continents: Drael and Sartor, north and south respectively, and to the west of them, Goerael and Toar, the latter of which was depicted Mearsies Heili as a small blotch near the northeastern corner.

"Once we clear this here big Sartor land mass, the current is gonna be pushin' us west. If we head straight south, the current will do our westing for us. But if we go southwest, see, we hit all these millions of islands between the two continents. A lot of 'em have pirates and the like."

Arthur nodded. "South it is."

And south it was, for days and days and days, each day successively colder as they moved away from the belt of the world. You couldn't say it was the same, because the sea and sky were never exactly the same two days running. In fact it was this never-ending change, with no relief of land in view, which made the journey seem endless.

Just once Liere gave in to temptation long enough to catch Diana between their respective watches. Lyren had been especially fractious that day, cold, tired, and bored. "That horse. Made of lightning," Liere said. "The one you Mearsieans let me ride when I first got rid of Siamis's enchantment."

"Hreealdar," Diana asked, flinging back dark braids.

"Will Hreealdar come this far out to sea?"

Diana shrugged. "Hreealdar mostly only comes when Clair asks. Or Seshe. Sometimes, CJ. And not always then. Clair thinks Hreealdar lives in the jewel caves, which are . . ." She waved a hand, palm covered with calluses.

"I know. The Selenseh Redian caves don't respond to place and time in any way we can measure."

Diana nicked her head in a nod, and they parted, Diana to mend sail, and Liere to try to soothe Lyren's wailing.

Arthur spent his free time burying himself in studies, and writing about those to Hibern and Leander, the latter of whom had been studying ward magic with Arthur and Roy. Liere exchanged letters with Senrid twice, reporting only what they were doing and not her endless gnawing fear. She spent the rest of her time helping repair torn sails and tending Lyren, whose spirits returned as the days quieted. But she had closed her mental shield like a night-flower, leaving Liere wracked with guilt.

Arthur and Liere scarcely saw one another, as Liere was part of Joey's watch, and Arthur Diana's. Neither wanted to talk to anyone as the frigid winter days passed with all the speed of melting ice, and slowly the cutter began to get low on stores. Dtheldevor had told Joey to pack enough to feed them well for a month, but that month was now past. Many days they'd been too tired to eat more than a dry biscuit, so the food had stretched well, but it wasn't infinite.

Arthur would risk magic rather let them starve. But if he did that, he might as well risk transfer. He watched the bags and boxes dwindle, struggling within himself, until, at last, Joey reported a hump on the horizon.

Whatever continent it was, Arthur promised himself, as soon as he touched land, the rest of the journey would be by conventional means.

"Heh!" Joey called down, after climbing to the crosstrees, where he perched precariously. "Delfin!"

"What's that?" Arthur asked.

"Islands," Diana said. "I know those islands. Between them and us in Mearsies Heili is the Pink Sea."

"Pink!" Lyren called, hopping down the deck. "Pink water?"

"Water's same color as everywhere," Joey said as he slid down a rope to the deck. "Gets its name from rose coral, big as mountains, undersea."

Arthur was glad of the conversation, because it gave him time to get control of disappointment so sharp it felt more like anger. There was no use in losing his temper. Islands instead of a continent were a disappointment, but they were a vast improvement over unending sea.

He said, "Then shall we sail on? Can we make it on what we've got left in the galley? I'm willing to eat once a day."

Joey shook his head. "Sails are near rags as is. This cutter wasn't meant for long cruises. We'll have to work to get supplies."

Arthur gritted his teeth. How dangerous, really, was the threat if he transferred? Every time he asked himself, he remembered handing his own magic books, with all his thoughts, discoveries, and learning, over to Roy to study.

He kept silence as he took his turn at the tiller so they could sail in on the tide. As he watched Liere and Diana handling the sails, he reflected on the irony of having become an expert sailor in time to hope he would never again set foot on any vessel, ever.

The cutter was small enough, and the season late enough, to win them a slip along one of the outer piers. Walking over the plank to the solid wooden pier was such a sweet relief he stood there looking around in euphoria as the sturdy wood seemed to heave beneath him.

"Let's get to the Wanderers' inn so's we can grab good beds," Joey said. "At least this ain't summer, when the beds're gone before midday, as like as not. But then, summers ain't so bad, sleepin' on the beach under the stars."

As he led the way with assurance through narrow alleys toward the city the hill behind the bay, Arthur reflected on Dock Talk's distinctive accent that one only seemed to find in harbors all over the southern world. Maybe even in the north, too.

As expected, there were plenty of bunks in the weather-worn building. The chalk board that every Wanderer inn sported out front also offered a goodly list of places willing to hire wandering youngsters. Arthur scanned the list, knowing he could work as a scribe if necessary, and as a translator. Or he'd replace roof tiles if he had to. He stood there scowling at the board and fingering the notecase in his pocket—until he heard a familiar voice.

"Wait, is that Sartora? Um, Liere? And wow, the sprout is really sprouting!"

They turned to find familiar figures walking up, all grinning broadly.

"Puddlenose?" Liere's high voice sounded the happiest Arthur had heard for a long time. *"Rel?"*

Puddlenose rubbed his hands, as Lyren danced around him, squealing for a piggyback ride. "Come along. I'll show you where to get the best food in the harbor. Cheapest, too," he said as he swung Lyren up onto his shoulder. "Looks like we got us some stories to tell."

Norsunder

Punishments usually began with beatings, floggings, and the like, but ended with the scut work that nobody else wanted to do. Denizens ignored those on work details, unless they wished to exercise their senses of humor; the prevailing attitude was, if you were stupid enough to get caught, you deserved what you got.

It was astonishing how much Erol heard, just by virtue of having a broom or hammer and nails or message in his hand. Most of it was gossip, retailed to the rest of the boys when they were safely alone, but every once in a while he overheard useful information.

Such as the day he glimpsed outside the Destination chamber Arech and the three surviving members of Wan-Edhe's inner guard. They were waiting for the mages to indicate it was safe to transfer back to Norsunder-Beyond. Though Erol remembered nothing of the half-destroyed ship he had been abandoned on to live or die after a failed Chwahir maritime attack, he had along with the Chwahir language somehow absorbed the Chwahir hatred of Wan-Edhe's dungeon master.

He'd heard gossip all over the Base when Arech had been

brought out from the Beyond that he was going to Chwahirsland for a run. He hoped it had failed. Since he was there with his bucket and scrub brush, he decided that the mildewed wall outside the chamber needed sprucing up.

Arech and the guards, confident that no one in the command building spoke Chwahir, spent their wait working on getting their stories straight. They talked until abruptly they began vanishing one by one, leaving behind the metallic burn smell of transfer.

Erol sneezed. He checked that he was alone, then tucked his bucket and brush in an alcove to wait for next time, and ran for the stables. It had been a grim winter, with few enough moments of entertainment, mostly a lot of painful transfers and useless searches, so he was very surprised to arrive to a circle of triumphant grins.

"Heard s-s-something," he began, then, "You g-go. First."

A glance at the map David had pinned up on the wall showed the lined-through sites of failure on the Liere-and-dyr search, but one spot remained untouched:

"Leef spotted them, just arrived in the Delfin Harbor. Get this. Puddlenose, and Rel the Traveler, already there."

"Rel?" Erol yelped. "He's in Ch-ch-wahirs-s-s-land!"

All attention turned from Leef's slashing grin in his dark face to Erol, who jerked a thumb over his shoulder. "Heard. Arech. S-s-ent to put blood mark on Jilo. Did. But Rel g-got him away."

David turned to Leef. "Your sighting was just now, right?"

"Saw them eating breakfast. All in a bunch."

David turned back to Erol. "How long has Arech been back? Last night? Doesn't matter. My guess is, that old mage Rel took up with must have sent him off. Rel travels with Puddlenose, doesn't he?"

"Often," Adam said—with regret, as he'd traveled with them, too.

"So we transfer in and grab Liere?"

David held up a hand, thinking. "There's something missing here. And I can guess what it is." To Adam, "What exactly did that Mearsiean girl say about the bloodknife mark on her when Kessler Sonscarna showed up to sting Dejain in Chwahirsland?"

Adam, who had written out the details in his journal, shut his eyes and pictured the page of code. Then recounted CJ's story in her own words.

"Right." David smiled, leaning back in his chair, his sleepy brown eyes wide. "There's a lot missing between what Erol heard and Rel's turning up in the Delfin Islands, but I'm guessing Kessler, and removing the bloodknife spell off Jilo, are the connection."

"You want to grab Rel?" Laban asked doubtfully. "He wouldn't tell us it was day if the sun was shining in his eyes."

"Yes," Adam said with gentle regret. "Intimidation would only make him go silent as a rock."

"I know that." David waved a hand to and fro. "I'm thinking in another direction altogether. Look, what do you want to bet they're heading for Mearsies Heili? What better place to hide Liere than a collection of farms at the ass end of nowhere?"

"Not taking that bet," MV said.

David grinned. "They're avoiding magic transfer, so we've got some time while they sail. Let's use it effectively. Here's my idea . . ."

Eight

Spring, 4747 AF
Mearsies Heili

ALL OVER THE SARTORAN continent, there was usually some
version of Flower Day celebrated on what was generally
regarded as the first day of spring. In many lands, the colored
ribbons tied to bare tree branches on the first day of the new
year were ceremoniously brought down to salute the
expectation of swelling buds.

In Colend, Flower Day was traditionally a day to announce
engagements, or hold Name Days for recently born infants, as
flower boxes nurtured through winter would be set out in
windows — and at the nighttime celebrations in and out of
doors, all distinctions of rank vanished behind masks.

In Sartor, the winter conservatories were opened, and
plants brought out to gardens. The spring social season began
with spring colors worn.

In Bermund, those who were not quite human, but had
assumed their shape, brought chosen summer blossoms out
from the vases kept in water all year, and planted them, where
they immediately took root, so that young flowers sprouted
everywhere seemingly overnight.

In Mearsies Heili, which eight centuries ago had been a

colony of Tser Mearsies next to Bermund, Flower Day had its own tradition centered around bringing out plants people had rooted all winter and putting them in the soil, after which people celebrated with bonfire dances.

Encouraged by Mearsieanne, the governors of the provinces invited the guild chiefs and community leaders to crown-sponsored formal spring festivals, at which the new militia captains were feted, and afterwards everyone danced.

To CJ, dances had always meant going out and moving to the music, even if that just meant twirling or jumping up and down and flapping one's arms. Whatever felt good. Or watching Dhana twirl and leap and flutter, thrilling at her breathtaking grace.

But these parties were different. Everyone dressed in their best. The musicians played the old-fashioned melodies that pleased Mearsieanne,. And the grownups had relearned old-fashioned dances.

What's more, it was apparent that they loved it.

But they weren't the only ones. As CJ watched with a mixture of envy, disgust, and a distinct sense of betrayal, Irenne joined Mearsieanne—each dressed in elaborate gowns of embroidered velvet with floating ribbons down the sleeves and at the waist—and danced. Sometimes with each other, and sometimes with *boys*.

Mearsieanne had obviously taught Irenne, who moved with assurance in the intricate steps, her long brown ponytail bobbing at each step, her grin wide as she clasped hands to twirl or go round.

Falinneh—of course—clowned off in a corner, mocking the movements, as her best friends looked on, doubled over in mirth. But they were in a corner, separate from the dancers.

Separate.

That's it, CJ was thinking aggrievedly. The girls weren't a gang anymore, they were a bunch of people who happen to live together. And Diana wasn't even doing that. Her "short trip" with Dtheldevor had now taken up most of a year.

CJ walked outside the governoral villa in Wesset North, glaring up at the stars.

When at last the party ended, she was silent until everybody was back home again.

Home, but . . .different.

After a restless night, she rose and padded out to the main

room in the underground cavern, aware that she was alone. In the old days, at least some of the girls would have been up early. And they would have been planning something fun after patrols. But Diana was gone, Irenne almost always slept in the white palace, as did Clair out of a sense of duty, and Mearsieanne had never slept in the Junky. She hated to even step in it, everyone had figured that out by now, though she never said a word against it.

Dhana had risen as usual, but she'd gone out to enjoy the rain, now that it wasn't so cold out.

Seshe walked up from the lower level, tall, thin, serious in face. She favored a long, ankle length sleeveless robe over a tunic top and loose pants, always in soft colors like eggshell blue, or pale rose, or gold-tinged yellow. Today she wore different shades of lavender.

"At least *you* haven't changed," CJ burst out.

"My clothes?" Seshe looked down, her long locks of ash blonde hair swinging against her lavender robe. "This is a fresh outfit."

"Changed into someone else. Some-*thing* else. That dance last night. It's all different now. And Irenne was out there, acting like . . .like I don't know what."

"Oh." Seshe moved to the kitchen alcove, and began putting together the fixings for hot chocolate. "Want to hear what I think?"

Though CJ was (used to be, another change!) Clair's second in command, Seshe really should have been, CJ had decided long ago. She had the bearing that people felt princesses should have, and she was smart, and kind, and she knew a whole lot about the mysteries of protocol. The girls had convinced themselves that she was a runaway princess, but one thing for certain, she wanted no titles, or special treatment.

More to the point, when she talked, everybody listened. Even Mearsieanne.

"There are two things going on," Seshe said as she uncovered the stone jug and poured milk into the pot set over the little stove with a firestick burning cheerily beneath. "One, Irenne was showing off."

"That's nothing new! She always does. Who was it who said about us that Irenne lives on a stage, and the world is the audience, and we're actors but she's the star?"

"I think . . .I think she wanted attention from boys." Seshe looked down as she measured in the ground cocoa powder.

"Boys?" CJ repeated in revulsion. "Why?"

Seshe dropped in some honey, then glanced consideringly at CJ. "Have you ever considered that not all of us will keep the Child Spell? Or do we have an unwritten rule, and any girl who decides to grow up has to leave?"

"She wants to *grow up?"* CJ squeaked, and then, an even more horrifying idea, *"You* want to grow up?"

"Not yet." Seshe held her stirring spoon out, then returned it to the pot. "Not yet, for me. Of course I speak only for myself. Not yet. Someday, yes. It feels . . .right. You can see that, can't you?"

CJ gritted her teeth as she struggled with the ready rage that was almost always her first reaction. "It will never feel right to me. Never." She breathed hard through her nose, then said slowly, "But I know I shouldn't judge for anybody else, and what happened to me on Earth might . . ." She waved a hand, loathing any mention of her early years of abuse. "Clair always wanted us to have our freedom. All right, so Irenne — maybe — wants to grow up. But you said two things."

Seshe looked away a long time then back. "Haven't you ever wondered what she talks about with Mearsieanne, up there in the white palace?"

"History, she said once. She likes hearing about the olden days."

"Yes . . .specifically, what the reward was for service to the crown. If you went out, and, say, led people . . ."

Irenne wanted a title? CJ couldn't even say it.

"There is nothing wrong with people wanting a reward for service," Seshe said as she stirred the mixture. "We're human. We like such things, or history wouldn't be full of queens and counts and duchases. Even Clair admits she liked being queen."

CJ knew the rest of the sentence that Seshe wouldn't say: she realized how much she'd grown to like it after it was taken away. And CJ couldn't squawk because it was Clair who had made her a princess.

That is, she liked being a princess who could go barefoot, and play games, and travel. "But to start that nobility and court stuff all over again here . . ." There were too many things wrong, beginning with what that would mean to Clair, to have the old ways imposed over her ways . . .

Seshe poured out chocolate into two mugs. "CJ, I don't

think anything is going to change overnight. Including Irenne. I could be wrong. She's never once brought up ending the Child Spell, and you know Mearsieanne never lifted it. Nor will she, she's said several times. And as for the other matter, Mearsieanne and Clair still agree on important things, before either of them act. And finally, you have to remember that we're too small to ever turn into Colend, or some of the more elaborate courts further down south of us."

CJ was silent as she sipped gratefully at the warm chocolate, which tasted perfect. But this time it didn't fill her with the expected sense of well-being, and excitement for a new day. She drained it in three defiant swallows, then declared, "I hate change."

"But we always —"

Their attention caught at the flicker of magic over the little desk set between the kitchen alcove and the tunnel leading down to the bedroom. On the desk sat the blotter that Clair had made to mirror a similar blotter up in the throne room, one of her first major magical projects.

Come see who's here!

CJ grabbed up the blunted quill pen sitting beside the blotter and scribbled:

On our way.

CJ and Seshe transferred to the white palace, and ran to the antechamber that Mearsieanne had designated as an informal receiving room, where they heard voices.

"Diana's back! And you brought Puddlenose! Christoph! Rel? *Liere?*"

When all the exclamations had ceased, they discovered that the travelers had spent most of the winter on the Delfin Islands, at first waiting out a series of bad blizzards, and then waiting for the *Berdrer* to catch up with them, in hopes of discovering what had happened to Dtheldevor.

The mood of hilarity dampened at the news of her capture and Carsen's death. Then the newcomers were swept off to the dining room, where Janil, the steward who had pretty much raised Clair while Clair's mother drank her life away, took immediate charge of rambunctious Lyren, not missing how Liere's shoulders relaxed almost immediately.

Over the meal, stories were exchanged — or listened to, on

Rel's part. When Puddlenose slewed around in his chair, and exclaimed, "That's right. Someone or other said you met Rosey, our old villain pal who wasn't any villain," Rel's gaze went to CJ, who stared back, fork halfway suspended between her scrambled eggs and her mouth.

He understood then that she still kept his secret, and giving her a nod of thanks that caused her to redden, he said, "I visit up there once in a while. He's sent me on a couple of interesting trips."

"Like all the way to the Venn? Isn't that what I heard?" Puddlenose asked. "Much as I've traveled, I've never dared go that far. What was it like?"

As Rel gave a curtailed description of his trip—describing the Venn homeland and the pirate battle, and excising Kerendal's offer—the talk shifted to Adam, and thence to reviling Detlev's boys.

In the midst of that, Clair walked up to Rel. He looked down at those steady green eyes in that square face framed by white hair. "Did you come to help guard Liere?" she asked quietly.

Rel said, "I was sent to the islands, where she happened to be. I don't know why. We all decided to travel together. But if you think she needs the help, sure, I'll stay." As he said it, a sharp pang of regret lanced through him. Until that moment, he'd been trying to figure out how to ask to be sent to Sartor, if it could be done without Norsundrian tracers.

"I think we could use your help," Clair said.

And when she walked away, CJ sidled up, giving such furtive looks all around that Rel suppressed a laugh. No one was paying her the least attention or she would have drawn all eyes. "Was I wrong? About Rosey?" she whispered, eyes huge.

He was tempted to say yes, but suppressed that, too. "You were right."

She flushed with pleasure, then gave him a wary look. "But you didn't tell anybody?"

"Not yet," he said. "Still getting used to it."

CJ let out a sigh. "Clair said I shouldn't say anything. I'm glad I didn't."

Then she flitted away before he could say anything excruciating.

Liere had forgotten how difficult it was to corral a lively

almost three-year-old in a huge space, after so long on board a ship, then in a small harbor. She spent an anxious time running after Lyren, who took "No" as a challenge.

Liere vigorously controlled the urge to scold her on the mental plane, after that terrible incident during the storm. Lyren seemed to have weathered it fine, but Liere still cringed inwardly with guilt. She had promised herself to raise a sister, a best friend. And she knew that Lyren couldn't bear Liere to be angry. Exasperation, she didn't mind, and worry, she ignored as thoroughly as she ignored Liere's careful explanations.

But then Steward Janil stepped in, catching Lyren up. "You, child, are getting a bath, and going to sleep," she said.

Lyren gazed at her, her eyes, golden in that light, round and wide. "Bath?" she said in a small voice.

"You will like this bath," Janil stated. "It's like a pool. And we have a lot of toys."

Liere watched, amazed. Here was someone who knew how to handle a smart, willful child who could hear on the mental plane, or shut the world out expertly when she wished. Proving that yet again, Liere wasn't any better as a sister then as a mother. She had so much to learn!

After two days of seeing Lyren behaving like a model child for the stern Janil, Liere's sense of failure sharpened, which in turn intensified her worries about what she was going to do, and how to solve problems she couldn't even articulate.

Arthur had gone off with Clair to study. Rel and Puddlenose, Christoph, and several of the girls were riding down to the coast to visit the *Berdrer*.

Liere poked around in the library without much interest while Mearsieanne dealt with crown business in the throne room. As the day waned, Liere wandered out the wide front doors of the white palace, which were open to the cool spring air, and she sat on the top step, chin in her hands. She didn't dare even write to Senrid, busy in Marloven Hess. His life was purposeful. Hers wasn't. No amount of scolding, or well-meant uplifting exhortation, would alter the truth.

Mearsieanne had been watching from a distance. After sending off the last petitioner, she went looking for Liere.

When she spotted her drooping form on that top step, she marched out onto the terrace and knelt down in a welter of embroidered skirts. "Liere," she said in a crisp voice. "Wait until you've been Norsunder's dupe for the equivalent of ninety years, after which they kill everyone who matters to you, and then you'll have reason to mope."

"I'm sorry," Liere said, blushing to the ears. "I know I'm being stupid."

"Not stupid, but mopey. It's time for dinner. Join us?"

Some of the girls stood talking on the terrace outside the kitchen, waiting for the servants to set the table. On her former visits, Liere had enjoyed how they all sat informally in the kitchen to eat. But now it seemed they used the formal dining room, which still had Mearsieanne's own furnishings in it, unused for two generations.

Irenne reveled in the new formality. Seshe adapted, as did Sherry and Gwen.

Worried about her manners, Liere took tiny helpings. Janil, the steward, looked on in dismay until Mearsieanne leaned over and dumped extra rice onto Liere's plate. Then she reached for the bowl of onion-braised chicken-and-gravy and lobbed extra of that on, followed by the cabbage.

"Now eat that," she said. "You're too skinny. You need strength."

And Liere picked up her fork.

CJ had resigned herself to using her best manners when she couldn't avoid that formal dining room, but when she did, she always got a smile from Clair, who liked harmony among them. With good will, CJ said to Liere, "So, what have you been studying?"

Liere sighed. "I've been trying again with magic. But I don't have enough . . . control."

Everybody gazed at her with variations of surprise.

Clair felt sorry for her, having witnessed occasions when people, finding out that Liere was Sartora, the Girl Who Saved the World, really did expect her to open her mouth and let diamonds of wisdom fall out. Liere didn't even remotely act like a girl, but she didn't act like an adult, either. What she had, Clair believed, was the worst of both worlds.

A little like Mearsieanne, in fact.

Liere ate a bite of gravy-soaked rice, her expression clearing. The food was delicious. Then she looked at all those faces, and sighed. "Being born with one talent doesn't make you smart. But people seem to expect it, and I hate to fail them."

"Does Senrid say that to you?" Sherry asked, looking

puzzled.

Liere finally smiled. "No. He tells me I'm being a fathead to pay any attention to what other people think, or want, or expect."

"He's right," Clair stated.

"Except look at him. And you, Clair," Liere retorted, without any heat at all. "Both of you daily live up to responsibilities many adults would have trouble with. So why shouldn't I live up to mine?"

CJ felt on slightly surer ground now. "*You* can't take responsibility for Siamis coming back again," she exclaimed. "Especially when there were armies stinking up countries all over the place, like in Everon. You can live a million years and you're never going to be able to defeat *armies*."

"That's what Senrid said as well." Liere flashed a grin, that for a moment almost made her seem less teeth-grittingly controlled. "Also said when I'm humble and arrogant at the same time it makes his brain hurt." And when they laughed, "Humble I don't mind. I always need to work on that. But I don't want to be arrogant, and that brings me back to learning magic, and failing."

Clair sighed. "Well, when I consider that the worst villain of all time must be thirsting for revenge for what you've done, I guess you're right to learn as much as you can as fast as you can."

"You mean Siamis?" Liere asked, looking puzzled.

"Oh no, his wicked uncle, Detlev."

Mearsieanne said crisply, "We will not have that filthy name introduced at the table. When we share a meal we shall be civilized."

Nine

AFTER LIERE HAD GONE to join Lyren in sleep, Mearsieanne turned to Clair, saying with a smile of satisfaction, "Just as well we've been putting the new patrol system in place. Liere's safe here. The child is doing well under Steward Janil's eye. I thought we might invite her to remain here until Tsauderei, or Erai-Yanya, or the northern mages, say it's safe to return."

Clair knew "I thought" was the civilized form of "I've decided" — which called for nothing but corroboration. Since she agreed, she smiled and said, "I think staying with us will be good for them both."

Life settled to a semblance of normal only because everyone was trying hard to make it seem that way. CJ struggled inwardly with the prospect of the girl gang breaking up. There was no villain to fight here, just . . .change. That she didn't want. She took off for long rambles in the woods to get her moods away from everyone, while Liere did her best to be a good guest, looking on wistfully at how successfully Lyren had charmed the castle people.

One morning Mearsieanne again found her sitting on the terrace brooding. She whisked herself away, startled a servant by a demand, then returned, thrust a dust mop into Liere's nail-bitten fingers, and pointed back through the open double doors into the great hall, so bare, but so perfectly proportioned with its arched ceiling and windows and the way the light slanted down, the entire spectrum of light diffuse in the soft glow, it never seemed barren.

Liere looked from the dust mop to the room, puzzled.

Mearsieanne said, "Every time I see you moping I'll put you to work cleaning the castle. At least then you'll be doing one thing that's practical."

Liere gave her a wistful attempt at a smile. "I wasn't really moping. It's just that Senrid thinks we'd be safer in his country, but Arthur won't get on another ship and we dare not transfer with the dyr."

Mearsieanne's face tightened at the name Senrid. "*He* most certainly can stay right where he is. *You* are very welcome to stay here as long as you wish."

"Thank you. And I would be happy to sweep, if it's needed. I learned housekeeping when I lived in Imar."

"Don't be sorry, Liere. Be active."

Liere shook her head. "That's my problem. I don't see how. I can't do anything helpful with magic or military things. But I do know how to clean."

Mearsieanne sighed and took the dust mop away. "Never mind. It was a terrible idea. We have a staff, and if you look, you'll note that the room is spotless. I understand that you cannot learn magic. Find something you *can* learn. Just don't be mopish, because it makes everyone else mope because they aren't being good hosts."

It struck Liere then that Mearsieanne was another who had done the Child Spell and the Birth Spell. "I'm afraid I'm doing a bad job with Lyren. That I shouldn't have . . .it was so different in my mind," she whispered.

Mearsieanne's eyes widened. "Ah!" And gathering her skirts, she sat down next to Liere. "The very first thing I did when I returned here was look up records of my son Tesmer, whom I had raised so carefully, with the best governesses and tutors I could find. But I've since learned that though you can stuff a child's head with knowledge, you cannot make him wise. He wasn't a terrible king, but he was a lazy one. Did you know that he had children by four different consorts?"

Liere said innocently, "Puddlenose's mother was an adventurer, was she not? And Clair respects her aunt Murial a great deal."

"Who lives as a hermit, refusing any sort of family life.

From what I can gather the children were all very close in age, brangled constantly, like their mothers, all of whom wanted to take precedence by being crowned queen. Though there was this great palace to get lost in, no one got along. And Doume turned out to be a nasty piece of work. Rather like my grandfather." Mearsieanne abandoned the subject of Tesmer's sybaritic rule, and tried another tack. "Arthur said something once that makes me wonder if you're like your father."

Liere stood up, face contorting in horror. "I am nothing like him! Nothing!"

"Sit down, sit down." Mearsieanne patted the air. "I ought to have said, in wanting everything just so. But life can't always be just so. Of course, civilization means we try. And so I try to have things civilized around me." She smiled up at the softly glistening walls. "My point is, the ideal is a family in which all love one another, and I'm certain we all start out that way, or why would we have children at all? But still people like Wan-Edhe, and Detlev, get born anyway."

Liere turned a dismayed face outward, and Mearsieanne saw that she'd again taken a wrong tack. "Your Lyren will not grow up to be a Detlev or a Wan-Edhe. She's far too happy." She rose. "I must return to my duties, but think about what I said!"

She walked away, afraid she'd only made things worse. Mighty mind powers seemed to point the way to madness. She hoped that did not lie in Liere's future, but one thing she did know was everyday civilization. Maybe living a semblance of it would settle Liere into the practical world.

Liere was still sitting there, debating what to write back to Senrid, when Clair and a few of the girls found her.

Falinneh looked at her expression and snapped her fingers. "I know just what to do. Down to the Junky. Time for the battle of the pies!"

Liere had enjoyed the pie fight on her first visit, but Clair knew Mearsieanne would say that it was not an appropriate way to treat guests. "How about this? Let's go down to the Lake and have a picnic."

"Of course," CJ exclaimed.

Clair said, "I'll arrange the food."

Liere remembered the broad pool below a waterfall at the base of the mountain, and was glad for the distraction.

They transferred down, and Liere found it even more

beautiful, and stranger, than she had remembered. Their lake was no bigger than a pond, but the place was pretty, surrounded by greenery. Most interesting of all were the shifting lights in the water, which were live beings.

Lyren crowed as a gigantic bubble rose in the air, wobbling before it fell back and vanished.

Dhana, who at a careless glance looked like an ordinary brown-skinned, brown-haired girl of about twelve, was slight and graceful as a deer in her smock-like top and loose knee pants, leaving her lower legs and feet bare. People thought she moved like a dancer—and she loved to dance—but humanity was a temporary skin for her.

When she saw Lyren crouching on a rock, peering intently down into the water, Dhana's thin, freckled face lifted with a small smile, then she leaped into the air, arced in a perfect dive, and vanished into the water without a splash, changing form in an eye blink.

Then a hundred, two hundred bubbles rose into the air—small, large—all rainbow sheened. It was such a beautiful sight that Liere's breath caught, and her chest shuddered. She wanted to laugh and cry at the same time, or maybe just sit still and watch forever. They were so *beautiful*. It hurt in a way she couldn't explain because it was so generous and joyous and she loved a world that could have such things in it.

Lyren crowed with delight as a bubble trembled in a slow circle around her, shimmering with rainbow colors.

Liere knew it was Dhana, though how she knew she could not have explained, for there was no human thought from the bubble in the mental realm. She watched as the bubble dropped to the water and popped, then Dhana splashed up on-to the shore, shook herself, and the water seemed to vanish from her skin and clothes. Inherent magic, Liere thought: had to be. She had never heard of even senior mages making material things like clothing vanish and reappear like that without the careful controls of transfer magic, and yet Dhana did it as casually as anyone else would brush a strand of hair back.

Liere looked at the trees tossing, the wind-swirled early blossoms landing lightly on the water, the bubbles frothing up, and said to Clair, "There is such very . . .*old* magic here."

How could she have forgotten? Some of the strangeness she heard on the mental plane was the Selenseh Redian deep inside the mountain beyond the waterfall. "I have so much to learn."

She sighed.

Clair said, "How about a sandwich?"

Presently Liere and Clair sat apart on one of the flat rocks, as Clair told her the little Dhana had said about the indigenous beings, there being few words in human vocabulary for them.

When clouds blew overhead, turning the wind chill, they returned to Junky, where a note had appeared on the desk blotter.

> *Come upstairs. Senrid is here. And a surprise!*

Within a short time, the group assembled in the white palace interview room, greeting Senrid, then turning to the tilt-eyed boy who grinned sheepishly. CJ scowled, trying to place him: badly cut thick, wavy dark hair, worn tunic-shirt and riding trousers worn by travelers in nearly every kingdom, rangy build, bandaged right hand, healing bruises under brown skin. A familiar sword hilt at his side —

"Dtheldevor," Liere exclaimed. "You're here! You're free!"

Puddlenose blew on his fingernails. "Told you if anybody could escape Norsunder Base, it'd be her."

"Except I didn't —"

"What happened to your *hair?*" Irenne exclaimed in horror.

Dtheldevor hooked a thumb back behind her shoulder and parodied a bully's strut, sticking out her jaw. "Pretty, ain't I?" she said then, and plopped down onto one of the dais steps. "Yep, it's me, by damn, and you c'n bet yer murderin' boots those soul-eaters enjoyed whackin' me braids off."

"What happened?" several of the girls exclaimed.

"Aw, later. Boring."

"No! No! Tell now!"

"You really want the whole rip-throat mess?"

"Yeah!" Diana exclaimed, laughing soundlessly.

Falinneh bounced forward. "Don't leave out any parts where you booted any of those stink-brained eleveners."

Dtheldevor smacked her hands on her grubby trouser legs. "Here goes. We was on the ship, then some o' sweetheart Detsie's cute little murderin' poopsies come along an — Falinneh, belay that puke-sniffin' cackle. No one c'n hear me story!"

"P—poo . . ." Falinneh wheezed, purple-faced. "Poopsies!"

"So anyway that soul-blasted MV, well, he bumped off ol' Carsen. He said he didn't, not that I believed the pinch-faced soul-sucker, but when I got to me ship just now, Sharly sez Carsen didn't die o' no stab wound. But still, it's his fault! Anyhow, we was fighting, and he whupped me. I'm shite-fire outa serious practice, an' so they put the grab on me an anchored-up by magic fer Norsunder Base."

Liere mumbled something sympathetic.

Dtheldevor gave an awkward shrug. "Oh, I been through worse. Notta lot happened, actually . . ."

She paused, bending a hairy-eyeball on Falinneh, who had collapsed against Gwen. From them occasional whispers issued forth: "Poopsies . . .Detsie's poopsies . . ." And, finally, "Detsie-poopsie-potsie." That one finished them off and they ran from the room, half-bent over, almost strangling on their laughter.

"Why did they take you?" Clair asked Dtheldevor. "What could you know that they wanted?"

"Nuttin'!" Dtheldevor shrugged, hands out wide. "Worst insult of all! Bully-boys whacked me braids, as you can see, and such-like shite. Then ol' Detsie hauls me in and jaws a little, makes no sense, then sends me down to stew for a couple thousand years. Then finally came a time when that jug-eared one, whassname, Roy, he comes slinkin' in and sez, I've orders to get you out. And I sez, why, thinkin' there's gotta be a catch, and he sez, there's trouble brewing here . . ."

The room had gone silent, and Dtheldevor, who wasn't used to talking so long, took a sip from the cup set before her.

She shut her eyes, her mind back in that stuffy, miserable cell, where she had never let herself give up hope of escape. The guards had respected her—or Detlev, who had issued specific orders—enough to have two sword-drawn guards standing behind the one who brought the twice-daily meals.

After every meal, Dtheldevor had forced herself to run knees high, around the cell two hundred times one way, then the other, to do handstands until her arms shook, and to practice sword drills in the air. If she got another chance to escape she had to be ready to take it.

But time had ground on, measureless in that place underground, until Roy showed up, half in shadow, half lit by the ever-present wall torches kept burning by magic. "Orders," he said. "There's trouble between factions, and we've giving Henerek a setback. Your going will point in the wrong direction."

So she was a decoy. Whether this was only a ruse to break her spirit or a fast trip to execution, she didn't care. She slammed out of the cell, glad of all that knee-high trotting because they ran full out through the dusty, rank-smelling corridors till they reached a place that smelled like stable. On the floor someone had chalked a Destination, which already smelled like burned metal.

Dtheldevor saw that they were not alone in this room. A thin figure stood against the opposite wall, wearing a ragged, blood-stained battle tunic and trousers, grimy, unkempt hair hanging in a bruised face, the one visible eye closed, the other hidden by a filthy rag tied slantwise around the head. The shadows over one eye-socket looked curiously flat.

Roy said to this figure, "Carl."

The thin, taut face lifted.

"Where to?" Roy asked.

"Everon." The voice was no more than a whisper.

Dtheldevor sighed, and faced her listeners. ". . .and next thing I knew, that poor wight was gone, in a breeze what smelt like home, and then Roy sez at me, where, and I sez, can ye send me to me ship, because I know he knows it. He sailed with Arthur times enough, the soul-rotted sneak. Then he shuts his eyes and then sez, I can do that. And did."

She paused to swallow more listerblossom steep, then clanged the cup down on the saucer, making Mearsieanne wince. "So I had me a reunion with me crew, got a good meal in me, an' rested up, then I figgered, I oughta come up here an' report, so I set out walkin' and when I got on the mountain I found this here Senrid just comin' up in offa that Destination square outside, and so we walked in together, and here I be."

She heaved a sigh. "So I 'spect yer gonna wanna put a heap o spells over me, like maybe Roy put some nasty tracers or somethin' on me, and I'm good with that because I don't want none of Norsunder tricks on me, before I go back to me ship and get back to sailin'. I get itchy bein' so long on land."

"We shall do that right away," Mearsieanne said briskly. "Who was the person who wished to go to Everon?"

"Carl," Dtheldevor said, wiping her eyes on her grubby sleeve. "Roy said, Carl. Kinda a popular name down there, isn't it, these days?"

Mearsieanne's face blanched, and Liere also blanched, her eyes closing.

But all Mearsieanne said was, "Come along. Let us make certain there are no tracers or wards on you."

Ten

DETLEV FACED THE GROUP. Despite the still, stuffy air, the windows were closed up tight, and he glanced around in that narrow-eyed way the boys had learned meant he was scanning on the mental plane. Then, "Report."

"They're both gone, now," Roy said. "And Henerek and Bostian's toadies will be accusing each other because the entire Base knew that Dtheldevor was your special prisoner. But who was Carl?"

"That," Detlev said, "was Henerek's personal prisoner." He leaned forward, his voice low. "You're aware that he's positioning himself to make a try for this Base from Dejain and the mages."

Everyone knew that, so they waited for the real point.

"Henerek is backed by Yeres," Detlev continued. "She might assume I don't know as she's cooperating with me in preparing Aldau-Rayad for Theronezhe's strike troops. She and Efael have been warded from Songre Silde for centuries. They have very long memories there. Because the Norss is communicating with me, Yeres maintains her pretense of cooperation. But she's given Henerek the wherewithal to lure Benin."

"Benin? The mage?" MV asked. "I thought he was

Dejain's."

"We've been avoiding all the mages," David added. "As a defensive strategy."

"Which is why I find you alive," Detlev observed, so drily the effect was far more chilling than mere threat. He waited while they put together the clues: the unexplained disappearance of underlings here and there, that number steadily increasing.

That meant the rumor was true. Benin was grabbing live victims to create a soul-bound army.

"Another reason is that Benin and Dejain are each trying hard to find sources of blood-magic. Both have hunters out looking for Kessler. I believe it's time to find him first—"

"Let me." David's sleepy gaze raised. "Tokens are done. We've a plan that should net all three of our targets."

Detlev sat back, hands on his knees. "Then carry on. I need to be back at Five, where I've found traces of Lilith the Guardian's interference." He vanished.

Laban grimaced, flung wide the window, and drew in a deep breath of the dust-laden stench of stable. "Ah, nothing like fresh air." He turned a derisive glance to the others. "Siamis renegade, Henerek lurking somewhere with an army of soul-bound, to which he'd probably love to add us, Bostian and Henerek readying for a command fight. Detlev dancing around Yeres at Five. And here we are. What now?"

"We carry out our plan," David said. "And then . . ." He closed his fist.

Firejive, Erol thought, but didn't speak. None of them did. Somehow their code word was no longer a solace, and had never been a protection.

David turned to Curtas and Roy. "You two go to the rat-hole and lay in supplies. In case we need a fallback."

MV snapped his fingers and jerked his thumb between Adam and Laban. "And you two, let's smoke."

Adam sighed. "I really have to do this?"

"You know we'd never break those wards in that Mearsiean palace unless they invite us in. Which they won't. And you're the only one who's been to that underground hideout."

"But anyone could find it," Adam said.

David didn't answer. He turned to his trunk and carefully removed a dagger whose edge gleamed with a greenish tinge. "It's time I met Senrid, but if he's not there it's also got Rel's name on it."

Laban didn't answer as he took the knife carefully by the hilt. Unlike MV, he preferred wearing shoes, or mocs for woods work, but for this mission he had put on riding boots. He carefully tucked the bloodknife into the sheath fitted into the boot, then shook his trouser leg over it.

MV went first, then Laban, then Adam.

When the transfer reaction cleared, Adam gazed around the forest, breathing in the scent of spring foliage, grass, and water.

"Where to?" MV asked.

"If David put us in the middle, we should go a little north and a little east, I think," Adam said. "But you'll see the trails. They're all over the place."

"Yeah, but I don't want to be doubling back all day."

Adam shook his head. "They all lead inward."

They began walking in silence, Laban contemplating the differences between this continent and Drael's southeast coast, and Adam wondering who of those they were likely to meet he'd least wish to see.

Thad, at least, would not be there. He was grateful for that. Arthur, maybe? Adam had traveled longest with Rel, but so much of their travel had been in companionable silence or talking about what they saw. With Arthur there had been sometimes difficult conversations, as with Thad, and especially Karhin. Like the time they'd talked about what defined evil and how easy it was to dismiss someone — in that case, Siamis — as evil.

"Is evil, or good, ever a single action?" he had asked Arthur, whose face had gone thoughtful. Adam remembered biting back words about how the "evil Detlev" in Adam's memory was the patient hand guiding steps, the calming in a night of violent nightmare, the soothing drink of listerblossom in fever, the fingers placing that first piece of chalk on Adam's palm, that had been bloody-raw with Adam's effort to rub off the intense invasion of memories gained through touch.

Adam shook himself, hard, and shuttered his mind. "This is not going to be fun," he said with regret.

MV clipped him on the side of the head. "We'll make it fun. Ah! A trail, just as you said."

Mearsies Heili's white palace

Late afternoon, Mearsieanne and Clair were busy with
Dtheldevor, whom they promised they'd transfer directly back
to her ship as soon as she was pronounced tracer-free.

Arthur and the Mearsean girls ran up the stairs with
Puddlenose, Christoph, and Rel to look at the big map in the
library as the boys recounted their latest adventures, little
Lyren trotting along behind with a basket of chalks. To her, the
glistening white walls in the hallway outside the library were
an invitation to almost-three-year-old art experiments.

Finding themselves alone, Senrid said to Liere, "Have you
thought about what you want to do next? My offer still stands."

Liere cast a quick look around, her shoulders tight. "Let's
go outside."

They slipped through the glass doors beyond the kitchen to
the garden terrace. It was chilly, and the leafing trees still dripped from the earlier rain, so they stood under the balcony of the
structure above. She faced him, arms crossed tightly across her
scrawny middle as she said, "I know you'll try to talk me out of
keeping the dyr, but I can't stop trying to figure it out. I just
can't."

He said, "You've learned to use the thing?"

"No. With elementary magic, it's even worse than before.
Arthur and I tried a lot of experiments on board the ship when
we didn't have sail and tiller duty."

Senrid tried hard to understand why Liere found it necessary to take on duties that were mainly self-imposed. Duty, he
understood. He was born to it. Duty guided his every day, and
he liked it that way. It gave his life, which so often had seemed
laughable, a sense of purpose.

But Liere never seemed to get the reward of a sense of purpose, because all these duties she clung so desperately to were
too much for one person.

She watched him closely and saw conflict in the furrow of
his brows, the twist to his lips. She said, "Nobody else is going
to figure it out because the dyr depends on Dena Yeresbeth first
of all. Which I have. Nobody else does. This should be a thing I
can do, don't you see?" Her voice rose anxiously.

He said, "What do you have to go on, figuring it out?"

The tension in her forehead eased to a perplexed furrow. "I
think . . .it's like a code, or a key. No, those words are wrong. I
don't have the right ones. Yet."

"I get that Lilith wasn't a dyranarya, whatever that actually means. But I don't get why she doesn't take that dyr and use it somehow, instead of leaving you here struggling in total ignorance."

"Maybe it's more like a new language, one she might not know, or have the time to teach me. Just because she's from Ancient Sartor doesn't mean she knows everything. She says so herself. And maybe the dyr won't help against Norsunder. It might be something that contains magic to . . .to . . .fix roofs. Or it has magic that paints pictures. Or perhaps it's lost all its magic over time. Except it did work, sort of, remember, when we freed it that day in when Siamis was chasing us?"

"Which brings me back to asking why the Norsundrians are after it."

"Don't know that either. But the mages on our side no longer seem to care. Lilith and the mages are all worried about what Siamis is doing. Yet I still feel I have to try. I have to do *something*."

He let out his breath in a long sigh, seeing her knotting up again. "Got it. So let's go catch Dtheldevor before they set sail. If you're afraid Norsunder can trace the dyr through magic transfers the way Jilo does with the enemies book, I wager anything she'd be willing to sail you over to Marloven Hess. And I promise, by the time you get there, I'll try to get anything Tsauderei has about dyr history."

"I've already done that part," Liere said. "There isn't anything. Or, what we have, it needs the code, too. None of it was any use. Erai-Yanya spent months on it. With Hibern's help. Erai-Yanya said her mother spent *years*."

"Got it. But what about Dtheldevor and the ship? My offer still stands. What now?"

Liere said with renewed anguish, "It was because of me that Dtheldevor got captured, and Carsen killed. I can't do that to them again."

"Then we'll figure out something else," he said. "Maybe it's disguise time."

"I don't know." Liere struggled to put a lid on her annoying, disgusting *useless* emotions. "Let's go find the others." She tapped her forehead, trying for a light tone to match his. "Lyren heard someone say something about hot chocolate."

CJ stayed behind, unnoticed by the rest.

She'd begun to move with the others until she saw Irenne following the boys up the stairs. In the past, it had never occurred to her to think that there would be any other reason besides hearing Puddlenose's travel stories, which were sure to be funny. He never talked about the bad ones.

But ever since Seshe had said that about the dance, and boys, CJ couldn't help but wonder if Irenne had another motivation. She so loathed the thought of change, especially mushy teenage stuff, she wanted to yell and stamp.

Much better to take her rotten mood away until she could improve it. After all, even if Irenne had more interest in Puddlenose, Christoph, and Rel as boys than their stories, everyone would say it was normal, it was natural.

But she *hated* anything about growing up.

Since all her favorite rooms had people in them, and even the garden outside had Liere and Senrid, she decided to transfer down to the Junky to get over her bad mood.

But as soon as she got there, she looked around the empty caverns that were usually filled with the sounds of the girls' voices, and her mood worsened. She retreated back up the tunnel and decided to go for a roam in the forest to clear her head.

It was just cold and wet enough after the previous night's rain for her to consider going back for shoes. But the afternoon was so still, so perfect, with the westering light gilding the white castle on the mountain with a fiery outline, and glimmering warmly through the branches in a lacework of light.

She began to sing, head thrown back as she listened to her voice reverberate through the trees. Now she felt warm enough to move.

But she hadn't gone fifty steps before five steely fingers closed on her arm and yanked her off her feet. Her breath whooshed out in a squeak, and before she could draw in air for a yell for help, a hard hand clamped over her face, squeezing the sides of her jaws so tightly she could not move her head.

She started to fight, but got tucked under an equally hard arm, her arms pinned to her sides, her legs uselessly kicking out behind. Her long black hair spilled over her face, obscuring her vision as she was carried for a short distance, then abruptly set on her feet.

She shook her hair back, trying to catch her breath. She stared into unfamiliar light brown eyes with amber flecks, below black brows set into a sharply planed face in whose contours there was utterly no hint of friendliness or kindness at all. He was vaguely familiar . . .from Everon?

One of Detlev's gang!

He let her go, and she flopped onto hard packed, magic-smoothed dirt. She looked up in horror and dread, recognizing the familiar mural, woven rug, desk and chair of the main room of the girls' underground cavern.

Their secret hideout had been breached.

MV grinned, thoroughly enjoying her undisguised indignation when she recognized where she was, until boiling over with rage, she bounced to her feet and began to shout insults in an ear-rending screech, hands fisted at her sides.

He slapped her. It was a casual slap, the sort he'd often given to Noser and the others, but she was a lot lighter than Noser, and sprawled on the rug again.

She sat up dizzily, hot tears of pain blurring her eyes, as her face throbbed.

"Which one are you?" he asked.

She'd die before giving a bully the satisfaction of showing her fear. To hide her trembling, she crossed her arms and curled her lip.

He turned his head. "Adam!"

CJ fought the rage and horror and pain that made thinking near impossible, as Adam appeared from the lower tunnel, wispy brown hair curls wild over wide-spaced, merry brown eyes.

So that's how they got inside. Of course Adam would remember how to enter the Junky. CJ gritted her teeth in fury.

Adam's arms were full of weapons that CJ recognized as Diana's trophy collection, swiped over the years from various villains. He looked delighted. "This place is better than I remembered," he exclaimed in Sartoran, with genuine enthusiasm. "I never saw the adjunct rooms. They've got *everything* — even one of our practice knives."

MV jerked a thumb in CJ's direction, and asked, also in Sartoran, "Which is this?"

Adam smiled his friendly smile that CJ remembered so well, and said cheerily, "Oh, hi, CJ. She's one of the fun ones." He waited, but when she didn't return his kindly greeting (and it was, too, without a trace of mockery or nastiness, which somehow made the situation feel a whole lot worse) he shrugged and wandered back down the tunnel to poke about some more.

"Huh," said a new voice, one CJ belatedly recognized. "Fun for what? Isn't this the one who can defeat Norsunder one-handed?"

There stood Laban, his expressive blue eyes bright with disdain, and CJ remembered all the pompous bragging Kyale had made in her name.

"Get out of here," CJ snarled, reddening to the ears.

Laban waved a hand as he said to MV, "Don't waste your time looking for the rest. Big Mouth here knows everything we want."

"Well you are a waste of time, Laban-lice," CJ said promptly, then remembered that they didn't have lice on this world. "In fact, you're a mistake. And a miserable, stinking excuse for one at that. *And—*"

MV rolled his eyes and said to Laban, "You want to, then?"

"Naw. You can," Laban said, flicking dismissive fingers in CJ's direction. He disliked interrogation at any time, though they'd all been trained to do it. He knew MV was the best at it — and Laban still had his own orders ahead. He wandered off toward Clair's room, picking things up, looking at them, then tossing them carelessly as he cursed under his breath.

As soon as Laban turned his back, CJ tried to make a break for the exit, but once again five steel bands clamped on her shoulder and yanked her easily back again. Then, with a careless shove, she was propelled into the desk chair, which skidded back, ruching the rug.

"Where's Sartora?" MV asked, giving the name a sarcastic twist.

"Who?" CJ shrilled, clamping her arms tightly across her chest.

"Who who?" he retorted, so promptly CJ was startled.

"Who did you ask about?" she returned, shifting bully-resisting tactics, sensing that blankness and stupidity would be the most annoying.

But he didn't look annoyed. "Did I ask about anyone?" He looked surprised.

"No!"

"Then why are you talking?" He grinned and patted CJ on

the head. "Just want to converse with me?"

"UGH no!" she retorted. And since this tack was not goading him in the least, she started talking fast, straining to fill the air with words as she tried to buy time. Someone surely would come . . .or she would think of a plan. But rambling out nonsense was harder than it seemed. Desperate and angry, she veered between languages, tossing in insults from the miseries of her schooldays mixed with headlong commentary. ". . .and you're stupid if you think that Liere and Sartora are indeed the same person, which is thought by all *stupid* parties of the first part, second part, and third part, we—in corpus, which in the *stupid* language called Latin means 'in corpse,' meaning a dead body, which we wish you all were . . ." On and on, total gibberish, keeping at it until someone came—or she saw her chance at escape.

MV had waited at first to see how long she could keep it up, until it became clear she was completely crack-brained and could go on like that forever. He was getting bored, and besides, they had orders. Best to wrap this up and smoke before real trouble turned up.

He loomed over her, but instead of quailing, she got even angrier, so he dropped a knife from his wrist sheath and held it at her throat. At least that got her attention.

"Yecch!" she yelped, hating her own fear, and screamed the worst insult she could think of: "Go to Hell! Oh, wait, you just came from there!"

"Where?" MV grinned, then moved away as she shakily wiped her neck off with her skirt, trying to calm her jangling nerves. "Never mind that. Where's Liere?" he asked.

"Where you'll never find her!" CJ snapped, and she decided it was her turn for some answers. "What's firejive?"

His head jerked back, his expression tightening, then he sneered, "It means the runny shits. How far away is 'where we'll never find her'?"

"Travel a million miles and it'll do you no good," CJ gloated.

"She's got the dyr, right?"

"You're an idiot."

MV gave her a kind of dispassionate snort and turned his head. "Laban!"

"Yeah?" came the far-off cry.

"Both of 'em are hiding somewhere here. Any maps, ours

or theirs?"

"Hang on."

CJ glared, wondering how he'd figured that out. Did he have Dena Yeresbeth? If he did, why go through the questions? It was because she hadn't lied, she thought in disgust. She'd buried the truth in snotty answers, thinking herself so clever.

Time to warn the others.

When MV went off to see what Laban wanted, she jumped up, bolted to the desk with the blotter, and slammed her hand on it, hoping someone was in the throne room and would see her handprint on the message blotter up there. She didn't dare linger to write — and even then, she wasn't fast enough to get to the tunnel before a hand clamped on the collar of her shirt and yanked her back. "I didn't tell you to move," MV said, and thumped her back onto the chair.

She launched up again, squawking insults, and he smacked her again, the way he did Noser when he was at his most annoying. She was annoying in exactly the same way, and just as crazy. "Stay put," he said, and went to roust Laban.

CJ got shakily to her feet, the familiar pain of a beating throwing her emotions all the way back to early childhood. *Hide, hide, hide,* her mind sang.

She was alone in the room. She catapulted up the exit tunnel and despite swimming vision made it out on the first try.

As she ran outside, the dizziness began to pass — though not enough to keep her from stumbling over a tree root she'd known about forever, and landing full length in the grass.

She got up, started to run, and fell again, this time deliberately tripped by Laban. "Back inside, twit," Laban said as she scrambled to her feet, dizzy again. "We're not done with you."

Her screech reverberated through the forest.

MV appeared behind her, then muttered an unheated, "Oh, shit," as he yanked out a knife.

Then sunlight glinted off a silver streak, and MV whipped his hand back, but not fast enough. A knife blade scored across his hand then vanished in the bushes behind him.

MV glanced from the blood across the back of his hand to the trees, and this time he grinned, a real grin, as he shook the welling blood off his hand. Rel emerged from the shadows, aiming straight for MV, Senrid right behind him.

CJ looked around wildly. Nearby Rel and MV fought hard

and fast, MV still occasionally wringing his bleeding hand while Puddlenose closed in from the other side, Christoph right behind.

Laban hovered about, loathing what he knew what was supposed to come next. To his surprise, he saw MV backing up, hard-pressed by Rel, who seemed impervious to MV's hard strikes. The few that landed.

Laban said in a sharp voice, "Rel!" and Rel's head turned.

MV hammered a third punch to Rel's gut, then a round-house kick to his jaw.

Rel went down and didn't get up, as Senrid tackled Laban, and the two went rolling into a nearby shrub. CJ sucked in a breath and let loose a throat-scraping scream as she hooked her fingers and went straight for MV's face.

He opened his hand, knocked her back into a tree, and ran off, Adam at his heels.

Eleven

CJ FOUGHT DOWN THE nausea and twinkling lights, leaned back against the tree and drew a few shuddering breaths. The enemy was gone and she had survived. It had been far worse when she was small. Far, far worse. No wire hangers or belt buckles this time, only some slaps, and all from an enemy she could hate instead of from her own father, who was supposed to keep her safe. She could hate Detlev's poopsies freely, and did; the worst pain had been when she crashed into the tree. But she could still move. She should move. Get help. While her fingers felt cautiously over the sticky spot on her scalp, and the aching side of her face, she looked around.

The clearing was a spectacular mess, with spring grass gouged up and flattened everywhere. Rel still lay on the ground, and near him Laban, both unconscious. Christoph and Puddlenose bent over Rel. Senrid stood near Laban, looking down, his hair in his eyes, one hand absently wiping at a nasty trickle of red from his nose.

Dhana was also there. She was the only one who didn't look like she'd been through a hurricane, which meant she'd arrived from her patrol too late to help.

"Here, let's wake Rel up, in case they come back for that." Dhana pointed down at Laban.

CJ turned blearily to see who Dhana was talking to and

discovered Falinneh, who began shaking her finger and insulting the oblivious Laban, daring him to get up and fight. Despite the distortion of a rapidly swelling eye, Puddlenose snickered at Falinneh's bluster.

Senrid didn't notice. Of all those on their feet he looked the worst, and he was probably trying to collect his wits.

"What happened?" CJ asked. "How did you know they were here?"

Dhana came over with her quick, graceful step. CJ watched with a detached pleasure, wondering if it was possible for her to do anything awkwardly as Dhana bent and lightly touched the side of CJ's head with a finger. "Who did that?"

CJ winced. "Hands off," she said, even though Dhana's touch was barely felt. "That clotpole MV. Rel okay?"

"Waking up now," Christoph said.

Rel stirred and sat up right then, wincing as he pressed a hand to his ribs.

"What happened?" CJ asked again. "How did you know?"

"We didn't," Irenne said, hands out wide. "We decided to come down to the Junky for hot chocolate. The boys went first, and heard you scream."

"Two of them got away," Christoph said, then grinned and nudged Laban's unconscious form with a bare toe. "This one tried to. Senrid dropped him."

"They'll probably be back," Rel said. "If they didn't find what they were looking for."

"What do we do about Laban?" Sherry asked.

Everyone turned to where Laban still lay motionless.

"If they even care," CJ put in. "I wouldn't," she said as Laban's unconscious body was picked up and borne back down the tunnel by Puddlenose and Christoph. Rel followed slowly, wincing at each step, but when the others stopped in the main room he kept right on going down to the next level.

CJ pushed forward the chair that she'd been stuck in a short while before, and they plopped Laban into it.

"Well, if we're going to do it, let's do it right," Senrid said. "Anyone got any rope?"

"Will sashes do?" Irenne asked.

Senrid shrugged.

Irenne vanished and reappeared with a handful of pretty silken sashes. Senrid tied Laban into the chair.

Just then Clair came up the tunnel from Diana's room, with

Diana frowning as she said, ". . .and everything has been rooted through. All my knife collection is missing."

Clair sighed, wiping her hair back off her brow. "I'd better get upstairs and help Mearsieanne with the extra wards up there. We still don't really know why they were here."

"Of course we do," Sherry said, looking surprised. "They wanted the Junky for their very own! CJ even said Adam liked it."

"Then why didn't they stay and defend it?" Clair asked. "No, I think they were here for something else." In a lower voice, "Or someone else."

Everyone turned to CJ, who muttered through numb lips, "Liere. Dyr."

Liere emerged from Seshe's room down the tunnel, her face serious.

"Is Rel okay?" Clair asked.

"Says he's fine besides a couple cracked ribs," Liere said, wincing. "He's going to lie down for a while, if you don't need him for anything. He seems to be in awful pain from them."

"Not just that," Senrid said. "It's the headache. Kick to the jaw like that. He's probably half blind."

No one wanted to ask what kind of experience made him such an expert on that reaction; Liere seemed to hear some sort of threat in Senrid's quiet voice, because she said, "What do you intend to do with him?" She pointed at Laban, who was now securely tied in the chair, his head drooping forward.

"What do they intend to do to us?" Senrid retorted.

The others watched, startled. No one else ever talked to Liere like that.

She put her hands on her hips, her face mottled. "So you want to be like them?"

"'Course not," Senrid retorted. "But we can hostage him against further attacks, maybe. And in the meantime have a little fun."

"Fun," Liere repeated, her tone not the least bit humorous. Then she turned her back and walked into the kitchen alcove.

Senrid rolled his eyes.

Puddlenose said with a thoughtful air, "I take it she won't like it if we cut him into bits and send the pieces back to Detlev."

CJ turned her glare at Laban, whose head still drooped forward. "Sure he'd want him? Betcha he'd send him right back," she cracked, and everyone laughed.

"What happened?" Gwen asked.

CJ embarked on a highly colored version of her experience, peppered with plenty of commentary on the enemy, while her audience cackled most gratifyingly. . .until they all heard a derisive snort from the other side of the room.

Everybody swivel-necked to take in Laban, who was very much awake. He stared back with a challenging sneer, despite being mud-covered and disheveled, his hands bound fast behind the chair back.

"How'd you find this place?" Senrid asked him.

Laban's eyes were a bright blue, vivid and derisive as he sneered, "I didn't."

"Told you it was Adam," Falinneh chortled. "Oh, did he play us! And he was so nice while doing it."

Laban's tone was indifferent. "You've left trails all over a blind man could follow. Staked out a trail crossing. Waited for one of you to come along."

Diana scowled. She'd been nagging the girls for ages about that very thing.

Arthur's brow puckered. "Where is Roy?"

Laban's lip curled, puffy as it was.

Gwen snorted. "Too much for his tiny mind. His Majesty answereth not." She said that last part in Laban's voice, but with a babyish tone.

Laban looked startled, which brought a big laugh. Then Christoph leaped up to bow and scrape, offering Laban all kinds of ridiculous things, served in goblets of gold and so forth, laying on the Your Majestys.

Falinneh had to jump in. Any kind of word game got her going. "Wouldest thou like some royal pea soup?" she warbled. "Or prefer a pinch of imperial prune pie?"

"A more comfortable throne?" Christoph bowed again.

"Or a more comfortable palace — at the bottom of the sea?" Irenne drawled, nose in the air.

Laban looked bored, though there was a telltale flush along his cheeks.

Then CJ got an idea. She loathed love songs, but had heard popular ones enough to have learned the typical patterns, which she turned into parodies to entertain the girls. In her best voice, she sang,

"Oh my dear I loathest thee

so do me a favor and abandon me . . ."

Puddlenose and Christoph clapped and cheered. Then Seshe, who distrusted the ugly mood of the listening circle, came out with a tray of root brew in fine porcelain mugs, hoping to distract her friends.

> *". . .oh my dear I'd die at thy will*
> *And thou hast already made me deathly ill!"*

Christoph, who never took anything seriously, raised his mug. "Let us drink," he proclaimed, "to the great Laban, Prince of Poopsies!"

As everyone made flourishes with their mugs, CJ heady with triumph at having at last pleased everyone, stepped up to Laban, sneering with righteous anger. "Want to be crowned?" she asked Laban in a loud voice, and as he stared back with a curled lip of scorn, she snarled, "I now anoint thee King of the Chuckleheads!"

And crashed the mug over his head.

The mug shattered.

She stood in shocked hilarity and apprehension, staring at the mixture of crimson-streaked brown liquid that ran down his face to puddle with ceramic shards on his lap, as her fingers clutched the handle.

"Cherenneh Jennet." Liere's voice hit her like an ice-ball in the back of the neck.

"I didn't expect it to break," CJ mumbled.

Puddlenose gave CJ a thump on the shoulder that made her stagger. "Nice one," he said.

Liere ignored them all. "You are acting like *them*." She pointed at Laban.

"Oh, lay off," Senrid said in a hard voice. "He's all right. We'll clean him up."

Liere gave Senrid a look of perplexity as CJ stole a guilty glance at Laban. She saw a gash on the side of his head, which was bleeding in a garish trickle. One of his eyes squinted, the other gazing at her with contempt.

Guilt warred with anger, and anger won. "You deserved that for what you creeps did to Karhin, who never hurt anybody in her life."

She threw the broken mug handle on the pile that Sherry

had silently picked up from Laban's lap, and ran out, shaking with reaction.

She wandered around purposelessly, trying hard to convince herself that her action was justified — that knot on her own head was still throbbing sullenly. Then she drifted back to listen in on the talk, braced against hearing herself described as a villain all over again.

But every conversation she overheard was about *them* — their purpose, and what to do.

Somehow, though no one was blaming her, the sick feeling inside hadn't abated, so she went to look in on Rel. They'd put him in Seshe's room, as nearest one with an empty bunk. He looked completely incongruous, lying there on top of her blue-and-white patterned quilt, his feet dangling over the edge of the bed. His bruised, swollen face was almost unrecognizable. He squinted at CJ like he had the king of all headaches, and CJ began to tiptoe backward.

Rel opened his eyes and flipped up fingers to stop her. "How many of 'em?" he asked.

"I only saw three. MV, Laban, and Adam the painter." She scowled. "I wonder if all those good drawings of his are all fake?"

Again the flip of dismissive fingers, as if to say, who cares? "Tell me what happened with MV."

She related the story, though by now she was thoroughly sick of it. At the end, she said, "What did you get out of that?"

"They are definitely after Liere. We have to get her out of here."

"I know, but they still can't decide where she ought to go. Senrid wants to take her to Marloven Hess, but Clair is afraid that a magic transfer might be compromised."

"Then we need to keep a sharp eye on Laban. The others have to be coming back for him."

"You're going to patrol?"

He gave a tiny nod. "Soon's I can stand without puking."

Laban was transferred up to the white palace, which everyone felt would be easier to guard, now that Detlev's boys had breached the hideout. They'd even untied him, which CJ really resented, but didn't dare speak. She was glad that Senrid sent off some fast notes to Keriam back in Marloven Hess, saying that he needed to remain longer. Senrid, Puddlenose, and Christoph trailed Laban around, never fewer than two of them, usually all three around, as elsewhere in the white palace, debates about what to do with their prisoner were fierce.

CJ slunk along the perimeter, hating the fact that however she justified her actions to herself, those she respected most among her friends felt she'd acted the part of a villain. She wanted Laban gone, and the evidence of her action gone with him. She avoided the discussions (while noticing that no one asked her opinion) until she finally cornered Clair. "Can't we get rid of him?"

Clair looked pained, her gaze shifting away. "That's just it. Arthur says that Tahra has been writing a stream of letters insisting that we send him to Everon and execute him as a murderer, for Glenn's death."

"But I thought one of the others actually did it."

"Yes, and it was a duel, and Glenn forced it on that boy. Even Canold—one of the Knight trainees who saw what happened—admits it. But Laban is one of the group, and she feels they share responsibility."

"A group of poopsies," CJ said. "I love the name, because it's the opposite of ominous and wicked, which I'm sure they love being thought of as. What villain wants to be called a poopsie?"

Clair spread her hands. "But finding a suitable insult doesn't solve the problem of Laban."

"I *wish* we could get rid of him. Um, some other way."

"So do I." Clair sighed. "We took a prisoner once before, remember?"

"Jilo," CJ whispered. "But we let him go!"

"Yes," Clair said. "And he's done good things for Chwahirsland."

CJ burst out, "But he wasn't a villain!"

"We thought he was," Clair reminded her.

"That has nothing to do with Laban," CJ retorted. And ran out.

Later, when she drifted back to listen, she heard Falinneh say to Laban, "So what does Detlev do in his free time?"

Laban's brows rose. "What free time?"

Gwen crumbled a biscuit, her brow puckered. "You mean he works all the time?"

"Works!" CJ exclaimed, forgetting that she meant to stay on the periphery listening. But indignation boiled over. "You call attacking people and countries *work*? I call it villainy!"

"When we see him, he's working," Laban said. No mistaking his amusement at these questions. "We don't see him much. Run independently."

CJ was so disgusted that she pushed past Senrid and went out to walk off her temper. But later on, she spotted Laban in one of the high towers of the white palace, to all appearances enjoying the view. Puddlenose and Christoph sat at the bottom of the stairs, playing cards.

CJ'd thought that Norsundrians couldn't get into the upper stories. Maybe the wards had been broken, or were fading, after the strange magic that had brought the city down from its cloud. She wondered what evil Laban was perpetrating. Maybe he was trying to signal Detlev somehow! Except he didn't have a lantern or anything.

She backed out and climbed the narrow, pearlescent stairway (more like a ladder) to the turret directly above Laban, though it was scary to be so high, where the wind blew through, icy cold. It was scary and thrilling at the same time.

Far below the setting sun touched the autumnal leaves of the forest to fire, while above, the wispy clouds threw back a glory of delicate colors. The only time CJ liked pink was at sunset, especially contrasted with the deep indigo of the night sky to the east, with the first stars glimmering.

What was Laban looking at? There wasn't a military thing in sight, and no Norsundrian could possibly be watching a sunset. CJ squirmed with conflicted feelings, wanting to be rid of him, to keep the purity of the night sky, and the tower, to those who deserved it.

Gripping the weird white stone with all her strength, she leaned cautiously out and peered down at the balcony below. Laban leaned on the rail, his shoulder-blades poking past the wind-ripples in his shirt, his dark hair blowing wildly around the bandage over the side of his head.

She scanned the view more carefully as the sun vanished, deepening the colors. He could be trying to spot the Junky! The girls had experimented and knew the exact location that broad sea of foliage. But his profile was turned elsewhere.

She began to sing the prettiest, most heartwarming and uplifting song she knew, all about harmony and accord and how Norsunder would dwindle away to nothing, leaving peace and plenty. She fully expected him to clap his hands over his ears and run. Or maybe shrivel up and blow away.

But his head lifted, and he actually was listening, so she shifted to an insult song, with his name added in. He listened to that, too—and when peeked down and saw his shoulders shaking with suppressed laughter, she slunk away, furious with herself.

The next day, Laban insisted on taking the bandage off.

CJ met Senrid outside the kitchen. "How long are we going to be stuck with that idiot?"

"Don't know." When he saw CJ's grimace, Senrid made a disparaging gesture. "Puddlenose and Christoph think they're guarding him, but I think he's loitering. I don't know why."

"So he can grab Liere?"

"That's what I think. What else could it be? Seshe seems to want to think he'd like to switch sides."

CJ hooted with laughter. Then, "So that's why the girls are sticking to Liere like glue."

Senrid flashed that toothy grin. "I better go see if they want a break guarding."

CJ retreated, leaving Laban to the boys, and holed up in her room.

Next morning, Sherry woke everyone with a horrified screech. They stampeded out of their rooms to discover Senrid lying on the floor with a knife in his right shoulder.

Not that CJ had to go far.

Senrid lay right outside her door.

Twelve

CJ SAT DOWN ABRUPTLY on the embroidered hassock in her room as Puddlenose and Christoph carried Senrid away. For an endless time all she could think was, *It's all my fault.*

Gradually she began aware of one of Steward Janil's nephews mopping up the blood smears from the white stone flooring.

CJ felt faint again, until she was aware of Sherry leaning over her, curls almost brushing her forehead. "He's breathing, CJ. Boneribs is okay. Can you hear me?"

Clair spoke from behind Sherry. "The healer just left." CJ blinked up at her as she wiped a shaky hand over her eyes. "Says he didn't lose much blood, and the wound missed anything important."

"Not much blood? It looked like *buckets*," Falinneh exclaimed, her face so blanched her freckles looked like they'd been drawn on.

Seshe appeared, her long ivory gown splashing with sunlight as she passed the window in the hall. She looked as sick as everyone else. "Liere is sitting with him. She is trying to find him by that whatever-it-is." She touched her high forehead.

"I think I'm going to take up my archery again," Clair said grimly.

The others were silent, though everyone there knew she did

not mean for sport. Even Seshe did not mention the Covenant, which after all had been an agreement between kingdoms to confine warfare to handheld weapons only.

Nobody made Covenants with Norsunder.

Liere came downstairs. "He's awake," she said quickly. She looked skinnier than ever, and tired. "He's awake. The wound in his shoulder healed up with a bloodknife mark."

"That's not true healing." Mearsieanne appeared in the doorway of the magic chambers. "Lyren is playing upstairs," she said quietly.

Liere flushed guiltily. "Thank you."

"You were up all night reading. Go sleep," Mearsieanne said. "And try not to be absurd."

Liere flitted away, and Irenne said, "What was that about?"

Mearsieanne's blue eyes flicked upward briefly. "Steward Janil is a grandmother, and used to babies. Lyren has so many people watching out for her, she is perfectly fine. But Liere feels that as a rebuke, for some reason."

"Typical." Falinneh mouthed the word, but at least she didn't say it out loud.

Later on, CJ lurked by Senrid's door to see how he was doing. He lay with his eyes closed, and she turned away, still gnawed with guilt, until his voice arrested her.

"I'm bored. If you sneak away again I'll have to get up and strangle you."

CJ breathed in relief, and walked inside. "With what?" She pointed to the mass of bandages keeping his right arm to his side.

"My toes."

"You look like you fell off a thousand foot cliff. I just hope you gave Laban-lice something to remember you by."

Senrid grinned, the puffy bruises on his visible skin distorting horribly. "I think his pretty face will impress his friends. But he won that scrap. I don't remember him dragging me to your door. Little message to us both, eh?" He touched his bandaged shoulder.

Christoph and Puddlenose showed up, Puddlenose saying, "I told you not to be alone with him! Why didn't you wake me up?"

"I thought he was asleep," Senrid admitted.

CJ slid out and began to wander the palace.

Something was wrong, she was sure of it. Then she

remembered why MV and the other two had attacked in the first place.

"Liere," she breathed.

She tore off to her room — empty. Neat as if she'd never been there.

Library — nobody there.

Magic chambers? Empty, Clair and Arthur studying, and of course Mearsieanne was downstairs with petitioners.

CJ remembered that comment Liere had made — *She's safer with you than she is with me* — and realized that Liere meant it.

Of course she did. She never said wild things, unlike the rest of them.

Feeling even more that everything was her fault, her only thought was that she had to be the one to find Liere. She transferred to the Junky, just in case.

Empty.

Where now? Liere didn't have transfer magic, or if she did wasn't using it, which meant she was on foot. Dtheldevor's gang had sailed away already, so the sea was out. Westward was forest, and if you went far enough, desert. South to the rest of the continent, but north? Eventually you could reach Bereth Ferian . . .

CJ began to run. The sky was beginning to cloud over when CJ spotted the lone, forlorn figure in the middle of the road ahead, clusters of chestnut and oak to either side framing meadows of tall spring grass.

CJ panted up, then said hoarsely, "Why are you running? Sartora, you must be the dumbest Ancient Sartoran alive!"

Liere recoiled as if she'd been slapped. "I am not an Ancient Sartoran," she said softly.

CJ panted, then shook her head, her uncombed black hair falling in tangles around her. "I don't even know what Ancient Sartoran means, except that Dena Yeresbeth — "

"Which you have."

"But mine doesn't make me smarter. It doesn't even work half the time."

"It's exactly the same for me." Liere's thin fingers pressed to her collarbones, her face distraught. "You feel like you're emptying a pool with a spoon, I feel like I'm emptying the sea with a spoon. We both fail. They nearly *killed* Senrid, and because of *me!* I've put you all into danger just by my presence."

"Horse manure!"

"I have." She crossed her arms, hugging her scrawny elbows against her ribs. "We all know I'm what they are after, me and this thing." On her palm lay the shiny, faintly gleaming round silver object. "Therefore I put Senrid in danger."

CJ backed away from the dyr, though she knew it was pointless. "Um, maybe it's time for you to learn some self-defense."

"Senrid keeps saying that. But how can I?" Liere shook her head. "Senrid takes lessons, and look what happened to him!"

"Puddlenose said Senrid should not have been alone with Laban." CJ realized too late that her protest actually proved Liere's point, kind of. But that was no reason not to *try*.

Liere began to walk again, and CJ had the uncomfortable feeling her words only sounded like nagging. They stopped beside a stream, and CJ bent to slurped up a handful of water, then wiped her fingers down her skirt, and tried again. "Liere, Senrid wanted to stay and help. Everybody did. You have to let them do it. Or you'll just feel bad forever."

Liere raised her gaze as an arrow of long-necked birds winged across the low sky toward the desert in the west. Tears gleamed along her lower eyelids.

CJ tucked her hands into her armpits and began flapping them as she did the chicken-walk. "I know I am a chicken, bucka-buck, have always been a chicken, *squawwwwwk!* And always will be a chicken, and I have to figure out chicken ways to get away from villains—"

Liere's lips twitched. CJ felt as if she'd won a battle, and continued clowning in a desperate venture to jolly Liere out of that distraught, lost expression.

The sudden patter of rain nearly obscured footsteps approaching from behind.

Liere sensed danger first, and her hand took CJ's, pressing a cold thing into her palm as MV sauntered up. "And there you are, right on schedule. A twofer!"

They whirled to run, but Adam was right behind them, having come from the other direction. He got between the girls as MV slapped a transfer token against Liere. Adam, MV, and Liere vanished.

CJ had failed again.

She kicked a boulder as hard as she could with her bare toes, sobbing with fury and pain. She reached for her medallion to transfer back home, then remembered the dyr in her hand—

possibly loaded with tracers — and began hobbling back as rain pelted down.

She scarcely noticed. The horror of imagination was far too vivid. In her mind she stood there beside Liere in Norsunder with Detlev and Siamis gloating and slavering over who got to kill her, or maybe they argued about who would question her first, a table full of torture instruments at hand.

The truth was far less sanguinary.

MV, remembering the lesson about prisoners, gave Liere an effective, impersonal search, and not finding the dyr, hauled her by the collar to Detlev's office in the command wing.

Of course Detlev was not there. So MV waited for the next patrol, and told them loudly that this was Detlev's prisoner, and to stash her until his return.

Then he returned, and grimly started making new transfer tokens.

Everon

A wave of cold spring rains kept everyone off the streets in Everon's royal city, except those who had patrol, or to do business.

Roderic Dei, Commander of the Knights of Dei, made his own round of the palace, leaving patrol to the Knights. He noted sadly, though he was not surprised, that each week saw fewer of Glenn's recruits gathering at the enormous salle that was the only building Glenn had ordered put up after ordering the destruction of the old royal garden. Much of the rest of the royal palace still wore its fire scars from Henerek's attempted attack, and Kessler Sonscarna's successful assault, almost five years previous.

Rain splashed down, running in the gutters as he made his way to his home, where his wife had left a fire burning in the central stove, and a baked pie cooling on the brick shelf next to it.

From a far room echoed the high voices of his younger daughters. It was a good sound, a cheerful sound — youth and life. He needed that, he thought as he sank tiredly into his armchair. Soon . . .eventually . . .he would get up and change, and eat, but not yet . . .not yet . . .

"Roderic."

The soft, low voice seemed at first to come out of the world of dreams.

He would know that voice anywhere. "Mersedes?"

But then a cold touch on his hand startled him, and he gazed up into a ruined face whose lineaments had been dearest to his heart for most of his life.

"Mersedes?" He started up from his chair, then fell back, waves of shadow nearly blotting her from his vision.

But that passed, and he stared up at the queen, missing for so long, in an agony of horror at her appearance.

"I've been walking around this past day," she said. "Even one-eyed, I can see . . .how difficult it has been." She let out her breath in a short sigh, and her gaze wandered around the room. "Do you know, this is the first time I've ever set foot in your house? And yet I've always known where you lived."

Roderic and his wife Seiran—now a duchas in her own right—had married with the knowledge that the queen would in a sense always exist between them. Seiran had understood Roderick's passion for the queen, for half the court had been in love with Mersedes Carinna, in addition to the wayward king. But she had married him anyway. In return Roderic had felt that his home ought to be Seiran's citadel; the fancy house on the main avenue that the king had insisted on giving them, burned to the ground in the Norsunder attack, had been merely for social occasions. They had never lived there.

None of that seemed to matter anymore. Nothing did. His wits had flown.

"Mersedes, sit down. Your majesty. Please. Let me send for the healer," he said, his stuttering mind reaching for sense.

"No," she said as she sank into the opposite chair.

"But . . ." He stared helplessly, the emotional agony as intense as if he, and not she, had endured whatever had happened to render her so desperately thin, with bruises and scars new and old, her fingers gnarled from healing badly after being broken. She kept two fingers curled under, to protect the finger ends with fingernails no longer there. His stomach knotted as he perceived this, and knotted again when his gaze returned to her face, and the rag tied around one eye. "The healer," he repeated.

She lifted a shoulder. "Healers cannot replace what no longer exists. I can see well enough on this side, so I have walked about to find out how much of what I overheard while a prisoner was distortion, how much truth, and how much outright lies."

Roderic let out his breath. "I am so sorry I couldn't find you. We searched—"

She waved a hand. "You could not have saved me. I was in the Beyond for a time—no light or air, no sup or sip. And then Henerek came to try to force me to make a writ signing the kingdom over to him, with the result you see before you. Until a power struggle at Norsunder Base, in which one enemy turned on another, and so I was freed. I see great changes here, where the Knights once lived. I know my son is dead. Henerek crowed over that."

Roderic gave her the shortest, blandest report possible. Then, "Tahra laid emphasis on law and former royal decree, which I supported with my most imposing manner while standing at her left side. But always, always, everything in your name. They long for your return."

"They long for the old days," Mersedes said. "As do I. But those days are gone forever. And so my longing is to join Berthold, and Valenn, and all those who wait beyond the world."

"But we need you—we need a queen, until Tahra can learn—"

"Roderic. I am so tired. Please do not make me argue. We both know that she is better educated than I ever was. I was a fighter, and a lover, and I merely reigned over a merry court. Berthold ruled. Tahra will learn to rule. None better, with her penchant for numbers. And with you safely at her left side, as you said. The guide and guard." Mersedes's smile trembled. "Roderic, I know you would cut your own throat before assuming the kingship."

He bowed, though they both knew that he was in effect king. But he would relinquish it when he could.

"How does Tahra on her own?" Mersedes asked gently.

"She's learning," he said. "In her way. She needs to recover from so much grief. Which will be the faster with you back—"

"No," she said. "Do not tell her that I am here."

Roderic stared, stunned. "What?"

"Roderic, I am broken in more ways than you can see. I survived with a single goal: killing Henerek. Did you know that he is assembling bands of outlaws in the western mountains?"

"No," Roderick breathed.

"He took great pleasure in describing, in detail, how many he has, where they are, and how he'll come against us. And of course what he'd do to all you." Her voice dropped to guttural fury. "Which I shall visit upon his own body if I possibly can."

"But—"

"He's coming back, now that Tahra is alone. It's *always* going to be this way," she said, low and fierce. "Norsunder is always going to come back, and there will be war, again, and again, and again. That is the nature of evil. There is no room in me for anything but my vow of vengeance."

Roderick's nerves chilled when he saw the rage distorting her one visible eye: he shied from the notion that Norsunder was indeed already here.

But she saw it in his expression, and the ferocity smoothed from her expression, her smile crimped with more pain than amusement. Her head dropped back, as a tear filled her one eye, and ran unevenly down her scarred cheek. "The dawnsingers speak of the never-ending mercy that awaits us beyond death. I've never believed in justice, though I tried to live as if I did. I certainly never believed we could find it after death. But now, with every breath, I hope for that mercy because the one gift I can give my poor daughter, whom I never understood, and who never understood me, is to destroy this one threat."

"But . . ."

"She already believes me dead."

"She refuses to admit to it. She speaks of you as alive."

"I suspect that is her habit, her stubbornness, her penchant for order. I want her to believe I'm dead, so that once I save her kingdom from Henerek she will not mourn twice."

"Your majesty . . ."

"This is an order. Perhaps my last, as a queen. And here is a suggestion from my heart: don't leave Tahra alone. I mean, give her people her age. Surround her with your girls."

"But that is not seemly. Your majesty." He took refuge in protocol, because he knew he was arguing with her

She sighed. "You are really using rank as a defensive thrust?" She waited for him to remember that she was the daughter of a not-very-successful wandering con man, and leaned forward to touch the top of his hand. "You and Seiran are raising smart girls with clean hearts. They are what Tahra needs, more than advisors. Though she needs them, too. But principally she needs friends who understand her, who will be patient with her ways. Your Carinna has always been good to her."

Roderic forced himself to bow.

"You are to order the Knights to scour out that infestation on our border, and I shall ride along as a scout. When the time comes, I'll deal with Henerek on my own. I have just enough strength to carry out this last plan, if there truly is justice. Or mercy. It is my will."

"Mersedes, I hate this plan."

"I know, Roderic, dear. But you shall do it."

She waited, compassionate but immoveable.

At length he said slowly, "I shall do it. But I warn you, I will exert myself to talk you out of it."

"Talk to me, Roderic. It will help me remember the good days. But when you begin to ride, Carl will join you."

His breath caught: that was the name she had first adopted when she had disguised herself as a boy to escape her father, and joined the Knights, a lifetime ago, when they were all young.

Thirteen

Mearsies Heili

CJ REACHED THE WHITE palace very late at night, and found herself promptly surrounded.

As soon as the others understood that Liere was gone, and that CJ had run after her to try to stop her, they began pelting CJ with questions.

"Where's the dyr?"

"They got her? How?"

"Why didn't you come to get one of us?"

At "What are we going to tell little Lyren when she wakes up?" CJ screamed, "Tell her I'm *stupid!*"

She threw the dyr down on the marble floor and ran to her room, leaving red smudges behind where her bleeding toes made marks.

Clair stepped out to pick up the dyr, saying, "Let her alone for a bit. I think I know what to do with this thing."

Arthur said, "I could take it back to Erai-Yanya."

Mearsieanne stepped out, arms crossed. She was polite, but adamant as she said, "You in the north had it, and almost lost it. I think we can find somewhere here to keep it."

Clair glanced from one to the other, and Arthur saw tension in her usually smooth brow. "My idea was to put it in the

Selenseh Redian, before anything more happens."

Mearsieanne grimaced slightly. "You know I dislike going in there."

"Everybody does," Falinneh put in, rolling her eyes.

"I don't," Clair said. "I like the caves. Always have. I know just the place, and best of all, Norsundrians can't get in there. When the mages decide what to do with it, we'll know where it is."

Before anyone could speak—or argue—she closed her fingers around the dyr and transferred.

Arthur looked at the spot where she'd stood, then at Mearsieanne, who had already turned away, her skirts sweeping the floor as she summoned a servant to clean the blood stains.

Arthur decided that he'd had enough. The dyr was gone. Liere was as well. Clair might once have wanted to talk magic studies, but now she had Mearsieanne, who had no use for anyone in Bereth Ferian, nor did she have much interest in the matter of the Venn, which was Arthur's current favorite project.

Further, Detlev's boys had gone. They had their target, and he didn't believe anyone had tracers lying in wait for him. At least at home, he could change out these books and get on with his project. Be useful.

He forced himself to follow Mearsieanne and thank her for his stay. She gave him a regal nod, and said nothing about safety or staying.

He transferred home, then stood in the quiet Destination chamber, looking out at the autumnal beeches. Nothing stirred that he could see, so he hefted his worn bag of books, and retreated to the sanctuary of his study.

From the shadows back in the hallway, Ferret, who had waited patiently for the past three weeks, touched two fingers to the top shank on his shirt. The magic glowed blue for a heartbeat, and he knew Siamis would have received the message: Arthur was back.

And just in time.

Mearsieanne forgot Arthur the moment he stepped outside the door. She was furious that the Norsundrians had managed to snatch Liere, furious at Liere for running, and furious at CJ for not warning anyone. But what could you expect of youngsters with no experience?

The rest of the company had dispersed in various direct-ions, some airing their views to anyone who would listen, except for CJ, curled up in a miserable ball in her room until exhaustion claimed her and she slept.

She woke abruptly with a pounding headache. She lay in the morning light, staring up at the blue and silver and white ceiling in her room, but even this haven of safety was no longer safe. Her eyes were sore, and her foot throbbed, but she felt miserably that she deserved every pang.

Then Irenne strode in, her rose and pink flouncy skirts swaying from side to side.

"I knew it." She proper her fists on her hips. "You're worse than Liere!"

"I'm scum," CJ said morosely.

"Don't you *dare* blame yourself," Irenne declared, hazel eyes wide. "Stick that foot out. I'm going to bandage it, so you won't have to have any grownup healer fussing at you."

"But it's my fault—" CJ began.

"Senrid said you were smart to keep that dyr thingie away from them. Mearsieanne agrees."

The fact that Mearsieanne would agree with anything Senrid said was more convincing than any argument. CJ knew that Mearsieanne distrusted Marlovens, and didn't like Senrid visiting, though she didn't *say* anything. The rare times Senrid had come since Mearsieanne's return, she simply wasn't around until he left again.

"But Lyren . . . I guess I should be the one to tell her, so she'll be mad at me—"

"Lyren already knows," Irenne said. She tapped her head. "She woke up saying that Liere is far away, but she'll come back as soon as she can. Kids that age, they only pay attention to what's right in front of them. And Lyren has a castle full of nannies."

Leaving CJ nothing to say, except to feel guilty for her sag of relief.

Irenne pulled a tiny pot of salve from a pocket and rubbed it gently over CJ's toes, as CJ hissed and groaned. When she was done, she wrapped CJ's foot in a bandage as she said, "Senrid wants to talk to you. About those horrible bloodknife things."

CJ gasped. "That knife Laban stuck in him. It was enchanted?"

"It sure was."

A short time later she reached the room Senrid was staying in. When he saw her, he unbuttoned the top two shanks of his shirt and yanked the neck opening over to show no bandages. There, amid a couple of healing bruises, was the horribly familiar smooth faintly shiny white line, like a slug track—a wound closed by dark magic. "Laban could have killed me," Senrid said, shrugging the shirt back into place. "There has to be a reason he didn't."

CJ's mouth pressed into a flat line. "Because they want to get at your mind by magic."

"That's what I thought." He rubbed his shoulder, his forehead tense. She waited, but he stayed silent a long time, and when he looked up, it was to ask, "Did yours itch?"

"Numb." CJ hated remembering her experiences with an enchanted knife, but if it helped him to talk about it, she would. Only if he asked. Because in a weird way she couldn't quite figure out, it felt almost like bragging. "Burned at night. Cold and hot."

Maybe they'd already started their attack. If so, no wonder there were dark smudges under his eyes. And as the memories she'd worked hard to push away resurfaced, she exclaimed, "That horrible Kessler knows how to get rid of the enchantment."

Senrid's breath hissed in. "Does he?" His eyes widened, then narrowed. "But how does one get hold of him?"

She sighed. "I dunno, but ask Rel. He was there when Kessler made mine go away, just to get back at Dejain. And, didn't somebody say something about Rel and Jilo and bloodknife wounds, right before he got to Delfin Island?"

Senrid's tense forehead smoothed out. "I'm glad you told me that. I think I'll move on before Laban shows up to finish the job. He's welcome to make another try in Marloven Hess. *If* he can get past my wards, he'll find half an army waiting for the first cut."

CJ laughed humorlessly at the thought of Laban trying to sneak past Senrid's billions of guards—just to get lost in that maze of a castle. "I hope he does, and I hope you stick him in a dungeon to rot. After dumping a barrel of horse manure over his head."

Senrid paused in pulling on his boots. "Can't promise the second one, but the first one? That's the plan." He grimaced against the pain in every joint, and the cold, weird numbness in his shoulder.

CJ flitted out, limping on one foot. Senrid followed more slowly. He found Rel with Puddlenose and Christoph eating breakfast, their travel gear heaped in a corner. "You're leaving?" he asked the three.

Rel said, "They got what they wanted. I don't think they're coming back."

"They didn't get the dyr."

"They have to know it's hidden by now."

Senrid assented to that. "Where are you going?"

"Back to Sartor." Rel tapped a pocket, where he'd stashed a transfer token.

Senrid's brows snapped together, then lifted. "You know how to rescue Liere," he said, his tone lightening. "You were the one who came for me, when I was a prisoner at Norsunder Base. Let me go with you."

Rel held up a hand. "First, we don't know that she's even at Norsunder Base. Second. There's no way to be sure that the tunnel exists anymore. Norsunder has to have figured out how we got out that time, and done what they could to plug up the breech. Third. I won't take you to Sartor with that mark."

Senrid smacked his hand over his numb shoulder. "Right. They can trace my movements. So I get rid of it first, then I'll come. I'll do anything needed . . ."

Rel's puffy face shifted as he made an attempt at a smile. "Unless you know the magic to get in and out of there —"

"No."

" —then leave it to us. There are . . ." He looked up as if trying to figure out what to say.

"Your morvende friends, and their secret caves. I learned a little about them when I traveled with Liere, back when Siamis tried the first time. All right. But tell Atan, and Tsauderei, and . . .no, I'll write to them myself." Senrid turned from him to the other two.

Puddlenose leaned back, hands crossed behind his head. "Christoph and me, we're staying for now, to do some patrols in case they come running back to grab Lyren. But we're moving down to the Junky to operate out of there." His usually cheerful brown eyes narrowed to hardness. "If you hear anything about Detlev's little poopsies, don't forget us."

Senrid said, "Right. I'll remember that. Meantime, you

might suggest to Clair that they send Lyren away altogether. If they have nowhere else, send her to me—once I get rid of this bloodknife mark." And back to Rel, as he jerked his shoulder. "I was told you know who can remove it."

"I don't. But." Rel looked around. Senrid laid a silent wager he was looking to see if Mearsieanne was in earshot, then he tipped his head toward the long doors to the garden out back. When they reached it, Rel lowered his voice. "Have you ever been to Jilo's castle in Narad?"

"Yes," Senrid said, having expected almost anything but that. "Several times."

"Then there wouldn't be any wards against you from the old king. And Jilo won't have warded you." Rel's expression had hardened when he mentioned the old king, an effect with those deep, dark eyes in that carved bone structure that was truly impressive, and Senrid wondered what emotion lay behind it.

Rel brought his chin down in a short nod. "Go to Jilo's castle in Narad, and walk the halls in the middle building, third floor. Maybe Jilo gave you a Destination? That would take you to the right place. I'm told Kessler's got the place filled with tracers. He'll find you."

"Thanks," Senrid breathed.

Detlev had not attacked him on the mental plane yet, but Senrid knew that was only a matter of time. He'd told CJ that he was going home, but that wasn't true. He knew he could never withstand a mental barrage from Detlev, especially over time, and his greatest fear was being made a puppet while someone ruled Marloven Hess through him, ordering his army out to slaughter for someone's pleasure.

He would cut his own throat before admitting it out loud, but he was terrified of going home before he got rid of that enchantment. He was even afraid of sleeping. Tired as he was, he took out the transfer token he kept in his pocket for emergencies, and worked the magic to shift its Destination to Jilo's castle.

Then he braced himself, and transferred.

He tried not to breathe in the stale, suffocating stink of old stone, uncirculated air, and far too much dark magic. Every nerve twanged with danger. The hairs at the back of his neck rose as he stepped forward cautiously, hands outstretched in hopes of sensing lethal wards before he walked into them.

He never would have risked himself in this dangerous place
to confront a very dangerous man, if he had not been afraid of
Detlev more. He walked toward the magic chamber Jilo had
shown him before, hoping that Jilo was there. Though he knew
Jilo would be no backup in a fight, his magic — especially in this
benighted place — was formidable, and he knew this place well.

But Jilo didn't seem to be around.

Senrid sensed . . .something. Had to be one of the silent
servants moving slowly about their affairs, half-bound in time.
Everything was skewed: his sense of time, of distance. Hearing
and sight. The place made his skin crawl.

He reached the empty the magic chamber, which seemed
darker and more suffocating than ever. Light flickered, and the
air stirred sluggishly from a transfer, revealing a slight young
man, pale, dark curly hair, his droopy eyes unexpectedly
bringing the Delieths and Atan to mind.

This had to be Kessler Sonscarna.

"You are?" Kessler said.

"In need of bloodknife spell removal," Senrid said. "Rel
sent me."

Kessler's lips tightened at the corners. "That is supposed to
be a recommendation?"

Senrid lifted his good shoulder. "No idea. But I want this
thing gone. If you want some kind of trade —" He opened his
hand.

Kessler uttered a short, voiceless laugh. "What I want," he
said, "is no more disturbances. I'll teach you the spell, which
you may do what you like with. I'll not be back again for that,
no matter who they mark."

Senrid was too tired for a magic lesson, especially blood
magic, which could so easily burn one in agonizingly
permanent ways. But he steeled himself, because he sensed that
this strange fellow meant exactly what he said.

Kessler went through the spell twice, phrase by phrase, and
Senrid recognized patterns in it, which made it somewhat
easier to master, though even those broken patterns evoked
that acrid burnt-metal stink of too much volatile power. The
rest of it was unsettlingly new, indicating (as if he wasn't
already aware) yet another area of dark magic he was
completely ignorant in.

On the second repetition, Kessler nodded, as if Senrid
should now remove the bloodknife spell himself. As soon as

Senrid had successfully done so, and felt the heat-snap of magic over his arm, the shadows behind Kessler and to his left shifted.

A boy stepped out. Kessler whirled, a knife appearing in his hand. The boy moved as fast, slapping something metallic to the arm descending in a lethal strike, and Kessler dematerialized a heartbeat before his dagger could reach the boy's throat.

Leaving Senrid standing face to face with a tall boy with waving blond hair much like his own, but in every other way totally unfamiliar. He wore an old tunic, half unlaced, baggy riding trousers, mocs. He seemed to be unarmed.

"Senrid," he said in a voice of appreciation. "I've wanted to meet you."

Though he did not speak with a Geth accent, Senrid suspected whom he faced. Closing his fingers on his transfer token, he said, "Not mutual."

He transferred back to Marloven Hess, leaving David to sink into Jilo's chair, laughing to himself as he worked to summon enough strength for a transfer.

How did Jilo endure this poisonous atmosphere? David had walked in from the border, and every step within the city seemed to gather an invisible weight.

Detlev had once taken him to a castle destroyed by magic centuries previous, inhabited only by spiders now. In the darkest areas, the castle had housed generations of spider webs in thick layers. The tracers and wards in this castle reminded him of that, except far more lethal than the spiders, impressive as they were.

It had taken all his concentration to find and remove all Kessler's tracers, so that the confrontation, when he happened, would take place in this room. The remainder of his strength had been spent in holding the shadow illusion quiescent.

Result? David had survived meeting Kessler, though he'd felt the tip of that knife a hair's breadth from his flesh before the transfer disintegrated it. And he now knew the bloodknife antidote.

He pulled his sword from the corner where he'd set it when he realized he wouldn't have been able to defend himself in this thick, airless atmosphere, and he, too, transferred.

Fourteen

SENRID DROPPED TO HIS knees, shaking from reaction, and snapped the glow-globes to light. Yes, he was home. His study. Alone. Safe.

Safe, but his nerves wrung, not only from the throbbing in his arm from Laban's stab—which now was returned to its fresh state—but from awareness that he had walked straight into a trap. The only reason he wasn't in Norsunder right now was that the trap had been set for Kessler.

His memory, unflinchingly clear, gave him back the speed of Kessler's twist with the knife and David's equivalent speed. That had to be David. The description had been specific. The only thing he hadn't seen was the old-fashioned saber with the dark steel, but that could have been there in the shadowy murk.

It was also clear that David and Kessler seemed to have some inhuman ability to resist the toxic magical residue in that place, judging by how fast they'd both moved. Senrid crowed for breath, filling his lungs again and again, until the floating spots faded from his vision. Senrid knew he wouldn't have lasted a heartbeat in a fight.

Only why did David wait until the bloodknife spell had been removed? Maybe he wanted to learn it, too. What was that Dtheldevor had said about trouble in Norsunder?

It was too much to hope that they'd all murder one another.

And even if they did, the winner would just send the rest out as soul-bound. It was never going to end.

But that didn't mean you stopped fighting.

When he heard footsteps approaching at a run in the corridor, he forced himself to his knees, and then his feet. It was only then that he noticed it was dark outside the windows.

Aching all over, he waved off the roaming sentries come to check on the sudden light, and forced himself to sit at his desk. Only every joint hurt so very much. He clapped his free hand to his now-bleeding, throbbing shoulder as he blinked his eyes into focus.

On his desk in the center lay duty reports from watch captains and a note in Keriam's neat hand listing decisions, requests . . .his mind couldn't take any of it in, but the overall impression was that no armies had invaded while he was gone. Or, far more likely, no jarls had taken it into their heads to attack the capital.

Now it was his turn to keep promises. He flexed his aching hand, then dipped a quill into ink, and wrote out the blood-mage spell while it was clear in mind. This lethal a spell could have no errors.

That done, he picked up one of the small pieces of paper he had waiting for notecase correspondence, and quickly composed a three-sentence report about the Kessler and David encounter in the Chwahir capital. At the end, he added, *Will you ask Tsauderei to write to me about rescuing Liere from Norsunder Base?* and sent it to Jilo.

That done, he made it to his bedroom, where he dug some bandaging out from a trunk — a habit he'd formed during his uncle's violent days — and wrapped it around his shoulder over his ruined shirt.

Then he flopped onto the bed and slid into uneasy sleep, waking every time he tried to move. Bad dreams intensified with the increase of hot pain in his shoulder, until he woke with a start, his mouth dry, his skin sensitive in the way that came with fever.

He blinked sticky eyes, registering a row of faces gathered around his bed, the foremost Keriam, whose bristling brows met in a thunderous line. "Awake. Good." And to someone else, "Go ahead."

Hands reached for Senrid. He recognized the palace guard's chief Healer. "No . . ." The word was more of a groan of pain.

In any case, Keriam, the Healer, and the aide ignored him. With the assurance of moral superiority, the Healer motioned to the aide to strip off Senrid's clumsy bandage and his shirt, and then the coverlet, which Senrid noticed with dismay was spotted brown with drying blood.

After an agonizing couple of centuries, he lay back as the aides laid a fresh coverlet over him. His ribs shuddered for breath. Then someone pressed a cup of listerblossom in his hands and held the back of his aching head so he could drink. Gradually the red-hot iron spike poking into his shoulder lessened the intensity of its throb as lassitude seeped through him.

The aides took away the bloodstained clothes and bedding and the Healer said he'd return at night to bring fresh keem leaves for the bandage, leaving Senrid alone with Keriam, who sat silently during the entire business, tight fists on his knees, his countenance grim.

"I went to Mearsies Heili," Senrid said. "Because Liere went there. On the run. I thought . . ."

He gave as concise a report as he could, and finished, "I *have* to know what's going on if I'm not going to walk into any more traps by trying to break her out. The dyr, Siamis assassinating Sartorans and the king of Colend, those boys chasing Liere, one of whom managed to nail Kessler Sonscarna and send him off, probably to Norsunder—don't you see? It *all* leads back to Detlev. When it comes to him, I *have* to know. I *can't* let myself be taken by surprise. I can't risk letting him get to me to use against Marloven Hess."

His unsteady whisper, the hectic spots of fever in his cheeks, his sunken eyes, and the way his tense, restless fingers plucked at the bedclothes forced Keriam to muzzle the objections piling up in his mind.

Dyrs — magic — Detlev: all matters beyond his knowledge or control.

He said, "I understand your reasoning. But if you get wounded like this again, I hope at least you'll send for the Healer, and give him a short report. We had the entire palace guard, and half the city, rousted out of their racks searching for assassins, once word passed about you leaking blood from an obvious stab wound. They woke me up not quite an hour after I'd retired. I issued the order to lock down the city, and I presided over said search."

Senrid winced. "I'm sorry. I didn't think."

Keriam went on in his precise voice, "I had half a wing guarding this floor while you slept, until I was certain we were clear. And then I found the Healer to bring up to you."

Senrid thought of all those people out late at night, searching for a danger that didn't exist — every bit of it unnecessary. "I'd better get up and . . ."

"And? Senrid, I hope you won't compound your error by going downstairs only to end up falling flat on your face. Once they understand you weren't attacked on their watch, that it happened beyond our borders, they'll settle down, and you may be certain the watch commanders will turn the search to good account by reviewing performance and procedure. A practice emergency that isn't one is useful in its own way. But."

"But," Senrid said. "I need to think ahead. Oh, I need to think ahead about *everything*."

Keriam heard the note of panic not very far below the surface. He got to his feet. "My advice, Senrid-Harvaldar, is to first put in some rest and recovery time." He opened his hand toward the bed. "Get your wits back."

Both were unanswerable, in particular the implication of witless actions.

Keriam was right, and he was safe. Senrid laid his head back and closed his eyes.

When he woke again, fever's stabbing fire had left his shoulder a smoldering throb, and the rest of him the normal ache of joints and muscles after a severe beating. He'd known how to deal with pain since his uncle had declared himself Regent when Senrid was five, and made certain Senrid knew who held the whip hand.

Move slow, hot bath. Listerblossom instead of coffee.

Over breakfast he mentally ordered his day. First thing, his notecase. It was heavy.

One of those, he hoped, would be from Tsauderei. Senrid winced when he remembered his feverish determination to hammer the old lighter mage with communications, even visits (assuming he could get past the wily old man's considerable wards) to make certain that Liere was not shoved to the bottom of anyone's priority list.

But as he turned the case over in his hand, he remembered Keriam's description of how much trouble the entire castle had been put to on his behalf. It was so easy to fall into king thinking — as if everything, not just state matters, but personal, too, would cause everybody else to drop what they were doing and jump to his will.

To put it more bluntly, if he started harassing Tsauderei, or Atan, or any of those people on Liere's behalf, he'd probably only annoy them.

He had to shift focus to alliance thinking. Right. The alliance was back. They had to maintain an inside line of communication, which meant he had to make certain checking and reporting was a first priority.

The first note was from Arthur:

> *I transferred home. Nothing happened to me, so I think they got what they wanted. And I'm just in time. Tsauderei is going to meet with the Venn mages here in a week.*

Senrid set that aside. The next was Tsauderei's.

> *I have been in communication with Atan, who got a report from Rel, now in Sartor. This is not the first time this problem has occurred . . .*

Senrid looked up and grimaced. He could just hear the gruff old voice reminding him sardonically that other important people had been taken prisoner at Norsunder Base since his time there.

> *. . . If you surmised that Norsunder acted to plug up the escape route after Rel brought you out, you would be correct. The morvende say that Siamis oversaw the wards and traps himself, but it was well after they had already dismantled the tunnel from their end. They have other ways to watch, I'm told, that neither you nor I will ever find out about.*
>
> *You may be certain that whatever we can do shall be done.*

After cursing under his breath, Senrid wrote back a fast note to thank him, and offer any help Tsauderei thought he might be able to give.

A note from Leander followed, detailing his latest studies in border wards, obviously added to over a few days, with a hasty addition at the bottom:

*Arthur says he's home, which you probably already
know. He also said you got stabbed with one of those
knives. Where are you?*

Long answer or short? Senrid looked past that to the next
note, spotted Thad's familiar graceful handwriting, and set that
letter aside to write a quick note to Leander:

*Home. Let's meet, I'll report. Also teach you the
bloodknife antidote. We need to spread that around.*

Then he took in a deep breath before opening Thad's note.

The sight of Thad's handwriting was always a punch in the
gut. Senrid knew that hindsight blame was stupid, but he
couldn't help feeling that if he'd pursued the conversation
Karhin had sought with him at the Selenna heir's Name Day,
she might still be alive. That memory was painfully vivid: her
flyaway red hair gleaming in the light, her freckled, earnest
face, her graceful Colendi hand gestures as she groped for
understanding.

Senrid even got a clue right after, when he saw Adam catch
that knife — evidence of considerable training. But he'd still
missed it by seeing what he expected to see.

*Senrid: I would never presume on our friendship,
but Terry insists that you are the one to aid me. He
said he would write to you as well.*

Senrid lifted the last letter, opened it, saw Terry's scrawl, set
it back down, and returned to Thad's.

*My situation is this. I made a promise to our prince,
now king, that I would write to him, and I have, but
receive no answer. I promised I would come to him,
but I am consistently denied a meeting. Even our
rose garden meeting place is under guard, ever since
King Carlael's assassination.*

*Three times I've gone to Alsais. Each time the
heralds tell me he is elsewhere, or engaged with royal
affairs, and though they always offer me the opportunity to leave a message I am beginning to believe
these are taken straight to the fire. Terry says he
tried once to visit, as I believe he told you. He insists*

that a Marloven king arriving in force, as appar-
ently your ancestors once did, might make a
difference.

If this is an imposition, I will understand. You have
your own royal affairs that must take precedence. I
gave my promise to Terry I would ask, and I would
like to keep one promise.

Thad Keperi

Senrid read it through twice, trying to sift his reactions.
He'd liked Thad from the start because of the way he accepted
everyone on their own terms, though he was very much a
Colendi in all other ways. Even Karhin had been gradually
giving precedence to rank. Senrid had seen it in her letters.

And yet here was Thad talking of royal affairs. Resentment
might lie beneath that. No, not Thad. Resignation. That was it.
He expected to be shouldered aside by rankers, as his own
countrymen were obviously doing. So the question was this:
Thad was denied an interview or communication with
Shontande Lirendi on the prince's orders, or by someone else
on his behalf?

Senrid threw Thad's letter down and scowled at his open
windows, through which drifted the sounds of young voices in
cadence. His own nightmarish existence under a regency that
was anything but protective or guiding made him restless, even
irritated on behalf of this Shontande Lirendi, whom he didn't
know at all.

Time to find out.

Terry's letter pretty much repeated what Terry had said at
that meeting in Roth Drael, but at the end, he wrote:

I've got an idea. I know you aren't going to march a
couple of wings across the continent to go bang on
Shontande's palace door, but how about this? If you
send Captain Forthan back to us, my mountain
guard is pretty enthusiastic about having him here
again. And I've talked to a couple of my captains,
both of whom love the idea of putting on whatever it
is your people wear and riding down the mountain
looking stern and pretending to be Marlovens if it

would scarify those Colendi snobs guarding Shont-
ande, the way your ancestor did a few centuries ago.

"Your ancestor."

That meant Ivandred, the king no Marloven talked about. Even the toughest heavy cavalry front-line brute was uneasy at the thought of Ivandred riding back out of Norsunder at the head of his elite, unbeatable First Lancers, partly because no one knew why he'd gone over to Norsunder in the first place.

The only thing the records pointed at for certain was that Detlev was around, in one of his many guises.

Senrid looked around his study, mentally reviewing the archives. So little was left from that time. He'd been forbidden to read any of it, which of course made it a challenge when he was young. He knew Ivandred had married a Colendi princess, Lasva, whose attempts to render the castle less barren and somewhat more livable still existed here and there. But Senrid remembered little else about that bit of family history. There certainly hadn't been any war, or he'd have recollected *that*.

He thought about it off and on through the remainder of the day, as he dealt with the usual round of matters. He paused once to write to Leander, inviting him to meet that night.

The tacit agreement was that Leander came to Choreid Dhelerei, as meeting at Crestel inevitably involved Kyale, who regarded a shut door as an invitation, and whose conversational skills tended to revolve mostly around herself.

When Leander showed up, he thoughtfully said nothing about Senrid's battered appearance.

Senrid handed him the bloodknife antidote paper. Since it was dark magic, he had to explain a lot of it to Leander, but once they finished, he said, "You know we have almost nothing about my ancestor Ivandred. But I do know that his wife was given Vasande Leror when her son took over as king. It was one of her descendants who decided the principality was a kingdom, since she's been a queen, and crowned himself."

Leander grinned, not denying it. That descendant was related to them both.

Senrid went on. "So they must have preserved Lasva's stuff to seed their royal archive. Did she leave any written records about Ivandred coming to Colend?"

"She didn't, but some of the others did, mostly about life after Ivandred's day. The only one who wrote about that period was Emras—"

"But there's nothing about Ivandred in the *Emras Testament*. Hibern made me read it when we worked on ward magic. It's a book on ward magic," Senrid exclaimed. "With a long, boring scold about the dangers of learning magic outside the Sartoran mage school."

"That's the version the Sartoran Mage Guild has," Leander said, shrugging. "Maybe you don't realize that Emras lived right in the Tannantaun house with the Colendi queen. They built it."

"You never told me that," Senrid said.

"Because I never thought about it until Terry wrote to me." Leader spread his hands. "It was four centuries ago! I went down to Tannantaun with Kyale once and spent a couple days rooting through old trunks in the attic. Found some old account books. There's a lot about life then, like, did you know that one of the household was an ancestor of Thad's? Or at least, in his family. Maybe Keperi is a common name in Colend." When Senrid didn't respond, Leander said, "Anyway, there's a note tucked into one of the household account books from Emras's cousin saying, basically, that she knows that a former scribe wouldn't be able to resist making a book, and if Emras was going to publish, to think of her. That's it."

"That's not evidence of a second book."

"Well, it is, considering Emras wasn't released from Sartoran Mage Guild custody until after she'd written and relinquished the testament. But the cousin's letter is dated some ten years after that. That plus the household accounts for ink and paper for 'Aunt E.' kind of indicate she wrote a lot, but it hasn't been handed down to us."

"All right, I didn't know that, either."

"No one did." Leander spread his hands. "If she did write a secret book, it might be hidden. My ancestors weren't like yours, destroying things right and left. That is, except for Kyale's mother, but her destruction was all in Crestel, and had to do with establishing her legitimacy as queen. She didn't touch anything at Tannantaun. I doubt she was even there. That's where Kyale's household was kept. It's been a family retreat, you know, all these years."

"Dead end, then," Senrid said. "Unless Terry has something that we don't. Which he might, since he brought it up."

Leander and Senrid agreed to visit Terry two days later.

Terry's favorite room was at the top of a bulky castle built to withstand mountain storms. Senrid had visited a couple of times, mostly when negotiating early in the alliance days to send one of his recently promoted academy cadets to advise in reorganizing Erdrael Danara's mountain guard.

"Hoo, Senrid, I hope whoever you tangled with looks worse," Terry said on greeting him.

"Laban," Senrid said, shrugging his bandaged shoulder.

"At least it wasn't the one they call MV," Terry commented as Leander and Halad agreed.

"He went for Rel," Senrid said.

"And?" Terry asked, brows up. "Tell me Rel thrashed the shit out of MV. Though that would leave nothing behind."

"MV knocked Rel flat, but I have to say, the one time I managed to look their way, he was having a tough time doing it. Back to Laban. Here's the antidote to the bloodknife spell, written out, with Leander's emendations for light mages. Spread this around," Senrid said, handing across a paper. "As for the reason we came. I don't seem to have any records of my ancestor's visit to Colend. Everything that exists about him is about what he did at home."

Terry grinned, the scar down his face corrugating. "It was Lad who found it, while I was at the coast trying to learn more about shipwrights."

Terry turned to his friend Halad, who had set a book on one of the tables all around a room designed for comfort rather than fashion: low chairs piled with pillows, books stacked everywhere, a field glass sitting by a window, various other leisure-time items on hooks or shelves.

"What you have to know first," Lad said in his soft voice, "is that Princess Lasva was not raised to statecraft —"

"Like me," Terry said with a twisted grin.

"The Colendi queen always expected to have a child. When that happened, and she made it plain that the child would inherit the throne, every prince on the continent, and a few on the other side of the strait, came courting Lasva, who was beautiful and graceful and hoola loola loo."

Senrid said skeptically, "I can't believe Ivandred of all people went galloping across the continent to chase a princess, however pretty. How would he even hear about her? If nothing else, my ancestors were notorious for ignoring everybody they couldn't actually conquer. I always thought the Colendi sent her to us."

"No, he definitely came to Colend. I think he was already outside the country," Lad said. "There was another prince along, an Adrani one?"

"Ah." Senrid hit his knees with his palms. "My very distant cousins over the mountains. All right, it makes slightly more sense. There used to be a lot of visiting back and forth between us and Enaeran Adrani."

"The gossip," Lad said, brandishing the old book, "was that they made a bet over who would win her. Or kiss her."

Terry noticed both Senrid and Halad looking impatient. Leander was too polite to express boredom. Terry still had maybe a year or so before he'd need the beard spell, but he'd been noticing girls ever since he was ten. And Karhin was the first one he'd ever felt . . .serious about, something he'd kept to himself, not even telling Lad. It still hurt far too much to think about, and made him savage with anger at the murderer and those who sent him.

Lad had gone on. ". . .so Ivandred — you said Ih-*van*-dred? It's spelled Ya-van-dred in the old records. Anyway he and his riders galloped up to the throne room door in Alsais. I guess you could ride up to it in those days, though you sure can't now. Anyway, he did it, and asked to court her. The queen then asked for an alliance. And when the Chwahir attacked, he —"

"Wait, wait, wait," Senrid said. "He rode up, and she made an alliance? Just like that?" He snapped his fingers.

"That's what it says here. Let me read it to you. He was an eye-witness."

Senrid listened with increasing skepticism to an otherwise accurate description of the long coats the Marlovens wore back then, and their long hair, and the complicated gown the queen wore and how far she descended from her throne to meet Ivandred, and even what was painted on the shield held by the queen's consort. All symbolic, Senrid was certain.

Even the fact that Ivandred had put his entire company in Montredaun-An black and gold, and had them carrying his personal flag — the Fox Banner, never used again after he rode it into Norsunder — instead of wearing their own House colors and carrying their House flags, was suspiciously symbolic, by someone else's design.

"No," he finally said. "Impossible it just happened. There has to have been some dickering back and forth beforehand. No Marloven, especially Ivandred, would have allied with someone out of hand, and from anything I know of those Colendi, they wouldn't, either. There was something else going on, and my guess is, the Chwahir are somewhere in there. The ride to the throne room was all for show, for someone to witness."

Terry bobbed his head in nods on each point, then said, "All true, I'm beginning to learn as I get better at kinging. But here's what caught my eye. All those princes? They didn't get near that princess, except at court affairs. But your Ivandred rode smack up to the door." He clapped his hands. "There may or may not have been some hidden haggling, but nobody stopped him when they crossed the border, though everyone was talking about him and his riders. And when they got to Alsais, they got action. There are too many witnesses to deny it."

Lad leaned forward as he carefully set the book aside. "Don't you see? The Colendi knew the Marloven rep, same as now."

"Yeah," Senrid said. "All right. I get that much. We're bad and bold. Mostly bad. That brings me to the situation now. How difficult is it, really, if nobody is being threatened with dungeons or death? Everybody tells me the Colendi are so polite they can't even say the word 'no' without wringing their hands, and they jump away from their own shadows. It sure seemed true enough for Thad and Karhin. Why go to all this trouble?"

Terry's grin vanished, and Lad shook his head slowly. "There are other ways to smother someone into doing your will," Terry said. "I think they keep Shontande so close because of what happened to his father, and so busy that he can't turn around without one of them coaxing and flattering him into what they call his duty."

Lad added in a low voice, "We know this from some exchanges before everything happened, he believed he had only two friends, outside of a cousin he likes, who he rarely got to see. Those friends were Thad and Curtas."

"One of *them*." Leander raised the back of his hand.

"Two friends, and one turns out to be an enemy spy," Senrid said grimly. "Right. I'll talk to Ret Forthan. Let's see what we can put together. Maybe," he added, "this will turn out to be fun."

They were all thinking they could use some fun, and success, after all the recent disasters.

Fifteen

Land of the Venn

KERENDAL SOFAR, PRINCE OF the Venn, begged his mother untiringly to be permitted to travel beyond the border again.

"I will be safe," he insisted. "Send any number of the Arm along with me. I promise I will stay within their boundaries."

"No," the queen said just as untiringly.

The Arm of the Crown might be able to protect him, but that meant fighting someone outside of the Land of the Venn, which could have nothing but bad repercussions.

"The Eyes of the Crown could not protect you," she said. "It is their abilities we must regain, and the only way we will make that come to pass is to prove that we are no threat. You are not leaving our border again, my son, until who we appear to be in outlander eyes becomes more like who we really are."

Kerendal made his bow of acceptance, but everyone there could see how unhappy he was to be confined.

Including the queen. Because of his desperate, unsuccessful journey, she spared him the knowledge that the faraway queen who held the Venn captains of ancient days would not relinquish the ancient mariners to sail home. The Venn reputation from centuries before was still too threatening, apparently.

Liut of the Eyes was a silent witness to these conversations with the prince, by the queen's order. He was never invited to speak, which meant he was only to hear.

He had already begun to wonder why he, of all the possible candidates, had been selected to travel to Bereth Ferian to meet with the outlander mages. Though he was very well trained in magic, he was not the best. And he was certainly not the most prepossessing in appearance. Far from it, with his one-legged hop aided by a crutch under his arm. They could say it was because he was well-spoken (and he had been called Silver-tongue since childhood) except he was not to speak.

Swirling spats of snow lifted hair and robes as they gathered at the windswept bridge that was guarded at either end, and glimmered faintly blue, orange, green, and yellow to all who could see the heavy layers of wards and traps laid by either side.

Cold as it was, old Sloda, who had functioned as emissary to the outlanders for five decades, turned his white-frosted head, his bone-colored braids swinging as he fixed Liut with a narrow gaze.

"Give no indication of what we hold until I say. Further, do not lose sight of the fact that this moment is less emendation than amelioration. They are desperate. We are desperate, for separate reasons. They do not wish to be invaded anymore than we wish to find ourselves the inadvertent means of invasion."

Liut had already heard a great deal of warning from his superiors and from the queen, but he touched his palm to his heart in acknowledgment, vouchsafing no answer.

Then Sloda said, "Leave the ceremonial to me, until I give you the signal to bring forth what we have. Until then, bend your focus to the periphery of what they wish us to see."

Liut touched both palms to his heart: orders received.

Sloda's craggy face shifted to an almost-smile, and they approached the bridge. The coalition of Federation guards at the far end saluted the Venn guards escorting Liut and Sloda. The Venn crossed the bridge spanning the blue-icy abyss as bitter wind spiraled to catch at their robes, then they were over, and walking to the Destination the Venn had used for centuries when dealing with the Federation.

It was outlander magic that transferred them, by twos, with as much of the familiar joint-and-muscle jarring jolt as their own magic, proving to Liut that their two branches of magic were essentially the same at root.

The Destination in Bereth Ferian deposited them in a warm room, from which they were led to the Hall of Light, a vast chamber made of marble with a dais at one end, on which rested two throne-like chairs.

One of the thrones was empty, and in the other sat a blond boy, his head inclined, face in shadow. Liut already knew that this boy was only a titular king, with no powers whatsoever, and the empty throne belonged to the mysterious girl who had removed the enemy's world enchantment a few years back.

The true outland power in the room was divided between the squat, fierce-faced, gray-haired old woman in the light blue robe and the gaunt old man with the long, silky beard and braided hair who sat in an ordinary chair at the side.

This man spoke. "Emissary Sloda, I believe we've met sufficiently to forego the speeches of good intent."

Sloda touched his fingertips to his chest politely. "As you speak, so we concur, Magister Tsauderei."

Liut eased his stance slightly, glad that the ceremonial seemed to be curtailed. Sloda had declared that refusing to sit reminded the outlanders that the appearance of cordiality was just that. To stand was to remind the outlanders that the long defeat was in no way an acknowledgment of subordination.

"Then permit me to state, for the record." Tsauderei opened a gnarled hand toward a scribe and a mage student in blue robes, both busy writing, at the other side of the room.

"By the sworn and signed agreement of the following governments of the Federated Northern Kingdoms, we are agreed that selected members of your Arm of the Crown, understood to be searchers, in company with one of your mages for advice purposes, and one of our mages should magical protection be necessary, shall be permitted to search for the Arrow, and whoever holds the Arrow, until it may be found."

And he began to read off the names of all the monarchs who had been brought to agreement.

Well, Liut thought, it seemed that the ceremonial was to happen after all, as everyone there knew that the outlander mages had been very busy with these other rulers. Whatever they had had to promise to get their signatures was no affair of the Venn; they had agreed to nothing, and would not, until the Arrow was released.

As the names of the rulers were read out and recorded by the busily scratching quills of the record-takers, Liut remembered Sloda's last order, and shut out the voice as he raised his magical sense.

He did not believe he would find anything amiss. The outlanders were clearly as determined as the Venn to hunt down the renegade Siamis. And he sensed no new magic beyond the ever-present weight of the lethal mirror ward that would rebound on any Venn mage who tried the smallest spell beyond the Venn border.

He let his attention wander about the room, taking in the decorations in their muted colors, so much less vital than similar rooms of formal purpose in and under the Venn capital.

A small smear caught his attention, so ephemeral he nearly passed it by. He would have, had he not been under orders to note peripheral anomalies. This was the boy on the throne who sat so quietly, his eyes distant as though he dreamed.

Perhaps he was bored. After all, he had no power here. His position, as Liut understood it, was entirely symbolic. But the boy looked more tired than bored, and Liut could not blame anyone for sinking into reverie as the list of names droned on.

Liut continued his gaze around the room as the old mage worked through the list, his voice betraying by the shortness of his breath a diminishment of strength.

The outlanders had to have been working hard indeed to have garnered these names in relatively short time. Perhaps the reading was an expression of triumph. Well earned! Getting kings to agreement, so said the records, was akin to the ordering of cats, requiring a great deal of effort, coaxing, perhaps a threat or two, certainly an exertion in surpassing ratio to the result.

But at last the list ended, and they moved to the crucial part of the meeting: deciding who was to go where, with whom, and how to communicate.

That brought Liut's attention back to the proceedings, as this was the portion that directly involved him. Sloda was now merely adjunct, as he would be with Head Magister Oalthoreh, coordinating the communications. And when all was agreed, the outlander mages turned expectantly to Sloda, who gestured to Liut.

It was time for their revelation, establishing them on an equal footing. Liut reached into his carryall, and removed a wrapped shard of black, shiny stone, one of many from the conical mountains along the most difficult part of the border.

"We have his blood," Liut said, holding up the preserved rock. "With our help, we can hunt him by this."

Liut continued to hold up the rock, but his attention was on the new allies. Instead of resentment or distrust, he saw the old magister laugh and thump his fists on bony knees. "Hah!" he exclaimed. "First piece of good news since this sorry business began."

Magister Oalthoreh sent a stern look his way, then said, "I must put forward a question, if no one else will: is this dark magic?"

"No," Liut said, having expected some such question. "The coercions of dark magic are as forbidden to us as they are to you. The forms of blood magic we use are for protection, and for tracing."

"So the blood on this rock will lead you straight to him?" she asked.

"It will lead us to his blood, if any has been shed, even with fragments of dead skin, though that must be recent. Everyone's blood is distinctive," Liut said. "There is no masking it."

Tsauderei noted the rigidity of the non-Venn faces as the listeners tried, like his did, to conceal their instinctive revulsion.

"Very well," Tsauderei said.

Arthur jumped as if startled, then blinked rapidly. Liut thought, yes, the boy had been half-asleep during the ceremony, while Arthur looked around, not quite disoriented, but off-balance. He couldn't believe how his mind had wandered during the most important meeting in years. Maybe centuries.

Arthur resisted the impulse to rub his eyes; he wished he'd been able to sleep the night before, but every time he'd tried, his dreams had poked him awake again . . .

At a safe location on another continent, Siamis withdrew from below the surface of Arthur's thoughts. He scanned the mental plane once again. Nothing. Detlev was still far distant, busy at Five. Anyone else who could hear on the mental plane was in the Beyond.

He opened his eyes, reestablishing the connection between body and mind. Blood hunt, he thought. Then he had left blood behind in that damned valley. How they'd found it in that continuous howling blizzard was a cause for wonder, but of course they had arcane methods.

His lead was shortening. At least he understood the nature of the hunt.

Sixteen

Mearsies Heili to Everon

CJ STAYED CLOSE TO her room in the underground hideout, trying to keep her rotten mood to herself. She veered between It's All My Fault and It's All *Their* Fault—the latter gaining the edge, because if there hadn't been a poopsie invasion, Liere would be just fine.

But she still could have saved her. Should have. Somehow.

When she finally slunk up the tunnel to the main room, she found Puddlenose and Christoph eating toast-and-cheese for breakfast.

"Clair was looking for you," Puddlenose said, poking bread in her direction.

"Okay," CJ said. Hope flared. Adventure calling? But after all her flubs, they probably just needed some dumb chore done, one an idiot could do.

Puddlenose could easily see the trend of her thoughts in her expressive face, and added, "I think she wants you to go to Everon."

CJ's head came up. "Everon! Euw —" Then she remembered that Glenn was no longer there, and blushed. To hide it she dashed into the kitchen alcove, which had a firestick for cooking, but also a carved wooden box with transfer codes for specific foods written on a chalk slate next to it: if the white palace kitchen had made the food, the spell worked. And if not, nothing would be there, so you went down the list trying the spells for things you wanted to eat.

It looked so simple, but it had taken Clair a lot of work to get it right. CJ paused to consider that, remembering her own eagerness in learning magic. It was she who had written out the spells, and had even figured out two of them. That was change, she thought. But it was change they'd all wanted, it wasn't change forced on them.

She backed into the main room, and said, "Any sign of the poopsies?" She spoke just to be saying the word.

"None," Puddlenose said, leaning back on his elbows. "Too bad, too."

"You want another fight?" CJ asked in disgust. Her face was still mottled colors from her smash against the tree.

Christoph gave her a sleepy smile. "We want to have a talk with Adam. Puddlenose doesn't believe he's a Norsundrian."

"He can't be," Puddlenose said breezily. "I've spent time with him. Curtas, the same, but especially Adam. He used to do nice things for people when they didn't notice. You don't have that kind of nature and join Norsunder."

"But they're kids." CJ's stomach lurched. "What if Norsunder is all they know? Ugh, what a horrible thought, Detlev as a dad. And I thought Earth parents were horrible. I bet Adam and Curtas get extra villain lessons. Maybe they get into trouble every time they do something nice!"

At the name Detlev Puddlenose waved a hand before his face as if encountering a noisome stench. "MV, I could see *him* being raised by Detlev. Laban, too. But Adam? Nah. Maybe he's a hostage."

"Or under some kind of weird spell," Christoph offered, his messy blond hair looking slept on.

"If mind control spells worked, Senrid would have been a robot ages ago, and his uncle would still be stinking up the Marlovens," CJ said.

"A what?" Christoph asked.

"One of her Earth things," Puddlenose said dismissively.

Christoph didn't bother reminding him that he had come from Earth, too. Robots were clearly one of those possible-worlds things, or maybe different times things.

CJ transferred to the white palace.

Long habit had prompted her to transfer as she was, but when she walked into the kitchen with only servants and heard voices from the dining room down the hall, she remembered that breakfasts were now dining room and manners. Porcelain dishes and silverware and shoes required.

She looked down at herself, fingered her long, straight black hair back neat, and shrugged. Mearsieanne had never come out and said she disapproved of bare feet, and CJ had gone through the cleaning frame first thing out of bed, so her green skirt, white shirt, and black vest were perfectly respect-able.

Bare feet weren't. But she hated the thought of another transfer just to get sandals, and though her bedroom upstairs had shoes in the trunk, those were for winter. The thought of having to wear them indoors made her feel hot and itchy — and would press on the ones she'd injured. She took tiny steps to keep her toes behind the hem of her skirt as she entered the dining room.

Clair, dressed in a blue gown, sat across from Mearsieanne, who wore lavender and white with pale peach ruffles. Irenne and Lyren sat nearby, Irenne with bright yellow ribbons braided into her hair, and a fancy gown with cream-colored lace on the bodice. She was playing some kind of game with little Lyren, who watched Irenne with parted lips, ready to laugh, as Irenne ate daintily with a duchasy air, little fingers arched.

Lyren tried to pick up her porcelain cup with only three fingers as CJ entered. Irenne was quick to rescue the cup and right it.

"Puddlenose said something about Everon?" CJ asked.

"Good morning, Cherenneh," Mearsieanne said with gentle reproof.

CJ suppressed a sigh as a servant set a plate before her and spooned out fluffy eggs and crispy potatoes. "Good morning, everybody," CJ said, making an effort to keep annoyance out of her voice, and saw her reward in Clair's smile.

She thanked the servant and ate quickly, mindful of her manners. As soon as she'd cleared her plate, she turned to Clair. "Everon?"

"Letters have gone back and forth," Clair said, and looked Mearsieanne's way.

Mearsieanne said, "Commander Dei thinks that Tahra needs the company of girls her own general age. She's been grieving deeply."

"They want someone to help her smile again," Clair said. "The Knights will be going on some kind of trip to their border, and we are invited to keep Tahra company back in her capital. Would you like to go?"

Mearsieanne added, "I have corresponded with the Sandrials, the palace stewards. They are well set up for children, and so I think you ought to take Lyren along. The enemies would never think to look for her there."

The child looked up quickly at her name, then returned to her game of prissy manners with Irenne.

CJ noticed distractedly that Lyren was doing surprisingly well for a toddler-aged person. But then Lyren had Dena Yeresbeth in a way that CJ didn't, even though she was very small. Lyren, though nearly three, was already more well-behaved than most five-year-olds, and CJ wondered uneasily how much mind-reading Lyren did. As she watched Lyren carefully use her fork to cut her pancakes into tiny bites, CJ concentrated on her mind-shield, which most of the time she forgot.

"Of course," CJ said, especially if someone else would be responsible for Lyren. She liked small ones for a little while, but it got boring chasing them around, picking up after them, and trying to keep up with all the "Why?" questions. And that was without any poopsie threat.

"I'll go," Irenne said. "It sounds like fun."

Mearsieanne said approvingly, "I think you would be excellent company for Tahra."

Irenne was startled by that. She had been thinking of going as Lyren's companion. Irenne loved palaces, and being around people with rank, but equally she loved long acting-out games, and Lyren adored these. They'd spent the entire afternoon the day previous going through trunks of old-fashioned clothes they'd found in one of the tower rooms, trying things on, and dancing around in them.

"Find out who else might like to go," Mearsieanne said. "It's early evening in Everon, so don't transfer too late. And take your shoes and coats, as that side of the world, while it has the same seasons as we do, is generally chillier."

CJ turned immediately to Clair, who half-started up, then sank back when Mearsieanne's brows went up. CJ could feel Clair's ambivalence. Clair no longer had any real duties, but Mearsieanne seemed to expect her to stay.

As always, CJ gave in to the urge to escape a situation she

couldn't possibly fix. She gulped down the last of her hot chocolate and said, "I'm off to see who else wants to go."

CJ wasn't surprised to hear Diana instantly volunteer, and of course Irenne. But the rest spoke up, too. Everyone wanted to go. The only one who thought about packing was Irenne — and perhaps Seshe — but seeing the rest pronounce themselves ready, she sighed, glad that she'd put on a favorite dress if she was going to be wearing it for a week or two, stepping through a cleaning frame once or twice a day.

CJ grumped about shoes, but went along as the others did.

They began the transfers, CJ last because she was the only one would could sense whether the whatever-it-was between the two Destinations was getting that dangerous hot-metal smell from too many transfers.

The weather in Everon was indeed much colder, and the royal palace at Everon looked as dreary as ever in the lamplight. They still hadn't repaired some of the fire damage. Only cleaned around it.

The other girls waited in an uncomfortable knot, except for Irenne and Lyren, who had gone off somewhere with the servants.

CJ was about to ask why they all stood around outside Tahra's favorite room when she heard Tahra's voice, high and angry. "If *that's* why they're here then they can go back. I *won't* stay behind."

Seshe stepped near and whispered, "Commander Dei came to welcome us. Said we would be good company for Tahra while they're gone, exactly as Mearsieanne suggested. Perhaps you ought to talk to them."

As CJ walked in, two faces swung her way. CJ said to Tahra, "Mearsieanne said we should come. You don't want us?"

Tahra flushed, poking an anger-stiff hand at the tired-looking older man. "*He* thinks I should stay here like a baby, when the *more important* people go to the border."

Roderic Dei said, "Tahra — your majesty — "

Using her title was exactly the wrong thing to say. He knew it the moment the words were out.

Tahra's long face drained to the color of paper as CJ watched, aghast.

"*If*," Tahra's thin voice vibrated with passion, "I am *really the queen*, then my decree is this: I'm *going*. And if *anything or anybody* keeps me from going, then it means I am *not* the queen.

And *you* can be king since you're *really* in charge."

CJ crossed her arms across her front and faced the commander. "Wherever you're going, we'll guard her."

Roderic looked from one to the other, making a tremendous effort to smother his frustration. All very well for the Mearsiean to make that meaningless offer in that high tone of self-righteousness. That gaggle of girls couldn't defend anyone against a real threat. Then his gaze rested with fresh horror on the three-year-old. Even worse!

He was in an impossible position, acting as regent to a sixteen-year-old girl who in so many ways acted more like ten. And yet in other ways was responsible and hard-working; she had an unnerving ability to recollect streams of numbers, and how they related. Born with another family name, she would have made a superlative quartermaster or tax minister-in-chief.

He wished Carl would appear and tell him what she wanted.

Then the thought occurred, if mother saw daughter, maybe it would be good for both. He would have to tread delicately, and let nature act. He could not break his word and interfere directly. But if he surrounded Tahra with these loud visitors, and then again with a silent ring of his best, they would be safe enough. The trouble lay in the mountains, and there was a long, grim slog between here and there, a march at a pace that would test trained warriors. If Tahra got tired of that . . .

Yes, he thought, taking in Tahra's lifted chin, her attitude of conviction. He kept his face schooled as he swiftly trashed and rearranged all the careful plans he'd laid with the senior Knights, and Carl.

"As you wish, your majesty," he said, and nothing could prevent him from adding, "I can see my advice is not wanted." He bowed.

He could see the remorse that struck Tahra, but he knew he could not relent. He'd failed spectacularly with Glenn, and here was his last chance. "With your permission I will remove myself at once, and see to all the necessary alterations to our preparations."

Tahra's mouth opened and closed like a carp.

Roderic Dei bowed again and withdrew. He'd intended to send scouts out soon . . .why not begin with a taste of what a march was really like? He turned at the door. "We must depart no later than midnight."

Tahra's mouth opened again, but she nicked her chin down in an affirmative, and Roderic Dei went off to find his staff and issue a stream of new orders as Tahra turned to her waiting maid, and said in triumph, "Tell Jenel to get camping things ready, for all of us, and people to set up the tents and fix meals. I'll pack my own study materials." And to CJ, "Thank you. Mearsieanne was right to send you. I'm so glad you came."

CJ walked out into the hall, wondering what had just happened.

Seshe approached, looking worried. "Did Mearsieanne say anything about a journey?"

"Nope. Only that Tahra needed company, and we should get Lyren away from home in case the poopsies came back. I guess we're going."

Seshe's lips twitched in a smile at the word poopsies, which CJ was still trying to get people adopt.

"At least we brought our coats," CJ said.

Seshe said, "I've always wanted to see the forestland here. I've heard so much about the dawnsingers. I hope we'll get to meet some."

Each of the others expressed characteristic enthusiasm: Diana, like Seshe, enjoyed woodlands, Irenne was interested in people and foresaw being important as companion to the daughter of Sartora, the Girl Who Saved the World; Dhana had her own motivations, which went unexpressed as she agreed with everyone else. It was easy to forget she wasn't actually human, until they encountered bodies of water and saw her flicker into rainbow form then reappear again on the other side, but the Mearsieans were used to her, and few others noticed.

Falinneh, Gwen, and Sherry, as always, saw this as an opportunity for fun, and little Lyren picked up their mood.

They set out at midnight, as ordered.

The Mearsieans, for whom midnight was really mid-afternoon, spread their feeling of excitement to Tahra, who actually smiled. Torches flared, lanterns swung, and lamps were relit in the city as the cavalcade, including the remainder of Glenn's recruits, rode slowly down the royal road toward the western edge of the city.

Quietly, with no fanfare, scouts raced ahead to assess and secure.

The western road was well-traveled, easy for night maneuvers. Roderic and Carl had settled it that the scouts would continue on after the main body camped somewhere before morning for a rest.

Thus, Seshe woke on their first day of travel in a forest she found beautiful and yet very strange. She had never seen ancient coppice-oak, venerable remnants of days when the western volcanoes occasionally sent rivers of fire down the slopes, burning trees above the roots, which lay beneath ground that eventually became richer until they burst into leaf again, guided and protected by the wandering dawnsingers' ancestors.

These were not even the oldest, biggest trees, which housed the dawnsinger platform cities, but that surprise was to come.

Diana and Seshe together wandered as far as they dared until CJ scampered up. "Time to move on!"

"Will we see more like this?" Seshe said, pointing.

Tahra had followed behind CJ. Her somber face lit with a smile. "Oh, yes. More. And older."

"Older?" CJ exclaimed, listening to how her voice echoed in the densely layered forestland. "I already get this weird feeling like, if I lie down on that mossy grass for a nap, I might fall into tree dreams and sleep a hundred years."

The sounds of cadenced voices reached past shafts of sunlight, and Seshe was distracted by the thick overhead canopy shining goldy-green and hazy with moisture.

"What's that counting?" Diana asked, her dark eyes narrowed, her head cocked.

"Knight practice," Tahra said, waving a hand in dismissal.

CJ pursed her lips, and as the girls wandered back, she slipped next to Diana and whispered, "You thinking what I'm thinking?"

"What's that?"

"If we're supposed to protect Tahra, maybe we need to get in some practice now and then."

Diana liked weapons practice. "Good idea. Tomorrow? Sounds like they're finishing up."

The camp was soon dismantled by Tahra's small army of servants and Roderic Dei's equerries. The travel order was: older Knights in front, Glenn's most promising recruits (now back to being called squires) around and behind the girls, who in turn surrounded Tahra. Another patrol behind.

They progressed steadily west, cheered by villagers who lined the road as they passed. CJ watched Tahra carefully, glad to see a small smile as she nodded back at the smiling faces.

"Do they know where we're going?" CJ asked. "This isn't supposed to be secret, is it?"

Tahra turned her way. "I don't know what they know. Maybe they think we're on a progress. I don't know anything about military planning. That's for Uncle Roderick." She squared her scrawny shoulders. "I just know I have to be there."

CJ had no argument to make to that so they rode on, she gazing at the stone houses, most with round roofs, here and there castles in the process of being repaired from the earlier war.

Travel was only as fast as the wagons, which enabled Carl, who had ridden ahead with the scouts, to return as the sun was setting. Now that the company had reached unfamiliar territory, they camped as the sun vanished.

The scouts who had reported back were given time to sleep, but Carl was far too restless for that. She had been appalled to discover her daughter using the weight of her rank to insist on accompanying the Knights, but then, she reflected, she ought to have foreseen exactly that.

And she had to admit that this gave her a chance to see a little more of her daughter, though always safely from afar.

Lanterns were hung from tree branches all around as Jenel Sandrial, now the head of Tahra's household—under her mother's stewardship—oversaw camp.

Carl stood uncertainly well outside the reach of the lamplight, peering at a lone figure crouched on a boulder, her half-eaten dinner sitting on another rock. It was Tahra, her lank hair hanging in unkempt tangles as she studied a paper.

Carl longed to approach, to talk to her. This separation of a few paces caused her more anguish than anything she'd endured at the hands of Henerek's bored, malicious guards. But this anguish was a very old battle: her deepest desire, to take her skinny, knobby-shouldered daughter into her arms, had had to be smothered ever since Tahra turned four and writhed impatiently against being held, being touched.

Carl took another incautious step, then rocked back on her heels when a figure flitted between the trees, and there was CJ, mindful of her duty to keep Tahra company.

"What's that?" CJ said. "Times tables?" she exclaimed aghast. She wanted to add, "Who's making you do that?" but caught herself in time. Her indignation on Tahra's behalf might be one of those queen things.

"Ratios," Tahra said softly.

She lifted her head enough for CJ to see the tear tracks on her long, sallow face.

"Tahra? You okay?"

Tahra sat upright, her narrow face pinched with grief.

"No," she said, "I'm not. I know I ought to be studying. Before she left to go home Mearsieanne said I'd be glad one day to be able to do maths in my head when a group of arrogant guild reps are standing before me . . ." She gestured helplessly at the paper. "But it keeps reminding me I'm alone now. They're all gone. Except me. And what good can I be? I'm just a target. That everybody has to protect. I wish . . ." She looked away, and then said fiercely, in a low voice, "I wish there was a spell for growing up faster. Then I'd know what to do."

CJ's revulsion showed on her face, but she saw Tahra's shoulder jerk up under her ears. So all she said was, "Some of the grownups seem to be as confused about what to do as we are."

"My mother wasn't," Tahra said, squeezing her eyes shut and turning away, but not before CJ saw tears drip down her cheeks. "She. Always. Knew. What to do."

CJ looked helplessly at Tahra's averted face, not sure what to say, as in the background, Carl took a step closer.

Unaware of being watched, CJ struggled to find words. Tahra's parents were just names to her and she hadn't liked Glenn much. But she knew that to Tahra Glenn hadn't been merely a snobby prince who'd like mean, rough games, he'd been her brother, and in his own way he'd watched out for her.

"Well," she said in a false voice meant to sound hearty, "one thing you can do for sure is to make Detsie-potsie boiling mad by staying out of his clutches, him'n his twinkle-topped popsie-poopsies."

Tahra gave her a watery smile. "That's what my cousins Carinna and Merewen say."

"They're right!" And then, with heroic good intent, "If you want to practice maths, why don't you come back and be with us and we'll make a game of it?" *Somehow*, CJ thought to herself. "You'll get your practice and have some fun at the same time."

That was what Carl wanted: Tahra surrounded by friends. It was much better this way, was it not?

Unnoticed by either girl, Carl moved back softly, softly, and vanished among the trees.

Seventeen

ON THE FOURTH DAY of their journey, as Tahra's company commenced the upward climb toward the mountains, the long shadows had begun to diffuse and blend when a young man's voice echoed through the trees. A girl's voice created a counterpoint, the two chasing up and down a melody like birds braiding upward in flight. A woman's golden contralto joined, and a boy's clear soprano. One by one other voices joined, old, young, singing the main line, harmonizing, the high voices in descant.

Dhana froze, mouth open. Seshe grinned in delight. When the last of the sunlight vanished the voices faded out one by one.

"That was dawnsingers, bringing down the sun," Tahra said to the Mearsiean girls, after the last notes had died away in the cool air. "That means there are platforms ahead."

"Tree houses?" Falinneh bellowed.

"I want to be in one," Gwen yelled.

"Tree houses," Sherry whispered, her light blue eyes huge. "That's even better than secret underground caves. I mean, if they're secret."

"Some of them are," Tahra said, glad for once to be able to give information instead of always being told. "They travel from branch to branch so there're never trails on the ground, and you cannot see the platforms even when you're under them, unless you know exactly where to look."

Diana cast her friends a significant glance, but for CJ's sake, she didn't point out that she had been warning the other Mearsieans for a long time about laying down trails around their hideout that anyone with a modicum of woodcraft could follow.

They watched some young dawnsingers clamber happily up the vine ladders to the tree platforms, made from planed fallen wood, with vines trained round as rails, connected along broad branches, and here and there, vine bridges. Once Diana discovered that one could swing from knotted vines from branch to platform, she had to try those out, CJ following more cautiously, her light body twirling around haplessly until she learned how to twist in the air to keep balance.

Seshe marveled at how the thick vines had obviously been trained. Platforms had all been built among spreading branches which not only formed roofs, but hid the platforms from sight below.

It was quite late when at last the guests settled down to sleep. CJ lay peering down at the twinkling lights like golden stars amid the trees, glowing in patterns far below.

When she woke to the singers singing to welcome a weak sun, it was to discover that the whispering leaves that had lulled them to sleep had actually been the patter of rain. The dawnsingers praised the rain in their song, and the Mearsieans were charmed by the easy way the singers chimed in or stopped when they wanted.

High above in the western mountains, the dawnsingers brought up a stronger sun, their voices echoing down the misty valleys. By then the entire camp was awake. Cooking smells began to drift in the air, as the light slowly strengthened, touching dewdrops into tiny lights.

Carl, knowing that the end was near, fought against riptides of emotion. The deep fury that had sustained her through her imprisonment abated only when she heard again the soaring voices ringing through the trees, singing of peace, beauty, and the striving for harmony in all things. But the rage never went away. It had poisoned every ill-healed scar and broken bone.

That morning, far to the west, the scouts had located the invaders, who arrogantly assumed they were undiscovered as they made their way slowly down a mountain, following a trickle that gradually widened into a stream.

The course Carl had determined on was not peaceful. It would not be beautiful. Perhaps it was not right. But it was the only way she could see to protect all those precious things, and all her remaining strength sharpened into anticipation.

Back at the camp under the platform city, Roderic summoned his defenders for practice as breakfast was cooked and bedding was packed up by the servants and equerries.

The Knights' squires formed up for the easier drill. At Roderick's command, his daughter Carinna, one of the older squires, invited the Mearsieans to join them. CJ led the girls, but when it was time to get some breakfast, she realized she didn't hear Irenne's voice. Wherever there were people around to be an audience, Irenne was usually at the center, often with little Lyren, who chattered to a couple of the servants.

She looked back, and there Irenne was, poised on a low tree branch, her head tipped a little so her light-brown ponytail draped over the branch as she watched a knot of older boys practice their duels. CJ whirled around, boiling—not sure who she could get mad at—then spotted Diana on another branch, also watching.

The little gestures Diana made with her fingers, the tiny shifts of shoulders and knees made it clear she was memorizing moves. CJ snorted out a breath, knowing that one shouldn't be justified for watching and the other not. But she was glad when it was time to form up for travel.

Over the next couple of days, as some of the dawnsingers traveled with Tahra's company, the Mearsieans discovered that storytelling for them was an art form, carried out in song.

At night campfires, music became a regular thing, but no one seemed to know songs as long—or as entertaining—as the dawnsingers.

After one of these, CJ whispered to Seshe, "I bet they've been at it for ages. All those rhymes in the middle of lines and at the end?"

Seshe huffed a soft laugh, as firelight played over her face, and turned her long blond hair to gilt. "I would think so!"

CJ said sagely, "They must have to invent all those poetry tricks in self-defense. I mean, how nasty would it be to have all that history told by a bore and a snore? But it's not the rhymes, it's how they make you see and hear things, and the melodies make you feel it."

Seshe had noticed that the Mearsieans were not the only ones drinking in the songs. The Everoneth all had, but Tahra in particular. Seshe would have thought that girl, so preoccupied with rules, and numbers, and order, would pay little heed to music, but she was glad to be proved wrong.

Sure enough, on the third night, for the first time, Tahra volunteered to join the campfire music-making. "Not singing," she said in a mumble. " I can't sing. And I'm not good with the woodwind, though I did practice, but my father taught me this song." From her pack she drew a much battered flute, and began to play.

It was a slow, pretty melody, and people listened politely. But CJ and Seshe both noticed after the polite applause that the mysterious scout they called Carl spoke for the first time, in a gruff voice, "Play another."

Tahra did. It was once popular, causing heads to bob and hands to tap on knees. At the end, one of the Knights said, "I remember Berthold whistling that before battle."

After a laugh, someone else said, "Remember camping on the hills above Ferema during our training days, and the nighttime tent raids?"

More laughs.

Tahra played one last tune, then said firmly, "Someone else ought to have the chance to be a bad musician."

But when she sat down, she wore a small smile when Seshe whispered, "I liked those songs, especially the second one."

Tahra thanked her seriously, then said, "I thought music would be easy. It's so much like numbers. It *is* numbers. But it's not *just* numbers, and that part I could never get. I like to play for myself, but I never make anyone listen. Usually." She sighed. "That was my father's favorite."

As the two girls began comparing songs, and names of songs, CJ looked around for the scout who'd asked Tahra for a second song, in order to suggest making that a regular thing, as it had cheered Tahra to be asked. But the scout seemed to have gone away.

They pushed westward, climbing steadily into the hills that soon would be mountains.

In spite of the spring weather, the heights were still cool, and presently they reached areas where the deepest valleys still had patches of blue-white snow. The nights got colder, making the young ones glad of the dawnsinger sleeping platforms, cocooned in their cozy quilts.

Around them the trees were just beginning to bud as they ventured deeper into wild woods where no roads existed. Only tracks, made by animals and humans who didn't claim land or build cities.

When a cold breeze started rustling up dancing spirals of withered leaves, Dhana twirled through them. Lyren, riding on one of the horses with a Sandrial aunt, clapped her hands and crowed.

After a morning of song, the dawnsingers faded off into the wood, and they trudged up a steep path in silence. CJ toiled along, thinking about music, and history, until she noticed that the Mearsieans had clumped up behind her, with Tahra in the middle. She said, "Are we ever going to be famous?"

Irenne batted her skirts down, then grinned sideways. "You mean people singing songs about us. Not just us making up our own songs. Right?"

CJ's face burned, leftover humiliation from her early days when girls got smacked for being pushy. "Does that sound stupid?"

"Yup." Diana didn't say it meanly. It was her opinion, given honestly, her black eyes narrowed. "Famous just means other people nosing into your business, and like as not putting their own reasons for doing things into your head. Hate that."

Everybody turned Seshe's way. She had wound her long pale blond locks around one wrist so the wind wouldn't tangle it. She saw the others waiting for an answer. "It doesn't sound stupid."

Irenne walked backward. "So do you want to be famous?" and then in a quick voice, "I suppose you'll say that that's arr-o-gant, that we should be glad to be helpful, and blah blah."

"No I won't say that," Seshe retorted. "Sounds like . . .someone I once knew."

CJ's wayward Dena Yeresbeth sensitivity caught the words Seshe suppressed: *my chief tutor.* But she knew better than to speak.

Irenne crossed her arms, which meant she was waiting for a real answer. Diana took off running, vanishing in the sha-dows.

"I like to see surprise and appreciation in people's faces when I do something right. People I know. Not strangers," Seshe finally said.

CJ snorted. "Better than wanting the attention of *boys*." Then she wished she'd kept her mouth shut.

Irenne looked around with a dramatic air. "Who wants the attention of boys?"

CJ sighed and kicked at grasses as she walked.

Later on, she felt better when they gathered around the campfire to sing, and her funny songs got laughs and claps from many of the squires and younger equerries. She also noticed Irenne singing as loud as any of the girls the chorus to the parody with which she'd serenaded Laban :

> *Oh my dear I loathest thee*
> *So do me a favor and abandon me!*
> *Oh my heart I'd die at thy will*
> *And thou hast already made me deathly ill!*

The adults clapped politely, a few exchanging covert eye-rolls, but Tahra erupted in a sudden laugh, and CJ regarded that as a victory.

Roderic Dei watched all this from enough distance to observe Tahra's alterations in mood, though he could not hear what was said. He hated this plan all the worse because he could see that those children had no idea what war really meant. He longed to get rid of them; he'd hoped that Carl would provide the means, but she lingered on the edges of whatever group Tahra was in, her battered face intent. Then she'd ride off to scout yet again.

Roderic Dei faced the fact that the final decision was going to have to come from him. He scrutinized the Mearsieans. Out of all of them, perhaps Diana could ward blows enough to permit Tahra to escape — assuming she'd actually throw her life in the way of a girl she scarcely knew, queen notwithstanding. But no one should want one youngster to sacrifice herself for another. Putting weapons in the hands of children was obscene outside of the training field. Even that he was beginning to question, and yet, if they didn't train, how to defend themselves against invaders?

When they nearly reached the summit of the slope above the King-Slip waterfall (also known as King's-Lip for a particularly unpopular monarch), they called a halt as the low clouds overhead began to spit rain.

The enemy had to know their location. Carl's order had been to continue the campfire singing; Roderic wondered if that was an emotional response. He hated to bring the company over the top of the rise, which he knew from his youthful travels would expose them to view for a significant distance in all directions.

He called a halt as the rain pelted down, reducing visibility to scarcely arm's reach. The trail became soup, dangerous to footing.

A hail, barely discernable above the roar of the rain, passed from throat to throat from above. Roderick bent into the downpour and slogged uphill, to where he made out movement in the gray curtain of rain.

His lead scout appeared, shouting above the roar, "Carl says it's clear ahead. Says, it's safe to go on up to the ruin and camp."

The scout, a lanky man Roderick's own age, was the only other person who knew Carl's identity. Roderic gritted his teeth, turned to his waiting aide, and passed down the order.

Wondering what Carl had discovered, he walked next to his mount, using the animal as a buffer against the worst of the downpour, as the horse would be catching it anyway. We'll soon have you under some shelter, he thought as the hooves splurped into the sucking mud.

An endless stretch later the trail broadened, flattened, then curved up to the pale stone ruin of what had been some kind of enclave centuries ago: it was a ruin in the oldest records in the kingdom.

"Is this Roth Drael?" he overheard one of the Mearsieans ask another, their high voices carrying over the weakening rain.

"I think so," CJ said. "Roth Drael has a big terrace like that."

Roderic could have pointed out that Roth Drael lay on the other side of the continent, beyond the mountainous belt of the world, and that this ruin was made of a limestone that might have been quarried because it resembled the weird pale stone of the Ancient Sartoran ruins to be found here and there., but it was a ruin of a few centuries, not thousands of years.

He left them to their surmises as the work of setting up tents was carried out, the animals taken to the shelter of one of the remaining overhangs. Somehow the youngsters being so wrong about geography underscored how very little they understood the dangers of the situation. He would strengthen the perimeters, already two deep—not counting the Mearsiean girls—around Tahra.

He walked away to issue the orders, and found Carl waiting, her hood pulled well down. "It worked," she said. "The soul-bound have been diverted in this direction."

Alarm flared through Roderic.

Carl said steadily, her one eye gleaming in the pale light, "When I am successful, it will fall to you to be merciful."

He grimaced. The word "mercy" had no meaning in this contest. The soul-bound were an abomination, the worst sort of strike force, as they were compelled by the magic that controlled them to ignore wounds and keep coming until they couldn't.

"You will know when Henerek's magical hold is broken."

"Carl," he began.

She turned away, and slipped behind a group of equerries leading a string of remounts, leaving him to oversee the last of the camp setup. His last order, "There will be no singing tonight. Fires only inside the two buildings."

And to the elder Knights, as he watched little Lyren hopping over the patterned stone tile inside one partially ruined building, "I want three perimeters tonight."

Eighteen

leaving cold, pure air. Tahra and the girls had been given the centermost building, with four walls, a partial roof, and a good fire burning. It was late when they finally bedded down, the Mearsieans warming up and drying off by prancing around the fire doing pantomimes since they weren't supposed to be making noise.

CJ had felt every laugh of Tahra's as a victory as Falinneh clowned about, braids flapping, freckled arms and legs wild. Irenne was perfect as the prissy, snotty butt of the other girls' clowning, pretending outrage and affront in a way that even had Lyren laughing, though few of the adults seemed to find the girls entertaining.

Well, everyone knows adults have no sense of humor, CJ thought sleepily as she burrowed into the borrowed sleeping bag. Tahra laughed. A lot. That's what counts.

When she was alone like this she wrestled with worry about what would happen when it was time for the attack. They'd had pretty good luck so far against villains, but as far as she was concerned, it was luck. Even if nobody in this world understood the idea of luck. CJ wasn't sure she believed in good luck, but she was utterly convinced that bad luck lurked at your heels like a nasty ghost, waiting to get you when you least expected.

She had positioned herself along a wall so she could look through the keyhole windows up at the stars. From that angle she almost missed the quiet entry of a new figure, no more than a shadow against the paleness of the walls.

CJ blinked, trying to get the firelight glare out of her eyes as the silhouette moved among the recumbent lumps of her companions. She wondered if she ought to yell. She was drawing in her breath when the figure changed direction, firelight briefly revealing the scarred face of — Carl the scout?

As CJ struggled with questions, Carl bent down, and kissed Tahra's brow. Then straightened up and swiftly moved away.

That was weird, CJ thought. And gross. But since nothing worse had happened, and nobody else came in, she turned over and went to sleep.

Carl moved swiftly away, fighting to keep the sobs locked up tightly inside her. In spite of the never-ending pain that burned with every breath, her body wanted to live, and fought her will, expressing that duel in the frantic race of her heartbeat singing in her ears.

But that moment with Tahra, which her daughter would never have endured waking, had strengthened her resolve. She would buy Tahra as much peace as she could.

She reached her chosen scouts, gave a nod, and picked up a waiting jug.

They faded silently into the night.

At the same time, on the other side of the deep valley between the lakes that filled ancient calderas, Henerek's two mages followed behind the phalanxes of soul-bound tramping stolidly down.

The soul-bound endured the whiplash of seedling trees and scrubby brush that could not be seen in the darkness, trampling it all flat so that the two could ride in relative peace. But chunky, grizzled Benin, the mage controlling the soul-bound, was exhausted after four too many transfers between Norsunder Base and Everon, just so that Henerek could maintain the illusion of his constant presence at the Base. The younger, Vasz, long-nosed, bony-shouldered and stooping, was furious.

Benin snorted, distracted from his almost-snooze by Vasz's angry breathing and muttered curses. "Shut up. It's only a sidestep. That town will still be there when these witless finish off Roderic Dei's old men and boys."

"Easy for *you* to say. You haven't spent two long nights

bespelling tracers and traps, just for a postponement," Vasz snapped back. "After a damned winter of being treated like a supply clerk."

Which is exactly what he was, Benin thought with contempt. Sometimes he wished he'd stayed with Dejain, but she'd a bad habit of pushing all the really tedious magical chores onto him, while hiding her search for those missing blood magic texts. He knew she never would have shared.

So thoroughly did he trust his magic compelling the masses of tramping soldiery ahead of them that he closed his eyes again as his horse plodded slowly. Vasz glowered, contemplating a nasty little spell to jolt Lord Superior Benin over there, who had a habit of pushing all the really tedious magical chores onto him so he could play with ways to make soul-bound faster, or maunder on about the ancient blood magic texts that no one had actually seen.

Vasz raised his hands, engrossed in the tiny red glow as he whispered a spell—

Zip!

Benin rocked in the saddle, an arrow in his throat. Vasz drew in a breath to curse, but then pain flowered through his chest, and he couldn't seem to catch his breath . .

Thud. Thud.

The soul-bound marched on, oblivious to Siamis emerging from the brush, slinging a bow over his shoulder.

He loped across the clearing and caught the reins of the skittish horses, calming them and tying their reins to a sapling. When they stood still, only their ears twitching back and forth, he continued to touch their minds with calming thoughts as he searched through both mages' packs for their magic books. Then he stripped one horse of its gear, dumped that gear into a nearby mass of marshy weed, and smacked the animal's flank to send it off to a different life.

Last, he pushed up his sleeve, examined his lacerated arm, then slid the sleeve down again and pulled up the other sleeve. Using his left hand, he sliced into his right forearm and counted the drips of blood as they splatted to the mushy ground.

He understood the theory of Venn blood hunt magic, but had not seen them practice it. Knowing that the Venn were hampered by having to coach ignorant northern mages through their process, he'd been counting between ten and twenty drips at each location. But here, where rain soaked the already sodden ground, he counted double that before pulling a length of cloth from his pocket, binding it around his arm, and yanking his sleeve down again.

Then he carefully opened a linen square, which held the seeds he had bespelled as tracers. He pressed one into the middle of the blood splatters, then refolded the linen square and returned it to his pocket.

He untied the reins of the remaining horse, mounted, and rode back up the trampled trail.

Dawnstar glimmered behind the low clouds pressing down on the mountain, though no one in Everon could see it or the sun an hour behind it. As rain rolled in at a roar, the perimeter guards outside Henerek's camp began to shout, causing the rest of the sleepy night guards to stumble to their aid—and drop, one by one, as arrows sped out of the surrounding gloom, one shot to a man.

In the center of the camp, Henerek woke, disinclined to get out of his warm bed. His hand-picked men could deal with whatever it was—

He sneezed, and sneezed again. Linseed oil? His tent door flapped open. A hand moved into the heavily pungent air. Ruddy light flickering over the ruined face of Mersedes Carinna, Queen of Everon.

She had been running words through her mind during the long trek in the pouring rain, words about justice, evil, trust, and vows, but events moved too fast for her, even faster than the thrill of fear that she'd never been able to entire banish.

He sat up, right hand snapping out for his sword a heartbeat before the air exploded into white flame as she tossed the torch at him. His soaked clothing caught fire. The queen threw herself onto him to keep him from escape as the entire tent erupted into flames, and white agony enveloped them both. She had feared that, too, but as the tent exploded into steaming fragments, hot steam seared her straight into oblivion as the rain poured in, and Henerek bellowed in inarticulate pain.

"Attack! Attack!" someone howled.

From elsewhere came the sound of a trumpet, followed by a shout, "West company, to the flank! North company, on me!"

Everoneth scouts ran among the tents, shooting fire arrows

into tents splashed with oil. Flames broke out, most instantly extinguished by the rain, but the smoke, fires, and most of all the zipping arrows from the surrounding darkness caused Henerek's brigands, who had never been molded into a unified force, to get in each other's way as some fought and others ran for the hills, angry that the promised easy pickings had been a lie.

When the camp was empty except for the dead and a few smoldering linseed-oil fires here and there, the grim search began.

A young scout called, "Found her."

Mersedes Carinna had not really understood how fire would work, and by flinging herself on her enemy, she had extinguished the flames between them. But his extremities had been unprotected, leaving him writhing in agony, the queen's dead weight pressing down on him.

The lead scout mercifully slit Henerek's throat. And on the other side of the valley, the soul-bound faltered to a stop, the magic binding them to Henerek's will broken by his death. Because there was no mage to respell them onto a new will, they stood silently, minds caught in the twilight world between life and death as rain pelted their bodies.

When the dawn's light began outlining the mountains, Roderic and the Knights—ranged along the ridge beyond the ruins—stared down, weapons gripped in sweaty hands. They made out the silent army at the foot of the slope below, standing still as stone.

Roderic had not slept all night.

He lifted his gaze to take in the waiting lines of his Knights, three deep. His voice carried above the rain. "Skirmishers, on me. This might be a trap."

"No," his oldest Knight said, hoarse with disgust. "These are true soul-bound. They'll stand there until either another mage takes command, or you cut them down."

"How?" asked the youngest.

"The surest method is beheading."

The Knights ranged up, every face reflecting horror.

"Do they suffer?" Roderic asked.

"I don't know." The old Knight shook his head slowly, hands out. Then lifted his somber face, running with rain. "What do you think you would feel?"

But an older Knight said in a gruff voice, "It's a mercy. They are only held alive by dark magic, which never bothers to mask pain. Release them."

Some turned away and others flinched, all perceiving that "release" in this situation meant killing them with steel.

Roderic raised his sword. "Make every blow true."

He had ordered the recruits, squires, and the other youth to form that third ring around Tahra, exhorting them to remember that they were the first line of defense in protecting her. His motivation here had been to spare them whatever was to happen as long as he could.

And so the young squires and the girls never saw the work that would haunt the dreams of the senior Knights for the remainder of their lives.

The rain lifted mid-morning.

Diana of the Mearsieans, having clambered to the highest roof as a volunteer lookout, yelled, "They're coming!"

From the outer perimeter, Canold, captain of the squires, peered up at Diana. He and his small troop held the southernmost part of the perimeter, where surely attack would come first. He gripped his sword as he shouted, "Ours or theirs?"

After a time, she called down, "I can't tell. They're all muddy . . .Oh, they're carrying people."

Murmurs back and forth, then Carinna called up, "Carrying how?"

"On things. Like beds. Between horses."

"Like wounded?"

Again, everyone looked at one another, unsure whether to slide downhill in the muck to help, or stay where they'd been told to defend their queen to the last.

But presently Roderick's horse, well splattered with mud, climbed past the front rows, head down. Roderick's head was bare, his hair streaming in the rain.

Canold and Carinna registered all the bared heads, and realized what it meant. "It's over," someone said in surprise.

"And they're bringing back the dead," someone else breathed.

"And a lot of captured horses," a third muttered, hurrying toward the area they'd set aside for mounts.

The youngsters broke ranks at once, crowding around their

elders as they rode into the ruins, carefully setting down their burdens. The wounded, relatively few, were borne into the ruin where Tahra and the girls had slept.

Roderic found his chance to take aside the scout leader. "And so?"

"It is done. He's dead. I finished him myself." The man looked around, wiping straggling gray hair off his high forehead. "I'm not certain what to say. It was very chaotic, all the smoke from the fires we started." He faced his commander. "We were good, but outnumbered. Someone had already taken out the sentries. Someone who's a dead aim. Kept on shooting them as they tried to run off."

He brought out an arrow, washed clean by the rain.

"That's not one of ours," Roderic said.

"No." The scout waited, question in his eyes.

Roderic shook his head. "It could very well be an internal matter, someone within Henerek's ranks who thought to take control. Say nothing now. We've enough to deal with."

The scout bowed his head, and both turned to watch as the dead were laid in a row. As it happened, though most of her body had been burned, and was swathed in a concealing cloak, Mersedes Carinna's face had been scalded by that burst of steam, but not consumed in the fire.

"That's Carl," CJ exclaimed. "The scout." And turned to Tahra. "He kissed you right before they left. Did you know him?"

Tahra recoiled, mouth thinned with disgust and resentment. "Kissed me? I don't remember that."

"It was while we were sleeping," CJ said. "Only I wasn't asleep."

Tahra repeated, "Carl?" as she stared down at the rain-washed face, then shock lengthened her face.

In death Mersedes Carinna's face had smoothed out, the scars mere shadows.

Tahra's eyes widened, stark with horror. She shoved violently through the people gathering around, sobbing as she looked for Roderic Dei.

"You knew," Tahra screamed at him. "You knew."

He came to stand at the foot of the makeshift bier, looking old and haggard and defeated, though the kingdom was safe, the young queen was safe. He waited until Tahra sobbed for breath, then said, "Your majesty. It was by your order you

accompanied us on this mission. It was by her order that I kept
her identity secret."

"But where was she? I thought she was . . ." She shied from
the word *dead*, now so true. "A prisoner."

"She was. During some trouble in Norsunder, she escaped.
When she came to me, it was with this plan. Her orders. Her
last orders as queen . . ." His voice hoarsened with grief and his
eyes closed, but Tahra saw the tears escape, then he forced
himself to continue. "She had inside information. And knew we
had to act at once. Everything. Was on her orders."

Tahra gulped, fists clenched. Then she wiped her snot-
smeared, teary face on her sleeve. "If I'd stayed in Ferdrian.
Would you ever have told me?"

"I don't know," he admitted, his helm held in both hands in
spite of the dreary rain. "But this I do know. I would have seen
to it that her heroism went into the records, that she would be
remembered by future generations. She said to me she did not
want you losing her twice."

Tahra gulped again, then said in a weird, tight voice, "She
died fighting Norsunder. So will I."

"No, child," Roderic said, and now he came around to her
side, but halted an arm's distance away from the stiff,
distraught girl. It was for her to reach for human comfort if she
would, but his voice was that of Uncle Roderic, not
Commander Dei. "No, you must not do their work for them,
nor let your mother's sacrifice be rendered worthless.
Disappoint Norsunder by thriving, and take the gift she gave
you, which is peace. Your duty is Everon. Not death."

"Yes," Tahra mumbled dully. "Yes. Everon is my duty."

Roderic lifted his gaze and dispersed people with glances.

The Mearsieans gathered around, uncertain what to do.
Even little Lyren, sensing grief on the mental plane, sat quietly,
one hand clinging to Jenel Sandrial, her small face troubled.

The wounded were tended to, the animals fed and curried,
food prepared and served to the tired, sodden company. By
noon the rain had lifted, and the dawnsingers, who had
vanished the day previous at Roderick's behest, had returned.

When the sun's fiery rim touched the western mountains,
the dawnsingers began to hum softly. No words. A rising and
falling melody so beautiful it hurt. The dead had been
straightened on their biers, hands that the night before had
gripped weapons now still. Eyes closed that had last looked on

the enemy's camp.

Tahra knelt at the head of her mother's bier, shivering, though Roderic had directed the equerries to set a fire behind her.

As the dawnsingers hummed a threnody, one by one people came forward to say words of remembrance over those close to them. Two sang songs, or tried, the second managing a few words, tuneless with grief, as in the background, the melody rose and fell, rose and fell.

At last Tahra stood up, and everyone else stopped moving. The last rays of the sinking sun struck highlights on wrapped wounds, tired, dirty faces, on Tahra's red nose and puffy eyes, and on Mersedes Carinna's long and sallow features that, with all the humor gone, now looked so much like Tahra's.

She turned her head, and slowly brought out her flute. She played her father's song, which she knew her mother had loved. It wavered, breathy at times, a lament that caused choked sobs, as Roderic stood with his eyes tightly shut, his breathing harsh: for the first time in her life, Tahra played with heart instead of head.

When she was done, in a sudden, violent movement, she threw the flute on the fire. "I'll never play again."

Then she touched her mother's forehead, whispering the words of Disappearance as somewhere behind, the dawnsingers took up the song and wove it into their own tribute to the queen who had been their friend.

The voices brightened, the melody lifting like birdsong, causing CJ to raise stinging eyes skyward to where the sunlight glinted on the edges of leaves, her vision blurry, so that for a heartbeat it seemed a veil between the worlds rent.

Others blinked tear-blurred eyes, seeing the faces of those lost in the earlier war. Others saw the golden glow of sunset, almost too beautiful to bear.

And then the sun vanished, the dead were gone, and it was time to turn about and make their way back down the mountain.

Nineteen

Norsunder Base

IF ONE WAS WISE, Dejain often reflected, one made the effort to cultivate Lesca, the steward of Norsunder Base. Most of the idiots who thought they would command the Base, and thence the southern front in the coming war, ignored Lesca, except when they threw supply commands her way.

She cooperated. If she didn't, her life would be short. But she could contrive things so that crucial supplies were a little late, and not quite right. There were always convincing reasons.

That was for the petty would-be warlords. For the ones who demonstrated considerable reach, Lesca's retaliation was more subtle: she had spy windows all over her private chambers, most of which Dejain herself had made for her.

These spy windows drew appreciable magic, which had its cost elsewhere, but Dejain—once she'd discovered how far Lesca had gone beyond the expected limits—had worked her own arrangements. It had taken patience, but she had agreed with Lesca that security was important.

And so from time to time Dejain joined Lesca in her comfortable inner room, sat back to enjoy fresh food transferred in straight from Colend (would these shopkeepers ever be surprised if they knew whom they supplied!) and watched those who had no idea they were seen.

Most enlightening it was, too.

Lesca knew quite well that Dejain was using her as a handy tool for spying, but she found Dejain entertaining, unlike most of the current crop of brutes. She said, on Dejain's appearing, "Henerek is gone again."

"Again?"

"Walked into his chamber, stepped into the chalk Destination that that slimy Benin made for him, and transferred."

"When was this?" Dejain sank carefully onto a low cushion. She appeared, in forgiving light, to be somewhere in her twenties, but dark magic could only do so much to preserve one. Her bones were very brittle. At least it was not winter, which caused her continuous ache.

"Last night. He's usually back by now. Did you find out where he's been sneaking off to?"

"Benin and Vasz have successfully warded any tracers, but it has to have something to do with Everon." Dejain sighed. "It's always Everon with Henerek."

Lesca shook her sleek, well-groomed head. She was a large, indolent woman, who favored Colendi styles. Her half-lidded eyes crinkled in amusement. "Someone," she drawled, "should encourage him to consider the benefits of variety."

Dejain returned a suitable answer, and stayed the length of time it took to drink one of Lesca's spiced concoctions. Then, making an effort not to hurry, she claimed work awaited and departed.

Dejain never made the mistake of thinking herself spared from Lesca's spying. She assumed that those windows were curtained off by illusion magic when Dejain entered her lair, and to search would be to gain Lesca's enmity.

Much easier to live as though she were always being watched. She made her way to the Command Center to look up at the markers on the big map; she could check the dispatches later, when she was fairly certain that Lesca was asleep, or entertaining a lover. Though Detlev hadn't received any of those Ancient Sartoran reports for a long time, Dejain still hoped to find those blood mage texts.

Kessler Sonscarna lay bound and gagged and blindfolded in his cell, his existence kept a secret by strict orders. As no one on the

detention staff wanted to be mindripped by Detlev, they obeyed his orders even when he wasn't there. The thought of him
suddenly appearing out of the Beyond and killing with a glance
kept them scrupulous: everyone remembered what had happened to the torturer Janek, found dead outside Dtheldevor's
empty cell, blood leaking from nose, eyes, ears.

Kessler was left alone, except for water and food once a day.
For Kessler time was measured by the humiliation of being fed,
not at all gently, by guards who refused to untie him.

He didn't even try to convince them he would not do magic
if he were free. He used his time planning his actions once he
faced Detlev.

But it wasn't Detlev who came for him after all.

When the cell was unlocked by magic—he sensed the
distinctive singe before hearing the iron clatter—the blindfold
came off to reveal light hair framing a familiar face: Siamis.

Steel gleamed. Kessler braced for attack, then the knife
sawed through the gag in two quick strokes.

"Kessler. You want to escape," Siamis said. It wasn't a
question.

Kessler eyed him, trying to think past the headache, then
hazarded a guess: "You want a diversion."

"And so? Your answer?"

"You're turning on Detlev?"

"Yes," Siamis said.

Kessler smiled.

Siamis dropped the keys on the bare floor. "Detlev's other
priority prisoner is the girl across from you, who reportedly
knows where the dyr is."

Siamis tossed down the knife and walked out, leaving the
cell door open.

Kessler rolled over to get his fingers onto the knife. It was
extremely sharp. He freed himself from the ropes, hefting the
knife in one bloody, nearly numb hand as he clumsily picked
up the keys with the other.

He freed as many prisoners as he could find, going last to
the cell that revealed a short, skinny girl.

Liere had been listening on the mental plane, once Siamis
was gone. Nearly frantic with fear, she got to her feet. Kessler
only had to jerk his head at her, and she stumbled toward the
door, but to her surprise he pushed her back inside, shut the
door, and said, "I've an escape route. But this is difficult. Hold

onto me, and don't let go."

Having studied the map a good, long while, Dejain leisurely made her way to Henerek's chamber, because she knew Lesca would expect that. She stripped the wards, and poked her head in. Nothing to be found, of course. She left, murmured the spells to replace the wards—glad that Vasz was as lazy as he was unimaginative—and walked on until she reached an area that she had made certain had no spy windows.

From there, it was simple to cast an illusion over herself. It didn't really make one invisible, just a blur, but from a spy eye, it was difficult to catch such blurs because of the distortion the spy window magic could not entirely prevent.

She wandered to Benin's chamber, and threw an echo spell: no one inside. At least no one alive. He had always made certain to be present in the mornings, as if no one would notice his being gone most of the night, which meant Henerek was definitely executing some plan, and Benin the Betrayer was (at least so far) working the magical part of Henerek's plan.

Dejain took her time with Benin's wards. His one claim to expertise was in soul-binding. A trap missed would mean another victim. She snapped the last binding and smelled the hot-metal singe of heavy magic dissipate. She unlatched the door and stepped cautiously in, feeling for more traps. Nothing. Benin had clearly not expected trouble.

Dejain looked around, ignoring the tumbled, sour-smelling bed, the trunk of clothing. The shelves and desk were bare. She approached, carefully testing. No wards, which meant his magic books were elsewhere.

"He's dead."

She whirled around, and froze, alarm chilling her nerves when she recognized Siamis leaning in the doorway. He was dressed entirely in black, the only color his visible skin, and his light hair, which lay in damp strands across his forehead. Reflected light gleamed in his light gaze, and on the polished hilts of knives at the top of each boot, at his belt, and up one sleeve as he gestured toward the barren shelves.

His sleeve fell back as he moved, and she caught a glimpse of a brown-stained bandage. She saw the hilt of his famous sword behind his shoulder.

"Benin's books," Siamis continued, "are elsewhere."

She said, "How did you get in past the wards?"

"Through the prison." His chin lifted, the hall's torchlight playing over the beautiful bone structure of his face. Youth was also beauty. He had both, and she loathed him for it.

"Why are you telling me this now?" she asked.

"Because among the other alarms shortly to break, Bostian's mage spies are about to discover the traps laid for them, which are going to point your way. Oh yes, and there are three layers of a trap waiting for you up in Command Center at the Dispatch Tray, that Vasz has been laying down each time he fetched messages. He won't be finishing it. He's dead, too. But you might as well remove it and get the credit."

Lesca had to have seen some of that, Dejain thought. *Why didn't she warn me?*

"Because," Siamis said — reminding her that he was a mind-reader — "Surprise makes far better theater. You should know that," he finished in a tone of mild reproof as he pulled the bandage from his sleeve, and blood ran down his hand to drip on the floor. "To Lesca, you're all puppets on strings."

"Then I had better —"

The words *start dancing* died on her lips when she heard the clangor of a bell in quick threes that meant prison break.

Her first thought was Kessler Sonscarna, the most dangerous prisoner down there, kept in secret. Or so they thought.

She hurried away, shock jolting at every step from her heel bones to her teeth.

Of course Siamis told her so that her actions would draw Kessler, but if even half of what he said was true, she already had a target on her back. And he'd never had lied to her outright. He — like Detlev — told the truth, though only as much as suited their purposes.

Siamis watched her scurry away, then leaned against the wall. He shut his eyes briefly, scanning the mental plane. The blood hunters, undeterred by having to hide their transfers, were now one jump behind him. This latest trace at Norsunder Base ought to give them a setback.

He opened his eyes and steadied himself.

Far more dangerous would be Efael's Black Knives, who should be appearing right about . . .

The whisper of steel, an in-drawn breath, and they came at him from both sides, two pair, as expected, long knives in both hands.

He swung up the illusion-hidden crossbow and shot. The lead assassin recoiled, but the distance was too short and the steel too fast. The bolt pinned his arm to his ribs as Siamis swung the bow in an arc and slung it wheeling at the opposite pair.

They dove apart to dodge the blur, which ruined their approach for a heartbeat, permitting him to draw his sword and drop a knife from his sleeve into his hand.

Then the three closed in, lethally trained, but leading with the edge of the blade because Efael likes his targets cut up before the kill.

Four thousand years ago, when Siamis was twelve, once Efael was through proving that Siamis had no hope of anything but humiliation, no expectation but of pain, no value except as entertainment, he had given him back to Detlev. And when the two were finally alone, Detlev had said, *They want you alive to force me to their will. Hold to that. Whatever happens, however much you will wish to fight back, never let them see your training until you are done.*

Ever since then, every single time Detlev took him out into the world, after whatever arduous, sometimes excruciating, exercise he was put through, at the end, Siamis had always asked, *Am I done?*

And Detlev had always answered, *No.*

I'm done now, Siamis thought as the three charged.

Subtle and deadly they were, but Siamis had watched Efael's patterns long ago when kept off-world as his toy. Now, with breath, muscle and bone moving in perfect synchrony, his mind mapping the geometry of patterns in arcs of advance, deflect, feint and lunge, he carved through all three and moved on fast, knowing that these would have been the volunteers. Efael would send back-up.

Siamis knew where Bostian was by the rings of would-be defenders. A couple of these tried to fight him off, but most of them faded, probably to find reinforcements. Siamis flicked checks on the mental plane every few steps, dangerous as that was. Efael wouldn't come without at least one team as backup. And his sister with her bag of magical cheats.

Siamis ran Bostian down in the map room as he monitored the search for escaped prisoners. The big man had defenders at his back.

At that moment the entire fortress lurched — massive transfer, not just at the Destination, plus points all over the fortress. That would be Efael's Black Knives. There'd be no using the Destination for months, now.

Bostian's men began to advance on Siamis, but betrayed in grips and shifty eyes and subtle jockeying a reluctance to be first.

Siamis spoke past them to Bostian, "Do I really have to send you after Henerek?"

"He's dead?"

"Fire," Siamis said, smiling, "*and* steel."

Bostian stilled. "So . . ."

"You had your orders. Clean this place up, and prepare for the shift to Five when the rift magic is won from Songre Silde."

Bostian lifted a shoulder, then his eyes narrowed on either side of his broken nose. "You're still running to Detlev's leash?"

"Who says," Siamis asked, "he'll be commanding at Five?"

Bostian's teeth showed in a broad grin, and Siamis, sensing the footsteps one floor above and one below as Bostian's group closed in, stepped outside the door and used the transfer-slide to Norsunder Beyond, and then back to where he had left the Arrow.

Twenty

KESSLER HAD PRACTICED THE spells over and over, so there was no hesitation as heat built.

Liere nearly lost her grip on Kessler's arm as vertigo and nausea shook her in violent vibration, worsened by the stench of hot metal. Kessler took a step, jolting her almost off her feet, as she found herself in still, stale air, then another step into a dank cold that smelled equally stale, shot through with mildew, mold, and the tang of overcooked cabbage.

Kessler shook off her hand, and pushed her into a wooden chair.

"Where am I?" she asked in a thread of a voice.

"Chwahirsland," he began, then stilled, the knife held along his forearm, blade out, in a way Liere had seen Senrid practice.

But then his arm relaxed when Jilo walked in. Liere recognized him, and let out a thankful breath.

"Prince Kessler?" Jilo exclaimed, and then, "Liere?"

"I used Wan-Edhe's back door out of Norsunder," Kessler said. His lip curled. "Which will no doubt be closed up soon."

"Is he there?"

"No. In the Beyond, somewhere on the borderland. Not at the Base."

Jilo sighed. "I've begun laying wards on this entire floor against that David."

"Don't bother." Kessler shrugged. "My guess is, he'll never be back. He was here to trap me. But I'm not coming back to undo bloodknife magic. Send her off," Kessler said, nodding at Liere. "I don't know what kind of wards might be on her."

"Tsauderei," Jilo said. "I have a token."

Liere was too bewildered to speak, and Jilo said with a fumbling attempt at kindness, "You'll like it in that palace of Atan's, I think. And it's safe."

He had no mind-shield, so his memory flooded Liere's tired mind: the fascination of ancient ovals worn in steps by people unafraid to walk about. Keyhole windows here, arched ones in that wing, trefoil windows down below, round ones over there, all from different centuries as the place was slowly added to, or knocked partially down, redesigned, some old things painstak-ingly replaced thread by thread and paint stroke by paint stroke, other things swept away to some cellar or attic and new stuff put in place. Because the Sartorans, Jilo had discovered on his short visit, never threw anything away. Everything had a history, and people had a tendency to want to tell you those histories.

He'd half-listened to Mondros and Tsauderei's truncated conversations about magic and the Venn hunt while he looked around the walls with their age-smoothed carvings and won-dered how many scenes of wonder and laughter, triumph and tragedy, loss and greed and mercy and discovery the walls had framed. And he'd wondered if he scraped hard enough at a column all carved with stylized bird shapes, worn by the touch of countless hands as they turned that corner, if bits of time would peel off.

These images flooded Liere in the time it took to take two breaths, which steadied her enough to say, "Please."

Mondros and Tsauderei had each given Jilo transfer tokens to use in an emergency after talking to him about the import-ance of keeping himself—and the enemies book—out of the hands of Detlev's boys.

Jilo pulled the tokens out, picked one, and put it into her resistless palm. "Say Tsauderei's name twice together."

She did, and once more transfer magic jolted her. But this time she smelled green things, and some unfamiliar herb scent. A dark-robed mage student entered the Destination, where she stood swaying as she stared at the elaborate golden dragons writhing up toward the rayed sun in the middle panel on the opposite wall.

The mage student on duty took one look, gave Liere a polite third circle bow and said, "Please come this way." And to someone else, "Send a message to the Chief Mage."

Liere set the token into a waiting box, and warm steep was pressed into her hands.

She was so tired, hungry, and light-headed from the bewildering changes, that she was unaware of time passing until someone said kindly, "This way."

She discovered that she had drunk all the steep, and some of the light-headedness resulted from the cottony effect of listerblossom. Someone else led her to a cleaning frame, which took away all the grimy nastiness from the clothes she had been wearing since she and CJ had run so uselessly.

And then she entered a chamber where Tsauderei sat, white brows knit into a line as he took her in. "A lot of people will be glad you're free," he said. "How about you tell me what happened, so I can deal with the questions they'll ask?"

"My daughter?" Liere asked. "I know she's all right. I visited her in the dream realm. But quickly. So I wouldn't be caught. So I don't know where she is, because she doesn't know."

Tsauderei considered how much to tell her about recent events, and decided simplest was best. "She is in Everon. The Sandrials, the stewards of the royal palace in Ferdrian, are taking care of her. It seems that Tahra finds her presence diverting as well as comforting."

"Oh yes." Liere looked away. "She is still mourning her brother."

"There's more recent news than that, but it can wait. How did you get free?"

"Prince Kessler, Jilo called him. Siamis said his name, too."

"Siamis?" Tsauderei exclaimed, leaning forward.

Liere repeated the entire conversation, which she had easily heard from the cell across from Kessler's. Tsauderei listened all the way through, his eyes narrowed. Then someone opened the door, looked in, and shut it again.

He said, "You remember Atan, do you not? You're currently a guest here. There is a meal waiting, and a bed. I'm going to write to Erai-Yanya and Arthur to let them know you are free. They'll spread the word, and no doubt plans will be made to reunite you with your small one. You're safe here. Eat. Rest."

Liere was beyond question, beyond plans, beyond any

thought or emotion except for gratitude as she did exactly that.

As soon as she was gone, Tsauderei took out his hated scrystone, and soon had Mondros's grizzled face staring at him through the rounded glass. Mondros waited through the entire explanation, then said, "What do you make of that?"

"First thing to consider is the fact that the Venn hunters had all been converging on Siamis, and now he's beyond tracing."

"So you think he knew about the hunt?"

"I've been sure of it as soon as all those blood traces were reported within a matter of days on four continents."

Mondros sighed.

"Second, he wanted that girl to hear that conversation, or he could have conducted it in privacy."

"Even if it's true, and he's turning on Detlev, that doesn't make him anything but a traitor to his own kind. Certainly not an ally of ours," Mondros said, his rough voice almost a growl.

"No," Tsauderei said, but he drew the word out, almost a question.

They ended the scry session then, and he sat back, thinking. Then gave a grunt, and reached across the desk for a rolled map. This he unrolled, and bent over it, looking at the random spread of sightings reported by the hunters.

The speed with which Siamis moved argued that he knew he was being hunted. His movements might be random, but Tsauderei didn't think Siamis was the random sort. There had to be some sort of pattern. But what? Nothing magical, of that he was fairly certain. So it was time to consult someone trained in military thinking.

Senrid had been sleeping badly, in spite of his resolves to keep busy until he fell into bed exhausted, his last thought firming his mind-shield.

Too often ever since Liere had been taken he slept like he'd dropped under a stone spell until the night watch's single toll, which ordinarily he rarely noticed. But he'd begun jolting awake, vaguely aware of bad dreams, and then find it difficult to get back to sleep.

He'd finally sunk back into to that heavy-limbed state between waking and sleeping when the dreamscape flickered and there was Liere.

"I'm free," she said, and, "Don't lose the dream. Stay."

He floated, concentrating on her image. She'd done this before, so it could be real, and not just him wishing —

"It's me," she said. "I'm in Sartor." And she let the dream fold around her, but he woke up anyway, sitting upright as he gazed around his darkened bedroom.

The urge to transfer to Sartor seized him, but he resisted it. The watch change bell had rung not long ago which made it barely dawn in Sartor. Since Liere was safe, there was no emergency. No one in Sartor would consider his wild curiosity anything but an annoyance.

He lay back down, shut his eyes, composed his mind-shield — then shocked himself upright again. If Liere could get past his shield and into his dreams, couldn't Detlev?

How did all that work anyway?

He slammed his head back down on the pillow. Nobody had invaded his mind through dreams yet, only Liere. Maybe the mind-shield had a hole in it for a specific person?

He couldn't stem the flow of questions, and he was wide awake, so he got up, dashed through his cleaning frame, and bolted out of his room. When he saw the roaming guard at the other end of the hall, he yelled, "Can't sleep," and dashed on.

When he reached his study, he checked his gold case, finding letters from Leander and Terry, both about archive searches of four centuries previous.

A third, from Arthur, reported that Liere was safe, and he was also keeping his promise with the latest about the Venn hunters. Senrid whistled when he saw how many Siamis sightings they'd found. Disturbing, considering they were tracing blood.

The latest sighting pointed to Norsunder Base.

No surprise there. He decided to start at the top of the magic hierarchy, wrote, *What happened with Siamis and the Venn?* And sent it off to Tsauderei.

He sat back, the notecase turning around in his hands as he blinked tired eyes. He might have slept a whole hour. How could he bore himself back to sleep?

The internal 'click' of a letter arriving in the notecase furnished a reply:

*I am here in Sartor for now. Use the palace
Destination.*

Tsauderei had had little experience of Senrid, and a great

deal of secondary information about Senrid's kingdom, none of it inspiring of trust. On further delving, he'd discovered that Senrid's father had attempted to redress some of that sanguinary reputation, until (it was rumored) he was murdered by his own brother. That was some years after another brother tried a palace coup, then ran for the border ahead of assassins sent by his own father.

Definitely less than inspiring. But Tsauderei liked mavericks, unless they proved to be malicious; he'd been rather a maverick (some used the word troublemaker) in his young days. He liked what he'd seen of Senrid so far, and more important, others with more experience of Senrid both liked and trusted him. The two did not always go together.

He remembered Senrid's nervy manner, headlong questions, and habit of launching into action, so when Senrid was brought to the chief mage's chambers (Tsauderei refused to think of them as his, and intended to find a replacement as soon as events permitted) he had everything ordered in his mind.

Senrid found himself greeted by the aroma of fresh baked goods riding the cool early morning air in Sartor.

As soon as he walked into the room where Tsauderei sat, the old man said, "Liere is here. Arrived the night before last. I understand she's awake this morning. She can tell you the details, but the gist is that Siamis, for his own unstated purpose, sprang Kessler Sonscarna from Norsunder Base prison, and he took Liere."

"Siamis did that?" Senrid repeated.

"Yes," Tsauderei said, and handed across a rolled map. "There's something else I thought you might want to know, but first I wanted to thank you personally for seeing to it that the antidote to that bloodknife enchantment got propagated among us."

Senrid opened his hand, a gesture that Tsauderei interpreted as assent. "Arthur says the Venn have been finding Siamis's blood all over the world?"

"If you'll take a look at that map, you'll see them marked. I've kept a careful count, though I could not make out any sense in so many."

Senrid glanced at the markers. Then uttered a short laugh. "Back of the hand?"

Tsauderei's white brows lifted in sardonic humor. "That

occurred to me. It also occurred to me that he found out about the search somehow, though we were very careful in choosing witnesses and warding the meeting place. Nobody could have come near that room without our knowing."

He waved a gnarled hand in dismissal. "But that's the past. Because of the number of sightings, which might constitute a pattern, I decided I'd better consult someone with military expertise. It certainly makes no sense from the magical perspective."

He paused, remembered that Senrid also studied magic, and thought, yes, this was the right person, young as he was. "As you probably know, light mages are forbidden to involve themselves in governmental matters, and are seldom invited to. There is an even greater divide between mages and military. I've a very few trusted advisors left alive, one of whom is Roderick Dei, Commander of the Knights in Everon. But this is not the time to disturb him."

"Why?" asked Senrid.

"Did you hear that the queen of Everon had escaped Norsunder?"

"I did. So she's home again?"

"Yes, and no." Tsauderei gave a brief, blunt report, watching Senrid for reactions—a grim expression at Mersedes's end, which tightened to a grimace when Tsauderei finished, "And so Commander Dei had to deal with the soul-bound, as well as console and advise the new young queen."

Tsauderei paused, then continued. "Roderic Dei sent the recruits back to the capital, and remained behind with a couple of experienced companies to make certain they'd cleared out the worst of the Norsundrian hirelings. Two days ago, about the same time your friend was freed from Norsunder Base, the Venn hunters arrived at that very site. They discovered the remains of two men, who had the residue of dark magic still clinging to them. They weren't armed, so the surmise is they were mages."

Senrid leaned forward. "Controlling the soul-bound? Why was Siamis there? Was he running the attack through Henerek?"

"All I can report is that Commander Dei ordered a new search of the area. And what he discovered was a significant supply cache, far more weapons and long-lasting goods of various types than made sense for the numbers they'd met."

Tsauderei leaned out and tapped the green marker on the map between the two lakes on the western border of Everon. "So they searched farther out. Discovered two more."

Senrid looked down at the map, recognizing a pass between the two lakes. "Enough supplies for an invasion and occupation," he said. "Hold the pass . . ."

Senrid pulled the map closer, his gaze rapidly moving over it. First, of course, to Halia, where he spotted a marker at the western edge of the Askalhan Mountains tucked under the Nelkereth Plains, affording a relatively short march southward into Toth and Perideth ". . .and north into Marloven Hess."

Could that be where Detlev had hidden that advance troop when Senrid first became king? Only Norsunder hadn't been able to make the rifts to bring in backup.

Senrid let out a shuddering breath, then moved his gaze from there to the other sites as the truth hit him. "These are all prime spots for hiding a strike force, to launch in at least two directions. And in mountains, where you could stash the supply caches to feed and arm them." Senrid looked up at Tsauderei. "Every one. You say Siamis's blood was at each?"

Tsauderei nodded on each point. "Yesterday a couple of mages, accompanied by government officials from various kingdoms, checked on five of them, and all five revealed supply caches in some state. A couple of them full, some barely begun."

"This is far too big for one army. It has to be for Norsunder's invasion," Senrid said slowly, his gaze moving rapidly over the map.

Tsauderei grimaced. "So it's not random."

Senrid flicked his hand away, palm down. "Do you want me to guess at the strategy here?"

"No," Tsauderei said on an outgoing breath. "I think I've got the idea."

Senrid returned his gaze to the map. "And Siamis betrayed them? Why?" He got up and paced around the room, unaware that he was doing so. "If that's true . . .then he has to be lying up somewhere. Waiting for you to figure it out?" Senrid whirled and walked the other direction, fist thumping from object to object. Then he stopped again. "He sprang an important prisoner from Norsunder Base."

"Two, really. Liere heard him tell Kessler Sonscarna that she was in the opposite cell."

Senrid whistled, remembering David lurking in Jilo's

fortress. "Detlev's prisoners," he said. "Oh, this is . . ." Thump, thump, thump, turn. "Unless he's got his own plan running. We know he likes playing around with magic experiments."

"So has Detlev," Tsauderei said. "Historically."

"Not enough facts." Senrid glared at the map again, and that supply site so close to his own kingdom.

"Agreed." Tsauderei lifted his head to listen to a pleasant-toned bell. "That chime means breakfast. Why don't you go join Liere and her daughter? Lyren came back with me from Everon, and everyone here is making her a favorite," he added.

"Of course they are," Senrid said. "That happens wherever she goes."

Senrid opened the door to find a page waiting outside. As he was conducted along a hall full of mosaic patterns, he thought about Lyren. She seemed to know instinctively how to get people to like her, young as she was. If it ever became conscious, she'd be insufferable. And Liere would be the last person to know how to fix that, if it could even be done.

That was the danger of having children. Hard on that thought was regret, and longing for a family of his own. But any thought of trying the Birth Spell brought back memory of Detlev's threats.

End of subject.

Twenty-one

THE PAGE OPENED THE door to a light, airy room. Liere started up from a long table, smile beaming as bright as the windows. Nearby Lyren chattering to a scrawny girl with brown hair and the distinctive droopy gooseberry-eyes that marked relatives of the Landis family.

"Who's that?" Senrid sat down next to Liere. "Oh yes, the little brat cousin who followed Siamis around when we were at Geth-deles."

Liere shook her head. "Julian stopped being like that. Atan thinks something awful happened to her in Old Sartor, before the enchantment, something about Julian's mother, who the old folks say was real ambitious. And awful."

"Looks like Julian and Lyren are pals," Senrid said.

Liere smiled proudly. "Lyren makes friends with everybody she sees."

Before she could switch to apologizing for her own awkwardness — Senrid sensed it coming, a habitual response he couldn't talk her out of — he changed the subject. "Where's Atan?" He waved at the table with its several empty places.

"She walks in her labyrinth, the Purad. In the mornings. Well, so did I, yesterday, then I went back to sleep again," Liere confessed.

Senrid could still see the effects of being a prisoner in Liere, who was skinnier than ever, but all he said was, "So Atan goes in this labyrinth thing?"

"Every day. In regular clothes. Then after she has to wear her queen clothes."

"Purad—'blessed circle'—whatever that means," Senrid said. "I think I remember something about those. Some kind of garden, right?"

"It's more than that, a path in four loops of threes. It's . . .very peaceful," Liere said, her gaze going distant. "They call walking it the *napurdiav*."

Senrid was already bored. "Tell me about your escape."

Liere's expression closed to the old fearful look, and Senrid regretted his question, then regretted it more when she couldn't tell him anything of use.

Twice she told him in a nervous voice that Tsauderei had promised that the palace was now warded against Siamis entering it unless Tsauderei himself removed the wards. "And best of all, Tsauderei said he would try to determine why my magic studies always go amiss."

"Sounds like a visit here will be a good thing for you," Senrid said. He'd intended to ask if she wanted to come to Marloven Hess to lie up, but it was clear she felt safe and happy here. Which was as well, because he still had to go back and follow up with Terry and Thad about excavations into their archives.

Senrid stayed long enough to greet Atan, then returned to Marloven Hess, where it was still dark.

He walked to his room and lay down to shut his eyes . . .and dropped straight into the first good sleep he'd had in weeks.

Retren Forthan was the youngest captain in the Marloven army. And not just any captain. He was a cavalry captain, understood among Marlovens to be the elite among the elite. He still had to work his way up the chain of command, and so his current post was night-watch captain of South Army's cavalry, which was stationed at the border between Marloven Hess and Toth.

This was not the most sought-after posting, as it had mostly been understood to be glorified sentry duty. But that was before Forthan found out about the constant horse-thieving brigands ghosting up from the plains below Toth, some said with the full knowledge of the Marloven-hating king of Perideth, south of

Toth. Marloven horses were renowned for their speed and smarts, and horses trained by Marlovens fetched staggering prices outside of Marloven Hess.

There may or may not have been Marlovens winking at the raids, and receiving their own cut, but Ret Forthan took brigandage in his territory personally. He led night raids, chasing thieves with the same vigor he had successfully commanded war games during his years in the academy. A year after his posting, a great many former brigands were now wanding out stables, and working off their sentences with other menial labor: the local roads, bridges, and army posting houses had not been in such excellent shape for years.

As a result horse theft had vanished, and any local brigands left over had decided to move elsewhere. Subsequently Ret Forthan's highly trained night watch was now h back to sentry rounds and drill. When Senrid summoned Forthan to the capital to discuss Terry's plan, Forthan and his own particular cronies in his guard, most of them friends from his academy days, were enthusiastic about the prospect of dressing up and swanking into faraway Colend, of which even they had heard.

The only problem was the logistics.

Senrid had gone through his archives with no success. Then he and Terry met at Thad's. Senrid had not seen Thad since before Karhin was killed. From the moment he transferred to the familiar house in Wilderfeld, he felt Karhin's absence sharply. She had always been the one to glide out to their little Destination in order to welcome new arrivals.

Thad's room looked unchanged, but he had gotten taller, and thinner. The tightness of grief still marked his face, leaching it of the old humor. Because Senrid had no language for these situations, he got right to business as soon as the greetings were over.

"First of all," he said, "you can't transfer a horse. That is, you can, but you aren't going to be able to use that Destination for anything but non-living things for an appreciable time. And that doesn't even go into how useless the horse is for a good while after."

Terry grunted. "Didn't think of that." Then his brows lifted. "But really, what does it matter? Are your horses so different? Four legs, tail, mane, right? More important, will the Colendi notice the difference?"

Senrid spread his hands. "I think ours are the best in the

world." He felt obliged to add, "But maybe everybody thinks that about their own."

"Your people can ride other horses, I am certain?" Thad said, hands at an open angle.

"They can ride anything," Senrid said, this time with total confidence. "Whether the horses will be skilled enough for the sort of riding we do is another question. I'll send Forthan over to begin scouting and training some local mounts. But I have to point out that the Marloven uniform doesn't look all that different, except in color, from what is worn at this side of the continent. It's designed to be practical, traditionally gray because it's easy to dye. What exactly would your court expect to see? I mean, to have an effect? I hope not embroidery and lace."

"If you will pardon what I am about to say — it reflects upon what I read in scribe records, which I believe are more forthcoming than the official archives — they will be expecting barbaric threat." Thad made an apologetic gesture, head bowing slightly.

"What exactly did Ivandred do while he was here?" Senrid asked. "I think I mentioned before that we haven't many records of events outside our border."

Given Ivandred's history, Senrid half-expected to hear that his ancestor had waded in among the Colendi, the sword he'd wielded so well lopping off heads left and right, but Thad said, "He taught the royal consort something of war strategy, and led his company against the Chwahir invaders."

"And won, I take it?"

"Oh, yes. Then let the Chwahir king return to his land, at the prince's behest."

Well, that didn't sound so barbaric. Senrid wondered how much the Colendi had cleaned that old story up, then shrugged as Thad went on, "Your ancestors all wore black."

"Black and gold is my House colors. They actually used to wear their own House colors back then."

Thad accepted this interruption with a graceful open-handed gesture, then continued. "They wore black, except for golden belt buckles."

"No sashes?" Terry cut in. "In our records, they wore sashes."

"That was earlier," Senrid said.

Terry went on, "In another record, they wore coats tight

through the chest. Long, with full skirts, down to their boot tops. High collar. Helms with human hair suspended."

Thad's upper lip lengthened. "Really? They really did that?"

"They really did that," Senrid said. "Cut right to the scalp. Some of them took the scalp, when they wanted to leave extra threat."

Like killing people wasn't enough? Senrid heard the question clearly on the mental plane, and tightened his mind-shield.

"They still wear horsetails on their helms," he said. "But they cut a few strands from the tails of horses they've ridden to victories. The horses don't mind." He didn't mention that the number of hairs corresponded with enemy kills or wounded. He already knew the speeches he'd hear about bloodthirsty barbarians.

"All right, those helms sound promising," Terry said, his enthusiasm returning. "But what about those long coats? I saw some sketches. Though it might be the way they wear them, somehow, that makes them look . . ."

"On the strut." Senrid flashed a grin. "We do wear similar coats, only in winter. You really wouldn't want to wear 'em in summer. The riders would drop off the horses and croak in pools of sweat." He paused. "Here's an idea. How about if I borrow some House tunics? The jarl families wear these at Convocation, weddings, memorials." *And executions.* "They won't be black and gold. Different Houses still wear their own colors. Eveneth, as tough a family as you could possibly want, wears violet and yellow, for example. Is that barbaric enough?"

The other two had brightened, but at the mention of purple and yellow, both faces fell.

Then Thad said cautiously, "If you will pardon my hesitation, I feel I ought to explain that colors are symbolic here. Purple is a Sartoran color, and yellow is favored by one of the duchases. In Colend, the one color not claimed is black, as it is considered . . .warlike."

"And you need barbarians. Right. Maybe this is why Ivandred put his boys in his own colors." *Under the fox banner, yet.* "I'll offer my volunteers Marloven black and gold, over their riding clothes. And we can add a lot of weapons as decoration. They won't mind that. It'll be a lark. What's the next step?" Senrid asked.

Terry turned to Thad, who tapped a scroll. "The protocol

would be to send a herald with a letter to the new king, saying you are coming to call on him, king to king."

"But then we're right back to the problem of intercepted letters." Senrid thumped his fists on his knees. "I thought Karhin told me he had a notecase."

"He did. He made it himself. They must have taken it from him, or else amended the magic in some way."

"That can be done, unless the wards are very well bound," Senrid said.

"I don't know how much magic he knows, or what occurred, but this I can promise. Even the highest among the council would not dare to interfere with king writing to king, a letter sent by a herald and thus witnessed. They will of course see the letter, especially if you send it first with a company, but they will have to share it with Shontande."

"But you did that, right?" Senrid said to Terry.

"My first mistake was to just go. I told you about the nine musicians and the duchas. Then I tried writing, but got back a letter signed in Shontande's name by some other duchas, apologizing most humbly, hoola-loola-loo. Our thinking is, if you let them know you're arriving with this force, see, and make it plain that you intend to talk king to king, and won't leave until you do, they'll have to let you see him."

"Got it," Senrid said.

"Thad. Which gate does this herald use?" Terry asked, one hand rubbing over the other with its missing fingers.

"The Gate of the Lily Path, of course —" Thad stopped. "Ah-ye! That is for diplomats already within the hierarchy, and of course for Colendi..." His old smile briefly brightened his face. "It must be the Gate of the Gold Crown. But not at early hours, for that is petitioners, or Lily or Cup, for artisan parades. They must arrive between the Hour of Stone and Noon. They will take note of *that*, to be certain."

"I take it these things mean something."

"Everything means something in Colend," Terry said, as the sound of singing drifted through the open window.

"Why am I coming?" Senrid asked. "We can't claim border problems from the other side of the continent, nor do we trade with Colend."

Terry shook his head. "The language of diplomacy makes everything sound a lot more pompous than it is. Or threatening. Or peaceful, whatever you want them to believe. You're going to be riding down after a conference — "

Thad caught on. "May I suggest, a *congress*."

Terry put his palms together and bowed exaggeratedly. "A *congress* between two kings. We'll even invite Jilo over and make it three kings, two known for their military. It's good for him to get away, breathe real air, taste good food."

Senrid believed that. "But Jilo doesn't call himself a king."

"That matters little," Thad said. "Anything to do with the Chwahir shall get the council's attention, that much I can promise."

Twenty-two

Summer, 4747 AF

SENRID SENT CAPTAIN FORTHAN to Erdrael Danara, where he
was welcomed back by Terry's mountain guard. He also pulled
in a couple of army tailors and explained what was going on,
figuring they would enjoy the ruse, especially as they'd be paid
out of crown funds.

This, the tailors thought, was almost as much fun as an all-
city war game, and enthusiastically put their heads together to
design a suitably barbaric battle tunic to be worn over shirt and
riding trousers, that wouldn't stew the wearers in summer
weather. Forthan picked out his company, and each, as soon as
his tunic was finished, found himself transferred to the other
side of the continent to begin preparation for the expedition.

The days slipped into weeks, and a month, as elsewhere
Tsauderei moved between Sartor and his retreat up in the
heights above Sarendan, scowling the more as the hunt for
Siamis abruptly dried up.

He's out there, Tsauderei thought repeatedly. Waiting for
something. For *him?* Such an idea ordinarily would cause him
to laugh at his own presumption, except for the peculiarity of
the timing of Siamis's many transfers to those supply caches.
When these were lined in order of appearance, they spiraled in

straight toward Norsunder Base, on the south side of Sartor. That timing suggested . . .something. A message to mages, most assuredly. A message, or a threat.

As summer ripened, at the opposite end of the world, winter howled over the mountains and across the landscape. Behind the doubled panes of winter windows, Arthur — returned to his studies at last — wrestled with a moral dilemma.

He kept in close contact with the Siamis hunt, scrupulously reporting the status to the rest of the alliance, but he had another motive. When the Venn returned to their homeland, he hoped that the mages chosen to travel with them and perform the actual magic would have learned enough of that magic for their own hunts.

Because Arthur wanted them to find Roy.

And?

That was the problem: and then what? All very well to fume over Roy's betrayal every time he laid eyes on the books he'd shared with Roy, or entered a room they'd spent so much time studying in, or even talked to people they'd laughed with.

He'd burned Adam's sketches, but put the one of Roy aside for the hunters . . .if.

The first *if* was the blood question. As far as Arthur was aware, Roy had never bled up at Bereth Ferian's mage school. When Arthur had dutifully gone over to the exercise arena, Roy had never gone with him. Arthur had thought him entirely sedentary.

Then the news arrived through Tahra that Dtheldevor's ship was home again, and Arthur was hit by memory of that stormy ship journey that he, Roy, and Clair had shared. So fun at the time, full of history talk and magic practice. How could he overlook that — it was the turning point in their relationship, from acquaintance to friendship. Deep friendship.

And memory was so vivid. That storm, their struggle in the small boat, and then, when Dtheldevor caught up and they climbed aboard in choppy seas, in keeping Clair from smashing into the hull, Roy had taken a glancing blow to the head. As they climbed aboard the *Berdrer*, he'd bled all over the deck.

Arthur did not examine why he might overlook that episode. He brooded instead about consequences: assuming they could find traces of Roy's blood on Dtheldevor's well-scrubbed, weather-scoured deck . . .what then?

Western Wnelder Vee

Roy and the rest of the boys had been ordered by Detlev to retreat to their lair and lie low after Siamis's raid ignited trouble at Norsunder Base. Roy sat in the boys' new rat-hole, which was what they called their retreats.

This rat-hole was a stretch of land in the southwest corner of Wnelder Vee, far from human habitations. Plenty of fishing in the streams, and good forest cover, but it was newer forest, free of dawnsingers. Roy had swapped off with David and MV in laying down tight wards.

They'd made their rat-hole here as a fallback to avoid Henerek's roaming brigands, and any patrolling Knights of Dei poking their noses over the border. Since the hypothetical retreat was now fact, the boys alternated between three domiciles: an abandoned hermit's cottage tucked up against a forest-shaded hill that would be perfect at the height of summer; a long-abandoned dawnsinger tree platform; and a wood-gatherer's cottage at the extreme west end, so old it was mostly flimsy supports holding up a sagging roof. Curtas headed a work party in reinforcing it enough to keep off the rain.

Curtas loved everything about building, from design to refining the labor. He found work over the border in Everon, where repair was still going on at the farthermost towns and villages, and Silvanas — recently arrived — had easily landed a job in the stable in Veiford, the border city where two rivers combined into one.

The two boys swapped off bringing home a knapsack of supplies every other day, as well as news garnered from travelers' talk. As Detlev was still far away on world matters, they were reduced to sifting truth from rumor.

Roy often thought about Arthur, but he never spoke any more than Curtas did about Thad Keperi or the new boy king of Colend. Roy and Curtas both knew that they'd done what trained spies are never supposed to do: permitted themselves to reach past their personas. A trained spy made certain that friendship — or any other type of relationship — stopped where the persona ended and one's true self began. But their personas had been . . .them. They'd been assigned to people they genuine-ly liked.

Mistake, Roy thought bitterly, and Curtas with intense regret.

There was no point in talking about what they couldn't fix, so Roy and Curtas kept quiet, even with each other. Only Adam seemed blithely unperturbed, talking as if they were all still great friends with the lighters.

MV found that increasingly irritating.

MV found everything irritating. The last of them had arrived, Ferret bringing a superficially chastened Noser, who whined about getting stuck doing wood all alone, no one else, and *why-y-y-y-y?* Ferret's story about having to go to Bereth Ferian to await Arthur's return, after which he was summarily sent back to Norsunder Base with no explanation, capped the irritation. The rumors about Siamis raiding the Base — freeing prisoners — casting wild spells — dueling Black Knives — was infuriating because no one knew the truth. The boys were on the outside of the outside, shut out from any communication except with one another, and MV was bored as well as irritated, a very bad combination.

David put him in charge of the drills. Laban had chosen the place partly for its secluded location, but also because the inner portion was ground for a prime obstacle course, and the wider area was a perfect stalking ground. With very little work to augment it, they had a tough two hour run before breakfast every day, and after breakfast, sparring and weapons' practice.

Afternoons, MV ran stalks: team stalks, all against one, blindfold. Evenings were for individual pursuits, unless they decided on a night run.

One afternoon, as Noser's shriek echoed through the maples, hickory, and oak, Roy looked up from his writing, wrung his hand, and gazed out from under the sagging roof to where MV had a bunch of them in a circle as knives flashed and glittered between them, thrown from hand to hand.

MV had, as usual, picked Adam to receive, but Adam was used to the constant challenge, and skillfully passed the knives on, even when Noser, snickering shrilly, tried to speed things up.

"Knifey-whizz," Roy said to David, who stood nearby, hands on his hips, brow knit.

The name for this dangerous, pointless game had been

invented by them at ages eight to ten, when it seemed there was nothing better to do than to invent ever more dangerous games in the constant state of competition that had existed under their former, unlamented boy leader. To play it now, when it obviously didn't hone any usable skill, was evidence of MV's restlessness.

Roy said, "Can't you send him to find a boat? There are a million islands off the coast to hide one among."

David flicked a narrow look his way. Roy sustained that, reflecting on how David's volatile moods had begun to settle, after those last very bad days in Geth—during which, with everything else going on, David had been struck by what they called marsh madness. It had heightened his Dena Yeresbeth suddenly and intensely, nearly past endurance.

But Roy had been practiced with a mind-shield since he could first speak. He flexed his hand once more, then picked up his pen.

David said, "I'd do it, but I think we're better off sitting tight until Efael gives up his hunt for Siamis. We don't want to draw his attention."

"Efael," Roy breathed, his neck prickling. Even sensed from behind a mind-shield, Efael's mental signature was so toxic that Roy had worked hard to avoid ever catching Efael's notice the few times they were in the same space. It was the only time he ever thought about his appearance: he was grateful to be so homely. Efael's cruel eye was primarily drawn to pretty boys and to girls with equivalent strength and skill, but they all understood there was nothing even remotely romantic in that preference.

"Hep," MV called, and the circle tossed the knives spinning into the air, caught them, and went to slide them into the rack.

"Time to think ahead to dinner," David said. "MV, you and Rolfin cook."

MV squinted at David, who stood loosely, hands at his sides. "I cooked yesterday."

"And you can today, and tomorrow, and every day until you find something else to do with your free time."

MV stilled, and so did the rest at the prospect of a scrap between their two leaders, who were fairly evenly matched.

MV assessed David's mood with the expertise of a lifetime. He could usually whip David except when the latter was angry. He could see the annoyance curling the corners of David's mouth, and tightening the skin of his forehead.

He turned away, jerked his chin at Rolfin, and was soon chopping vegetables as Rolfin went to scour wild herbs from the overgrown garden, abandoned a couple generations ago. The sun had sunk behind the tree line by the time those appointed to clean up got that done. Then most of them went off on a night run.

MV stayed behind, seated on an upturned bucket, one knee jiggling as David took out a carving knife and began working on a larger flute. Finally, MV said, "I'm going to Norsunder Base. Find out what's really going on."

"We were ordered to go to ground," David reminded him.

Roy, working by the light of a glow-globe, sorted the tones: MV's statement not quite a question (or he would have just gone) and David answering with the obvious as he probed for the underlying reason.

"To keep us safe. But we're not nine anymore. We've proved we can hold our own." MV's shoulder jerked up. "Nothing happened to us at the Base."

"That was before whatever shitstorm we got out ahead of."

"That's ended." MV surged to his feet. "I made a transfer token, in and out of Detlev's office."

"Which will have half a dozen tracers on it to see who comes through."

"So? I'm as fast as any of those idiots there."

The fact that MV had made the transfer tokens obviated an answer.

David sighed. "Be faster."

MV cracked a laugh. He loaded up on weaponry, and was gone before the runners came back.

Roy returned to his work, and David to his carving, the knife quickening in its soft hiss as curls of wood shaved from the instrument forming under his tense hands.

At Norsunder Base, MV stayed in Detlev's office until the transfer reaction faded — an extra hard reaction, suggesting that the air, or whatever it was, still roiled from too much use the day Siamis showed up, followed by massive transfers of the Black Knives. The Destination chamber had to be hot and toxic. The office transfer had been rough enough.

MV gulped breaths to fight down nausea and vertigo, and when he regained his wits, reeled out the spells he'd prepared to disintegrate basic wards and tracers. Of course his appearance would have set off some tracers, but so far no one had shown up, and he didn't plan to stay long enough to wait for ambush.

He didn't bother glancing at the stack of written reports on the desk. Those would be standard, if not outright misleading, and the boys had learned that if anything important was ever in them, Detlev already knew.

MV walked out to find out who had come out on top after the ruction. He made his way in a circuit around the pits where the head snakes usually hissed, gauging attitudes in the few who recognized him. At the first sign of a knowing smirk, he'd be out of there. They all knew who would love to get at Detlev through his boys, pets, brats, pick your slur.

"Hemmin," he addressed a runner who was often seen outside the mages' area. "Where's Siamis?"

Hemmin, not much older than MV, rolled his eyes. "You tell me."

"We haven't seen him," MV said.

"Nobody has since he ripped through here, springing prisoners, taking out the off-world relay desk, and leaving a trail of bodies. Rumor is, he also did for Henerek and Benin somewhere out in the field. Whether it's true or not, they haven't been back."

MV whistled. "Who's up top?"

"Bostian's running the west side" — meaning the military wings — "and Dejain's got all the mages busy repairing the relay desk magic."

Hennin's shifty gaze had been taking in the surroundings, but MV had been watching as well, keeping his back mostly to a wall. Mostly.

When Hennin's gaze stilled and his expression blanched, MV's shoulder blades tightened, and he whirled, hands pulling knives.

Efael had stepped up noiselessly from behind, bare steel in either hand.

From the right and left corridors, Black Knives stepped out, boot heels ringing on the stone. Efael gave his chin a jerk, and Hennin's footsteps retreated rapidly.

MV's heart knocked against his ribs, but it always did before a hot scrap. He knew that Detlev despised Efael, but MV wavered between accepting Detlev's judgment and his own secret admiration for Efael's power of intimidation just by standing there in his black man-leather, doing nothing more than breathing.

MV's shoulders twitched, his hands ready with his knives. He was pretty much the height of a medium sized man, and though much skinnier, he prided himself on being fast. As for strength, only Rolfin and Leef were stronger, but they were built like bulls.

MV balanced on his toes, ready for anything.

Efael's sharp face sharpened even more in a not-quite-smile. "You think you can take one of us?"

"I can try," MV said, easing his right foot back. They were all bigger than he was. Four on one was going to be a smash, but maybe he could do some damage before he could transfer. Though he'd been warned about Efael's proclivities, what he didn't know he didn't fear. Efael wouldn't make it a killing matter, not until he was sure he could also defeat Detlev and Siamis, that much he believed. That meant at worst they would beat the living shit out of him. Well, that had happened before, and he'd survived.

Efael took the time to run his eyes down MV in a leisurely way that made MV's hackles rise. Then he licked his lips.

"I think it will be fun to let you try," Efael said in a voice husky with anticipation of a kind that MV had never heard before, and that instinctively warned him to run—but as he dropped one of his cherished knives to retrieve the transfer token, Efael moved faster, and slammed him into the black of the Beyond.

Twenty-three

WORD RICOCHETED AS FAST as Hennin could talk: Efael had taken one of Detlev's boys.

From there it radiated outward, caught by Siamis, who checked on the mental plane each night when his chosen vessels slept. He entered through the dream realm, touched the jumble of the day's memories, and withdrew.

Efael was making a move, and MV had blundered into becoming a piece in his game. Siamis opened his eyes and regarded the Arrow, glittering coldly in the near-darkness of the ancient dragon cave, where once dragons had lived, long, long ago.

Siamis buried his chin in the yeath-fur coat that barely kept out the frigid cold, despite the season being high summer far below, and stood staring down at the wind-scoured rock. He had set this course. It was time to finish the journey.

He shut his eyes, cleared his mind, whispered a spell . . .

. . .and on the other side of the same sky-scraping range of mountains, Tsauderei started when his scry-stone flickered with the gray-blue light of a high-mountain sky.

Nobody had the skill to do that.

Or so he'd thought.

He whispered a couple of protective spells, and hitched his chair closer to the side-table where the stone rested so that he could look down without touching anything.

Shock pooled in his belly when he recognized Siamis's face. "I understand you're looking for me."

"Everyone is," Tsauderei said, hand fumbling across his table for one of his protective tokens. Then his fingers froze when Siamis spoke.

"A trade," Siamis said. "The Arrow for asylum."

"What?" Tsauderei exclaimed. "No," he responded with instant loathing.

"You really want me to toss the Arrow back out there so that Efael and Yeres will get it?"

Tsauderei expelled his breath. "This is a damned Detlev ruse."

Siamis's eyes narrowed, but otherwise he did not protest, exclaim, curse, plead, or laugh. He waited.

Tsauderei breathed out again, aware of his old heart laboring against his scrawny ribs under his fine robe. He was getting too old for these games.

But he was not about to funk. Old as he was, Siamis had come to *him*, when—assuming he'd want not only asylum but treasure or position or the sort of thing kings could offer—he could have gone to any number of rulers with mages trained enough to not only know what the Arrow was, but would be panting to use it to effectively control a powerful nation's mages. Even Oalthoreh, head of the northern school, might be tempted, for the Venn's own good of course, to keep some kind of control, because so much northern history had focused her view on local political and geographical dynamics.

But Siamis had come to Tsauderei.

He had to be aware of Tsauderei's total disinterest in any plan that involved anyone else controlling the Venn but the Venn. Erkric the Evil was nearly a thousand years dead. The Venn were not the same as they had been back then any more than any other nation was.

He let out a third long breath. Detlev and a possible ruse? The response, Tsauderei knew, sprang from not just loathing but total distrust of Detlev. And yet he'd spent considerable time trying to winnow out the man's thinking from the scant footprint he left in records, and nowhere did it indicate Detlev would be willing to throw away years, possibly decades or even centuries of work for . . .what? What could he possibly gain if Siamis were given asylum? No one was going to trust

Siamis past his next breath.

"I'll need to put the question to my allies," he said, and noticed that Siamis did not ask who they were.

"You probably have a day," Siamis said. "Two, at most, before either Detlev or Efael catches up with me."

"What does he want the Arrow for anyway? Anyone who tried to control the Venn might succeed on the surface, but from what I've been learning about them would be in for a lifetime of trouble."

"Not the Venn," Siamis said. "With some changes, the spells on that stone theoretically could be extended to control the Norss of Songre Silde. At which point it will be a relatively easy matter to make rifts from Norsunder Beyond to Five — what was once Aldau-Rayad, the fifth world — to garrison armies there, and to send them beyond when needed. Or, the spells could be extended to control, say, the Council of Ones on Geth-deles. Or the Sartoran Mage Guild —"

"You'll have your answer by tonight," Tsauderei promised, and the scry stone dulled.

He had enough strength for one more scry conversation. He chose Erai-Yanya, who could be relied upon to spread the word to the northerners involved in the Arrow treaty. Duty required him to write first to the Queen of the Venn to apprise her of what concerned her above anyone else, to discover that she had died during the night a couple weeks before.

He received a carefully written letter in not-quite-grammatical Sartoran:

> I trust the Queen of Sartor, because of the true word
> of Rel the Traveler queen champion. Venn abide by
> your decision.
>
> Kerendal Sofar, Venn-King

Ho. *That* was going to take some pondering!

But Tsauderei didn't have time for that now. He wrote to Mondros, then to the Sartoran Mage Guild in a letter that he instructed the duty scribe to share with everyone. Finally, he wrote to Atan, to discover that she had already heard from Arthur, whose fingers were faster with a pen.

After which came a flood of notes. Most of these expressed various degrees of horror and mistrust, but from Senrid came: *How do we know it's not a ruse from Detlev?*

Young as he was, Senrid thought strategically, that much Tsauderei had seen during their conversation after Liere's escape from Norsunder. He wrote back: *To what end? Are you seeing some military viewpoint that is invisible to me?*

While waiting for an answer, Tsauderei responded to a long, stiffly polite request for an interview from Oalthoreh, who seemed to have appointed herself chief speaker for the Arrow treaty members — who then wrote on their own behalf.

He dealt with all these while his stomach gnawed with hunger and his eyes burned. He'd half-forgotten Senrid until a response came back: *Nothing that makes sense.*

To which Tsauderei answered: *My conclusion as well.*

He wrote one last letter, and over it whispered a spell that Lilith the Guardian had given him many years ago, to be used only in the direst of emergencies, then shut his notecase, ignored the magical warning of further letters, and retreated to eat and rest.

When he woke, he tackled the pile of notes. First and most important was a short one from Lilith.

> *I dare not leave Songre Silde, especially now, unless Detlev does. But here is my suggestion: if Siamis is serious, then he must surrender himself at a Selenseh Redian.*

Tsauderei read that and his nerves chilled. He never would have considered that answer, but it was perfect. As far as anyone understood those caves, anyone with evil intent never walked out alive again.

He dealt with the rest of the notes, either with one or two words or by just pitching them into the fire. People could revile against Siamis (and Detlev) all they wanted. He didn't have to read it. It wasn't as if his thoughts were any different.

The rest of the morning he spent in doing his best to organize his affairs in case Siamis's communication turned out to be a ruse intended to remove one absurdly long-lived old mage from the world. His personal business took a morning, after which he transferred to Sartor's royal palace, and waited on Atan, preparatory to facing the mage guild.

She listened to his description of the conversation, her young face troubled, her brow tense. Then she said, "Assuming that it happens. What does asylum mean?"

"It can mean anything, or nothing." Tsauderei spread his

hands. "That is, I get north and southern mages to agree to leave him be unless he harms any of us. Governments, of course, I cannot interfere with."

Atan studied her old teacher and guardian, then said, "I hate him."

"So do we all."

"But I don't hate him as much as I do Detlev, whose damage to my family and kingdom we are still recovering from, a century later. Siamis's enchantment didn't harm us that much. Unless it really was him killing Chief Veltos and those others."

Tsauderei shook his head slowly. "We know from eyewitnesses in Colend that the killer was dark-haired, a description that matches Veltos Jhaer's assassin. Though it could have been Siamis in disguise. I'm still inclined toward Detlev's boys, who already were involved in a small killing spree. Or some other Detlev-trained assassin. If it was Siamis and he agrees to enter a Selenseh Redian, we may have the problem solved for us."

"That would be the best," Atan said. "Do!"

"And we have to consider this: if he really is bent on undoing Detlev's plans, who knows what other useful things he might disclose?"

"If we can believe anything he says." Atan gritted her teeth. "People are going to look to me, aren't they?"

Tsauderei said, "You are the Queen of Sartor."

"And we are people who, ideally, believe in freedom, and seeing the best in others. And . . .mercy." Her voice was low.

"If you offer him asylum," Tsauderei said, "It need not be forever. A symbolic gesture might go a long way toward some cooperation that we may well need, especially if Detlev is bent on bringing Norsunder against us. We have noticed that he's been seen more in the world in the last year or two than in the past century."

"Yes," Atan said. "Oh, Tsauderei, how I hate this!"

"I do, too. If it helps, I can make it clear that if he comes, he is going to be warded in certain ways, and I will remain here as long as he's here. I'm going to want to comb his brain as much as he's willing to talk. We really are going to need every advantage we can possibly gain."

Atan bowed her head. "Done." Her eyes lifted. "But only if he did not murder Veltos."

"I shall put that question. And hope that I can discern truth from misdirection, as I am given to understand that he and his uncle disdain outrights lies."

"And yet everything they stand for is the worst of lies," Atan said.

Tsauderei didn't disagree. They parted, she to deal with kingdom affairs, and he to face the Sartoran mages. By the time he was done with that, the day had sped, and he was hungry again. But when he checked his scrystone, which he had brought down from his valley retreat, he found the glow that indicated a communication.

When he looked into it, he found not a face, but a place that he recognized immediately: the dragon caves on the heights. Of course. In retrospect it was so obvious. And yet no one would think to search there. The northern mage school had ceased to send students there more than eighty years ago. Tsauderei had been among the last.

Cursing fluently, he retrieved his heaviest winter clothing, added a scarf to wrap around his head, ears, throat, and lower face, then braced for the transfer to the topmost mountain plateau in the world.

Here he found a slim figure waiting, equally bundled up. Good sign: the infamous sword was not at hand. Tsauderei did not make the mistake of assuming that Siamis was any less dangerous, but at least they were not beginning this interview over drawn steel.

Tsauderei made his way to a familiar low stone, and sat down with a grunt.

Siamis sidestepped, then sat beside him, looking up as his breath clouded, froze, and began to fall before dissipating. Then he said, "When I was small, I had a very old scroll. Written in some language none of us could read. Depicting the dragons. There was a sketch of this very cave."

"Early Chwahir," Tsauderei surmised, not quite a question.

Siamis turned out his hands.

"So, begin with why," Tsauderei said. "And make it quick. While I appreciate the symbolism, and the relative safety of this location, my body won't tolerate it long."

"Will you believe anything I say?" Siamis asked. His face was mostly masked against the bitter cold, but his eyes were clear, observant.

Tsauderei held consciously to his mind-shield, hoping it was good enough. "Try me."

"I always wanted out," Siamis said. "From the first day I was taken."

"Yet you have been very active on their behalf. Was that you, murdering Veltos Jhaer?"

"That was Efael, hot on my trail. I believe he also killed Carlael Lirendi of Colend, though I have had little communication with anyone who would know for certain."

"I know the name. The mysterious Efael of the Host of Lords," Tsauderei said. "Efael is tall, face broad at the top, narrow chin? Wearing some kind of black garment of a shiny, heavy fabric . . ."

"Not fabric," Siamis said. "Leather."

"Leather? What is that?"

"Tanned and dyed man-skin. When I was twelve, one of the first things he told me, and at excruciating length, was how he at my age learned the art of flaying in one piece."

Tsauderei recoiled. "That is abominable."

"You don't know the half of it."

Tsauderei said, "You understand, I trust, there are consequences to every action. And you'll have no easy time among us. You won't last ten breaths if you ever set foot in Sarendan."

"I know."

Tsauderei was shivering by now, but he could not resist. "Why did you shoot Derek Diamagan?"

"It was defensive instinct, one I immediately regretted, but I'd just transferred from Geth-deles and was still recovering from the transfer. Even so, Peitar makes a better king, and Diamagan a better martyr, than the reverse would have."

The even voice chilled Tsauderei as much as the frigid air. *What does that say about me, that we came to the same conclusion?* His voice sharpened. "Did you immediately regret enchanting most of the world, not once but twice? Did you regret siccing Norsunder on that small trade town in Wnelder Vee, which could not possibly have any military value?"

Siamis said, "Loss Harthadaun was going to happen anyway, as I had little authority over the captains present there. I used that episode to establish authority, let us say, or there would have been a far wider swathe of destruction."

"As in Everon in '42?"

"Kessler had already been loosed before I was released from the Beyond."

"And the enchantments?" Tsauderei leaned forward. "What excuse have you for those?"

"None," Siamis said, looking away for the first time. He seemed about to say something, then turned his gaze back. "Regard me as penitent."

Tsauderei snorted his disbelief. The hairs in his nose froze, stinging unmercifully. He needed to get out of there. "And I suppose you'll explain away hunting that poor child Liere Fer Eider from one end of the world to the other because of that dyr thing, which we still don't understand. Unless you would care to enlighten me about it?"

"I don't understand the dyr either," Siamis said blithely. "But I was under Detlev's orders to get it."

"You can always blame Detlev," Tsauderei observed with heavy irony. "What's more, you're more likely to be believed, if for nothing else. One last question, though it's probably the least useful of any, but what do you intend to do?"

"Make a place for myself in this world."

"On someone's throne?"

Mockery tightened Siamis's eyes. "Exchanging one set of chains for another? No."

Tsauderei grunted. "There is a great deal about the days of Ancient Sartor that is a mystery to us. So little survived. You might be useful to the archivists."

"I was twelve. From a fairly remote location," Siamis retorted. "I'd think you'd be better putting your questions to Lilith."

"Who is rarely seen, and never for long. And when she does turn up, tends to speak elliptically."

"As I've discovered."

"Very well. I can't stick it here much longer. I can scarcely believe I spent two entire summers up here when I was your age, studying the few traces left of those days that were ancient even when you were born. So. To Lilith again: we have all agreed to her offer, you surrender that Arrow at a Selenseh Redian."

Siamis spread his gloved hands on his knees. Tsauderei watched his brows lift, and his eyelids flicker, and wondered for the first time about the emotional cost.

"Done," Siamis said.

Twenty-four

Western Wnelder Vee

WHEN A SHORT TIME stretched to midnight, then morning, then an entire day without MV's return, David's worsening mood infected the others. Even Noser had the sense, or the instinct of survival, to keep his mouth shut and his head down.

David ran the drills, putting them through hard practice, and stalks in the afternoon during a pelting rainstorm.

No one complained, though Laban looked increasingly sardonic, and Roy wondered if David was trying in some impossible way to assure MV's endurance with their own. Assuming he was even alive.

When night fell again, Leef and Errol decided to do a late perimeter patrol. Laban and Curtas went off to sleep on the tree house platform. Vana collared Noser and said he was going to do some training with wild horses. They vanished, Noser's shrill laughter echoing back through the trees.

Roy stayed where he was, making up more ink from the tree sap and lamp blacking he'd collected for the purpose. Ferret and Adam played a game with tiles they'd learned on Geth, and Rolfin caught up on sleep.

David brooded, wrestling inwardly with attempting to reach Detlev on the mental plane, though he didn't like using the marsh existence (you couldn't call it a world, but it was vaster than a physical location) because coming out left him dizzy and disoriented for an appreciable time. Nor did he like practicing the exercises in the mental realm that Detlev had given him, which made his stomach worm with his efforts, his head throbbing.

It was somewhat easier when he could cut free of his body, but that wasn't going to happen unless he could be alone. The last time he'd done it, at the Norsunder Base, he'd come out of it hanging upside down from a wall sconce, completely naked, in the dead of winter, with his hands tied behind his back. It was—of course—Noser's brilliant idea.

He was sloppy, unskilled, and only anger or desperation gave him the wherewithal to reach . . .

And Siamis was there.

David startled into wakefulness, then shut his eyes and desperately extended his mental reach again. Siamis was still there, but instead of sending thoughts, he gave David a vivid image of a patch of ground. A Destination.

David opened his eyes. Siamis had always been older, better at everything, tolerant. Some had hated him for all those things, but David hadn't. The only times he'd resented Siamis had been those brangles with Detlev at Norsunder Base over the past few years, always public, increasingly bitter. It had been painful to see how avidly, even greedily the others at the Base drank it in, then slanged them both behind their backs, but you didn't tell your elders to keep their fights private. The rumors about Siamis were so wild and contradictory, even that he'd gone completely renegade. And here he was offering David a Destination.

Curiosity was compelling. With MV gone it was irresistible.

If he went at all, it would be better to go strapped. He slipped a couple of knives up his sleeves, and another through his belt, then picked up his sword.

"David?" Roy looked up from his makeshift desk, feet propped before their low fire.

"It's Siamis. I can't not go."

Roy rarely argued. He flicked his pen in salute and returned to his stirring.

David braced himself and transferred to the Destination Siamis had given him. Clammy wet air hit him. Mountain air. He rocked on his feet, then felt a hand on his arm steadying him.

He backed away, arm snapping up in a block. Siamis withdrew his hand. He looked down into David's face, his expression impossible to interpret. "We're in the outer cavern of a Selenseh Redian," he said. "We're not alone," he added, with a glance over David's right shoulder.

David saw that indeed they stood in a cave, not too far from the entrance, judging by the diffuse light and the slow-moving currents of air that smelled of wet grass and stone. He sensed others just outside, but they were standing there. Non-threatening.

Siamis said, "I'll speak fast. Efael took MV through the world-gate."

"For . . ."

"You boys were once warned. This is what it means." Siamis allowed enough memory on the mental plane – David was wide open – to shock David pale. Then, mercifully, shielded again as Siamis said, "He'll survive it. I did, and I was much younger. Efael won't dare cross Svir or Ilerian by killing him. He might even try to recruit him to the Black Knives. He's short a few at present." Siamis's teeth showed briefly.

As David tried to assimilate that, Siamis's expression smoothed into the familiar slightly rueful mildness. "I believe Detlev will want a witness."

"To?"

"Me, entering the Selenseh Redian." Siamis's gaze lifted to inner part of the cave branching off.

A different kind of horror suffused David. He whirled, hands crossing to the hilts of his knives as he glanced at the cave entrance. Daylight limned a gaunt, white-bearded old man, who leaned against the rock.

Siamis took something cloth-wrapped from a pocket, and tossed it. "Here you are, Tsauderei. As agreed."

"As agreed," Tsauderei repeated, and nodded to the darker tunnel beyond Siamis. "Your turn."

"What's that – is that the Arrow?" David demanded. "Why . . .what happened?"

An old woman stepped up to Tsauderei's shoulder; Roy would have recognized Oalthoreh, but David looked away, too full of questions to wonder about identities. He knew what was said about these caves, of which there were only seven in the world. Few came back out again after going in.

And reputedly they *moved.*

Siamis flicked a last glance at David, stooped to pick up his sword by the sheath, then walked quickly around the corner into the darker tunnel. David reached instinctively with his mind, to encounter a vastness that echoed his thoughts back at him, causing his head to ring.

Grief unspooled in his chest, and he reached for the ready anger to tighten it again. Anger enabled action: he whispered the transfer spell before any of the other threats could act against him, and jolted back to the quiet house in the rat-hole.

Most of the others had returned. Adam and Ferret dropped their tiles, Roy his pen, as Noser exclaimed, "Where were you?"

David waited until the transfer reaction ended, and he knew he had command of his voice. "The lighters got Siamis, and forced him into a Selenseh Redian. Before he went, he told me that Efael has MV. Maybe for recruitment," he added, to deflect more questions he didn't intend to answer.

"Efael?" Noser wailed, sick with jealousy. "MV? Why does *he* get to try for the Black Knives? Why can't *we*?"

David walked out, sucking down clean air. But nothing was going to cleanse Siamis's memories from his mind.

Sartor to Land of the Venn

Rel was surprised when a palace runner appeared at the newly refurbished garrison for the city guard of Eidervaen.

He still held off from committing to the guard as a profession, but everyone there accepted that he would serve when he was in Sartor. And they respected him enough that he had a small room of his own, now that the garrison had regained some of their old buildings.

It was barely big enough for the requisition bunk and trunk, but it was his. And of all the places he'd laid his head, it felt the most like his. It was almost . . .home. So slippery a word that he still couldn't define it, so he didn't try. Instead he drilled with the guard, and served as a patroller when he wasn't at the palace visiting with Atan, or taking a trip to the local geliath with old friends Hinder and Sinder, to hear the morvende sing to their own echoes in the great caverns.

He'd settled into a pleasant routine, so receiving notice from the palace that Atan wished to talk when she was supposed to be dealing with court came as a surprise. The first thought was something wrong, but the city seemed peaceful enough as he walked with the page back through the first district to the palace, everyone busy in the mellow summer air.

The page, a youngster of about twelve and quivering with self-importance on this her first order directly from the queen, brought him straight to Atan.

"It seems," Atan said, holding out a smooth sheet of what they called silk paper, " that the new King of the Venn has requested your presence at the ceremony for the returning of the Arrow."

"Me?" Rel said. "Ah. That has to be Kerendal."

"Who? Oh yes, the prince you met. Tsauderei said we need to dress up. The Venn are very formal."

Rel really wanted to see Kerendal again. "Let me know when to break out my good tunic."

Atan grinned. "Rel, the treasury is not completely empty. I think we can manage to provide a more suitable garment."

He shook his head. "I've put in enough time laboring over repairs to know how much work goes into the weave and the making. It seems so wasteful to go to the trouble for something I might lose, and probably won't need again until after I've grown out of it."

That reference, oblique as it was, left her with nothing to say. She colored a little, and he said more gently, "You haven't changed your mind?"

"No. Especially now. It's time. Come New Year's, I will relinquish the Child Spell. And you?"

Rel dipped his head in a nod. "I'd promised myself I would after I found my father. I've found him." He'd told Atan that much, knowing that she liked Mondros, rough as he was. But then her first fifteen years had been spent in the company of a plain-speaking palace guard and crusty old Tsauderei. "As you say, it's time."

By the next day, he'd borrowed various items from among his garrison friends to put together a formal robe of deep blue linen of finest weave, embroidered with red berries worked into gold trefoils down the front edges, sleeves, and hem. Under it he wore a white shirt embroidered with red acorns, over loose trousers and his best pair of walking mocs.

Over the robe he wore a baldric that Atan had found in one of the family closets, which held up the sword she had given him.

She wore violet, white, and gold, the Sartoran colors, her brown hair worked into a coronet of braids that kept the Star Chamber golden circlet from pressing into her scalp.

Tsauderei looked as good as he could make himself in a brocade robe, his pure white hair brushed over his shoulders and his beard neatly trimmed for the first time since Peitar's coronation.

They transferred one by one to Bereth Ferian, where they were met by Arthur, who said, "Just so you know, as soon as you sent the communication about the Siamis deal, the Venn burned all their magical materials."

Tsauderei whistled. "No chance of discerning their fundamentals?"

"Nothing." Arthur rubbed his eyes. "We know no more than we had before the first contact."

It was in a suitably chastened spirit that Arthur helped organize the party to transfer to the Venn capital, a first for centuries, in rank order. The impassive Venn mages provided the magic tokens themselves.

When they'd recovered, they were brought into a vast chamber with a vaulted ceiling high above, dominated by the glittering mosaic of a huge tree — stories tall — on one wall.

The Venn did not waste time on speechifying. They had arranged things so that Oalthoreh, as representative of the northern mages, Arthur, as representative of the Federation (now to be rendered utterly purposeless), Tsauderei because he was Tsauderei, and last, Atan as Queen of Sartor, would each release one layer of the spells.

Rel was the only one who had no purpose, but it was he who Kerendal sought out, smiling with real welcome. Karendal had grown, looking impressive in black and white with golden knotwork down the sides of his garments, his light hair bound back under a circlet, and a golden torc at his throat. Rel was glad that he'd taken the time to borrow his finery to honor the occasion. He could see in Kerendal's flush how much their appearance meant to him, he who had so longed to travel.

Then a Venn mage gestured Rel to back up under the great tree, as Arthur was motioned to stand opposite Kerendal. Atan took her place at Arthur's right, next to an old Venn whom Arthur had never met, which meant he was probably the senior noble. At his left, Tsauderei stood with the chief of the Venn mages.

When the mages had everyone placed, each moved to a Sartoran to coach them in the spell he or she was to say, as Kerendal held the Arrow on his palms.

Vast as the chamber was, the magic intensified until it buzzed along the skin. Each spoke unerringly, until Atan pronounced the last words, followed by a nearly blinding blue flash that glittered up that fantastic mosaic as if lightning flashed under the vaulted ceiling.

The stone left lying on the new young king's hands had turned colorless, except for the fires in its center, reflecting light with the intensity of the sun on water.

"It is finished," Kerendal said.

"It is finished," echoed the white-haired Venn mages, in the husky voices of deep emotion. "And so, we rejoin the world. Come! Let us celebrate."

Off to the formal meal in another room filled with color, gilt, and bright mosaics. Using his new rank, Kerendal cut Rel out from the rest, chattering non-stop as he introduced him to various cronies, who had waited in the far room.

He added in a low voice, "Once it was understood that the Queen of Sartor herself had agreed to the treaty, and would come in person, suddenly the diplomats of Goerael have become all smiles, and our lost kinsmen from days of old shall sail home at last. There will be so much to talk about!"

Rel smiled and nodded and agreed to everything, while still pitying the boy king who would still be effectively a prisoner, for what Kerendal did not say was that he would now be able to travel. He was, Rel perceived, as hemmed about by well-meaning counselors as Atan was.

Twenty-five

Colend

THE GENERAL MOOD OF good will at that historic meal
(dutifully sketched by scribes of three kingdoms, as well as
written up with painstaking exactitude) was matched by
another royal meeting that nobody wrote up, taking place at an
outpost on the border between Chwahirsland and Erdrael
Danara, attended by Jilo, Senrid, and Terry.

The herald bearing the letter Thad had written for Senrid
(duly copied out in Marloven as well as the original in formal
diplomatic Kifelian script, on the finest mulberry paper) had
already been dispatched two days before.

The chief topic of gossip at their meeting was Siamis being
caught by Tsauderei, of all people, and forced to a Selenseh
Redian, after he tried to escape by summoning one of Detlev's
boys—according to Arthur, who had got his information
through Oalthoreh, head of the northern mages.

"I figured they'd gone to ground," Senrid said. "Too bad
they didn't think to slap a tracer on David before he smoked."

"Agreed," Terry said grimly. "So we'll find out where they
are when someone else turns up murdered."

Senrid turned to Jilo. "I don't suppose they get any mention
in your enemies book?"

"Except for one of them, MV, going to Norsunder Base a few days ago, no. They don't seem to be using Destinations warded with tracers by Wan-Edhe."

Terry flipped up the back of his hand. "Enough of them. Senrid, before you and Retren ride down the mountain, let's see that demonstration once more. I promised my mountain guard they could invite their friends and family . . ."

Retren Forthan had had no problem finding excellent local horses. These were taller than the Marloven breed, mostly white as they were descendants from the whites of the north of Drael, which caused Senrid, who had seen Hreealdar once, to wonder if these animals' ancestors had mixed with the mysterious creatures who'd chosen horse form.

Which still didn't even begin to explain what kind of being Hreealdar was, or why (he? She? It?) lived in the Selenseh Redian at Mearsies Heili. He wondered if there were lightning "horses" at all the Selenseh Redians — and if Siamis been trampled or burned by one.

No one could answer those questions, so Senrid mentally set aside useless queries and made himself watch the demonstration. Young animals, human and equine, had obviously taken to one another at once, all strong and good-natured. The horses had picked up what was expected of them with agreeable speed, and so Marlovens and then some of the more adventurous Danarans put together trick riding, shooting, and acrobatics demonstrations.

After the excellent demonstration, Danarans and Marlovens celebrated, posturing and swanking about in their new battle tunics, laughing with anticipation of a prime caper, for the Danaran hosts had not stinted in describing the snobbery of their Colendi neighbors.

That very day, down the Alassa River at Alsais, Terry's herald and his guide arrived at the correct hour at the Gate of Gold, which caused a flurry among the Colendi royal heralds.

Before the Hour of the Lamp, when ordinarily the regency council would be attending various court festivities, the seven members of the regency council had each received a written copy of the astonishing letter and were meeting in secret to discuss what to do.

Until now, they had all agreed that they would take turns

writing on behalf of the young king, after they all agreed on the content. None wanted the others to become the habitual voice for the king. They strove in the most polite way possible to gain influence over Shontande, thence one another.

But here was an entirely new situation: a king with a formidable reputation writing to their king. Except for despised Chwahirsland, none of Colend's immediate neighbors were considered formidable; Khanerenth might have been, but they were largely involved in civil strife.

It would set a terrible precedent to keep this missive from Shontande. If the kingdom found out — and there was every possibility that they would if this barbarian really did come riding over the border as he promised in the letter — then there would be an uproar all through court. And as much as the regency council intended to gain total control of the young king, they were watched by the rest of the court, whose equally strong intent was to prevent that.

The letter raised a storm of talk of the kind the regency council most deplored.

"Our primary desire," everyone was assured, " is that our young king, until he gains maturity, ought to be kept from anything that might place undue stress upon him."

In other words, keep him from going mad as his father had.

The court mages had always insisted that the king's madness had been magical, but the lovely, petite Count of Ariath, used to courtly insinuations, didn't believe that for a heartbeat. She had been groomed from birth to marry a king, but Carlael had demonstrated his madness before that could happen, in refusing her. She fully intended to marry her daughter to Shontande before any possible madness manifested. (And if it did, why, so much the better: then Alian would rule as well as reign.)

The tall, formidable Duchas of Desentis, ostensibly the Count's closest friend, was equally determined to scout the Count's overweening power plays at every turn, ably aided by her seemingly sleepy and slow consort, commonly regarded as the handsomest man in Colend.

Presiding over this council was the elderly Duchas of Gaszin, who was granted not a jot more power by the others than calling their meetings to order.

And finally, the last of the important figures of this council was the big, handsome Duchas of Altan, whose family had traditionally jostled with the ruling family for power — when they were not intermarrying.

"Precedent is clear," the old Duchas of Gaszin murmured. "I am certain you will concur, precedent is clear: a letter from a king must be seen by the king."

"Even," the Duchas of Desentis cooed, "when both are understood to be underage?"

"This king of the Marlovens speaks for himself, without benefit of a regent," the Duchas of Altan said as he idly fanned himself, the silver paint on his nails subtly underscoring the royal blue of the fan's underside. "This missive is clear enough about that."

"If it were that obstreperous young fellow from up north again," the Count of Ariath whispered with a graceful gesture, palm toward the north and Chwahirsland, "I might regard this as a situation outside of precedent. Our king, so young, has so much to learn of the intricacies of statecraft . . ." Her voice drifted as she waited for someone to concur, so that she could put herself forward to write on Shontande's behalf. Or, she could suggest with a little laugh that her daughter, as Shontande's most devoted friend, might write for him —

"Perhaps," the Duchas of Altan said, gesturing with fingertips touching his heart (he had very fine hands, and displayed them often)," if it were such, but as we see, it isn't. Marloven Hess, though located on the far side of the continent, is quite as large as our own kingdom, and it is further said to be as influential in its way through the west."

"So, uncouth, the west," the Duchas of Desentis commented, fan at the angle of Regrettable Truth.

Heads turned toward the black-haired, black-eyed, irascible Duchas of Alarcansa, whose attendance at these things, and at court, was intermittent. But it would be as big a mistake to overlook him as it would be to try to manage him.

With Alarcansa being tucked right up against Chwahirsland, the duchas's chief interest was foreign affairs. "I imagine," he drawled, "they say similar things about us."

Silence met that, some amused, some offended.

The second oldest person there, a vague count who had married Shontande's grandfather's younger brother, observed, "His was letter was diplomatically correct to the most formal degree."

"True," said the Duchas of Desentis, with a slight bow.

"This suggests awareness of polite usage, whatever their reputation elsewhere, and this king promises a visit in person."

"Then we must encourage his majesty to welcome the guest in royal style, with a series of splendid entertainments," the Count of Ariath stated, her fan at the angle of Art.

And all understood her meaning: limiting the time the two young royals would actually spend together.

And, of course, *never* alone with one another.

The weather cooperated, adding pleasant breezes to the ride into Colend. The Marlovens found the terrain pleasing to the eye, the roads well kept, the plinths with carved towns and cities indicating direction well marked. Marloven Hess did not use signposts, or street names in the cities, a centuries-old tradition dating back to when their ancestors first invaded Iasca Leror and decided that such things would only be an invitation to the next wave of invaders who had never actually made it into the kingdom. (Though the Venn had tried, and everyone knew that the absence of signposts would not have stopped them.)

None of the Marlovens had been outside of their own borders, except for occasional horse-thief chases into Toth, which was not all that much different from Marloven Hess. In fact, for centuries had been part of it. The single drawback was how difficult this land would be to defend, a land of gentle hills bisected by pleasant rivers fed by the mountains dividing them from the Chwahir to the north.

Word ran ahead. By the time the river they rode along began to curve down toward the capital, interest among the Colendi prompted the curious to come out. When they saw straight-backed, well-built young men riding easily on the backs of prancing horses, the result was gifts of flowers, and entertainments of every variety offered when they stopped. Colendi always appreciate beauty, grace, and style, and though not all these Marlovens were accounted beautiful by Colendi standards, grace and style they exhibited in abundance.

The inns were comfortable, the food excellent, the stables clean, and the Colendi knew how to have fun. The only one not carousing was Senrid, who spent the evenings quietly in his room, writing and reading reports and letters.

By the time they'd reached a trade town a night outside of

Alsais, Forthan's group were united in agreeing that so far this was the best ruse ever, topping even the all-city war games in Choreid Dhelerei.

Senrid's first impression of Alsais was that it would be a nightmare to defend. A single glance at the direction of Forthan's gaze made it clear he was thinking the same thing. From there it was too easy to picture those artfully shaped windows in white-plastered walls with trained trills of flowering vines, the decorative ironwork and patterned tile steps and walkways, the curving canals, all destroyed by Norsundrian strike troops with fire and sword.

Senrid tried to shake off the mood as they trotted in column up a neat brick carriage-road toward Crown Gate on the east side of the palace complex. This required crossing the city, as they'd entered from the west, but Thad had given Senrid a map with carefully drawn landmarks: they'd passed the white-blossom garden bordering the Gate of the Lily Path, and over there was the bell tower with its polished carillon, which would presently ring noon.

Colendi and visitors to the city stopped to watch the Marlovens in their black and gold, each rider bristling with steel — they'd had vigorous bets going on who could fit the most weaponry about their persons — the two riders behind Senrid and Forthan carrying the Marloven gold on black screaming eagle banner. The black-clad riders and their cream, ivory, and fog-gray spotted horses drew the eye. The horses knew it, arching tails, ears alert, stepping with confidence.

Kings had visited so seldom in recent years that Crown Gate had begun to be regarded as the artisans' gate for mastery parades at the Hour of the Lily, but today the heralds had made certain a royal welcome had gathered well before noon.

Senrid had to admire how skillfully they were guided to where the Colendi wanted them: horses led away to a distant stable area, screened from sight and smell, the riders to the herald-guards' own wing, and Senrid and Forthan into the palace proper.

Conversation with Thad had convinced Senrid that he would never be able to master the intricacies of Colendi manners, which the natives had been raised with since birth. Other than avoiding outright rudeness, he wasn't going to try.

The shadow thing was serious, he could see, but at noon shadows were small, and the smiling guides glided to either side, keeping their shadows well out of reach of barbarian blackweave riding boots.

The palace appeared to be a confusion of greenery, glass, marble, and diffuse light, everything in curves around fountains and pools. Color was supplied by the many varieties of blooming flowers and aromatic herbs in pots and plots and windows, broad doors opening onto more gardens, which encouraged the summer air to flow in a cool breeze. Square rooms in a row on one level were apparently inelegant. Senrid knew he'd get lost quickly, and followed along, glad of the guide.

There's little to be said about the official meeting, all very formal. Senrid likened it to some kind of dance. Shontande Lirendi was small and thin, almost frail in his layers of embroidered silks, his fingernails painted an eggshell blue to match his eyes. He reminded Senrid of the spun sugar treats seen in his kingdom's bakeries.

The ritual played out exactly as Thad had predicted. By then Senrid was beginning to sort out the various Colendi in their layered silks. They were too smooth to be caught being condescending, but he felt corralled all the same, maybe because he'd been warned. He was a guest, on his best behavior, so how one stepped relative to others who were busy inviting one with word and gesture made it seem natural to go along.

But as the food, music, art, and conversation blended one into the other, one thing became clear: the sardonic, black-eyed, brown-skinned old duchas, the pretty little woman with the dark blond hair, the big duchas with the dark brows, and the tall, red-haired duchas were not about to leave him alone with their boy king.

Plays in Marloven Hess were mostly ballads, dances, and battle pieces strung together with words the actors made up according to their mood, but he knew about written plays. He'd seen a few while visiting friends. When the time came for the formal conference (as the carillon played a new melodious pattern in the background, and they moved to yet another marble-walled room) Shontande Lirendi's invitation to speak about Senrid's treaty congress came out sounding like a written script in a play.

Well, Thad had coached Senrid in what to say, refined by Terry, so his words were also rehearsed. That was all right. This was all an excuse. Nothing that affected either kingdom would come of it.

But toward the end, after the ever-present nobles uttered their pretty palaver about peaceful progress and hope of good trade with neighbors near and far, Senrid sensed that he was about to receive a silk-clad boot to the butt, and decided his moment had come.

He said to Shontande, "I regret that I must soon return to my kingdom, but before I leave, I would like to return your hospitality with a demonstration."

Shontande, who had been feeling more and more caged by the endless demands of obligation, duty, training, and expectation, had been surprised by Senrid's letter. His first thought had been Thad's alliance, but there was nothing in the letter about Thad. He'd read it through twice.

Though he could not imagine why Senrid, king of a country at the other end of the longest continent in the world, would want to visit, he'd found himself thinking about it and hoping it had something to do with the alliance, though he'd feared that was forever killed along with Karhin, and Glenn of Everon.

Before he could speak, the pretty count bowed, making a graceful arc with her fan, and said smoothly, "If we may be permitted, it would be our pleasure and honor to arrange an appropriate day and place for such a rare delight."

"And I concur, Honor," began the black-haired duchas.

"No," Senrid said, pleasantly, but distinctly.

They had the word, though it was not done to utter it. But what would they do to a foreign king, pull out sword and fall on him?

"No," Senrid said again. "I must return home tomorrow. Why not now?" He spoke directly to Shontande. "I saw a grassy area off the canal that is exactly the right size. If you want to see it, we want to show you what we can do."

Senrid watched the younger boy's pupils dilate. *Come on, don't rabbit on me.*

Shontande did not look at his nobles. He said softly but distinctly, "I would like that very much."

Senrid was aware of a subtle stir from a couple of those adults, no more than a shimmer of light over silk, a fan closing here, one pointing downward there, but he ignored them. "Captain Forthan, can you ready your company?"

"Instantly, Senrid-Harvaldar," Forthan said, his free hand

closing into a fist and thumping his chest.

Shontande made a two-fingered gesture to one of the silent servants standing against the wall. "Lehlas, my steward, will arrange things, if you will go with him," he said to Forthan.

Another fist to chest salute, then Forthan put his helm back on, one hand to the cavalry sword at his side, and said to the gray-robed man who had stepped forward, "Lead on."

Shontande turned to Senrid. "That sward is where the final performances of the yearly Music Festival are held. It is an excellent place. I'll show you where I always sit." He then turned his grave face to his nobles. "Anyone who does not wish to observe the demonstration need not feel compelled."

He rose from his cushion, his layered silk robes rustling like water. He reminded Senrid even more of a doll, not the least because of his lack of expression. Senrid wondered what kind of friendship could this doll of a boy and Thad could really have, then laughed inwardly. He knew there were some who could not understand his friendship with Liere. Sometimes he didn't either, except that they had been through so much when they first met. But sometimes friends just . . .were.

Shontande was afraid to let himself hope. As he led the way through the linden garden to the waterfall grotto, he reflected on how there would never again be a kingly visit with this much freedom. The regency council would see to that. It had felt so good to act, because there was no protocol for a visiting king saying *no* like that. So they could not say Shontande had done wrong.

But by tomorrow the regents would all be gently explaining new protocols, and how careful he must be, how much he required guidance. So he hoped that today—whatever it brought—would be worth it.

And he would forever treasure the memory of their faces when King Senrid had said, *No*.

They reached the lawn that served as an outdoor amphitheater, trees hiding the walls bespelled to reflect back sound from below.

Shontande led Senrid to his favorite spot in the middle. There had not even been time for servants to spread covers over the grass, or to bring food and drink that he didn't want—or to surround him, except for the two herald guards who always followed at a discreet distance, staying out of earshot.

He had not invited any of the regency council to join them,

so they must perforce stay back unless he brought them forward. His heart pounded at his daring. Oh yes, they would cage him even closer now, but if . . .if . . .

"Your majesty." The low voice belonged to one of the Count of Ariath's servants. "I am enjoined for your safety to remain in your proximity, if you will permit."

Senrid turned his head. "I'm not armed, as you see." Actually he was. He always wore knives up his sleeves, but nobody was going to know that. "And I want to talk to your king privately."

The man turned to Shontande, who now could say, "He is my guest. His wish shall serve as my will." There was protocol for that!

And the steward had to withdraw.

Then out came two of the Marlovens with hand drums. They began a rolling beat in counterpoint, moving slowly up the grass until the sound seemed to come from everywhere.

Colendi were gathering in twos and threes along the perimeter, their soft voices lost in the martial beat.

The thunder of horse hooves rumbled under that beat, and Forthan's company appeared, riding two by two at the gallop.

The formation was not the tight nose to tail of home. These horses had not had enough time to train in the really complicated tricks, but they separated off smoothly into two circles, one riding inside the other in opposite directions as the riders stood in the saddle and began leaping back and forth from horse to horse.

It was the sort of trickery they all learned while young, meant to train horse and human to know one another so well that they did not have to think about riding, before they learned archery on horseback, spear, sword, and lance.

Shontande stared, his lips parted, as the drummers took up stances behind the two kings. Senrid, who had been seeing much better demonstrations all his life, said in Sartoran, "I'm here for Thad."

That got Shontande's attention. "Thad Keperi? But he has not written back to me." He answered low-voiced in the same language, facing forward.

"He says the same thing," Senrid replied. "You've never written to him."

"But I have! Many times, though not of late. I thought he must have decided against our correspondence, though I couldn't understand a reason. I was afraid that Curtas might've killed him, too, and I sent someone to ascertain his welfare. But the servant I sent merely reported that Thad was sent away by his family."

"He was, but now he's back. He said you made a notecase."

"Yes, I did. But after my father was killed, they took it, to make certain no evil spells were on it. They gave it back, but the only letters I get in it now are from the regents."

"I thought that might be true," Senrid said. "So I made you one. It'll be much harder to tamper with it, but it'd be best if you keep it hidden."

"How?" Shontande said. "There are people with me from waking to sleeping, and two herald guards outside my bedroom door when I retire. If they see light, they always come in to find out what I need."

"Then you find a way to block the light," Senrid said. "And write at night."

Shontande stared back at him.

Under cover of the galloping hooves and the rumbling drums, Senrid said, "I don't know if it makes any difference, but Curtas didn't kill Karhin. She was dead before he and Thad got back to Wilderfeld."

"But he is one of *them*. And another of them did the deed. As a third killed Glenn, and possibly our own king, my father."

"Your king was killed by one of the lords of Norsunder. But yes, Detlev's boys did for the rest. They nearly destroyed the alliance, but they haven't. We've reorganized to share information about them." Senrid touched his pocket. "You can write to me, too, if you want, in this thing. I put a paper inside with the sigils for all the other rulers under age, with or without regency councils. Including the queen of Sartor. Jilo, too. He wants to bring the Chwahir out of the bad years, and is working hard to do so."

Shontande looked down at Senrid's hand, which rested on his thigh as he sat there cross-legged on the grass. "Not yet," Senrid said as the riders shifted to choreographed sword fights on horseback. "I don't have to turn my head to know they're watching us. When I was your age my uncle was my regent. He was a very bad king, but a worse regent. When I got caught crossing his will I paid for it for days. So I learned not to get caught."

Shontande said slowly, "My regency council says their first

purpose is to hand me a harmonious kingdom, and their second to train me to keep Colend prosperous."

"They're doing a good job with the first, at least from what I saw riding in," Senrid said. "But Thad can tell you more."

"I miss Thad so very much," Shontande spoke almost too low to hear, and Senrid didn't have to have Dena Yeresbeth to sense the intense loneliness of the boy king surrounded by fabulous beauty and wealth.

Out in front a company of herald guards kept off a massive crowd ringing the grass where the horses and riders formed circles, Forthan in the lead, watching Senrid for signals.

At a lift of Senrid's forefinger on his thigh, Forthan gave a nod. Seemingly without warning the circles broke open and the horses trotted up the sward toward the rear, the riders doing acrobatic tricks from horseback to ground and up again.

They passed close by the nobles, who could not resist turning, and in that moment Senrid pulled the new case from his inner pocket and slid it under one of the peach-and-silver edges of Shontande's outer robe.

The boy king turned to watch the riders, and as he did, his hand moved the case inside the robe to some pocket hidden in another of his layers, then out came his hands.

The riders finished up by forming one large circle, and as they rode past Shontande each saluted with his sword before sheathing it and then riding back down to the canal path, and toward the stables.

They were followed by waving fans and soft voices of acclaim.

"That was splendid," Shontande said, rising. No sign of the note case. "I am truly grateful." He put his palms together in the peace.

"Glad you enjoyed it," Senrid said, laying his fist to his heart, the Marloven salute to a king.

The nobles closed around again, for it was time to fall back into their carefully planned evening. Shontande went through it in a far better mood, that case secreted next to his skin.

The next day early the Marlovens departed, and Shontande had readied his words for the expected inquiry into what the two young kings had talked about—Marloven Hess, Erdrael Danara, and Chwahirsland—following which the regency council met to discuss their having been outmaneuvered.

They agreed that no harm had come of that interruption in

their harmonious routine, the Marlovens, peculiar barbarians that they were, had merely exercised some sort of barbaric whim, but they would get the heralds to find suitable protocols from historical records so that nothing would threaten their good order again.

By that time, Senrid and the company had left the outskirts of the city behind them. Once they reached an empty stretch of road, Senrid climbed down from his horse, stuffed his fancy House tunic into his saddlebag, and handed off the bag of transfer tokens he'd made to Forthan. One by one the company would shift back to Marloven Hess, leaving the last two to bring the string of horses to the waiting Danaran mountain guard at the border.

Dressed once again in his plain shirt, trousers, and boots, Senrid transferred to Wilderfeld, where he gave Thad a report on everything that had been said.

At the end, Thad's face lit with his old smile for the first time since Karhin's death. "He wrote to me last night."

Twenty-six

Western Wnelder Vee

SUMMER WAS WANING WHEN MV appeared by transfer outside the one-room cottage at the eastern end of the boys' rathole, on the Destination David had scratched into the hard-packed ground.

The four who were in the process of repairing the cottage according to Curtas's directions stopped hammering and stared in shock as MV walked in stiffly, a mottled mess of bruises and dirty bandages around his head, one arm, and above one knee. His hands were a mess, his knuckles raw and purple.

He fell face down onto the nearest bed, and when of them approached to ask if there was anything he could do, MV said savagely, "Touch me and I'll kill you."

David jerked his chin at the door. Everyone withdrew outside, out of earshot, under a spreading tree whose foliage rustled and hissed in the heavy rain. Lightning flickered at a distance, revealing his set expression. "Move to the stone cottage. Stay there."

They took off. David walked noiselessly inside, put a water jug by MV's bed, and set about making some food.

For a long day MV neither ate nor drank. The next day, he drank water. And on the third day, ate something, still unspeaking, while David briefed him about Siamis. The morning after, the summer broke with the first cold, sleety storm of autumn, leaving the leaves turning brilliant colors.

MV dunked his head in a basin of water, dug around in the trunk for fresh clothes, then walked out of the house as if nothing had happened, though the fresher bruises were just beginning to purple and the older ones to fade. He whistled for the others to line up. He then rousted them into a run in the cold rain.

When they got back, some arguing about which cottage needed repairs the most, assuming they were stuck for the winter, MV pulled out his whetstone, sharpened all his already-honed blades, and when he was done, he said to David, "I'm going to snuff Tsauderei."

"What?" David exclaimed.

"We all know where he holes up: Delfina Valley, Sarendan. They kill one of us, we kill them. Simple."

"But we don't know that Siamis is dead. Selenseh Redians could be a time shift."

MV didn't answer. He was already gone, having made a transfer token while David was out of the cottage.

David rolled his eyes, mentally composing his report to Detlev.

MV was a fast learner with a tenacious memory, but his magic studies had been conducted in fits and starts because he could never sit still long. He'd learned best when the need arose, or when he became curious. Then he'd descend on David, who strove to be the best in all things out of a sense of self-preservation, or Roy, who was absorbed in magic studies. He'd work furiously for a day, or a week, or a month, however long it took to master what he was after. After that he'd be field training again, or in the old days, sailing.

He'd paid attention to briefings on the most formidable mages the world could bring against Norsunder. Of them, he found old Tsauderei the most interesting—the loner who cleaved to no hierarchy. The lighter world came to him.

MV didn't bother looking into his motivation. He needed action. Tsauderei had done for Siamis, about whom MV had felt the ambivalence of admiration and envy.

Reckless as always, MV transferred straight south to the Destination Kessler had established in the forest below Delfina Valley, without checking to see if it had been warded, or even if it still existed. His contempt for lighter magic made him a ready candidate for surprise, and sure enough, he was caught by a ward when he appeared.

He found himself seized by magic and drawn up into the air. Fear warred with fascination as he zoomed over the treetops, then higher up a slope impossible to climb by anyone but goats.

As magic drew him inexorably farther up, as on the other side of the mountains in Sartor, an internal alarm warned Tsauderei that someone had breached the old forest Destination, which existed at the extreme edge of his boundary.

He sighed as he put down an ancient Sartoran Mage Guild record, and reached for his scrystone. A few whispered words, and a tall boy in black swam into view, an escarpment falling away below him. A Marloven?

Carlael's killer, Efael of Norsunder?

He cursed as he looked around, then remembered that Atan would still be at breakfast. He hoped Rel might be there as well. Between the two of them, perhaps the mystery guest might be identified.

He thought about that long walk, then summoned the first year mage student studying in the next room while on page duty. A short time later, both Atan and Rel entered, along with Hinder the morvende, his white hair like cobwebs in the autumnal morning light.

"You know who this is?" Tsauderei asked, pointing.

Hinder and Atan both said, "No."

"That's MV." Rel grimaced. "One of Detlev's boys."

"Here?" Tsauderei asked. "Is he the one who killed young Prince Glenn?"

"No. But according to witnesses, he was there, and certainly did nothing to stop it."

"Interesting," Tsauderei said. "I wonder what madness prompted this visit?"

Atan said, "I hope you'll be careful. Their reputations are awful."

Tsauderei grinned. "He'll be coming to my cottage, where he won't be starting any sword fights. I've got about an hour to prepare." He watched as MV, who had not ceased attempting to gain control of his flight, discovered that he now had a certain amount of autonomy, though he could not fly back down the mountain. He could only go upward.

Tsauderei, Rel, Hinder, and Atan watched in the scry stone as MV began experimenting, swooping high, turning over and over in the air, then diving down like a falcon on the stoop before arcing up again. But when he tried to veer westward, the magic seized him again, and anger tightened his face, followed by a narrow-eyed determination.

MV arced down again, fast as a raptor, but he didn't pull up. Even in the small scry stone the determination holding him could be seen in his rigid body before the magic slowed him to a level float before he could crash head-first into the rocks.

Tsauderei grunted, brows up. "This one is very angry. I wonder if I will be using . . .the chair."

All three repeated, "The chair?"

Followed by Atan's, "Which chair?" She had spent the first fifteen years of her life going in and out of that cottage.

"Oh, it looks ordinary enough. All of you have probably used it numerous times. But you have manners," Tsauderei said.

Hinder sighed. "I should like to fly again."

"You may come back with me another time. This interview, I think, is better conducted alone."

Tsauderei transferred back to his cottage in the Valley while MV discovered that flying was as much fun as sailing, though not as dangerous, at least in the grip of this magic. He tried twice to crash himself, to be pulled away and up again past snow-covered peaks that probably never saw melt.

When at last he sighted the Delfina Valley with its plateaus settled with dwellings around a deep blue volcanic lake, he tried to fight the magic but it brought him gently and inexorably to a high plateau on which sat a single cottage with a great window on the lakeside wall.

The magic released him outside the door, to chilly mountain air. He kicked the door open impatiently and took in the single room with its wall-to-ceiling shelves packed with scrolls and books, except for the bow window overlooking the lake, framing a gaunt white-bearded man seated in a wing-backed chair.

MV curled his lip.

Tsauderei sat back, the diamond in one ear glinting as he closed his hands around a shallow bowl of Sartoran steep.

MV sauntered in, heels ringing on the stone floor.

"Come in and sit down." Tsauderei indicated a simple

wooden chair set before his.

"I'd rather stand," MV said.

"I'd rather stand," Tsauderei mimicked, then set aside his bowl and propped his fists on his bony knees. "Why is it every time I have one of you fools in my valley as my guest, do I hear the same surly refrain? Tell me! Am I supposed to find your standing before me a sinister prospect, or is this an example of what passes for etiquette in your little corner of the universe?"

MV shot him a derisive glance, swung the plain wooden chair around, and plopped down backward in it—

And the chair disintegrated, dumping MV on his butt amid pieces of kindling.

"Let's try that again," Tsauderei said, as MV got to his feet. "A little hint. In my house, we use at least a semblance of manners." He snapped his fingers, and the chair flew back together.

It looked good, of course. But anyone who knew some magic would know that it took a lot of spell-casting to set all that up. MV got the message about who was in charge, and so he gave Tsauderei a satirical salute and—carefully—sat down.

Tsauderei said, "What brings you to Delfina Valley?" He added with no change in tone, as MV's right hand shifted, "I don't play death games with children, so keep your mitt off the knife concealed up your sleeve."

MV's black brows lifted.

Tsauderei grinned. "Yes, some of your kind have refused to believe I mean what I say, and they stand as ornaments in my garden. You may visit them if you like. My stone spells generally last."

MV crossed his arms.

"I gather you're Detlev's latest experiment, and judging by the spectacular bruising in your visible skin, apparently as unsuccessful as his previous failures with various kings. Where'd he find you? Refuse heaps of the world?"

"Most of us, yeah," MV said. "A couple of us, he bought."

"So, again, what brings you to my valley?"

"You smoked Siamis. I was going to return the favor."

"You want me to ask you for asylum?" Tsauderei gave a crack of laughter as MV's mordant expression lengthened to disbelief. "No, no, it doesn't work that way. *He* came to *us*."

MV snarled, "No chance."

"But he did," Tsauderei said, not bothering to hide his

enjoyment. "If he can be believed, he always intended to, though admittedly he took a rather roundabout path, and in less of a hurry than we could have wished. Say, by a couple dozen centuries. But the consequences of his actions will wait for him, should he reappear from the Selenseh Redian that Lilith the Guardian mandated for his part of our . . .let's call it a truce for now. So. Look around. Any questions? Detlev has never been able to stick his nose in here. He'll be wanting a report up close and personal, I'm certain."

MV cocked his head slightly.

"No questions? Threats, even? Surely you concocted some splendid threats and curses on your journey up the mountain. Go ahead. Get them out. I'm listening. I enjoy a good threat, and I save up really inventive curses. I've heard some choice ones over my many years. No? I guess it's time for you to be on your way, then." And as MV tensed, "Next time, don't talk so much."

That surprised MV into a laugh—in the middle of which he found himself abruptly shifted to a rocky shore somewhere no doubt weeks from the nearest city.

When he recovered from that long transfer, he fingered his transfer token, which wrenched him back to the rat-hole.

Twenty-seven

Autumn 4747 AF

THE NEWS ABOUT TSAUDEREI'S agreement with Siamis propagated outward, in some places causing nearly as much reaction as a declaration of war.

The first sign of trouble was a letter from Peitar Selenna of Sarendan to Atan.

"You know how Peitar is dedicated to peace, but I can tell he's struggling to accept it," Atan said to Tsauderei as she shared Peitar's letter. "But Lilah's letter hurt to read, she feels so betrayed. Peitar admits that she's been crying for days. It's like she's lost Derek Diamagan all over again. I feel even more guilty because I never liked Derek."

Tsauderei rubbed his temples with his fingers. "If Peitar were the worst of it, I'd be content."

Atan flinched inwardly, wishing she could rescind the offer to extend sanctuary-with-boundaries to Siamis if he reappeared. But she'd promised. And when she wavered, she had only to think of those supply caches, as well as the Arrow and what Detlev would have done with it, to stay firm.

Some dismissed those gains as trivial.

In Mearsies Heili, Mearsieanne sat with a slight frown, listening to everything, until Clair was done reading her letter from Atan.

Mearsieanne didn't speak until Clair said, "And so Atan feels obliged to offer Siamis limited sanctuary in Eidervaen, with Tsauderei supervising."

Mearsieanne gripped her hands together, her blue eyes a contrast to the red in her face. "I must say I'm disgusted at Yustnesveas Landis's weakness. Well, she lives in Sartor, a continent away. Just keep that blood-smeared rodent from my sight," she said in a low, fierce voice. "I hope his midden-heap of an uncle comes after him and they kill each other."

Clair said, "It sounds like the thing he did for the Venn —"

"The Venn," Mearsieanne cut in contemptuously. "They could just as well have stayed as they were for another century or two. No one wanted them a thousand years ago, and we've done fine without them since."

Clair stared back, troubled, and for once CJ had nothing to say.

"As for *Detlev*." Mearsieanne spat the name out. "I only hope I live long enough to see him destroyed, so that I may dance on his dust." She stirred, then made an obvious effort to regain control, as Clair looked almost as pale as her hair.

CJ said quickly, "Did I tell you what I discovered in one of the rooms upstairs? It's a room we've never seen before."

Mearsieanne turned a determinedly interested face her way, knowing a peace offering when she heard it. She'd been the first to say that when she was young she used to explore the upper rooms in the white palace, some of which seemed to flicker in and out of time, though no one actually caught them doing it.

"They are magical portraits," CJ said, bringing out two golden picture frames.

She touched the first frame and stepped back. They all watched as a life-sized illusion formed on the floor in front of the enchanted picture. A boy dressed in a colorful outfit that seemed to be made up of slashed fabrics bound with ribbons danced and twirled, a trained bird flying from one of his wrists to the other.

"I don't know who he is or when he lived, but he must have been really important to someone, because that spells feels old," CJ said.

The second frame provided the illusion of a woman declaiming a poem in a type of old-fashioned Sartoran difficult to understand, but her stylized gestures and her expressive face conveyed a lot of the poem's story.

These prompted a search of the archives in hopes of identifying time and place, if not persons, and so amity was restored.

At least, on the surface, Clair thought to herself.

In Marloven Hess, a local truce between the silk-weavers of Vasande Leror and the Marloven miners on their mutual border absorbed Senrid and Leander more than foreign news.

"I think it's working," Leander said on a blustery autumn day, when they met together in Senrid's study.

"That doesn't mean another bunch might not be squabbling next week," Senrid retorted, but completely without heat. "I'm going to shift Forthan back here as cavalry commander. You can trust him to keep things reined tight." He paused, considering that. Five more years, and Forthan could be appointed his Harskiald, the commander of his army. Five years — assuming Norsunder didn't attack first.

And maybe Siamis had bought them that time.

"You heard any news?" he asked.

Leander said, "Nothing about Detlev's gang. They seem to have gone to ground, after one of them showed up in an unsuccessful try at assassinating Tsauderei."

Senrid gave a hoot of laughter. "Would have liked to see that. All I've been getting is a lot of righteous fuming about Siamis."

"Can you blame them?" Leander asked, looking askance, and Senrid reflected that Leander, so far, hadn't been one of those ranting on and on about Siamis hopping the fence.

Senrid wasn't sure how he felt. He hated Siamis unreservedly, but Siamis had apparently provided information that would seriously set Detlev's plans back. That meant something. Then there was memory. Senrid had spent plenty of time being reviled by the self-congratulatory peace-loving and harmonious lighters back in the bad old days, when he'd tried to make his way out of dark magic thinking. Therefore his ambivalence.

As if in parallel thought, Leander lowered his voice. "Been writing back and forth to Arthur. They're having debates about justice up there."

"Justice." Senrid snorted.

Leander's bright gaze narrowed. "You don't believe there

can be justice?"

"Depends on how one defines it."

"Arthur finding out about Roy being one of Detlev's boys feels it a personal betrayal. Even though so far, there's no sign that Roy has attacked anyone. Of course, that's so far."

And when Senrid shrugged, Leander said, "How would you feel if Liere turned out to be Detlev's mouthpiece?"

Senrid burst out laughing, then shook his head. "Arthur and Roy were that tight? Yeah, they were. What I worry about are Detlev's caches. I'm an idiot not to have thought about establishing our own caches. Of course we'll need weapons."

"For?"

"Fighting back." Senrid rapped his knuckles on his map case. "When Norsunder comes. Even if they beat us into submission, whoever is left is going to fight back. So my question is, where to cache? What's my fallback strategy? These hills seem an obvious choice, all those old mines. Which is why I want to bring Forthan back, so he oversee affairs with your Lerorans. Keep good relations. We'll keep our cacheing on our side of the hills."

Leander gave him a sideways glance.

"What?" Senrid said.

"I don't know, those caches, the way you're thinking, it seems a grim thing to be running your mind about."

"My mind never stops running. Don't tell me yours does."

"No," Leander admitted, remembering that blood mage text. "No."

Early winter 4748 AF
Western Wnelder Vee

Winter in the southern half of the world struck early, slowing preparations for New Year's Week with a series of snow storms. Gradually interest in Siamis, who had not reappeared, gave way to more immediate concerns. But among the Young Allies, resentment against Detlev's boys smoldered, ready to flare into flame.

As for the boys themselves, reinforced walls were only part of what they needed: there were also basic necessities like warm blankets, coats, and above all, food.

One afternoon, as Adam stood with a paintbrush in one ear,

sighing over the ruin that Noser and Vana had made of one of his wall paintings as a joke, Roy laid his quill down carefully. "I'm done," he said, fingers tidying a considerable stack of closely written papers.

Adam wasn't paying attention. "Why couldn't they make their own painting? Noser actually has talent." He turned away, groping for his bag of paints. "I'll do another one."

David walked up to Roy, arms crossed. "That took a while."

Roy flexed his fingers. Accusation—curiosity, maybe. Of them all, David would be able to comprehend. Perhaps MV, assuming his ricocheting interest caught.

There were times when Roy felt sick of the secrets, sick of lies, sick of certain memories that he could not suppress. "It's there, if you want to read it over." He turned away. "I'm going for a run."

When he returned, the papers lay exactly as he'd left them, which didn't mean David hadn't glanced through them. But no one said anything as the day stretched into two, then a week.

With afternoons free, Roy trained Adam in the basic magic needed to make firesticks, which required endless repeats of a fairly simple spell as one gathered sunlight into the twig-stripped, sanded branches. MV took it upon himself to lead the forays to get supplies; on the surface he seemed the same as always, except there was a look to his fiery gaze and a snap to his drills that kept the others at a wary distance, David particularly narrow-eyed and watchful.

MV was systematic in varying his raid targets. First venturing well north, then east into cities and prosperous castle-towns, and then finally, after New Year's Week, south into Ferdrian, an irresistible challenge that had the added advantage of the terrain being well known to the boys who had spent so much time among Glenn's recruits.

On a bitterly cold night under intermittent sleet, MV and his party sneaked to the auxiliary supply storage at the extreme north end of the palace complex. The single sentry on duty, a bored recruit, had stopped walking during a spate of icy sleet, and retreated under an eave.

He crouched beside a stack of barrels, using them as a buffer between him and the wind. In his dark gray wool cloak he blended into the shadows, his hood pulled well over his face to keep his ears warm, as he waited out the weather before resuming a dull patrol.

Nothing had happened since the triumphant defeat of Henerek in the mountains. Some of those very supplies were now housed behind him, which no one needed this early in winter. When he heard a familiar snicker, at first he thought it was a bad dream. He glanced up as a series of figures ghosted by, barely discernable in the gloom. But dim light from the quartermaster's house on the other side of the courtyard caught on the light hair of the smallest figure, and he instantly recognized that obnoxious boy called Noser.

Shock rocked him to his feet, and he started out after them, hunching into the icy downpour. He shadowed the shadowy figures because it was duty, while his mind raced ahead. What could he do, one against all them? When they slid around a corner, briefly lit by a dim slant of golden light that caught the sharp, distinctive profile of MV, he stopped still, swaying. He only had a knife. He'd left his spear behind, as his hands even in knit gloves were too cold to hold it. And what could he really do with a stupid spear?

He knew what he should do. His heartbeat throbbed in his throat; no yelling, or they might turn around and fall on him. He ran back to the Knights' garrison.

By the time he had the Knights roused and following him back to the storage buildings, of course MV and the rest were gone, along with a wagon, and a well-chosen number of boxes and barrels.

"What this means," Commander Roderic Dei said the next morning to Tahra, "is that they must be somewhere in the vicinity, or why would they be raiding our stores?"

Since her mother's death, Tahra had fallen into a kind of numb dullness, which she'd turned into a strictly ordered routine once little Lyren went off to Sartor. But at this mention of Glenn's killers, all the old grief and anger boiled up again, bitter as acid.

"Search the city," she snapped. "The kingdom. If they are here, they *die*."

Roderic Dei bowed, disturbed by this first sign of real life in the girl whose flat affect had been as unsettling as her not-quite-under her breath counting of steps, sharp turns, carefully lined quill pens, and her upset if rugs were not absolutely squared, or anything else in the fire-scorched, shabby castle was slightly out of plumb.

Roderic took his worry to Captain Prasedes, one of the

senior Knights now. She was the current day watch commander.

She listened, then reddened with an anger to match the
young queen's. "I know you see a difference between
Henerek's Norsundrians and these boys, but I don't. The boys
are merely Henerek in a few years. The sooner the world is rid
of them, the less damage they'll be able to do. If you do not want
to search the kingdom, I'll do it with volunteers on our liberty
time."

Roderic did not like where their anger-driven thinking was
going, but maybe the anger would spend itself in this pursuit.
He said, "I relinquish charge of this search to you. Do as you
see fit."

Captain Prasedes reported to the palace, to discover that
Tahra, in her persona as Queen Hatahra of Everon, had written
her second royal proclamation, the first having been a day of
mourning for Queen Mersedes Carinna. This new edict put
enormous prices on the boys' heads, caught dead or alive.
Prasedes saw to it that the heralds sent out to read the
proclamation in every village and town square were
accompanied by either Knights or recruits.

It was one of the latter of whom who, a week later, on
glimpsing Curtas busy painting varnish on some new trim,
stopped her horse and squinted up at him. So far, it had been
so boring a journey that her first reaction was mildly inquisitive
when she said, "I know you. Aren't you friends with the artist
Adam?"

Curtas stared down at her, sun-lightened hair lifting in the
wind of an on-coming storm, as her expression changed from
puzzlement to a kind of intensity. She unrolled the
proclamation to reread the descriptions of the criminals
associated with Glenn's murder, Adam and Curtas having been
included, along with Laban. By the time she looked up, he was
gone from the ladder, having clambered over the roof.

"He's one of them," the recruit realized, her voice rising to
a shout. "After him!"

The Knight and the recruit gave chase, which raised the rest
of the village.

Curtas ran for his life.

For a time the danger was sharp, as the river land along the
border with Wnelder Vee offered little cover. But the weather
and his training got him far enough ahead of the hunt to go to

ground in a reedy marsh, where he lay underwater except for a reed straw as the searchers' circle widened outward and then vanished. At nightfall, muddy and shivering, he splashed his way out and ran hard for the rat-hole.

He reported to David, who turned to MV. "You were sniffed in Ferdrian. You didn't even realize it."

MV cursed as he honed a knife. He hated being sloppy. The cold was no excuse.

"That's it." David turned to the rest. "We don't want mages joining the search, and stumbling on our perimeter wards. Ferret, at first light you go make sure Curtas didn't leave a trail. Then we're sitting tight until the noise dies down."

It was good thinking, but he didn't comprehend how much hatred they had engendered. By the time Curtas had stumbled into the moss house, bits of caked mud falling off at every step, and his lips blue with cold, Tahra had written to Thad, Arthur, and Atan to complain bitterly about the murderers still lurking somewhere in Everon, no doubt to finish the job of eradicating Delieths from the world.

From there, word spread.

Meanwhile, next morning a company of Knights rode across the border from Curtas's village. They, like the previous hunt, ventured in widening circles, moving north far enough to find themselves enveloped by fog, which turned them about without their realizing it. Three times they attempted to push through the fog, to find themselves wandering in another direction entirely when they emerged.

When they reported to Commander Dei, Tahra listened intently, then said, "That fog is magic."

She insisted on going with a full company of Knights into Wnelder Vee, knowing that Wnelder Vee didn't really have any kind of protective presence like the Everoneth Knights. Morgeh Troiad, a fine friend and a superlative musician for someone so young, was pretty much king in name only. The kingdom was governed by a guild council, whose members relied on local governance. Any militia they raised would be no match for Detlev's trained killers.

When Tahra's search reached the spot that the Knights had marked carefully on a map, they discovered that the only ones who could cross the fog bank were Tahra and the young recruit who came along to hold the horses. "It's them. It has to be. They have this spell on Geth-deles," Tahra said angrily. "Only underage people can get through. They're in there, all right."

She left her company behind and transferred home to write to Arthur, who reported the news to everyone in the alliance, adding Tahra's request for the alliance to come to her aid in flushing them out.

In Mearsies Heili, Clair showed the letter to Mearsieanne, whose faded blue eyes widened. "Knowing Tahra, she'll go herself if no one helps her. In a situation like this, there's strength in numbers."

Clair studied Mearsieanne. "You think we should go?"

Mearsieanne, young and old at the same time, said with cut-glass precision, "If you don't, I will."

Clair summoned the rest of the girls, and explained.

"Great! I'm in," CJ exclaimed, rubbing her hands. After all the fun of New Year's Week, the boredom of winter stretched before them. Then she frowned. "But what's to stop them from just transferring somewhere else?"

Clair waved the letter. "Arthur right now is teaming up with Mondros to use their border against them. They can add a tracer over it, so if they transfer away, the tracer will say where. Maybe the senior mages will be able to do something with that part. Our part is to chase them out, into the waiting arms of the Knights."

Falinneh yanked on her red braids. "If it was just Adam, I wouldn't mind, except I feel bad to stick him in jail, or make him have to pave roads."

"I think Tahra wants to execute them," CJ said, knowing that Mearsieanne would highly approve.

Falinneh pruned her freckled face. "Kill Adam? Far as I know, he never hurt a gnat. And the rest of them scare me. I want to stay home."

"Me, too," Sherry said.

"Hey," CJ protested. "Someone has to go with Clair and me."

"I will," Seshe said. "I love the forest in Wnelder Vee. I won't be any better or worse at catching poopsies there then I would be here, but I can give the alarm if I see one."

"I'll go, too," Dhana said. "Same reason."

"Me too," Irenne said, fluffing out her long brown ponytail. "I really want to see Laban get caught."

"I'll stay here if Puddlenose and Christoph want to go. I'll guard our forest," Diana said.

"I'll talk to the boys," Clair said, and to no one's surprise, returned to say that they'd volunteered to help.

As always, the prospect of leaving Mearsies Heili made CJ feel homesickness before she even left. S he went out to enjoy the remainder of the afternoon in a good run.

The air was so cold it hurt to breathe fast, but she snuffed in the pine fragrance, her breath clouding. The sun set before she returned, starlight glowing off her breath. The snow crunched and squeaked underfoot as she sang and listened to the winter-sharpened echoes of her voice ringing back. Dhana danced by once, flitting like a shadow-spirit, light as wind-twirled snowflakes.

The girls by unspoken agreement all camped out in the main room of the Junky, before a cozy fire, with various hot drinks to choose from. Their talk ranged from "Remember the time . . ." to "What if?"s, brightened — always — by a steady bombardment of jokes.

The prospect of separation drew them together, and the possibility of danger made the fire brighter, the chocolate tastier, the jokes funnier. No one argued that night, or went to sleep angry, and while there may have been worries, no one was haunted by the thought that they would not all be together again when the adventure was over.

The only one who worried that there might be too much danger was Seshe, but she comforted herself with the reminder that Clair would be with them. The wilder girls always listened to Clair, and she was grateful that the girls who needed the most protection, Sherry and Gwen, were staying home.

And of course they all wore their medallions. Even if calling Hreealdar to their aid was an uncertain prospect at best, at least they all had a transfer spell, which would shift them straight back to the underground hideout.

When one woke, all woke, and Sherry said cheerfully, "Breakfast first!"

"What if it's mealtime in Everon?" CJ asked, and then remembered that it would be more or less the middle of the afternoon.

"Then we'll get two breakfasts," Irenne said. "How is that a bad thing?"

"Now *that* tempts me to go with you," Gwen said, and Falinneh nodded so hard her braids flapped.

"You can have two breakfasts here," Clair said, getting up

and folding her quilt.

"True," Falinneh said, wrinkling her nose. "Why isn't that as good?"

"Because it's more fun at someone else's place," Sherry said, round blue gaze earnest as always, her curls bouncing around her face. "If you have two at home, you're a pig. But if you have one at home, and one someplace else, then you're being a good guest."

Diana's brief, rare grin flashed. "I think it's because it feels like you're getting away with something."

The girls who had escaped from unfair or onerous situations flickered glances of agreement at that.

"We'll eat here first. In case." Clair's kitten laugh escaped her, then she added, "Everyone pack one change of winter clothes, and extra socks. They might have a cleaning frame, but that won't dry anything, remember. We'll begin the transfers to Everon when you're ready."

Twenty-eight

THEY ARRIVED IN TAHRA'S palace to find an atmosphere of tension that was all the more unsettling because of Tahra's fierce, triumphant grin, and Commander Dei's retreat behind scrupulous protocol. It didn't take much insight to guess that he had been doing his best to keep Tahra home, which she adamantly refused to do.

"I'm going," she said. "I *will* see justice! As for protection, Morgeh Troiad sent Dtheldevor. The pirates can protect me better than any of Glenn's silly recruits."

The privateers were newly arrived, along with Senrid, Liere, and little Lyren, the latter two having just arrived in Marloven Hess for a visit. Senrid had talked Liere into coming; in addition to her Dena Yeresbeth abilities, she was also, he recollected, one of the few people Tahra listened to.

Liere looked worried, as usual, but willing, as Arthur (also there) said to Clair and CJ, "We might need Liere to scout by mind." He tapped his head. "I think at least one of the enemy has Dena Yeresbeth."

"Adam," said Liere, surprising them all. "And maybe more. But I'm certain about him."

Senrid whistled. "He sure hid it well."

Everyone contemplated that, many still finding it difficult to equate Adam with sinister intent.

When Roderic Dei, feeling helpless to get Tahra to see reason, gave Lyren a significant glance, "We'll guard her," Senrid said. "And if it looks like she might be in any danger, a lot of us know transfer magic."

"Perfect," Tahra said stonily, her thin, sallow cheeks mottled. "If anyone else comes to help me, they can follow on. The Knights can ride with us as far as the fog, and see to it that we have supplies. All we have to do is chase the murderers out to be caught by the best of the Knights."

"We're going? Now?" CJ asked, having been almost the last to arrive, and in an undervoice to Clair, "I'm glad we ate breakfast at home!"

"Tahra does seem to be determined." Clair eyed the pack that Tahra had sitting next to her feet. From the looks of its pointy shape, there had to be at least one weapon in it.

"Let us go," Tahra said, and started determinedly for the door, everyone trailing after.

Tahra was anxious to reach the fog by nightfall, so that they could penetrate it while they still had light, and if necessary find a place to camp and get busy in the morning. She feared that if they delayed any longer, Detlev's villains would assuredly escape. If they hadn't already. In her mind, the enemy would be rounded up in a day, and on trial by the next. She had been planning her speech at their execution ever since they found the magical fog.

Because the trip was made on horseback, they accomplished it well before dark. But here they encountered the first setback. The company Commander Dei had left reported that the fog extended for an appreciable distance.

Tahra listened, white-lipped. She had assumed that the ward would be about the size of a village square, or perhaps the equivalent of the Knights' parade ground.

"We can still go in," Senrid said. "As a group. If we don't see them, we hole up until morning, then reconnoiter."

The word "reconnoiter" had an authoritative sound. Everyone agreed, and so the allies ventured past the thin fog, into a quiet meadow dotted with hickory, shrubs, and tangled old oak.

Puddlenose said, "There are trails here, though they aren't real fresh."

"Could be anything," Seshe said.

"Right. We don't know how long this ward's been here,"

Arthur put in.

"Whatever is going on with the magic, I see trails. They have to lead somewhere." Puddlenose elbowed Christoph. "Let's do a quick scout. I'm for a real bed if we can get it." They ran on ahead, vanishing among the trees.

Irenne pointed upward. "Snow coming, and tents never keep the wind out during a storm." She glanced meaningfully at little Lyren. "She'll freeze."

"Let's push on. See what we can find. Then lay down a watch perimeter," Senrid said. "There are enough of us."

"Listen this way, too," Arthur said to Liere, tapping his forehead.

"I am." She looked frightened but determined.

The clouds thickened overhead and snow had begun to drift down when Puddlenose and Christoph pelted back down a trail. "Found us a spot to camp!"

"It's clean inside," Christoph added, and Senrid's brows lifted.

They led the way down an adjacent trail into a thick oak grove, beyond which lay an empty, dilapidated one-room cottage that looked as if it had been repaired quite recently, with scavenged wood freshly fit together with shiny nails. The newer end boasted a sleeping loft snugged under the roof, directly above an old ceramic stove, into which a firestick was put at once.

CJ and Irenne exchanged mutters about poopsie cooties as the Mearsieans laid out their sleep rolls on the platform, but no one paid attention.

The stove, like most at that part of the world, had the usual shallow cook-bowl, but also a flat metal square that could be used for simmer-cooking. With practical efficiency, a couple of Dtheldevor's sailors got a huge pot of spicy bean-rice-tomato soup slowly thickening on the stove.

Lyren ran around and climbed up and down the ladder, stopping to stare, round-eyed, when Dtheldevor bawled genial curses. The Warren twins, whom Dtheldevor summarily appointed the evening's cooks, beat together some pan-biscuit batter and spread a sheet with olive oil. When it was sending up curls of steam, they put dollops of dough on to bake.

The aromas drew everyone inward toward the stove. That first meal balanced between awkward and interesting as the company tried to get used to one another. They'd scraped the last of the soup and scarfed the crumbs of the bread when CJ suggested they do storytelling.

Suddenly Puddlenose tipped his head, his hand halfway to his mouth with his last bite of bread.

Christoph cupped a hand around his ear and grinned, pointing upward.

"Poopsies?" Dhana whispered.

The three boys looked at each other, then Dtheldevor pointed each to a window or a door, scooping in a couple of the Warrens for backup. These six crept noiselessly out.

"I'll get ready," Tahra stated as she reached into her pack and pulled out a crossbow.

Several looks were sidled at Liere, who got to her feet, walked over, and crouched down by Tahra.

"Let me understand," Liere said very softly, so softly her voice didn't carry much past the two of them. "Are you really planning to kill any of them you see? I thought you were going to offer them a fair trial. If you are not, I want to know, because if so, then I'm going home."

Tahra flushed. "Then why are you here, if you don't think they deserve death for what happened to my brother? To Carsen, and Karhin, and her king, and all those people in Sartor, and who knows how many others?"

"I'm sorry for what happened to your brother," Liere said. "I *hate* what happened to Karhin. But if we start killing, what's the difference between us and them?" She put up her hand. "I don't mean if a fight turned into life and death. I mean picking that crossbow up, and going out and looking for any boy to shoot dead, including the ones no one has actually seen with a weapon."

Everyone had stopped talking. Liere's attention snagged on a glowing, glimmering thing hanging from Clair's medallion. She blinked away the distraction and said, "I don't know if it makes a difference. But for the sake of truth. The king of Colend, and the mages in Sartor, were not murdered by any of these boys."

Dtheldevor approached, having come back in halfway through this speech.

"Pinecones on the roof," she said, and elbowed her way toward Tahra, short hair swinging about her genial, sun-browned face. "Now lookit here. I don't hold no friendliness toward them spit-faced farts, but the fact is, after I was took, when t'others went to lay out Carsen for his Disappearance, they found he only had a small cut on his ribs. So he did die inna fight with that MV, but Sharly says it was its ol' heart, wore out by things all along, that done fer him. Further, he tole me long ago he always wanted to go in a fight. So there's that."

From the doorway, Sharly the centaur nodded her head.

Dtheldevor continued. "I did have me a fight with MV, and he's mighty quick with a blade. I'd like to have a second go, but I ain't yet going for to gut him. Not 'less he guts one o' us. If he does, then everything changes."

Tahra looked down at her gripped hands. "One of them did gut my brother."

Dtheldevor made a sharp gesture with her palm up. "That was a duel. I'm talkin' 'bout cold stalkin' and killin'. That's the sorta shite *they* do."

Tahra sighed, hating that everyone seemed to be against her. Against *logic.*

Dtheldevor jerked her chin at the door. "So, to tomorrow. I think we oughta go out in twos." She eyed Liere and Lyren, then amended, "Threes. Or more. But unless they come at us board 'an carry, take no prizners, we oughta agree on no killing."

Senrid's gaze flicked between Clair, Liere, and Tahra.

"Shoot 'em in the knee. And a trial." Tears of anger glinted in Tahra's eyes.

"Thank you, Tahra," Liere said sincerely.

Clair turned away, the thing on her medallion glinting then vanishing in the folds of her sturdy blue tunic. "Anyone have a story or song?" she asked, as Liere blinked at the medallion ornament. She could feel the strong pull of magic, but it was a slippery sort—utterly unfamiliar.

"I'll start," Sarmonwilda said. "Time to bring down the sun."

The rat-hole stretched between two rivers, one of which was fed by a ridge at the west end, curved around a waterfall. When they'd first considered adopting this spot, Adam had insisted on including this ridge because of its painterly prospects, though it would have made a natural barrier for that end of their territory.

Laban had united his voice to Adam's, his unspoken belief

the larger area they held, the better. MV agreed, though he'd have to help with the mage work. He pointed out that the highpoint of the entire territory lay on the ridge, and they might need a lookout in all directions. David and Roy, with MV helping, laid the wards down over the hilly area beyond, which had added a month to their work.

Before Curtas was chased back by the Knights, Errol and Leef tested the ridge, discovering that not that much could be seen beyond treetops in most directions, but there were a couple of caves on the west side that they'd overlooked on their initial exploration. Fallbacks were always good, and caves made great hideys during stalks.

Then Ferret, who had gone back to check on the success of his obscuring of Curtas's trail, appeared at a stumbling run. He stood before David and MV, hands on his knees, head hanging as sweat dripped off his nose. "Riding . . .Knights . . .trying to . . .find a way in."

David looked up sharply. "They have anyone underage?"

"Yep. Heard him . . .saying he . . .didn't see fog."

"Shit," MV exclaimed.

"They've found the magic." David threw down his carving knife. "Let's fall back to the moss house."

"But we just got done building," Leef protested, pointing up to the new sleeping platform.

"We picked this shack for the same reason it'll doubtless be the first place they'll find: it stands out. I'll scrape out the Destination pattern. Pack up."

At dawn the next morning they hauled their belongings away. Curtas and Laban remained behind to clean up any signs of their recent residence, and used brooms to obscure their footsteps as they began their retreat.

They hadn't gone far when they heard voices ringing through the trees. Both recognized those voices: Puddlenose and Christoph, obviously scouting.

Curtas worked silently next to Laban, who cursed under his breath; to him, being invaded was worse because he liked both boys.

When they reached the moss house and reported, David said, "That was close."

No one argued.

"First light, we'll divide up. Make paths leading them around and around, toward the boundaries. Maybe they'll go out again and keep going. Ferret, I want you to shadow them. Find how many besides the two Laban and Curtas heard."

Noser whined belligerently, "Why don't we just drop 'em?"

David's first impulse had been readiness for a war, but Detlev's words still stung. He took a moment to study Roy's shuttered expression, Curtas's averted gaze, and Adam's open dismay, then said, "If they come for blood, sure. Otherwise, no."

"Why not?" Noser demanded. "We're just gonna let them walk in and take over *our* rat-hole?"

"No chance, Nose," Silvanas said, gently thumping Noser's shoulder. "We gotta lie low. Until we get different orders."

Laban said to Noser, "Vana's right. Also. If Puddlenose brought any of the kings in their alliance and we drop them, we'll get whole armies sicced on us."

"But—" Noser began.

Roy said, "And mages."

"But we can—"

"What can light magic do?" Rolfin asked, looking askance.

"Yeah, that's just what I was gonna say," Noser shrilled.

MV remembered Tsauderei's promise of stone spells in his garden. "I wouldn't put anything past that old geezer in Sarendan. You kill any of them, and he'll be on us fast. He's the one that trapped Siamis, remember."

"Lie low," David repeated. "Those were our orders."

Noser sighed, slumping in surrender.

David eyed him. "If they crowd us, we'll give them enough heat to drive them off, at least long enough for Roy and me to break whatever wards they're laying over ours. Then we're smoke."

Noser saw everyone agreeing, including Vana, but he was thinking, there should be a way to make things fun.

Both invaders and defenders woke the next day when the sun began to blue the forest. Everything was frosty cold, sounds cracking like icicles, even laughter.

Arthur muttered to himself, testing any changes in the wards. Senrid was more quiet about scanning changes with dark magic, but stopped when Arthur said to Liere, "I feel some kind of magic, really strong, nearby. I don't know what it is."

"Is it bad?" Liere asked.

"No. But it's there."

Senrid figured he'd lay aside the dark magic unless it was necessary. Lighter magic was exasperating with its meticulous safeguards, and he wasn't nearly as adept in it, but he didn't want trouble with Arthur.

Seshe and Clair volunteered to cook for the day, and Puddlenose and Christoph offered to do the cleanup. The girls made pancakes, which everyone doused with honey or preserves. While they ate, Senrid said, "We don't know how big this territory of theirs is, or where it lies. I suggest we split into four groups, two feeling their way in either direction along the magical border to see how far it goes. I'll take one of them. Other two groups scout between, with at least one person who knows some surveying, so we can begin a map."

Liere said, "I'll stay here with Lyren and listen on the mental plane."

"I want to go!" Lyren protested.

"Snowdrifts are bigger than you are," Dtheldevor said genially.

Lyren had learned aboard the *Berdrer* that a captain was like a king. A loud king. So she gave up, especially when she discovered a set of chalks that Adam had inadvertently left tucked on a shelf behind the ladder to the loft.

Arthur said, "I'll take the border in one direction."

"Then we'll go inland," Clair said, swinging her hand to include her group. "Diana isn't here, but she's taught us something about surveying."

Seshe nodded.

"We'll go with Senrid," Puddlenose said, indicating Christoph and himself.

Dtheldevor said, "Then us is taking the other direction."

"I'll go with you," Tahra said to Arthur, determined to avoid the Mearsieans, because in spite of her words to Liere, she meant to kill David if she saw him. The lie was justified by the fact that the others hadn't lost anyone. They could afford to blather about justice and mercy and all that.

She sidled a glance Arthur's way, noting the sharp angles of his skinny shoulders and elbows, everything at odd angles, no symmetry. She was no good at reading expressions, but she knew from his letters how angry he was about Roy's betrayal.

She had to get him aside for some private talk.

Everybody bundled up, some covertly, or not so covertly,

taking weapons. Senrid matter-of-factly strapped on his wrist sheaths and put a knife in each boot top. Tahra was furtive about secreting her crossbow in the heavy, voluminous coat she had chosen for exactly this purpose.

They trooped out into the cold air. Senrid and Arthur split up, one venturing southwest and the other southeast. The rest stood in a clump.

Dtheldevor said, "Well, land pret' much looks the same to me, but Sarmonwilda here kin tell one tree from another, dawnsingers being raised up to land navigation, so she kin chart fer us, if it's all the same to you."

"We'll take the northeast," Sarmonwilda said in her high, clear soprano. She was small and dainty as well as flaxen-haired like the rest of the dawnsingers, quite a contrast to Dtheldevor's tall, rangy build, dark hair, and wood-brown coloring.

Dtheldevor considered the rest of her primary crew: Sharly the centaur, Joey Warren, nearly as tall as Puddlenose and as lean and tough as MV, pale-haired Ellen, the youngest of the Warrens, equally tall, and equally competent with knives and a bow, and the twin sisters, Gloriel and Peridot, short and sturdy, adequate with weapons. Gloriel wielded a mean knife in galley prep. Not so good with fighting, due to a soft heart.

Dtheldevor said to the Warrens in what for her was a low voice, "How 'bout someone stay to guard Liere. I don't think she could defend herself against a leaf falling, if them buzzards was to fall on this-here house."

Ellen said, "I'll stay."

That settled, they separated their various ways.

The Mearsieans headed straight for the ridge, visible to the northwest. On finding a path, they began to follow it, triumphant that they'd been the first to stumble upon the enemy. But as soon as they reached deeper woods, they began to lose their sense of direction, and the path seemed to double back without reason.

A couple of them were just as happy not to be encountering any enemies. The woods smelled so different from home. Seshe, sensitive to nature, recognized that this forest was far older. Not only were the trees ancient, but the things that grew on and around the trees were ancient. The layers of green formed a pattern that had long ago ceased striving to shut the other things out, as younger forests do. It all had reached a balance of infinitely slow growth that seemed meditative to her, despite the ebb and flow of seasons: the eternal tinkle-platt-rustle-hush of water here, and the creak and crack of ice there, depending on how the ground folded and air moved along it.

CJ moved determinedly, at first with dread that she worked hard to hide. She hated to admit that Detlev's boys scared her. Calling them poopsies and like insults was supposed to lessen their threat, and she pretended it did, but it really didn't work.

Being in a group meant she could watch over Clair and feel slightly more at ease. Surely no one would attack so many of them, but even so, she kept urging everyone to talk in a whisper if they had to talk at all, and she kept watching in all directions as she slogged along in the icy mud.

Dhana was the first to consider the trees. "This trail isn't going anywhere," she said.

Seshe glanced around, murmuring, "I agree."

"So let's leave it," Dhana said.

She leaped up onto a mossy low branch, pulling the others after as if by a magnet. The girls discovered that it was even easier here than at home to avoid the ground altogether, and travel from tree to tree. Up above, they could see the sun's arc better, which meant better orienteering.

They dropped back down into the snow when the light began to fade to shadowy greenish blue. Seshe took the lead, leading them unerringly back until they caught their original trail just after sunset.

They were the last ones to arrive back, Liere scanning their faces and listening on the mental plane. It was clear they had encountered no enemies, nor did they particularly care.

Senrid and Arthur had both transferred back from their stopping places, Senrid in his puzzle-solving mood, and Arthur with averted gaze. Liere knew Arthur well. One look at Tahra's compressed lips made it clear that those two had come to some kind of agreement that they were not going to share, and Arthur had a tight mind-shield. Tahra avoided meeting anyone's gaze, especially Liere's.

On the sailors' exploration, Sarmonwilda had used her early dawnsinger training to gather an abundance of fallen nuts, still accessible under the thickest trees this early in winter. She offered to cook dinner, to which Clair and Seshe gladly agreed. With Gloriel's help Sarmonwilda cooked up a stew with nuts, herbs, and root vegetables she'd scavenged from the picked-over garden out back of the house.

Dinner passed with a superficial mood of harmony. Toward the end, Irenne flipped back her light brown ponytail, and said, "What shall we do? My idea is, we perform one of our plays."

Clair looked up, her long, waving white hair swinging down to her waist in front, hiding her medallion, but Liere sensed it there. Odd. She had no success whatsoever with magic studies, but that thing hanging on her necklace next to the medallion felt like . . .a *little* like the dyr. And yet no one else seemed to feel it.

Her imagination, of course, she decided, as CJ said doubtfully, "Without Falinneh? She always does the funny parts."

"I can do both roles," Irenne said, chin up. "You know I can."

Irenne beckoned the rest of the Mearsieans up to the sleeping platform, whence fierce whispering issued as everyone else passed dirty dishware back, and Arthur and Puddlenose dunked and stacked.

Irenne led the way down the ladder with an important air, and the girls took their places in the center of the circle. "This is Laban meeting a goat and pig at a bridge," Irenne said, and straight-away hunched over, whining, "My name is Laban, and I'm a sinister and evil Norsundrian, so I have to go first . . ."

The play might have been funnier if there had not been quite so many private jokes, but the others sat politely, Senrid smothering yawns until his eyes watered, as he'd woken first and perforce lay still, his mind running possible plans, until someone else had finally stirred.

Then Dtheldevor's group offered some sea ballads. After these, everyone agreed that an early night would be welcome after a long day of slogging through the cold and finding little.

Senrid lay in his bedroll, mentally reviewing the emerging map based on what everyone had reported. Detlev's boys' hideaway was far larger than anyone had expected, involving months of magic, maybe longer than a year if Roy was their only mage. They needed more systematic reconnaissance.

Twenty-nine

Day Two

THE ALLIES' SECOND DAY was much the same as the first: exploration, while, unknown to them, Detlev's boys shadowed them from a distance. Curtas had spotted Arthur marking the magical traces of the rat-hole's eastern curve. He ran back to report to Roy, who spent the afternoon pacing Arthur unseen, trying to gauge Arthur's inner mind, which was protected behind a firm mind-shield.

That next morning, Arthur brooded along familiar mental paths as he tramped along beside silent Tahra, who had her crossbow out and cocked. Once they'd agreed that if they saw David she would shoot him and claim it an accident, and if they saw Roy Arthur could drop him with a stone spell, neither had wanted to talk much more.

Arthur found himself increasingly uncomfortable with that agreement. He felt dirty, rather than righteous. Sometimes he glanced at Tahra stumping along. He thought he could sense her murderous intent, but of course that had to be his imagination. He didn't have Dena Yeresbeth, because he heard no one's thoughts, and even his sensing of mood obviously couldn't be trusted, or surely he have discovered the falsity under Roy's guise of friendship.

When the day's close brought the allies back to the house, they found a surprise: three newcomers, Leander and Kyale in company with tall, dark-eyed Rel, whose appearance Senrid, Dtheldevor, and Tahra hailed with not-quite-sufficiently subdued relief. If (*when*, Tahra thought privately) things came to a fight, Rel would be of far more use than most of the others put together.

The Mearsieans welcomed Kyale among them, CJ looking at her with puzzlement. After time spent around Sarmonwilda, CJ found that Kyale's silvery hair, and her pale-colored eyes the same shade as a frozen lake, made her wonder just what lay in the Leroran princess's background, because she knew there were not any dawnsingers at that end of the Halian subcontinent.

The newcomers had pulled a cart packed with foodstuffs sent by the Sandrials. The prize was fresh bread and a cake that had been wrapped hot from the oven. Setting these on the porcelain stove restored some of the warmth, and they enjoyed a good dinner while catching up with one another's news.

Rel knew everyone there, so he took his time walking around to greet each friend. But when he sat down, it was beside Senrid, who said with a quick look, "I'm glad you're here. So far we haven't seen any of them, but that could change suddenly."

Rel grunted assent, then passed the bread to Senrid, his mind returning to the fog that the Knight guides had seen, and Rel hadn't. That meant he was still underage as far as the magic was concerned, but like that sun below the horizon before dawn, not for long. For a few breaths his mind ranged back to standing in the center of the royal Purad with Atan on New Year's Firstday, and the two of them removing the Child Spell.

Rel had expected more of a sense of great change, but he'd felt absolutely nothing. They'd stood there in the middle of the ancient labyrinth, braced against the piercing cold, the stars overhead glittering like shards of ice, then Atan had said, "I don't know what to expect next."

He'd agreed, wondering how their friendship might change as adulthood claimed them at last. For the first time he felt awkward with her, and wondered if she felt the same. But he wasn't sure how to ask without making things even more awkward. So they'd walked back in silence, welcoming the noise and music spilling from the New Year's party in Dragon

Hall.

Milestones, he thought, seemed to be sudden when acknowledged by one's community . . .

". . .with Rel here," Puddlenose said, splintering his thoughts.

"What can I do?" Rel tried to get his mind to make the shift from Sartor to Wnelder Vee.

Senrid leaned forward, wrists resting on his bent knees. He sat against a wall, with an unimpeded view of the windows and door. His profile was utterly unchanged from the summer up at Tsauderei's.

Rel wondered if Senrid would ever remove the Child Spell as Senrid said, "Scout with me. I'll ask Leander if he wants to continue with the border mapping. The others do their best, but Sarmonwilda thinks in tree patterns. Dtheldevor is useless for navigating on land. The Mearsieans are good enough at surveying, but I think they're looking for scenery more than enemies. You know something about scouting, right?"

"Enough," Rel said, understanding that by "scouting" Senrid meant hunting down Detlev's boys. Well, that was why he'd come. "Spiral out?"

Senrid flashed a grin. "Let's see how far we get."

Day Three

The third day saw changes, first perceived by Liere, with her long-honed instincts of the solitary person who never quite fits anywhere. But she said nothing, having known from the beginning that she was there because of the lingering reputation of The Girl Who Saved the World.

Siamis was not going to descend on them. There would be no handy dyra to defeat an enchantment. And Detlev's boys, if they were there, all had practiced mind-shields. As would be expected from anyone raised by Detlev. But the others seemed to like the idea of her being there, listening on the mental plane. Even though she heard nothing of use, while Lyren scrawled chalk drawings over the walls, whispering some kind of story to herself.

Leander and Arthur returned first that day, having finally met at the far side of the magical border. They transferred back and began to sketch landmarks onto Senrid's map. As they worked, Liere perched on the lowest rung of the ladder, knees hugged up tightly under her chin, and wondered if any of Detlev's boys got Dena Yeresbeth training. The idea filled her with a mixture of dread and envy. She was glad to be distracted by the return of Rel and Senrid, followed by Puddlenose, Christoph, and Leander.

Senrid walked up to the map and said to Arthur and Leander, "I discovered a training run up against the western end, by the ridge. Everything inland between these two rivers is prime territory for stalks. They have to have picked out this place ages ago."

"That can't mean anything good," Leander said, as Liere joined the group. "If we find huge weapons caches and supplies . . .Except it would be useless to Detlev as adults can't cross that magical border."

"Magical wards can be unmade," Senrid reminded him.

"Should we tell Tahra?" Leander asked.

"No," Liere whispered. "She is too angry." And I've failed with her, she thought miserably.

Arthur's expression tightened, and he glanced aside as Puddlenose shook his head. "Agreed. She's not toting that crossbow around underneath her coat for the fun of it."

"Right." Senrid turned his thumb up. "You can't unstart a bloodbath. We need to answer questions before taking that kind of action."

Then he grabbed the chalk to work on the map.

"Senrid," David said, "found our run. Anyone else?"

"Arthur and Leander finished tracing the border," Roy reported.

"Damn," David breathed. "What else?"

Erol said, "More. M-mear-s-siean girls. One l-looking this way." He gestured toward the upper pathway of the moss house.

As the others reacted with irritation, sighs, and expressions of *now what?* MV said, "Senrid put that together with us here?"

"I paced him," David said. "No skills in woodcraft, but it's to be expected he'd know an obstacle course when he sees one." Though they had been forbidden to even cross the border into Marloven Hess, they all knew about its famous academy. "He didn't find the start, much less figure out where we are."

"What next?" Vana said. "Invisible still?"

Ferret looked up from the moc he was repairing. "If they map the rat-hole well enough, they could bring in more searchers. Spread a dragnet. And we don't have any more winter shelters."

MV set down his whetstone and carefully tested the edge of one of his blades as he said, "Adam's waterfall hut is unlivable in this weather, but we can use it as an outpost."

David opened his hand in assent. "We'll fall back to the tree house for now. At the first sign of a dragnet, we'll shift to our secondary plan: make life so tough they decide to go back to their warm, comfortable homes."

"It's about time." MV went back to whetting his knife, slash, slash, slash. "It's about time."

Day Four

After breakfast, Senrid found Tahra crouched over the map, studying it intently. "I think the shape is off," she said.

"I'm sure it is," Senrid replied. "Until we can measure, I'm adding in landmarks, then more details in reference to those. Getting the ratios right will come."

"I'm good at measure," Tahra said. "I'll do that. I want to know where every tree and bush is, so they can't hide."

Senrid gazed at her determined face, the dull blotches of red in her sallow cheeks. Her angry eyes, with no vestige of humor. He'd mentally set aside a week at most for this exercise. He'd assumed if they were unsuccessful by then, that they'd turn the matter over to the locals. Tahra sounded like she was going to stay however long it took to get her target.

He realized he'd been staring when she colored even more, then said in a low voice, "Just the one."

Was that guilt? If she was fighting an inner battle, her thirst for vengeance seemed to be winning over any moral qualms. He didn't say anything to her. He knew she wouldn't listen to him anyway. He moved off, leaving her studying his map, and sought Liere, who lingered on the edge of the Mearsiean group as usual. Irenne was teaching Lyren how to stir batter, with the expected mess.

When Liere saw Senrid, she backed up, unnoticed by the chattering breakfast cooks, and joined him by one of the windows. "Do you sense magic on that necklace of Clair's?"

"Her medallion? All those girls wear them. They're transfer tokens, and have some other minor wards," he said. "And I guess they can summon that lightning-horse. Or, at least try."

"No, I mean the thing, whatever it is, hanging off of her medallion."

"Oh, that shell thing? Puddlenose gave that to her. I happened to be there when he got it from some old woman. It was in Everon, before the enchantment lifted, not long after I met them."

Senrid's mouth thinned. He still did not know who had wrenched him away from where he'd been and put him with the two Mearsiean boys, who he'd never met in his life. He hated the thought of an unknown someone (Lilith the Guardian?) interfering in his life like that, a casual display of power that disturbed his late night wakeful periods almost as often as Detlev's remembered threats.

Liere, seeing the tension in his face, dropped the subject as he unbuttoned his shirt pocket and pulled out a shank. She knew he usually used them for transfer tokens.

"Speaking of transfers," he said. "If things get serious, take Lyren and use this. It's got three transfers left on it. The word is 'Choreid' twice. It'll take you to Choreid Dhelerei."

"Serious?" Liere repeated, and glanced back at Tahra. Senrid watched Liere's golden eyes widen then shutter. She said, "I brought Lyren because I thought it would be good for Tahra to see her—and to . . .I don't know . . ."

"Help get her to forget Sartora?"

"Yes. She seems to like small children. And I thought, if we're just here merely to chase those boys out, it would be something like a game."

Senrid sighed. "Became a different game soon's we got them trapped."

"Why don't they leave?" Liere asked. "They have to know we're here."

Senrid said, "They put a lot of work into this retreat. Probably thought we'd look around, see no one, move on. They might still be thinking that."

Liere studied him, a slight pucker between her brows. "At your academy. They do this kind of thing, right?"

"Yep."

"So . . .if we stay . . .what would come next?"

Senrid opened his hands. "If they're thinking of this as a war game in which the goal is to hold the ground, they'll make it hot, and try to drive us out. Maybe grab prisoners. Make demands, if they want it badly enough. If the steel comes out, the goal is pretty much what Tahra wants: a body count."

Liere glanced at the Mearsieans. "This is a different game for them. Like hide and find. Clair won't want them to stay if things get horrible." She turned her considering gaze to Senrid. "What about you?"

His toothy grin flashed. "I'll play any game."

"Breakfast!" CJ shouted, causing a general scramble.

After the meal, they divided up once again, and as Lyren watched wistfully, wanting to follow, Liere wondered if she ought to take Lyren and leave right then. Senrid had been so very careful about his warning, not a hint of how Liere was not only useless, but would have to be defended.

All true.

She fingered the transfer token, then let out a breath. If Kyale could stay, she could, as well. Most of her friends were here, and she had to know what would happen. Until she was sent, or there was danger to Lyren, she'd stay.

While she brooded, the Mearsieans invited Kyale to join them, which she gladly accepted. They set out in a group, their intent more exploration than map-making or chasing.

CJ waited restlessly to get into thick forest again so they could resume the tree-branch road. When they began taking to the trees, Kyale was dismayed, but decided to follow. She didn't like dragging her skirts in the snow and getting them wet and muddy. She gained courage when she saw Irenne launch skillfully into a venerable oak, managing her frilly skirts easily with one hand.

Once she was on the tree branch, Kyale discovered the delights of moving through the air over ground. It wasn't nearly as much fun as flying had been in Tsauderei's Valley, but this was close, the broad branches easier to walk on than the thick snowdrifts.

They picked a new direction, led by Seshe, who had glimpsed a promising grotto the day before. From a distance they sounded like a flock of birds as they exchanged comments and laughed, swinging, jumping, and running along enormous branches; as no one had seen any danger, they'd forgotten about being silent, so they never noticed Leef shadowing them.

When the ground began to rise, the trees thinned, interrupted by mossy, vine-covered rocky outcroppings. Seshe breathed in the heady air, looking around in delight. There were enough evergreens to lend color to the grays and browns of winter-bare trees, with blue-white snow below.

"Ah," she said, and clambered down an ancient hickory.

Kyale froze on her branch, mouth agape when Dhana swung through the air from a branch overhead, turned a somersault, and landed lightly as a bird.

When Kyale finally made it to the ground, she found the other girls clumped up at the top of a narrow trail. Green-covered stones had been set into a steep incline below a hanging curtains of leaves held together by thorns.

"That is the best thing I've seen here yet," Dhana said, touching the leaf curtain. These were thick, waxy leaves, not unlike leddas, the marsh plant from which shoes and belts and harnesses were made.

With an eye to those thorns, they carefully parted the curtain and one by one descended the steps, to find a low cottage built into the side of the hill, its roof covered with snow and pine needles.

Seshe glanced back as CJ pushed past her to scout first, heart hammering in her throat as she clutched her medallion with one hand. She could transfer out if she had to. Of course so could Clair, but CJ hated the thought of her friend in danger. CJ loathed danger, but at least so far, she'd somehow managed to get out of it, probably because she was . . .not what anyone would think of as good. From early childhood she remembered a horrible saying, *Only the good die young,* and Clair was good. CJ made too many mistakes, due to her temper, her grudges, and jealousy, to ever be anything like good.

So she would always go first.

CJ eased down the last few steps to a low window, and peeked in.

The cottage had one room. "It's empty," she said to the others ranged up behind her on the steps, faces ruddy from the cold.

One by one the girls climbed in through the open window, and cautiously ventured into the low-ceilinged room centered around a fireplace carved out of stone to look like a tree. Clair noted scraped spots on the stone floor where furnishings, or trunks, had recently sat. Dhana closed her eyes, listening to the trickle of water somewhere nearby.

Seshe and CJ took in the stone-carved branches worked up the entire wall and reaching around one side of the room, where silken leaves had been made in a kind of collage. "Wow," CJ breathed. "I wonder who made *that?*"

"There has to be a good story," Irenne stated, but the giggle in her voice made it clear she was not talking about the stone tree.

CJ and Seshe turned. Before the opposite wall Irenne and Kyale stood laughing. Someone long ago had painted a historical scene, faded on one side, the faces merely blobs, the details flaked off. The other half had been restored skillfully in bright colors, each figure distinctive in expression. But in the middle, the central figure, a queen or hero, surely, had a wolf head somewhat roughly painted on her neck, tongue lolling ridiculously. To the right, a man holding a bow in a dramatic post had a pig's head painted over his, with drool dripping down.

"Someone went to a lot of trouble," CJ said, turning around to the others. "Adam?"

"No," Clair said, her eyes narrowed. "At least, not the pig and wolf. Adam is too good at painting. Those are sloppy compared to the rest."

"It's also mean," Seshe said.

"Mean!" CJ repeated. "He's a poopsie!"

Clair sighed, then said as she gazed at the pig head, "I can't remember Adam ever being mean. Roy, either. But he's one of them. I don't get it."

"We haven't yet discovered what mean things they've done," CJ said. "Except for Roy. Arthur says Roy snuck a lot of advanced magical knowledge while pretending to be one of us, which I guess is mean."

Clair nodded slowly. "It's not so much mean as sneaky. Maybe those two were raised to be spies."

"Adam knew Karhin," CJ said, looking at the wolf's long white teeth.

Clair's head dropped forward, her hair swinging down, but she couldn't hide the hurt caused by the memory.

"They were here," Dhana said, sniffing. "I smell humans on the air. And food."

"I think we'd better leave," Clair said, looking around. The delightful discovery now felt vaguely menacing, as if inimical eyes watched from beyond those thick pines, and the stone outcropping above the fireplace wall.

In reverse order they left the moss house and hurried up the stairs and away.

Full of their news, they started back, to be caught by an incoming snow storm. At first it was light flakes, but before long the world turned white. They rushed up into the trees again, figuring slippery branches would be better than floundering in drifts. CJ, Clair, and Seshe continued to feel as if they were watched, and everyone froze in shock when Kyale let out a shriek that would have reverberated through the entire wood had not the falling snow muffled it.

"Someone threw a pinecone at me!"

Dhana, behind her, shook her head. "Fell."

"Let's hurry, before this snow turns into a blizzard," Clair said.

Trusting to Seshe's woods sense, they slowly made their way back.

The light had begun to fade when they slogged through heavy drifts to the house and fell into warmth and light. They were the last ones in.

Dtheldevor bellowed over the noise of general chatter, "Anybody nail one of them chum-sucking pissbuckets? I got nuttin'."

"Saw a couple shadows moving." Leander turned his thumb to the northwest. "Not sure if that was animals or my imagination."

"One of them hurled a pinecone at me," Kyale said with a definitive air.

"I still think it fell out of a tree," Dhana muttered.

"Somebody dumped snow on me, and ran away cackling," Christoph said. "Almost sure it was the little blond one."

Everyone turned to face him, their varying expressions revealing surprise, dismay, worry, and Tahra's flicker of exultation.

Annoyed that no one was saying that snow had just fallen on *him*, Kyale dragged attention back to herself again. "We found a house. And Clair thinks they were *there!*"

"The stone floor was scraped in places," Clair said.

"That explains the snow," Rel said to Christoph. "You must

have gotten close without knowing it."

"I *still* think one of them threw a pinecone at me," Kyale stated, hands on hips.

Dtheldevor said, "Now we got 'em up against a lee shore, and we got the wind."

To the puzzled looks, Senrid said, "They're going to push back. The snow attack on Christoph might be considered the first—" He was going to say *arrow*, but a glance at Tahra made him correct that to, ". . .move in the game." And, with another glance at Tahra, "It could as easily have been a weapon. We know they're capable. But they haven't."

"Yet." Tahra bit out the word. "It's all a game to them, but Glenn is still dead." She glanced at Clair, then rubbed her forehead. "But our plan is to drive them beyond the magic border so the Knights can get them. We shall, *should*." She caught herself, remembering that she was not the only monarch here, and Wnelder Vee was not her country. "We should form into a line so we can see each other, and search."

Rel glanced down at the map, then shook his head. "Aren't enough of us for a dragnet."

Senrid said, "We have a general sense of what's where, except for this ridge over here. I suggest we go out in our groups but move fast. See if we can push a couple of them to the border, at least—"

The flicker of a transfer startled everyone, then surprise gave way to relief when they recognized Terry of Erdrael Danara.

As soon as he recovered, he looked around, and a flash of recognition—of acknowledgement—passed between Tahra, Arthur, and Terry. They all knew Terry was angry on Karhin's behalf; Senrid and Rel, who caught that look, suspected some sort of secret plan, and Liere looked away, oppressed by all that was unsaid.

Thirty

Day Five

ARTHUR WOKE AND IMMEDIATELY did a magic scan. Senrid, as usual awake long before anyone else, watched covertly, and noticed Arthur looking around with a puzzled expression.

Senrid sat up, miming question.

"I think there's something here," Arthur whispered. "But not like anything I've ever . . ." He shook his head. "Maybe it's just the wards. I can feel them changing."

"So can I," Senrid said. "But I don't sense anything else."

"Then it's my imagination. At any rate, it's not harming us."

Their conversation, soft as it was, woke one or two, who then woke the others nearby. They took turns walking through the cleaning frame Arthur had made, several wondering how much longer they'd have to sleep in the same room. Tahra hated it more each day, but that hatred was a mere candle to the sun of her dedicated hatred of her brother's assassin.

Leander, who had spent much of his early life as a forest outlaw, went out to dig through the garden in hopes of finding something he could use to add to the breakfast, as Seshe set about whipping up quickbreads from the bag of flour from the Sandrials' supply cart.

After eating, the allies divided into their usual groups, the plan of the day to make noise in order to push the enemy into retreat. They struck out in separate directions.

Seshe led the Mearsiean group, heading for a part of the woodland they had yet to see. Enough snow had fallen to make the tree highway a necessity for moving fast. Clair slipped along behind Seshe, her white head blending with the snow-dusted evergreens as she looked back and forth.

When they ran out of chatter, Irenne kept up running commentary, then switched to one of Falinneh's plays, speaking all the different parts, which kept Kyale in a trill of laughter.

When the trees thinned out before a rocky scree, they jumped down and began climbing. Kyale, in an attempt to mimic Irenne, started making up a long conversation about Detlev's boys on the run, scared of bugs, tripping over their own feet, mistaking a hill for a castle. Except for the conceit of the boys being the stupid ones, it was pretty much a repeat of Falinneh's play.

The girls laughed to be good natured, and Kyale, reveling in the attention, kept on, repeating herself tirelessly when she ran out of ideas until Dhana nudged Seshe in one direction. They all knew how responsive Dhana was to water, so Seshe obediently turned, pulling the others like beads on a string up a narrow trail.

On the top of the hill, Adam watched in both directions. To the right, the girls wound their way slowly, ducking gnarled old branches, as they worked their way toward the rise. On the other side of the hill, Leander, Terry, and Arthur made their way steadily into the older section of the forest, where the boys' treehouse retreat was located.

Adam sighed. He didn't know a lot of magic beyond the basics, but he had spent enough time around mages to recognize that Arthur was repeating some kind of tracer, which would probably lead straight to Roy, busy fighting the unseen mages over the rat-hole protections.

Adam stood, faced left, chopped his hand, then stabbed three fingers in the direction Arthur and his two companions were going. Then he sat down again, mostly hidden, to continue his watch until Ferret came to relieve him.

Down below, MV and Rolfin slipped through the trees, shadowing the three boys until they made a turn up a narrow path above the stream feeding the river.

MV jerked his chin, two fingers thrust out.

Rolfin eased around and down the slope above the stream. There, he chose a fallen branch and stomped it.

Crack!

Up above, Leander stilled, and faced downslope, the other two copying him as he said, "That was deliberate. I *thought* someone was pacing us —"

He didn't get any farther than that because MV took three steps through the soft snow and palm-heeled Leander into a rock fall, Terry into a tangle of reeds, and Arthur straight into the stream. By the time Leander and Terry had picked themselves up and slogged over to haul shocked, shivering Arthur out of the water, MV and Rolfin were gone.

From the lookout post on the hilltop, Seshe's voice echoed back, "Oh! Oh! Oh!"

Utterly unaware of being seen from above, the girls stared down into a little valley so sheltered that it had escaped winter so far. Trees, bare above, here brandished leaves with the glowing-ember remains of scarlet, pumpkin, orange, umber leaves, contrasting with the dark evergreens.

Noser appeared on their trail, silently laughing a challenge up at Adam. Then in quick, soundless steps, he followed the girls who, in turn, followed Seshe into a tunnel of tree branches arched overhead. Another sharp turn toward the plash of water. Ice rimed the edges of the stream, not yet frozen. Icicles hung here and there, glowing with crystal drops, and at the bottom of the stream lay a king's ransom in jewel-colors, leaves of maroon, four different reds, amber, and emerald.

"Wow," CJ breathed.

But Seshe wasn't done with her discoveries yet. "Look here," she called from farther down the trail.

Little runnels of water, or melt, made the trail slippery. Irenne held her skirts up as she followed Clair and CJ, from her manner lost in some gracious-lady daydream, judging from her poised walk and faraway expression. Kyale watched her with a mixture of admiration and a little resentment, as Irenne was not a princess, but she was acting like one. But she reminded herself that the Mearsieans never paid the least heed to distinctions of rank. In Irenne's story world, she was a runaway princess.

Kyale wished sourly that she could get people to remember that she was a real one as she heel-toed behind, using her most poised walk in case they might be seen.

Dhana vanished ahead with a skip and a leap, soundless and printless.

Another slanting turn brought the explorers to a low stone house set into the side of the hill, overshadowed and sheltered by ancient trees. Its broad window overlooked a spectacular waterfall.

"Wow," Dhana breathed. "Who lives *here?*"

"Abandoned, looks like," Seshe said. "Though maybe it belongs to someone in the warmer seasons."

CJ crouched down on her toes, and poked at bits of matte color that turned out to be tiny fragments of drawing chalk. This had to be Adam's chalk. She looked up. As the girls stood about chattering and gazing out at the magnificent view, CJ said, "I'm going to climb up on the roof. Wouldn't this make a great hideout for us?"

She didn't wait for an answer, but clambered up the far side and reached the summit of the cliff, which was sheltered from the wind by a thick tangle of blue-green cedar.

She stood at the very edge of the cliff, admiring the waterfall tumbling down to shatter into foam. She lifted her gaze to the rest of the wooded ridge, drawing breath to call to the others when two small hands smacked her shoulder blades and shoved. Her head snapped back as she catapulted out over the rocky scree, screeching and flailing toward the water.

But then a rainbow streak flickered into a slim brown girl's hand that clasped CJ's wrist and swung her in an arc before letting go. CJ tumbled on the rocky stair cut into the slope the little hut had been dug into. In summer clothes, she would have been badly scraped, but her thick woolen trousers and heavy coat and muffler protected her somewhat.

She rolled over and blinked up at the row of startled faces a few steps above, as Clair scrutinized the edge of the cliff above the hut.

"Someone pushed me," CJ squeaked, and rolled to her feet, her neck throbbing. "That was mean!"

"And could have been dangerous, in that cold water," Seshe said, "if it hadn't been for Dhana."

They turned toward the waterfall, where rainbow flickers of color flashed up and down the cascade: Dhana playing.

"Laban," CJ snarled, though she wasn't sure Laban's hands were that small. "Maybe he pushed with his fists?"

"I think it's time to go back." Clair turned in a circle, stiff and wary. "There might be more of them."

Seshe cast back one last regretful look. "Why would someone mean-spirited choose to stay in such so beautiful a place?"

"They can't *possibly* see beauty," Kyale declared.

Clair stuck her mittened hands in her armpits. "Perhaps this is a good spot for some military reason invisible to us. It's certainly hidden."

"Adam saw beautiful things," Dhana said, having rejoined them. She alone didn't wear a coat. "And painted them."

Clair looked down at the trail. "Roy saw beautiful things, too. Curtas as well."

CJ remembered that Clair had traveled with Roy and Arthur, talking of history and magic, during that horrible time CJ had been grabbed by Dejain. She hated remembering any of that, and stayed silent for the entire walk back, her shoulder blades crawling as if the handprints had left invisible marks on her.

Clair walked next to her, hearing shrill cackles on the still air, so faint she was not certain they were real or her imagination.

The wind had come up, sharp and bitterly cold by the time the girls struggled to the house. They tumbled inside, exclaiming in relief, as several people shouted, "Shut the door!"

They discovered Arthur crouched before the open stove, the firesticks inside blazing at maximum height, though that used more magic.

Terry explained that Arthur had been knocked through the thin ice to a chilly drenching. Whoever it was vanished into the swirling snow as Terry and Leander struggled to haul Arthur out of the water and get him back to safety. By the time they'd reached the house he was half-unconscious, his mouth blue. They got his icy clothes off and wrapped him in three bedrolls while Liere boiled water for Sartoran steep.

Arthur clutched the hot mug as Clair reported what had happened to the girls. Kyale and the Mearsieans were uncharacteristically silent while Seshe hung their damp coats and hats and scarves over every available surface, filling the air with the heavy aroma of steaming wool.

Senrid turned to Liere. "Can you hear cackling in the mental realm? Can they project it somehow?"

Liere considered the mental realm, knowing that it was not

quite the same for everyone. And it wasn't always minds she sensed. The dyr had been a presence, a blue glow. That ornament of Clair's gleamed like a dragonfire heart in the mental realm, though its material form resembled a shell with a spiral pattern, and not any kind of gem.

Liere said finally, "I can sense them, oh, think of it as a light through a keyhole, but completely shielded, mostly late at night. I think one is Adam," she said finally. She suspected another might be Roy, but she was so unsure. The third was unfamiliar.

"Does he know as much Dena Yeresbeth as you?" Terry asked in a low voice, as if brain-scraping mystery powers might strike him down if he spoke too loud.

Senrid flat-handed impatiently. "You don't talk about how much, like a pile of bricks. It's what you can do, like any other skill."

Liere said with care, "Their shields are very good, but . . .the one I don't know . . . The first time I sensed him, he was listening for Detlev, so I withdrew very fast. The other two times, I couldn't even sense that much. And he wasn't there very long."

"Which one is he?" Arthur asked.

"I don't know him."

"They are our age," Arthur said. "It figures Detlev must have scouted out children with DY. As well he missed Liere. You said once that Lilith was guarding you, from the time you were a baby?" he asked, as the door opened and Dtheldevor and her gang stamped in, followed by Rel.

"Yes. She taught me to shield my mind when I was very small," Liere said as soon as the door was shut.

"Then why didn't she guard the poopsies?" CJ asked from behind Clair.

Senrid glanced up. "Probably because DY can hit you at different ages. Liere got it early on. Maybe they didn't."

"Who knows? Who cares? We want to find 'em and thump 'em," Terry said.

"Thump 'em back," Dtheldevor retorted, coming up to hold her hands out to the fire, a bruise forming on her forehead. "Pegged us with pinecones," she said. "One of 'em has piss-stinkin' good aim as well as a good arm."

"They're trying to drive *us* out." Senrid glanced toward Lyren, now busy showing Irenne what she had been drawing, then lowered his voice as he turned to Liere. "I think it might be time for you two to go."

Liere listened, sick at heart. Here it was, what she'd dreaded. She was useless, a liability only.

Lyren cried out, "I don't *want* to. I *like* it here."

Senrid said to her, "There are some mean boys out there who might hurt you."

Lyren put chubby fists on her hips in mimic of Irenne. "I know some," she said with precise consonants in her soft-palate lisp. "Roy won't be mean. Adam won't be mean."

"You knew them when you were a baby, and they were pretending to be friends," Arthur said to her.

"How old is she?" Christoph whispered.

"Three going on thirty," Rel whispered back, smiling a little.

Lyren's lower lip came out — and she was three again.

"Adam," Rel said, glancing from Liere to Senrid, "has Dena Yeresbeth?"

Liere's forehead puckered. "Yes. Almost all of them do. Their control is very good. But yesterday, oh, the image was of the sky . . ." She fumbled for the words to explain how perception of them was somewhat like an eclipse, but she didn't have the words for that, either.

"Adam's harmless." Dtheldevor's shoulder jerked up. "I'd be more worried about one'a them ones handy with the weapons."

"But don't you see?" Rel said. "Adam sitting there in Wilderfeld with the Keperis, who probably never had mind-shields. Even if he wasn't in the room, he could have heard everything. Which no doubt Detlev then learned. And as for my trip to the Venn . . ."

He shut his eyes against the unsettling paradigm shift. Now the coincidences seemed deliberate: the drakans, the foolishness in the harbor, even the cooking, all to get them to the ship that Kerendal, as Cor, sailed on. Because if you had Dena Yeresbeth, you could hear all those minds on the mental plane, right?

Even Adam spilling his drawings all over the deck, to catch Cor's attention with the sketches of the drakans. Adam had been making friends with all the rulers in the alliance.

Kerendal had to have been his target.

Right?

Rel opened his eyes, to find everyone staring at him. He backtracked mentally, remembered what he'd last said, then gave his head a shake. "I don't know if it's true or building a false picture from a few coincidences, but he seemed to be going for . . ." Rel then remembered he'd told no one about his experiences with Kerendal. So he finished, "The Venn, but in any case, the pirate attack ended that. I suspect it was Detlev who pulled him out of there, and left the rest of us to die, sink, or get captured."

"That," CJ said forthrightly, "sounds *just like* Detsie!"

"Well, we already figured they were spies," Leander said.

"That's true." Rel tried to shake off the feeling he'd missed something important. Adam — Kerendal — the Venn — at the same time of that search for the Arrow. It all seemed connected, or maybe that was just . . .

Unnoticed by the rest, Liere got to her feet. She could not bear for anyone to see how heartsick she felt. She had failed to influence Tahra, and she was useless for anything else. She began mechanically to gather her things and Lyren's toys. If she didn't find out who she was and what she wanted to be, she would always be the one sent away for safety.

And because she couldn't bear the falsity of farewell chatter, as soon as her things were piled, she took hold of Lyren's arm, fingered the token Senrid had given her, and the two transferred.

"Wait, what just happened?" CJ asked, whirling around.

"Liere took Lyren off to Marloven Hess," Senrid said.

"Because of *Adam?*" CJ asked. "Wow."

"Because of the pinecones," Leander said. "All that about Dena Yeresbeth is a sort of double threat."

Senrid turned up his palm in agreement. He didn't mention the third transfer on the shank-token, which Liere could use to return if she wanted. There were plenty of people in his castle who would gladly watch Lyren. In fact he'd never known any child with so many willing minders all over the world. He knew some of Liere's inner struggles. They'd talked in circles about her self-doubts. The only thing he could do would be not to add to them. She had to decide whether to stay away or return.

"Just as well," Tahra stated. "I don't know what would be worse, Lyren as a target or a hostage."

Thirty-one

Day Six

ARTHUR AND SENRID GOT up early as usual, and worked through their list of magical tracers, one light magic, one dark. Arthur still sensed the mystery magical presence, but didn't mention it since nothing about it had changed. It didn't help or hinder.

He ignored it, began his tracers, then sat back, letting out a pungent curse.

"What?" Leander sat up in his bedroll a couple lengths away, and Terry a heartbeat later.

Senrid turned. "Maybe it was Liere's and Lyren's transfer away, maybe it's coincidence, but they've laid on a ward, a bad one. No one transfer out, all right? Because it'll send you somewhere else."

"Who wants to bet it's Norsunder Base?" Puddlenose shook out his bedroll.

"Not taking that bet." Terry put one palm out.

"One of 'em knows a lot of magic." Senrid rapped his fingers absently on the dusty floor. "Or more than one, because this ward would have taken me a week if I was still using dark magic."

"Roy." Reflexive anger tightened Arthur's his mouth.

"And David." Senrid remembered the incident at Jilo's castle. "At the least."

Rel sat up, his deep-set eyes mere shadows as he said, "Suggest tactical shift: they seem to be abandoning hiding. We'd better post a watch. If they know when we're leaving this cottage, there's nothing to prevent them from coming in behind."

"And destroy our camp and supplies." Senrid snapped his fingers. "Right."

"We'll be getting another cart delivery in a few days, if we're still here," Tahra reminded them.

"That means we'll have to defend our supply line as well, because they'll have thought of that." Senrid turned to her.

"Draw straws," Terry suggested. "If no one volunteers."

They did, and the Mearsieans lost. "Let's use the time to put together a play," Irenne suggested, mentally reviewing stories she liked acting out, with herself in the central role.

"I'll help," Kyale volunteered, also mentally reviewing her favorite kind of stories, in which she could play the central role.

"I think I'll make a cake," Seshe said after a quick look at their stores.

This suggestion earned enthusiastic endorsement from all sides.

Since an entire boring day stretched ahead of them, CJ decided to scrub away Lyren's scrawls so that she could draw some caricatures of poopsies. If the allies did lose the house, she intended all the poopsies she knew, especially Laban, to see themselves lampooned.

Clair and Dhana dutifully volunteered to watch at the windows for the first part of the day. None of them expected anything to happen, so a short time before noon Clair was startled when a couple of figures emerged out of the light snow.

Adam and Curtas had been ordered to scout the abandoned house, which they knew the invaders had taken over. "If they were stupid enough to leave it unguarded, take what you can and destroy the rest," David said.

"And if it's guarded?" Curtas asked.

David shrugged. "Use your imaginations."

They'd talked it over as they slipped through the trees into the softly falling snow, which muffled their footsteps. If Rel was on guard, they'd retreat, and come back in force. Best case: someone like Senrid or Dtheldevor left on guard, so they could have a dust-up, and see which way things went.

As they covered the final lap, they discussed the potential scrappers. Dtheldevor's gang? Fun. No fun: Arthur, Liere, or most of the Mearsieans. They weren't sure about Leander, and both had been dismayed to discover that Terry had joined the alliance. Neither Adam nor Curtas wanted to scrap with Terry, who they both still liked, though it was clear from what Ferret had overheard the day before while shadowing them that Terry hated them all.

Curtas said, "Maybe Liere ought to be in Rel's category. Couldn't she do something nasty on the mental realm?"

As he ducked a low branch, Adam considered his answer. Liere was strong with potential, and subtle when she wanted to be, but so very untrained. As always, he refrained from discussing Dena Yeresbeth. "Perhaps," was all he said.

When they sighted the house, light glowing in the two windows, they slowed. The curtain of snow made it difficult to see details, but heads moved about inside.

"Shall we see who we've got?" Adam asked.

Curtas nodded, and they took a few steps, trying to make out faces.

Inside, Clair recoiled away from the window. "Girls." The urgency in her voice caused everyone to drop what they were doing, and crowd to the windows.

"What do we do? What do we do?" Kyale asked worriedly. "Don't let them close!"

"We don't have any weapons," Clair said, glancing inside. Rel's sword leaned in a corner, but none of them could wield that in a fight and expect to win.

"But we do have pies," CJ said, forefinger upraised.

Dhana stayed at the back window, in case more showed up there. "How can pies do anything? They aren't even real, just dust and dirt and water taken from surroundings, and given illusory stinks and colors and textures." She was very proud of her knowledge.

"It takes an hour or two for them to fade to nothing," CJ reminded her. "That's enough time in this weather for those smells and the stickiness to feel really, really awful."

Clair jerked her head in a nod. "We want them to go away. Maybe that will work. Let's try it. Better than nothing." The boys had approached close enough in the swirling snow for her to make out Adam's curly hair, and Curtas's pleasant face, though he looked wary now. She was aware of her worry easing a little, as neither of these two had ever seemed threatening.

Seemed. "Quick, CJ."

CJ had already begun muttering the spell. The girls had perfected the illusory bad pie magic long ago, coming up with disgusting combinations that no one would ever eat even if they were real. Perfect for pie fights.

The boys had slowly advanced until they were maybe ten paces away, when Adam called out something. His voice was too faint to hear through the shut windows and door.

"Okay," CJ said, indicating the array sitting in a circle around her, as glutinous aromas wafted in the warm air. "We each have three."

"Get ready." Clair swept them with her gaze. "On my count, open the windows. CJ, since you're left-handed, you take that side of the door and I'll take the other. Throw as hard as you can."

The girls carefully carried the soupy, pungent pies to their positions, Kyale muttering, "This smells horrible."

"It's a spoiled-banana-sauerkraut supremo," CJ said, ranging herself at one side of one window, Irenne opposite her. "I worked long and hard to fake up that stench."

". . .three . . .four . . .*now*." Clair jerked the door open.

Adam raised his hands to his mouth to shout again a moment before the windows flew up.

Out whirled globby fake pastry. He and Curtas danced back, unable to identify the projectiles hurtling their way. Most of the pies missed, but one caught Curtas down the front of his coat, and Adam got clipped on the shoulder by one that broke apart, splattering his face.

Curtas gave an inarticulate yell, and Adam scraped the mess with his hands, smearing it into stickiness that began to string in the cold. Looking up at Clair, who peered through a crack in the door, he called, "Are you going to invite us in to clean that off?"

"Come close and see what happens," she called back, with no friendliness in her voice.

"This stinks," Curtas said, trying to wring the freezing oozes off his hands, with no success. "I'm out of here."

Adam agreed. They whirled and ran, vanishing into the lazily drifting snow.

The girls shut the windows and door again, adrenaline making them fizz with hilarity as they exchanged *what-ifs* and *we-should-haves*. When they'd calmed down again, keeping watch had become the favorite activity. But no one appeared until Puddlenose and Christoph stamped in, sending a swirl of freezing air around the room. They muscled the door shut then thumped the caked snow off their feet.

Irenne said, "What happened to you?"

Puddlenose said, "Chase. Flushed the little one potting us with icicles." He indicated a raw scrape on the side of his face. "Ran till we reached that big ravine we spotted that way." A thumb jerked westward. "He nearly led us into a trap."

Christoph said, "We would have fallen into it, except he started slowing and looking around. We figured it out about a heartbeat before Rolfin, Leef, and one I don't know showed up, and then it was us on the run."

"All the way across the forest," Christoph said, cracking his knuckles. "Might have caught us but for snow getting heavy. They sheared off."

"Probably have a long run back, and visibility was nothing. So here we are," Puddlenose said, and noticed a tray Seshe set on a makeshift table. "Ah, cheese breads."

"Didn't you want to ask us what *we* did?" Kyale asked.

"We had a pie fight," CJ crowed.

They told their story, the boys laughed, and everyone settled down to wait until the stragglers showed up.

When the door banged open, the sight of Arthur and Terry with blood crusted in the snow on their faces shocked the group into silence. Arthur had a cut over one eye that had dribbled down to pool in his eye socket, his eyelashes stuck together because of the cold. Something had sliced deep along Terry's jaw under his ear.

As people leaped to help them, Rel said, "We were on our way back just now. It was that little one, Terry says is called Noser. Slingshotting icicles melted to points."

"He did that with us, too," Puddlenose said, fingering his cheek.

"Tell them what you did," Arthur said.

"He bunked, but I caught up with him." Rel's voice was flat. "Dislocated his arm."

Angry cheers went up at that, but Rel looked away. He'd done what he could to stop the brat, but the fact remained that even though Noser had struggled mightily, and would have attacked viciously had he had more reach, he was much smaller and lighter. There was nothing remotely to be proud of in disabling a small boy; Rel had made it as quick as possible, in hopes of getting Noser out of action until everyone could leave.

But the way certain of the others carried on, it was like he'd won a duel with Detlev. He was considerably relieved when noise outside meant that the sailors had returned. Dtheldevor banged the door open, and her crew streamed in, flanked by Leander and Senrid.

Once again the stories were told, finishing with the pie fight, which caused laughter, except from Senrid, who shook his head.

"What?" CJ asked, handing Senrid a cup of hot cider. "You don't think it was funny?"

"Don't you see? That was a reconnoiter," Senrid said.

Noser screeched all the way back to the tree house, though Silvanas and Leef carried him as fast as they could.

MV heard more rage than pain in the shrill, hoarse screams, but he said nothing until he'd grasped Noser's arm. Ignoring the boy's babble of threats, curses, and pleas, he said to Silvanas, "Hold him down."

The rage-shrill scream escalated into pure pain, then died away abruptly as MV moved the bone back into the socket. "Neat job," he commented. "Who did that?"

"The shit-faced big one." Noser mopped his nose on the sleeve of his good arm.

"Rel," Leef said.

MV's amusement hardened to mordant appreciation, but all he said was, "Come on, Nose. Let's get that wrapped up."

"Shit, shit, shit," Noser droned endlessly as Leef held him up and MV briskly and expertly bandaged his shoulder, then bound his arm to his side. Then, "Give it a few days. You'll be fine." Over his head, MV said, "Slingshot?"

Silvanas shrugged. "He nearly put out Arthur's eye."

MV said nothing else until David got back from his scouting run. "Things are hotting up a little," he told David. "If today doesn't send them running, and I doubt it will, I think it's past time to hit the south house in force. Turf 'em out, take their stuff, let 'em go hungry a day or two. All within orders. And I," he added, "want to have a little talk with Rel." He cracked his knuckles, then reached for his whetstone.

"You already dusted Rel once," Noser said belligerently.

"Nope. Laban distracted him. I want a one on one. No interference."

David said, "Roy and I had better scout the house first. If they don't put up wards, I'd be surprised. After that, sure."

As their dinner simmered, they quickly divided up and sketched out the morrow's plans.

Thirty-two

Day Seven

THEY WOKE TO CLEAR weather, the world smooth and white.

Tahra insisted on everyone going out at once, in force. "We know most of them seem to be at the hills, and it takes half the morning to get there," she argued. "If enough of us go, we will outnumber them."

"I'll stay," Arthur said, blinking one-eyed, the cut one swollen and purple. "I can't see much out of this eye, but that won't stop me from doing magic if they try anything here."

"I 'm not nearly as advanced as you with ward studies, but I know some handy tricks they might not expect," Leander said to Arthur. "I'll stay with you."

Arthur stared at him in fascination. Raised by an elderly, serious mage, overseen by benign but equally serious adult mages, Arthur had spent his childhood working. He loved his work, but until he met the Mearsieans, he'd never known what play was. "Tricks like . . .?"

"To begin with, the side-step Destination," Leander said. "It's tedious to set up, and of course the spell won't last much past nightfall, but we lay down tiny Destinations surrounding the house so that anyone who steps on one gets his feet transferred sideways the length of a foot." Leander demonstrated with one hand jerking from right to left.

Arthur grinned. "Let's get started!"

"We'll lay down a path for the others to follow to get out, then do it last . . ."

As they loaded on coats and gloves, Senrid walked up to Rel. "How about if we scout the wings? A big group like that, I'd send someone to skulk on the flank. Attack if they see an advantage."

"All right," Rel said, and in a low voice, "Do we take weapons?" He glanced at his sword.

"Let's," Senrid said, and for the first time, reached into his gear to pull out a composite bow, weapon of the Marloven light cavalry, and a full quiver of spiral-fletched arrows. "Don't have to use them unless we have to. But why not look serious?"

After a quick breakfast they departed.

Dtheldevor's sailors, the Mearsieans, Kyale, Terry, Puddle-nose and Christoph joined Tahra in walking in a wide line straight through the center of the territory. Tahra led, scanning eagerly for a blond head. But as they floundered through heavy drifts without seeing anyone, her glee began to erode. By early afternoon, she would have been glad to find *someone* to shoot at.

Rel and Senrid split to flank the allies, right and left.

Rel was the first to catch a stalker, spotting a shadow slipping from tree to tree, exactly as Senrid had predicted. Despite his size, Rel could be stealthy when needed, and the snow helped; even so, he got within about five paces of Adam, recognizable by his long, wild curls and the chalk behind his ears, before the latter whirled around, then took up a defensive stance, his startled expression smoothing to question.

As a distant branch cracked, and far off, a bird cawed, they regarded one another. If it had been MV, Rolfin, or Leef, Rel would have come in swinging. But to Rel, Adam wasn't all that much larger than the blond brat they called Noser, just taller. So Rel said, "Are we going to scrap?"

"Not," Adam said, "unless you want to."

"I take it you can hold your own?"

Adam lifted a shoulder.

"And yet you abandoned us to the pirates when we were sailing. Did you take my transfer token?"

"No. I didn't know you had one. I had one of my own." And Adam confessed, "I don't touch anyone's things if I can avoid it."

Rel heard the sincerity in this rare personal admission, then suspected he was being side-stepped. He said, "Why did you chivvy us onto Cor's boat? Because you did. Then flung those drawings in his face. What for, to get him killed?"

"No." Adam's brows rose. "Orders."

Rel remembered being told by different people that Detlev always had long plans. And it was entirely possible that he didn't explain them to his underlings any more than a war commander bothered illustrating his grand strategy to a flatfoot.

"Take off," he said. "If you bring friends back, I'll swing first and ask questions after." He held up his sheathed sword.

Adam saluted airily, fingertips to forehead. Then the only sound was the chuffing of Adam's retreating footsteps in the snow, and the thump of his knapsack on his back.

Not long after, on the left flank of the line of searchers, Laban and Senrid spotted one another. Laban pulled his knife at the same moment he saw Senrid's nocked bow. And at least four knife hilts in view.

They stilled, assessing one another. They were the same size and knew they were fairly equally matched in a scrap, both trained in close combat. And both would have welcomed a scrap. Elsewhere. Not in snowdrifts the height of a man, far from either HQ.

"The knife," Senrid said, twitching his shoulder. "That was a ruse to get at Kessler?"

Laban flicked his hand up.

It all fell into place, then: Laban could have killed Senrid, but hadn't. The rest had been bad enough, but Senrid had survived. Whereas he wouldn't have survived a knife to the heart.

So Senrid whipped up his bow and shot Laban in the shoulder.

Laban fell back in the snow, then rolled over to his knees, his good hand gripping the haft. His head jerked up as Senrid approached, another arrow ready. But when he reached Laban, he said, "Beat feet. Tahra and Terry want blood."

"Terry?" Laban said tightly, red along the cheekbones, white at the lips, his blue eyes stark.

"Karhin was Terry's friend," Senrid said.

Laban got to his feet, swaying. Senrid didn't move. Laban

turned and began walking, one hand holding that arrow. Senrid had to give him this much—he didn't look back, and he managed to keep his legs moving, though Senrid knew from experience his knees had to feel like they'd been replaced with water. When Laban had vanished among the trees, Senrid lowered the bow.

Senrid returned to the hunt, heightened awareness causing him to check in all directions, including in the trees. He even risked brief listens on the mental plane, though that threatened vertigo, and by the time he saw Tahra and half of the group beginning the long trudge back, he had a pounding headache. But he didn't relax until they were safely back. He knew that the next meeting pretty much guaranteed a step up in stakes.

Unaware of any of this, and with mutual and unspoken relief to get a break from Tahra's single-minded intensity, the Mearsieans were glad to have an excuse to separate off when Dhana said, "I found something. I think you should see it. Not far." She pointed backwards, through a stand of trees.

When Dhana said she'd found something, it always meant something beautiful, usually having to do with water. Clair was delighted with anything that would get them away from poopsie hunting, and Tahra's thirst for what she insisted was justice. "Show us, then we'll catch up with the others."

Dhana took the lead, skimming lightly over the snow. CJ ran with her, pounding along grimly but enjoying the wind on her face and the blue of white-etched bare tree branches dappled by the late-sun shadows.

Dhana stopped short. CJ nearly crashed into her, looking about wildly for threats—weapons—then she spotted what Dhana stared so fixedly at, as the other girls closed in behind.

The smooth snow had gently dipped, coming to the edge of a cliff. Below, catching the edge of the sinking sun, lay a lake. At the far end the rocky ridge rose high, bisected by the glow of a frozen waterfall, ochre in the slanting light. The light changed the frozen water to a thin dragon stone with fire in its heart, blue with molten gold in its center. The light filtering through the trees caught tiny icicles with the reflections, so they looked like sun drops above the deep blue waters of the lake.

"Wow," CJ breathed.

A shifting noise below was their first sign that they were not alone.

CJ edged closer to the cliff's rim, and discovered Adam

sitting on another, narrower ledge maybe twenty feet below her. He sat on a rock, sketching the waterfall on a pad resting on his knees, chalk in his fingers and behind both ears.

He smiled up at the girls. "Ever seen colors like that?" he asked.

Irenne nudged Dhana. "Wreck it," she breathed. "He doesn't deserve it."

"Do it," CJ added, a hot ball of rage in her middle.

Dhana turned from one to the other. "It'll form again."

"But he can't draw it now," CJ said, struggling against a vast, inchoate sense of unfairness, as if Adam was getting away with something.

Dhana knew that breaking the waterfall would cause no harm, and it would be fun. She flung up her arms and dove out past the icy shore. Midway she flickered from human to her other form, no more than a ripple to human eyes, and vanished before she hit the water. The waterfall glowed with rainbow hues, then cracks fingered out and it exploded, ice shards falling to tinkle with almost musical ringing on the half-frozen lake below.

She reappeared, human again, her hair wet and slicked back, her cheeks mottled with color.

"Go back to Norsunder," Irenne shouted down at Adam, hands on her hips.

A slow clapping from the trees directly behind the girls caused them to whirl around, aghast. MV sauntered out from behind the bole of a wind-twisted cedar, tossing a huge snowball on his gloved hand. "Nice touch," he called derisively. "I love lighter hypocrisy, don't you?"

Adam appeared not ten paces away, stuffing papers into the knapsack the girls had seen countless times. "Dhana probably thinks I was mocking it."

MV snickered as he advanced slowly, and from the other trees Rolfin, Curtas, Leef, Erol, and Ferret appeared, all holding huge snowballs. The girls backed slowly toward the edge of the cliff, except for Dhana, who had vanished.

The first one caught CJ right in the face. It had no rock in it, but hurled at maximum strength, it hurt almost as much as a rock-snowball would have. Lights flashed across her vision and she staggered back, gasping. Her face stung with a thousand tiny cuts as she whirled around yelling to the others, "Run!"

She scrambled down the trail, the others following in a hail of snowballs.

MV and the rest waited at the top of the trail long enough for the Mearsieans to realize they had just trapped themselves between them and the water before bending to make more ammunition.

CJ remembered Arthur's shivering form, and knew they were in serious trouble. And she was the one who'd stupidly managed to back them into a trap.

Then Dhana popped up from the water, human again as she called, "CJ, here."

A massive green-brown surge of water stopped the boys in their tracks, as a group of enormous fresh-water turtles climbed onto the icy shore.

"Come on," Dhana exclaimed, leaping onto the back of a turtle.

CJ gulped and jumped up beside her. The rest of the girls, with many grimly fearful glances, clambered onto the backs of the turtles. The creatures moved slowly into the water as MV and the boys began pelting them, but distance soon caused the snowballs to fall harmlessly into the water.

The turtles glided gently toward the opposite shore, forming into a line as the boys began running back up the slope. CJ surveyed the shore fearfully, relaxing marginally when she saw the rough terrain MV would have to cross to catch up with them. Dhana showed the girls how to step from one broad turtle-back to another until they reached the shore. And vanished among the trees.

MV and the boys stopped at the top of the rise, looking back; they knew they hadn't a chance of catching up.

"That was the weirdest thing I've seen in a while," Rolfin commented, studying the deceptively placid water.

MV's answer was as succinct as it was crude.

As for the girls, they ran their hardest, breathless with reaction. CJ laughed out of relief rather than real humor. When they neared the safe zone and no one leaped out at them, they slowed.

Finally Clair said, "He wasn't doing anything to that water-fall."

"No." CJ gritted her teeth. "But he was there."

Irenne tossed her ponytail. "Why should he be free to destroy things and people, then pause along the way to help himself to beautiful things? I hate that!"

"Maybe it'll turn him," Seshe said earnestly. "He's not doing anything evil when he's looking at waterfalls. If he's drawing, he's not hurting anyone."

"He was drawing everybody, including Glenn and Karhin. You can't say *they* didn't get hurt," CJ muttered. "And Arthur, and I know nothing happened to him, except all that magic stuff. I just . . ."

"I know," Clair said. "We've heard enough about justice."

Clair's tone was even, and CJ knew Clair was talking about Tahra, Arthur, and Terry, but she felt rebuked just the same.

David and Roy never got anywhere near the house. They'd begun by checking the wards over the rat-hole perimeter, to discover a couple of nasty ones laid over theirs. They put in some time destroying those, then set out toward the south house, but they hadn't gotten a hundred steps before they both sensed tracers warning them that the wards had been replaced.

"There are at least three mages outside the perimeter," David said, eyes closed as he sifted magical signatures.

Roy shook his head. "Four. One at a distance. And we've got two inside, who've been laying magic traps over the south house all morning."

They hiked back to their tree, every step sinking to the thigh, to hear Noser wailing and cursing from his bedroll, bored and restless, but as yet hurting too much to defy orders and go off looking for trouble. By the time they got a hefty dose of green kinthus into him and he sank into sleep, the others began drifting back, Laban last, his face blanched, and his coat dark with blood.

David's mood was savage. The two semi-disabled were not as intimidating as the fact that their lines of escape were vanishing. If they had not been given specific orders to go to ground, it would be such a relief to go on the attack. He could feel the others waiting for the least sign. MV might not wait. The whetstone was constantly in his hands.

David kept silent until the others had eaten, ignoring all the after-action "We ought to . . ." barracks grievance. At least Liere was gone, and none of the others seemed capable of attack in the mental realm. He'd sensed Liere's absence the last time he'd made an unsuccessful attempt to reach Detlev.

He was tired of failure, and angry enough to challenge his

own fear. Though he'd been told that the mental plane had no physical component, he could feel the pull of the world when he tried to send his focus out of it. Perhaps that was a limitation of the Geth Marsh, though he was not certain, because when one was physically present in the Marsh it felt somewhat like a link-point between an infinity of worlds, with no true up, down, or sideways. It was only with extreme concentration that he could maneuver in and out of it, and it was an inescapable presence in his mind, reshaping the mental realm.

He sat cross-legged, hands on knees, head back against the smooth bole of the tree, shut his eyes . . .And there was that limit, perceived as a curve of air keeping him safe inside a bubble. If he pushed beyond, his mind might tumble forever . .
.

Furious, desperate, he fixed on an image of Detlev, familiar all his life, and again *reached*.

:David.

:Detlev! We're up against it. David struggled to contain the stream of emotion-laden images and confine himself to words.

:Let me give you a focus.

Abruptly—David didn't know how Detlev did it—they stood in a gray space, simulacra of their physical selves facing each other. David knew his symbolic self was false. It was a bit like Norsunder Beyond, but he could move, breathe, and most of all, communicate in words.

"Summary," Detlev said. "Without justification."

David grimaced. It was useless trying to hide anything from Detlev. "We're trapped by the alliance in our rat-hole. We could fight our way out. Magic will be more difficult. They can't break our Geth ward, but they're using it to lay on wards that Roy and I keep having to trace and break. There are four mages on the outside ranged against us. On the inside, led by Arthur of Bereth Ferian, Senrid Montredaun-An, and a third I don't know."

"Where is your retreat?"

David knew Detlev was not going to be pleased. "Southwest corner of Wnelder Vee."

"You let Laban choose the locale." It wasn't even a question.

"It was convenient while we were in Everon on your orders."

"Which result we have discussed previously. You were taught how to construct a safe Destination. You could have made your retreat anywhere. And I told Laban to stay away from that area."

When Detlev stated the obvious, he was really annoyed. He went on, "The most pressing matter here is a Norss snare formed around their rift magic, and also Yeres's bid to take control of Five for garrison building."

"Take complete control of Five? But the Den!"

"That's one of my current priorities. You have two orders. First, you will make world-transfer tokens and fall back to the Den."

"And?"

"Tell Laban he may select one of the allies to bring along, but it will be no one from that region."

"As hostage? Prisoner?"

"As an experiment. Now, let me give you the magic for the transfer tokens . . ."

When David recovered, and had managed to catch his breath and blink the world back into alignment from its nauseating spin-shift, spin-shift, he said, "I found Detlev."

The others paused in the process of handing around flatbreads and a thick pepper soup made with potatoes, cheese, and the last of their withering greens.

"We're falling back to Five," he said.

Through the cheers and curses came Noser's hoarse sarcasm, "Shit*fire*."

"Wooo-ooo!"

"Grass ass!"

"Shut up," MV snapped.

David cut through the noise. "It's going to take time to make the tokens to shift worlds. Roy, you're going to have to break the lighters' wards on your own. MV, I might need you, so don't range far. The rest of you fend off the invaders. Laban. You have a special order."

Everyone quieted.

"You are to choose one of them to take with us. For an experiment. No one from this region."

"What sort of experiment?" Laban asked, as everyone else exclaimed, laughed, made suggestions of the sort of experiment that would be most fun for them and least for the target.

"I don't know, but his mood didn't improve when he asked about our location. That may or may not have influenced his decision to assign that order to you." David turned to Roy and began a detailed magical discussion.

Freshly bandaged, with keem leaves laid over his shoulder wound, Laban said to Curtas, "What do you think he means?"

"I don't know, but I suspect in there will be a reminder about strategy," Curtas answered, not without sympathy. "I like this location. I could easily have wintered here. But you probably could have found as good a retreat over the mountains in Daraen, or anywhere that's not Wnelder Vee, Everon, or Imar."

That was irritatingly unanswerable.

The only one excused orders was Noser. Laban drank down a dose of listerblossom before he and Roy went off on perimeter duty for the first half of the night.

Once they were out of earshot of the tree, he put his question to Roy, "What do you think he means?"

Roy took his time thinking, as he usually did. They'd checked out a noise in the shrubbery that turned out to be a fox, and had reached the turning point for the sentry walk, before Roy said, "I think if I were you I'd pick someone interesting."

"Interesting!"

"Yeah. You might end up spending a lot of time with this person. Experiment sort of suggests that, doesn't it?"

Thirty-three

Day Eight

HUNTERS AND HUNTED ALIKE woke to a clear dawn.

Clair woke early. Her quiet rustles and whispers of spells eventually roused CJ, as their bedrolls lay side by side. After trying to talk by hand gestures and moving lips, they decided to get their coats, mittens, and hats, and take a walk until the others began to stir.

The snow lit with the pearly-yellow-peach colors of dawn as they crunched their way out of the house, breath puffing vapor in the still air. Chill tried to worm into up inside CJ's sleeves and down her neck so she swung her arms and stamped to stay warm.

Clair hunched into her coat, her white hair blending with the background. Her profile wore that inward look.

After a while of aimless walk, CJ said, "I hope you're not worrying about home."

"Not a bit. I know Mearsieanne is doing a great job," Clair stated with such heartiness that CJ flicked her a side-eye.

"Then?"

"It's this mess," Clair said after another twenty steps or so. "I think we'd be better off giving up and going home. We could leave right now if we wanted."

"I thought we couldn't magic out."

"I tested this morning," Clair said, fumbling at her neck to pull out her medallion, and was distracted by the shiny stone hanging next to it. "It's weird. Liere kept looking at Puddlenose's shell. No one else has ever noticed it before."

"You hardly ever wear it."

"True, but also Arthur said something about a magical thing he could sense. I thought that was just . . .well, I like touching it. I like looking at it. I sense magic on it, too, but not all the time. But last night, my dreams got weird. Like something was reaching for it, not quite a tentacle, not quite . . .oh, you know how ink looks when you pour it into water and give it one stir?"

"Yes," CJ said, looking around the quiet winter forest as if she expected to see tentacles of doom writhing toward her.

"It was like that. Only the ink thing was reaching for me. And . . .*it*."

"Ugh," CJ said, and shivered.

"So I tested magic, figuring it's always best to try with something not live. I sent the shell back to its carved box in the white palace. Then I brought it back to make sure it really worked. So I think our medallions would transfer us safely home."

"And let the poopsies win?"

"I don't like Tahra walking around with that crossbow."

"Boneribs carries a bow."

"But I don't think Senrid wants to kill anyone with it. I don't believe Tahra when she said she'd shoot David in the leg. I think she and Terry both want to kill him, or Terry wants at least one of them dead for what happened to Karhin. And if our side starts that . . .who do we become?"

CJ shrugged, her shoulders up under her ears. She hated Clair being upset. "I don't want the poopsies making *us* target practice. Even if we had bows, not all of us could use one. Except you." She groaned. "I guess I wish we could make them go away for good."

"I don't think running around like this is going to make them go. I'm afraid it might do the opposite. If they do attack for real, we'll be the losers whatever happens. At least—" Clair paused, then looked around. The stand of pine to the left stood tall and still in the cold air, the pristine white ground sloping away toward the other trees, deeper into the forest. She whispered so softly CJ could barely hear it, "I think I have to tell you something I never told anyone."

CJ hugged her elbows against herself, instinct warning her that this couldn't be good. And yet Clair was the girl who had traveled all over looking for kids who nobody else wanted. "Sure."

Clair gave her a funny sideways smile that made her look like Puddlenose when he was making cracks about his very bad days in Chwahirsland. "It's about Siamis. The first time he came. Before he put that enchantment over me. I didn't know who he was. I thought he was a visitor, so we were talking. Then even after he told me who he was, I was still talking to him."

"A villain?" CJ flung her hands out wide. "What could you think he'd say but evil things?"

"That's just it. He talked about the golden days of Ancient Sartor, and the glorious future if we could get all that back. I had to know if he really wanted to make us like those old days. So I said, *How can you do that?* He said, *That's simple, yet profoundly difficult: to lead this world to peace.* I said, *That's more of a goal, isn't it?* He said, *It might be, for some. But I see it as a duty, not a choice but an obligation, that my experience makes me particularly fit to fulfill.* He wasn't making fun of me, or threatening me, so I said, *What if your duty is harder to define?*"

CJ made a face.

"Then he said, *If I didn't know how to define my duty, I'd seek as wide a variety of experience as I could. Eventually my perspective would be clearer.* And then the next thing I knew, the enchantment broke, and all you were there."

"And so you told me now because . . ."

"Because the snow is cold, and I had a bad dream, and that . . ." She shrugged. "And while some of those boys are exactly as horrible as you'd expect of Norsundrians, some others aren't . . .what I expect."

They walked back in to discover everyone awake. The breakfast volunteers had made berry biscuits for breakfast. Arthur and Leander, disgusted that no one had shown up the day before to fall into their magic traps, were consulting with Senrid about planning more elaborate magic traps to be put farther out from the house. Dtheldevor and her sailors offered enthusiastic if impractical suggestions.

CJ sat with Irenne and Kyale, who described their play in low voices. It sounded good, actually, one of the old Peddler

Antivad stories, only with a girl at the center. She did not understand what all the mean or greedy or grabby people around her were saying, causing them to get into trouble because she accidentally spoke what they really thought. Irenne had enthusiastically embraced the lead villain, leaving the central role to Kyale. Gloriel and Peridot had joined in.

"We'll do it tonight after dinner," Kyale whispered, and CJ glanced at Clair, wondering if they would be around to see it, much less perform.

A rope of Seshe's long hair hung over her arms as she lifted the last tray of berry biscuits off the stove. The privateers and Kyale hung around her like vultures, eyes picking out the biggest biscuits.

Clair beckoned the Mearsiean girls closer. Only Dhana didn't join them, but lay back, her face turned slightly so she could watch the flames. They danced in her huge pupils as Clair whispered, "I think it's time to go home."

Kyale's voice rose in dismay. "No! You *can't*! That's so *unfair*! Not until we do our play!"

Irenne huffed. She had finally put on her prettiest dress, in expectation of doing the play. She said in a wheedling tone, "How about going home tomorrow? We don't have to . . ." She lowered her voice. "We'll walk around today. We don't have to look for fights."

"I agree with that," Seshe said, joining them. "I'll fix a really good meal while you look around one last time. How's that?"

CJ had stayed out of the discussion because her feelings were so ambivalent. She knew a good person would want to go home, and a bad person wanted to see the poopsies get . . .

She always stopped there, holding her breath against those roiling emotions in her gut whenever she thought the word *justice*. She kept hearing the whisper *hypocrisy*. She firmly substituted *justice* with *turned into cactus*.

Dhana waited until Kyale bustled away to find out what her brother was planning, then she said to Irenne, "If Clair wants to go home, we should go home. You can do a play at home. It'll be even better with Falinneh in it."

Irenne tossed her ponytail back, her hands twitching at the lavender lace on her gown. "Kyale —"

"She can do plays at her home."

"No, she can't." Irene stopped fussing with her lace and crossed her arms. "She's *alone* there. Except for her cats. Which don't do plays."

"It's all right," Clair said, looking from one to the other. "We'll do Seshe's suggestion. Another day won't hurt, if we spend it walking around."

"I don't see what's stopping *you* from going home," Irenne said to Dhana, "if you're in such a hurry."

"I'm not," Dhana said. "But I think Clair wants to go."

Irenne's wrists hit her hips, elbows akimbo, fingers curled outward, her shoulders twitching as she tossed her hair. "And *she* just said she wants to *stay*."

"No, she gave in because you flounced."

"I don't *flounce*."

"I learned the word because of you," Dhana stated.

Their argument was nothing new, and they blew over as fast as they hit, but Clair—who got upset whenever anyone argued—felt especially anxious on behalf of the others, so she said, "I want to leave tomorrow. One last walk, then Seshe's feast today. And the Peddler Antivad play tonight, our last one."

"Eeeeee," Kyale squealed softly. At last she would get to be the center of a play—of course everyone was going to be enthralled.

Dhana said, "Okay," and turned to roll up her bedding, leaving Irenne sighing dramatically, as she hated not having the last word.

The residual tension between the two girls, plus the other tensions as people loaded up with weapons, caused Clair to long for some privacy. Only for a short time. That walk with CJ had not been enough, not after a long week of everyone jumbled together every single night.

As the others pulled their winter gear on, Clair's fingers fumbled at the bump beneath her warm tunic where the shell lay against her medallion. That dream about ink-tentacles prompted her to pull the necklace out, and unhook the shell again. She tested the transfer magic, and once again it vanished safety. So transfers still worked. She's summon it back on the morrow to test transfers before she sent everyone home.

Having a deadline and a way out was enough of a relief to enable Clair to fasten her coat and join the others at the door. They filed out, already separating into twos and threes, not-quite-arguing, but in no spirit of amity. Definitely time to go home.

When they reached the trail head, they began splitting off along different trails. Clair headed off by herself to the extreme right, where no one had ever encountered anyone.

No use in worrying, she scolded herself. Irenne and Dhana would be fine by midday. Their quarrels never lasted. But the memory stirred up memories of unspoken resentment, such as Diana's staying in the Junky in spite of Mearsieanne's regarding it as a place to be ignored, or as a suitable place for the boys, Puddlenose and Christoph and Ben, the latter of whom had been traveling more and more, ever since Mearsieanne's arrival.

Clair knew Diana had not come along because Dtheldevor's group was coming—and she would be divided between the two. The truth was, Clair suspected only loyalty to Clair and CJ kept Diana from leaving Mearsieanne's Mearsies Heili altogether and joining Dtheldevor's crew permanently.

How that hurt! It shouldn't, but it did.

A bird exploded from a tangle of branches overhead, sending down a fine dust of white snow. It hit her face, stinging her cheeks with the cold. She watched the bird winging through the trees, until it burst free of the high branches and disappeared against the white clouds overhead.

This was a chance to think things out, painful as it was. Like: why was it that everyone tried extra hard, yet there always seemed to be some kind of invisible line dividing Mearsieanne from the rest of the gang, as if they were being watched, and she was a judge? Mearsieanne seemed to love them all, she never criticized anything the girls did—and she could get pretty fluent about what displeased her in other countries and other rulers—but still, the girls were . . .different around her. Polite, careful. Mearsieanne was a great queen. She would surely make Mearsies Heili a great kingdom again.

Clair sighed. Where did that leave her? As one of the girls, of course. And they had good lives. CJ, who couldn't hide her real feelings even when she made villains extra mad, was genuinely glad to have Clair with them.

So why do I feel lost?

Thirty-four

THE REST OF THE group had split into several parties. Tahra forged ahead, the sailors going with her; as Dtheldevor said privately to Joey, "The way she keeps stalkin' around, stompin' every twig, I 'spect them fart-faces to hop out at her any time. I think she wants 'em to. Let's see if we kin keep anyone from becomin' target practice."

Leander and Senrid, with somewhat the same idea, flanked Tahra's group on one side, and Terry and Rel on the other side.

Arthur stayed behind to guard the house, and began a silent, determined ward duel with Roy, who worked in the tree house at the northern end of the territory, and immediately recognized Arthur's magic signature.

For the first time, the Mearsieans split up.

Seshe had seen Clair separate off. She, too, suppressed worries about the group splintering, but if Clair didn't want to talk, then she deserved privacy. Since they were getting low on flour, Seshe figured the best thing she could do would be to crush nuts for some nutbread, and she returned to the house.

Dhana danced off alone, vanishing from sight. Sometimes being human overwhelmed her, especially surrounded by others day and night. She understood that the other girls saw her interactions with Irenne as quarrels, when Dhana simply saw them as truth butting up against pretenses she could not understand. Most of the time she found Irenne good company, but she would never understand her craving for attention, especially certain kinds of admiration. To Dhana clothing was something humans did, but the desire to hang ribbons and lace and sashes and gems about oneself to draw notice to one's phys-ical self was never going to make sense any more than humans would understand bird talk, though they listened to them season after season.

That left Irenne to her chief admirer (and rival, though she did not know it): Kyale.

As for their enemies, they, too, had split up, knowing that the end was nigh. MV stayed at the tree house long enough to make transfer tokens, adding in an extra, then took off with Rolfin and Curtas. He was not going to forego a chance to scrap with Rel before they had to vanish. More than scrap, heh. He had his own plan for experiments.

He was pleased when the crunch of small twigs echoing among the evergreen boles indicated two someones ahead, two people who didn't care about being heard. He figured that Rel wouldn't tromp around like that a heartbeat before the hoped-for pair of weapons-loaded scrappers turned out to be a pair of prissy girls who caught themselves short, both faces with rounded eyes and mouths.

Kyale let out a shrill squeal, followed by Irenne stamping her foot and yelling, "How *dare* you!"

Her voice rang through the trees downslope, where it start-led Clair out of her funk. She whirled around, and started run-ning in the direction of those voices, as in the clearing, MV said to Curtas, "This might not be a dead loss after all. What you want a bet we might effect a trade?"

Irenne put her hands on her hips. "How *dare* you?" she demanded again, before whirling to run.

In the play of her life, boys wouldn't harm her if she didn't harm them. Even in the bad old days, Jilo had been a nuisance, not an actual danger. And so far, CJ, or Dhana, or Clair had effected the best exits for their adventures.

So when the big one closed the distance between them, grabbed her and held a knife blade at her neck, saying over her head, "Find Rel—" she didn't panic.

Irenne had never been in the grip of a tall, strong boy, any more than he had held a girl in his grip. Neither understood the body language of the other, only instinct. She bridled, twitching

her shoulders and flinging her hair back, as his hands instinctively tightened.

And the knife blade, razor honed, sliced cleanly through the
artery at the side of her neck.

Clair stumbled right into a holly bush in time to see MV
back up, red-edged knife jerking away as Irenne stood, fingers
distended like starfish, shrieking as blood pulsed from her neck
to splatter down her gown.

Kyale's shrill squeal for attention scaled up to a genuine
scream of terror. She screamed again as she ran blindly straight
into a tree branch, which whipped across her face. She recoiled,
sobbing, and staggered past the holly bush where Clair stood,
white lights pulsing and twinkling across her vision as Irenne
crumpled slowly . . .slowly . . .

MV bent over Irenne. Was that surprise, or triumph? Clair
saw the flare of magic, fighting the white things that unaccoun-
tably had become roiling shadows across her vision.

When she could see again, they were gone. All of them.
Leaving only Irenne's blood turned to dark rubies in the snow.

She stumbled away, her head an aching ball of ice, until
three figures loomed out of the stinging blur of her vision: Terry
limping, expression worried, Senrid, gray-blue eyes watchful,
mouth tight and hard, Puddlenose saying something repeatedly that she could not comprehend.

She lifted her hand and pointed back. Her throat worked,
but she couldn't find any words.

Senrid said, "Who was that screaming?"

"Irenne," Clair managed. "Irenne . . ." Her throat locked
tight.

All three boys took off in the direction she'd pointed. Clair
turned to follow, but the haze blurring her vision blocked her
path and she bumped face first into a tree, thoughts coming
from far away: must not cry, the tears would freeze, find the
girls, she had to be the one to tell them, but what? Not yet, not
until she had the right words, because she hadn't been there in
time, she hadn't stopped it —

She stood in the snow with her arms locked around her
middle, rocking back and forth as the first sob ripped up from
deep inside her. Then another, and another.

Her feet had nearly gone numb before she could get her
breathing under enough control to look around, to see that she
was lost. She pushed one foot in front of another until she

reached a rock. She sat down put her hands over her face, but the image would not go away, over and over, Irenne's hair flying, her startled wide eyes staring upward, then drawn with pain as crimson splashed the white world red . . .

. . . and then she crumpled, slow and cold as drifting snow.

The numbness creeping up Clair's limbs was just turning to a weird non-cold when footsteps crunched toward her. It hurt to move her hands, to look up. But she forced herself to. "Senrid?" she said.

"No." It was Laban of the curly dark hair and bright blue eyes, swathed in a black cloak, one arm in a sling. "You're even better than he is, come to think of it. Less annoying. Come on."

"No," she managed, but she couldn't get her muscles to move. She was shivering too hard.

He reached with one gloved hand, took her arm, and pulled her to her feet, which made every muscle in her body protest.

"Walk."

She did, just so she wouldn't fall face-down into the snow. Presently she became aware of warmth, a different kind, an immediate kind, with weight on her shoulders. She raised a hand and encountered the heavy folds of a warm black cloak. He wore a light coat.

"You look half-frozen," he said.

She said nothing. Saw again Irenne falling, falling, so soundless and pale, surrounded by living red splatters on the snow, and the pain was so agonizing she tried to sink back into the fog. But noise forced her back to the here and now. She discovered they had reached a tree house with a rope ladder hanging down. Their hideout. She had found their hideout.

And, bitterly, laughed at herself. *Their hideout has found me.*

Either way, nothing seemed to matter anymore. *Irenne — how can I tell the girls?*

Laban said, "Up you go."

She whirled, pushed violently at him and tried to run, but tripped over the dragging cloak. Laban caught her one-handed, keeping her from doing a facer in the snow. Hands reached from above, grasped her wrists, and she found herself pulled up onto the platform in spite of her struggles. She dropped onto splintery wood, the cloak twisted about her, and gazed up uncomprehendingly up into Roy's big-eared, homely face. "The firestick is over here," he said.

"I want to go home," she said numbly.

"Orders," Laban said. "We're already in enough trouble."

Roy dropped onto the platform on his stomach, doing something with papers. Laban sat on Clair's other side. Clair then registered a noise she'd been half-aware of for some time: wind, and snow. Building toward a blizzard. She stumbled to her feet, her feet pins-and-needles with merciless intensity. She tripped over the long cloak, and fell to her knees.

Wind howled through the trees high overhead, sending flurries of snow swirling across the platform to pile against a low wall someone had hammered together. The fire danced violently, hissing and steaming as snowflakes tumbled into it and perished. Roy's papers lifted and scurried toward the fire. He smacked and scraped them together as several white-dusted figures hauled themselves up and stamped onto the platform, two helping one who sank down, cradling a broken arm.

Clair blinked, and the figures resolved into a group of dark-coated boys, with one familiar face: Clair recognized Terry, his hair plastered wetly to his forehead, his eyes dazed.

MV slammed Terry onto the platform next to Clair. The rest of them stamped to get snow off boots, and hands brushed at sleeves and cloaks as they joked back and forth in Geth-deles.

"What is this?" said the last arrival, a blond one Clair had never seen before. Clair found herself staring into curious brown eyes, set in a face vaguely familiar, except Clair was sure she'd never seen this boy before today. His expression was thoughtful, the emerging bones making his age somewhere around MV's. Only his wary brown eyes belied the smile.

"My orders," Laban said, thumb turned toward Clair.

"*My* experiment," MV said, smacking the top of Terry's head. MV was furious. The one possible interesting fight had been denied him, instead he'd tangled with that girl, that damned *stupid* girl, who cut her own damned throat—but it was his arms that had tightened—

He snarled, "Terry jumped Ferret. Did a pretty good job, too." He jerked a thumb at Ferret mopping his bloody nose, one arm hanging limply. "I made an extra token."

"All right, then," David said, rolling his eyes, Detlev could deal with MV's temper. "In order. You first."

Laban closed his hand on Clair's arm, and before she could try to pull away, he pressed a square of metal against her and magic wrenched her from the world.

Thirty-five

"NO," CJ YELLED HER loudest, hands clenched at her sides, her face crimson. "No, no, no! You shouldn't *say* stuff like that, you're *stupid!*"

Senrid looked as sick as he felt. "Clair must have seen it happen. She said Irenne's name, and we ran to the site. Saw the blood. Someone must have Disappeared her. We can search again, but . . ."

"But we did," Puddlenose said, low-voiced, the humor so characteristic of him utterly gone from his face. "We searched until the blizzard got too bad. We're pretty sure we found their hideout. It was a treehouse, and there was stuff left behind. But they're gone. Irenne's gone."

Christoph said softly, "And we can't find Clair."

Dhana's pale face swam into CJ's view. "We all looked. None of us could find her."

That snapped CJ back into the present, and she sniffed the bread that had burned, and heard Kyale sobbing noisily in the corner, unnoticed. CJ sank to the floor like a string-cut puppet.

Seshe stepped up to her, robe smelling of cinnamon, then she stood up, fingered her medallion, her eyes wide, her pupils so black they seemed to swallow her irises as she said, "I promise I *will* find her—"

To everyone's astonishment, the room filled with white,

blinding light. They ran to the windows, and saw the lightning coalesce into a shimmering white horse. Seshe thought, astounded almost witless, *He came. He will take me to Clair.*

As CJ yelled, "Wait, wait," Seshe ran outside, threw herself over Hreealdar —

And they vanished.

"*What* was *that*?" Arthur gasped.

"How'd she *do* that?" Kyale squawked, her tears forgotten.

Sick as she felt, CJ managed words. "That," she said, "was Hreealdar."

Dhana said, "Hreealdar is . . ." She scowled, her round, bland light brown face shuttered. "Sometimes a horse, sometimes lightning. A little like us." She patted her scrawny chest. "Not human, I mean."

Senrid snapped his fingers. "When Liere destroyed Siamis's spell, she was on the back of a huge white horse, but it didn't gallop, it . . ."

"Transformed into lightning," CJ said, getting slowly to her feet, and turned to Dhana. "I never thought Hreealdar would come all the way *here*. Clair put this spell on our medallions, which calls to Hreealdar, not that it always works. This is the first time he came in a long time. And not at home. Is it because Clair is missing?" She turned to Dhana. "Do you think he can find people?"

Dhana shook her head. "I told you Hreealdar is a little like my people. But not from our world, the way we are."

No one else spoke. They were too stunned by all that had happened so quickly.

CJ stared through the window at the spot where Seshe and Hreealdar had vanished. Hope began to melt the ice around her heart.

Then Tahra startled everyone by slamming her crossbow to the floor. "They're really gone?" The caustic emphasis on *they're* made it clear she meant Detlev's boys.

Rel spoke up for the first time. "There's no sign of them anywhere."

"Then they escaped justice *again*."

Rel shut her out, looked around at the piles of gear, at friends and some who should be friends, and thought, *Farewell to childhood.*

He gripped the token Atan had given him, and transferred.

CJ and Dhana were the next to leave. CJ could not bear to

say goodbye, not without Clair, and Dhana came and went as lightly as she danced.

As soon as she saw the familiar surroundings of home, CJ burst into a shocking crying jag that lasted until the others had gathered. Dhana gave a succinct report, and for a long time they stood in a circle regarding one another without being able to say anything.

Mearsieanne's face looked old, despite the youthful contours. Tears gathered in her eyes and began to overflow as she walked away and shut her door. With her gone, the girls by unspoken but mutual agreement desired the oldest comfort and retreat, their underground hideout. But there was scant comfort to be found. Right in the main room lay one of Irenne's lacey shawls, reluctantly left behind at the last moment because her carryall was already bursting.

"What do we do with Irenne's things?" Gwen asked tearfully as she picked up the shawl and held it to her chest.

"Leave 'em," Dhana said. "We won't touch them. Clair can decide if she gets back."

"*When* Clair gets back," CJ corrected fiercely, her swollen eyes aching. "They didn't see any . . ." She couldn't say the word *blood*. "They didn't see any evidence that what happened to Irenne happened to her. So maybe the poopsies did take her. And you know she'll try to escape, if Seshe doesn't find her first."

She scrubbed her sleeve across her eyes. "If they went to Norsunder Base, maybe the morvende can rescue them, like they did Senrid that time. Or Kessler can get her out. I'll write to Jilo to ask him. Yes, that's what I'm going to do. I'm going to write to *everyone*, until we get her back."

When Siamis emerged from the Selenseh Redian, he found Lilith waiting.

She sat on a low stone as if she'd been there for some time.

"When is it?" he asked.

"Winter, 4748," she said. "You've been in there a few months."

He sat down across from her, hands on his knees. He noticed that his sword still stood where he had left it, leaning inside the cave entrance a few paces from where Lilith sat. "And you are here to . . .?" he prompted.

"Get you caught up, to begin with," she said, her years of effort in the world over the centuries aging her face in lines of sorrow and pain, but no anger. "Detlev failed in Songre Silde. He seems to have withdrawn to your citadel on Aldau-Rayad, which I believe you call Five. Yeres of the Host has withdrawn altogether from Aldau-Rayad," she added. "Thanks to you, their plans seem to have been set back a generation, if not more."

Siamis shook his head. "There are other plans."

"I understand that," she said. "I said seem. So now we come to you."

He shut his eyes. "When he went over to Norsunder, I was in Efael's grip. I don't know if you realize what that means."

"I do indeed." Her voice was soft. "I know what Efael was, and who made him what he is now."

"The one thing he respects is power." Siamis opened his hands. "As much as he craves it. As for Detlev. I was the only one of the family remaining. His surrender bought my life. But when Svirle said, 'Come now, you have left as sanguine a trail as any of us,' Detlev said, 'Yes.' I always remembered that, during the ensuing years; we were angry with one another for an appreciable time, an anger they encouraged. He, the anger born of guilt for a wrong he was helpless to avoid, and I was angry because I had done nothing to deserve it, and he had done nothing to save me."

"But you learned he couldn't, right?"

"Of course I did," Siamis said gently. "But at the same time I learned that I had to hide every insight, and to act as expected. I was still their performing puppet, but at that moment the sense of agency was born. It began with lying to the masters of lies."

"I am sorry I was too late." Her voice trembled with sincerity.

"You are human, and you lost as much as I did." He lifted a shoulder. "Erdrael was not much older than I. Further, I did find the moral touchstones you left in the world during various times when I was permitted to emerge. Such as Isa Cassadas."

"I discovered her nearly lost in the dreamworld, when I was elsewhere at the time. She was a joy to teach."

Isa Cassadas had already been far-seeing when Siamis met her. He'd discovered that she was a daughter of Adamas Dei of the Black Sword's line. He said, "I got a year with her before I sensed them coming, and ran. I was not permitted out again for centuries."

He still did not know if his precious, life-changing year with Isa had produced children. When next he had been able to escape Norsunder, he'd discovered that the Cassadas family had blended with the Marlovans, and many of their records had been destroyed. Not all. It was one of his private goals to find them.

But he kept that to himself as Lilith said, "I'm to tell you that Tsauderei has extended a diplomatic invitation for you to visit Rive Dien in Eidervaen, capital of Sartor."

"No doubt within boundaries and wards."

"Of course. It will take time to earn trust. If that is your intent. And I'm certain you will not wish to remain there any longer than they will attempt to keep you. Someone needs to train the youngsters making their unity, for they are struggle-ing."

"So," he said, "am I."

Fifth World from Erhal, Norsunder Base

In the central building of the compound known as the Den on Aldau-Rayad, Detlev sat at a desk watching over a serious-faced boy of two whose small fingers gripped a pen as he slowly traced out letters.

At the sound of noise from the outer room, both pairs of hazel eyes looked up. "The boys are back," Detlev said, smiling.

The child, barely out of toddlerhood but deft far beyond his years in movement, slid off his stool and vanished out the door, writing materials clutched under his arm.

About the Author

Sherwood Smith writes fantasy, science fiction, and historical fiction. Her full bibliography can be found on her website at https://www.sherwoodsmith.net

About Book View Cafe

Book View Café is an author-owned cooperative of professional writers, publishing in a variety of genres including fantasy, science fiction, romance, mystery, and more.

Its authors include New York Times and USA Today best-sellers as well as winners and nominees of many prestigious awards such as the Agatha Award, Hugo Award, Lambda Literary Award, Locus Award, Nebula Award, RITA Award, Philip K. Dick Award, World Fantasy Award, and many others.

Since its debut in 2008, Book View Café has gained a reputation for producing high quality books in both print and electronic form. BVC's e-books are DRM-free and distributed around the world.

Book View Café's monthly newsletter includes new releases, specials, author news, and event announcements. To sign up, visit https://www.bookviewcafe.com/bookstore/newsletter/

Made in the USA
Las Vegas, NV
31 January 2022

42751491R00340